SHIRTALOON
HE WHO FIGHTS WITH MONSTERS
BOOK FIVE

www.aethonbooks.com

HE WHO FIGHTS WITH MONSTERS FIVE
©2022 SHIRTALOON

This book is protected under the copyright laws of the United States of America. No part of this publication may be reproduced, stored in a retrieval system, or transmitted, in any form or by any means, without the prior permission in writing of the publisher, nor be otherwise circulated in any form of binding or cover other than that in which it is published and without a similar condition including this condition being imposed on the subsequent purchaser. Any reproduction or unauthorized use of the material or artwork contained herein is prohibited without the express written permission of the authors.

Aethon Books supports the right to free expression and the value of copyright. The purpose of copyright is to encourage writers and artists to produce the creative works that enrich our culture.

The scanning, uploading, and distribution of this book without permission is a theft of the author's intellectual property. If you would like to use material from the book (other than for review purposes), please contact editor@aethonbooks.com. Thank you for your support of the author's rights.

Aethon Books
www.aethonbooks.com

Print and eBook formatting by Steve Beaulieu.

Published by Aethon Books LLC.

Aethon Books is not responsible for websites (or their content) that are not owned by the publisher.

This book is a work of fiction. Names, characters, places, and incidents are the product of the author's imagination or are used fictitiously. Any resemblance to actual events, locales, or persons, living or dead is coincidental.

All rights reserved.

ALSO IN SERIES

HE WHO FIGHTS WITH MONSTERS

BOOK ONE

BOOK TWO

BOOK THREE

BOOK FOUR

BOOK FIVE

BOOK SIX

Want to discuss our books with other readers and even the authors like Shirtaloon, Zogarth, Cale Plamann, Noret Flood (Puddles4263) and so many more?

Join our Discord server today and be a part of the Aethon community.

1
TOO VALUABLE TO LOSE

The Chinese village had been levelled by a powerful earthquake, and the villagers watched as an alien figure used beams of energy to cut through the girder blocking the hole in which a child was trapped. The strange being was inhuman in nature, a dark, floating cloak, containing not a person but an energy that looked much like the Helix nebula—the Eye of God. Floating around the cloak were eye-like orbs, which fired the beams that sliced through steel like it was soft cheese.

At first, the villagers had been afraid of Jason Asano and his terrifying companion, but as the pair rescued person after person from the rubble, they went from wary to welcoming.

The beams of Jason's familiar, Gordon, made short work of the collapsed girder, revealing the narrow hole underneath. Jason could easily see through the darkness to the top of the little boy's head, and extended his shadow arms to pluck him out of the hole. As soon as the boy was free, his mother rushed to embrace him as the villagers looked on. In the midst of the relief efforts, they were all as dirty and caked with dust as Jason was under his cloak.

In her office, back in Australia, Sydney Network branch committeewoman Annabeth Tilden was watching the latest video file delivered by the branch's new Director of Operations, Ketevan. It was news footage, intercepted before ever going into public distribution. It had been sent by the Beijing Network branch, along with an angrily worded message.

"...took responders several hours to reach more isolated areas in the wake of the catastrophic earthquake. The collapse of the bridge you see behind me devastated this small village, but the villagers themselves attribute the low number of casualties to a number of mysterious individuals, several of which they describe as appearing supernatural in nature. This is not the first..."

Anna closed the video file with a sigh and added it to a folder with the others. One of the more disturbing elements was that the reporter had been speaking not in Mandarin but in English. Not only was Jason being far too prominent in his actions, but clearly someone wanted to publicise them in the west. None of the videos had made it to broadcast, but several had been appearing online.

"Jason may be playing rather loosely with the secrecy provisions of our agreement after our people attacked him in Hanoi," Ketevan said, "but at least he hasn't been showing off the stars in his cloak since then. No one has connected the stories to the Starlight Rider."

"Yet," Anna said. "And they weren't our people in Hanoi."

"How many times have we had to explain that the people who went after him were Network but not *our* Network?" Ketevan asked. "I'm not so sure he'll still see us an ally once he's done with his journey of self-discovery or whatever it is he's off doing."

"I swear, I want to fire a missile at the Hanoi branch."

"The International Committee more or less did," Ketevan reminded her.

A month earlier, in Hanoi, Jason had underpriced the yacht in order to sell it off quickly. He started his trip by playing tourist but quickly sensed the people following him.

The capture team had two category threes and a dozen category twos.

They realised that Asano had clearly sensed them and had been forced to shed slower members as they pursued their elusive target through the city.

They finally tracked him down in the Hong River Slum Town, a bizarre hodgepodge of urban, industrial and rural. Illegal dwellings were bunched in with small farm plots, stores and even factories. Dirt roads and irrigation ditches defined the thoroughfares, with everything from the buildings to the very ground marking poverty, pollution and dilapidation. It was a backwater oddly located in a city of seven and a half million.

Without streetlights, it was a dark and dangerous place at night, more for the environment than the residents. For the capture team, though, darkness was not an issue. Only one of the category threes, Thanh, had managed to maintain the chase all the way, courtesy of speed powers granted by his light essence. The same light essence was able to illuminate the area with his aura.

Thanh's aura didn't simply radiate light. Over a wide area, all darkness was banished. It seemed to have no source and was simply everywhere, filling every nook and cranny with soft illumination.

When the space lit up, Jason was revealed to be standing right in front of the capture team. The only remaining patch of darkness was inside the hood of his cloak, in which only a pair of silver eyes could be seen.

"I'm surprised anyone was this stupid," Jason said in Vietnamese. His skill at actively using his translation power with specific languages was improving, although he was stubbornly clinging to syntax that gave an odd mix of perfect pronunciation and deeply odd grammar. Rather than try to adapt, the way Farrah had so quickly, he had made it into a rather obnoxious signature.

"I didn't think anyone would be stupid enough to cross the International Committee after they gutted the Lyon branch like a fish," he continued.

"You no longer need to concern yourself with things like that," Thanh said. "You belong to us now, so you don't make decisions anymore."

"It could be the Chinese," Jason mused, ignoring the man. "They may be using you as a cat's paw to test my capabilities without it blowing back on them. Maybe the EOA, looking to take me off the board before I start looking for them over their part in holding my friend prisoner. It could be that there's no one and you really are this dumb. I mean, you let me lead you by the nose until half of your team was left behind. Your trackers kind of suck, by the way. I had to aura project like a lighthouse for them to keep up and it was still hard to avoid escaping by accident."

"You are arrogant," Thanh said. "That is your Japanese blood speaking."

"Strewth; racist enough for you, mate?"

"We have studied your methods, Asano. You are a creature of the shadows. Without them, you are vulnerable and exposed."

"You've got me there," Jason said. "I definitely didn't train with someone from a family of essence-user instructors the equal of anyone on two worlds who laboriously drilled me on how to fight when I was caught out of my element."

"You like to jabber and distract," Thanh said. "We know this about you. Quick words cannot change that we hold the advantage in numbers, in power and in the environment. There are no shadows for you to cower in."

They were on a dirt road, with a heavily polluted irrigation ditch running along one side and a ramshackle slum house on the other. The six category twos were arrayed in front of Thanh, with Jason standing before them in his combat robes and cloak. With the appearance of the light, the attention of the locals had been grabbed. They were variously hiding, fleeing or even recording the proceedings from behind cover.

"Can you blur me in those videos?" Jason asked Shade, under his breath.

"I'm sorry, Mr. Asano. This silver-rank light is having an extremely deleterious effect on my capabilities. I will be unable to manifest any of my bodies or run interference on detection abilities. I can only remain in the hood of your cloak, which remains impervious to the shadow deletion. Otherwise, I would not even be able to speak with you."

"No worries," Jason said. "Part of why we left was to throw ourselves into training, right? This should push our limits nicely."

"This may be throwing ourselves a tad hard, Mr Asano."

"Maybe, but that guy in Lyon left a lingering unpleasantness. I'd like to—"

"You have the nerve to stand in front of me and talk to yourself?" Thanh yelled, anger scoring his face. His aura blasted out, but immediately slammed to a stop against Jason's, like a truck ramming a concrete wall. While Jason wasn't powerful enough to suppress the silver-ranker's aura and the light it produced, his was discernibly the stronger aura, despite Jason's lower rank. The disparity left Thanh visibly unnerved.

"KILL HIM!" Thanh screamed, forgetting that their purpose was to take Jason alive.

A grab-bag of powers was hurled Jason's way. One of the bronze-rankers underwent a bizarre transformation, his arms turning into snakes and his legs into those of a grasshopper. He pounced at Jason, who intercepted the snake fangs with his cloak as the man landed in front of him. He then pushed into the man's space and rammed a conjured dagger up under his jaw to pierce his brain.

Bronze-rankers couldn't fight through what should have been lethal blows the way a silver-ranker could. The man with a dagger penetrating his head was tough enough to cling to life but fell limp. Jason grabbed his collapsing body and used him as a shield to soak up other attacks coming his way. A fire bolt spell, a spiked ball on a chain and a laser beam of light from the silver-rank Thanh all impacted against the slack body.

The bronze-ranker in Jason's arms did not survive the attacks and Jason rushed forward, still using him as a shield. He rammed the corpse into one of the other bronze-rankers, leaving them both to topple over as Jason spun away, positioning himself so the group was obstructing one another's sightlines as much as possible. His dagger, in a backhand grip, ran across the next victim's throat before jabbing back into the side of the neck. Jason let him go as the man stumbled backward, clutching desperately at his throat with one hand as the other scrambled for a healing potion.

The shock of Jason's counter-blitz only lasted moments and a fresh wave of attacks was already on its way. To an observer, it might seem that Jason was dangerously outmatched. From Jason's perspective, his opponents' attacks were the inexpert flailing of amateurs. That was not to say they were without strategy. The elimination of the shadows had a large impact and it wasn't the only trick that seemed tailor-made for him.

Clearly, the enemy had learned of his fight against the last silver-ranker and the tether power that had pinned him down. One of the bronze-rankers had a similar ability and Jason had neither shadow nor cover to avoid it. Jason tossed his dagger into the air and a shadow hand emerged from his cloak to snatch it. His normal hands each pulled a throwing dart from the sheaths on his chest and flung them.

The first was an explosive dart, thrown directly at the tether rod. The blast from a tether rod being destroyed had caused him to lose his last fight against a silver-ranker, but this time, he was triggering it himself. The second dart was thrown at the ground, right in front of the rod. This was the dart Jason had developed after that same fight, using the artifice knowledge he gained from a skill book. When the dart hit the ground, a door-sized wall of magically reinforced ballistics gel sprang into being, right as the tether rod exploded.

The force from the blast sent the person who used the ability flying, along with another of the bronze-rankers. It didn't kill them, but Jason knew for himself how disorienting that blast could be. It would give him some breathing room with the other three who, like Jason, were protected as the blast hit the gelatin wall. Gobbets of harmless ballistics gel rained thickly as the wall exploded.

As the fight resumed in the wake of the blast, Jason's cloak protected him from some attacks, although its shadowy substance was also negatively impacted by the light. Its true value was to obscure his true body position, causing many attacks to simply miss. He had long ago incorporated unexpected movements into his technique, with hours upon hours of flexibility and balance training. Between that and his cloak's ability to spread out and dance to Jason's whims, it was tricky to pinpoint his body's exact location at any given moment.

Jason's magical senses tracked incoming magical attacks before they were made. This included conjured and magical weapons, while mundane weapons would be useless. Sensing where the attacks would be, he was constantly moving to where they wouldn't, never stopping still.

He seemed impervious to attack, moving like a ghost through projectiles and weapon swings. Part of it was that he truly did avoid many blows. Another part was that his cloak masked the blows that did land, and he gave no indication of being harmed.

For his part, his dagger flashed out to land again and again. His shadow arm extended at need, giving his dagger no less reach than the guy with the spiked ball and chain. It flailed like an unattended hose with the water turned to full, yet in the seeming randomness, his dagger bit flesh time after time, riddling the enemy with afflictions.

Jason also pulled out the hydra whip he looted from his very first bronze-rank monster, wielding it with a second shadow arm. The semi-autonomous heads thrashed wildly as they lashed out with savage teeth. The whip couldn't pile on bonus afflictions like the dagger, but a single special attack could be delivered once for each of the five heads. The targets were somewhat random amongst whichever enemies were in range, but that was only a minor disadvantage.

The whip could also be used to intercept attacks. As it had the hydra's property of regeneration, it quickly recovered from most damage. Only the fire attacks of one of the bronze-rankers and the searing light from the silver-ranker's attacks left lingering damage.

Jason largely left the silver-ranker alone. Thanh hung behind the others, making ranged attacks instead of diving in, which was exactly what Jason wanted. He only made occasional feints in Thanh's direction to keep him on his toes. So long as the silver-ranker didn't plant his feet to play rapid-fire turret, Jason could handle it. He was careful, luring the bronze-rankers into interrupting the silver-ranker's sightlines, even intercepting some of his attacks.

Jason had seized the momentum of the battle and was not letting go. The enemies' problem was not that they didn't know how to fight; they had clearly received meticulous combat training. The problem was that combat training was derived from Earth methodologies. The way they moved, the way they fought, even the way they thought was based around the paradigm of a baseline human, with the powers incorporated as an addendum.

At iron-rank, that wasn't too much of a liability, but bronze was the point where an essence user truly became more than human. If they continued to think and fight like a human at that point, they were tossing away their potential.

Jason had been trained as an essence user from the ground up. The confluence of his attributes, perception and powers comprised a series of force multipliers, the results of which demonstrated exactly what made Farrah and himself so valuable to the Network. It wasn't just improved meditation techniques to get people off cores but a holistic method of going from ordinary warrior to magical weapon.

Jason's enemies suffered a disconnect between their powers, their physical abilities and the way they sought to use them. They looked buffoonish next to Jason, who was combining and interweaving powers. He relied on his enhanced perception over his ordinary senses. His every motion made use of his superhuman agility and flexibility. Each physical attack was delivered with an appreciation of the power he could put behind it and the strain his body could take in landing it.

His enemies had the potential, but they squandered it. They were humans using superhuman abilities while Jason was a superhuman, through and through. The results were stark. Even without shadows or pulling out his familiars, he gave the bronze-rankers a brutal education on the differences in approach.

Even so, a less-than-stellar silver-ranker was still a silver-ranker. The ability to banish shadows truly was an impediment to Jason, even if it wasn't the defining factor his opponent had anticipated. Like his subordinates, Thanh squandered much of his potential, but a silver-ranker had far more potential to squander.

Thanh was a ranged attacker, staying back and flinging beams of light and crystal shards in Jason's direction. He clearly wasn't as secure as he should be in his silver rank resilience, wasting his silver rank strength. If he had moved in hard on Jason with his superior strength, toughness and reflexes, he could have at least prevented Jason from going wild on the bronze-rankers. Instead, Jason used the bronze-rankers as cover and shields to intercept Thanh's ranged attacks.

The ability to use the bronze-rankers as human shields was just the beginning. Jason loaded them up with afflictions, hitting them with spells even as he danced amongst them. They were incubators for the afflictions building up, each one charging the protective power of Jason's amulet.

Despite his superiority, Jason went far from unscathed. As many hits as he avoided, there were just too many enemies. Much of his fight was about minimising hits that couldn't be dodged. The relatively weak-but-rapid attacks from the silver-ranker alone packed a dangerous punch against Jason, even in his magic armour.

If Thanh had challenged Jason without the bronze-rankers, he would have had a very good chance of winning. With silver-rank powers, silver-rank attributes and the ability to deny any shadows, he had no shortage of advantages. The bronze-rankers seemed like another advantage but they were, in fact, the equalisers.

More than just being human shields, the key reason the bronze-rankers were liabilities to their leader was that they allowed Jason to endure hit after hit. Each affliction Jason incubated on the bronze-rankers added a shield to Jason's amulet. Not only did his Amulet of the Dark Guardian give a weak shield for every affliction he delivered, each shield that was broken became a healing effect.

As Thanh punched through the shields, they transformed into healing that was added to Jason's own life-draining power. His Leech Bite attack drained health to further top him off and, when that wasn't enough, his Feast of Blood gave a large burst of drain-healing. If it still wasn't enough, he drained the afflictions from a bronze-ranker. His Sin Eater power turned every affliction he drained into ongoing recovery of health, stamina and mana, while leaving holy afflictions in place.

With each bronze-ranker that he drained, Jason's regeneration grew stronger. The downside was that as each enemy succumbed to the holy afflictions burning them from the inside out, it became easier for Thanh to land hits.

Once the bronze-rankers were all dead, there were no more obstacles to Thanh's attacks. In spite of this, the precision of his attacks dropped as his frustration rose. Jason's armour was ragged and he should have died a dozen times over. Instead, he had fed on the life force of the bronze-rankers and used them to build up an absurd level of regeneration. If Jason didn't have them to use, Thanh's chances would have been far better.

Despite all of that, defeating a silver-ranker was no mean feat. Even if Thanh was getting sloppy, Jason was out of human shields and Thanh's attacks were outpacing his healing. Jason focused on trying to take down Thanh, but the man had a number of slippery movement powers. It slowed down his attacks to use them, but it didn't stop them altogether.

If not for extensive training with the lightning-quick Sophie, Jason would have been at a loss to counter the man's speed. As it was, he wasn't landing hits. He struggled to apply as much pressure as he could, employing every trick he knew for combating faster opponents. The key was finding the limitations of their speed, which hopefully they had.

Jason's pressure exposed Thanh's weakness, which was a need to slow down when making rapid, sequential shifts in direction. It not only made him easier to pin down but accelerated his exhaustion, even as it decelerated his speed.

Energy attrition was not wildly effective against Sophie, whose endurance almost matched Jason's, but Thanh lacked her absolute dedication to speed. While any silver-ranker's endurance was formidable, Jason could sense Thanh slowly but surely tiring. For his part, Jason was like Sophie in being an endurance fighter. The same effects continually restoring his health were keeping his mana and stamina topped off.

Jason's goal was to exhaust the silver-ranker, forcing him to pause long enough that Jason could employ his most powerful weapon. If he could spray the silver-ranker with Colin, Jason's leech swarm familiar, it would move the fight into the end game. This man clearly knew Jason's tactics, however, and would be aware of his most dangerous ally. Jason knew Thanh would not let himself be caught out easily. Only by forcing the situation could Jason use Colin effectively, and missing would mean the silver-ranker could easily avoid the sluggish familiar.

Things were not going Jason's way; Thanh had his own plan. While Jason was trying to run out the clock of Thanh's mana, Thanh wanted to overwhelm Jason's health regeneration before that happened. The silver-ranker had the attribute advantage, and with the bronze-rankers gone, the fight was slowly turning in his favour.

Amongst Thanh's suite of powers was a burst of ultra-speed, such as Sophie, Rufus and Danielle Geller all shared. Thanh appeared to lack any big-hit powers to maximise the burst of speed, but it allowed him to queue up an array of projectiles to fire the moment the power ended. From training with Rufus and Sophie, Jason recognised the telltale blur and threw himself out of the way, but there was no truly dodging that level of speed. Each time it happened, Jason was ravaged with attacks. The only blessing was that each use was a devastating drain on Thanh's mana.

As Thanh landed hit after hit, Jason felt the jaws of death growing ever closer. Rather than let them feast, Jason chose to turn the tables and feast on death instead. He paused, startling Thanh enough that a light beam missed wildly as Jason chanted out a spell.

"*As your lives were mine to reap, so your deaths are mine to harvest.*"

Ability: [Blood Harvest] (Blood)

- Spell (drain).
- Cost: Low mana.
- Cooldown: None.

- Current rank: Bronze 6 (09%).

- Effect (iron): Drain the remnant life force of a recently deceased body, replenishing health, stamina and mana. Only affects targets with blood.

- Effect (bronze): Affects all enemy corpses in a wide area.

The bronze-rankers were half-rotted away with necrosis and half dissolved by the transcendent damage of holy affliction. Jason had not used his finisher on any of them. Thanh watched in horror as the blood-red glow of their remnant life rose from their bodies and was siphoned away, a series of bloody trails moving through the air and seeping into Jason's body.

Thanh's senses told him that under the ragged armour and bloodied skin, Jason was more than just physically recovered. Jason's mana and stamina had already been diminishing far slower than Thanh's own and now both pools were completely replenished.

Thanh was not yet fully exhausted but had thrown no shortage of mana at Jason in the form of magical attacks. The damage from his hyper-speed burst attacks had been undone, leaving only Thanh's mana deficit behind. As he watched Jason fully restore himself using the ruined carcasses that had only minutes ago been his team, Thanh's will broke.

Jason felt the moment his opponent's morale crumpled—the man's aura turned to glass. Jason slammed his own aura down like a hammer, shattering that glass to pieces just as Thanh had been activating a movement power in an attempt to flee. Instead, his aura, now a paper tiger, collapsed under Jason's assault.

Thanh felt a sensation unlike any he had experienced, like a knife pressed against the throat of his soul. He could sense that it would dig in if he moved even the tiniest bit in the wrong direction, flooding him with fear.

Thanh froze on the spot, hearing footsteps slowly approach from behind on the gravel road. His aura no longer banished the shadows, but motes of light flew out from Jason's cloak to bathe the road in starlight.

"I think we need to return to our previous conversation," Jason said, his voice a glacial inexorability. "Tell me why you violated the International Committee's edict."

"I don't know," Thanh said. "The Hanoi branch director just told me to capture you."

Jason only jabbed a pinprick against Thanh's soul, but it was the most violating thing the man had ever experienced. He shrieked in fear and pain, even though the sensation lasted but a fraction of a second.

"I really don't know!" Thanh begged. "They tracked your boat; that's how they knew you were coming. That's all I know, I swear!"

Thanh still couldn't see Jason standing behind him and his aura senses were clamped down by Jason's aura suppression. As for his magic senses, with the absence of the light, Shade was once again masking Jason's presence. Thanh's nerves rose towards panic, as all he could sense was the razor claw gripping his soul.

"I'm not going to kill you," Jason said finally. "You should be doing your real job, which is not trying to hunt me down. It's protecting people from the dangers they don't even know are there. Your power is too valuable to lose from that fight, so you get to live. I suggest you go back to your job and be very, very diligent about carrying it out."

The pressure suddenly vanished from Thanh, who immediately shot off like a rocket. A path of light spread out under his feet as he fled with all the speed he could muster.

"Shade," Jason said. "Have Farrah tell the Network what happened. Make sure they buy up the recordings of all these on-lookers. Tell them to be generous about it too. These people could use the money."

"I imagine the Network will want to speak to you."

"I don't want to speak to them. Remind them that part of the agreement was that the Network would stop coming after me, and let them know that if they are going to be sloppy about the terms, then so will I."

"I don't think they'll like that," Shade said.

"I'm done caring about what people like," Jason said. "If they want something from me, they can pay for it."

The stars from Jason's cloak that were floating around him returned to the cloak, then dimmed down to nothing. The street was once again plunged into darkness.

"…should be doing your real job, which is not trying to hunt me down. It's protecting people from the dangers they don't even know are there…"

Adrien Barbou closed the video file with a sigh, created a folder and moved the file into it. He pressed a button on his desk.

"Fiona, please arrange a meeting with Mrs West at her earliest convenience."

2
ALL I CAN DO IS MY BEST

Jason walked down the single street of the dilapidated West African township. Buildings of clay brick and rusted, corrugated iron were silent and the streets empty. The only people he saw were amongst the tents set up at the far end of the town, where people in hazmat suits were bustling about. They had too much to do, too few people to do it and too little resources to do it with.

He made his way down the dusty street, the heat pounding down like a blacksmith's hammer. It wasn't until he drew close to the tan tents, set up in neat rows, that the busy humanitarian workers noticed him. A hazmat-suited woman rapidly approached and started yelling at him in French.

"What the hell do you think you're…"

She trailed off as she met his eyes, seeing their silver colour.

"Are you him?"

"Yeah," Jason said. "Who are you?"

"Dr Chloe Baudrillard. What do I call you?"

"It's probably best I don't leave a name. It's one less thing you have to tell when people come asking about me."

"You seem certain they will."

"Once you see what I can do, you will be too."

"I've heard the stories. From people I trust, but it doesn't seem possible."

"A place like this could use a little impossible, don't you think?" he asked.

"You're damn right it could. If you can do what they say…"

"I can. But only for as long as people don't come looking for me," Jason said.

"I was told that keeping quiet was your rule, but I can't promise that we can stop people from talking," she said. "I was told to give you whatever you need and stay out of your way, but people talk. Obviously, or I wouldn't have heard about the Eurasian man with silver eyes."

"I'm not looking to build a legend," Jason said. "I'm just looking to help people. The goal is to do as much good as we can for as long as we can, right?"

"Yes," she said. "Yes, it is. So, what do you need?"

"Some privacy and all the sick people you've got."

She led Jason, but after a short distance, he stopped.

"Is there a problem?" she asked.

"I need to see someone," he said. "Go to where I need to be and I'll find you."

She frowned, turned to look at the tents and then back to Jason, but he was already gone.

"What the… does he think he's Batman?"

Elsewhere in the camp, Jason stood outside a tent and let a little of his aura show. Shortly thereafter, another hazmat-suited woman appeared, this one with a bronze-rank aura.

"You're here," she said. "You're Jason Asano?"

"Yes."

"You realise that the Network isn't slacking off on this, right? We are helping. We just aren't making a spectacle of it."

"I respect that," Jason said. "We're both working in secret, only at different points on the scale. If we aren't more direct in using what we can do, though, secrecy will cost lives."

"If the secret comes out, you think it will make things easier once the world descends on us?"

"This isn't a hospital full of camera phones and media saturation," Jason said. "We have leeway here and we should use it."

"You think we don't want to march through here, raising people up off their sickbeds? We have to look beyond today, to the next outbreak and the next one. Plus, there's only so much mana to go around."

Jason plucked a wooden box out of the air, sliding off the lid to reveal stacks of bronze-rank coins.

"Would this help?"

The woman didn't answer for a moment as she looked at the coins, then shook her head as if to clear it.

"You're willing to just hand these over?"

"You want some iron ones as well? Actually, give me a list of everywhere I can find Network personnel working on this and I'll make some drop-offs."

"That's very generous," she said. "It doesn't change the fact that what you're doing puts us all in jeopardy."

"You could look at it as a safety precaution," Jason said. "If anyone latches on to your activities, you can pass it off as the work of the magic healer roaming around."

"It's not as simple as you make out."

"It never is. All I can do is my best, based on what I know and what I can do."

"Well," she said. "I don't like what you're up to, but it's not like I can stop it. And I am going to take these coins."

Jason walked into the large tent, Chloe beside him in her hazmat suit. There were people laid out in rows, letting out a discord of feeble moans.

"Are you sure you want to see?" he asked. "Once you do, you'll never see the world in the same way again."

"You think I should choose ignorance?"

"As a rule, no, but it's not so easy to pick up your regular life after peeking behind the curtain of the universe."

"Just do what you came here to do."

"Alright," he said. "So be it."

Jason moved to the first patient, who was agitated and delirious. The man's aura was in chaos and Jason used his own to guide it back to calm. After months of practising, his aura control had eclipsed his abilities of the past.

From Chloe's perspective, Jason's mere presence calmed the man, lulling him into sleep. Then that presence passed through the room like a wave, the pitiful moans dropping away. Chloe felt it herself, like being in the presence of a benevolent dictator. Then Jason raised his hand, speaking words in a language she didn't recognise.

Red light started glowing from within the patient. Chloe's attention transfixed. Looking at the light felt like looking at the man's beating heart, although it was stained with black taint. As she watched, the taint seeped out of the light, streaming up into Jason's waiting hand. It only stopped once the red light was clean, at which point it retracted into the man's body. Still unconscious, the patient looked immediately better.

Chloe looked on in disbelief as Jason went through the patients, one by one. He didn't so much as glance at her until he had gone through every patient.

"You have more tents, right?"

Despite their misgivings, the aid workers had cleared out to let Jason loose on the patients after getting implausible but emphatic word from other camps. Now that he was gone, they were swarming over the patients, running tests multiple times out of raw disbelief. Chloe suspected that she herself was in some stage of shock, the unreality of it all completely disorienting.

"What you did in there, I can't explain," she told Jason at the edge of the camp. "It looked like you were healing people with a magic spell."

"It did, didn't it?"

"You were right," she said. "I'm not sure how to just move on after what I saw."

"I imagine you'll be busy in the next little while. By the time you have a chance to stop and think about it, you can just pass it off as some weird trick."

"I don't think that's going to work. Not if you really cured those people. Was that you in Sydney last year? Healing all those kids at the hospital?"

"I try to be more circumspect, now, but…"

They both turned to look at the frenzy of activity in the camp.

"Sometimes people just need helping," she said.

"Yeah," Jason agreed.

"Are you going to more camps?"

"Of course."

"I won't keep you, then," she said. "There's no shortage of people that need you."

He narrowed his eyes at her. "You're really not going to ask, are you?"

"Ask what?"

"You know what."

"You can tell?"

"I can feel it in your aura."

"Oh, my aura," she said sceptically.

"You just watched me heal the sick with a magic spell, but auras are where you draw the line? I'm not talking about the aura photographs you can get in a new age shop. I know you felt mine."

Jason let his aura gently brush against hers, showing off the delicacy of his aura control. She felt the domineering nature of his aura power, Hegemony, along with the unyielding resolve that came from all that his soul had endured.

"So that's you," she said after recovering from the strange sensation.

"I'm not as serious as my aura might imply. I'm actually pretty funny."

"Most people who say they're funny, are not," she said.

"Ouch."

"I think it's time for you to go," she told him.

"Why didn't you ask me to heal you?"

"You've given us miracles enough. What's a little cancer next to what these people are going through? I can go home and do all the chemo I like. All they can do is lie there and hope not to die. You should be moving on to more of them."

Jason gave her a warm smile. He held up a hand, repeating the chant in the language she didn't understand.

As with the patients before her, her red life force was brought out, cleansed and returned to her. She felt like a fresh breeze had just passed through her whole body.

"You're a good egg, Chloe Baudrillard."

He plucked a pen and notebook from thin air, scribbling a note and tearing out the page before handing it to her.

"You'll be busy with this for a while, but when you're done, come find me. I'll show you how to heal in ways you never imagined. You do want to do what I just did, right?"

"You're saying I could…"

"Some variation on it, yes. If I show you how."

She looked down at the paper in her hand.

"Jason Asano," she read.

"That's my name," he said. "I'd appreciate you keeping it under your hat."

She looked up from the paper, her eyes searching his face for answers.

"Why me?"

"Because you didn't ask," he said.

A black UTV, something between a quad bike and a car, was moving along a road of red dirt, between vibrantly green bushes and trees. The man in the driver seat was not driving but instead narrating to the recording crystal floating over his head.

Losing power due to low levels of ambient magic was a problem for magic items, especially weaker and cheaper ones like recording crystals. Fortunately, Jason's inventory was able to replenish the depleted magic of objects, so long as Jason himself wasn't mana-starved. Since the transfiguration of his body and soul through the World-Phoenix's blessing, Jason no longer needed spirit coins to keep his magic levels up, or even consume them for food, so that was not an issue. The steady trickle of power from the astral he now enjoyed sustained him both physically and magically.

"You could use a non-magical recording solution," Shade suggested as Jason put the recording crystal away.

"Recording crystals adjust to the movement of the vehicle so there isn't a jiggled image."

"Are you suggesting my suspension system is insufficient?"

"Not in the least," Jason said. "This is as comfortable a ride as I could hope. As always, Shade, you excel."

As they continued on, a magic item on the passenger seat began glowing with silver light and made a low hum. It looked like an oversized compass.

"It's not even two o'clock and this is the second one today," Jason said, picking up the device. Farrah had devised the compass after digging into the nature of the Network's detection grid. There was some resistance to giving her access from certain elements of the Network, but that changed as sections of the grid started experiencing failures. At that point, Farrah became a valued part of a multi-branch investigative task force.

When it started happening, Jason had offered to return immediately.

"Not wanting to seem rude," Farrah said, "but you won't actually be able to help. This is an array magic thing and you just don't have the expertise."

"The grid involves astral magic too, right?"

"Yes, but the astral magic part works fine. It's the bones that need looking at. Not everything is about you, Jason."

The grid compass alerted Jason to proto-space formations in the vicinity by tapping into the grid. At the pivot-point of the needle was a crystal that glowed different colours, according to the strength. Smaller crystals gave a rough indication of distance by how many lit up.

"Seventy klicks," Jason said. "Silver rank too."

The UTV pulled to a stop and Jason got out. The vehicle transformed into a cloud of darkness, most of which disappeared into Jason's shadow. The remainder took the form of Shade.

"My supply of coins is getting low," Shade said. "I'll need more if we're going to fly."

"Ask and ye shall receive, my friend," Jason said, producing a box of coins.

Neither Shade nor Jason needed coins in the low-magic conditions, although Jason still needed coins if he wasn't consuming large amounts of food. He had no shortage since he was interceding in proto-spaces at least once, and often two or even three times, daily. Shade needed coins to supplement high-energy forms like flying vehicles. Only once he was silver-rank would Shade be able to fly in an energy-efficient manner.

When he jumped in on proto-spaces, Jason was leaving behind the bulk of the silver-rank loot for the locals and satisfying himself with bronze-rank spoils. Leaving behind the best goodies with no work required made for exasperated responses from the local branches, but no actual complaints. Not since leaving China anyway.

"Actually," Jason said, pulling a completed recording crystal from his inventory, "take this too, please."

Shade put the coins and the crystal in his own dimensional space. It was significantly smaller than Jason's but could be accessed through any of his bodies. This meant that Jason could send his recording to his niece Emi via Shade. She sent him back gifts in return, like biscuits she made with her mother.

Shade then took the form of a new vehicle, an ultralight trike. Not much more than a seat with a motor behind it, with glider wings over the top, it was also black with a few white embellishments.

"I'm not sure black is especially safety-conscious," Jason said.

"I could transform into a regular tricycle instead," Shade suggested.

"No, this is good."

Using the road as a runway, they were soon soaring over the landscape. Seventy kilometres would be roughly a half-hour trip.

"I know it's probably time to be looking towards heading home," Jason said, enjoying the wind flowing over him. "I'm having an absolute blast, though. I would love to bring Erika's family on a trip like this. Minus the monster-slaying and horrifying misery of the plague camps, obviously."

"You have responsibilities, as vaguely defined as they are, right now," Shade said.

"Meaning that I don't even know what they are," Jason said.

"I believe that Dawn will eventually contact you again for further explanation. The failures in the grid may not be unrelated."

"I was thinking the same thing. I don't want to leave while this Ebola outbreak is still ongoing, though. It's nice to use what I can do to help solve a non-magical problem that affects so many people. It's exactly what I imagined back in Greenstone."

3
A MODERN MYTH

"...SPOKESPERSONS FROM MÉDECINS SANS FRONTIÈRES AND THE WORLD Health Organisation have both dismissed claims of miracle healing, stating that the success in containing the outbreak is due to experience and the protocols established during the 2013-2016 outbreak. Evangelical aid group Samaritan's Purse has officially echoed these statements, but unnamed sources within the organisation have referred to what they describe as divine visitations—"

Mr North paused the recording playing on the wall monitor. The Four Cardinals of the EOA—Mr North, Mrs South, Mr East and Mrs West—were seated around a square table. Lined up on the opposite wall to the large monitor were their various subordinates.

"Preparations are taking longer than expected," Mr North said. "We need to reassess our response to Asano's activities."

"Before we start looking towards action, we need a revised time frame for our agenda," Mrs South said. "When will we be ready to act?"

"Disabling the grid is proving more difficult than anticipated," Mr East said. "To date, we have been successful in shutting off only localised areas."

He glanced at Adrien Barbou, who was standing against the wall with Mrs West's other flunkies.

"The information provided by Mrs West's new subordinate has been useful in accelerating our progress in that regard. Our problems have come in enacting a wide-scale loss of grid functionality."

"Surmountable problems, I assume, or you would have reported your inability to complete your task to us," Mrs West said.

"Our original estimates were based on the scale of the grid," Mr East explained. "Only once we attempted to scale up did we discover the key issue. The grid appears to have some manner of self-repair function. Whoever originally devised it apparently anticipated localised failures and developed a system by which surrounding areas compensate and restore the damaged areas. The Lyon Network branch had to repeatedly disable the grid to hide the astral space that formed in Saint-Étienne."

"And the solution?" Mr North asked.

"The same thing that is impeding us will also enable us to achieve our goal with less direct intervention than originally anticipated. We have been making attacks on grid infrastructure, disabling various sectors around the world as we mapped out the nodes critical to the self-repair function. Once we've identified them, simultaneous strikes on these critical nodes will cause the entire infrastructure to fail."

"What about the risks of this mapping process?" Mrs South asked.

"Obviously," Mr East said, "this has come at the risk of exposing our activities to the Network. Their response teams are active, but our agents within the Network have kept them from intercepting our teams thus far. Mrs West's new associate maintains a number of Network contacts and has been useful in this regard."

The cardinals glanced at Barbou.

"If the Network traces your activities back to us before we act, they will intervene," Mrs South said. "Again, I ask for a timeline. Our original intention was to have made our move by now. How much longer do we have to risk discovery?"

"I anticipate two more months," Mr East said.

"Very well," Mr North said. "Mrs West, you will add your resources to Mr East's efforts, in order to keep the Network from drawing too close while he completes his work?"

Mrs West nodded her acknowledgement.

"Then that leads us back to the issue of Jason Asano," Mr North said. "Now that our time estimates have been extended, we need to revisit the impact of his activities on our intentions. He is far more brazen than the

Network about employing his capabilities and that is entering the public consciousness. Thus far, the attention has been minimal and contained, but we need to formulate a response before that impacts our own goals negatively. I know you have each had your people analysing the issue, so I suggest we listen to the potential responses they have devised."

The other cardinals nodded.

"Very well," Mr North said. "Keenan, we'll begin with you. What is your proposed response?"

One of Mr North's subordinates stepped forward.

"The mistake that every person to antagonise Asano has made," he said confidently, glancing at Barbou, "is that they have always employed half-measures. Asano needs to be dealt with using direct and overwhelming force. I have developed a proposal by which we incite the Network branches here in the US to eliminate Asano using their own category threes. We already know that the US elite operatives have superior capabilities, commensurate with Asano himself, but they are above his current rank. Unlike the category threes of the French and Vietnamese, Asano will be unable to overcome one of them, let alone multiples."

"You advocate elimination," Mr North said.

"I do, sir. If you'll allow, I can elaborate on my plans to spur the US branches into action, predicated on Asano's known anti-American prejudice."

"Perhaps before that," Mrs West interjected, "we might hear from an alternative perspective."

"Agreed," Mrs South said.

"Very well," Mr North said.

"Adrien," Mrs West said. "Please share your proposal."

Barbou stepped forward, throwing Keenan a glance as Mr North's subordinate stepped back.

"To contextualise my proposal," Barbou said, "I feel I should first respond to the idea of employing direct force against Asano. Frankly, that is the most idiotic path we could conceivably pursue. Every man, woman or thing pitted against Asano has fallen short, myself included. He's been outranked, outnumbered, ambushed, suppressed and blown up. The last category three we know to have confronted him not only stood above him in rank but possessed specific counters to Asano's key abilities. That man did not suffer so much as a scratch at Asano's hands, yet to this day, he remains terrified at the idea of ever encountering him again."

Barbou threw another look at Keenan.

"I'm not saying that I believe Asano could defeat a team of category-three elites from the US Network."

He turned his gaze back to the cardinals.

"The point is that I neither over nor underestimate Asano. Putting him down might work. Might. But that uncertainty is not a reliable basis on which to move forward. Assuming nothing goes wrong in my associate's plan to push the Network into mobilising some of their most powerful assets, Asano would definitely not defeat them. But does he need to? Victory may not be possible, but escape is. We already know that he is highly elusive, even from category-three senses."

Barbou panned his gaze across the cardinals.

"Asano can demonstrably poach from any dimensional incursion at will and seems to be doing so for the purpose of growing stronger. Right now, he's remaining relatively predictable, but if he wanted to be more evasive about it, he certainly could be. I can't speak for you, but I don't want that man out there going hardcore guerrilla warfare, building up his strength in the darkness, waiting for the moment to hit back."

He once more looked to Keenan.

"What do we do if we strike out and miss, only for him to come back stronger than ever? Right now, his power is limited but incredibly strong for his rank. Do you want to take that man on at category three? I don't. What do we do if it reaches that point? Convince the US Network to bring one of their category fours out of stasis?"

"You know about those?" Mr North asked. "The Americans were only participating in the debate over creating category fours to hide that they already have them, knowing that they're useless without gold spirit coins. I didn't realise the international branches were aware of this."

"It's not widely known," Barbou said. "There have always been rumours within the Network. I just happen to know that they are true."

Keenan snorted his derision.

"You're so well informed about the US branches?" he asked. "You French are a bunch of second-raters compared to the Network branches here. Why would we believe that you knew anything?"

Barbou gave Keenan the smile he would give an obnoxious child he was trying to indulge so they wouldn't throw a tantrum.

"As a whole," Barbou explained, "Americans dislike the French. Individually, however, Americans find the French quite alluring. Their operational security is far less stringent than the United States branches like to tell themselves."

A smile played across Mr North's lips.

"An issue the Americans have had with multiple countries," he said. "Their field operatives are solid, but their management has had… issues."

"My proposal," Barbou said finally, "is the exact opposite of bringing the hammer down. We help Asano."

Aside from Mrs West, that earned raised eyebrows from the cardinals.

"I'm intrigued," Mrs South said. "Please expand on that."

"We don't need to stop what Asano is doing," Barbou said. "We need to change the way we look at the situation. We're worried about him stealing our thunder, but there's plenty of thunder to go around. So long as he isn't forced to go public before we're ready, he's laying the groundwork for everything we need to do."

"You're saying we use him as a stalking horse for the public revelation of magic," Mr North said.

"Exactly. When the time comes, we reap the benefits of every child he rescues from earthquake damage and camp full of sick people he cures. All we have to do is make sure that he remains a rumour while still working his way into the public consciousness."

"A modern myth," Mr North said.

"Precisely. The Network has all the government influence, but we have the media power, which is exactly what we need. We let him prime the pump for when we draw the water. And if he needs to be dealt with then, we let the public do it. We have footage of Asano killing people in nicely graphic ways."

Mrs South narrowed her eyes at Barbou.

"You're the one who prompted the Vietnamese to go after him, aren't you?"

"I have no idea what you're talking about," Barbou said with a smile. "I was just fortunate enough to get ahold of the footage before the Network eliminated it all."

Flying through the sky on Shade, the ultralight trike, Jason felt it as he approached the region coterminous to the proto-space and put away the grid compass.

"Alright, Shade," he said as his cloak manifested around him. Shade's vehicle form turned into darkness and returned to Jason's body. The starlight cloak swept out like wings of night and Jason started gliding. Shade could not transition into the astral space, even hidden in Jason's shadow as he normally was. Only when they were fully unmanifested could Jason carry his familiars across.

Gliding through the air, Jason let his aura bleed into the ambient magic. Spending time around proto-spaces had been excellent for his aura control. His aura was the means he used to insinuate himself through the dimensional membrane. He felt out the dimensional barrier separating Earth's physical reality and the proto-space, then passed through it like it was a curtain of water.

As he glided through the air, the African landscape sprawled out below him blurred and then was replaced with an entirely different vista. The terrain below him was now a snow-strewn taiga, looking more like Russia than Africa, although with one feature native to neither. Odd, alien ziggurats dotted the landscape, dusted white with snow.

Shade re-emerged, retaking the form of the ultralight trike, already in flight. Settling back into the seat, Jason pulled out a computer tablet. This was the standard-issue magitech tracker that the Network used to track the anchor dimensional entities that were the key to containing proto-spaces. Shade did the flying as Jason navigated them in the direction of their targets.

Shelia was the Director of Tactical Operations for the Network's Monrovia branch and was first through the aperture once the ritual team cracked it open. The taiga terrain was fairly hospitable, albeit cold after arriving from an African late summer. She immediately organised the teams that followed.

After the sweeper teams secured the area around the aperture on the inside of the proto-space, the support teams were brought in and set up camp. Assessments were quickly made.

"Director," one of Shelia's subordinates said as he approached. "The detectors aren't registering an anchor entity. We can move straight on to farming the rest of the monsters. Also, the stability readings say the space will hold for more than sixty hours."

"He's still here," Shelia said. "Was there any indication that anyone else had opened the aperture?"

"None. I would go as far as to say that there was definitively no prior use of the aperture."

Shelia sighed.

"How is he getting in and out?" she mused.

"I could just leave through the aperture you've conveniently opened up there," Jason said, emerging from the shadow of an awning set up by the support teams. A dozen guns were instantaneously pointed at him.

"Harsh," he said. "Lovely to see you again, Shelia."

"I take it that you have dealt with the anchor dimensional entity, Mr Asano?"

"Actually, it was a triple, so I snagged a few silver spirit coins for myself. I still left most of them for you, of course. They were all on top of those weird ziggurats, so you shouldn't have any trouble finding the loot. I did scoop up an essence, though. I didn't realise that a hair essence was a thing, so I couldn't help myself. I did leave you that sun essence the other day, so I don't feel super bad. Do you think I could do a Medusa confluence with this hair essence? Probably add in snake and earth, is what I'm thinking."

Shelia plastered on a transparently false smile.

"We've been instructed to extend you every courtesy, Mr Asano. By all means, feel free to immediately depart via the aperture."

"Well, gee, Shelia. You almost make a guy feel unwanted."

"I've been specifically directed not to express that sentiment."

"Oh, you have?"

"Yes."

"Someone felt the need to go out of their way to tell you to not tell me that my presence was unwanted?"

"They did."

"They mustn't be aware of our great dynamic."

"Actually, I've been quite clear on that issue in my reports, Mr Asano. The aperture is right there, so please go ahead and use it."

4
BREAKNECK PACE

"Do you have any idea of the disarray you've thrown my life into?" Chloe asked.

Outside of her hazmat suit, she had plain, blockish features and light clothes chosen for the Moroccan heat. She was sitting with Jason at a teahouse in Marrakech.

"Oh, I'm well aware of how magical revelations in the middle of a crisis can throw you off. Whether you sink or swim teaches you a lot about yourself."

"Well, thank you," Chloe said. "While I may have felt like I was going insane for a while, I can't begin to express our gratitude for what you've done. For me, obviously, but the outbreak went from potentially years down to months."

"I'm just a man who happens to have a useful gift," Jason said. "It's the people who don't have my advantages yet throw everything into helping others that truly warrant praise. The ones working day in and day out, putting themselves at risk. You and your colleagues can't just magic away sickness. Not to mention that there are others like me, working on less self-aggrandising and more long-term efforts."

"I was surprised that you found me here," she said. "I intended to go find you in Australia, once I'd been home."

"I just happened to be in Marrakech and sensed your presence."

"You sensed my presence? One person in a whole city?"

Ability: [Midnight Eyes] (Dark)

- Special ability (perception).
- Base cost: None.
- Cooldown: None.

- Current rank: Silver 0 (00%).

- Effect (iron): See through darkness.
- Effect (bronze): Sense magic.
- Effect (silver): Enhanced aura senses.

- Ability [Midnight Eyes] (Dark) cannot advance further until all attributes have reached silver rank.

Perception powers were always the first to rank up and Jason's ongoing aura control practise had caused his perception power to outpace his other abilities even further. The effect of a silver-rank perception power enhancing his aura senses was far more impactful than he realised. Combined with the raw strength of his soul and his semi-spiritual nature both enhancing those senses already, the effect had been a level of sensory overload that left him almost debilitated for the better part of a week. He was only now recovering as he got a handle on his new level of perceptual strength.

The attribute that governed perception was spirit, and while Jason's was in the upper echelons of bronze rank, it wasn't enough for him to handle the explosion of sensory input when his power crossed the threshold into silver. Fortunately, it had taken place as he meditated in a random patch of African wilderness, far from prying eyes and ill intentions.

It had been like going from black and white to colour as he realised that the aura senses he already had were crude and oblivious to his surroundings, however sharp he had thought them to be. He could now sense the auras of everything around him. He had thought that only thinking beings with souls had auras, with some magic-based exceptions, but now he learned that the trees, grass, and even the wind had echoes of aura.

It wasn't the true auras he was already aware of but some kind of intrinsic nature related to the interplay of physical reality and the astral that lay hidden beyond it. He suspected that his own nature gave him some unique insight that others might not share.

His familiars had stood guard as he spent days acclimatising to his new senses. After so long working on aura control, he found his senses to be powerful enough that he now required sensory control. The advancement of his perception ability did more than enhance sensitivity. He now had much more control of how all his senses operated. This only added to the disorientation as he grew used to it.

As he adjusted to the changes, he realised just how much of a difference it would be. His hearing could filter out sounds and focus on distant noises. His vision could adjust to see or ignore different light spectrums. His smell and taste could block out specific sensations, which was critically useful given his new sensitivity.

The most overwhelming aspect of his new aura sense was the sheer range. His unique advantages and the raw soul power he possessed allowed his senses to spread over a huge distance. If he had been in a city instead of the empty wilderness, he would have half-expected a brain aneurysm.

After the initial onslaught of sensation, he spent hour after hour, day after day in meditation as he brought his senses under control. The initial experience was like being in a kaleidoscope at a heavy metal concert held in a compost silo. Over the course of a week, he learned to draw back and filter the raw sensations, then started to explore the potential of his newly enhanced perception.

Auras, he discovered, were far more sophisticated and nuanced than he previously realised. He had become satisfied with his aura control after months of practise, only to realise that he was only beginning to master it. His new awareness revealed how far he had yet to go.

In the week he spent in the wilderness, working on his sensory control, he had dropped off the radar of those tracking his activities. He stopped poaching proto-spaces and appearing at humanitarian aid stations. He decided it was for the best, at least regarding the Ebola outbreak.

The outbreak was being brought under control. His contributions would no longer be worth the attention they brought, especially as there was an increasing movement on the internet connecting his various activities. Despite not using his cloak, the connection was being made between his camp visits and the Starlight Angel persona that had dominated the Australian media nine months earlier.

Jason refocused on developing his abilities, starting with his new sensory power. He made quiet appearances in larger and larger population centres, learning to balance the sensitivity so he wouldn't get overwhelmed. He worked his way up to Marrakech and was getting ready to meet people when he had recognised Chloe's aura and decided to say hello, inviting her to join him in a tea house.

"No one is sure what to make of you," Chloe told him. "None of the testing we've done in the wake of your activities makes any kind of sense. If we tried writing papers on it, they would never pass peer review. On myself, included. It's like the cancer was never there. I keep waiting to wake up and realise that it really is impossible and I dreamed the whole thing."

"I know how you feel. After I was introduced to magic, I was semi-convinced it was all me going insane until my friend died and brought me down to Earth," Jason said. "Although I wasn't actually on Earth at the time. You'll meet her soon; she's on her way here now."

"I'll meet who?"

"My friend who died."

"She's not dead anymore?"

"She got better. Eventually. I come back much quicker than she did every time I die."

"What?"

Jason had pulsed his aura like a beacon as he sensed the plane carrying Farrah and the others arrive. He also sent along enough bodies that Shade could take the form of a car large enough to carry them comfortably.

As they arrived outside the teahouse, Jason assessed their auras. Farrah was still in the early stages of silver rank, although her progression would largely stall until they found their way back to her homeworld. Erika and Ian were both midway through iron, having taken cores regularly in the time he'd been away. Emi's aura was still normal rank, but he could sense some lingering magic attached to it.

Emi had frequently talked with Uncle Jason via Shade. She was especially excited about her ritual magic lessons with Farrah, which had taken the sting out of not being old enough for essences. She had recently moved on to some very basic practical elements, the residual effect of which Jason could sense.

Prior to his aura senses being enhanced, that wouldn't have been possible. He was even able to recognise that elements of her aura were still in flux. He suspected that once they stabilised, she would be ready for essences. He would need to examine her aura further to get a sense of how long that would be. He knew a simple ritual that could check, but he wanted to ask Farrah if high-rankers could just tell through their aura senses.

Farrah and Erika's family entered and spotted them; Jason and Chloe rose to greet them. Emi lunged to trap Jason in a hug. As he wrapped his arms around his niece, he gave the others a bright smile.

"Dr Baudrillard, let me introduce you to my family," Jason said in French. "This is my sister, Erika, her husband, Ian, and their daughter, um…"

Jason took on an absent-minded expression, then his face lit up with recollection.

"…Ellie," he said. "This is my niece, Ellie."

"Bête comme ses pieds," Emi said to him.

"What do you mean, dumb as my feet?" Jason asked.

"It's a French insult," Chloe said after snorting a laugh.

Jason turned to Ian.

"Sorry, I didn't ask," he said. "How's your French, Ian?"

"It's fine, isn't it, dear?" Erika said in French.

"Er... oui," Ian said.

"I'm fine with English," Chloe said, using the language in demonstration. She had only a slight accent.

"This is actually our daughter *Emi*," Erika correctly introduced. Emi was glaring at her uncle but had to lean back to do so, unwilling to relinquish her grip on him.

"And this is Farrah," Jason said, "who is my friend from an alternate reality."

"What?" Chloe asked.

"You know, Jason," Farrah said, "I think I'm coming around on not letting you introduce people to magic. You just love throwing the wildest stuff at them and watching them get confused."

"You should probably leave it to the professionals and just satisfy yourself watching reaction videos online," Emi said.

"Hey," Jason said, mock-hurt. "Oh, and family, this is Dr Chloe Baudrillard, of Doctors Without Borders."

"Lovely to meet you," Erika said, shaking her hand, then moving over to hug Jason over the top of her daughter.

"You know, Jason," Farrah said, "the Network doesn't like you just arbitrarily offering magic to people."

"Tell them that I don't like that they occasionally try to kill and/or kidnap me," Jason said.

"She told them to stick it up their—"

"Emi!" Erika scolded.

"At this point, I think they're happy you told them at all," Farrah said. "I think Anna sees you as a puppy resistant to toilet training."

They settled in and arranged for drinks, Emi boxing Jason against the wall like she was afraid he'd run off. They had remained in contact via Shade, but it wasn't the same as meeting up in person. Farrah had been heading to Greece to investigate a grid failure and she had brought along her new apprentice, since Jason was only a hop across the Mediterranean. Emi's parents were not going to just let their daughter traipse off to Europe, so they decided to make a family reunion of it, after which they would return to Australia together.

Jason was eager to discuss the grid failures with Farrah, who had largely shut him out of the investigation to let him focus on getting his head right. In the wake of her captivity, he had supported her as much as he could as she slowly opened up. She, in turn, recognised that what he needed was space to settle himself.

He could have made an issue of inserting himself into the problems with the grid, but he knew she was doing what was best for him. He trusted her to call on him if he was actually needed.

Chloe departed, having her own travel plans. Before they parted ways, Jason reassured her that there were secrets and wonders waiting for her in Australia.

"She seems nice," Erika said.

"She's been sick," Farrah said. "Did you heal her of something?"

Farrah's senses were also enhanced enough to notice the lingering turbulence in Chloe's aura.

"She had cancer," Jason explained. "She decided to use what time she had to help people, which is why I wanted to help her."

"She's been vetted by the Network now," Farrah said. "They didn't turn up any problems."

"Gladys is actually excited to work with her," Ian said. He himself had been working with Gladys at the clinic following Jason's departure.

"Let's forget about all that for now," Jason said. "I've planned a family trip to the Ouzoud Waterfall. No monsters, no Network. Just some quality family time. I've seen some beautiful things while I've been out and about, and it'll be nice to see some more of them together."

Alone in a sleeping cabin on the Network's private plane, Jason contemplated the journey now coming to an end. He had two goals starting out, the first of which was coming to terms with the feeling of being caught between two worlds. His need to reconcile the person he had become in the other world with who he needed to be in his original one was his main impetus for starting the journey.

Moving across Asia, through the Middle East and into Africa, it was fighting the outbreak where he finally felt things coming together. Bringing magic from one world to another in a way that wasn't about violence and death was exactly what he needed. It took him back to his early days in the other world, using his powers to heal people.

As his adventuring duties grew more pressing and the Church of the Healer started living up to their responsibilities, that early motivation had fallen to the wayside. Now he had come back to that place, reclaiming some of the innocence he had drowned in blood. Not all the changes he went through in the other world were good ones.

It would take time and pressure to know if he'd really found the balance he sought when his journey started. For the moment, he felt that he had, which was enough to be going on with. That left the secondary goal of advancing his abilities.

In the other world, whenever things got too much, he would head out into the delta, clearing every adventure board he could find of monsters. It allowed him to channel all his negative feelings, venting them in a way that was at least a little productive. Those were the times he pushed himself the hardest, always rushing to the next monster.

This journey had not been exactly the same, but the ability to chase down proto-spaces instead of monster notices had the same side-benefit of grinding out the advancement of his abilities.

He had been back in his own world for nine months and bronze rank for a year. Contrary to his expectations, being on his homeworld had not stalled out his advancement. The magically saturated proto-spaces on Earth had even more monsters than the astral space in which he had reached bronze rank. The problem was that, unlike in the astral space, they weren't disastrously escalating in power to match his growing strength. Few bronze-rank monsters posed a threat to his current skills and abilities.

JASON ASANO

- Race: Outworlder.
- Current rank: bronze
- Progression to silver rank: 72.5%

Attributes

- [Power] (Blood): [Bronze 7].
- [Speed] (Dark): [Bronze 8].
- [Spirit] (Doom): [Bronze 7].
- [Recovery] (Sin): [Bronze 7].

RACIAL ABILITIES (OUTWORLDER)

- [Party Interface].
- [Defiant].
- [Spirit Vault].
- [Tactical Map].
- [Nirvanic Transfiguration].
- [Dark Rider].

ESSENCES (4/4)

Dark [Speed] (5/5)

- [Midnight Eyes] (special ability): [Silver 0] 00%.
- [Cloak of Night] (special ability): [Bronze 8] 97%.
- [Path of Shadows] (special ability): [Bronze 8] 42%.
- [Hand of the Reaper] (special ability): [Bronze 8] 76%.
- [Shadow of the Reaper] (familiar): [Bronze 9] 04%.

Blood [Power] (5/5)

- [Blood Harvest] (spell): [Bronze 7] 68%.
- [Leech Bite] (special attack): [Bronze 8] 86%.
- [Feast of Blood] (spell): [Bronze 7] 37%.
- [Sanguine Horror] (familiar): [Bronze 7] 98%.
- [Haemorrhage] (spell): [Bronze 8] 84%.

Sin [Recovery] (5/5)

- [Punish] (special attack): [Bronze 8] 84%.
- [Feast of Absolution] (spell): [Bronze 7] 66%.
- [Sin Eater] (special ability): [Bronze 7] 79%.
- [Hegemony] (aura): [Bronze 8] 24%.
- [Castigate] (spell): [Bronze 8] 83%.

Doom [Spirit] (5/5)

- [Inexorable Doom] (spell): [Bronze 8] 89%.
- [Punition] (spell): [Bronze 8] 50%.
- [Blade of Doom] (spell): [Bronze 8] 66%.
- [Verdict] (spell): [Bronze 7] 11%.
- [Avatar of Doom] (familiar): [Bronze 7] 91%.

Jason had spent about a year and a quarter going from iron to bronze—a completely normal timeframe. The standard progression from bronze to silver was three years, although that was a highly flexible number. The two most impactful factors in the speed of advancement were opportunity and dedication. Monster surges could shave months off that time and Jason had experienced a private monster surge that had lasted for months. If it had come at the end of his progression through bronze instead of the beginning, he probably could have broken some kind of speed record. He wondered if Farrah knew what the record was.

The latter stages of a rank were much harder to push through than the early ones. If he kept up the pace he had taken during his journey, then he could probably close out bronze rank in half a year. A year and a half for the entire rank was already a breakneck pace to reach silver, which he would be extremely happy with.

His concern was the warning they had received from Dawn. He needed to solve an issue that, ironically, would give him exactly what he needed.

If the magical density of the proto-spaces escalated, he would have the monsters he needed to halve his time to silver.

The repercussions, however, were not worth it. It would take time before the Network was ready to handle more powerful monsters; failing to shutdown proto-spaces would only accelerate the problem. He was concerned enough with the grid blackouts, and now that his time away was over, it was time to involve himself. As if in answer to his ruminations, there was a knock at the door.

"Come in," Jason said, having sensed Farrah on the other side of the door to his private cabin. She stepped in. "Alright. Time to catch me up."

5
GRAND TOUR

"It's definitely sabotage," Farrah said. "The Network is convinced that the EOA is behind it, and I have no reason to doubt them. They know the local politics a lot better than me."

"As it was explained to me," Jason said, "the EOA's agenda is built around the knowledge of magic going public. Are they tired of waiting and trying to accelerate the process?"

"That's the prevailing assumption," Farrah said. "Our best guess is that they're trying to get lucky and have a proto-space go uncaught while the grid is down in an area. That happening at the bottom of the ocean is one thing; we have crazy sailor stories in my world too."

"But if it happens in the middle of a city…"

"Exactly. The grid has a self-repair function, so the blackouts don't last more than three or four days. If we don't start intercepting these attacks, though, sooner or later, a proto-space will appear in an area where the grid has gone dark and we won't know until it's too late."

"I'm curious about the actual infrastructure of the grid," Jason said. "How does that work, exactly? Are there a bunch of secret chambers buried all around the world?"

"It's quite fascinating," Farrah said. "At least to someone with my specialty. It's unlike anything I've seen before. The locals barely understand it and neither do I. The more I study it, the more I learn and, world-ending consequences aside, I'm loving it. The principles on which the grid is built are as revelatory to my understanding of formation magic as those books you have are to astral magic. Probably more so."

"That's quite a claim. What makes it so unique?"

"The grid infrastructure isn't like a normal formation array of permanent ritual circles. Each node is enormous and not made from a ritual circle at all. It's like the landscape is somehow operating as a series of interconnected rituals, creating a magical array from the natural features of the world itself. We're talking about nodes the size of cities, with elements made up of mountains, hills and rivers to form a magical array covering the entire planet."

"Like feng shui or ley lines or something."

"Exactly," Farrah said. "I've been reading up on those since I started investigating the grid. That Li Li Mei who tried to rope you onto China's team sent me some materials on Chinese geomancy."

She gave Jason a wry look.

"What?" he asked.

"She asked about you, you know."

He shrugged his shoulders, looking smug.

"What I have can't be taught," Jason said.

"Nor should it be. What about Asya?"

"That's not so easy," Jason said with a frustrated grimace. "Yes, she's smart, gorgeous and I must have been blind back in school. But there's an unfair dynamic when I can constantly sense her emotions."

"That should be less of an issue," Farrah said. "I made her a bracelet that gold-rankers with no aura control use to keep their auras from popping regular people's heads like pimples. She can't use her aura and it tamps down her own aura senses, but if she wears it around you, you shouldn't be able to read her. Not unless you actively try, anyway. Your aura senses must be monstrous now."

"You've got no idea," Jason said. He went on to explain his troubles adapting to his new sensory strength. Afterwards, they got back onto topic as Farrah continued to explain about how the grid functioned.

"These giant nodes in the landscape have the nuance and flexibility to adapt as the landscape shifts over the centuries. I'm still only starting to get my head around it. The brilliance it would take to devise a system like this is staggering."

"How do you build something like that into existing landscape?"

"I suspect that whoever built the grid actually shifted the landscape to make it work."

"That's possible? I know earth-shaping is a thing, but that kind of scale? Again and again, all across the world?"

"A gold-ranker with the right powers and enough time could manage it. Eventually. The records the Network have of their founder indicate it was a process of many years."

"The grid is low-level magic, though, right?" Jason asked.

"Yes. The power level is low, which allows it to operate continuously with your world's low magic. The principles behind it, though, have a level of subtle sophistication that screams that the designer was diamond rank. The way it blends into the ambient magic so undetectably. Even you can't sense it, right?"

"I can't," Jason said. "What you're describing reminds me of the Mirror King's aura. That had the same property of blending in with the ambient magic. I drew inspiration for my new aura control techniques from that."

"You met the Mirror King?"

"Only briefly. If the grid really was designed by someone on his level, how does that work? Dawn said that a diamond-ranker here would be a huge problem."

"My guess is that the designer was not the same person that put the grid in place. It's more likely that a diamond-ranker designed it and someone else brought it here and adapted it. Even that much suggests an incredibly capable expert, and they would have to be gold rank to alter the landscape like that. It would still take years, probably decades, and they would need a stockpile of gold spirit coins. When the magic is as low as it is in your world, substituting higher numbers of lower-ranked coins wouldn't be enough."

"What do you think happened when they ran out?" Jason wondered. "Left the world again? It was hundreds of years ago, but a gold-ranker can live that long, right?"

"If they're still alive, they almost have to be gone," Farrah said. "An essence user needs three coins a day in the course of normal activity. A low-ranker can get away with lower-rank coins or lots of regular food, even in this world, but not a gold-ranker. That's over a thousand gold coins a year. If they're largely inactive, they could probably cut it by a third, but that's still hundreds of thousands of coins if they've been here since the grid was put in place."

"You think someone brought that many coins with them?"

"It's not totally inconceivable, but I have to imagine even a diamond-ranker would have trouble collecting that much as a lump sum of coins. At that rank, they operate on more of a barter system for valuable items and materials. Only a fraction of what Emir gets paid is in spirit coins when he works for diamond-rankers."

"They're probably not here anymore, then."

"More likely they either left this world or got magic-starved and died. I've heard it's a rough way to go, but it almost never happens in my world. There's usually magic enough and gold-rankers don't have trouble finding work. I've only heard stories of it happening to outcasts, like people with restricted essences."

"So, what is the Network doing about the sabotage?" Jason asked.

"The problem is that for all the adaptability of the grid that prevents incidental disruption, a concerted effort can shut things off fairly easily."

"And if the nodes are as big as you say," Jason said, "there's no way to guard them."

"Exactly," Farrah said. "What's worse is that we don't know if we're even registering all the blackouts. The Lyon branch was able to mask their suppression of the local grid for years. The International Committee is still riding herd over the French branches, but a lot of their members have mysteriously vanished."

"Has Adrien Barbou resurfaced?" Jason asked.

"No, but we think either he or others from the Lyon branch are helping whoever is behind this, based on their knowledge of the grid."

"He's worked with the EOA before," Jason said. "What's the Network doing about the EOA?"

"Piling on the pressure, but it's going nowhere. The EOA claim that they're too cellular in nature to coordinate systemic attacks on the grid."

"But you think they're lying."

"There's a growing sense that the EOA might not be as fractious and scattered as they appear. We've seen indications of an underlying authority guiding their actions."

"I really hope it's not the Builder," Jason said, shaking his head.

"You think it could be?"

"I don't know," Jason said. "I've seen some of the EOA's modified people. The process seems to be different, but I've seen the Builder modify people as well. Maybe Dawn knows more. Have you seen her since…?"

"Since you punched her so hard she died? No. I don't think I'd want to see us after that either. Once I found out that she hid where I was from you, I wanted to punch her too."

"Maybe we should try and contact her," Jason suggested. "If proto-spaces start dumping monsters into the world, not only does the world turn into chaos, but the timeline for world collapse gets accelerated. Some more direction might help us onto the right path."

"I suspect she'll contact us when she feels like it and not before," Farrah said. "For now, leave investigating the EOA to the Network. You and I may have the edge in a fight, but we're out of our depth when it comes to the interplay between sprawling global organisations. I'll keep studying the grid and you focus on hitting silver as quick as you can. You'll also need to catch up with the Network and what your family has been up to."

"Oh?"

"Your father and your uncle have been industrious."

"This is incredible," Jason said.

Although Ken and Hiro were his ostensible guides through the new family compound, it was Emi who was dragging him by the hand, pointing everything out. It was hard to believe that, six months ago, this had been undeveloped bushland. Now there was what looked like a whole resort village nestled amongst the trees. The construction was all wood and tile, blending magnificently into the winding gardens and thick bushland. Given how all the plant life was thoroughly grown in, it looked like everything had been in place for years.

There was a main village thoroughfare, with sprawling buildings of rustic wood. Their huge windows only seemed to reflect the gardens and never the other buildings. It added to the feeling of being integrated with nature; Jason could sense the minor but effective magic responsible.

Making their way down the thoroughfare, Jason's guides pointed out multiple gathering halls, an administration building, a food court. Atop the food court was a restaurant, although it was as empty and unused as everything else, thus far.

"A food court and a restaurant?" Jason asked.

"Sometimes you want a communal experience and sometimes you want something fancier and intimate," Ken said.

"I see your lips moving, Dad," Jason said, "but I'm hearing Erika's voice come out."

"Of course we consulted the family chef on dining arrangements," Hiro said.

"Down there are the training facilities," Emi said, pointing out a side street off the main thoroughfare.

"There's also some magic facilities down there that Farrah said we probably won't need for a long time but are best incorporated into the core design of the compound."

"The Network office is down there too," Emi pointed out.

"The Network office?"

"It's just Asya and Auntie Farrah," Emi explained.

"Oh, it's Auntie Farrah now."

"She's reliable," Emi said. "*She* doesn't keep vanishing for months or years at a time."

"That's a little hurtful," Jason said. "Can you still call this a compound? You built an entire small town."

"Pretty much," Hiro said. "All this is just the communal facilities, branching out from the main thoroughfare."

He pointed out some of the streets leading off between the large main buildings.

"Sports facilities down that street, recreational facilities like the spa and gym down that one."

"The spa is huuuge," Emi said. "There's saunas and massage rooms and creepy old man balls bathhouses."

"Emi!"

"What?" she asked. "Every time you see those bathhouses in a movie, it's full of saggy old men in the nude. It's gross."

"What kind of movies is your mum letting you watch?" Jason asked.

"The saggy old man bathhouse is Hiro's personal project," Ken said.

"I am not a saggy old man," Hiro said, and not without reason. Both Ken and Hiro had regained the healthiness of their youth after absorbing essences. If they were able to rank up to bronze, the body transformation might even turn back the clock somewhat.

"The medical centre is down with the spa too," Ken said. "Ian is in charge of that one, although we had a lot of input from his new friend Gladys when we were putting it together."

"We've had useful input from various Network people," Hiro added. "They've got families who've been working with magic for generations, so they helped us avoid a lot of pitfalls. They tried to slip in some surveillance too, but Farrah gave them a sharp slap on the wrist for that."

"All the buildings there behind admin are storage facilities," Ken said. "Farrah wanted to make sure we had plenty of storage for food, construction materials and magical supplies. All magically enhanced, not just warehouses and refrigerators. Once we've stocked up, we can hole up here by the hundreds for months, if need be."

"Here on the main thoroughfare, we have a three-storey pub," Ken said. "It's directly connected to the cinema behind it so you can have a meal and a beer while you watch a movie."

"Once you get away from the central part of town," Hiro said, "you start getting to the residential areas. Only the main family house is here on the thoroughfare, which is that building there."

"That's a house? It's huge."

"The other residential areas have been built in clusters. There's three bushland pods, two beach pods and the clifftop pod. We ended up buying every scrap of land we could here. There were a few residences and holiday homes, but they were happy to sell at the prices we offered. We knocked them all down and worked from scratch."

"How did you afford all this?" Jason asked. "Even with my gold money on top of your original capital, this is way more than what you were talking about when I left. That's even without the magical infrastructure, which may not be visible, but I can sense it. You must have forked over quite a bit to the Network for all this."

"Actually, a lot came from Craig Vermillion and his mysterious sources," Hiro said. "Farrah has been in charge of acquisitions and knows more about that side of things than I do. I do know that she traded off most of the magic coins you left behind. She didn't keep much more than a supply for those of us with essences."

"Using our abilities also saved us a lot of issues," Hiro said. "I've been pretty much doing as I'm told with the magic parts. Farrah has been teaching me, but I still only understand part of what she's doing. As for the physical construction, buildings and landscape, Ken has been an absolute beast."

"The ability to move earth and facilitate plant growth is incredible," Ken said happily. "I'm like a one-man landscape and construction company with a time machine."

After taking Jason through the core section, they took him to see the residential areas. The homes there consisted of more wooden buildings that blended into the bushland, a series of small housing estates built in clusters. Each home was unique, rather than built to a template, giving each area a natural and eclectic feel.

There were beach homes in a row, fronting directly onto the sand, as well as multi-story houses surrounded by lush bushland. His favourites were the slightly more remote clifftop homes that had been dug into the rock, with balconies that emerged from the cliff face.

Farrah joined in to guide Jason through the magical aspects, replacing Ken and Hiro. Emi understood the magical elements better than her great uncle, despite only a passing instruction in array magic. She accompanied Jason and Farrah.

Farrah explained the security features of the compound, with some of the design choices making more sense as they went. The nodal nature of the layout, for example, was a defensive measure. Rather than a singular area with traditional fortifications, the central area plus each of the residential hubs was an individual core of magical defences. If one of the nodes had its defences compromised, the others were able to reinstate and reinforce them.

Farrah also took him through the more secretive aspects that only Ken, Hiro, Emi and she were aware of. Neither the Network nor any other members of the family knew that the clifftop excavations had been a front to establish a tunnel system. It linked the various compound nodes, as well as serving as secure service tunnels for the magical infrastructure.

Each of the subway-sized passages contained a two-way tramway combining magic and technology. The tramway was currently inactive, as were the lights. Emi was delighted as Jason used the floating motes of his star cloak to light their way as they travelled on foot.

"Seriously, how much did all this cost?" Jason asked.

"The Cabal was very interested in accessing some magical resources," Farrah said. "I brokered some three-way deals with the Cabal and the Network. You are going to have to do an awful lot of looting now you're back, by the way."

"That's fine," Jason said. "I want to keep up the monster-hunting anyway."

"I really mean a lot," Farrah said. "I made some promises."

"It's okay. You did an amazing job with all this. I can't believe this was all done in six months."

"Don't underestimate your uncle's and father's contributions," Farrah said. "Your uncle found us a lot of very discreet construction workers who didn't ask questions, which we needed them not to. Your father's contacts with experts in your world's construction and engineering fields were invaluable during the design stages. As for building it all, Ken's talent for building with magic is every bit the equal of yours with aura control. Also, I've seen construction golems who don't work as hard as him."

The single biggest secret of the compound Farrah saved for last: another secret tunnel, separate from the others. A long passage ran from the main residence out into the ocean. Like the other tunnels, it had a two-way tramway that was not yet active, leaving them to go on foot.

A few hundred metres out, the underground tunnel ascended into a glass one that ran along the seafloor. It was like being at an aquarium; there were numerous sea creatures floating near the tunnel and Jason could sense the subtle magic attracting them.

"That's a nice touch," Jason said.

"That was my idea," Emi said.

"It was?" Jason asked.

"It really was," Farrah said. "I did a little neatening up of their design, but that's all. Emi and Hiro designed and implemented the fish attraction together."

"Good job, Moppet," Jason said to a beaming Emi.

Two kilometres out from shore, the glass tunnel ended, not with any kind of sealed environment but simply stopped, terminating at a vertical sheet of water beyond which was open ocean.

"What is this?" Jason asked.

"A discreet place to put your cloud house," Farrah said. "You can set it up right at the end of the tunnel. Air-sealing magic like this is very efficient when set up correctly. Even on your world, it can just run off the ambient magic."

Jason walked up to the wall of water and poked it with his finger. It was rather cold.

"That's pretty awesome," he said. "I've wanted to test the cloud house out underwater since Emir told me it could work like that. I was half-tempted when I moved back to Casselton Beach."

"Having it all the way out here will also stop your cloud house from disrupting the magic of the compound with its vortex accumulator."

"I wanted to ask about that," Jason said. "I could sense the magical defences and utility magic hidden throughout. Is there enough ambient magic to fuel all that?"

"No," Farrah said. "I actually used some of what I learned studying the grid to create a version of your cloud flask's vortex accumulator, except less potent and much larger. I set up several of them in empty areas offsite and the power feeds into the compound."

"We should just be calling it a town," Jason said.

"Even with the magic we have feeding it, it still isn't enough," Farrah told him. "I've made accommodations accordingly. For one thing, the town's entire magical infrastructure can operate at various levels. The town is uninhabited at the moment, so we're running at no magic. No ordinary power either. We're still finalising the design on the magically enhanced solar panels that will power it all. I'm working with a Network magitech expert, provided by Asya."

"Will the magic need spirit coins to run once it's all going?" Jason asked.

"At the lowest level of actual operation, only specific functions will require spirit coin supplementation," Farrah explained. "I've also designed it from the onset to adapt as the magical density of the world goes up."

"So, the worse things get, the more ready we are to face them."

"Exactly."

"What's going to get worse?" Emi asked.

"Don't worry about it, Moppet," Jason said, tousling her hair. "Uncle Jason and Auntie Farrah are going to save the world."

6

NEW GROOVE

Jason, Farrah, Emi, Ken and Hiro stood on the thoroughfare of what Jason had started thinking of as Asano Village. He was about to open a portal to Casselton Beach when Farrah's phone bleeped.

"Category-three incursion," she said after checking the message. "Ready to get back in the saddle?"

"Listen to you, category three," Jason said. "You've gone native."

"I've gone native? You were frying giant worm meat in a village stall on your second day in my world."

"So, how do we get to Sydney?" Jason asked. "I have the range to portal straight there now, but I can't send a silver-ranker."

"Don't worry," Farrah said. "I have a guy."

"You can portal the rest of us, though, right?" Hiro asked. "You're our ride."

"Wait, this is your guy?" Jason asked as he sensed the approaching aura.

"You can sense him from that far out?" Farrah asked. "What kind of crazy perception do you have?"

"That's not normal?"

"No," she said, turning to look at a growing dot in the sky. "See how fast his conjured helicopter is? His partner bought out Kaito's half of their helicopter charter and he's been working for the Network instead. They pay better."

"He has Greg and Asya with him," Jason said. "They're making their way towards bronze, but I'm not sensing cores from them. It's very quiet for a helicopter."

"You can tell that from here?" Farrah asked. "I can barely hear it and I have silver-rank perception. It's quiet for a helicopter, but it's still a helicopter."

Jason gave her an odd look.

"What?" she asked.

"I was just thinking about our time together in your world. The fact that you now have a basis for comparison on helicopter noise blows my mind. You're wearing jeans."

"I like jeans. I see you finally stopped wearing the clothes you picked up on the other side."

"I kept getting into fights. There's only so much damage that basic self-repair can do, and I only have a couple of suits left. Why are Greg and Asya not using cores? Do you have Greg fighting monsters?"

"He wanted to fight monsters."

"Of course he wanted to fight monsters. He's a huge nerd."

"He's actually pretty good. Not at, you know, stabbing, but he's got a versatile flex-support power set. It's more about timing and judgement."

"I have one of those on my team," Jason said. "I wonder how she's doing. I'm not sure I approve of Greg going out in the field, though. What about Asya?"

"The Network has been gearing up for problems ever since the grid blackouts started. They've been putting anyone willing to do it up for training. We have three training streams now. One for core users looking to retrain, one for people going from scratch using our methods and one for core users focused on unconventional approaches."

"Unconventional, how?"

"Like your brother. We're using cores to raise his abilities while his training is being adapted from military pilot training. He's doing great as utility and air support."

"He's going into proto-spaces?"

"It's fine."

"He has kids. Little kids. What if something happens to him?"

"What if something happens to you?" Farrah countered. "You think Emi is ready to lose Uncle Jason again? And look at everything going on here."

She gestured around at the village that had been built in his absence.

"You are the pillar on which all this rests. With time, the Asano clan will be able to stand on their own, but they aren't there yet."

"We're not a clan."

"Tell that to the Japanese."

"What do the Japanese have to do with it?"

"You really need to talk to Keti."

Kaito's helicopter swooped over the village to settle on the helipad on the roof of the main residence.

"Should there really be just this one big residence in the middle of the village?" Jason asked. "It's a little elitist, isn't it?"

"We've been calling it the Mayor's House," Farrah said.

"Who's the mayor? Please don't say Amy."

"No, it's Erika. She wrapped up her TV show and she's kind of taken over family affairs."

"Okay, that's good," Jason said.

The pair leapt up the several stories to the rooftop helipad, Jason with bronze-rank strength and his cloak and Farrah with raw muscle. The side of the helicopter slid open to reveal Greg and Asya inside.

"Aren't you worried about hitting the helicopter blades, jumping up like that?" Greg asked loudly over the spinning rotors.

"No," Jason yelled back. "If you're doing your mobility training properly, that should never be a danger. Farrah, have you been letting him skip out on mobility training?"

"Of course I haven't."

Jason and Farrah stepped into what seemed more like the passenger compartment of a private jet than a helicopter. Jason even focused his senses to check there wasn't any dimensional manipulation going on. The door slid shut behind them on its own, completely silencing the exterior noise. Greg and Asya were already seated, wearing the black fatigues standard for Network tactical response teams.

"You need to take that off," Farrah said to Asya, who glanced awkwardly at Jason before nodding and removing a black cloth bracelet.

Jason had been able to sense the basic properties of her aura, but with the bracelet's removal, Asya's emotions became plain. It was mostly nervousness.

"G'day," Jason greeted as he sat down opposite her. A smile played on the corners of his mouth.

"Hi," she said.

"Sure glad this isn't awkward," Greg said with a grin as he shifted into the seat next to Asya.

"Go away," she told him, and he moved back out.

"I am never getting out of high school," he grumbled.

Emerging from the aperture into the proto-space, Jason looked around. Craggy cliffs of dark grey stone rose to his left and right, while the line of sky between them roiled with storm clouds and rumbled with thunder. He immediately moved deeper into the gorge as more people streamed from the aperture. The bottom of the gorge was a trickling stream running over loose rocks.

- You have entered an unstable physical reality. Your presence will decrease the rate at which it will destabilise.

"Not a great spot for base camp," Jason observed.

His cloak appeared around him and he jumped straight up. Shadow arms extended from his cloak on either side and he used them to grab the rock walls and fling himself higher. In the last six months, he had used them more and more independently of his real arms.

During his time away, Jason had done more than simply advance his abilities. Just as he had worked on his aura control, his proficiency with his other powers had improved. This wasn't just advancing his essence abilities but enhancing his skill in wielding them.

Shooting over the top of the gorge, he looked out over the landscape as he slowly drifted down to one side. It was a blasted land of dark soil and bare stone, with only a few blackened trees dotting the landscape. From what he could see, the gorge he was standing atop was part of a greater spiderweb of crevasses and gullies.

Farrah flew out of the gorge on fiery wings, flanked by a handful of Network scouts who shot away immediately. Farrah's flame wings were not great for flying, lacking strength, control and speed. She generally avoided flying with them once she armoured up, as they were barely able to lift her. The wings had other virtues, however, and Jason's power had given them a solid indication of who was responsible.

Ability: [Wings of the World-Phoenix]

- Transfigured from [Outworlder] ability [Wings of Fire].

- Conjure fiery wings that allow flight. While wings are active, add disruptive-force damage to all fire and heat damage inflicted. This effect consumes mana.

- The wings can be detonated to inflict fire and disruptive force damage on nearby enemies while subjecting self and allies to a powerful healing effect and a cleanse that affects magic and poison. The strength of the healing effect on yourself is significantly higher than on allies and highly effective on catastrophic damage and wounding effects.

- Subsequent conjurations of the wings will have diminished bonus, slowly recovering strength over 24 hours. Wings cannot be detonated again until ability strength is fully recovered.

The wings made Farrah's flames much more effective against incorporeal creatures and magical defences, although it further added to her mana-consumption issues.

"There's a lot of silver-rank monsters in this space," Jason said. "Are we sure this is a silver-rank space?"

"It is," a silver-ranker said, rising out of the gorge on a gust of wind. It was Koen Waters, the Sydney branch's Director of Tactical Operations. "Non-ADE cat-threes started appearing in category-three incursion spaces before you two came along. It's been escalating over the last year, though, especially while you were off playing David Carradine."

"Who?" Farrah asked. "I've been here a year and I still have no idea who you people are talking about."

"You haven't seen *Kung Fu?*" Koen asked.

"Is that another old TV show?" Farrah asked. "What is wrong with you people? Jason's sister made me watch some *Airwolf* and it was terrible."

"What makes you think there are a lot of cat-threes?" Koen asked Jason.

"I can sense them. And your people down in the gorge. You're earth-shaping space for a base camp?"

"We'll set up on top as well," Koen said. "It'll be a little bit before we secure the space and get to sweeping, but your being here means we don't have to rush. The extra time you extend incursion space stability, plus the looting, makes it worth having you here even if you spend the whole time in a lounge chair."

"I think I'll skip the chair and go clean up some of those silvers," Jason said and dashed away.

Koen sighed as he watched Jason zip over the ground at a fleeting pace.

"I see he didn't work on his collaborative skills while he was away. Can he really sense monsters from here?"

"Did you just sigh?" Farrah asked.

"Er... no."

"Are you still breathing? You shouldn't still need to breathe at silver rank. Have you not been doing those exercises I taught you?"

"I'm going to check on how the camp setup is going," Koen said, gesturing with his thumb and then jumping back into the gorge.

Jason could have used Shade for transport but decided to set out on foot. During his time away, he had worked on his ability use, but not everything was new. Back in the Mistrun Delta, Jason had developed a running technique that used his cloak to increase speed, conserve energy and navigate terrain. With his speed attribute at the top end of bronze, he revisited that technique with the enhanced agility, reflexes and straight-line speed that entailed.

The result was that he moved across the rough ground of the protospace like a ghost, all but skimming through the air. The hopping, slightly uneven gait of the past was now smooth like a hovercraft on a cushion of air.

As he approached the first silver-rank monster, Jason sensed a gaggle of smaller, weaker iron-rank monsters around it, along with a few bronzes. The main monster turned out to be a giant black lizard with silver-white glowing eyes, while the supplemental creatures were elementals. Wind and lightning elementals danced on the air like dandelion petals, while earth elementals swarmed around the creature's feet.

"Gordon," Jason said, not slowing his approach. The familiar appeared next to him. Gordon's ordinary floating speed could not match Jason's, so he kept pace by chaining his dash ability.

The monsters sensed their approach as soon as Gordon appeared, the elementals stirring into a frenzy. They rushed forward and Gordon gave up dashing as they entered his considerable range. Four bright beams of energy, two orange and two blue, swept through the iron-rank monsters with annihilative force.

The blue beams of disruptive-force were doom for the amorphous wind and lightning elementals, disposing of them with a crackle like insects hit with a bug zapper. The orange resonating-force beams dug into the earth elementals like they were drilling for oil. The few bronze-rank elementals lasted a little longer, but Gordon was at the high-end of bronze and the perfect weapon against such creatures.

Jason ignored the elementals, moving directly on the lizard that was the size of a school bus. Jason sensed the magic precursor of an attack and juked sideways, not slowing as lightning erupted from the lizard's eyes and flashed past him. He arrived in front of the lizard as he conjured a dagger into his hand.

"Shade."

Several of Shade's bodies surrounded the creature. In the past, Jason would have used them to stage hit-and-run strikes, landing a couple of special attacks and then backing off to cast spells before moving on and letting his affliction suite do its work.

This was not what Jason did to the lizard. His dagger flashed out to make sewing-machine strikes: quick, shallow, in an unceasing staccato. Hit after hit, each one delivering the afflictions of a special attack plus the afflictions of the dagger. Instead of pre-emptively dodging with shadow jumps, he relied on his skill to avoid the lizard as he kept attacking.

The oversized lizard thrashed and tried to bite at him, but Jason used its size against it, staying tucked in close, his dagger never stopping. It repositioned to get a better angle on Jason; only then did he shadow jump to one of Shade's bodies, the needlework of his dagger barely pausing.

Although Jason had seized the initiative, the lizard still posed a threat. It did not have the reflexes of a silver-rank essence user but was still devilishly quick for its size. Its strength would have given even Farrah pause. When it caught Jason with a tail lash, it shattered the accumulated shields from his amulet and hammered his torso like a speeding car.

He was sent careening through the air before the lightness of his cloak let him drift to a floating stop. The healing from Colin and the converted amulet shields went to work as Jason floated in the air where he'd been slapped. He extended his hand towards the monster.

"*Your blood is not yours to keep but mine on which to feast.*"

Life force drained out of the lizard and into Jason. The lizard retaliated by opening its mouth and spitting out a ball of lightning that floated towards Jason, who was exposed as he drifted in the air. Jason used his cloak as a shadow to jump through, right before the ball of lightning exploded in the space he had just occupied. He emerged from one of Shade's bodies as a new cloak manifested around him, immediately resuming his attacks.

The rapid-fire strikes from his dagger represented a fundamental change in Jason's approach to combat. He had long ago given up on rapid

58 | SHIRTALOON

kills as impossible due to his lack of immediate damage attacks. Instead, he consigned himself to the slow and steady path to victory. As he took the time to reassess his abilities, Jason had reassessed that presumption as well and developed a new combat dynamic.

From the very beginning, Inexorable Doom had been Jason's signature ability, with only his familiars more iconic in his repertoire. It had been critical to his combat style, allowing him to back off while it piled on more of every affliction he levied. He used it now on the lizard, along with other affliction spells, chanting the incantations even as he dodged limbs and the lizard's bite. This time, however, it was merely an addendum.

Jason didn't care if his sewing machine attacks were weak, so long as they riddled the lizard with afflictions. The monster was staggering already as a tide of necrosis washed over it. Jason leapt lightly up and then kicked off the lizard with both feet, sailing back thanks to the lightness from his cloak while he cast another spell.

"*Suffer the cost of your transgressions.*"

Punition dealt damage based on afflictions in place, which devastated the lizard. It was a stumbling wreck. Even so, silver-rank fortitude persisted. Sensing its demise, the lizard made a final play. A third of the elementals were yet to be swatted by Gordon. They suddenly drew closer to the lizard, like dinghies caught in a whirlpool. They struggled to escape, but the force pulling them in didn't allow it and they were absorbed into the lizard's body.

Jason sensed the power building inside the monster and returned to his normal weight, dropping agilely to the ground and opening the portal arch to his spirit vault. He ducked inside, Gordon and Shade's bodies following quickly behind. From inside his spirit vault, Jason sensed the destruction of the archway. The darkness inside the matching arch inside the vault vanished, leaving the archway empty.

- You have defeated [Lesser Stormchar Lizard].

Jason used his portal ability, Path of Shadows, on the empty arch. On the battlefield Jason had just left, an archway rose up from the floor of a newly formed crater. Jason stepped out and looked around. Extending his senses, he found a scrap of blackened flesh and brushed his fingers over it.

- Would you like to loot [Lesser Stormchar Lizard]?

Striding out of the crater, Jason turned his eyes to the sky, looking at the distant drone Koen had sent to follow him. Behind him, rainbow smoke rose from points around the crater like streamers, from every place an exploded piece of monster had scattered. Then he skimmed off over the ground in the direction of the next silver-rank monster.

At the base camp. Koen was rewinding the footage from the drone.

"What are you looking for?" Nigel asked him.

"The timestamp," Koen said, pausing the footage. "We just watched a solo category two wipe out a swarm of elementals and a cat-three the size of a train car in forty-three seconds."

7
GET TO THE CHOPPER

KAITO HAD BEEN SUPPLIED WITH A VARIETY OF AWAKENING STONES loaded towards producing useful complements to his main power. Koen Waters had seen potential in Kaito's abilities. He had the Network recruit him and provide the stones to complete his power set. They started with common stones, like awakening stones of the gun and various elemental stones. Less common were the awakening stones of vision and reach.

The result was a comprehensive suite of abilities that turned Kaito and his helicopter into a high-utility asset for the Network. His helicopter was not well-suited to confronting powerful monsters but was highly effective at escaping pursuit and handling the kinds of weaker enemies that appeared in greater numbers than their more powerful counterparts.

The true value of Kaito's contribution was twofold—neither factor being the hunting of monsters. One was that he could swiftly and safely deploy tactical units or supplies throughout an incursion space. The other was the improvement it brought to the command and control capabilities of the incursion response team.

Kaito's vehicle was sized in between a military transport helicopter and a large commercial helicopter while being both faster and more agile than either. He was able to modify the helicopter literally on the fly, reconfiguring the interior to meet his needs moment to moment. From luxuriously spaced passenger transport to efficient troop seating to cargo space, complete with loading platform, the helicopter could perform whatever role was asked of it.

What really excited the Director of Tactical Operations was the helicopter's value as a mobile command relay. The helicopter had a communication system that was as useful, if not more so, than Jason's party interface. It was able to augment ordinary comms technology to operate reliably in magically saturated areas. It could also serve as a sensor platform, courtesy of Kaito's powers. His abilities were able to collect and relay video feed and sensor data from the helicopter itself, as well as remote auxiliary units.

Those auxiliary units were the two semi-autonomous drone variants Kaito could produce with abilities from his vehicle essence. One type was a trio of small attack units, mounted with infantry-grade guns. The more useful consisted of a half-dozen observation drones that had no weapons but could travel extended ranges at high speed. They carried high-grade video and audio systems, along with the sensor capacity to track magic and auras.

Kaito's observation drones were an improvement over the two varieties the Network used. The non-magical ones they employed had significant reliability issues in magical zones. The magical ones were much better but were fuelled by spirit coins, a limited and costly resource. Kaito's drones used his mana and could reliably transmit video, audio and sensor data to the helicopter, the base camp, or both.

The sensor suites available to the drones and the helicopter itself came courtesy of Kaito's perception power. It was akin to something many summoning specialists gained access to. Rather than enhance his own senses, at least at iron rank, it bestowed the perception power on something else. Instead of a summon, as was typical, the subject was the sensors of his helicopter, providing magic and aura senses that outstripped a normal iron-ranker. More mundane sensor systems came as part of the helicopter conjuration power, although those systems were magically enhanced.

Drone control and secondary system management were all controlled from the cockpit. Rather than a physical dashboard of displays and screens, there was only a sleek, minimalist dashboard of controls. All systems were monitored through augmented reality glasses that could provide or eliminate any and all displays as needed, from drone feeds to helicopter systems.

Control of the secondary systems could be carried out by the pilot, but they were most effective when managed by a co-pilot, for which reason the Network had supplied the helicopter with a crew. Kaito's three-person crew ended up being Asya and Greg, who had both known Kaito for years, along with a category three whose job was to step in when something big and nasty appeared.

Greg took the co-pilot slot. Kaito had been teaching him how to fly a helicopter, but his true role was to manage the drones, sensors and comms. He had been chosen both for his existing connection to Kaito and his prodigious talent for multitasking.

Asya was combat support. She was somewhat superfluous, with the category three on board, but in addition to being groomed for higher rank, her power set gave her a useful niche. With her gun, gathering and adept essences forming the master confluence, she was rapidly becoming an expert sniper and general support gunner.

She had finalised her own repertoire of abilities with this role in mind, completing her power set only after being assigned to the helicopter. She had chosen some awakening stones specifically to add heavier weapon options to her original precision sniper approach.

The silver-ranker wasn't a ranged attacker like Asya. Ruth didn't look like a Russian bodybuilder so much as like she'd eaten a Russian bodybuilder and wanted to fist-fight a bear to work off the carbs. It would have been a one-sided victory, given the silver-ranker's abilities. Her might, swift, and hand essences combined to form the onslaught confluence, making her a powerhouse of speed and strength with battering ram fists. She excelled in intercepting and putting down dangerous attackers, which was exactly her role on the helicopter's crew.

Despite having arms the thickness of Greg's head, Ruth was incongruously sweet and friendly, with unassailable confidence that her lower-rank companions found reassuring.

Kaito's helicopter moved high over the ground in the proto-space, with a section of Network troops in the back. An occasional wind or lightning elemental would approach, at which point Kaito's supplemental abilities came into play. An expensive awakening stone of dimension had given Kaito a retractable gun for his helicopter that fired rapid streams of disruptive-force ammunition, which was effective at dissuading even the bronze-rank elemental variants from approaching. It wasn't enough to kill them, but it convinced them to veer off in search of weaker prey.

"I've got a category-two flier, coming in fast at ten o'clock," Kaito said as a signal appeared on the cockpit sensors. The current cockpit configuration had four seats for the crew, with a bare-bones troop transport set up in the main compartment.

"Fast or tough?" Ruth asked.

"Fast," Kaito said. "You're up, Asya."

A small panel next to Asya opened, letting in a rush of air. Asya conjured a sniper rifle and slid the barrel out through the panel, eyeing down the sight.

"Altering trajectory to give you a shot," Kaito said. Soon after, a black lizard with huge wings fell into Asya's sights.

Asya had an ability to ignore rank disparity that was more like Farrah's than Jason's; it was an essence ability, rather than an evolved racial gift. Even so, getting a one-shot kill on a bronze-rank monster was unlikely given the toughness of monsters.

Asya still could have gone for the kill, her power set allowing her to gather and condense ambient magic for a single potent shot. If she could land the headshot, it could be enough to drop the creature, given that flying monsters weren't usually as tough as their land-bound counterparts.

Instead of risking a high-impact shot on the monster's relatively small head, however, she aimed for the broad wings. She used a special attack that erupted in a proximity burst. The power didn't match a direct hit, but it tagged one of the creature's wings. The monster wasn't crippled, but was injured enough to drop away, rapidly losing altitude.

"Nice," Kaito said.

He noticed Greg staring into space.

"What is it?" Kaito asked.

"I just watched Jason through one of the drones," he said. "I'd only seen him fight in some patchy drone footage from before he left. It doesn't seem like him, all black-clad and ominous."

"That's exactly like him," Kaito said. "Such a melodramatist."

"I'd like to see that footage," Ruth said. "Can you send it to me?"

"Sure," Greg said.

Ruth put on the augmented reality goggles hanging on the back of Greg's seat in front of her.

"Cancel that," Kaito said. "We're coming up on the drop point."

Greg radioed the section of troops in the rear, telling them to prepare for deployment. Kaito dropped the helicopter to two hundred metres and brought it into a hover. Normally, he would go lower, but there were a lot of flying monsters in this particular proto-space.

In the rear compartment, the side of the helicopter slid open as a panel on the floor slid away to reveal what looked like a small wind turbine pointing up. It started blasting air, which oddly collected in front of the open side panel, shimmering in place.

"Go!" the section leader called out, and the first trooper dashed through the shimmering air and out of the helicopter, falling away. Some of the shimmering air attached itself to him as he passed through it. The whole section jumped out, one by one, plunging towards the ground.

Right before they landed, the shimmering air around them tightened into a cushion, depositing them softly onto the ground before dissipating in a rush of wind. Back on the helicopter, the side door closed itself and Kaito set course for the next objective.

"I have to say," Jason said from the rear of the cockpit, "I'm kind of annoyed at how well this worked out."

The helicopter crew all turned to look at him in surprise.

"I was going to give you the rat, snake and skunk essences," Jason continued. "I wish I had now, to be honest."

"How did you get in here?" Kaito asked.

"I've got magic powers. How do you not know that at this point?"

"I have security abilities," Kaito said. "Sensor abilities."

Ruth chuckled, sharing an amused look with Jason.

"The tyranny of rank, little brother."

"You're the little brother," Kaito said.

"That may be true out in the world, Kai," Jason said, "but not here. This is my kingdom."

Jason and Asya walked along the Castle Reach shorefront. Grass led down to white sand on one side of the street, while the other had cafés and storefronts. Asya and Jason were heading for the ice cream shop.

"This is my kingdom," Asya quoted. "Really?"

"A bit much?" Jason asked.

"A bit? That was cringeworthy. Not as sad as Greg constantly telling people to 'get to the chopper' in a sketchy accent, but not good."

"I thought it was cool," Jason said.

"It was not. It was also rather mean."

"Kaito deserves it."

"That's a boy's complaint. It's time for you to be a man."

"Ouch. Greg thought it was cool."

Asya gave him a flat look.

"I'm not helping my case here, am I?"

"Greg is great," Asya said. "But he's also a little bit twelve years old. The man wears Ninja Turtle shirts to briefings."

"To briefings about fighting monsters from another dimension using magic powers. Ninja Turtle shirts should be the uniform."

"I don't think Ketevan is going to like dealing with the both of you at once," she said with a laugh.

"What's going on with Greg's abilities, though?" Jason asked. "Wasn't that combination meant to give him the magitech confluence?"

"It did."

"Every magitech guy I've seen in the Network is all about high-tech gadgets and stuff. They're half James Bond and half Iron Man. How did Greg end up all steampunk Tesla?"

"You don't like his electrified nail turret?"

"No, it's awesome, I'm just wondering."

"You know, we still need to talk about Network business. That is technically what we're meeting about."

"Are you sure I can't tell you another heroic story about my trip away?"

"Alright," Asya said with an accommodation Jason immediately found suspect. "Did you happen to run into Li Li Mei while you were passing through China?"

"Who?" Jason asked innocently. "Oh, the Network rep who came here that one time. I don't recall her being super-pretty at all."

"Who said anything about her being pretty?"

"So," Jason said, his voice half an octave higher. "Time to dig into that Network business, you say?"

"No," Asya said, pointing at the shop they were now standing in front of. "It's time for ice cream."

"Right, yes," Jason said, pushing open the door.

"How long were you in China for?" Asya asked as they went inside.

"You know, I might just go vanilla. People look down on it as a plain flavour, but a proper vanilla can be really delicious."

"That's the attitude that had you following Amy around like a puppy back in school."

"Twist the knife, why don't you?"

On the roof deck of the houseboat, Asya and Jason were sitting next to one another at a table. Asya was taking him through the important things he had missed during his time away.

"…escalating rate of manifestation, which you've already seen for yourself. The new training programs are starting to pay off, but it's going to take time in areas outside of Australia. The new training protocols we've developed with input from Farrah are showing their effects here, but the international partners now have to go back and work with their own people. Even then, we're talking about training programs that have been developed and implemented in a critically short time. The largest deficit is experience."

"There's only one solution to a lack of experience," Jason said, "and that's to go out and get it."

"We're projecting significant problems. In the short term, we're anticipating a sharp increase in casualties."

"That's realistic," Jason said. "The Network is never going to fight the way they do in the other world and they'd be foolish to try. They need to learn from what Farrah can teach them but find a way to use it that works for them. All Farrah was really trying to impart were principles, as well as things like improved meditation methodology. She can't turn the whole Network into adventurers in six months."

"No, it's on us now. You know, the original idea was for you to do the teaching."

"You're better off, believe me. It's a matter of temperament."

"Oh, I believe you."

"Hey…"

"The last thing we need to discuss is the image you built up during your time away."

"I was trying to avoid building an image."

Asya opened a video depicting a man in starlight cloak fighting people in a Vietnamese slum.

"For the most part," Jason added. "If the Network doesn't want me showing off, you should stop trying to kidnap me."

"We came down on the Hanoi branch the same way we did Lyon. Disturbingly, we got the exact same result once we started digging."

"Meaning what?"

"Adrien Barbou."

"You're kidding. I thought he hadn't resurfaced."

"We're keeping it quiet, for now. We believe he's working with the EOA, feeding them information from his old Network contacts. We're currently attempting to infiltrate those contacts to get something concrete we can slap the EOA with. We can't just accuse them of orchestrating the blackouts and go after them with no evidence because the Cabal won't stand for it. The Network is the strongest of the world's magical triad, but we aren't stronger than the other two put together. If we start acting unilaterally against the EOA, the Cabal will side with them out of fear we'll go after them next."

"Why are you even telling me?"

"Our analysts think that Barbou has taken it upon himself to become your publicist."

"What?" Jason asked.

"We constantly monitor media for potential breaches," Asya explained. "When you went more overt after Hanoi, we paid additional attention to any media attention related to your activities. We realised that someone was putting the pieces together and quietly dropping breadcrumbs for others to find."

"Why?"

"We don't know. We stumbled into the idea that Barbou might be the man behind the curtain because we've been looking into his old contacts. As for his motivations, the best we've come up with is that a magic man secretly running around the world doing good deeds fits the EOA agenda of bringing magic into the light. They might have seen us not clamping down on you and tried to run with it."

"He's making me look good?"

"That's arguable. We're seeing a lot of fringe chatter around the Starlight Angel/Starlight Rider persona, but conspiracy types don't tend to look at things in a positive light."

"I was healing the sick."

"But did you make them sick, as an excuse to implant tracking devices? Were you testing a bioweapon for use when your people start the invasion?"

"They think I'm an alien?"

"You are an alien."

"I am now, but they don't know that. I'm from the Mid North Coast, not the mid-north of Andromeda."

"You really don't know anything about astronomy, do you?"

"Because I'm not an alien!"

8
WHAT'S LEFT OF YOUR PRINCIPLES

"Chloe, it's good to hear from you," Jason said as the video chat opened. "How've you been?"

"I've been staying with my sister," she said. "It's been nice, but I am increasingly ready to go."

Jason chuckled. "As a guy who ran away from his family for six months, I completely understand."

"Well, whatever your reasons, the entirety of West Africa benefited, even if they don't know it. Which is actually why I called you."

"The outbreak is flaring back up?"

"No, it's about you. I've been talking to my colleagues and a lot of them have been contacted by an investigative journalist."

"I didn't think they had those anymore. Isn't it all just ideologues and regurgitated press releases now?"

"It depends on who is willing to pay, and someone is putting up for some airline miles on this one. The people talking to me aren't talking to them, but sooner or later, someone will."

"I'm aware of someone pushing me into the spotlight from the shadows," Jason said ominously. "He's an enemy I picked up along the way."

"I have to think that someone like you has a different kind of enemy to someone like me," Chloe said. "My biggest enemy beat me out for the good parking space at the hospital where I used to work."

"My enemy held my friend prisoner and… let's just say yes, different kinds of enemy."

The meeting room of the Four Cardinals of the EOA seemed cavernous, with high ceilings and wide walls while being almost entirely empty. There was a large monitor on one wall, a square table in the middle that seemed diminutive given the scope of the room, and an exterior wall, made entirely of glass.

Two men, Mr North and the new Mr East, stood in front of the wall, taking in the panoramic view of Los Angeles. They were awaiting the arrival of Mrs West and Mrs South.

"You realise," Mr North said, "that if we tie you or Mrs West to the demise of your predecessor, the consequences will have a resounding finality."

"I do," Adrien Barbou said.

"Then let me compliment you on your thoroughness, Mr East. My investigators rarely find themselves at such a loss."

"I'm sure I have no idea what you're talking about, Mr North."

Mr North gave a saturnine smile.

"I do so hope there won't be any problems stemming from a leadership change at this critical time, Mr East."

"I think you will find, Mr North, that a change was exactly what was required. I called this meeting for a reason."

"I'm positively dripping with anticipation."

Mr North did not probe further, awaiting the remaining members of their collective. He had long ago schooled himself out of dangerous curiosity and exploitable impatience. When Mrs West and Mrs South arrived together, the four took their places around the square table. Their subordinates were not present at this meeting and the four were alone in the large room.

"The meeting is yours, Mr East," Mr North said. "The agenda is yours to set."

"In the process of auditing the activities of my predecessor," Barbou said, "I have come across a number of unfortunate irregularities."

"Oh?" Mrs South prompted. "What manner of irregularities?"

"It would appear," Barbou said, "that the previous Mr East had rather drastically overstated the problems in enacting the final stage of our plan. It seems that he was stalling the process to give certain factions within the Cabal time to prepare."

"What factions are those?" Mr North asked.

"Unknown. I have only just made these revelations and immediately moved to lock down all of the previous Mr East's subordinates for investigation and table this meeting. I felt it prudent to discuss these issues before launching an internal investigation and enacting inquiries into the Cabal."

"A choice wisely made," Mrs West said.

"You have evidence of these improprieties on the part of your predecessor?" Mrs South asked.

"I do," Barbou said. "As the materials are sensitive, rather than digital transmission, I am having the full details hand-delivered to each of you on secure drives."

"Prudent," Mr North said. "If Mr East truly was stalling, then do you have a revised time frame in which we can enact the next stage?"

"We could begin immediately," Barbou said. "I would recommend, however, that we wait two weeks. This will give me time to root out any more surprises the previous Mr East left behind and vet his people. It would also allow me to bring to fruition the project that was delayed by my rise to the seat of Mr East."

"You're ready to move forward with that?" Mrs West asked.

"Yes, although I won't make the final move without consensus. This will go further than the Network is willing to tolerate."

"And will prime the world for our next move with a conversation of what is and is not possible," Mrs West said.

"There is another problem the late Mr East was either hiding or unaware of," Barbou said. "One that potentially means cancelling everything."

Eyebrows raised all around the table.

"Go on," Mr North said.

"I've been personally re-examining every aspect of the grid blackout program, now that I have control of it. Mr East's grasp of the magical mechanics involved was not as comprehensive as either we would like or he portrayed. In addition to the fact that we are ready to go, he failed to grasp the full ramifications of dropping the grid in its entirety."

"Which are?"

"My predecessor indicated that it would take the grid between one and two weeks to reactivate following a total shutdown. Enough time for dimension incursion spaces to deliver monsters across the world and definitively proving the existence of magic. We already know that the results of this will be damaging. The reality is that the grid will be down for months. At least two, most likely three or four. It could be longer, or even permanent. That's a low but real probability. This is all assuming that the Network fails to find a way to repair the damage and return the grid to functionality, which would alter our timelines, obviously."

"Months," Mrs South said. "That wouldn't be damage. Months of monster hordes being spewed into the world would be an apocalypse."

"That's a little dramatic," Mrs West said.

"No," Barbou disagreed. "Mrs South is right. I've seen the dimensional spaces, the armies of monsters. Months without the grid to intercept them will change civilisation forever. It could potentially end it."

"Assuming that the Network can't get the grid active again," Mrs West said.

"How likely is that?" Mr North asked.

"A year ago, I would have considered it highly likely," Barbou said. "The outworlders have changed that. My contacts tell me that the outworlder once in my custody has been advancing the Network's comprehension of the grid in leaps and bounds."

"Farrah Hurin," Mrs West said.

"It doesn't matter what her name is," Barbou said. "Only what impact she has on our plans."

The other three looked to Mr North, the first among equals. They waited as he sat in thoughtful silence, tapping a finger against his lips. Then the finger stopped.

"One week," Mr North said. "If we can move now, then we go at the earliest reasonable opportunity. Is that sufficient to root out any further problems regarding your predecessor, Mr East?"

"If you are willing to loan me some of your excellent investigators, Mr North. I am still building my own cadre of reliable people."

"Done," Mr North said. "Mrs South, please coordinate with Mr East and take charge of looking into the Cabal's activities."

"Are we truly going to gloss over this?" Mrs South asked. "Our goal was to forge a place in a world turned to magic, not to burn that world down."

"A wide-scale collapse of civic and social infrastructure does not obviate our objectives," Mr North said.

"You would leave us ruling over a pile of ash?" Mrs South asked.

"So long as we rule," Mr North said. "The complete collapse of the systems on which the Cabal and the Network have built their power bases will, at the last, bring us to parity. As the world rebuilds, we will finally stand as one of the tallest pillars."

Mrs South took a long, slow breath, then stood up.

"We are not the people we set out to become," she said. "In the beginning, our goal was to democratise magic. To take it from those who were hoarding it for themselves. Somewhere along the way, instead of defeating them, we became them. I have no illusions that I am good and I can live with that. I gave up on pulling down the tower for the chance to live on top of it, looking down at others like ants. But there is a difference between looking down on ants and using a glass to burn them. I may have given up on making the world better, but I won't be party to burning it down."

In the wake of her monologue, the other three shared a look, then turned their gazes back to Mrs South.

"Are you certain?" Mr North asked. "You understand the consequences of standing on what's left of your principles. You won't affect change. You won't make anything better for anyone except whoever end up inheriting your seat. Someone who we will make sure does not share your compunctions. Only if you participate do you have any chance of steering events in the direction you want them to go. You can't stop it, but perhaps you can ameliorate it. Only by standing with us will you have the chance."

"Mrs South," Mrs West said, her face filled with reluctance. "Audrey. If you go against us, you change nothing. You won't leave this room and you know that. I understand that staying the course might feel like a stain, but do you want to die clean or actually make some kind of difference?"

Mrs South turned around, placing her back to the table.

"I'll die clean."

"…amateur footage of a figure that looks to be wrapped in an eerie garb made from the night itself. It doesn't move like a human and what it does to the people in this video is not something a human can do. Perhaps not even something any human would, given the horrific results. The Vietnamese government denies this incident took place, claiming the video is a hoax, but we have found what we believe to be the site of this altercation and spoke to local residents. As you're about to see, these people claim the impossible is not as impossible as most of us believe…"

Anna sighed, pausing the footage. She was in her office with Asya and Terrance Tilden, Anna's brother and also the Sydney Network branch's media director.

"How much traction is it getting?" Anna asked.

"It's getting a lot of promotion amongst susceptible demographics," Terrance said. "The mainstreaming of conspiracy rhetoric in the US is helping this along, and with their cultural influence, it's spreading far and digging deep. Most outlets are dismissing it, but they're all playing it because it's content that gets people talking. The footage from the rolling gunfight here in Sydney is getting more play than ever."

"How bad is this?" Anna asked Asya.

"The International Committee is throwing a fit," Asya said. "Not the local office in Canberra, but Brussels, Berlin, Shanghai, New York, Johannesburg, Cairo…"

Asya shook her head in resignation.

"There's an emergency video conclave going on as we speak," she said. "It was decided that there wasn't time to convene in person. I'm not privy to what they're discussing, but the preliminary directions they're issuing speak volumes."

"Which are?" Anna asked.

"All branches are being instructed to prepare to enact breach protocols."

"This is it, then?" Aram asked. "The IC is ready to bite the bullet and go public?"

"The consensus is that the Engineers of Ascension will do it if we don't. Expect direction soon, and in the meantime, get ready to start working with local government officials. Those channels are going to be critical now."

"I think I always knew," Anna said, looking at the frozen image of a cloaked Jason on the screen, "from the moment that lunatic popped up, he was always going to be the one to bring it all down."

"I don't think that's fair," Asya said.

"Of course you don't," Anna said. "It's hardly a secret that you're looking to be the coulis on his panna cotta."

Asya's body language closed off.

"I'll thank you to show some professionalism, Committeewoman Tilden. If I have any further directives from the International Committee, I'll see you receive them."

Anna winced as Asya stiffly left the office.

"Stress," Anna said, pinching the bridge of her nose, "is not improving my work performance."

"You need to go see Susie, Anna. A good hard shag will knock the tension out of you."

"Get out, Terry. But organise me a car. I'm going to catch up with Susan while I have a free moment."

Terrance shot her a grin and left, but a few moments later came rushing back in.

"I take it this isn't about the car," Anna said.

"The grid went down," he said.

"A blackout here in Sydney?"

Blackouts in major cities were always the most dangerous.

"Not a blackout," Aram said. "The grid went down. The whole grid. Everywhere."

9
CONTINGENCIES

"I'm sure Uncle Jason will be here soon," Erika said to her sullen daughter.

"I don't see what the big deal is," Emi's friend Ruby said. "You're always talking about your uncle, but he's never around."

The beach birthday party was going well, although the ongoing absence of her uncle was increasingly ruining the birthday girl's mood.

"Mrs Asano, Miss Emi," Shade said. "Mr Asano is on his way."

"Who said that?" Ruby asked, looking around. "Is there a British man hidden somewhere? Is it a birthday surprise, because that would be weird."

"Shade," Erika hissed. "What are you doing?"

"The time for secrecy is over, Mrs Asano," Shade said. "Mr Asano is coming to bring your family to the compound. Prepare them to go."

"What are you talking about?"

She looked up, hearing a commotion. Her eyes followed the startled gazes and pointed hands to the street that ran along the beachfront. A huge black motorcycle hurtled along at a pace well outside the speed limit, a cloak of stars trailing behind like a comet's tail.

The bike swerved off the road, over the grass and off the grassy embankment. Instead of dropping down to the sand, the bike erupted into a cloud of darkness. The rider glided through the air, his cloak swept out like wings of night, absorbing the cloud of shadows. The rider landed in front of Emi, the cloak draping around him. In the middle of the sunny day, surrounded by colourfully clad children, it looked deeply incongruous.

"Sorry I'm late," Jason said. He ignored the crowd of people pulling out their phones to record.

"What are you doing?" Erika asked as her husband rushed up to join them. Ruby's parents likewise rushed over the sand, protectively standing in front of their daughter.

"Questions can wait," Jason said. "Right now, we go."

Erika opened her mouth to ask a question, processed what Jason had said and then paused.

"Alright," she said, nodding.

"What is going on?" Ruby's father asked. "You're that thing from the news. The one that kills people!"

A pair of silver eyes, shrouded in darkness turned on him, and the man felt a weight pressing down on his soul.

"Then you should probably watch your tone," Jason said in the voice he normally saved for people about to die.

"Uncle Jason, that's my friend's dad!"

He looked down at his niece, then pushed the hood back off his head.

"Sorry," he said. "Happy birthday, Moppet, but we have to go. We're all moving to the compound. Today."

He opened a portal arch, which drew an audible reaction from the crowd.

"I need to round up the rest of the family," Jason said. "I'll explain later, but things are about to get very, very bad."

Emi pushed past Ruby's parents to grab her friend by the arms.

"They have to come too," she insisted.

Jason looked at the fierce determination on his niece's face and grinned.

"I have to get the rest of the family, so the portal closes in one minute," he said. "You have until then to convince them to step through."

"I am not letting my daughter step into whatever the hell this is!"

More of the Asano family were rushing up as Ian tried to calm down Ruby's father and Erika spoke to her mother. Some of the Asano family knew what was going on, but others did not and were startled to see Jason clad in magical darkness.

"Son, what's going on?" Ken asked as he ran onto the sand.

Jason had rushed right past him earlier, up on the grassy embankment that bordered the beach. He had been with Hiro, who was following close behind his brother. Behind him was Taika, who had made an executive decision after seeing Jason in full regalia, as well as the portal he opened.

"I've got the cake!" he yelled out carrying the box containing the birthday cake Erika had made. He took it straight through the portal without bothering to wait for anyone else.

Jason turned to Ken and Hiro.

"Help me get the ones who don't know about everything through the portal," he said. He was struck by the family resemblance as the brothers both nodded and got to work, turning to the still-gathering family members.

Every Network facility on the planet was a frenzy of activity and they were not alone. All around the world, military units that had worked with the Network scrambled to expand their readiness for what was to come. Government bodies globally were enacting protocols developed with the Network, attempting to set logistics into place, rapidly introduce emergency legislation and accelerate a program of public awareness that the world was about to face an unprecedented threat.

The public awareness component was the first to face a crucial impediment. As governments tried to broadcast public service announcements, media companies resisted, unleashing a barrage of legal challenges.

Those challenges didn't completely shut down the flow of information, but it was inflicting critical gaps in the knowledge that was going out to the public. With genuine information patchy and inconsistent, those gaps were being filled with speculation, conspiracy theories and outright disinformation. In different parts of the world, the results ranged from social media flame wars to panic on the streets.

The legal obstructionism of the media barons was clearly not going to hold up, with the first cases being struck down in hours. Every delay was costly, however, as proto-spaces appeared undetected around the globe. In less than three days, they would start spilling monsters directly into the world.

Farrah had been part of an international task force with hundreds of members from Network branches all around the world to investigate the blackouts. While they had considered a complete collapse of grid functionality a low-probability outcome, contingency plans had been put into place and were currently being carried out.

The core of the response was a program to actively search for proto-spaces by getting Network ritualists out into the field. Farrah's expertise and her studies of the grid had made her a lead in the contingency project, and she had developed a ritual for just that purpose. It had to be simple enough to be employed by those with minimal ritualism skills, efficient enough that it wouldn't break the spirit coin bank, yet wide-area enough to actually be worth using.

Farrah had given Jason an item for his trip that allowed him to track proto-spaces, but replicating that item was not a viable solution. On top of the cost to mass-produce it, it was only able to find proto-spaces and not the apertures into them. Only Jason had the power to enter the spaces directly.

Although it was only a side project to the investigation into the grid blackouts, Farrah had taken the contingency ritual through several iterative improvements before disseminating it. It was simple enough that a ritualist in every branch had been made proficient in its use, which was paying off as they taught it to others in turn.

The contingency plans being put into action were a poor substitute for the grid. In addition to tying up personnel and consuming resources, they could only monitor tiny slices of area compared to the coverage of the grid. Instead, they focused on thorough scanning of population centres over maximising total coverage. Network ritualists could be deployed prioritising population centres. Major cities were critical both for population and infrastructure, which made preventing monster outbreaks critical.

The trade-offs for this approach were not easy to swallow. The Network had the people to cover major cities in most of the developed world, but rural and isolated areas would be left unprotected. The impact on agricultural regions would be extreme once hordes of monsters were roaming the countryside but covering expansive regions with minimal population wasn't a viable option. The problem was the food shortages that this would eventually lead to.

Some areas of the world lacked the proper Network coverage to cover even the major population centres. The area most impacted by this was Russia, which was largely dominated by the Cabal. The Network branches there had always been operating in a borderline state of effectiveness and they were not equipped to meet the new challenges. The International Committee was working to remedy this, but there were already too many fires to put out.

The situation in Russia was part of the impetus for the Network to reach out to the Cabal. The places where the Network was weakest were often those where the Cabal was strongest and the idea of supplementing Network assets with Cabal resources was being actively explored.

"Asano," Anna called out as she emerged through the rooftop door. Kaito turned from where he was directing people as they loaded crates onto his helicopter.

"Committeewoman," Kaito greeted after jogging from the helipad to meet her.

"I heard that some of my fellow committeepersons had conscripted you to take their scattered family members to their family compounds."

The members of the Steering Committee were all old family Network, including Anna herself. The kind of work the Asano family had done on their own compound, the old families had put in place decades ago. They didn't have the expertise of Farrah as a guiding hand, but the accumulated knowledge and resources of generations was not to be dismissed.

"You have your own family," Anna continued. "Things are going to get rough and you should make sure they're taken care of."

"Jason is dealing with that," Kaito said. "He'll see them right and then come here to help with logistics. Right now, I'm needed here. There's a lot more people than just our families who are going to need help."

"No kidding," Anna said. "I can't help but notice that you aren't ferrying committee family members, in spite of their requests."

"Farrah told them all to go jump," Kaito said. "She scares them."

"She should. You're moving resources for the dimensional space detection contingency?"

"People, resources, whatever it takes."

"I'll let you get back to it, then," Anna said.

"Jason said he'll come here once our family has been rounded up," Kaito said. "He can move a lot of people through those portals of his. Let him sort out those committee people's families, if only to stop them throwing their weight around and making trouble."

"Can't your brother only portal to places he's been before?"

"Farrah had him scope out all the Network family compounds for reference before he went on his trip," Kaito said. "He can portal right to them."

Kaito turned and headed back for the helicopter. As he approached, he snapped his fingers and it started spinning its rotors.

Anna returned to the chaos of the operations centre where Ketevan was marshalling the chaos like a general in the midst of battle. As Director of Operations, she had a lot more to do than Anna, whose oversight role had been reduced to Asya looping her in on International Committee directives as she passed them onto Ketevan. It had always been the case that the IC didn't have actual authority over the branches, but with a global crisis, any branch not getting with the program was dooming the people they should be protecting.

Anna waited for a rare lull and made her way into what used to be her own office.

"Keti," Anna said. "I'm pretty much useless at this point. Do you have anywhere I can make myself useful?"

"Absolutely," Ketevan said. "We've got a bunch of people coming in from the EOA looking to defect."

"Defect?"

"The rank and file didn't know what the people in charge were doing. Once the grid went down, orders started coming in and a lot of them didn't like it when they realised what was happening. They've started to approach Network branches all over looking to contribute."

"Isn't there a concern about infiltration?" Anna asked.

"Of course there is," Ketevan said. "Right now, though, we need warm bodies and information, and they have both. I'd love for you to take that whole mess off my hands."

"Alright," Anna said. "Point me in the right direction."

While the Network was in chaos, in a quiet, still and largely empty stretch of Arizona desert, an old shed sat a few miles from a town that wasn't much more than a gas station, a bar and a pervasive sense of having been left behind by life.

No one had gone to the old building in years and the gate lock on the chain-link fence had long ago rusted shut. None of the locals remembered it being anything but abandoned. The only surprise was that it hadn't fallen down yet.

The building was largely empty, which made the two things that were present stand out. One was a 2002 Pontiac Firebird in pewter metallic, covered by a dusty car sheet. The other object was significantly more extraordinary, and likewise covered in a sheet. It was a glass cylinder filled with a liquid that looked like water, radiating cold despite not being connected to any kind of cooling device. The truly unusual part was the naked woman floating in the liquid, neither truly alive nor truly dead.

What the sheet did not cover was the magical diagram that had been cut into the concrete floor, seemingly with a saw, in a circle around the glass cylinder and its bizarre contents. It was covered in dirt and dust, as were the piles of spirit coins placed in locations around the circle.

The small town did not have anyone with magic, regardless of what old Raquel would claim about her psychic powers. There was no one to sense the disembodied soul approach from the west, enter the building and slip into the body in the tank.

After sitting dormant for many years, light shone from the lines of the magical diagram on the floor. One by one, the spirit coins within it disappeared and the liquid within the tank started to glow. Finally, the now-embodied soul opened her eyes. The glass shattered, sending icy liquid flooding across the floor and she staggered out, eyes blinking in confusion. She moved to the car, leaning heavily on it as she worked her lungs for the first time.

Eventually, her mind and body came into sync as her soul imprinted her memories onto the still-pliable brain. She was disoriented, uncertain as to how long the process had taken by the time she regained lucidity. She had never really expected it to work, but after what happened, she knew it was her only chance. If she had played along, they would have watched her every moment, ever-ready to swing the axe. Better to take the risk and seize the initiative before they dug out her contingencies.

She pulled the cover off the car and peered into the side mirror, seeing a face fifteen years younger than it should be looking back. It was not the face of Mrs South, which was a name she had now surrendered. She was once again Audrey Blaine, and she was hungry.

10

HUMANITY

"…BROTHER OF CELEBRITY CHEF Erika Asano, shown here, actually appeared on his sister's cooking program. He was declared legally dead for a year and a half after an explosion in his apartment building, which the Victoria Police at the time put down to a gas explosion. Subsequent enquiries have revealed that the building in question had no gas service, pointing to a quick and quiet cover-up. This, in turn, leads to questions about how long authorities have known about Asano and what appear to be his extraordinary abilities…"

"You're more famous than Eri now, little brother," Kaito said. "Why did you make a big display on the beach like that? It wouldn't have taken you that much longer to do it quietly. Hell, with the commotion, it probably would have gone faster. Then you show your face with all those people using camera phones."

Jason and Kaito were watching news footage with the augmented reality goggles provided by Kaito's helicopter as they flew rapidly over the Australian outback. A passive ability from his swift essence let Kaito's helicopter outpace any ordinary helicopter, even at iron rank. He had several active abilities that could give it a further boost, but he was holding off on those.

Endurance was the theme of the day as they used Kaito's helicopter to sweep the country for proto-spaces. Even at Kaito's speed, they couldn't cover the whole country, but while Jason was busy shepherding the Steering Committee members' families around, Kaito and the operations team were plotting out a plan that maximised coverage. Instead of a grid sweep, they would hop from one population centre to the next through inland Australia.

The Network ritualists would stick to the coast, which required the least travel and had the most people. All in all, Australia had it quite lucky. Despite a landmass comparable to the contiguous United States, Australia had only a fraction of the population, almost all of which clung to the coast.

The logistics of sweeping for proto-spaces wasn't easy, but it was less troublesome than if the country wasn't mostly empty. The simplified search ritual Farrah developed was being deployed alongside anyone with even a rudimentary grasp of ritual magic. Even Emi had been roped in, with Taika, Greg and the silver-ranker, Ruth, as her protection detail. The now thirteen-year-old, courtesy of Farrah's personal instruction, was a better ritualist than many in the Network.

Jason and Kaito weren't the only ones being sent inland to patrol the smaller centres, but they were the most efficient. Kaito's speed and Jason's ability to duck into a proto-space, assassinate the anchor monsters and leave again allowed them to cover more space than any other team in the country. Their schedule was to go inland across New South Wales, up through the Northern Territory, back east into Queensland and then loop back south through New South Wales to Sydney. They would be covering as much as a quarter of the country, or at least as much as they could before monsters started turning up.

The grid compass Farrah had given Jason for his walkabout originally worked by tapping into the Network's grid, alerting him to nearby proto-spaces. She had modified it to directly sense proto-spaces itself, which diminished its effectiveness, but not so much as to make it useless. It continued to trade off range for the inability to detect apertures, making it mostly useful to Jason.

Other teams were roaming around, some of which had been given replica dimensional compasses. They were markedly less effective, however, lacking both Kaito's mobility and Jason's ability to enter a proto-space directly. This forced the other teams, on finding a proto-space, to take the time to hunt down the aperture and open it. Only then could strike teams move in to hunt the anchor monsters and negate the threat.

Fortunately, the strike teams had been retrained by Farrah and were able to act with speed and confidence. It wasn't a match for Jason entering the astral space directly and hunting the anchor monsters with Shade's vehicle forms, but it was better than what had been possible a year earlier.

"I don't understand why you let people film you with your hood down," Kaito said.

"What I can do is terrifying," Jason said. "Even in the other world, the way I fight had people comparing me to the monsters. In a very short amount of time, this world will start seeing monsters."

"You don't want to be lumped in with what's coming," Kaito realised. "You're using this time before the dimensional entities start arriving to have the media humanise you."

"Yes. For whatever reason, the EOA had been playing me up instead of shutting me down in terms of media coverage. I might as well use it."

Audrey Blaine felt odd as she drove along an Arizona highway. Her new body had been in stasis for more than a dozen years, the last remnant of a secret program whose progenitors were all dead. That was something she had made very sure of, a long time ago.

Thirty years ago, a top secret collaboration of personnel from the Network, the Cabal and the Engineers of Ascension had been enacted, without their parent organisations being made aware. Researchers from each group came together in an attempt to take projects from each faction that had plateaued in their development and push them forward using the knowledge and the resources of the others.

The resulting advancements in EOA and Cabal projects benefited both groups without either realising the source of the breakthroughs. The comparatively limited advancement of the Network programs proved the group's downfall as disgruntled Network researchers leaked the group's existence.

The three factions had proceeded to eliminate the group with Audrey in charge of the EOA purge contingent. The EOA was delighted with what the group had delivered to them but were unwilling to allow the potential security risk should their long-term goals be compromised. The work done already was enough for the EOA to move forward on their own.

That assignment had been the start of her rise as she ruthlessly excised the researchers. Her ambitions led her to assemble her own team to poach what they could, even as she was praised for destroying everything. In the wake of the program's seeming destruction, Audrey's hand-picked people continued.

In the end, she became wary of her own researchers as her rising career brought increased scrutiny and their skeletons remained buried out in the desert. She purged everything except for the body she now inhabited.

The body in the tank was based on a research path the original team rejected due to the extreme incorporation of Cabal and Network materials and methods. As this meant it couldn't be introduced to the mainstream EOA, the research path was redirected, despite the promising results. Audrey's own team had no such compunctions.

The body in the tank was cloned from Audrey's own DNA by her team, who accepted means and methods that the original team had rejected. Biological material provided by the Cabal was heavily incorporated, its mystical properties maintained by processes learned from the Network.

The EOA's modern converted people were much more advanced than the early version developed by the original secret research collaboration. The ability to create stable, silver-rank converted was the impetus for finally putting their plans into motion—plans that had originated back with the crude, early, iron-rank converted.

Even so, the converted remained relatively simple and almost synthetic in their powers and development. They were the result of external forces being applied to individuals, rather than building such individuals from the ground up.

The key to the EOA methods had been the soul modification methods developed by the original team. Once they discovered that the critical element to accessing the soul was consent, the secrets of the Cabal and the Network allowed them to unlock the path to change, transforming ordinary people into magical powerhouses.

Audrey's body was new to her but of an age with the early, iron-rank converted. Unlike the converted, though, her body's abilities were more holistic, inherent and exotic, courtesy of the biological material provided by the Cabal. She didn't know what had gone into the inception of her body, and even its creators had been unsure of what it would be capable of.

Audrey had kept this one project hidden away after eliminating even her own team because of the magical connection she had to it. She was the basis for the bulk of the body's biomass. The magic matrix that governed it, something possessed by all living things, was based on Audrey but reinforced using Network methodology.

Audrey's team believed that the result was a latent bond that would allow Audrey herself to occupy the empty vessel should anything happen to her original body. This was similar to an ability some members of the Cabal enjoyed, creating empty vessel replicants of their bodies to be inhabited after death.

So long as their souls never made it to the astral, this did not draw the attention of the Reaper. Once a soul entered the astral, it was the Reaper's to govern, but until then, it was the affair of the local death god, if any. The Reaper's concern was not with cheating death but coming back from it once the soul passed on to the astral.

The bond served as a tether for the soul, guiding it to the new body. It was the reason she had refused the magical augmentations that her position in the EOA offered. Although the potential of the bond was untested, she did not want to risk severing it. Without these augmentations, she had looked the eldest of the Four Cardinals, despite Mr North and Mrs West both being her senior.

After all those years, Audrey had finally tested it out, with success that both surprised and relieved her. Her new body felt strong and potent, although it was possessed of an unnerving power that she was yet to understand. She felt like a child wearing new clothes that had been bought for her to grow into.

She was very aware that her new body was hungry for power. The car had contained a small fortune in spirit coins taken from the Network years previous, mostly bronze coins but even some precious silvers. The first thing she had done after steadying herself enough to move around properly was to shove bronze coins into her mouth, one after the other. Each left the electric tingle on her tongue of licking a battery, but their power felt hollow, like diet soda of the soul. Ten of the coins vanished into her mouth before she was sated. She felt a craving for the silver coins but steeled herself to keep them in reserve.

Her senses were far more powerful than those she had had in her old body. More than once as she drove along the highway, she had been forced to pull over with vertiginous sensory overload. Even the monochrome, empty desert could overwhelm her. She saw things far in the distance, colours she didn't know existed. The dry air on her skin told a story of the weather and her location that she understood on an instinctive level. She had the concerning sensation of the instincts behind that sense not being entirely human.

Sitting in the driver's seat by the side of the road as her dizzyingly overwhelmed senses settled once more, she considered her options. The smart move would be to stay dead, collect the resources she had hidden away and live quietly on a beach somewhere. However, with the complications likely to arise from her new body and a world facing a monster apocalypse, this was not a viable approach.

The EOA's plan was precipitously close to the next phase; the media interference prevented the Network from effectively seizing the initiative before the monsters started to appear. She couldn't go back to the EOA, nor would she. There was the Cabal, with whom she had contacts, and they might even see her as one of their own now. She had no idea what their response to the EOA's actions would be, though, and she would be tarred with the same brush, even after leaving them.

That meant the Network. She didn't have as strong connections there, but she did have leverage. The information she possessed was exactly what they were going to need. Even so, she hesitated. They would likely be even more hostile than the Cabal, and there was an outside chance some local goon might decide to torture what she knew out of her. It was unlikely anyone would take the risk with what was currently at stake, but it was something she was wary of.

She thought about what she had done, standing up to the other cardinals. She was not a decent human being. The decent part was long gone and now the human part was gone with it. But there had to be a line. She wasn't going to become a monster. She could not tolerate letting civilisation crumble in a grasp for power.

She'd had to walk to the gas station to get the car running. The petrol in the can in the shed had long since degraded. Fortunately, the money stash had not. She'd bought a cheap burner phone while she was there, but she didn't have any of her contacts saved. Like everyone else, she had given up memorising phone numbers years before. She did know where to find the Network branch in Phoenix, though, so once her head cleared, she started up the car and continued on.

Jason and Kaito were flying over an Indigenous community in the Northern Territory that wasn't large enough to be spared a Network presence, which was true of most of the outback. Jason blurred and vanished from the passenger seat of the helicopter as he phased into the proto-space. That continued to unnerve Kaito, even when he knew it was coming.

Kaito landed to rest and recover some mana, consuming an iron-rank coin for himself and feeding one to the helicopter through a slot on the outside of the vehicle. The slot had originally been in the cockpit, but every person who saw him use a spirit coin on the helicopter made a coin-operated joke. Now, when he conjured the helicopter, the coin intake was located in a discreet spot on the exterior.

Twenty minutes later, his helicopter detected a strong aura burst a few kilometres away and he moved to pick Jason up. Jason had emerged from the proto-space after hunting the anchor monsters.

"Any problems?" Kaito asked as Jason stepped aboard.

"Nah, the anchor monsters were only bronze. No flyers, either, so Shade just flew me right over the trash. It would be nice if I could bring you into the spaces with me."

"We both know that won't be happening."

Jason could only transition into proto-spaces alone and there was no way Kaito trusted Jason enough to enter his spirit vault.

"Mr Asano," Shade said. "There is an issue that has arisen at the family compound."

"Didn't we decide to call it Asano Village?"

"That proposal was rejected," Shade said. "Discussions are ongoing, although the situation is generally too chaotic for such organisational concerns. There is still some contention as to the necessity of moving to the compound, despite your warnings and demonstrations."

"People have been watching the stories that say I'm either a hoax or a killer?"

"They have," Shade said. "The latest family-related problem is quite different, however. A woman has arrived from Japan claiming that she wants to test your worthiness to carry the Asano name."

"Bugger that," Kaito said. "No one gets to tell us if we can carry our own damn name."

Jason glanced at his brother and they shared a nod.

"Damn right," Jason said.

"What would you like me to do until you get back, Mr Asano?" Shade asked.

"Find that lady and tell her to park her worthiness where the sun doesn't shine."

"Very well," Shade said. "If you do not mind, however, I would prefer to paraphrase."

11
MEDIA BLITZ

JEREMY WESTIN WAS SURPRISED TO FIND A FRESHLY SEALED ROAD LEADING all the way into the isolated bushland area. He followed it to a gate in a chain wire fence, where a sign marked further progress as a private road. There seemed to be something off about the fence, but he would need to look closer to identify what it was.

Next to the gate was a security booth. It was circular and made up almost entirely of mirrored glass that didn't allow him to see inside, giving it an unnerving panopticon effect. The fence intersected the circle in the middle, leaving half of the building on each side of the fence. The glass building was incongruously modern amongst the pleasant bushland surrounds. He wondered about the legality of something that could throw off blinding reflections, although it didn't seem to be doing that at all, despite the sunshine beaming right onto it. Taking a second look, he realised the lack of glare coming off of it was quite unusual.

Jeremy pulled up in front of the gate, turned off his car and waited. No one came out and he wondered if the small building wasn't the security station he assumed but some kind of art installation. He stepped out, looking closer at the fence. Instead of the traditional chain-link pattern, the wiring on this fence was deeply varied, as if someone had tried to make a tapestry from a wire fence. The fence also looked a little different in texture and colour to steel mesh he'd seen in the past, but that could easily be a matter of the galvanisation process.

The wiring was shaped into what looked like ideographs from a language he didn't know, and not the same ones in a loop. He suspected that someone who knew the language in question would be able to read the fence like a book, although what language that was eluded him. The closest thing he had seen was hieroglyphs developed by Catholics trying to convert First Nations people in Canada.

He heard a helicopter faintly overhead, although he didn't spot it when he craned his neck to look for it. He walked up to the glass building, of which the only non-glass portion was a steel section on each side where the fence terminated against the wall. There did not appear to be doors. Walking around as much as he could, the building seemed to be made from two complete, unbroken glass curves, one on each side of the fence. He tried cupping his hands to peer through the glass, but its reflective surface was impenetrable.

In fact, there was a door, so seamlessly integrated that Jeremy had missed it entirely. A panel of glass retracted, slightly, with a quiet hiss of air, before sliding out of the way. It would have revealed the interior of the building if not for another wall behind it made of Māori.

"G'day," Taika said. "Who are you, and why can't you read the sign? It's a private road, bro. How about you bugger off so I can go back to looking up photos of Jason Statham with hair?"

Jeremy opened his mouth to speak, but a voice behind him beat him to the punch.

"He's a journalist. Telling them to leave just encourages them."

Jeremy turned around to see the person behind him. He recognised the face of Jason Asano from the storm of media surrounding the reveal of the two personas, the Starlight Rider and the Starlight Angel. First had come the Angel at the children's hospital, then the Rider in a rolling gunfight on motorcycles. From the beginning, there was debate over whether the two were the same, given that one brought life and the other death.

Rumours linking them to events across Asia and then Africa only fuelled speculation, culminating in the West Africa EVD outbreak. Despite denials from humanitarian workers, rumours persisted of a man who passed through the camps like a miracle healer.

The person healing people in camps was not draped in starlight but described as an Eurasian man. The parallels with the first stories of the Starlight Angel were obvious, however. It was in the wake of this that a small team of journalists put the pieces together and brought all the events to light. They dug up amateur phone footage, suppressed news stories, and myriad firsthand accounts.

Debate flared as to whether the reported events really did—or even could—take place. The stories and footage were so fantastical that most of it was dismissed as hoaxes and film manipulation. Was the Rider, filmed horrifically killing groups of people, the same Starlight Angel being praised as a merciful messenger from God? The reported appearance of other figures, including the dark riders shown in the helicopter news footage from Sydney, only muddied the waters.

When the government started releasing a series of inconsistent and ominous public announcements, suddenly there was an explosion in new information about the enigmatic man of starlight. New stories, new footage. A whole slew of reports from China, reportedly suppressed by the government, of a man with superhuman powers helping earthquake victims.

Then the Rider revealed his identity in a small coastal town in New South Wales, captured in a bevy of phone footage. It was so blatant that there was little doubt that the Rider had revealed himself to the world on purpose, but he literally vanished. Recordings of the incident showed many people, primarily Asano's family, appearing to vanish through a magic archway.

Once again, there were claims of hoax and doctored footage. Even so, the media immediately turned piranha, descending on the sleepy beach town in a frenzy. What they discovered was that every member of the Asano family had decamped from the town entirely, leaving reporters to scour the town for whatever they could find.

Information came in thick and fast. Jason Asano was the brother of a celebrity chef, and footage of his appearances was being juxtaposed with footage from his activities as the Rider. The joking man bantering with his sister as they demonstrated recipes together was a world away from the one massacring drug-fuelled bikers or fighting like a demon when cornered and outnumbered in a Hanoi slum. There was no recorded footage of him ever healing anyone, despite the repeated stories.

The fact that Jason Asano had been declared legally dead in a hastily covered-up explosion was a key focus of media analysis. Some even postulated that the current Jason Asano was actually an impostor, citing physical differences from his television appearances before and after his reported demise.

Jeremy had sent one of his junior reporters to Casselton Beach, along with the gaggle from other outlets, where unusual stories were turning up from interviewed townsfolk: Asano driving around in a variety of black supercars or being filmed performing elaborate feats of parkour in a park. Some local teenagers found their view counts hitting the stratosphere as their recordings of Jason's parkour antics were revealed in the mainstream media.

Those videos fuelled further speculation regarding an unknown woman apparently putting Asano's young niece through a rigorous training program, including after Jason stopped appearing. That the timing coincided with the activities around the world only cemented Jason as the man of mystery.

Interviews with locals revealed that Asano had been living on an enormous houseboat that appeared out of nowhere one morning and was now gone, just as mysteriously. The houseboat seemed to be a hub of strange activity, from a science-fiction-looking helicopter coming and going to strange lights at night to people flying over the water in jet suits that had yet to be released anywhere in the world, let alone Australia.

The sum total of all these oddities was a media vortex that threatened to swallow up the public warnings being issued as people tried to find the man who could reportedly perform miracles. As a professional participant in the media landscape, Jeremy recognised that someone with a lot of power was pushing the Asano narrative hard. There was a lot of interest in the story, to be sure, but his seasoned sensibilities told him that someone wanted the story painting over whatever else might be going on.

Even so, investigating that meant, like everyone else, investigating Asano. Doing his legwork, he managed to dig up some information about land purchases by Asano's uncle. Looking into Hiro Asano, he discovered that Hiro had been connected to organised crime in Sydney, until just before Jason Asano rose from the grave. At that point, he completely extricated himself and moved back to his hometown, living on Jason's houseboat.

Further digging led Jeremy to well-buried records relating to a construction project on the expensive chunk of bushland Hiro had purchased. Suspecting this to be the location of the vanished Asano family, Jeremy had come to investigate and now found himself face-to-face with Jason Asano.

There was no indication of how Jason had arrived unnoticed. There was no other vehicle and they were standing in open bushland. At a glance, he seemed a world away from the stories surrounding him, leaning casually against Jeremy's car in shorts, sandals and a Decepticons t-shirt. He had a look of amusement on his face, but something in his silver eyes left Jeremy unsettled. It left him feeling naked, as if Asano was staring directly at his soul.

"Hello, Mr Westin," Jason said. "Taika, this is Jeremy Westin. He runs an independent news website called *The Westin Front*, one of a handful trying to squeak around the media monopoly and do some actual journalism. His speculation about the terrorist readiness exercises has been way off the mark, but he's usually pretty good."

"You're Jason Asano," Jeremy said.

"So people keep telling me, but I saw on the news that I'm actually someone else."

"Are you?"

"No. Everyone changes, Mr Westin. I'm not exceptional in that regard."

Jeremy heard fake coughing behind him.

Cough "—load of bull shi—" cough.

Jeremy turned to look at the giant Māori. Then he turned back to Asano to see that his car had vanished in his brief moment of distraction.

"What happened to my car?"

"We'll take mine," Jason said.

"Yours?"

A terrifying cloud of shadows erupted from Asano, then coalesced into what looked like an oversized black hypercar that would not have seemed out of place in a Batman movie. The gullwing doors opened of their own volition and Jason ducked into the driver's seat. Jeremy stood frozen on the spot, eyes like poached eggs. He almost stumbled over when Taika gave him an encouraging slap on the back. Jason leaned over in the car to speak to Jeremy through the open door.

"Mr Westin— can I call you Jeremy? Jeremy, I don't have a lot of time, for reasons that will become apparent with tragic alacrity. That means that I need you to make a choice now: either get in and learn the single biggest secret on this planet or I give your car back and you leave. You're the first to find us, but your contemporaries will be close behind and I can give one of them the story instead."

Jeremy blinked, still getting over the one-two punch of overt magic and a back slap that seemed to have realigned several vertebrae. He warily entered the car, looking around at the interior like it would chomp down and bite him. The gullwing doors closed and his face showed a trapped expression.

"So what do you think of the security booth?" Jason asked.

"What? Uh, it's an odd piece of glasswork. That reflective treatment seems unusual."

"It's not actually glass," Jason said. "That's the cool thing. It's an aluminium-based ceramic. With a few tweaks."

In front of them, the gate rolled aside and Jeremy's eyes fell on the fencing again.

"Tweaks?" he asked. "Like the wire on the fence?"

"Good eye," Jason said as the car started moving. Jeremy noticed that Asano wasn't touching the steering wheel or the pedals, but he'd conjured the car out of solid shadows, so those minor details weren't really worth mentioning.

"Things are about to get crazy," Jason said. "The big news companies are using me to mask the very important warnings trying to go out, although I think the government announcements are doing better in countries where more than two companies own ninety percent of the media. I don't have to tell you that."

"Why are you showing me these things?" a rattled Jeremy asked.

"Because either today or tomorrow, an interdimensional war with an endless, unrelenting enemy is going to start across the world."

"What?"

Jason drew into the main thoroughfare of the family village, parking in front of the large residence. Erika was waiting for him out front. The street was awash with activity, with many stopping to look as Jason pulled up. Mostly, they were Asanos, but not all. Jason spotted Taika's mum loudly directing people as she organised something inside of the gathering halls. She gave Jason a wave and then went back to yelling at some of Jason's cousins who had paused in the process of carrying a table.

"What's up, Eri?" Jason asked as he stepped out of the car.

"Shade tells me you've been explaining magic to a reporter."

"Someone is clearly building up a specific narrative. I figure that we use the attention on me to put our own out there."

"Ignoring the fact that what you just described is the Network's job, not ours, Shade told me that you were doing the explaining yourself."

"Who else was going to do it?"

"Shade. Hiro. Me. Ian's tennis partner, Glenn. Anyone that isn't you."

"He needs to know."

"Even assuming that's true, you're literally the worst person to explain it to him."

"I'm not that bad."

"So you haven't been dropping bombs with zero context just to see how googly you can make his eyes go?"

"Shade, you're a traitor," Jason said.

"Fun is for people with time, Mr Asano," Shade said from Erika's shadow. "We have very little of it, so I decided that your sister would be the better introduction for Mr Westin. All you did was unnerve the man for your own amusement."

Jason groaned his concession and he and Erika turned to where Jeremy was still in the car. The journalist yelped as the car dissolved into darkness around him and he fell to the ground while the shadows were being drawn into Jason's shadow. Jason helped Jeremy to his feet as a motorised scooter came zipping along the thoroughfare.

"Uncle Jason!"

Emi didn't fully stop the scooter before stepping off, allowing the momentum to carry her into a power hug.

"G'day, Moppet," Jason said, returning the hug. "I thought you'd be off working for the Network."

"Farrah had them assign me to Coffs because it's closer to home. I have my own security escort!"

"Someone reliable, I hope."

"It's Ruth and Greg, since they aren't working with Uncle Kai right now."

Jason could sense them both, meandering in the direction of the main thoroughfare. Emi didn't need constant guarding when she was with family.

"Speaking of Kai," Erika said, "Jason, how long before you two are back in the air?"

"Enough time to sleep," Jason said. "Once Kaito is at full charge, we'll be back at it. The goal is to set up a series of potential teleport destinations so I can get around the country by hopscotching portals. I can portal to anyplace I can halfway remember, so I'm just hanging out in various places while Kaito takes a break."

"Let me take care of the journalist," Erika said. "Emi can take you to our other guest and then I'll bring the reporter back to you for an interview before you hit the sack."

"The other guest being our Japanese visitor?" Jason asked. He could already sense an unfamiliar silver-ranker. She was a core-user, but her aura had none of the usual sloppiness; it was clean and sharp.

"Yes," Erika confirmed.

As Jason's thoughts drifted to core users, he noticed the absence of his sister-in-law.

"Amy's not here?" Jason asked.

"She's still organising civic preparedness for when things kick off," Erika said.

The Casselton region was too scattered to warrant a permanent Network-scanning presence. The Network had foisted the area onto Jason, despite his having evacuated his family. It wouldn't take too much of his time to portal in and check the area for proto-spaces every couple of days between patrols. The concern was that a manifestation out of his dimensional compass range could lead to a dimensional breach in a neighbouring area. Once the monsters arrived, there was nothing to stop them from wandering in.

For this reason, Amy, as mayor, was preparing to commandeer all the accommodation in the tourist towns of Casselton Beach, Castle Reach and Casselton North. They all fell comfortably inside the range of the compass, if used in the central town of the three, Castle Reach.

Once people started realising the new reality about to descend on them, Amy would be ready to collect most of the regional populace into the three towns. It wouldn't prevent monsters arriving from out of range but was better than just leaving people to their fates. Few small towns had as much protection.

"Alright, Jeremy," Jason said. "I'm going to leave you in the capable hands of my sister while I go deal with the Next Damn Thing. Emi, lead the way."

12

GRANDMOTHERLY ADVICE

"We've got her in the guest wing of the main house," Emi said.

"There's a guest wing?" Jason asked.

"It's better than the holding cells, plus only Farrah would be able to get her in there."

"There are holding cells?"

"Farrah thought we would need somewhere to handle intruders until we figure out what to do with them. Plus, a drunk tank. We even have a magically reinforced divvy van. It's all in the administration quarter."

"That's thorough planning, I guess."

"She's up here," Emi said as she pointed at the section of the main residence ahead of them. Jason stopped walking.

"No, she's not," he said.

"She's meant to be," Emi pouted.

Jason ruffled his niece's hair and she shoved his hand away, annoyed.

"It seems she wanted a look around. You run off, Moppet, and I'll sort it out."

"I want to see."

"Shade," Jason said.

Shadows emerged out of Jason and Emi's shadows, wreathing Emi in a jet suit that took off and flew her away with a yelp.

"I'll get you, Uncle Jason!" her voice rang out of the village as Jason laughed, giving her a wave as she disappeared over a rooftop.

Asano Akari watched a girl spitting invective fly past the rooftop on which she was crouched. She frowned at the unusual sight.

"There are dark days ahead," a voice said.

She stood up, whirling to face it. She hadn't sensed his presence at all, despite her silver-rank hearing and aura senses. She still couldn't make out his aura despite his being close enough that she should be able to smell him, which she couldn't.

"We should take our fun where we can get it," Jason said. "There's sadness enough to come."

"You are Asano Jason."

"Seriously, what is with people? Do I have amnesiac tattooed on my forehead?"

"I am Asano Akari."

"G'day. I know we named this place Asano Village, but you came an awful long way to visit."

Examining the woman, Jason was struck by how much the woman resembled the sword at her hip. Her body and aura both were lean and sharp. The way she moved was swift, precise, and efficient. Her hair was cinched back in a practical ponytail, her clothes were sleek and fitted while her face had the polished perfection of silver rank. Although they did not look the same, Jason couldn't help but be reminded of his first encounter with Sophie. This woman was all sharp edges.

He glanced at the sword hanging from her belt. It was a chokutō, a Japanese straight sword, and his magical senses told him it wasn't conjured. It was a genuine magical item of exquisite craftsmanship, at least physically. To check the quality of the magic, he would need to look closer.

People with weapon essences fell into three camps. One conjured their weapons, usually with multiple options for multiple situations. Another used the best weapon of their type that they could find, using their abilities to enhance them further. The last type did both, using their real weapon personally and employing conjured weapons for various unusual attacks and abilities. The weapon essence users Jason knew well, Valdis and Gary, fell into the second category, although he had met individuals of all three types.

"I've been told why you're here," Jason said, "but that didn't come across as very flattering regarding your intentions. How about you tell me about why you're here before I go judging and we figure things out from there?"

She looked Jason over. He looked like anyone off the street with his casual clothes, but his undetectable aura belied that. He seemed to be standing at ease, but she could spot his careful balance, ready to move in an instant.

"You are of the assassination type," she said.

"Maybe, if you call a man with an axe a tree assassin," Jason replied. "It takes some hacking away to get the job done."

"You accumulate damaging effects instead of making a decisive strike. Unusual for someone with a focus on stealth."

"Really? When you're waiting for a monster the size of a traditional rustic cottage to die, good stealth is exactly the thing you want. Trust me."

"Many believe that our powers reflect our true natures. Your way of fighting throws away your face."

"Yep," Jason agreed with a chuckle, looking at the sword on her hip. "Honour is how people with fancy swords fight people with sticks and claim it's a fair fight."

"That is a poor characterisation of honour."

"And you came to my house to tell me I have none, which is a poor demonstration of courtesy."

Akari nodded, acknowledging the point.

"I passed the first test, then?" Jason asked. "Something along the lines of not flipping out when provoked?"

"The assessment is ongoing," Akari said.

"Then the next question is what gives you the right to come here to judge me and mine?"

"My family has been part of the Network for centuries. When you rose to prominence, we investigated your background and we do, indeed, share an ancestor."

"That's a fun fact that doesn't answer my question. How far back is this ancestor, out of curiosity?"

"Early Edo period."

"The seventeenth century? Not exactly second cousins, then, are we? Which makes me wonder again why I should give a damn about anything you have to say about how we do things here."

"My family—"

"Doesn't matter. You keep talking about your family, but I didn't ask about them and I don't care. State your business."

She gave him a flat, steely glare backed by her aura. When it had no discernible impact, her eyebrows raised in surprise.

"We have neither the right nor any interest in telling your family how to behave," Akari said. "How you handle your affairs is your concern and your concern alone."

"Glad we got that settled," Jason said. "I don't know where you parked, but the guy at the gate will let you out. I think they'll start closing airports pretty soon, so you might want to get a move on."

"My family is well known in Network circles," she said.

"Aaaand we're back to the family. If there's any kind of point you're edging up on, that would be great. It's kind of a busy week for me."

"You have started to shape your family into a clan," she said. "How you conduct yourselves is not our affair, but you share our name. If you flounder and collapse, that reflects on us, fairly or not. With your new prominence, Jason Asano, it is not just your own face you discard with your actions. It is ours as well."

"If you think you can decide what we do or how we do it, you're sorely mistaken, Miss Asano."

"We understand that your culture is not ours. Right now, your nascent clan stands or falls with you. It has been decided that so long as you yourself have the strength to earn respect, we shall not intervene."

"How generous. So, if I have the goods to prevent my family from collapsing in a pile and make you look bad, you'll leave us be?"

"Yes."

"And how do you check that? We fight?"

"That would be pointless," Akari said. "Your capability in that area is well-documented, but you cannot carry a clan on the strength of arms alone. You need leadership. Management. Foresight. You need to choose subordinates well and raise your people up as a whole. You must weather setbacks and resolve challenges. Know when to stand firm and when to bend. This last one is something we have heard may be your weakness, yet can be the most important."

"That doesn't sound like the kind of assessment where you do a quick few interviews and a multiple-choice test," Jason said.

"No. It will be extensive, carried out in a time of challenge and transition. If you can thrive in the coming days, then we will be satisfied."

"And why should we put up with any of this?" Jason asked. "You have no authority over me or my people and acting like you do is kind of giving me the irk."

"For the duration of the assessment, you will have something that your fledgling clan very much needs: an additional, expert category three."

"You'll come work for us while you're doing your little checks?"

"Yes."

"And you'll actually do what you're told? We already have the obnoxiously independent leadership position filled."

"I will act as directed, within reason, and make clear beforehand when asked to operate beyond the limits I am willing to tolerate."

"Alright," Jason said. "I'll take it to the family and we'll talk it out. What happens if we tell you to take a hike?"

"Then I will leave and we will hope that your clan is consumed in the coming crisis, which is an acceptable outcome that will not reflect poorly on us. Should you survive, once things have settled, then further action will be considered."

"Good to know."

Jason sought out his paternal grandmother. Her name was Yumi, although anyone that used it got a glare that stung like a slap across the ear. Yumi had been fully versed in magic during Jason's time away, through the Network's induction program.

She had one of the bushland residences, nestled amongst the trees. Jason sensed her up on the balcony and leapt two stories up with his cloak floating around him, which disappeared as he alighted on the wooden floor.

"Polite people knock," Yumi told him from over a cup of tea. She was sitting at an outdoor table made from native wood.

"I was hoping you could help me with something, Grandmother."

"This is about our visitor?"

"You're the only member of the family who was actually Japanese. I was hoping you could share some insights."

Yumi had come over from Japan with her late husband, shortly before their first child was born. Things had not been easy for Japanese immigrants in the seventies, but they had thrived, eventually becoming naturalised citizens.

Jason talked Yumi through his conversation with Akari.

"Honour is more a western concept than an eastern one," Yumi told him. "You said she spoke of face. The Asano clan does not care about our behaviour, so long as they are not shamed by us."

"What do you think she really wants?" Jason asked. "There's no way the Japanese Network gives up someone of her skill and power now, just over public relations."

"It is possible you are underestimating the importance of face to this clan. But you suspect something deeper?"

"Yeah," Jason said. "Grandmother, things are about to get bad. As bad as they've been since World War II, and maybe worse. Even if Akari was already on her way here when the grid went down, her clan should have had her on a plane home immediately. They definitely shouldn't be offering her up for some open-ended service to a fledgling Network family in a different country."

Yumi had quietly taken in Jason's explanation and did not respond immediately, sipping delicately at her tea.

"Jason, I have heard it said that you and Miss Hurin are extremely valuable to the Network. Without your usual braggadocio and nonsense, how valuable are you, exactly?"

"Priceless," Jason said. "So long as we cooperate, we represent knowledge and resources that doesn't stop paying off. We've been offering it on the cheap too, because protecting the world from monsters is the goal, not something to profit from."

"There is your answer, then," Yumi said. "The Asano Network family in Japan want to use our connection, tenuous as it is, to gain advantages from you."

"Then why come in so aggressively like this?"

"To save face. Their intention is to offer you a service in providing an expert when you need it most. They most likely believe that you will feel obligated to return the favour should their darkest day come to pass. This woman is not here to judge you but as an overture. How she is conducting herself is simply a show of strength, so as for her Asano family to not show weakness in front of ours, maintaining their face."

"Do you think we should accept that overture?"

"That depends," Yumi said. "Would she truly be an asset to us?"

"With the state the family is in and what is about to happen? Absolutely. It will be years before we produce our own people even close to her calibre."

"Then are you willing to reciprocate, when the time comes?"

"I think that's something I can live with," Jason said. "Provided there aren't any unseen dangers lurking below the surface."

Yumi nodded her approval.

"Yes," she said. "Make sure that this isn't an attempt to lure you into some specific troubles."

"If I find something out, we turn her away, then?"

"No," Yumi said. "If she's hiding something, then we don't reject her. If they are dealing with us in bad faith, we close our fist around them."

"Ah," Jason said. "We don't turn her away but demand more."

"Exactly," Yumi said. "So long as you are confident of handling whatever mess they want to bring you into, we milk them for all they're worth."

Jason nodded. "I'll call a meeting of the family to make a final decision, then."

He moved to jump off the balcony, when his grandmother spoke, and he paused, turning back to look at her.

"Jason," she said. "Did I ever tell you that you were my favourite grandchild?"

"No, Grandmother."

"Good, because you're not. You are coming along, though."

Jason chuckled and leapt over the railing, leaving his smiling grandmother behind.

13
A BLOKE WITH VAST COSMIC POWER

ON A BUSY SYDNEY STREET, AN ARCHWAY FILLED WITH DARKNESS ROSE UP in the middle of the footpath. The crowd backed away. Some quick thinkers immediately pulled out their phones, so when, after a few moments, two figures emerged from the arch, they were able to capture it. One wore dark robes, impossibly draped in a starry void, while the other was dressed normally but looked rather shell-shocked.

Jason pushed the hood back from his head as he looked around.

"I didn't pick very well," he said. "Nowhere to park. I feel bad about disrupting traffic."

He walked into the street where the cars were only crawling along, and stood in the path of a car so it stopped. The car ahead slowly moved forward to allow a full car length. Jason took Jeremy's car from his inventory, which dropped about thirty centimetres to the road with a crunching sound.

"Oops. How's your suspension? Never mind, just hurry. We're holding up traffic here."

He turned to Jeremy, who was throwing up in the gutter as more people pulled out their phones.

"Get it together, mate," Jason said. "You've got a story to do. Time to get moving, cobber."

Jason helped Jeremy to his feet and led him into the driver's seat of his car. While a queasy Jeremy was getting settled, Jason looked at the car he had forced to stop. The driver had opened the door to half get out and was also filming with his phone. Jason wandered over to him.

"Sorry about this, mate. You know what it's like finding a park, yeah."

"You're really him."

"Yep. What's your name, mate?"

"Sanjit."

"Nice to meet you, Sanjit. Sorry about Jeremy, there. It's his first time teleporting and he's not handling it all that well."

Sanjit was shaking his head in disbelief as he looked at Jason, Jeremy and the car Jason pulled out of thin air.

"How do you do those things?" he asked.

"I've got magic powers, Sanjit. Seems crazy, I know, but the spectrum of what constitutes crazy is about to be drastically realigned. There might be some panic, and people always hoard toilet paper when that happens, so I'd advise stocking up now and beating the rush. Hang on a sec."

Jason moved up to Jeremy's car, where the reporter had finally settled into the driver's seat, wide-eyed.

"Time to get a shuffle on, bloke," Jason said through the window.

Jeremy gave a dazed nod, started his car and slowly edged it forward. Jason went back to Sanjit.

"I'm suddenly worried if he's okay to drive," Jason said. "Looks like I've caused bit of a hullabaloo, so I'm going to make myself scarce. It was nice to meet you, Sanjit."

"Uh, you too. You're not what I expected."

Jason chuckled and shook Sanjit's hand.

"I'm just an ordinary bloke with vast cosmic power, trying to get by."

Jason flashed him a grin and then went back to the portal, where people were experimentally poking it with their fingers.

"Excuse me," Jason said. They moved aside, as he stepped through it and vanished. The portal descended into the ground, leaving a line of darkness that then too disappeared.

Returning to Asano Village, Jason was ready for some overdue rest, but first arranged a meeting of the family decision-makers to take place after he woke up. He took the secret tunnel tram from the main residence, out under the water to where his cloud house now sat at the bottom of the sea. The hidden tram system had been brought online with the rest of the village's magic infrastructure as soon as the family started occupying it.

Farrah's systems were collecting and delivering magic from elsewhere to fuel the infrastructure, but certain systems had to be supplemented with spirit coins. Fortunately, Jason had no shortage of iron and bronze coins. The handful of systems in the village requiring silver coins remained dormant.

When Jason had emptied the cloud flask into the water, the cloud house had taken the form of a series of domed rooms, connected by short tunnels. The cloud-stuff domes could be shifted between opaque and transparent; Jason preferred to leave it transparent. When the sun was bright and at the right angles, light reached the depths of the water to illuminate the rooms with a constantly shifting blue light that Jason loved. Other times, the cloud house produced downward-directed glow lamps that floated over the domes to produce a similar effect.

The reaction to Jason's lighting solution was mixed amongst the few who knew of the cloud house's location. Erika found it distracting while Emi shared her uncle's love of the cool, shimmering colour.

Dealing with the reporter and Akari had bitten off a couple of hours of what should have been Jason's time to sleep, or his personal equivalent. Under Farrah's direction, instead of sleeping, he now entered more of a recuperating trance state that enhanced recovery and maintained a subconscious awareness of his surroundings, even passively expanding his senses. It wasn't the same as being fully alert, but he was easily roused by unexpected stimuli.

It was the middle of the day, but Jason was far from the only one whose sleeping patterns had been thrown out of whack. All around the world, Network personnel and others were in a mad scramble to prepare for what was coming. Their efforts were impeded by the chaos in the media, of which the news vortex surrounding Jason was only a part.

One of the larger problems was mixed messaging. Some countries had media alerts going out with physicists talking about dimensional invasion to general disbelief. Others were trying to promote readiness in the population while being vague on the nature of the threat. Add in obfuscating media companies across the globe, and it was a giant mess that failed to prepare or inform. There was no way that the media obstructionism would last, but the clock was running down before monsters started appearing.

The first recorded incident of monsters manifesting happened in Angola, while Jason was resting. Gem-like monstrosities and blighted earth elementals appeared en masse at a diamond mine. By the time footage of the creatures reached the internet, there were incidents on every continent. Even an Antarctic science team recorded monsters from afar as they evacuated their research station.

In most places around the world, the Network's plans to protect the major population centres proved to be effective. Active searching for proto-spaces around population centres was working and the spaces were being shut down. Public messaging was finally becoming clearer, just in time to get people heading for the major centres, although that presented logistical issues of accommodation and overcrowding.

Fortunately, the Network partnerships with civilian governments and the military over the last few years had put in place contingencies that were being immediately enacted. This included logistical efforts in the safe zones and Network-supported military response to the monster waves.

It was far from enough to handle the events without loss, however. The death toll rapidly climbed as monsters appeared in isolated and rural areas. The populations were smaller than the cities, but whole towns were wiped from the face of the Earth before the overextended response teams were able to intervene.

On the day the first monsters arrived, the course of human history was irrevocably changed. Those protected in the safe zones watched monster movie footage play across the news as people flooded into the cities. Then, an entirely different kind of movie started playing out.

All over the world, individuals with abilities beyond those of ordinary people appeared to fight the monsters. These were not the black-fatigued essence users of the Network but colourfully garbed people who appeared in small teams, acting independently of the military and government response.

"Superheroes," Jason murmured as he watched. "That's genius."

In the media room of the main residence of Asano Village, Jason was observing a bank of monitors, alongside his closest family members.

"Genius?" Erika asked.

"Think of all the garbled coverage leading up to this," Jason said. "All the uncertainty and confusion. Now the monsters have come and magic is out there for everyone to see. How are the world governments going to explain this? Are they going to walk people through the complexities of the magical secret societies? The Network, the grid, the secret history? All while people are panicking as monsters emerge from the countryside to slaughter them?"

"People are idiots," Yumi said. "They always choose a simple lie over a complex truth. Someone wanted this chaos so they can take control of the messaging by giving people a simple answer."

"Exactly," Jason said. "The world just went crazy and people aren't ready to hear about a complex history of secret conspiracies. Superheroes are a paradigm that people can get their heads around. All you need is someone with magic powers, well-defined abdominals and some bright, stretchy fabric."

"Who are they?" Erika asked.

"The Engineers of Ascension," Jason said. "The EOA defectors already let the Network know that the media meddling was in preparation to seize control of the narrative with big moves once the monsters started appearing. Now we're seeing how. What has been the one consistent thing in the news over the last few days?"

"You," Erika realised.

"Exactly," Jason said. "They've been slowly building up public awareness of me for months, in preparation for today. They were priming the world to accept people with extraordinary powers."

"How powerful are these superheroes?" Hiro asked.

"We've gotten word from a major defector to the American Network that the EOA has reached a new threshold in their magical enhancement program. It's a process to enhance people with magic other than essences and it's significantly more intrusive. Caustic alchemy baths, surgery to engrave magic runes onto bones. Magic tattoos are the easy part. The result is people who are strong and fast, with a few extra abilities from the magic tattoos I mentioned. These new ones will be silver rank, and based on what we've seen in the past, probably able to boost themselves higher temporarily."

"They won't have the experience that Network people have," Yumi assessed. "They're going to lose some, but that might work for them. A few heroic sacrifices will go a long way."

"Most likely," Jason said. "There's a reason all those old comic books had the hero looking defeated on the cover."

"There are teams of these heroes appearing all over the world," Erika said. "They have this many?"

"I don't know how many of them will be at this new level of power," Jason said. "When they were mobilising them in preparation, a lot of the EOA caught wind that something bad was happening and either fought against it or completely defected to the Network. None of these new silver-rank ones, though. Whether through loyalty screening or brainwashing, they knew which side their bread was buttered on and kept their mouths shut."

"If the EOA had so many defections, it sounds like they messed up," Ken said.

"No," Yumi said. "They knew the price and were willing to pay it. They came in ready to make sacrifices in order to grab the initiative."

"Which is exactly what they've done," Jason said. "Their so-called superheroes are dominating the narrative."

"Piggybacking off of you," Erika said.

"I'm only a part of it. They used me out of opportunism. If I hadn't come along, they would have just done something else."

"So, what now?" Erika asked.

"The Network has me on standby right now," Jason said. "They want me ready to go when silver-rank monsters appear. They also want to establish that the government response can be effective by publicising operations against lower-rank monster swarms, which, in fairness, they are the best at. They don't want to play into the EOA's narrative."

"Does it matter who is telling the story?" Ken asked. "Shouldn't everyone be out there, doing what they can?"

"No," Yumi said. "Public reaction is going to be critical in how the long-term response is formed."

"This is too big for small groups of people to be the centrepiece of the response, even people with powers like Farrah and myself," Jason said.

"That's the outcome the EOA wants because a broad, military-based response favours the Network. They want to use public opinion to push governments into directing resources their way."

"This seems like the worst time to be haggling over political points," Ken said.

"It is," Jason said, "but the EOA set this into motion, to the point of a revolt forming in their own ranks. Expecting them to act in the public interest now is futile. People are dying and the ones with power are fighting over more power. Some things even an interdimensional monster invasion can't change."

"Jason," Yumi said. "We should have that meeting you scheduled."

"I don't think now is exactly the time," Erika said.

"Yes, it is," Jason said. "We need to discuss a powerful new asset that we may very well need in this new world."

After bringing the extended Asano family into the village, along with a handful of others, a village committee had been formed to manage the village's affairs. It had originally begun as a meeting to decide on a name for the village, ultimately settling on Asano Village. Jason's second choice —'Jason's Magic Buff Emporium'—was resoundingly overruled.

Under Erika's direction, the committee subsequently evolved into a formalised management group. Specific roles were introduced and membership underwent some early shifting as people took up or begged-off various responsibilities. Erika controlled food logistics, Ken had land development and Hiro was in charge of magical infrastructure. Jason's paternal grandmother, Yumi, oversaw medical. A retired doctor, she managed the administrative aspects while Ian led operations. There were numerous other roles, held both by Asano family members and by other families also in the village.

The extended Asano family made up the majority, but there was a scattering of others as well. This included the family members of Asya, Taika, Greg, and Emi's friend, Ruby. Kaito's best friend and former business partner, Benny, had also brought his family as had Erika's old producer, Wally. Although many of them were left confused, they had all been strongarmed into heading for the village by their family members in the know.

Asya's mother, Rabia, was the member of the village committee representing the non-Asano families and had been working with her daughter over the last few days to introduce everyone at the village to magic. They were using a heavily accelerated version of the Network's induction program.

Jason's role on the committee was not as a permanent member. Although he had become the de facto patriarch of the nascent Asano clan, he was too busy to be involved in the day-to-day management of the village. His formal role was to break voting deadlocks on the committee and set the direction for the family as a whole. He anticipated more than ample outside input in this regard. Generally, the committee would only call on him as needed.

In the meeting Jason had called, he presented Akari Asano's proposition of remaining in Asano Village to the group. Debate went around the table but was dominated by Yumi, who highlighted the lack of downside to such a potentially important gain. Consensus was swiftly reached.

"We'll accept her provisionally for the moment, then," Jason said.

His phone alarm went off.

"Grandmother," he said as he checked his phone. "I'll have you deal with Akari for now, if you don't mind. It looks like I have work to do."

14
A VERY LONG TO-DO LIST

Strategy meetings to develop effective responses to the monster waves were taking place all over the world. At one such meeting in Sydney, Network and military personnel were discussing the responses still being rolled out, less than a day after the monster waves had begun. Sydney's Director of Tactical Operations, Koen Waters, spoke in a meeting held in a large briefing room.

"In most instances, we anticipate tried and tested methodology to be effective. Existing sweep and clear tactics are the most effective means to rapidly exterminate waves. We foresee three main scenarios where alternative approaches will be more effective. One is when the monsters are clustered together even more than usual and in wide-open spaces. This is a best-case scenario for us because a small number of high-category-operators specialised in area coverage can clear these scenarios. After that, a small team for mop-up will be all we need."

"How often can we expect to see this best-case scenario?" Annabeth Tilden asked.

"In the outback, quite frequently," Koen said. "There's an awful lot of flat and empty out there and those are the areas with no dimensional space patrol coverage. This is good news. Australia's geographically condensed population will see us through this far better than many other nations."

The government's liaison officer, Gordon Truffett, interrupted.

"What's your opinion on the best way to spin this to make us seem in control?"

"Shut up, Other Gordon," Anna said. "This is a strategy meeting, not a political one. What's scenario two, Koen?"

Other Gordon fumed. He was about to retort when he felt the oppression of Koen's aura, leaving him flustered.

"Scenario two is when the landscape is just the opposite. Complex terrain, poor sightlines. It's a bug hunt where the bugs are the size of a bread truck and setting up ambushes."

An Army major spoke up. "Military vehicles are much easier to use when not trying to get them through the apertures. To what degree do you anticipate that compensating?"

"We're rolling out the magically enhanced heavy ordnance program that has been in the works since the category-four incident in England. Major, you should see magically enhanced, vehicle-mounted weapons arriving at bases before the end of the day. Numbers are still limited, but we expect them to have an increasing impact as more enhanced weaponry is mobilised. At the end of the day, though, the best solutions are the small-group special strike teams we've been training up over the last nine months. The ones we're training from scratch aren't ready for deployment, but the retrained teams are already showing positive results."

"You anticipate things being under control, then?" Other Gordon asked.

"Not even close," Koen said. "I'll be discussing the key problems after outlining the scenarios, the third one of which is the problem of power. High-category dimensional spaces contain primarily category-two dimensional entities, along with one or more category threes. Our specialist strike teams have the strength to handle them but not the numbers, while our combined military/Network sweeper teams have the numbers but not the strength."

"Couldn't this scenario be combined with either of the other two?" Anna asked.

"Yes," Koen said. "A scenario one and three combination is harder to deal with than a one, but still manageable. It's combining two and three where things get rough. As we speak, that is the exact situation we're facing at a location in the Blue Mountains. We have multiple strike teams en route, plus Jason Asano."

"This is the man from the news?" the major asked.

"It is," Koen said. "With every analysis we've made of Asano's capabilities, he has turned around and outstripped our projections. Personally, I'm hoping that he never stops, because we do not have what we need to meet the challenges ahead. Too few people, too few resources, too little power."

"I'm assuming this meeting wasn't called just for you to explain how buggered we are," the major said.

"It was not," Koen said. "There is a response that is being tried in other parts of the world. Africa and Russia are already reporting positive results, only a day into the monster wave. They've been drawing on external support."

"Please tell me you aren't talking about the EOA and their bloody superheroes," Anna said. "League of Heroes, my arse."

"No," Koen said.

"I think we need to consider that option," Other Gordon said. "They're getting a lot of positive traction."

"Not an option," Anna said. "Even if we were willing to overlook that they were responsible for this in the first place and then responsible for neutering an effective response in the lead-up, they aren't willing to work with us. Even in situations where we have arrived together at the same events, they overtly operate alone, with their media teams in tow."

"Their numbers are actually smaller than their media presence would suggest," Koen said. "They do not present the kind of help we need. The Cabal does, and they already have strongholds in the kind of remote, isolated areas where we need increased strategic options."

"So they can claim the credit too?" Other Gordon asked.

"Actually, just the opposite," Koen said. "The Cabal's concern is that their members will get lumped-in with the monsters. If we help keep them hidden until the world has a better handle on everything that's going on, they're offering their secret support."

"Then as the government's representative, I approve," Other Gordon said. "Further, we should be pushing the narrative with our own media teams."

"Absolutely not," Anna said.

"Actually, I agree with Mr Truffett," the major said.

"Who?" Anna asked.

"Me!" Other Gordon roared.

"Oh, right," Anna said. "But no to media."

"Mrs Tilden," the major said. "Your organisation is used to secrets, but the time for secrets is over. Mr Truffett is not wrong that we are fighting a war on multiple fronts, one of which is public opinion. If we let the Engineers of Ascension control the narrative, that is a beachhead from which they'll launch their invasion. The military has long had protocols for embedding press. We'll use them and show the real face of this conflict."

Anna sighed unhappily but didn't argue back.

"We're willing to discuss it," she said.

A flight of transport helicopters flew over forested mountains. Jason and Akari Asano were just two of a gaggle of essence users, mostly bronze and silvers from strike teams trained by Farrah. Jason and Akari were in Kaito's helicopter, along with one of the strike teams.

The helicopters were en route to where an advanced team had been setting up a landing zone ahead of the monsters' predicted path. The monsters were spread out over a large area, which they were currently flying over. It would be a lengthy and laborious task to dig them all out.

The silver-rank section leader leaned over to Jason.

"I know you do best working independently. You want us to drop you off here?"

"That'd be great." He leaned to Akari. "We're going to jump out here." Jason then turned to the cockpit door. "HEY, KAI. OPEN THE SIDE DOOR."

The cockpit door slid open. Kaito's flight crew, Asya, Greg, and Ruby were in front with him.

"I can hear you," Kaito said. "No need to shout."

"WHAT? I CAN'T HEAR YOU OVER THE HELICOPTER!"

"What are you talking about?" Kaito called back. Switching the helicopter controls over to Greg, Kaito got up and stood in the cockpit doorway.

"I THINK SOMETHING IS WRONG WITH YOUR HELICOPTER," Jason yelled into the near-silent helicopter. "IT'S NOT NORMALLY THIS LOUD."

Kaito frowned at him in confusion.

"I WAS WONDERING ABOUT THAT MYSELF," Greg yelled from the front.

Kaito looked questioningly at the Network strike team, who all put their hands over their ears and shook their heads.

"What the hell is going on?" Kaito asked, looking around at his helicopter with worry. "I can't hear anything. Is it a magic thing?"

Then he saw the confused expression on Akari's face and turned a glare on Jason.

"You're an arsehole."

The helicopter was filled with laughter as a grouchy Kaito went back to his seat. When he slapped a hand on the console, the side door of the helicopter opened up. Still moving at speed, it filled the space with loud, rushing air.

"GET THE HELL OFF MY HELICOPTER," Kaito yelled back, then the cockpit door slammed closed, cutting the cockpit off from the rushing air.

Jason nodded at the door to Akari and they jumped out. Jason made sure he stayed close to her as they dropped, since the cranky Kaito had not activated the slow-fall power of the helicopter. Despite not having a slow-fall power of her own, Akari had leapt from the helicopter with no hesitation. As they closed on the ground, Jason reached out to grab her with a shadow arm and pulled her into his body, using his cloak to arrest their fall.

Jason dropped them lightly into an area with lighter tree coverage and they both turned their heads to the right. A silver-rank monster had sensed their descent and was making a swift but silent path through the trees.

"Let's see what you can do," Jason said.

Akari nodded, moving forward.

Despite being a silver-rank monster, it was smaller than most iron ranks at half the length of a person. A thin, dark green lizard, it had four long legs with feet almost like hands and a flexible tail that ended in a spine-covered bulb. It was quick, jumpy and did a decent job of hiding its aura. There were other silver-rank monsters nearby and it seemed to have tried to use their auras to mask its own. Once it was close, however, they were able to differentiate it.

Jason faded into the shadows as the creature sprang to the attack, engaging Akari in a battle of mobility, speed, and quick defences. Physically weak for such a powerful monster, it boasted a suite of special attack forms instead. It shot venomous spines that rapidly regrew on the bulb tail and spat clouds of poison gas that lingered, complicating the environment. It could also spit out a trio of barbed tongues to make flexible, piercing attacks.

Akari was a swordmaster, in the vein Jason was familiar with from the other world. She had the ubiquitous combination amongst such essence users of the sword and adept essences, in her case matching it with the magic essence to produce the master confluence. Forgoing other common choices like the swift or foot essences denied her the selection of mobility powers they offered, but her adept essence had clearly enhanced her agility. She sprang around the trees almost as easily as the lizard, both treating the trees like solid ground and barely putting a foot to soil.

The advantage of her magic essence was that it expanded her repertoire in the face of more exotic abilities. Like other swordmasters, she met attack with attack, her magic essence giving her more interesting options. It also provided her with a blinking teleport, compensating for the lack of a dedicated mobility essence.

Jason was familiar with the power, which was better in a close-range fight than the teleport Humphrey had from his own magic essence. Akari's ability did not offer long-range travel at higher ranks. Instead, it became more and more effective as a combat ability than Humphrey's or Jason's teleports. Akari left behind after-images that exploded with force and appeared, phasing through the lizard, to inflict damage as she passed through it in a briefly incorporeal state.

Akari's sword sliced through the clouds of poison, which split with the blade's passage and dissolved into nothing. Clusters of spine projectiles were deflected by force waves from her swinging sword. The tongues only made one attempt to stab at her, which she nimbly dodged before bringing her sword down on them. It didn't sever the silver-rank flesh, but it did leave the tongues cut and bloody. The lizard snapped them back into its mouth and didn't send them out again.

The silver-rank monster was trickier than most, but at the trade-off of much less fortitude. Its silver-rank body was bizarrely tough for its size, but it couldn't take the punishment of a larger monster and Akari eventually landed enough clean hits to take it down.

Akari was a classic swordmaster, the type that was very popular on Adventure Society teams. If a swordmaster had the ability that matched their high-skill power sets, and Akari certainly did with hers, then their balance of strength and endurance were always welcome. She couldn't frontload damage like Farrah or Humphrey or have the endurance of Jason, but she occupied an efficient middle ground of power and longevity.

"You'd do very well in the other world," Jason told her.

She gave him an inquisitive look.

"You really went to a whole other reality?"

"Yep," he said with a sad smile. "I miss my friends, but I don't know when I'll get back to them. I have responsibilities here."

"You're going back?"

"Someday."

"How?"

"Figuring that out is on a very long to-do list, and not at the top. Ready to loot your first monster?"

Akari was connected to Jason through his party interface. With Kaito on site, the interface was not needed to provide comms for the response team, so it was just the two of them. Since they weren't in a proto-space, the lack of magic made the range of Jason's power too small anyway for effective communication or for looting.

Akari touched the monster and the loot prompt appeared in front of her.

- Would you like to loot [Toxic Hopper Lizard]?

"Yes."

She grimaced at a face full of rainbow smoke, followed by a huge sack of coins landing on her head, staggering her. They were closely followed by a pair of green lizard-skin boots.

"The trick is to move away before activating the loot power," Jason told her. "Also, if you don't have a storage power, be sure to dodge."

"You could have told me those things beforehand," Akari said, leaning against a tree.

"Is that some humanity poking out from that taciturn exterior? 'Look at me, I'm a very stern clanswoman with a sword. I'm very good at stabbing.'"

"I am very good at stabbing," Akari said. "You would do well to remember."

Jason let out a chuckle.

"You don't seem too sloppy, so let's split up a little. I'll keep you in loot range; we won't run out of monsters."

Akari jabbed at the bag of coins at her feet.

"I don't have anything to keep these things in."

"No worries," Jason said, tossing her an empty dimensional bag.

"What's this?" she asked, picking it up.

"Dimensional bag. Bigger on the inside."

She held it up in front of her, looking at it with a sceptical expression.

"You're telling me that this thing is a bag of holding?"

Jason narrowed his eyes at her. "Do you play *Dungeons & Dragons*?"

Her face froze for an instant before she schooled it back into a mask.

"No."

15
ANOTHER STEP FORWARD

AKARI WATCHED IN HORROR AS THE LEECHES CRAWLED OFF THE DRIED-OUT remains of what had been, a short while ago, a very intimidating monster. The leeches formed a pile from which a bloody rag shot out to wrap around Jason's hand. The pile then rapidly melted into blood that flowed up and through the rag to finally seep into Jason's skin and disappear.

"Colin can't pop in and out as easily as my other familiars," Jason said. "It's likely as not on account of him being physical, as opposed to incorporeal. When he does come out, though, everybody sure does know about it. Am I talking like a cowboy? It feels like I'm talking like a cowboy. A magic cowboy. That's pretty cool. I bet you could do a great quick-draw combo. On the cheap too. Gun and swift essences, obviously, but what about the last one? Eye or hand would both work, I reckon. What do you think?"

"Are you an insane person?"

"Probably. This whole ninja warlock thing doesn't seem very plausible."

"We just watched a leech monster devour a two-headed dinosaur."

"That doesn't seem very plausible either," Jason acknowledged. "Good point."

"We just saw that," she said, pointing at the huge, ruined monster, "and you're casually discussing some hypothetical essence combination?"

"Lady, you're silver rank. Category three, whatever. Please tell me they didn't just pump you full of monster cores without ever putting you in front of an actual monster?"

"Of course not. I'm just not used to someone who fights like you. You're worse than the dimensional entities."

"Well, that's downright rude, ma'am."

"Stop talking like a cowboy."

"Counter proposal," Jason said in an increasingly sketchy American accent. "What if I double down and get a big hat?"

"What is wrong with you?"

"It took the Network a while to figure that one out. It turns out that once you pass a certain threshold of handsomeness, it starts affecting the ambient magic."

"You are the most aggravating person I have ever met."

"You're not even top three for me. At least you've calmed down some."

"You think I'm calm?" she asked incredulously.

"Perhaps calm isn't the right term. At ease, maybe. At least you've stopped thinking about the fact that every other time you've gone on a monster hunt, there were a lot fewer monsters around you and a lot more allies."

"You're trying to be supportive? You aren't very good at it."

"You're not the type to respond to regular sympathy, especially not from a man famous for his lack of sincerity. You're not my first tsundere."

"I am not... are you looking to get buried in the forest, never to return?"

"Oh, you can bury me in the forest, but I wouldn't be so confident on the never-to-return part. Resurrection is kind of my thing."

"You're saying you can't be killed?"

"Oh, I can be killed just fine," Jason said. "It does make me a little cranky, though, so I'd advise against it. Now, I'd love to keep on chatting away, but we do have to deal with the monsters bearing down on us right now."

"What?"

"You haven't sensed them yet?"

Akari concentrated on extending her senses, detecting a swarm of weak but multitudinous auras coming their way. She recognised them as wisps from their aura, creatures she had encountered in the past. They normally appeared in one of two circumstances: in swarms or as bait, luring victims into ambushes by more dangerous monsters.

Individually, wisps were feeble and frail creatures whose only attack was a mana drain. Their level of threat was based on the combination of their rank and numbers, as well as how well-equipped their would-be victims were to fight incorporeal entities. Any form of magic attack could affect incorporeal creatures to some degree, but only specialised attacks were truly effective.

Akari had attacks effective against such creatures. The approaching auras were universally bronze-rank, so they posed only a limited threat to her, even in massive numbers. Her concern was Jason, who was no higher rank than the monsters. He was also known, from her family's investigations, to specialise in fleshy enemies with few area attacks.

She shifted a tense gaze from the direction of the approaching swarm to glance at Jason. She went wide-eyed when she spotted him standing with a sandwich in one hand and what looked like iced tea in the other.

"What are you doing?" she asked.

He looked down at his hands in confusion.

"Do you not know how sandwiches work? How sheltered was your upbringing? Were you raised in some isolated mountain fortress? Was there a hot springs episode?"

"I am not an anime character," she said through gritted teeth.

Jason flashed her an impish grin.

"Boys, why don't you go out and save the nice lady the trouble?" he asked.

Gordon and a handful of Shade's bodies emerged and dashed off into the trees. Akari tracked them by their auras and magical emanations as they clashed with the approaching swarm. Gordon's beam attacks vaporized the creatures as they repeatedly passed through the swarm, while the Shades eradicated every one he encountered with a touch. His ability to mana drain outstripped theirs easily; the wisps were highly susceptible to their own form of attack. As each was drained in an instant, they dissolved into barely perceptible motes of dust.

Akari sensed the pair of familiars methodically eliminate the wisps like they were painting over an exposed wall until there was nothing left to sense. She and Jason moved to the location of the startlingly brief battle as Jason's familiars returned.

"Good job, blokes," Jason said as the familiars disappeared back into him. Still eating his snack, a pair of shadow arms emerged from his cloak to trail their fingers through the dust as he walked over the battle site.

- Would you like to loot [Greater Forest Wisp]?

He left the area before triggering the looting so the rainbow smoke wouldn't impair the enjoyment of his sandwich. Once he did, the colourful mist rose up and out from the tree canopy over quite a large area.

"I reckon we swing east next, where those things came from," he said. "I suspect we've pretty much cleared out this direction. What do you think?"

After regrouping with the main Network force, Jason sent most of Shade's bodies out to sweep the region for monsters. The Network teams were regrouping and switching to a mop-up protocol as they hunted down any straggling monsters. They were easy to miss in the sprawling forest region, so Jason coordinated with other essence users deploying their own scouting abilities, like Kaito and his drones.

The base camp was packed up, although the tactical teams remained on standby in case they needed to move rapidly if the scouts found something unexpected. Jason sat in a quiet corner, meditating to consolidate the gains of his latest experiences.

Akari joined him in meditation, though hers differed in that she had laid out a mat with a ritual circle stitched into it and held a monster core in her hands. After joining up with the Network team, her reserve that Jason had cracked open went back in place, although she was not quite as cool with him. That was not the same as friendly, though, as she remained wary of the strange man who mixed absurdity, power, and horror in equal measure.

Individual essence abilities each felt different as they ranked up. As another of Jason's crossed the threshold to silver, he felt an icy cold within the depths of his soul, although it did not offer pain or discomfort. It was a part of him, and a part he felt warmly about, despite the chilly sensation.

- Ability [Shadow of the Reaper] (Dark) has reached Bronze 9 (100%).
- Ability [Shadow of the Reaper] (Dark) has reached Silver 0 (00%).

- Ability [Shadow of the Reaper] (Dark) has gained a new effect.

Ability: [Shadow of the Reaper] (Dark)

- Familiar (ritual, summon).
- Cost: Extreme mana.
- Cooldown: None.
- Current rank: Silver 0 (00%).

- Effect (iron): Summon a [Shadow of the Reaper] to serve as a familiar.
- Effect (bronze): Summoned familiar has bronze-rank vessels with additional abilities.
- Effect (silver): Summoned familiar has silver-rank vessels with additional abilities.

- Ability [Shadow of the Reaper] (Dark) cannot advance further until all attributes have reached silver rank.

Akari sensed the shift in Jason's magical state, even catching a glimpse of his normally hidden and rather intimidating aura.

"What ability was it?" she asked.

"One of my familiar summons, Shade," Jason said. "I'll need to resummon him before he can use his new strength. I've been trading resources in preparation for resummoning all my familiars ever since I first started working with the Network."

"Is it resource-intensive?" she asked. "I've known very few essence users with familiars, most of them ritualists in support teams."

Jason nodded; that was typical across the Network.

"I have most of what I need," he said. "Silver-rank materials are still somewhat thin on the ground, though, and the materials for Gordon are proving especially tricky."

"Which one is Gordon?"

"The one who looks like he has the God's Eye Nebula inside him."

"And he's called Gordon?"

"He doesn't have to let what he is define him," Jason said. "Unfortunately, it does define how to summon his silver-rank vessel. I'm pretty sure the Americans and the Chinese have what I need, but I'm not on great terms with either of them. I kind of hauled off on Americans when they tried to recruit me."

"Why?"

"I made some implications about their policies as a nation."

"You think your government would be any better if they had America's global power?"

"No," Jason said, like a child admitting he hadn't made his bed.

"What about the Chinese?"

"There have been allegations that I may have filmed some things while I was passing through their country. Footage that possibly might have mysteriously found its way to the international press."

"What kind of things?"

"Camps, mostly. Not the toasted marshmallow kind. You might have seen some of it on the news a few months back."

"Is there anyone who doesn't immediately dislike you?"

"What are you talking about? People love me."

"I'm still not sold on this idea," Jason said.

He was back in Asano Village, walking alongside Farrah. He had placed the cloud house back in its flask and set it up in a grassy field just outside the village for a special event, at Farrah's insistence. It was set up in the form of a single hall, with an open space and amphitheatre seating.

The vortex manipulator sucked ambient magic in through the building's roof, disrupting the village's magic, but it was a temporary necessity. Conducting a silver-rank ritual would otherwise require heavily charged mana lamps.

As they left the village thoroughfare, Jason and Farrah were far from the only ones walking over the grass towards the hall. Members of the Asano family and other village residents were collectively moving across the field to head inside. Many of them pointed out Jason to one another since he was now a celebrity who many of them had barely met.

"Most of these people haven't seen some proper magic," Farrah said. "They've seen magical effects on the news and here in the village, but now they can see a proper ritualist at work."

"I'm a proper ritualist?" Jason asked.

"You're adequate."

Jason grinned at Farrah's disapproving expression, knowing how demanding her standards as an instructor could be. Her adequate was high praise.

"It means a lot coming from you," he said. "Thank you."

"Don't let it go to your head."

"I'm not sure that resummoning Shade is the ritual to introduce them with, though."

"It'll be fine," Farrah said. "It can't be as bad as with Colin, right? You're not going to bleed out your butt hole and pass out, right?"

"I didn't bleed out my butt hole."

"You bled out of everywhere. We thought you might be dead."

"It went a lot better when I resummoned him at bronze rank."

"You know, having a familiar of higher rank than you can be strenuous," Farrah said. "It's one of those awkward aspects of being close to a rank-up. You should be fine, given your soul strength, though. Maybe not when you're pushing up against diamond, I don't know, but that will be a good problem to have."

"Yes, it will," Jason agreed.

They went into the hall where people were being organised into the seating. Managing the villagers was the responsibility of Jason's Nanna, who was very lively after months of recovery from her Alzheimer's. She had a small staff who made sure people found places to sit without contention.

The villagers watched as Jason and Farrah set up the ritual circle on the stone floor the cloud house had replicated for the hall, tracing out lines with chalk. It was a large and complex ritual circle with silver spirit coins and silver-rank dark quintessence gems set out in many small piles.

"You know you can get ritual bowls to hold those things," Farrah said. "Kind of like those little bowls Greg uses for board game bits, except magic and expensive."

"I don't think those can be sourced locally," Jason said.

"Probably not," Farrah acknowledged.

"Okay, I think we're good," Jason said as they completed adjustments to the ritual diagram. Farrah moved over to Erika, who took over crowd control, telling everyone to settle down as Farrah subtly quieted the group with her aura.

"What you're about to witness is magic," Erika announced. "Proper wizards and spell-book magic. You are all going to watch in silence, or There Will Be Repercussions."

Farrah emphasised Erika's words with a slight aura surge and the audience felt like gravity was pushing them into their seats. Farrah and Erika took their own seats at the front, next to Emi, leaving Jason alone in the middle of the hall with the ritual circle, in total silence.

He started chanting, his intonations cold as the merciless void of space. As he chanted, the ambient magic was stirred up to the point that even normal people could feel it, but Jason's aura projected out, leaving them frozen in place.

"*I call to the realm beyond cold and darkness, where death has no meaning, for life has no place. Let mine be the dark beyond darkness, falling on the final road to the end of all things. Let mine be the shadow of death.*"

The shift in the ambient magic started to affect physical reality as the hall grew dim. With the final word of the chant, the hall was plunged into darkness, yet not a sound disrupted the ritual, the onlookers still arrested by Jason's aura. A point of cool celestial starlight appeared on the floor and started slowly tracing out the magic diagram until the ritual circle was shedding dim light throughout the hall.

In the darkness between the lines, the piles of coins and quintessence sank into the floor like they were melting. Jason's aura faded; a new one took its place, spreading out from the ritual circle. It had the feel of an infinite void, inexorably waiting for all things to enter, patient with the certainty that they inevitably would.

A dark figure rose from the centre of the circle. Then another and another, shadowy forms barely visible in the light of the glowing circle at their feet. The only truly discernible features the dark figures had was that they seemed to be wearing cloaks, and from within the hoods shone bright, silver eyes.

Jason could see much more clearly than the others and was startled by what he saw. Not only were the eyes mirrors of his own, but Shade's new bodies kept coming and coming. At bronze rank, Shade had seven bodies and Jason had expected around a dozen or maybe fifteen at silver. But now, bodies kept rising up to crowd the circle until thirty-one Shades stood in the room.

With each new body, Shade's intimidating aura grew stronger, until the last body finally appeared and his aura vanished, like a magic trick. The light returned to the hall, the ambient cloud house lighting that was familiar. The dark bodies rushed in a wave, vanishing into Jason's shadow until only one remained, standing in front of him.

"Another step forward," Jason said.

"Yet many are to come," Shade answered. "This world is large and not the only one demanding your attention. And beyond them lies the infinite."

"That's a little above my rank, right now," Jason said.

"Since when did that ever stop you?"

16

TACTICAL FLEXIBILITY

The residents of Asano Village spilled out of the hall into the blessed sunshine, freed from Jason's domineering aura and the unnatural darkness they had been plunged into. Even though the darkness had faded, reaching sunlight under open sky still felt like an escape.

Once outside, many made a beeline for the village, putting the amazing but unnerving demonstration of magic behind them. Others stopped to watch as Jason returned the solid building they had just occupied to a flask, like putting a genie back into a bottle. Jason's other close friends and family had seen it before and had already paused their other activities longer than they should, thus were rushing back to resume them. The exceptions were Farrah and Emi, who stood by Jason as the building slowly dissolved into cloud-stuff that snaked its way into the bottle.

"You got the recordings for the Network media relations guy alright?" Jason asked.

"I haven't checked them, but it should be fine," Farrah said. "Once I get back to Sydney, I'll give them to Terrance. You really need to rank up that portal ability, Jason."

"One power at a time," Jason said. "I'm going to put Shade through his paces, now that he's ranked up. You're higher-rank than me now, Shade, so I'm anticipating you doing most of the work while I slack off."

"Miss Emi," Shade said. "If you find yourself in need of a shadow-based familiar once you obtain essences, I think you and I should talk."

"Traitor!" Jason exclaimed.

After returning the cloud house to its hidden location underwater, Jason wanted to go out and explore Shade's expanded limits and capabilities. In the village thoroughfare, Shade took the form of a motorcycle. Jason climbed on and they took off.

The front gate at the edge of the property was around three kilometres from the village proper and there was a large crowd on the other side. Jason pulled to a stop. On either side of the road, tents and campers had been clustered.

Once the location of the Asano compound had been released in the press, panicked people had come seeking the Starlight Rider's protection rather than head for the designated safe zones. Mixed in were some with fringe opinions about him that Jason had no interest in engaging. As he pulled up behind the closed gate, he spotted signs and placards welcoming the messenger of God, decrying the Antichrist and an oddly large number mentioning chemtrails.

"Has Kaito been leaving condensation trails with his helicopter?"

"No," Shade said.

"What's the chemtrail thing about, then?"

"I don't know," Shade said. "Something I have learned in my very long life is that not all knowledge is worth possessing."

"A font of wisdom as ever, Shade."

Aside from the would-be refugees and the loons, there was a contingent of press present, in what Jason suspected to be one of the least coveted jobs in the current media landscape. He looked over at the sketchy portable toilets that someone was charging for the use of and confirmed that suspicion on the spot.

Numerous people had attempted to bypass what seemed like the simple security of a chain-link fence, even if it was a rather odd one. What they had discovered was that anyone who attempted to climb over the fence fell unconscious, courtesy of the mana-draining field Farrah and Hiro had built into it.

In one instance, a press helicopter had attempted a flyover of the property, only for the pilot and passengers to wake up in a different state with no helicopter, no recording equipment and no idea what happened.

Those who tried to cut their way through the fence suffered considerably worse—the fence wasn't so much electrified as it shot lightning bolts.

The village largely ignored the people gathered outside so long as they adhered to two rules: leave a space around the security room and keep the road clear. This second rule was currently being broken by the press gathering in front of the gate to shout over one another, firing questions at Jason.

"You're obstructing a public thoroughfare," Jason said.

His voice was soft yet somehow carried across the whole group. They fell into silence as Jason's aura descended. Frantic eyes lit up with the desire to mob-rush the gate as it started to slide open, but Jason continued to use fine aura control to not just keep them in place but have them scramble back off the road.

Before he set off, Jason looked around the reporters for the one that was holding up the best against his suppression. He relaxed the strength of his aura against that one person to almost nothing and the man fought through the fear to yell out a question.

"You haven't allowed press into the compound since before the dimensional invasion began. What are you hiding?"

Jason turned, his silver eyes falling unerringly on the man despite his position at the back of the pack. Then he grinned.

"What I'm hiding is my family. I don't know if you've heard, but there are monsters about."

Without waiting for a response, Jason's bike shot off like a rocket.

"...but there are monsters about."

Anna muted the television on the wall of her office with a groan.

"Why does he keep running into the press?" she complained. "He has magical stealth powers."

"Because I asked him to," Terrance said.

"You did this?"

"Of course I did," Terrance said. "The EOA went to the trouble of legitimising him, after all. We've been doing the faceless government response thing and I get it; we want to show everyone that there's a system in place and that society isn't crumbling around us. Yet. But the EOA has been kicking us up and down the street with the good-looking superhero act and we need a human face for people to get behind."

With the Network transitioning their Media Interdiction department into the more traditional Media Relations department, the new Director of Media Relations was Terrance.

"Publicity is a secondary concern at this point."

"Right up until it isn't," Terrance said. "Did you know the superheroes are claiming credit for the grid?"

"They're admitting to taking it down?"

"No, they're claiming that they were secretly keeping away the monsters until terrorists took down their early warning system."

"They're claiming to be us?"

"Anna, if they convince the public that they're us, it's only a matter of time before governments start switching their support from us to the EOA."

"That's insane. The governments know the truth."

"Yes, but they don't care. If public sentiment sways in favour of the EOA, the governments will follow. Everything is unstable now and they're going to follow the path of least resistance out of pure desperation. The EOA know that we're busy protecting the world with a massive outlay of people and resources. They're busy taking credit for it using a few flashy idiots in spandex with dedicated media crews."

"They're not actually wearing spandex, are they?"

"No, their costume design is actually pretty fabulous," Terrance conceded.

"You do realise," Anna said, "that if you go with Asano, your human face of the Network is not actually human."

"He's from a small town, sweetie, not space."

"Never mind. He's not actually Network either."

"Look," Terrance said. "Asano is charismatic, great at handling the press and he has this light and dark thing that plays amazingly with most of our test demographics."

"You've done focus groups?"

"Of course we have. He tests low with older people, which is partly racism and partly a religious-based backlash to everything going on. He does great with the younger demos, though, because he has these dichotomies that balance each other out across the board. The lefties love him because he's not white, so they can feel superior by supporting him, but he's also not so ethnic it makes them uncomfortable. That also helps with conservatives who are on board because of the footage we've leaked of him riding around the outback on a motorcycle, tearing through monsters."

"You've been releasing our combat footage?"

"Don't worry about that. He's got that easy-going larrikin thing that makes him relatable, but he's also shrouded in mystery. His powers are dark, dangerous, which brings in the edgelords, but he's also running around healing people like emo Jesus. Actually, Farrah should have some footage for me that will let us show off that dark power thing a little more."

"You want to play up the dark powers when people are scared of monsters running around?"

"People need to know that someone is going to save them right now. The EOA has been selling this superhero narrative and people are eating it up, so we have to sell it better. They've been showing off a bunch of second-rate supermen but they've forgotten that people like Batman more. Asano is an Australian, multicultural, yobbo Bruce Wayne."

"And you can sell this? I've met the man and he's mostly pushy and weird."

"You think I picked him on a whim?" Terrance said. "I'm a professional, Anna. I watched every bit of footage we have on him, went over action reports, and interviewed anyone I could find who has dealt with him. Then I interviewed him."

"And?"

"He becomes what he needs to get what he wants. He might seem off-kilter to you, but that's because he wants you off-kilter. With regular people, he's relaxed and charming. When he needs to be in control, he's fierce and domineering. He's confident, he's handsome and he's exactly what we need right now."

"Handsome," Anna groaned, slapping a hand over her eyes.

"Oh, he's a tasty treat, alright. I mean, those eyes; it's like he's hunting you. Gives me the shivers."

"Oh no."

"The sexy shivers."

"Terrance," Anna said disapprovingly.

"And have you seen his brother? We should get some publicity shots of them together. Maybe after spraying them with water."

"Terry…"

"I'd be the creamy filling in that sandwich any day. Plate me, I'm done."

"Do I have to call HR again?"

"Don't be such a prude, sis. It's just you and me."

"Do you want me to tell Mum how you've been acting at work?"

"Oh, you wouldn't."

"I damn well would," Anna said.

"You know, Anna, she keeps complaining that you're never home for dinner. She likes having everyone together, but you're always here."

"Yes, well, sometimes I have to work late. It's the monster apocalypse."

"You know the nomenclature guidelines don't like that term," Terrance said.

"I will not be lectured on appropriate language in the workplace by you."

Jason could have easily tested Shade's new abilities in Asano Village, but a motorcycle ride in the warm sun of late summer was a balm after the intensity that followed the grid's collapse. Jason had spent almost every waking moment patrolling for proto-spaces or flying off to help put down monster waves. He would inevitably be called up again, but for the moment, he enjoyed the simple pleasure of the wind on his face.

Jason took advantage of the respite, riding to a little coastal town that made Casselton Beach look big. Normally, there would be a few tourists and locals enjoying the white sand and clear water, but the town had been evacuated. No small number of them were now in tents in front of Asano Village's main gate.

He stopped riding at the edge of town and walked down the only street. The only noise was the sound of the ocean; the quiet emptiness in the middle of a bright, sunny day was eerie.

"My world is never going back to the way it was, is it?" Jason asked.

"No," Shade said, a body emerging to glide along the ground next to Jason. "But you will have to become far stronger if you want to hold those responsible to account."

"Assuming I ever reach that kind of level, who will I have become? Sometimes I look at the way I conduct myself and feel like I've become a caricature of myself."

"Magic pushes people to extremes," Shade said. "Power gives people the chance to be what they truly desire. It strips away the layers they place between their deepest selves and their behaviour."

"I'm not sure I like what that says about me."

"You could have done far worse, Mr Asano. The perfectly righteous man is a myth. I've encountered people on myriad worlds and beyond the truly good ones are those doing their best, in spite of their flaws. I've seen gods consumed in pettiness and rank villains become vaunted messiahs. What I have never seen is a perfect person, from base mortal to great astral being."

"You're saying to stop worrying about what I've done in the past and focus on doing my best in the future."

"I am. I have high hopes for you, Mr Asano."

"But higher hopes for my niece."

"If a better ship comes along, it's only natural to board it."

"It's talk like that that makes me like Colin and Gordon more than you."

They made their way down to the beach.

"It's not a new ability," Jason said, "but what kind of vehicles do you think you can manage with all those extra bodies?"

"The existing rank restrictions on the forms I can take remain," Shade said. "The ability that lets me use such forms is yours, not mine, so flight and submarine forms will still take more bodies to achieve lesser effects."

"That's fine," Jason said. "What kind of limits can you hit with your new body count?"

"I can probably manage a small private plane by employing almost all of my vessels, although that would be forcibly using my higher-rank to push the limits of your lower-rank ability. The energy I would consume in doing so would make the spirit coin cost of that extremely prohibitive until you rank up."

"So, you're really waiting on me, then. I don't suppose you could manage a giant rotary cannon if we pulled up a tank or something?"

"We've been over this, Mr Asano. I can mimic attack forms that are a permanent part of the structure, but not special and projectile attacks. I can create claws or a battering ram but not poison breath, shooting spines or projectile weaponry."

"I thought maybe with the rank-up…"

"You want to replicate your brother's entire power set with one racial gift, I know. I strongly recommend you temper your expectations, Mr Asano. Perhaps we would be better served turning our attention to an ability I actually do possess?"

"Fine."

Shade's new plethora of shadow bodies meant that Jason could expand the people he kept a Shade in the shadow of. He could now include his father, his sister's entire family and Farrah without losing too many bodies for practical purposes.

As for actual new abilities, Shade had gained two on reaching silver rank. One was that any of his shadow bodies could teleport to any of his other bodies. This meant that Jason could deploy Shades all over and call them back at need, or send a group of them to help a family member should they run into trouble.

The range of this ability was equivalent to a portal ability of one rank below Shade's vessel. This meant that at the baseline of silver rank, the range was the same as Jason's portal had been when it first reached bronze, which was roughly forty kilometres.

Shade's other new ability had the same range limitation. Within that range, Shade was able to act as a medium for any of Jason's non-combat abilities. This meant that he could shadow-jump to one of Shade's bodies, ignoring the usual requirement of the target shadow needing to be nearby. This massively expanded his non-portal teleportation range, which could be critical when he ran into the cooldown of the portal.

During the motorcycle ride, Shade had left a shadow body behind every few kilometres. Jason stepped into the Shade next to him and appeared next to the most recent body left behind. He stepped back immediately and proceeded to hop from body to body until he arrived back in Asano Village.

"No portal arch, no cooldown," Jason said. "I can't bring people along —it ups the mana consumption and the range isn't ideal—but still, this is awesome."

"It does offer additional tactical flexibility," Shade conceded. "I will be able to go to areas you cannot see directly and provide you with shadow-jumping options. It is an adequate use of the power."

"Calm down, mate. Don't get too excitable."

Jason stepped back into Shade, jumping back to the beach and began testing other abilities. Another aspect of using shadow bodies as a medium for his powers was that Jason could use his non-combat abilities from Shade as if they were his own body, once again within the same range limit.

His perception power worked, so when he shared the senses of one of Shade's bodies, he had his full perceptual range. His Hand of the Reaper ability did not, as the afflictions it could apply apparently marked it as a combat ability.

The most unexpected result was when he manifested his cloak over Shade, for the simple reason that he was able to do so even while having one conjured on himself. To date, he could only have one cloak because he had to occupy it. With Shade's new capability, that was no longer a hard limit.

He had most of Shade's bodies teleport to him, aside from the ones attached to family members, then conjured cloaks on all of them. The mana cost of conjuring his cloak was only moderate but conjuring twenty-seven in short order had carved off a serious chunk of his mana.

"Strewth," he croaked, with a slight headache from dumping so much mana in an instant. It had been even more than an extreme mana cost spell, like summoning Shade in the first place cost him. Fortunately, he was near the peak of bronze and his mana pool was rich, courtesy of his high spirit attribute.

Once his cloak ranked up, it would cost a moderate amount of mana for a silver-ranker, which would make it more prohibitive until he had a silver-ranker's mana pool. It was one of the difficulties of being on the cusp of ranking up.

Jason popped a bronze-rank spirit coin in his mouth to help him recover.

"I think I'll go home for a rest," he said.

His phone started beeping an alarm.

"Oh, bloody hell."

17
BROKEN

Broken Hill was a carefully chosen target. One of the best-known locations in the Australian outback, its rich history and iconic desert landscapes had woven it into the fabric of Australia's soul. It was also one of the centres in which isolated people from across that region of the outback had been gathered, exploding the population from fewer than twenty thousand to almost thirty-five thousand.

The Network presence was minimal, with only a single tactical section to protect the support team whose core duty was to check for dimensional incursions. With resources stretched thin, only when a dimensional space was detected would a substantive force be brought in.

The personnel in charge of organising the massive influx of people were regular civil servants, military logistics specialists and no small number of volunteers. There were builders knocking up prefab domiciles and companies donating materials, tools, and machinery. Like in other safe zones being set up around the world, people were coming out to show how many were willing to step up and help one another.

Major population centres around the world were being turned into military green zones; the most rural areas were being abandoned. Broken Hill fell somewhere in the middle. It had been placed under Network protection but with only a fraction of the resources allocated to a major city.

The Network had become known to the public as the Global Defense Network in the weeks since the monster waves began. The terrorist readiness exercises were cited as preparation for the worst-case scenario now being faced. The sympathetic portion of the media referred to the 'supernatural task forces' the GDN fielded as the government response to an unimaginable threat. Their practicality and professionalism were intended to instil confidence, but this was continually being upstaged by the flashy antics and expert media manipulation of the EOA's League of Heroes.

The EOA's agenda of positioning themselves as a top power player that matched, or even eclipsed, the Network was built around taking a lead position in response to the monster waves. This involved a two-pronged attack—raising themselves up as they simultaneously tore the Network down.

The EOA's goal wasn't to convince the governments of the world that they were better than the Network. The governments knew full well that the Network's power, resources and reach easily outstripped the EOA. The EOA's goal was to swing public sentiment so ferociously in their direction that the governments were forced to give the EOA a seat at the table, shifting support, resources and influence away from the Network.

Various targets around the globe were selected to further this purpose; Broken Hill fit their criteria perfectly. It was under Network protection, but with minimal Network presence. They had a support team to scan for proto-spaces and a nine-person tactical section to protect them. Otherwise, Broken Hill was staffed by regular military, civil servants, and volunteers.

In addition, Broken Hill was geographically isolated in an enormous nation where the Network had limited magical transport options. All these factors tallied up to make Broken Hill a soft target for the EOA's plan. If the Network suffered a catastrophic failure in one of their supposed safe zones, only for the League of Heroes to step in, it would be a major blow to the Network. If it repeatedly happened worldwide, that failure went from a major blow to a crippling one.

While the Network had been scrambling to save as many people as possible, the EOA had been choosing their targets and carefully infiltrating them. The EOA's League of Heroes was the right hand distracting the audience; their clandestine operations were the left hand performing the trick. The volunteer staff and even the military personnel stationed at Broken Hill had no shortage of EOA plants.

The infiltrators in Broken Hill were meticulous and patient. The government and Network personnel were more wary of panic amongst the population than sabotage, leaving the EOA's people safely undetected. Not even Jason, briefly passing through, had picked out their duplicitous emotions amongst the tens of thousands in the overstuffed town.

The EOA played their roles well, not jumping at the first proto-space detected in the region. Earnest volunteers, they worked as hard as anyone to support the team that arrived to intercept the monster wave. That team even included the famous Starlight Rider, tearing across the desert on a motorcycle, his cloak of stars flying behind him.

They would only get a single shot. The EOA waited for the right proto-space, lucking out perfectly when one appeared right on top of Broken Hill itself. It was then that the EOA struck. Communications were taken over. The tactical section was ambushed and eliminated, as was any military personnel not already suborned. Black-clad paramilitary soldiers swept in from the desert on trucks to contain the town, claiming to be government reinforcements.

The civilian camp workers were not taken in by the obvious lie but were forced to go along. They had no choice, with the lack of outside contact and large number of armed soldiers surrounding them. They made various attempts to get word out, but every phone line was cut and every signal jammed.

In the general chaos of the monster waves, it took a full day before the Network realised that Broken Hill had become unreachable. They sent an emergency investigation team who managed to scout out the situation and get word back that someone had taken control of Broken Hill, but it was already too late. The EOA had stalled long enough for the proto-space to start disgorging monsters onto the town in flashes of rainbow light.

Kaito's helicopter flew directly inland at a pace no ordinary helicopter could match. Other teams approached Broken Hill from Adelaide, which was closer than Sydney, but Kaito would still beat them onsite. Jason and one of Sydney's strongest tactical sections were in the back, the mood sombre. Everyone on board was concerned for the tens of thousands of people they feared being too late to help.

The back section of the helicopter was in a utilitarian configuration with simple chairs for the soldiers to strap into. Jason sat with them, no one uttering a sound. Jason handed out spirit coins; none of the team had eaten actual food in weeks. With the agricultural areas ranging from under threat to evacuated to under attack, food shortages were already becoming a factor. Essence users were all under direction to live exclusively on spirit coins.

It was a small drop in the bucket compared to the food needs of the population at large, but every bit would help in what could be a long and harrowing ordeal. The regular consumption of coins would also help the essence users stay fresh and ready for their continuing struggles.

This drastically increased the need for coins, so China and the US opened their vaults to keep other parts of the world supplied. France was also contributing. They had converted the permanent astral space in Saint-Étienne to a dedicated spirit coin farm. There had been a lot of awkwardness when Farrah had arrived to help them set it up during Jason's sojourn, even with the original Lyon branch members replaced by the International Committee.

Jason was likewise pumping out as many coins as he could manage. When shutting down proto-spaces before they could pop, he was taking the time to wipe out any lower-rank monsters he could quickly knock over for the loot. In this, Gordon's sweeping beams were the most effective and the familiar was closing in on his next rank. Jason was still short on the resources required to resummon him, though, but it was hardly the time to seek them out.

A wall panel slid open to reveal a screen. Greg's voice came through a speaker.

"Communications just opened with Broken Hill, but our people aren't responding. What is coming out is a live news transmission."

The screen blinked to life, showing camera footage of a street filled with chaos, apparently shot by a reporter hiding inside a heavily damaged building. It was far from the only one. Some buildings had collapsed walls while others were on fire, sending up plumes of black smoke. Corpses lay bloody and burned in the street as screams of pain and fear filled the air.

In the middle of the street, a colourfully dressed man with steel gauntlets traded blows with a rock monster that had a glowing red gem in its chest. The monster had the edge in strength, but the superhero was faster, hammering steel-clad fists on the stone body of the monster. It was a long way from an essence-user fight, at least one Jason or Farrah would be involved in. No powers were on display, just two supernatural beings pounding away at each other.

As they fought, the reporter's commentary came through.

"…government's unpopular reliance on the so-called Global Defense Network has led to tragedy here in Broken Hill. Claimed as a safe zone, all they accomplished was luring people to their deaths. If not for the rapid intercession of a League of Heroes team, this reporter would already be counted amongst the dead…"

There were actual snarls in the helicopter as people who had thrown everything they had into protecting the populace were badmouthed even as innocents died. Jason opened his map ability, watching the kilometres tick down. Kaito was downing mana potions as quickly as he could while using his various powers to push the helicopter to its limits, yet their speed felt excruciatingly slow.

With his eyes on the map, Jason felt when he crossed the distance threshold he needed. His current portal range was four hundred kilometres. Once they got that close to Broken Hill, he released his safety belt and stood.

The others knew from the briefing that Jason would be heading out alone. He wasn't taking anyone else because he couldn't portal the silver-rankers, a good part of the elite section, and he wouldn't take the bronze-rankers and isolate them from the team.

They were quietly glad. For all their specialist training, they would not plunge into a high-grade monster wave with just their small group. The Adelaide teams would arrive not far behind them for a joint operation.

The side door opened, the influx of air at their incredible speed causing the helicopter to lurch. Jason kept his feet by gripping the seat belt he had just removed and then flung himself out the door. Gliding towards the ground, he spotted a pleasant enough spot running alongside a creek and rapidly descended there before opening a portal arch and stepping through.

The EOA's superhero program involved all their latest breakthroughs in human enhancement. Their bones were engraved with magic sigils in a series of deeply invasive surgeries. Their flesh was treated and retreated with alchemical baths, deep-tissue injections, and magical radiation therapy. Their blood was drawn out and magically altered using modified dialysis machines.

The body modifications were only a part of the procedure. Without similar changes to the soul, the massive bodily augmentations could not be endured by the subjects. Volunteers to the program were subjected to magical sensory bombardment while their bodies underwent the treatments. Those able to truly open themselves to the changes gained soul mutation. Many volunteers washed out of the program, however, unable to truly let go and open up their souls. These unfortunates were inevitably crippled by the incomplete enhancement process. It was hideous enough that most who didn't die asked to be killed. The EOA complied.

The EOA's methods were akin to some of what Jason had experienced inadvertently, although their methods were much cruder and lacked the months of treatment Jason received to help him through the trauma. They also lacked the strength his soul had already gained from ranking up. The results of the EOA's practices were souls that grew stronger but were warped in the process.

Decades of advancement had managed to reduce the impact on the mental state of the recipients, although the specific means were a closely guarded secret. The recipients themselves remembered only strange feelings, having been in induced comas through the process. Only echoes remained in their souls.

The earliest iron-rank subjects had suffered from twisted minds, which manifested in ways ranging from catatonia to malevolent and depraved tendencies. As the program developed, advancements were made. Later bronze-rank subjects showed significantly better results. While the successful subjects often lacked imagination and critical-thinking skills, they made for excellent dumb muscle.

The latest iteration of the process had entirely eliminated the mental problems through the production of a mysterious and extremely secretive implant. The silver-rank enhanced were mentally normal to all tests, without sacrificing any of the abilities the earlier iterations shared. They could even be produced in larger numbers than previous iterations, allowing for the heroes deployed across the world.

The silver-rank enhanced, like their lower-rank predecessors, were able to use alchemical boosts to enhance their rank temporarily but the key material for the boosts were spirit coins. Without access to gold spirit coins, the ability of the silver-rank enhanced to boost themselves was purely theoretical.

What they did have at full strength were magic tattoos. Unlike the magic tattoos Jason was familiar with, these were designed specifically to work with the enhanced, allowing them to carry multiples of each without the magic coming into conflict. Hidden away beneath their costumes, their magic tattoos gave the enhanced access to more exotic powers than just silver rank strength, toughness and speed. Each of the superhero-branded enhanced was given a standard suite that allowed them to project energy beams from their eyes and fly for short periods.

The enhanced had enough of each tattoo to put on a show or to use in a critical moment, but not to employ continually. Although an essence user could only use one tattoo, the silver-ranked enhanced were able to have eight. Even with this advantage, the lack of boost serum meant the superheroes were no match for an equivalent-rank essence user.

Once alerted to the appearance of monsters in town, the EOA's media teams moved in on a helicopter and in cars. The media teams were staffed with bronze-rank enhanced and would be able to handle themselves, whatever they told the audience. When the media were in place, the superheroes activated their first flight tattoos.

The heroes flew over a town of people who were fleeing and screaming in response to the multitude of rock monsters pursuing them through the streets. Some of the monsters were hulking, vaguely humanoid elementals with no heads and giant, opalescent crystals embedded in their chests. Others were basketball-sized flying creatures of crystal and stone, with crystals either blue or red. The smaller monsters with blue crystals conjured up icicles and shot them like arrows, while the red-crystal monsters sent out motes of fire that burned flesh and buildings alike.

The larger monsters, despite their larger crystals, seemed to have no attendant power. They were rampaging around using pure brute force, smashing through walls, and using cars as bludgeons. They seemed more interested in destruction than in killing, while the smaller monsters hunted people almost exclusively. Only the fire types would throw flames at the surroundings if no people were around to offer themselves as targets.

The silver-rank superheroes had strength and fortitude in the upper ranges of silver, but their speed was closer to the baseline. Even so, they were weaker but faster than the silver-rank monsters.

Each superhero wore magically enhanced metal gauntlets so as to not use their bare hands against monsters. Without their boost serum, they were equivalent to a mediocre essence user who never used their abilities properly. Only the occasional burst of eyebeams supplemented their brawling combat.

They simply did not have the strength or the numbers to handle the monsters. The proto-space they had forcibly unleashed on Broken Hill was a category three, and a strong one at that. The larger monsters were silver rank and there was no shortage of them. The smaller monsters were all bronze rank.

This was acceptable to the EOA, however. The objective was not to save the people of Broken Hill but to be seen stepping in when the Network had failed. They would pass off the death toll on the Network's failure, played alongside their own people fighting a desperate, but ultimately doomed battle. The EOA media teams were more than happy to make their narrative explicit; their target demographic were not strong thinkers.

"The valour of the League of Heroes is clear, but they can only do so much. If the governments of the world would offer them support, perhaps such tragedies could be avoided. So long as they continue to prop up the failing Global Defense Network, how many of the so-called safe zones will suffer the fate of Broken Hill? Is Melbourne or Sydney next?"

The armed militia of the EOA had already long fled, leaving the locals and refugees to their fate. The population of the town, scared and scattered, were buoyed by the arrival of the heroes, only to quickly realise that they were little help. Instead of going after the small monsters hunting people, the heroes rushed into visually exciting clashes with the large monsters destroying the town while leaving the people largely alone.

On the outskirts of town, an obsidian arch rose from the ground. Jason stepped out, his cloak manifesting around him as he surveyed the scene of death and destruction. Despite all the things he had seen, this was an apocalyptic display that gave even him pause.

"Shade, bring the bodies you have protecting the family here. We're going to need them all."

18

NEVER ENOUGH

Lauren Chamley and her family hunkered in their house with a family of monster wave refugees that the Chamleys had taken in, fearfully checking through the windows from time to time. Many of the families in Broken Hill had opened their homes, although there were never enough places. Most of the people brought in from the surrounding areas had been staying in a tent camp on the outskirts of town.

Lauren and her husband had taken in the other family, who were crammed into the bathroom with them after the house suffered damage. There were eleven people between the two families, with kids sitting in the bath and Lauren herself standing in the shower.

On one of her periodic checks, Lauren discovered that the house had been set on fire. They would need to flee. It would take both of their cars to carry everyone, so she checked the driveway. Of all the terrible crashing they had heard from inside the house, two of those crashes had apparently been the cars. One of them had the back end stomped into the concrete driveway, while the other had wound up in the neighbour's wall, upside down.

The two families reluctantly left the burning house on foot, aiming to get away from the town and the monsters ravaging it. They ducked through yards and took any cover they could find to hide their passage.

There were simply too many of them, though. They were quickly discovered.

Although the civilians didn't know it, the rock and crystal monsters were unusual for elemental creatures. Most elementals were an unusual type of monster. With their kind, the magical manifestation that would normally create a monster body only created a monster core before mindlessly animating elemental material around it.

These monsters were not actual elementals but true, fully manifested monsters. Although their bodies were of elemental substances, the crystal in their forms contained a motive spirit, the false soul that most monsters possessed. Rather than mindlessly aggressive elementals, the crystal monsters had minds, if animalistic ones.

Unfortunately, the minds of the small floating monsters had a deep-running vein of sadism, delighting in the pain and suffering of their victims. Rather than go for the kill, they played with their victims like a cat toying with a captured mouse.

The two families were not attacked immediately. The monsters that found them hovered ominously to delight in their fear. In that pause, a sleek, black passenger bus came smashing through a fence, ramming the monsters and sending them flying.

More monsters approached and the bus interposed itself between them and the families. It was a strange design, like a bullet train designed by a ninja. The bus door opened to reveal the friendly but anxious face of their neighbour, Griff, who ushered them aboard.

"Our car is in your house," Lauren told him as she waved her family inside.

"Yeah, that was the point we got out," Griff said.

The bus took off the moment the last person was in, at which point they noticed it had no driver. The bus was half full of townspeople and was already on the hunt for more survivors. Looking out the windows, they saw the monsters peppering the bus with attacks, only for black tendrils to rise out of the bus and intercept them.

"What is going on?" Lauren asked.

"Don't know, don't care," Griff said. "I've seen more of these buses running around, though. It looks like they're collecting survivors."

"Look!" Lauren's daughter yelled, pointing out the window.

Everyone followed her gaze to a figure of darkness and stars, dancing across the broken asphalt of a street infested with monsters. The figure moved through the monstrous crowd like a ghost, striking them down left and right with a sword shimmering with power. Despite being surrounded by monsters, the shadow-clad man moved with impunity, monsters dying with his every flowing motion.

"It's him, right?" Griff asked.

"It's him," Lauren said. "I saw him when he was here a couple of weeks ago. Thank God."

"I would not say that to his face, ma'am," said a voice that sounded vaguely like a British butler. "He has a thing about gods."

In the almost two months since Shade had reached silver-rank, Jason and Shade had continued to uncover the nuances of the familiar's new abilities. One of those discoveries was that if all the shadow bodies involved in creating a vehicle wore starlight cloaks, the properties of the cloak were bestowed upon the vehicle. This now protected the buses and the survivors inside from the projectile attacks of the monsters.

It took six shadow bodies to form a bus. This was enough for five buses and one body left over to be Jason's own shadow, allowing him to coordinate the others. Conjuring all those cloaks had been extremely draining, but the presence of so many aggressive enemies also provided a solution. Every attack against an ally within Jason's aura inflicted an instance of the Sin condition on the enemy making that attack. With all the attacks hitting the buses, that loaded up the monsters with afflictions.

Jason had been taking advantage of this more and more. A Shade body wrapped in a starlight cloak was hard to distinguish from Jason himself unless they were standing still in good light. This made them excellent decoys soaking up attacks and triggering Jason's aura's retaliation. On stronger enemies, this gave Jason a chance to frontload his afflictions, while he had another strategy for the weaker ones. It was a strategy that had sent two of his lingering abilities skyrocketing to the front of the pack.

One of the buses tore away, leaving behind the cluster of now-afflicted little monsters that had been attacking it. Jason tossed his sword into the air and caught it with a shadow hand as he threw his real arms out to the side.

"*Feed me your sins.*"

The rock and crystal monsters were immune to Jason's necrotic damage and bleeding powers, but they were subject to the curses levied by his aura. They could be drained away.

The unliving monsters had no life force, so the afflictions were dragged directly out of the crystals in their bodies. The Sin curses flowed out of all the monsters at once and into Jason's waiting hands, flying through the air like a black and purple spiderweb.

Ability: [Feast of Absolution] (Sin)

- Spell (recovery, cleanse, holy).
- Base cost: Low mana.
- Cooldown: None.

- Current rank: Silver 0 (00%).

- Effect (iron): Cleanse all curses, diseases, poisons and unholy afflictions from a single target. Additionally, cleanse all holy afflictions if the target is an ally. Recover stamina and mana for each affliction cleansed. This ability ignores any effect that prevents cleansing. Cannot target self.

- Effect (bronze): Enemies suffer an instance each of [Penance] and [Legacy of Sin] for each condition cleansed from them.

- Effect (silver): Increase cost to moderate to affect all afflicted enemies and allies in a wide area.

- [Penance] (affliction, holy, damage-over-time, stacking): Deals ongoing transcendent damage. Additional instances have a cumulative effect, dropping off as damage is dealt.

- [Legacy of Sin] (affliction, holy, stacking): You are considered more damaged for the purposes of execute ability damage scaling. Additional instances have a cumulative effect.

Jason had been startled at how swiftly the ability had climbed once he started using it in this fashion. Even though he'd had to use it on one monster at a time before it ranked up, no cooldown meant that he could fire it off in quick succession. Many fights had been nothing but his aura and his cleansing power, topping off his mana and leaving behind the transcendent damage holy affliction, Penance. That affliction now burned through the gathered monsters.

As the monsters were smaller and only bronze rank, without the immense vitality that came at silver, the transcendent damage burned through them in short order. They started dissolving into rainbow smoke. Since enemies wholly annihilated by transcendent damage were auto-looted, Jason had taken advantage of this every time he encountered weak, swarming monsters. As Gordon ran around beaming them down, Jason would take out as many as he could using Shade decoys, his aura and his affliction drain.

Feast of Absolution's ascension to silver demonstrated once again why it was arguably Jason's most potent ability. The often-overlooked passive it was paired with, however, gave Jason his first taste of true silver-rank power.

Ability: [Sin Eater] (Sin)

- Special ability (recovery, holy).
- Cost: None.
- Cooldown: None.

- Current rank: Silver 0 (00%).

- Effect (iron): Increased resistance to afflictions. Gain an instance of [Resistant] each time you resist an affliction or cleanse an affliction using essence abilities.

- Effect (bronze): Gain an instance of [Integrity] for each affliction you resist or remove using essence abilities.

- Effect (silver): Health, mana and stamina gained through your own essence abilities of the drain and recovery type can exceed the normal maximum. Excess health, stamina and mana deplete over time until the normal maximum is reached.

- [Resistant] (boon, holy, stacking): Resistance to afflictions is increased. Additional instances have a cumulative effect. Consumed to negate instances of [Vulnerable] on a 1:1 basis.

- [Integrity] (heal-over-time, mana-over-time, stamina-over-time, holy, stacking): Periodically recover a small amount of health, stamina and mana. Additional instances have a cumulative effect.

Now, instead of wasting all the mana and stamina that Feast of Absolution was feeding him, he could absorb it all, even if it started draining away immediately. More importantly, he could use his health draining abilities while fully recovered, stocking up hit points like a D&D character to absorb hits that would normally take a silver-ranker to survive. That would be less of an issue once he reached silver, but while he remained at bronze-rank it was potentially an immeasurable boon.

Jason had long employed a drain-heal method of staying alive in fights, but without the fortitude of silver rank, he was always running on a knife's edge. If not for Colin's regeneration, his incredible amulet, and his custom combat robe, he would have fallen many times.

As monsters disintegrated around him, Jason's shadow detached from his body and turned into a motorcycle. He leapt on and rocketed off in pursuit of another bus being harassed by monsters. As he went, he struck down the monsters he passed with his sword, like a hooligan hitting mailboxes with a baseball bat.

He could sense the silver-rank monsters and the superheroes fighting them. It was his first time encountering them in person and he made a startling discovery, but it was not the time to explore it. Since the silver-rank monsters seemed uninterested in the populace, Jason left them for the heroes and continued scooping up survivors.

The five buses could not be everywhere and had to head to Jason's still-open portal to empty themselves of passengers periodically. Jason did his best to shield survivors until a bus could arrive, shepherding them together in readiness to board quickly. He could only cover so much ground, though. Throughout the town, he sensed lives being snuffed out in quick succession. He had to rely on his meditative techniques to keep his mind clear. Bad decisions made in anger would cost lives.

On Kaito's helicopter, the passengers were still watching the live feed from the town.

"… Jason Asano, the Starlight Rider, has arrived to join the other heroes in trying to save the town. Despite his valiant efforts, however, the situation only serves to highlight how one hero has been propping up the failing Global Defense Network. Even as we watch, the—"

Suddenly, the cracked door they were filming through was swung wide open.

"Why is there a bunch of people with magic powers hiding in here, pretending to be a news crew, while people who don't have any powers are dying out there?" Jason growled. "You are going to get out of here and start helping people to safety."

He pointed to one end of town.

"Find anyone not on a bus and get them to the portal down that end of town. If I find you hiding again—and I will—you'll wish the monsters got to you first, you cowardly sacks of shi—"

The feed cut out, replaced by a pair of news anchors.

"Uh, we seem to be having technical difficulties, but I'm sure our news team will be fine with Jason Asano watching over them. Going to Michael for analysis of the unfolding situation…"

"…military and GDN personnel are rapidly setting up a camp to receive them, even as more Broken Hill residents emerge from the portal you're seeing on screen. We are standing some four hundred kilometres from Broken Hill, yet the people escaping are claiming that they travelled that distance instantaneously through the mysterious arch believed to be one of the Starlight Rider's many abilities. There seems to be a strong nauseating factor to the exotic form of travel as many of the escapees are demonstrating, right on the grass…"

Terrance was talking on his phone as he watched the coverage.

"Make sure the coverage highlights the difference between the EOA fighting monsters and Jason rescuing people. I want to see interviews with every person from Broken Hill with the power of speech. No, don't send a news crew to the town, you maniac. Take a footage feed from Kaito's drones and have a panel of analysts dissect how useless their superheroes are."

Just as he ended the call, Aram came rushing into Terrance's office.

"New development?" Terrance asked.

"We're pretty sure the EOA are responsible for the Broken Hill disaster."

"No kidding," Terrance said. "I do not want a single word of that getting into the press. No pointed suggestions, no leaks, nothing."

"Isn't it bad for them?"

"The moment accusations start, the EOA will turn it around to accuse us of setting them up. Salacious accusations going back and forth slide right into their tone of discourse, not ours, which will make us look desperate."

"We have proof!"

"So does climate change and how's that going? If I hear anyone on our side peddling a line about the EOA being behind this, I will personally have wild monkey sex with your father."

"My father's dead, you arsehole."

"Then he won't struggle, will he? Get back to work."

Jason was tireless as he went through Broken Hill, constantly draining afflictions to amass stamina and mana. He would lure monsters to a bus to draw them away from scattered survivors and then afflict and drain them in clusters, before sending the buses to collect those survivors.

His incredible senses allowed him to tag monsters and survivors on his tactical map ability, the sight of which constantly threatened to crush his spirit. As fast as he worked and as hard as he fought, it was never enough. Again and again, the red dots of an unfriendly intersected with the green dot of a friendly, which then blinked out.

The superheroes had finally finished off the silver-rank monsters and had started chasing down the smaller ones, but they were built for cinematic battles, not efficient sweep-and-clear. Only the arrival of Kaito and the Network strike teams would be able to carry that out successfully, their numbers and practised tactics outpacing what Jason could accomplish.

When reinforcements finally came into range of his voice-chat power,

Jason was filled with relief at the assistance and remorse that he couldn't do more. It hadn't been that long, but it felt like an endless slog as more and more lives faded from his senses. He opened a voice chat to relay the situation they were flying into.

Finally, hours later, Jason found himself in the remains of Broken Hill, every civilian in it either dead or evacuated. He had used his portal again and again as it reached capacity. At his current rank, a thousand normals could go through before hitting the limit, which put the survivor count, based on portal use, at fewer than twenty thousand survivors.

He had swept the town and patrolled the outskirts multiple times to make sure, as had Kaito with his drones. He stood amongst the ruins and the dead, feeling empty and at a loss. They didn't have hard numbers yet, but he could see with his own eyes the bodies piled up in the burned-out remains of the tent camp. Based on that and his portal count, he estimated somewhere between ten and fifteen thousand people had died.

Jason instinctually wanted to collect up the bodies instead of just leaving them where they lay, but there would be an organised operation to collect and identify the dead. He would only muddle that up if he interfered.

His gaze turned to the superheroes, standing together with their media team, who pointed a camera his way.

19

MEDIA LANDSCAPE

Smoke rose from smouldering buildings into an orange sunset over Broken Hill.

"Shade," Jason said quietly as he looked over at the EOA media team filming further down the ruined street. "Please find an ordinary handgun and discreetly leave it nearby."

Jason had spotted enough armed dead that it would not be a difficult task. He had seen the military personnel, mostly clustered around their post near the tent city. Many of them had been killed by firearms rather than monsters. Only a handful of the military had survived, isolated and armed with weapons that couldn't harm the monsters. He got them out with the other survivors, although a few had insisted on trying to fight. Rather than let them learn the hard way, he had Shade knock them out and then shoved them on a bus with the others.

He had also seen some black-clad corpses other than the Network's tactical section, which were likely part of the group responsible for the Broken Hill tragedy. Not all of them had managed to safely extract, whether due to monster attacks or the military and Network personnel not going down as easily as anticipated.

One of Shade's bodies slipped away, unseen in the growing shadows of evening.

Penelope was the leader of the EOA's media team.

"I don't know that talking to him is a good idea," she said.

"It's all upsides," said Garret, the leader of the superhero team. "You said yourself that we were having trouble finding stand-out personalities in our hero ranks. If we can associate ourselves with Asano, that might change. He's the face of magic right now."

"I don't think he's going to be very accommodating," Penelope said.

"That's fine too. If he accuses us of setting all this in motion, we use it to tar the Network. One way or the other, it's a win for us."

"We could make a point that he's a better fit for the League of Heroes than the Network," Penelope mused. "There's no way he jumps ship, but we have been working to paint him as being one of us who only works for them. An actual interview might help push that along."

"See?" Garret said. "We win every way."

They were speaking quietly as the face of the media team, Davina, was giving a voiceover for the live feed as the camera recorded Jason.

"As the sun truly sets on Broken Hill, we can only wonder if the historic town will ever see a new dawn after the catastrophe it has suffered. For all his valiant efforts, Jason Asano, the Starlight Rider, stands in the ruins of the Global Defense Network's failure. Again, we apologise to viewers for the graphic images on display…"

As Davina continued to narrate, Penelope silently grabbed her attention, communicating her intentions with hand signals. Davina nodded.

"We're going to approach Mr Asano with the head of the League of Heroes team, Garret Dunhurst, a.k.a. Skybolt. Skybolt, this will be your first time meeting with your fellow hero, is this correct?"

"It is, Davina, and I only wish it could be under better circumstances. Unfortunately, the crisis we all face means that every hero is facing terrible circumstances and the Starlight Rider is no exception."

Davina, Garret and the camera operator approached Jason. They could only see the silver eyes under his hood, the light on the camera failing to penetrate the shadow.

"Mr Asano, despite working side by side with your fellow heroes, the death toll is clearly in the thousands. Do you think that closer collaboration with your fellow heroes might reduce the impact should further GDN safe zones be compromised?"

Seconds ticking over in the dead air as they awaited Jason's response.

"Mr Asano?"

"You think we're heroes?" Jason asked in a voice of weariness-infused gravel. "Stepping forward is the absolute minimum to expect of people with our abilities. To do any less would make us nothing but worthless cowards. If you want to see heroes, look to the people who have no powers, yet they step onto the same field as us. And why do they do that? For no more reason than there are people in need of help. They don't have the strength to face what we can face, but here they are, making the ultimate sacrifice."

He gestured at the ruined town around them.

"If you want to find heroes, go digging through the rubble; they're piled high. You think we compare to them because we run around in costumes, fighting monsters?"

"We protect the people," Garret said.

"We aren't the ones that will get the world through this calamity," Jason said. "We can help some people, yes, but we're just a symbol. The people of the world will get through this disaster not by waiting for some fool in a costume like me to save them. They'll get through this by coming together, the human race united. A network of people who are heroes not for the powers they possess but their willingness to raise one another out of the darkness."

Garret could feel himself losing control of the narrative and tried to guide Jason towards making an accusation.

"Those people will need leadership and guidance. Heroes to show them the way. Surely you recognise that without us, the body count today would have been much greater, perhaps even total."

"Leadership and guidance," Jason repeated. "That's the kind of language you hear from dictators. In the free world, we choose our leaders, they don't choose us, but I can see why you would think that way, given where your powers come from. We may accept your League of Heroes because the monsters are here and we need everyone we can get. But I won't forget who unleashed those monsters in the first place so that you could run around playing super friends. There will come a day when the monsters aren't looming over us and the people hiding behind you will face a reckoning."

"Just to be clear," Davina said, "Mr Asano, are you claiming that there is some kind of secret cabal behind the League of Heroes who brought the monsters down on us all? That is quite the accusation, for which I assume you have some amount of proof."

The chuckle that came from inside Jason's dark hood could have frozen water.

"I don't need to prove anything or convince anyone. The day will come when the people hidden in the dark will die, alone and unknown. And no one will ever hear about it."

"You were just talking about dictatorship," Davina said. "Now you're talking about extrajudicial murder?"

"Someone needs to hold the men behind the curtain to account, but if you don't like it, who's going to stop me?" Jason asked. "Your heroes, here?"

A pair of silver eyes fixed on Garret.

"Are you going to stand in my way, Spybolt?"

"It's Skybolt."

"I don't care. I'll be the villain to your hero, but you'd best stop me now. You're as strong as you're ever going to get, while my power grows with every passing day."

He turned back on the reporter.

"What about you, Davina? You're one of the league's secret heroes. Are you going to stop me?"

"I don't know where you got this idea about me having powers came from, but you are completely wrong."

"Is that so? Shade, if you would?"

A shadowy figure emerged from the camera operator's shadow, taking the camera off his shoulder and focused on Davina. A shadow arm shot out from Jason and picked up a nearby pistol, which Jason then pointed at the reporter as Shades rose up behind her and Jason both. With silver-rank reflexes, Garret interposed himself between Jason and the reporter, but Jason was already disappearing into his own Shade.

He emerged behind the reporter, shooting her in the back of the head without hesitation. Davina staggered a few steps, groaning loudly as she held a hand over her head where she was shot.

"You're a maniac!" she spat at Jason, turning around to face him.

He pulled his hood back to reveal his face. His eyes were bloodshot, red and puffy from tears. In an instant, he went from faceless menace to a man shattered in grief at the tragedy around him.

"I'm sorry," he said bitterly. "If that bullet to the head left you with a headache, maybe you don't have powers. That's why you hid instead of stepping out to help these people, right?"

"You can stop your play, Asano," Penelope said. "The studio cut the broadcast."

Jason didn't bother to say anything more, opening a portal and stepping through.

He arrived a short distance from the camp containing the Broken Hill survivors. Jason started walking in that direction over the yellow, shin-high grass.

"You did grab the memory drive from the camera, right?" Jason asked.

"Of course," Shade said. "I am uncertain how it will help, though, given that the footage went out live."

"Never underestimate the value of the unedited original," Jason said. "There was probably a broadcast delay on the live feed, so there's no telling how much they managed to edit of our little play."

"I cannot help but notice that with your ability to control your physiology, as grief-inducing as the day's events were, you should neither get bloodshot eyes nor produce tears."

"The dead deserve tears," Jason said. "Your father best take care of them or he and I are going to have words."

"I don't think you are ready to threaten the Reaper, Mr Asano."

"Not yet."

He tucked his hood back up over his head as they drew closer to the camp.

"This is a wagonload of horse manure," Terrance said. "I have work to do."

"Not if you get removed from your position, you don't," Anna told him as they walked the halls of the Network office in Sydney. "Make no mistake, if this workplace mediation doesn't go well, you will be replaced."

As a publicity man, Terrance was forced to admire Anna's choice of tearing him down in the halls where anyone could and would overhear. It sent a message that the upper management was accountable, the general staff were respected and that family was not a shield against bad behaviour. That did not mean that he wouldn't argue back.

"We have more important things to deal with than someone's feelings getting hurt."

"Terry, you threatened to have sex with the man's dead father. I've worked with Michael Aram a long time and he's a good man whose father was incredibly important to him. You are going to apologise and you are going to god damn mean it or I will throw you out of the building myself."

"You can't force me to be sincere."

"Terry, we all need to be at our very best. If people refuse to deal with you, people that you need to rely on, then things are going to get missed. If they have someone who has authority over them and is free to abuse them, that is going to detract from their performance. This isn't you and me in the backyard. These are people that work hard, work well and are deserving of your respect. The problem here, Terry, is you, and I will excise that problem one way or another. If you can't get your head around that and realise that you need to do better, then I do not want you here. Which, in case you're not paying attention, means that you won't be."

"You're not the only member of the Steering Committee, Anna. Some of the others like the way I do things."

"And they'll interfere when I try to fire you," Anna acknowledged. "But do they have the stones to interfere when I throw you off the roof?"

"Oh, come on, Anna."

"You'll survive," she said. "You can go liquid form."

"It'll take me hours to pool myself back together after a fall like that. That's assuming I don't lose any of myself down a storm drain again."

"Don't worry," Anna said. "I'll have the stuff from your office boxed up and waiting for you in reception when you get back."

Jason quietly arrived at Asano Village in the washed-out light of predawn. He had spent the night in the survivors' camp but not to sleep. He hadn't been sure what solace he could offer the survivors, but all he had left to give was his time. He then spent additional hours in debrief and even more time talking to the press.

Erika, Emi and Ken gathered around him, catching him in a supportive embrace. They moved to the lounge of the village's main residence, Emi sitting on a couch between Jason and her mother, each of them holding one of her hands.

For all that Emi's intelligence and maturity was beyond her age, the things she had seen that day had been a lot for a thirteen-year-old. Erika had told Emi she shouldn't watch the news but hadn't stopped her. They had all been glued to the television, catching every glimpse of Jason amongst the violence and the ruins and the death.

Jason and his family sat in awkward silence. Like much of the country and even the world, they had been watching him on the news all day. It began with the early scraps of action captured by the hiding EOA team, then the interviews with survivors. Footage from Kaito's drones had been fed live to the press, showing Jason moving like a dark, flittering bug in his desperate striving to extricate survivors.

Many countries around the world had fought back against the EOA's media control, including Australia. The Emergency Communications Act passed with overwhelming support in Parliament, despite unprecedented pushback from the media on all fronts. Not only did the law enact massive emergency funds for the public broadcast network but required government information updates to air daily on all free-to-air networks and instituted an Office of Media Disinformation with fierce enforcement powers.

Privacy advocates pushed back against what they termed draconian measures against press freedom, which the media companies got entirely behind with complaints about editorial independence. The wake of tragedy, however, was always the easiest time to curtail civil liberties. Broken Hill was the largest of Australia's disasters, but not the first.

"I'm not going to keep Shade's bodies with you anymore," Jason said finally. "I like being able to communicate and know that he's there if something happens. It's become clear to me, though, that I need to stop splitting my power."

Shade had called his bodies back to Jason, but it had taken time for them to get into range. They could only merge from forty kilometres away and had merged into an unmanned surveillance plane, moving at speed before travelling the last leg through the portal. In the time it took, there was one fewer bus picking up survivors than there could have been. Jason couldn't help but think of the lives that he failed to save in that time.

"We understand," Erika said.

His mind kept going back to the waterfall village where he had fought the elemental tyrant as the villagers evacuated. He had saved everyone that day. Everyone. All it had cost him was a scar. He was so much more powerful now, yet he had done so much worse. He was unmarked, but thousands of people were dead. He knew that one monster was different from an entire proto-space worth, but that didn't offer him solace.

"I need to get stronger," he murmured, head bowed.

"You're already strong, son," Ken said.

"No," Jason said. "I've seen power so vast that my mind is too limited to comprehend the scope of it. I'm a grain of sand before that. A bug on a windshield."

"What will you be if you get that kind of power?" Erika asked. "You're talking about god-like power, right? Is that what you want for yourself? If you become that powerful, will we be the grains of sand to you?"

Jason looked up at her with tremulous eyes.

"I don't know."

"Power isn't everything, Jason," Erika told him, nodding at Emi's small hand in his. "Power can't offer you that."

He tilted his head as he sensed a familiar aura approaching.

"What is it?" Ken asked.

"Someone I know just arrived at the village gate."

"As in the gate three kilometres away?" Erika asked. She and Ken both had aura senses, but theirs barely covered the room.

Jason's senses had grown to incredible proportions. They were based in his aura strength, although they reached further than his aura, like a radar sending out signals. He was still getting a handle on them, though.

In the familiar calm of Asano Village, there weren't enough auras to be onerous on his senses. In Broken Hill, the monsters and the chaos had been overwhelming, but he'd pushed himself to endure, extending his senses to the limit. He had needed to know where the survivors needed him most.

Jason stood and opened a portal.

"I'll be back in a moment," he said.

Jason emerged from a portal arch outside the village gate. Most of the people camping there had long gone as food shortages became worse. They had been forced to the cities where the government was rationing out food after seizing control of the supply chains. Only the most committed and unhinged people remained outside Asano Village.

A car had stopped in front of the gate and the security guard on duty had emerged from the booth. It was some distant cousin Jason didn't really know, looking at him nervously.

"It's fine," Jason said. "I'll handle this."

Dawn stepped out of the car, an expensive but ordinary European sedan.

"I'm sorry about what you went through today."

"Save your sympathy for the families of the dead."

"Very well. I was hoping you might put me up for a little while. A normal-rank avatar isn't up to the rigours of an increasingly dangerous world, as you well know."

20

INSTABILITY

In the Sydney Network branch's media operations centre, Terrance was going through the footage Jason had stolen from the EOA at Broken Hill again, discussing it with his publicity staff.

"The key to what he's doing here is that he's not telling us what the EOA's secrets are, which would get people immediately calling bull. He's 'inadvertently' letting slip in his anger that he knows what the EOA's secrets are. Instead of people denying what he's telling us, he's got them wondering what he's keeping to himself."

He pointed at one of his staffers. "Hailey, what is number one on trending right now?"

"Which platform?"

"Just pick one."

"Alright, boss, just a moment… number one is #scottbaioeyebeams."

"Scott Baio? The *Charles in Charge* guy? You know what I'm looking for, Hailey."

"Number three is #wheredothepowerscomefrom."

"Where do the powers come from?" Terrance repeated loudly to the room. "When the monster waves started, people were asking about the powers, but it was one more thing in a world gone crazy. Now people are getting a handle on monsters and superheroes, so it's time to refocus that question, which is exactly what Asano just did."

The doors opened and Aram came in.

"The Steering Committee wants an in-person update," he said.

"Very well," Terrance said. "Hailey, take over the analysis. Pay particular attention to the way that instead of going against the EOA's hero narrative, Asano played into it to give himself the legitimacy he then used to undercut it. Seriously, I could kiss that man. I mean, I couldn't, he was very clear on that, but still…"

Jason and Dawn were riding the underground tram out to the cloud house.

"You're getting close to silver rank now," she said.

"Events have accelerated my advancement," he said flatly. "If I had the choice, I'd rather it go slower and not have all the death."

Globally, the death toll from the monster waves was over two hundred thousand, although those were soft numbers. The count was potentially much higher.

"You have a question for me," Dawn said. "One that you need to ask before we can move forward."

"Why didn't you tell me about Farrah?"

"You realise that you could have asked that instead of punching my nose through my brain."

Dawn's new avatar was indistinguishable from the one that Jason had killed and looted.

"No regrets," he said. "I bet you were all 'that little bastard' afterwards."

"Of course I wasn't," she lied. "I'm an ancient and powerful being, so I'm a little more mature than someone who just turned twenty-six. I noticed that you didn't celebrate your birthday last week."

"It's not a celebratory time. I never liked my birthday anyway."

"Because it's on April Fool's Day?"

"It might seem like a fun combination, but it's not," Jason said. "Why didn't you tell me about Farrah?"

"Because of you."

"Me?"

"If I had come to you when you first arrived back, what would you have done?"

"I'd have gone and got her."

"No," Dawn said. "You'd have died trying. Think about the state you were in when you got back. No local resources, no allies, no information, no understanding of the magical society of your world. You were also still very much caught up in a war mentality. Your first instinct to every obstacle was to murder it."

"I'd have found a way."

"You did, when you were ready. You had allies, information and a more balanced mindset."

"You could have shown me how."

"And would you have trusted me enough to listen?"

He grimaced.

"No," he acknowledged.

"She was sent here to help you, not just as a warrior but as a friend. She understands what you've been through because she has been through much the same. Most of all, she is someone you can trust. It took time to get there, even with your family. Except for your niece, but she couldn't offer you the support you needed."

"I know what Farrah represents," Jason growled, then his face softened. "And I am grateful that she was brought back."

"You can thank the Reaper for that," Dawn said. "It was the one who offered. It wanted to avoid the World-Phoenix sending your soul zipping back and forth across the astral with her tokens every time she needed you in one world or the other."

"And now I have to figure out how to astral travel fully intact or not at all."

"You will."

The tram tunnel emerged from underground into the underwater section.

"I have more questions for you," Jason said.

"The Builder did not violate the agreement," she said, anticipating what he wanted to know.

"Then how are the Engineers of Ascension making converted with his clockwork cores?"

"I don't know."

"You don't know?"

"I don't know everything, Mr Asano, and I can only tell you so much of what I do. What I can tell you is that the Builder has not intervened in this world any time in the last five centuries or so."

"Unless he found a way to sneak past you."

"Sneaking past me is possible," Dawn said. "Sneaking past the World-Phoenix is not."

"You're saying you can't help me figure out what's going on, then?"

"I am not saying that. I would direct you to the defector from the EOA leadership who is working with the American Network branches. She has insights into their enhancement program from its very origins."

"How exactly is it that you get your information?"

"I'm not going to tell you that."

"Is it just a bunch of people?"

"It is not just a bunch of people."

"You don't want to tell me who they are because then I could just go ask the bunch of people myself, right?"

"It is not just a bunch of people!"

"Sure, it's not. I totally believe you."

"I'm beginning to understand why the Builder was so caught up in killing someone as insignificant as you."

"Rude."

The tram came to a stop at the end of the tunnel and they went through the airlock into the cloud house. Jason looked around as he did every time he entered, still happy with the configuration of interlinked domes.

"This is rather nice," Dawn said, the air shimmering with light passing through the water outside. "It reminds me of home a little."

"And where's home?"

"The city-universe of Interstice," she said. "It's minute by the standards of a normal reality, but quite large by the standards of a city. More like a free-floating astral space. It is also profoundly magical, yet unique in that monsters do not manifest there. Many consider it to be the capital city of the astral, at least the portion of it that we know. The astral is more vast than even a diamond-ranker like myself can conceptualise."

"So, the astral has its own societies, then?"

"Many worlds are more familiar with astral travel than the one you have known. Pallimustus has rather undeveloped astral magic, although the Builder's intervention is changing that. Even now, your friend Clive is deciphering and disseminating more advanced astral knowledge."

"You know about my team?"

"They are all doing well. They do not know that you are alive again, however."

"Knowledge must know I'm not dead. She knew about the token your boss gave me."

"The deity knows. It just isn't telling."

"Bloody transcendents and their bloody games," he muttered, shaking his head.

They went through a tunnel into a lounge room, each sitting in a comfortable cloud armchair.

"I'd offer you refreshments, but I don't keep any on hand," Jason said. "Rationing, you know."

"…consistently gaining ground in defining the discourse," Terrance reported.

He stood in the Steering Committee meeting room giving his report.

"The EOA was always running on a clock before they lost control of the narrative," he continued. "We're seeing them pay for it now. Even in the beginning, certain areas were resistant to their obfuscation. In the US, for example, the EOA has incredible media dominance, but the Emergency Broadcast System cut through a lot of the noise. Now that countries are enacting media intervention laws like our Emergency Communications Act, the EOA can't muddy the waters so easily."

"We know the EOA have been insinuating themselves into states who have long felt that the Network was a tool of the west," Anna said. "Certain nations are even looking to oust the Network and have the EOA fill the role. This is the EOA's endgame, as far as we can tell. What is your assessment, based on media analysis, for further action on this front?"

"If the projections of the grid coming back up inside of two to three weeks hold up, then I think the EOA are pretty much out of steam in terms of infiltrating governments. I would be looking out for a reorientation of their plans moving forward. There is no way they don't know about the grid projections, so we're keeping a sharp eye for a shift in messaging that might indicate whatever new approach they're going for."

"Alright, thank you, Terrance," the committee chairwoman said. "So long as nothing else terrible comes up, I don't anticipate there being any problems."

"Oh, come on," Terrance exclaimed. "Why would you say something like that?"

"Why are you here, Dawn?" Jason asked. "I'm sure that you could find a nice, secure spot in any of the big cities."

"I warned you in the past of what is happening to your world as the magical density grows."

"You did."

"Most of the astral spaces on this world were already going undiscovered, under the water," she said. "With the deactivation of the grid, the rate of magic being introduced to your world increased by a third. That is a not-inconsiderable amount."

"It's accelerated the process," Jason said. "Not hard to surmise."

"It's worse than that, I'm afraid. I've been studying the effects on your world and the rate of acceleration seems to have crossed some threshold."

"Something's happened that won't get fixed when the grid goes back up? I don't suppose you ever considered helping with that. Or warning us what the EOA was up to?"

"I am an astral magic specialist, Mr Asano. While I am not unversed in array magic, I am used to operating with higher-order magic—higher-rank rituals in high-magic zones. Your friend Farrah is more conversant with lower-order array magic than I am and better suited to the task. As for warning you, there are rules on how much I am allowed to interfere."

"That seems like a convenient excuse for acting when you want to and ignoring us when you don't."

"Then where do we draw the line, Mr Asano? Where would you like the intervention of higher-order beings to stop? Do you want the World-Phoenix coming in and solving all your problems? Of course, then what constitutes a problem and an acceptable solution would be for us to decide. What if it was the Reaper instead? The Builder? How much freedom are you willing to give up? Knowing you, Mr Asano, I'm guessing not very much. There are lines that we do not cross and I recommend you be grateful for that. As it stands, my presence here is already edging that line. I am a servant of the World-Phoenix, whose authority is dimensional integrity, so I have some leeway on how free I can be with information pertaining to that. Anything else I need to be more careful with. I can help you connect dots but not draw the dots myself. Even then, I must be cautious."

Jason looked unhappy but nodded, acknowledging the point.

"If you're an astral magic specialist," he said, "how about you help me get my head around these books that Knowledge gave me?"

"Yes."

"Wait, yes? As in yes, you'll help me out without buggering about being mysterious?"

"Yes."

"Uh… great. Thank you."

"I will need some local accommodation."

"We can do that. The food won't be terrific; we're rationing the same as everyone else."

"This avatar can be sustained on spirit coins."

"No worries, then. Now, back to what you were saying about some kind of change that won't be fixed when the grid goes back up. Are you talking about direct manifestations, with no proto-spaces?"

"No, that is still a number of years away. A smaller number, now, but there is time for more pressing concerns. What I am talking about is something even I have not seen before. Do you recall that I told you about the previous Builder creating this universe as an experiment?"

"Something about making it using existing realities as a template instead of starting from scratch?"

"Precisely. I have been examining the dimensional integrity of this world and I believe that the increased magic from the current circumstances has triggered a unique symptom of instability based on templates from which your world was constructed. Once the grid is back up, the acceleration in magic will be arrested somewhat as the proto-spaces it detects are once more being intercepted. At that point, I believe the instability will show itself, like a dimensional whiplash effect."

"Show itself how?"

"By the flaws introduced in the way this universe was constructed manifesting directly. Pockets of reality, warping into patterns based on the templates on which this reality was designed."

"What will that look like?"

"Like an astral or proto-astral space. Different geography, climate, magical conditions. Except there will be no dimensional boundary. Instead of being connected to your world, these zones will be part of it, the space they occupied being reshaped on the most fundamental level."

"What about people in that space?"

"I don't know."

"Will there be monsters?"

"I don't know. What the previous Builder did here was drastic enough that he was removed and replaced. This is, as far as I am aware, unprecedented. If the World-Phoenix knows more, it has not shared that information with me."

"Doesn't feel great, does it?"

"No, it does not."

"So, what do we do?" Jason asked. "Farrah said the grid reactivation team is hoping to get it back up in less than two weeks. Until just now, I thought that was a good thing."

"All you can do is warn the world. I am not withholding information here; I truly do not know. You will need to discover how to deal with whatever comes for yourselves, although I have a place that you can start."

"You're going to connect some dots for me?"

"Yes," Dawn said. "It is time for Akari Asano to tell you why she is really here."

21

SUPERNATURAL

"Really?" Dawn asked. Shade's motorcycle form made almost no noise, but she spoke loudly over the rush of air.

"What?" Jason asked back.

"You have a portal power."

"Which I might need to use in an emergency."

"Your familiar can turn into a car."

"On a beautiful day like this?"

"Or more than one motorcycle."

"I don't know what you're complaining about," Jason said. "Emi loves the sidecar."

They were riding through the bushland separating the communal area of Asano Village from the residential clusters. In spite of Jason's light-hearted banter, Dawn understood what lay beneath it. Her senses relied on projecting her aura through her avatar, but Jason sensed nothing, even as his emotions were laid bare. As strong as his aura and senses were, Dawn was realms beyond him in this regard.

As well as Jason hid it, his tangled nest of grief, frustration, and shame were plain for her to see. She had been observing him long enough to know that banter was a key coping mechanism of his and she let herself fall into it, playing the game on his terms.

The roads were only months old but well made, the product of Ken's earth manipulation powers and a construction crew brought in by Hiro. The workers had been told that they were the day crew. The extra work they found done each morning was attributed to the night crew, who they never saw. They were paid well to not ask questions, so they overlooked the myriad incongruities that came from the night crew, being Jason's father and his magic powers.

Jason and Dawn followed the road as it wound through pleasant bushland and climbed to the clifftop residential cluster, the most remote of Asano Village's mini-suburbs. Jason pulled the bike to a stop, where a large yard spanned the gap between the road and the cliff-hugging house. Aside from a tiled path leading to the front door, the yard was all open grass.

There was an outdoor cabinet next to the door, up against the stone wall of the house. It had a magic lock that any essence user could open with a little mana. Jason did so, taking out a pair of silver-rank suppression collars, along with two swords covered in faintly glowing runes.

Item: [Practise Sword] (bronze rank, common)

Practise sword designed to allow full-contact attacks in safety (weapon, sword).

- Effect: All damage dealt by this weapon is negated, replaced with a mild stinging sensation.
- Effect: Inflicts [Minor Stun]. Strength of stun is based on the amount of damage that would have been dealt.

- [Minor Stun] (affliction, magic): Causes loss of function in the area of the body affected. Affects a larger area of the body when used against targets lower than bronze rank. Delivers debilitating disorientation when used on vital areas.

Dawn waited at the edge of the yard with Shade, who had returned to his natural form of a shadow with silver eyes. Jason moved to the middle of the yard, letting out a pulse of aura, even though he knew Akari would have heard his approach. He clipped one of the suppression collars around his neck.

The collars Akari brought with her from Japan were more artistically designed than others Jason had seen. Most suppression collars were thick, plain, and not designed with the comfort of the wearer in mind. These were more like jewellery, with elegant engraving and silver gilding. It would not be hard for him to shrug off the collar's effect, but he let it work.

Akari emerged from the house wearing a dark blue kendo gi. Her hair was in a practical ponytail that always reminded him of Sophie, despite Akari's hair being shampoo-commercial shimmering black instead of metallic silver. Jason wore track pants, sneakers and an H.R. Pufnstuf t-shirt. She wordlessly took one of the swords and the other suppression collar, snapping it around her neck.

Jason and Akari squared off in the middle of the yard, each watching for openings. When they had started practising together, they had been evenly matched. Akari was a specialised swordswoman but had been caught up in human fighting styles designed around human limitations. She made good use of her speed, but her superhuman body was capable of far more than she was using it for.

Jason, by contrast, made complete use of his peak bronze-rank attributes. They were not the equal of her silver-rank ones, but his were fully leveraged when he fought. Her highly aggressive approach was not inherently bad but was poorly suited to confront Jason's style, which heavily employed feints and counterattacks. Key to this was his use of aura manipulation, something that Akari vastly underutilised.

Jason was hard to read for the aggressive Akari, who found herself repeatedly baited into missteps and overextensions. After almost every loss, she admonished herself for becoming exposed.

Jason's strange chimeric style would shift from approach to approach in ways that should have been discordant yet were somehow natural and smooth. In one moment, it resembled kendo, and the next, capoeira. Bursts of direct, rapid aggression gave way to elaborate and outlandish movements that seemed more like dancing or acrobatics than combat. It shouldn't have worked, yet he leveraged his capabilities to turn what was impractical for a human into a powerful weapon for a superhuman.

As weeks and then months passed, Jason had arrived again and again at Akari's door to fight. With Akari's unflinching analysis and unswerving dedication, she rapidly addressed the flaws Jason had revealed in her combat style.

Jason was diligent in his swordsmanship, but for Akari, the sword was the core of her being. She learned to leverage her own attributes while modulating her forceful aggression into precision and care, improving her ability to read feints, avoid dangerous counterattacks and adapt to Jason's unconventional style.

Akari had been training in the sword as long as she could remember. Jason had little to offer in improving her technique, but the principles of the way he fought helped her to reforge herself with the tools she already possessed. A lifetime of training gave her the means to awaken her potential; Jason merely provided the impetus.

Jason had likewise learned from Akari. He tended to overcomplicate and get caught up in trying to be clever when clean, simple and direct was the superior choice. He did not share Akari's lifetime of immersion in the way of the sword, so he did not make the same strides as her, but she helped him work on the weakest area of his technique—efficiency.

Jason and Akari each grew into their respective strengths. After two months, Jason went from winning four in ten spars to one in twenty when they faced off in the open yard. That ratio shifted significantly upward when they moved into the bush, however, where, even without his powers, Jason moved like a ghost. The dedication Akari put into being a swordswoman, Jason put into being a predator.

As Dawn watched, they had a typical spar, with Jason infuriatingly hard to pin down. Akari was relentless, however, punishing every mistake Jason made with his wild combat style. Jason still managed to goad her into an opening, turning the tables with a flurry of counterattacks. Even on the back foot, however, Akari was calm, efficient, and precise. What had once been a desperate defence in the face of Jason's chimeric style was now clinical in execution, dismantling Jason's momentum as she inexorably turned the tables back.

Landing a clean hit on Jason's leg arrested his mobility as the stun inflicted by the magic training sword took effect. This signalled the end as Jason at his best was barely able to hold her off. A strike to his other leg dropped him to the ground and her sword came down on his head.

The magic of the sword meant he didn't feel more than a mild sting from any of it. Instead, he suffered a stun effect to his head that delivered a bout of debilitating vertigo. He lay on his back, giggling like a child who had spun themselves dizzy as he felt the world turn wildly around him.

Akari took Jason's sword and unclipped his suppression collar. The training device had a simple clasp to keep it closed, with no key. She looked down at him as Jason pushed himself onto his elbows, still grinning with a giddy expression.

"Sometimes I suspect you're losing on purpose just to get hit in the head with the training swords."

"No worries on that front," Jason said. "If I did that, you'd use your real sword on me."

"Just as long as you know," she said, helping Jason unsteadily to his feet, which pulled them close together.

"I should have been there," she said softly.

He gave her a smile devoid of his usual smirking undertone.

"It's not like you were taking a spa day. Broken Hill didn't stop every other threat out there and you had other people to help."

"You shouldn't have had to face that alone."

"I didn't. I just got there a little earlier. Once the troops arrived, I was pretty much reduced to opening portals and directing bus traffic."

Akari frowned.

"You don't always have to be self-effacing, you know. It's the most Japanese thing about you, but it feels wrong when you do it."

He flashed her a grin.

"I'll keep my shameless braggadocio completely unearned, thank you very much."

"Definitely wrong."

She shook her head, then turned to look at Dawn.

"Who's your friend?"

"Your new housemate. We don't have enough places to give every swinging single their own crash pad. Let's go say g'day."

They walked across the lawn to meet Dawn as Akari removed the collar from her own neck.

"Asano Akari," Akari greeted with a respectful bow.

"This is Dawn," Jason introduced. "She may seem ordinary, but I assure you that she is not. In fact, she is, quite likely, the most remarkable human being on this planet."

"May I ask how so?" Akari asked. Her demeanour around Dawn was significantly more respectful than her casual attitude with Jason.

"Well, for starters, she's not a human being. She's not even on this planet; what you're seeing here is basically a fancy telephone."

"I think I'll step in," Dawn said. "Jason is notoriously bad at explaining things. My name is Dawn, as he said, and I am a diamond-ranker from outside of your universe. This body you see is an avatar; a near-powerless projection of my true self, which is residing outside of your reality."

"To be honest," Akari said, "what both of you said seems extremely outlandish."

"It does, doesn't it?" Dawn said and held out her hand. "Give me a sword."

That got raised eyebrows from Jason and Akari both.

"Are you sure?" Jason asked.

"Quite," Dawn said.

"I'm just asking because of that time I punched you so hard that you died."

Akari turned to give Jason a wide-eyed look.

"It's fine," Jason told her while gesturing at Dawn. "Look, she's fine."

"My new avatar can leverage my senses much better," Dawn said, giving Jason a flat look.

"In case I try to punch you in the face again?"

"I was more worried about Miss Hurin."

"Good call. Farrah definitely wants to take a swing too."

"Miss Asano," Dawn said. "Would it be accurate to say that you learn what you need to know about a person through their sword?"

"It would," Akari said.

"What does my sword tell you?" Jason asked.

"That you always make the outrageous choice, even when the simple one is better. That you overcomplicate everything and will often make two moves when all you need is one."

"Meaning that you're all flash and no bang," Dawn said.

"Hey," Jason complained. "What did I ever do to you?"

"You killed me."

"So what? I've died twice; you need to get over it."

"I truly hope you survive to diamond rank, Mr Asano. I am looking forward to you and I having a very different conversation."

"Are you going to kick my arse?"

"Across reality and back."

"Like *Star Trek*, except the warp drive is a sexy lady," Jason said with a creepy smile.

"You are disgusting," Akari told him.

Jason flashed her an impish grin.

"Give her a sword," he said.

"Are you certain?" Akari asked.

"It's fine. I already killed her, so how bad can it get with stun swords?"

Dawn gave Jason another flat look.

"Very well," Akari said. She moved to put the collar back on her neck, but Dawn gestured for her to stop.

"It's fine," Dawn said.

Akari gave Dawn an assessing look, then nodded, handing the collars to Jason and the second sword to Dawn.

"It might be a little heavy."

"I'll manage," Dawn said, holding it in two hands.

The two women moved to the centre of the yard while Jason stood next to Shade.

"I would ask if you really needed to antagonise both women," Shade said, "but I have known you long enough at this point."

Jason responded only with a chuckle, then his face turned dark.

"What's the count?" he asked.

He had one of Shade's bodies keeping an eye on the Broken Hill death count as it was updated.

"Nine thousand confirmed, with an estimated total of twelve to fifteen thousand."

"Damn it."

"The survivor count came to over nineteen thousand," Shade said. "No small part of that is down to you."

"To us," Jason said. "Without your buses, that number would have been halved, easily."

Akari watched Dawn, standing in front of her, sword held in both hands. Every sense she had told her that Dawn was a normal person, but Jason had said she was anything but. Akari had learned that while Jason liked to lie frequently and transparently about inconsequential things, he was honest about the ones that mattered. As such, she didn't take the woman in front of her lightly.

With no collar, Akari opened by slamming both her aura and sword down at Dawn. She missed, without being entirely sure how. The fight that followed was the single most bewildering combat of Akari's life.

Dawn was slow and weak, yet she seemed to know every move Akari made, not just before she made it but before she even thought of it. Every action Akari took, Dawn and her sword were exactly where they needed to be, as if by coincidence or prophecy.

Akari's silver-rank speed and strength massively outstripped the other woman, but Dawn was always in exactly the right spot, in exactly the right pose. She could not block, yet her sword deflected Akari's just enough to turn hits into hair's breadth misses. Akari felt as if she were trying to cut down the wind, her blade passing through the air again and again.

Dawn even managed to slip past Akari's defences to land hits, although the damage was negligible. The magic swords translated damage into a stunning effect, but Dawn's damage was so light, it left Akari with barely a noticeable tingle. The pair clashed intermittently for several minutes, spending more time watching each other than crossing blades.

Eventually, Akari made a mistake and Dawn's sword came up under her chin. Even that was not enough, only the rank of the sword allowing for a mild buzzing sensation in her jaw. Akari stopped anyway, stepping back and bowing deeply.

"I am a magical swordswoman," Akari said, "yet I cannot find any word that better describes your ability than supernatural. Will you teach me?"

"I will," Dawn said, "but that will have to wait. The time has come to discuss your true reason for coming to Australia."

Jason wandered over, looking Dawn up and down.

"You let me hit you, didn't you?"

"It was something you needed to get out of your system. I didn't think you would do it hard enough to kill me, and I certainly didn't think you would loot the body."

"Well, I had been drinking. And I really, really wanted to punch you in the face."

22

ARMS RACE

Akari led Jason and Dawn into the clifftop house. What was remarkable about Asano Village's clifftop homes was that most of their space was underground, dug into solid rock. The underground portion then emerged from the cliff face with a glass wall offering views over the Pacific Ocean.

Without access to magic, the construction of the cliff houses would have been dangerous and the results unstable. Since magic was involved, it was simply impressive. Jason was reminded of this as he walked up to the glass wall in Akari's underground lounge room.

"This is nice," he said. "If I didn't already have a place, I'd definitely pick one of these."

"Where do you live, exactly?" Akari asked. "I thought it was in the main residence, but it's not, is it?"

"No," Jason said. "I have a little spot tucked away."

Jason turned from the window and they sat in the lounge chairs around a coffee table.

"As I stated outside," Dawn said to Akari, "the time has come for you to make plain your purpose in coming to Australia. Normally, I would not have revealed as much as I have about myself to you, but you are the gateway to preparing for the next challenge this world will face."

"Meaning what, exactly?" Akari asked.

"Meaning that the Tiwari clan's guardianship is coming to an end."

"Tiwari?" Jason asked. "That's an Indian name, not a Japanese one."

"Yes," Akari said. "Centuries ago, the Network founder came to Japan, creating the secret societies that today are Japan's Network branches. The founder brought with him the Tiwari family. They were the guardians of an ancient object of incredible power and he brought them to Japan to keep it hidden. After centuries of intermarrying the locals, while the name and bloodline remain, they are, by any discernible measure, Japanese."

"What is this object?" Jason asked. "Dawn has been maddeningly vague."

"A door," Akari said. "No one is exactly sure where it leads, only that it is a world not our own. Further, when the door is moved, it opens to a new location. As best as anyone has been able to determine, wherever it is, it leads to an equivalent point in another world."

"Is it Farrah's world?" Jason asked Dawn.

"No," Dawn said. "In fact, Akari is incorrect. The door does not lead to another world, but a hidden aspect of this one. It gives access to the building blocks with which this universe was constructed."

"You're talking about the templates that the original Builder used," Jason said.

"Yes," Dawn said. "The door is a tool for accessing the fundamental underpinnings of not just this reality but also the other to which it is connected. Should it be taken there."

"And this is some kind of space that can be physically entered? Is it some kind of sub-dimension?"

"The specifics are significantly above your current grasp of astral magic," Dawn said. "Sub-dimension is a sufficient explanation for now."

"That sounds like it would be dangerous to mess with," Jason said.

"Yes," Dawn agreed. "Your world and your friend Farrah's have always been connected. They were built that way. That connection is woven into the fabric of your two realities. It causes echoes from one to the other."

"I noticed from the start that odd things seemed to work the same way in both worlds," Jason said. "Everything from the people of that world appearing in our legends to the way we keep time being identical. Is that connection the reason, somehow?"

"That is a factor of the resonance," Dawn said. "Echoes between worlds constructed on the same model, imprinting on one another."

"Which is how you get a lion-man named Gary, I suppose."

Akari was listening in silence. She quickly realised that she was getting a peek at some of the greatest secrets that existed. While she was missing many of the specifics, she followed as best she could.

"Someone came to this world centuries ago," Dawn said. "They brought with them the door now in the Tiwari clan's possession. The connection between realities is a fabric that stretches across the universe. That door is a tool that can modify small portions of that fabric. On a universal scale, it can only affect a fragmentary space, but that is enough to strengthen the link between two connected points."

"Such as two versions of the same world," Jason said.

"Precisely."

"Why didn't you tell me any of this before now?"

"Because I did not know," Dawn said. "While you have been treating the symptoms of the problem at hand, I have been diagnosing the cause. The link connecting this planet, in this universe, to its equivalent in the other universe have been enhanced. It only affects the area around this planet, although if the link is not returned to its natural state, there could be catastrophic cascade effects as the fabric of reality begins to fray."

"I'm assuming that's a metaphor. Also that it's really bad."

"If this planet is lost, the rupture in this reality could potentially chain through your universe and cause it to collapse entirely. The other universe has a dimensional membrane supple enough to endure the backlash, but the rigid membrane of this one may break rather than bend."

"So the escalating magic is only here, on Earth," Jason said. "It's not affecting aliens and such, but if we lose the Earth, we may lose the universe."

"I have touched on this when we spoke in the past," Dawn said. "To return the link to its normal state, you must rectify the problems here, then return to the other reality and do so on the other side."

"Save the universe, no pressure. How do I do that, exactly?"

"The original connection between universes is an intrinsic element of the design by which the original Builder created both realities. When the templates on which it is based are made manifest, the components of that link are brought into physical being. The door is a tool that makes those templates manifest, allowing the collection of those components. Collect enough and the door can be used to modify the link."

"How exactly do you find this stuff out?" Jason asked. "Is there an online encyclopaedia for wizards or something? Is it subscription or can you just use a free account?"

"Do you know what an astral resonance imprint beacon is?" Dawn asked.

"It's kind of a recording probe, right?" Jason said. "It's sensitive to astral forces and if you're crazy good at understanding astral effects, you can interpret the readings."

"You've been studying your astral magic books."

"I've had to distract myself in my downtime somehow," Jason said. "Normally, I'd cook, but there's all this rationing going on. If I'm following all of this correctly—which is a big if—then this magic door can rewrite the DNA of the universe."

"Very broadly speaking and on a very small scale, but something like that," Dawn acknowledged.

"Which means the Builder made this door, right? The current Builder. Unless there's someone else out there who can fiddle with reality on that level."

"There is not," Dawn said. "That being said, I believe that it was not a follower of the Builder who brought the door here, however. It was an outworlder, like you, but one who had entered the service of one of the other world's gods."

"Purity has been working with the Builder."

"This outworlder likely modified the link in the other reality first, using the door, then came here and did the same. This set in motion the magic siphoning from the other reality's version of Earth, Pallimustus, to this Earth. The impact was slight, at first, but it's been escalating. Over the last century and a half, that escalation has become precipitous, leading to a rise in the number and the strength of the proto-spaces being formed."

"The person who did all this," Jason said. "Is it the same one who built the grid and founded the Network?"

"I believe so."

"Why?"

"Balance," Dawn said. "The architect of this plan does not want the planet destroyed, at least not until they are done with it. They need it in place to soak up the magic that would normally accumulate around the other world until it triggered a magic surge."

"Which is why the grid never covered the ocean," Jason reasoned. "It was never intended to stop all the magic, just regulate it. The grid—and by extension, the Network—is a safety valve designed to keep things under control once the magic started building to dangerous levels."

"This was my conclusion as well," Dawn said. "The grid could have covered the oceans if the original designer had wanted it to do so. Giving the Network the tools to traverse aquatic environments and confront monsters there would certainly have been within their capabilities."

"We're still soaking up the magic from Pallimustus that would normally become a monster surge," Jason said. "Is that why the monster surges have been taking longer and longer?"

"Yes," Dawn said. "With how much magic Earth is siphoning right now, the monster surges have stopped altogether. They won't resume until the enhanced link to Earth is reduced to its original state, at least on this side of the link."

"They haven't had the surge yet?"

"No."

"That makes it something like fifteen years now. They must be going nuts. And once we shut off the spigot on this end, won't they get the humdinger of all monster surges?"

"Yes. They have been on the cusp of a monster surge so long that once it happens, there will be an unprecedented breach in the dimensional membrane in the vicinity of their planet. This will allow the Builder's forces, which are already poised for an invasion, to come through with all the magical manifestations."

"I thought your boss and the Builder had a non-intervention deal. It feels a lot like he's still rummaging about in both worlds."

"That accord prohibits only direct intervention. It does not cover the use of mortal agents or events already set into motion."

"It sounds like he's already off to the races," Jason said. "That deal doesn't sound super-helpful."

"The deal more thoroughly prohibits intervention in your world. My involvement is pushing the boundary, even at a remove. If not for dimensional integrity being the direct purview of the World-Phoenix, I would not even be allowed this much."

"Yeah, I'm sorry. I know you're here to help."

Jason grimaced.

"If I'm following this correctly," he said, "to save this world, I need to doom Farrah's world to an interdimensional invasion."

"If it makes you feel better, letting your world die would have the same effect," Dawn said. "It would just take longer and the resulting effects on the other world would be all the worse."

"Oh, great."

"You will need to rectify the enhanced link on this side first, which will at least slow down the damage to your world as it exposes the other. Then you must go there and resolve the link on the other side."

"You told us we'd have to go back."

"Yes," Dawn said. "At the time, I had discovered that the link would need to be adjusted at both ends. Now I know why and how."

"I need to go get the magic door."

"The door is only the beginning," Dawn said. "To use it to modify the link, you must do what was done when the link was first modified. Collect the elements of the link left behind by the original Builder in the templates on which your world was constructed. Gather enough and you can restore the link to its original state."

"Oh, a fetch quest, great. If I kill ten boars, do I get a green-quality spear?"

"Originally, you would use the door to give us access to those templates. Circumstances have changed."

"The EOA," Jason realised. "They plugged the safety valve. You said that when the grid went back up, there would be a magical backlash."

"Yes," Dawn said. "The templates, and the manifested link components within them, will start to appear randomly, reshaping your world. You will no longer require the door to access them, although it will still be necessary to rectify the link."

"Isn't that good, in a way?" Jason asked. "We should be able to gather these link components more easily."

"As will anyone else. These components will be the most magically dense objects on your world. Do you think it is more likely that the magical factions come together for the greater good, or leap into a magical arms race?"

"Oh, crap."

Jason and Dawn took the time to fill Akari in on the broad strokes of what she had heard. They didn't go into too much detail, just enough to give her a general understanding of what was happening and what was at stake.

"You need me to convince the Tiwari to give you the door," she surmised.

"Yes," Jason said. "What I don't understand is what led to you coming here. I think we can safely put aside the pretence of assessing the worthiness of my family."

"That is not as much pretence as you may think," Akari said. "We take the dignity of our name seriously."

"Well, I have to save the universe and I take that seriously."

A throat-clearing sound came from within Jason's shadow.

"Relatively seriously," Jason said. "Also, you don't have a throat, Shade."

Jason turned his attention back to Akari.

"Why are you really here?" he asked her.

"The founder left the Tiwari clan with a prophecy," Akari said. "When monsters walked the world, a man of two worlds would close the door forever. They believe that man is you. Given your name, they came to us in the hope of approaching you. We have been Network allies for many years, but the revelation of the door and the clan's origin was news to us. I was sent to assess not your clan, but you. To see if you could be trusted with this secret."

"Which obviously I can, because I'm terrific."

"You are a hard person to like," Akari said.

"I have to assume this prophecy is another level of control," Jason said. "If they wanted to throttle the link back once it had served its purpose, the person most likely to have the ability and knowledge would be an outworlder."

"Yes," Dawn said. "The conditions for an outworlder to be sucked between worlds rather than simply annihilated are quite specific, but with the link in the state it is in, those conditions being met somewhere in your world were an inevitability."

"Are you sure?" Jason asked. "Seems like bit of a gamble."

"A gamble one might be willing to make if they were willing to live with your world being destroyed if it didn't pay off. Or perhaps they were relying on other forces recognising the danger and taking steps to rectify it. The goddess Knowledge gave you a trove of astral magic knowledge to take home. The World-Phoenix made sure you would get there. I don't think the Builder was happy that you were the agent the World-Phoenix chose, but it seems likely in hindsight that he did anticipate her actions."

"Meaning your boss got played."

"Yes," Dawn said. "The Builder, for all his seeming short-sightedness and frustration, seems to be getting everything he wants. Even you, saving your world, serves him by setting in motion his invasion of Pallimustus. The bargain that keeps him from intervening in this world limits the World-Phoenix's ability to act against him now."

"You're telling me that getting obsessed with me was all an act?"

"Perhaps, perhaps not," Dawn said. "The second Builder has always been erratic, to the point that many of us suspect it to be a problem with his being raised from mortality. The Builder leveraging that reputation to mask the depths of his intentions is certainly possible."

"So, what now?" Jason asked Dawn. "We go to Japan and take this door?"

"First, warn the Network about the template manifestations. There is no telling exactly what will happen, but hopefully, there will be a need for large-scale evacuations."

"Hopefully?"

"As opposed to people being dissolved into nothingness as the reality around them is reshaped."

"Yeah, that would be bad," Jason said.

"Next, we need to collect the door," Dawn said. "It needs to be in your possession before the templates begin to manifest. If the magic factions discover it and learn what it can do, they will fight over it."

Jason and Dawn both turned to Akari.

"What?" Akari asked.

"Are you going to warn your people about how important the door is?" Jason asked. "If they know, then they will extort everything they can for it."

"Only a few members of the Asano clan know of this and they will act with integrity," Akari insisted.

"And what about the Tiwari clan?" Jason asked. "Will they share your unflinching honour?"

Akari frowned.

"I would like to think so," she said, "but I cannot speak for them."

"I'd like to get in a room with that EOA defector at some point as well," Jason said. "I want to know where they're getting the Builder's clockwork cores from."

"That doesn't matter at the moment," Dawn said. "You don't have time to visit the United States. There are now larger concerns at play than the Engineers of Ascension."

23

SWORD-FIGHTING WITH NO SHIRT ON

"I know Broken Hill must have been rough," Ketevan said, meeting Jason in her office.

"Not as rough as it was for the people who lived there," he said.

"Even so, I understand if you need to take some time before getting back into action. That being said, if you are up to it, we could always use you."

"Actually, I came in to tell you that I need some time away from Network activity. Also, a flight to Japan and back would be good. With air travel restricted, I can't just go buy a ticket. I could use Shade, but until I catch up to him in rank, using him as a plane would leave me shovelling coins into him like an old-timey train driver."

"Japan?" Ketevan asked. "Is this a family thing? Something to do with Akari? She's been doing some impressive work for us, helping to shut down proto-spaces and clear dimensional entity waves. We can manage without you, but losing you both at this point will make a dent in our capabilities, I won't lie."

"It's a larger concern than family," Jason said. "We need to have a meeting. You, me, Anna and Farrah to start with. It's about preparing for what happens when the grid comes back up."

"We've been holding discussions about what happens following the grid-reactivation since it first went down."

"Those plans need revising."

"I shouldn't have agreed to this," Jason said as Kaito flew him and Farrah back towards Asano Village. They were in the cockpit, catching a ride as Kaito moved a load of supplies north for Network ritualist teams. "I should have pushed the issue and had us on a plane to Japan already."

"I don't think you realise how much attention is on you now," Kaito said. "They're saying that Broken Hill is the fifth-largest loss of life from a single incident since the start of the monster waves. There's been nothing else on TV. Interviews with survivors, footage from the evacuation. Every channel is looping footage of you taking out monsters and shoving people onto buses."

"Footage from your drones," Jason said.

"Don't look at me," Kaito said. "That was Terrance."

The cockpit seats had a two-by-two configuration, with Kaito and Farrah in the front seats. Jason was in one of the rear seats, with Terrance in the other.

"You should see the tracking data for your online footprint," Terrance said. "There's enough footage and interviews that people are doing deep-dive analysis of your performance vs. the League of Heroes. They went after the big monsters while you worked on helping people, which did not go unnoticed. I made very sure of that."

"I'm so glad that all those dead people were good for your optics," Jason snarled.

Farrah turned around in her seat, patting Jason on the arm. When he first arrived back on Earth, his anger would have let his aura loose. Months of renewed training let him keep it under control.

"I sympathise with those poor people, of course," Terrance said, "but we need to strike while the iron is hot. The press has been wanting access to interview you for months and now is a perfect time. After Broken Hill…"

Terrance trailed off as Jason turned a withering stare on him. He didn't lose control of his aura; instead, he used it with pinpoint efficiency. Terrance had never sensed Jason's aura before, but now he felt it like an icicle spike, pressing into his throat.

"If I hear the phrase 'thoughts and prayers' pass your lips," Jason said coldly, "you will not like what happens next."

"Of course," Terrance said with a visible gulp. "Obviously, the press will be instructed to be sensitive about it."

Jason had agreed to participate in a press day while the Network prepared to send him to Japan. The journey was more than just arranging a plane. There were diplomatic issues with Japan's Network branches and even the Japanese government. Jason had become a figure of prominence and, more importantly, power. If he wanted to move openly, it involved obtaining government permission; there was a level of nervousness engendered when a one-man army applied for a visa.

"How is this press day of yours going to play out?" Jason asked Terrance.

"We already have some selected press en route to Asano Village," he said.

"They get vetted at the gate," Farrah said. "By me."

"That's fine," Terrance said. "In fact, if you could make the magic as overt as possible, that would work nicely. Then you, Jason, give them a little tour. Your sister will make an appearance. A celebrity chef talking about rationing, making it clear that there's no special treatment."

"There's lots of special treatment," Kaito said.

"The idea is to make it feel like there isn't," Jason explained. "Our people really are rationing, so there's no catching us out on that."

"Make sure you go through the medical centre as well. Let them talk to your brother-in-law and that Doctors Without Borders lady you brought back from Africa."

"She brought herself from France," Jason said.

"Don't care. I want sound bites for Doctors Without Borders, Africa and Ebola. I want to hear the phrase 'experience with handling a crisis' on every nightly news program. I want interviews with the people being treated talking about how grateful they are."

The Asano Village Medical Centre was well staffed and well-stocked, so the Asano family had offered it up to the Network as a medical way-station for those suffering exotic attacks that couldn't be resolved by the people in the field. Many of the strange poisons and diseases monsters inflicted were easily remedied by Jason if he was on site.

"You're sure they'll say what you want them to?" Kaito asked.

"Very," Terrance said. "After the tour, you're going to do sit-downs with all of them, followed by one in-depth interview."

"With who?" Jason asked.

"Jeremy Westin," Terrance said. "He's independent but a friendly, and he's the only member of the press who has been inside the village before."

"Fine," Jason said. "What's the tone we're going for? Sober in the face of current circumstances but with enough lightness for a humanising touch?"

"That's exactly what we want," Terrance said. "They're going to ask you about the League of Heroes too."

"How do you want me to approach that?"

"Respect and solidarity while undercutting them with backhanded compliments."

"You want me to neg them."

"Yes, but don't go after the League of Heroes directly. Shining a light on the EOA itself works much better. Highlight the EOA as the organisation behind them, inferring that the league is a puppet organisation."

"They are, so it shouldn't be hard. Point out the shiny fruit of the league while letting people see the rotten tree they're growing on."

"To help with that, I've set up a video chat with the EOA defector in the US before you meet with the reporters. It should give you some ammunition."

"Yeah? Thanks, Terry. I genuinely appreciate that."

"Enough to consider how we introduce you to the press?"

"No. I do not practise sword-fighting with no shirt on."

"It'd be a great visual. Pouring a bottle of water over yourself after working up a sweat."

"I don't sweat."

"You don't sweat?"

"No."

"We could make it look like you sweat. I could rub oil on you."

"You know, I thought it was strange when your sister gave me the number for the Network's human resources department. Now I get it."

The Network office in Asano Village was not large but did include a secure communications room. One of the few areas in which Earth magical development outpaced that of Pallimustus was in communications, due to incorporating magic and technology together. As a security specialist set up the secure link with the Network branch in Arizona, Jason and Asya were in the main office area, leaning side-by-side against a desk. Between them, their hands gently touched.

"We haven't had a lot of alone time over the last couple of months," she said. "I can't help but think I moved a little too slow."

"Seizing the moments when you have them can be important," Jason agreed.

"How are you?" she asked softly. "Have you even slept since Broken Hill?"

"Not yet," he said.

Broken Hill had only been the day before. After hours of speaking with survivors in between debriefs at the evacuation camp, he hadn't gotten home until first light. Then Dawn arrived and they spoke with Akari before he portalled to Sydney mid-morning. Now it was late into the afternoon and soon the press would be arriving.

"You need to take some time," she said. "I know you aren't as fine as you make out."

"Oh, so you're interested in making-out, are you?"

"Time and place, Asano," she said, a smile teasing the corner of her lips. "This is a professional environment."

"Oh, I wouldn't call myself a making-out professional. More of a gifted amateur."

"Gifted, are you?"

"Well, enthusiastic, at the very least."

"There is something to be said for keenness."

"I have a whole book on sex magic."

"Actual sex magic, or just porn?"

"Actual magic. Farrah gave it to me. Kind of."

"She *what?*"

He held his hands up in a surrendering gesture.

"It's not what it sounds like."

The woman on the screen looked around Jason's age, although he knew that was not the case. Audrey Blaine, the EOA defector, inhabited an artificially constructed body. The result of some shady EOA/Cabal/Network joint research program from years ago. She had been forced into using the results of a long-cancelled resurrection experiment when the EOA killed her off. Refusing to go along with the plans that subsequently killed hundreds of thousands wasn't much of a moral line, but at least it was one.

A mothballed reincarnation program from years ago, she had privately left it in place as a personal contingency she was finally pushed into using. It had been a gamble at best and the body that had been pickled in a jar for well over a decade was apparently not without quirks. The Network was still trying to figure out exactly what she was and what she could do.

In the meantime, Audrey was being kept under comfortable but thorough guard as she coughed up the EOA's secrets. There was no question that the EOA knew about her revival by this stage and would kill her all over again if given the chance.

"It seems that you and I are in a very small club, Ms Blaine," Jason said, by way of introduction. "Not many people come back from the dead."

"I've heard that you claimed to have died," she said. "Your companion that Adrien Barbou was holding in France too. How did you manage to revive?"

"Oh, various means," Jason said. "A friend of mine's dad rules the afterlife, but he refuses to help me out, so I've been making other arrangements. Barbou really is with the EOA, then?"

"Yes, and he's very much in the ascendant. You know that he was playing with you in France, right? Exposing our people so you thought the EOA's objective was the astral space and your outworlder friends, while our larger plan came to fruition."

"You mean *their* larger plan," Jason said. "You're not EOA anymore, right?"

"Old habits."

"I did realise that I was a cat chasing a string," Jason said, "but only in hindsight."

"For such a stealthy man, you are very loud, Mr Asano. You make a useful distraction. I understand you're looking for some juicy nuggets to use against my former organisation in the press."

"Yes, but that is a secondary concern."

"Oh?"

"Tell me about the implants being used in the silver-rank converted."

"The what?"

"The superheroes."

"Oh, the category-three enhanced. How did you even know about the implants? Have you been pulling people apart, Mr Asano? Now you want to know what the implants are."

"I know what the implants are," Jason said. "I've seen them before and I know where they come from. I want to know why the EOA has them."

"You know what they are?" she asked, scepticism plain on her face.

"Clockwork cores," he said. "They're produced by artificial life forms called clockwork kings, which are themselves created by an entity called the Builder. He and I don't get along."

"Clockwork king," Audrey said thoughtfully. "Is that what it's called? It was dug up in the eighties, buried with a bunch of Assyrian relics more than two millennia old. The archaeologists thought they'd found an alien robot. It took decades before we figured out how to get anything out of it. Part of a joint program with the Cabal and the Network to advance our various research projects. That was the beginning of the human enhancement project, although we were never able to use the implants—clockwork cores, you called them? We were never able to use them properly until we advanced the other aspects of our enhancement program. We didn't get our enhanced to category three until around two years ago, at which point we were able to properly integrate the implants. It solved a lot of issues with the earlier iterations."

"The EOA isn't in contact with the Builder, then?"

"I don't know who or what that is. If anything, Mr Asano, you seem to know more about this than I do. I suspect only Mr North has the answers you're looking for. He's the true leader of the EOA and I'm not exactly sure what he is. He's far older than he seems and I don't think he's human. At least, not entirely. Of course, neither am I, anymore."

"Alright," Jason said. "Tell me more about this enhancement program."

"I have to go," Asya told Jason as he emerged from the secure communications room. "I'm been assigned to crewing your brother's helicopter again."

"I'm going to be busy as well," he said. "I may not see you for a while."

She gave him a resigned smile.

"Another time," she said sadly.

The people gathered outside the Asano Village compound gate knew something was going on, growing more riled up with the arrival of each additional news crew. Security let the press through the gate so as not to be harassed by the people outside it, but they were told to wait until all seven crews arrived. They got out of their vans to film B-roll and establishing shots of the gate, the mirrored security room, and the people on the other side of the gate causing a ruckus.

"It's actually not glass," the security guard explained, having been talked into an interview by the waiting press. "The whole building is made from an aluminium-based ceramic, along with some magic, but I don't know how that works."

"You're not well-versed in magic?" the reporter asked.

"I don't even have any essences," the guard said.

"Essences?" the reporter asked.

"Oh," the guard said, looking stricken. "I don't think I was meant to say that."

"It's fine, Toby," Jason said. "I'll take it from here."

Jason had been standing amongst the reporters, going completely unnoticed despite standing in their midst.

"Sorry, Jason," Toby said as he slunk back to the security room.

The reporters all turned to Jason, who wore a light, casual shirt and slacks. The camera people stopped filming the guard and B-roll of the gate and crowd to focus on him.

"Essences are the source of the powers possessed by members of the Global Defense Network," Jason said. "I'm not a member myself, but my powers also come from these essences."

He plucked a green cube from the air and handed it to one of the reporters crowding around him.

"You might say that essences are a natural form of magic. Human beings are inherently connected to magic of this type and develop powers in symbiosis with these essences after absorbing them."

The reporter stared at the object in her hands.

"Are you saying that anyone can gain superpowers if they have one of these?"

"Ideally, you'll have three," Jason explained. "Absorbing essences is an easy and actually quite exhilarating experience. You can look at it as the natural method of obtaining powers, without the time-consuming and invasive surgeries of the human conversion process that the EOA uses."

"The EOA?"

"Oh, I'm sorry," Jason said. "Once you get deeply involved in all this, it's easy to forget that the magic societies aren't common knowledge. The EOA are the Engineers of Ascension, which is the organisation behind the League of Heroes. The name comes from their goal of transhumanism—the desire to modify the human race to gain power. The League of Heroes is the result of their experimental programs."

"Then your powers come from an entirely different source?"

"Oh, goodness, yes," Jason said with a light laugh. "The EOA have spent decades overcoming the flaws in their human modification program, for which you have to admire their dedication. Most would look at the price of progress and give up, but they were unflinching in their resolve. Today, almost all their subjects survive the process and, without it, we wouldn't have the League of Heroes we see today."

"Where do these essences come from?" one of the reporters asked as they passed the plant essence around.

"We can talk about that as we head into the village proper," Jason suggested as darkness flooded out of his shadow to take the form of a bus.

After the footage of Broken Hill was broadcast everywhere, Shade's sleek bus form was intimately familiar to professional media personnel like the news crew. Although Jason said nothing about it, the bus invoked memories of Jason's actions during the disaster. The reporters had been warned that it was a delicate topic for Jason.

"Before we hop aboard, we do need to do a quick security check,"

Jason said. "My friend Farrah, whom you can see approaching, will be responsible for that."

The reporters looked around, not spotting anyone. Jason casually pointed up and the reporters followed with their gaze to see a woman descending from the sky with wings of fire. The reporters nudged their crews to aim the cameras upwards.

24
CANDID AND AUTHENTIC

Jason and Akari had arrived together in the main thoroughfare of the village, where Emi and Erika were speaking with one of the reporters. Jason was bringing Akari to be interviewed, but the reporter had been waylaid.

"That story you did last November on mining deregulation was an exercise in buffoonery," Emi said. "I don't even think you're a corporate shill; you're just gullible. Have you even seen the foreign ownership statistics or do you only look at press releases and regurgitate them like a mother bird?"

"Look, Little Miss," the reporter said, "clearly you've—"

"Little Miss?" Emi asked, nostrils flaring. "Do I look like the protagonist of a book written by a nice English lady in the fifties? At least I have the decency to use a person's name, *Mr Dennier*."

"Actually, you do kind of look like…" Jason started, trailing off as he received a weapons-grade glare from his niece. He held his hands up in surrender, but also flashed her a grin.

"Emi…" Erika said with the disapproving tone only a mother can truly master.

"What?" Emi asked, going from death glare to wide-eyed innocence like someone flipped a switch.

"What have I told you about listening to your uncle about politics."

"I have no idea what you're talking about," Jason and Emi said in unison.

"Emi," Erika said. "Isn't it time for you to go to Coffs Harbour and make sure there aren't any monster waves coming?"

"Fine," she grumbled. "I'll go find Uncle Kaito."

"Feel free to edit that out," Jason said as they watched Emi stomp off in the direction of the main residence. "She's a pistol, no mistake, but she can go off on political rants when she may or may not have all the facts at hand. No idea where she gets it from."

"Wait," Dennier said. "Is she really the one making sure that no monsters invade Coffs Harbour?"

"How's your dimensional membrane protrusion-precursor analysis theory, Mr Dennier?" Jason asked.

"My what?"

"That's what I thought. When you're better at magic than my niece, feel free to question her credentials. Until then, how about we stick to qualified opinions?"

"NOT REALLY HIS AREA!" Emi shouted from the steps of the house.

"That's enough out of you!" Jason yelled back at her. She stuck out her tongue in response and he did the same.

"I see you are as vigilant as ever about the dignity of the Asano name," Akari observed dryly.

"I didn't pull out my apocalypse beast, did I?" Jason asked. "And he loves eating new people. I mean, meeting new people."

"Did you just say apocalypse beast?" Dennier asked.

"What?" Jason asked. "No idea what you're talking about. Let's go take a look at the medical centre and you can talk with Akari along the way."

"That would be good," Dennier said as Jason led the way. "Miss Asano, as a relative outsider here, how have you found living with your Australian relatives?"

Akari cast a glance at Jason.

"Challenging."

Erika, being the experienced media personality, had attached herself to the tour. She wanted to at least reel in her brother's impulsive nature, which was going roughly as well as expected. As the reporters interviewed people at the medical centre, she leaned close to Jason.

"You did tell Craig and his anaemic friends to stay inside today, right?" she whispered.

"Of course," Jason said.

Vermillion had been unhappy about giving up his country mansion but turned out to be quite satisfied with one of the clifftop houses. Since it was not practical to keep shuffling blood donors up from Sydney, he had a sufficient retinue living with him to keep him fed, although he, too, was rationing.

The Cabal was keeping quiet in Australia, but in other parts of the world, they were more active. Individual factions assisted against the monster waves in places like Siberia and the South Pacific where the Network were at their least influential and spread the thinnest. Having Vermillion present gave Jason a line on Cabal activity, and while it didn't impact his activities for the moment, if the Cabal became a flashpoint, then he had the inside line.

Ian came over and kissed his wife.

"Any idea when the circus is going to shuffle out?" he asked. "We need to get these patients ready to transport."

"I think Terrance is around here somewhere," Jason said. "He's on press-wrangling duty, so I'll get him to play bad guy and kick them out."

"Actually, could you go do that, honey?" Ian asked. "Some of the patients wanted to meet Jason and I thought that might look good for the cameras."

"Why would they want to meet me?"

"Because you're the hero of Broken Hill."

"No, I'm not!"

The anger in Jason's raised voice caught the attention of the reporters.

"I do not want to hear that phrase spread around," Jason said, his voice low and fierce as he jabbed a finger at Ian.

"You don't always get to choose," Erika told him. He glowered but didn't say anything more.

After leaving the medical centre, Jason led the reporters back to the main thoroughfare where Taika stood in front of a series of vehicles, looking self-satisfied.

"What is going on?" Jason asked.

"Team Knight Rider," Taika said, extending his arms out proudly. "It's pretty sweet."

"No, it isn't. Shade, why would you even participate in this? Most of these vehicles aren't even black."

"I know," one of the cars said unhappily. "I lost a bet."

Jason ran a hand over his face and let out a groan before glancing at the camera crews, who were still filming everything.

"Did you really have to do this today?" Jason asked Taika.

"A bet's a bet, bro," Taika said, handing Jason his phone. "Take my photo."

"I don't think that's necessary," Shade said. "I'm certain that Mr Asano requires my services in some capacity."

"No, I'm taking the photo," Jason said. "A bet is a bet."

"This is all very undignified," Shade said.

Jason took the photo and handed Taika back the phone.

"Okay, Shade. Knock that off and come give these nice reporters an interview."

"You have been an enigmatic figure for some time now," Jeremy Westin said.

He and Jason were sitting comfortably, facing one another in the lounge of the main residence of Asano Village. The sun had long since set and the other reporters were gone. Along with Jason and Jeremy were the cameraman, Terrance, and Erika.

"Are you looking to lift the veil of mystery, Mr Westin?" Jason asked.

"I imagine you'll still have no shortage of secrets when we're done, Mr Asano. I'd like to start by going through some background and then what the public has seen of you, from your perspective. As you might imagine, there has been no small amount of inquiry into your background. Until just a few years ago, you were a relatively ordinary person, with an ordinary job. The most unusual thing about you was your occasional appearances on your sister's cooking program."

"I did see the interview with my old boss, Sadiq," Jason said. "That part where he was cranky about me not giving notice once he found out I was alive was classic Sadiq. Someone should make a workplace sitcom about that guy."

"That brings us to the key point," Jeremy said. "Your disappearance and apparent demise. The destruction of your apartment and the subsequent cover-up. Then you're gone, presumed dead, for a year and a half. You come back ten months ago, and immediately, we get the first appearance of the Starlight Angel, or Starlight Rider. Do you have a preference for either moniker?"

"Jason's fine. If you really insist, then I prefer to avoid the religious connotations."

"Yet, that does seem to be a problem for you. You've been variously hailed as a messenger of God and decried as an agent of Satan."

"Jeremy, I'm not interested in telling anyone what they should or shouldn't believe," Jason said, prompting a startled cough from Erika.

"Sister, dear," Jason said. "You're a professional. I think you know better than to step on the audio."

"Sorry," she said. "I thought I heard a bull defecating."

Terrance paced back and forth. He was in the main residence with Erika, Farrah and Jason. "What the hell is Team Knight Rider?"

"It's a TV show from 1997 that got cancelled after one season," Jason said.

"Why did you stage that scene? You did stage it, right? You didn't just lead a bunch of reporters into the middle of your farcical personal life."

"Of course I staged it," Jason said. "You think Shade goes around making dodgy bets? You wanted humanising. A little unexpected weirdness feels candid and authentic. If something or someone comes across as too polished and too perfect, people react negatively. I'm sure you know that better than me."

"I'm fairly sure you had not perfect covered. Using the Māori for diversity was a nice touch, though. What was that thing with your niece?"

"That was entirely her," Jason lied. "I didn't coach her at all."

"Seriously, mining deregulation?"

"What do you want me to say?" Jason asked. "Contemporary youth are demonstrating increased levels of political engagement across the board."

"That girl is a menace," Terrance said.

"Did you just call my daughter a menace?" Erika asked.

"Your daughter is—"

"...an unabashed delight," Jason interrupted, completing his sentence before the man finished digging a shallow grave. "She also has a doting uncle who gets very cranky when people say bad things about her. An uncle who, on an unrelated note, has killed dozens of people."

"You've killed dozens of people?" Terrance asked.

"I downplayed the number when they asked me about it in the interviews," Jason said.

"Why do people keep threatening me with violence?" Terrance complained, looking at Jason. "They don't threaten you."

"Did you not hear what I just said about the dozens of people? Everyone who has threatened me is either dead or a god-like being from beyond reality. Or had their power stripped by an invasive procedure. Oh, or had their soul devoured by one of those god-like beings I just mentioned. That was a rough way to go, but I wasn't directly involved. Actually, there is one guy who wound up fine. His name's Jerrick and I almost killed him, but I kept him alive for evidence on this thing I was working on. Then there was a political cover-up and he lost his job, but he's doing alright. Even helped me out once. My soul was being tortured and he let my friends know where I was because of the time I didn't kill him. There were these other guys I killed while I was bringing him back for questioning and I think it left an impression. They gave him his job back for that. Helping me, I mean, not watching me kill a bunch of people in a shopping arcade."

"Uh..." Terrance said.

"Invasive procedure?" Farrah asked. "Are you talking about skeletal suppression?"

"Yep," Jason said.

Farrah noticed the confused expressions on Erika and Terrance.

"It's a similar process to what the EOA apparently does as part of their enhancement process," she explained. "They cut you open and carve magic right onto your skeleton, except, instead of giving you powers, they enchant suppression collar magic right onto your bones.

Assuming you survive, it permanently suppresses all your magical abilities."

"That sounds horrifying," Erika said.

"It's not used very often," Farrah said. "Normally, if you've done something bad enough to warrant it, they just execute you."

"Even in Farrah's world, it's considered ethically sketchy, and that's saying something," Jason said.

"Are you saying that my world is immoral?" Farrah asked.

"Every time I killed people, I got rewarded," Jason said.

"That means you were killing the right people," Farrah told him. "I thought you moved past this kind of thing."

"I don't ever want him to move past that kind of thing," Erika cut in. "If he becomes a remorseless killer, he's not really himself anymore, is he?"

"That's true," Farrah acknowledged. "Who did they do skeletal suppression to?"

"Lucian Lamprey," Jason said.

"The Director of the Magic Society?"

"Yeah," Jason said. "He helped that crime boss to kidnap me."

"You didn't mention that in your recordings."

"It wasn't exactly the best time for me."

"That's understandable."

Terrance moved next to Erika as Jason and Farrah were talking.

"How much of this are you following?" he asked her.

"It's best not to try with Jason. Just let him run around, nod occasionally and wait for him to tire himself out."

"Kind of like a toddler."

"*Exactly* like a toddler."

"I don't suppose you know how to get your brothers into some kind of water fight?"

Erika turned to give Terrance a flat look.

"I had to ask," he said.

"It's time for me to get out of here," Jason said. "I have a plane to catch."

"Get a good night's sleep first," Erika said. "The plane will wait for you. I know you have magic stamina or whatever, but you still haven't slept since Broken Hill. Your amiable façade is getting a little pasted on."

"My amiable façade is fine."

"You just explained to your publicity guy how all the people that crossed you died horribly. Now he thinks that if he's mean to your niece, you're going to kill him and bury him out in the bush."

"That's actually not what I was thinking," Terrance said. "I am now, though."

"Don't be ridiculous," Jason said. "I wouldn't bury him out in the bush. I'd feed him to Colin."

"You didn't show Colin to the reporters, did you?" Farrah asked.

"Of course not; you know what Colin's like. He's super friendly but also a terrifying apocalypse monster that feeds on blood and flesh."

"What about Terrance's bones?" Erika asked.

"Colin's a little trooper, so I'm sure he'd manage," Jason said. "He's got all those teeth, remember?"

Jason forewent his semi-sleep trance for actual slumber. With Farrah nearby and secure in his hidden underwater cloud house, he was able to let go of his defensiveness and get some genuine rest. He had been half-expecting nightmares but mental exhaustion won out. In the morning, he called to say he was ready for the plane and meditated while it was prepared.

After Broken Hill, Jason's meditation pushed his abilities closer to the precipice of silver, with two of them tipping right over. The ability that allowed him to shadow teleport and open portals, Path of Shadows, crossed the threshold to silver. He could now portal a silver-ranker, albeit only one, and his range immediately doubled from four hundred kilometres to eight hundred. On the downside, portals beyond the bronze range of four hundred kilometres increased the cooldown from ten minutes to an hour, although after ten minutes, he would once again be able to portal at the shorter range.

His other ability was his aura, Hegemony. Already possessing a terrifying strength, it now reached new heights of potency. It also gained new effects with its new rank, one extremely useful and one much more niche.

Ability: [Hegemony] (Sin)

- Aura (holy, unholy).
- Base cost: None.
- Cooldown: None.

- Current rank: Silver 0 (00%).

- Effect (iron): Allies within the aura have increased resistance to afflictions, while enemies within the aura have their resistance to afflictions reduced. Enemy resistances are further reduced for each instance of [Sin] they are suffering from.

- Effect (bronze): Inflicts an instance of [Sin] on enemies that make physical or magical attacks against allies within the aura. Instances applied in this way cannot be resisted.

- Effect (silver): Aura can be extended over a larger area before aura strength becomes compromised. Transcendent damage dealt by enemies within the aura is downgraded to either resonating-force or disruptive-force damage, depending on the source.

- Ability [Hegemony] (Sin) cannot advance further until all attributes have reached silver rank.

Transcendent damage was rare below silver rank; Jason was unusual in that regard. Although it was an effect that would rarely see use, it could prove critical. One of the known properties of transcendent damage was that complete annihilation of the physical body would prevent most resurrection effects. Since such a revival ability was now one of Jason's trump cards, the prospect of transcendent damage negating it was a sizeable threat. Now, so long as his prodigious aura was not suppressed, that threat was neutralised.

Farrah had spent most of her time in Sydney and was happy to stay in a cloud bed once again. They had both slept until late morning, after which Jason was finally able to return Farrah to Sydney via portal, although she alone was the portal's limit. He had previously attempted to portal himself while Farrah resided in his spirit vault, but the portal had collapsed in the attempt.

Feeling buoyed by his new gains, when the call came to tell him the plane was ready, he cheerfully sought out Akari and Dawn in their clifftop house. Dawn immediately noticed the changes in Jason, congratulating him on his advancements.

Jason opened another portal direct to the Network's hangar at Bankstown airport. As portalling the silver-ranker Akari consumed all the portal's capacity, he sent her first while he and Dawn followed after waiting out the ten-minute cooldown. There they found Asya and Michael Aram waiting for them.

"Seeing us off?" Jason asked.

"Tagging along," Asya said. "Akari is a member of the Kobe branch, while you and Dawn aren't Network members at all. Michael is representing the Sydney branch and me, the International Committee."

"I hope this flight goes better than our last one together," Jason said, shaking Aram's hand.

"We've had the plane very thoroughly checked," Aram said, "but I'll be relying on you to save me again if things go awry."

"We're also here to help things go smoothly from a diplomatic perspective," Asya said. "We've prepared a gift for when you meet Akari's father, the clan head."

"Thank you, but I'm comfortable with the gift I've prepared," Jason said.

"May I ask what you've chosen?"

"Just a couple of things I picked up along the way," Jason said.

"He refuses to tell me," Akari said.

"It's a surprise," Jason said.

"I am deeply concerned," Akari said, getting a laugh from Asya.

"Uh-oh," Jason said. "I think they're teaming up. Mike—can I call you Mike?—I think we need to form a man alliance."

Jason threw an arm around Aram's shoulders and led him towards the plane.

"We can do manly men things, like talk about trucks."

"Um, I don't know anything about trucks," Aram said.

"Me either," Jason confessed. "Or fishing. Are you a fishing guy?"

"I'm more of a theatre guy."

"Yeah? I saw a great production of *Wicked Sisters* at the Seymour Centre just before the monster waves started."

"In the Reginald Theatre? I saw that too. It really was good."

Still with one arm slung over Aram's shoulders as they headed for the plane, Jason used his other arm to punch the air triumphantly.

"Manliness!"

25

WARMTH AND LEVITY

As the plane flew north over Queensland, Asya looked to Jason sitting on the floor, meditating, as he had been since reaching cruising altitude. Akari stepped up next to her.

"I know he seems frivolous," she said, "but I've discovered that he devotes much of his inactive time to training. His diligence in that regard surprises even me, and I was raised in a life of training."

"I rejected cores because I wanted to learn the right way," Asya said, "but I have other responsibilities. I've been through the tactical training program, but crewing Kaito's helicopter hasn't given me the chance to confront monsters that I need. I see people who gained their essences long after me hitting category two because they use cores. I'm the only one on the flight crew still category one."

"There is no shame in using monster cores to grow," Akari said. "The danger is in letting them be the only source of your strength. You must be vigilant that you do not let your capability flounder and make sure that you grow not just your essence abilities but your mastery of them."

"I'm sorry, I didn't mean to offend you," Asya said. "You're a core user and so much stronger than me."

"I understand," Akari said. "Like you, I have seen core users whose skill fails their power. There are more of them than there are of those who reach their potential. The training programs Miss Hurin instituted have been helping, but you can't turn a culture of decades around overnight."

"The current crisis is finally showing people what Jason and Farrah said from the beginning," Asya said. "Of course, not everyone needed teaching. Finding out just how many of the American Network members don't use cores has been revelatory."

The monster wave crisis had every Network branch pulling out all the stops. With that came the revelation that the US and the Chinese had been using some variation of Farrah's training program for as much as a century. They had inserted themselves into her instruction programs not to learn but to refine their techniques.

This was paying off as China and the United States demonstrated that, like Jason and Farrah, they had people capable of operating independently of teams. They avoided it where possible but in emergency situations, they could deploy individuals capable of facing groups of monsters alone. Both countries had silver-rankers who were not the failures Jason had so far encountered, but were around his level of skill. Given that they were also a rank higher, they were also demonstrably stronger. Some were even powerhouses on the level of Farrah.

Jason had become something of the face of magic internationally, but both China and the United States were pushing their own people. They weren't the only ones, but they were having the most success, courtesy of powerful rosters of essence users. This meant that, like Jason, they could overshadow the generic supers put forward by the League of Heroes.

Jason had been asked about his US and Chinese counterparts during his interviews, where he openly stated that many of them were more powerful than him. It was another tool he used to highlight the legitimacy of the Network over the EOA.

The two women felt a surge of magic come from Jason, who was still consolidating his development from the long, desperate intensity of the Broken Hill battle. He opened his eyes, which were sparkling with triumph.

"I'm so close to silver, I can taste it," he said.

"Another ability reached category three?" Akari asked.

"My cloak. Combining it with Shade's bus form really gave it a workout."

Ability: [Cloak of Night] (Dark)

- Conjuration (darkness, light, dimension).
- Base cost: Moderate mana.
- Cooldown: None.

- Current rank: Silver 0 (00%).

- Effect (iron): Conjures a magical cloak that offers limited physical protection. Can generate light over an area or absorb light to blend into shadows. Cloak can reduce the weight of the wearer, allowing reduced falling speed and water walking. Cannot be given or taken away, but the effect can be extended to others in close proximity, with an ongoing mana cost rising exponentially with each affected person.

- Effect (bronze): Cloak reflexively intercepts projectiles. Highly effective against rapid, weaker attacks, but less effective against powerful, singular attacks. Cloak allows gliding.

- Effect (silver): Cloak passively manipulates physical space, slightly shifting the trajectory of incoming attacks. Manipulation can be actively managed for more directed effect or to allow passage through spaces normally too small to physically traverse. Cloak allows flight for a low ongoing mana cost, increasing to a moderate ongoing mana cost while in direct sunlight.

- Ability [Cloak of Night] (Dark) cannot advance further until all attributes have reached silver rank.

Looking over his upgraded ability, Jason noted that the wording had changed from earlier iterations of the ability. Partly that was due to mana costs for lower-rank effects being removed. He couldn't help but wonder, however, if the changes were purely due to ranking-up or whether his perception of his own powers was impacting the description. His thoughts turned to Clive and how excited he would be to figure it out.

"What are you thinking about?" Asya asked.

"Hmm?"

He looked up, distracted.

"What are you thinking about?" she repeated. "You looked sad all of a sudden."

"I was thinking about a friend," Jason said. "We really could have used him in all this. He's probably the only guy I know as smart as my niece. She'd still eat him for breakfast, though."

Jason narrowed his eyes at Akari, then conjured his cloak around him.

"Punch me in the face," he told her.

"What?"

"I got a new ability I want to try," he said. "Punch me in the—"

Akari dashed forward, supernaturally quick, to jab Jason in the middle of the face, sending him reeling and letting out a nasal moan.

"Ah, you hit me in the eye."

"I was aiming for your nose."

"You clipped the nose pretty good," he said, the blocked-nose tone of his voice backing him up as he crouched over, both hands clasped over his face. "Clearly, I'll have to get the hang of this ability. Thank you, by the way."

"You just thanked me for punching you in the face," Akari said.

"Well, I was asking for it," Jason said. "I think I might just focus on the fact that my cloak will let me fly now. Can't wait until we land, and I can try it out, but honestly, I think I'll get more practical use out of flying with Shade. It's weirdly anti-climactic."

He looked at Asya, who was looking back at him with amusement.

"What?" he asked.

"You're kind of honking when you talk," she said with a giggle.

"I got punched in the face!"

"Also, you asked someone to punch you in the face."

Next to Asya, Akari snorted a laugh.

"Girls are mean," Jason complained.

"Jason," Asya said. "Didn't you tell me that you don't use breath and vocal cords to speak anymore?"

"That's right," Jason said, still holding his nose.

"So why would your voice go funny unless you were deliberately putting it on?"

"I have no idea what you're talking about."

Asya moved up through the plane and took the phone handset from the flight attendant. Her eyes went wide as she listened to the person on the other end.

"Give me the details," she said.

A while later, she moved back to the other passengers as the plane changed course. Akari and Jason were sat on the floor, meditating, while Aram was badly losing a game of chess to Dawn.

"You've really never played this before?" Aram asked.

Jason and Akari opened their eyes, focusing on Asya. Despite the aura-suppression bracelet that helped her mask her emotions from high-rank essence users, Jason and Akari both felt her inner turmoil.

"Why are we changing course?" Aram asked.

"We're shifting west, to Indonesia," Asya said, looking rather lost as she took a seat. "There's been an incident and we need to intervene."

"Why us?" Akari asked.

"Because they're calling in everyone on this side of planet," Asya said.

"That bad?" Aram asked.

"In Indonesia," Asya explained, "there's been something of a balance of forces between the Network and the Cabal. The Network has been protecting the urbanised areas and offering substantial support for the Cabal facing monster waves in remote areas."

"There's tension?" Jason asked.

"In most places around the world, either the Cabal or the Network is the dominant force," Asya explained. "The monster waves have seen unprecedented collaboration, with whichever force is stronger taking the lead, although that is usually the Network. The secondary force acts in support, which has been working so far."

"But you said balance of forces," Jason said. "The Cabal and the Network have been struggling for control in Indonesia?"

"Yes," Asya said. "Those tensions have been put aside during the monster waves, but they haven't been put away. Thus far, it's been fine, or that's what we thought. It turns out that the government there has been ramping up their support for the Network. They're trying to establish their authority in the magical community by picking a side, but neither they nor the Network branches affiliated with them realised how much hidden power the Cabal possessed. Some of the Indonesian branches got forceful, only to bite off more than they could chew. A lot of the smaller branches weren't happy, even throwing in with the Cabal."

"A Network civil war," Aram said, his expression troubled. "There's been actual fighting?"

"It's worse than that," Asya said. "The larger Network branches there knew the International Committee wouldn't stand for what they were doing with the monster waves going on, so they kept the whole thing under wraps. It's not like anyone was going around to check on them with things the way they are, so long as they kept reporting that everything was fine. None of this has hit the media, so no one was the wiser and they've managed to keep the conflict secret."

"Surely the smaller branches reported that the main branches were off the reservation," Jason said.

"They did," Asya admitted awkwardly. "It was passed off as the little fish complaining and the usual tension between the Network and the Cabal."

"Are you kidding?" Aram asked. "What is the International Committee doing?"

"Fighting the monster apocalypse, Michael," Asya said. "We're all stretched a little thin right now and things are going to fall through the cracks."

"It's a civil war in our own organisation!" Aram exclaimed. "That's a bloody big crack."

"Blame can wait until we have time to judge with consideration,"

Akari said. Despite her still being sat cross-legged on the floor, her calm voice carried an authoritative weight.

"Rather than look back with recrimination," she continued, "we need to look forward, to the challenges ahead."

"That's my concern as well," Jason said. "Asya, please tell me that what I'm thinking is wrong."

"What are you thinking?" Aram asked, having calmed down a little.

"If there's a problem with patrolling for proto-spaces," Jason said, "branches are under instruction to report to the International Committee and request immediate assistance."

"Oh, damn," Aram said, following Jason's train of thought. "If they have a problem with checking for spaces but don't report it to avoid scrutiny…"

"That's exactly what happened," Asya confirmed. "It's the worst-case scenario. Makassar, in South Sulawesi. One and a half million people. A category-three dimensional space started dumping monsters into it less than an hour ago. Network responders are onsite already, but the logistics of evacuating or protecting a population of that size and that density is a nightmarish quagmire. They were a million and a half before the city was declared a safe zone. Now we're looking at a sweep-and-clear operation through a city full of civilians and monster wave refugees."

Only Dawn kept her composure at the thought of monsters spilling into a heavily populated city. The others were pale and shell-shocked.

"It still gets worse," Asya said.

"How?" Aram asked.

"There's another dimensional space, practically on top of the first one. Between them, they'll box the city in. The second space is projected to cross the breakdown threshold within the next hour and start spilling out monsters within two."

"Twin dimensional spaces," Aram said. "That's rare."

"It used to be," Jason said. "I've encountered it a half-dozen times when sweeping for proto-spaces over the last couple of months. There should still be a chance to shut it down if they've detected it, right?"

"Early responders detected it, but there's no way they can shut it down in time," Asya said, then paused as if afraid to continue.

Finally, she spoke.

"It's a category-four space."

Silence followed Asya's revelation. One or more gold-rank monsters, surrounded by silvers, was not something that could be quickly readied for, certainly not within an hour.

"I can extend the duration of proto-space stability," Jason said. "Can we get me there in time?"

"We don't think so, but we're trying," Asya said. "We're en route to Darwin right now. We're going to throw you out of the plane instead of taking the time to land, and a portal specialist will meet you on the ground. He's been to Makassar and will send you directly. Forces are being readied to take on a category-four anchor monster, whether we catch it in the dimensional space or not. The Guangzhou branch is already preparing magically enhanced heavy munitions."

"It or them," Aram said. "Multiple anchor monsters are more the norm than the exception, these days."

Jason turned to Dawn.

"If you have any more tricks or secrets, now is the time."

Dawn frowned, her expression conflicted.

"You know I can't intervene," she said, "as much I might want to. The most I could tell you is that the USA and China branches of the Network have undeclared assets. Those assets are difficult and costly to field but could be critical. Perhaps you can pressure China into deploying them, but most likely, they will deny their existence. They will keep them in case what is happening to Indonesia happens to them."

"What kind of assets?" Aram asked.

"I've already said more than I should. I will not speak on it further."

"People are dying," Aram said. "This is no time for secrets and games."

"If she says she won't say more, trying to change her mind will only waste time we don't have," Jason told him.

"At this point, we'll take what we can get," Asya said, standing up. "I'll go see what I can do."

She headed for the front of the plane where the phone was located. Jason looked at Akari, both of them still sitting on the floor.

"Get your mind settled and whatever rest you can," he told her. "I don't think either of us are ready for what we're about to see."

It had barely been days since Jason had been desperately fighting to save lives in Broken Hill. In its wake, he had been seeking out warmth and levity while his insides were pulled taut like a bowstring. As he pictured the lives being lost at that very moment, the bowstring snapped.

26

AN INTELLIGENT KING

ONE PROTO-SPACE HAD ALREADY DISGORGED ITS MONSTROUS CONTENTS onto the city of Makassar. A second one, with even stronger magic, was on the verge of doing the same. This proto-space was a troubling reflection of the city it was about to open up on, except that the buildings were grown over with rainforest and the sky was cast with volcanic ash. The city was not as hot as its normal-world counterpart but was weighed down with oppressive humidity.

In the heart of the proto-space city, four figures stood atop a building. They were roughly the shape of a human but twice the height and covered in brown and green scales. Their faces were the most inhuman part, long and dominated by large, toothy mouths. Above the mouths were eyes filled with intelligence and cunning.

They all wore clothes and chitin-like armour, conjured by just one of their magical abilities. They could also conjure up various weapons, from swords to magical firearms, although none had chosen to do so at that moment. They were looking down at the aperture that the humans had opened, surrounded by the corpses of those same humans. Only a handful had managed to escape back through the shimmering circle.

The only living things in front of the portal were monsters. They had the appearance of dinosaurs, although not a species a palaeontologist would recognise. The toothy jaws of the long-necked quadrupeds made plain that they were not herbivorous. They also moved faster than dinosaurs were thought to, with silver-rank flesh stronger yet more supple than that of the prehistoric creatures they resembled. They looked like giant, single-headed hydras.

Although they were the largest and most numerous of the dino-monsters, they were only one type of many, each a monstrous variant of something someone from Earth might recognise. Featherless, bronze-rank raptors, a third the height of a human, that hunted in packs. Horn-headed triceratops variants whose beaked mouths were lined with pointed teeth. Tyrannosaurs whose tiny arms ended not in hands but puckered sphincters that shot poison darts to slow their prey.

Every type appeared to be a meat-eater, built to prey on the mammalian monsters that also populated the proto-space and were themselves not weak. Lanky, giant apes using agility, cunning and powerful fists to escape or even overcome their would-be predators were just one species struggling to survive in the unusually Darwinian monster ecology.

Monsters of any kind rarely preyed on one another, but the three varieties in the crowded proto-space seemed to operate in a hierarchy. At the bottom were the mammalians, either bronze or silver rank. Preying on them were the dino-monsters, ranging from the bronze-rankers at the bottom of the heap to the peak predators, like the tyrannosaurs. Those even went after some of their fellow dino-monsters, as well as the mammalian varieties.

At the top, above even the largest and most savage dinosaur monsters, were the humanoid dino-men. They were not as strong or as tough as the larger dino-monsters, and far fewer in number. What they did have was intelligence and unusual magical abilities. This ranged from the power to conjure weapons and armour to their most powerful ability: controlling the unintelligent dino-monsters.

One of the dino-men was not like the others. Standing above the intelligent silver-ranked dino-men was the only one of their number to be gold rank. Quickly dominating the others, he had chosen the smartest and strongest to serve him personally, while the rest were sent to gather the unintelligent monsters.

Under the gold-ranker's direction, they had pushed back the human incursion and held the aperture secure. They awaited the point where the proto-space delivered them to another world, more vast than the one they knew.

"Will more of the humans come?" one of the silvers asked. He had chosen the name Silha for himself. The other silver-rank male had named himself Kowal, and the female, Chesh. The gold-ranker they referred to as King.

King had been the anchor monster for the proto-space, the one the humans needed to kill to prevent the monsters from entering the human world. Now the proto-space had crossed the threshold past where it could be stopped from dumping its monsters into the real world. The proto-space was about to break down and King was no longer its anchor monster, but he retained a lingering connection to the proto-space.

"I don't know if more will come," King said. "We have passed the point of no return. Even if the humans managed to kill me now, it would change nothing. I suspect they know this and prepare for our arrival, instead of further, futile expeditions."

"What will we find on the other side?" Chesh asked.

"I, like you all, am less than two days old," King said. "I know no more than any of you. Not how I came to know what a day is, the language we are speaking or even the concept of a language. What I do know is that the humans will not tolerate our existence. If we are going to make a place for ourselves, we must carve it from their flesh and wash it clean with their blood."

"They will be many, won't they?" Silha asked.

"Yes," King said, looking down at the aperture. "And they will be gathered around the other side of the hole they made in the wall of this world. If we are close to that hole when we cross over, we will be overwhelmed. We must move, so that when we do pass from this world to the next, we do not arrive in their midst."

"If we leave, more may enter through the hole," Kowal said.

"It is too late for them to accomplish anything," King said, looking down at the dino-monsters teeming around the aperture. In range of the dino-men, they were under control and placid, despite their highly aggressive nature.

"Our unintelligent brethren will suffice to occupy any humans that enter, at least in the time it takes for this world to end and pass us into the one that follows."

Taking King's lead, the four quickly departed the vicinity of the aperture.

On the Network plane, Akari watched Jason, who hadn't spoken since the discussion on the Makassar disaster. He wasn't meditating. He was still sitting on the floor, just staring into space, stern-faced. She was struck by how different he looked without the usual lively eyes and perpetual half-smirk. Instead of looking at the world like there was a joke only he could see, there was a determination in his silver eyes that slightly unnerved her. Even without his aura behind it, which she couldn't sense at all, when his eyes flicked in her direction, it made her feel like a prey animal.

"We're here," he said, standing up. The action looked oddly inhuman as he rose straight up from his cross-legged position without using his hands for balance or support. The smooth, confident motion of it made Akari think of a camouflaged praying mantis, revealing its presence with sudden movement.

The Network plane boasted a feature uncommon in most private jets: a quick-deploy hatch in the floor. It was in its own small compartment so as to not disrupt the rest of the plane when the hatch opened. Jason strode towards it as the pilot announced that they were approaching the drop zone.

Asya joined the pair in the drop compartment, standing by the button for the hatch as Jason and Akari stood on top of it. Jason was shrouded in mist for a few seconds, his combat robes in place when it dispersed.

"Stay safe," Asya told them, her eyes on Jason.

"The objective is to keep other people safe," he said as he grabbed Akari's hand. "Hit the button."

Asya gave him a worried look, lifted the clear cap and slammed her palm onto the big red button. The floor hatch dropped open and Jason and Akari were dumped into the skies over Darwin. Jason let his shadow arm extended to keep his grip on Akari's hand when falling from the plane yanked them apart. He would need to pull her close when he decelerated their drop. In the meantime, they both angled their bodies into a streamlined free fall.

As they drew closer to the ground, Akari sensed the silver-ranker below them and they aimed for that spot, an empty beach. As they dropped further and further without Jason pulling out his cloak, Akari became increasingly concerned. The ground seemed to be lunging up at them.

"JASON!"

He didn't turn his head. She knew his sharp senses heard her despite her voice immediately being carried off in the wind rush of their fall. His eyes were locked on the ground below as she called his name again and again, not eliciting so much as a sideways glance.

She was about to flatten her body to slow the descent when he seemed to sense it. Instead of conjuring his cloak, however, he shocked her with a burst of overwhelming aura suppression that jolted her into holding her descent angle, along with a tug on her arm from Jason.

Finally, Jason yanked himself to her with his shadow arm and his starlight cloak came into being, unfurling like wings of night. Gravity's hold was drastically lessened and they rapidly decelerated, barely a hundred metres from the ground. They were travelling at ninety metres per second before Jason opened his cloak. Even magic could decelerate them only so much. It took only seconds before they crashed into the soft sand, their superhuman bodies soaking up the impact.

They landed on a beach that would normally be full of tourists, but the crisis had even the locals staying in their homes. Akari stood, stunned for a moment, before wheeling on Jason.

"What are you thinking?"

"Seconds matter," Jason said, providing no further explanation as he strode towards the man jogging over the sand in their direction, waving a friendly hand.

"Hi, I'm Remy. You two came in pretty hot."

"Portal," Jason demanded.

"Jeez, so much for small talk," Remy said and started drawing a circle in the air with his arm. "You're lucky I can even hit this distance. My ability only got stronger a little while ago. Normally, the Network stops giving out cores once you hit silver, but those of us with portals are the chosen few. Especially these days."

A shimmering sheet of rainbow light appeared in front of him and Jason marched through without hesitation.

Jason stepped out of the portal, which led to the inside of a ramshackle slum house in Makassar. It was largely empty, aside from a rotting mattress and the stench of urine.

"We're in a slum near Paotere Harbour," Remy said after coming through the portal behind Jason. "There's a command post there; you should be able to sense the essence users from here."

Jason was already moving, kicking the rotten door right off its hinges and dashing out. His cloak spread out like wings, whipping him into the air and then launching him over the rooftops. He did not pause to revel in the sensation of personal flight, his attention elsewhere.

- You have entered an area coterminous to a proto-space.
- The proto-space is in the final stages of breaking down and can no longer be prevented from purging into your current space.
- If you enter the proto-space, the breakdown will be decelerated and the manifested entities within will be purged into your current space at a reduced rate.

"A thank you would be nice," Remy called after him. He turned to Akari, who had been the last one through the portal. "Your friend is kind of a dick."

Akari followed Jason outside and leapt up, hopping rapidly over the corrugated rooftops of the slum. She chased after him, likewise detecting the cluster of essence users. She also detected essence users clashing with monsters all around. It seemed that the slum had already been evacuated as she didn't sense any normal-rank auras.

Jason quickly reached Paotere Harbour, clustered with wooden pinisi ships crammed against one another. The boats were being used to evacuate civilians while the open space of the docks had been occupied by a Network command post. Jason's distinctive appearance was well known and Akari arrived to join him as he was being shown to the camp's command tent.

"Is it true that you can stall out a dimensional space?" the commander asked after the briefest introductions.

"It's too late to stop the monsters coming out," Jason said. "I think I can slow down the rate at which they emerge, though. I'm not sure by how much."

"Whatever you can do, we'll take, but we haven't been able to secure the aperture. The other side is packed tight with category-three dimensional entities."

"Not an issue," Jason said. "I'll buy you as much time as I can."

"I don't suppose you have any of those magic buses on hand for moving evacuees?"

Jason closed his eyes, exploring his sense of the proto-space that none of the other essence users could even detect without rituals. In most cases, a proper astral space would cut Jason off from his familiars, while a proto-space would not. Jason had become familiar enough with them to tell if it would be any different which, in this case, it was not. He would miss Shade in the proto-space, but others needed what his familiar could offer more.

"Alright," Jason said, marching outside the tent. "Clear me some room."

The commander ordered space clear as Shades started emerging from Jason, only one remaining as Jason's shadow.

"I'm going to need some mana," Jason said.

He turned to where people were being evacuated by boat, then took to the air, his cloak winging him out over the water where he landed on the mast of a pinisi boat, perched like a dark bird. He had picked out the boat with the most wretched-looking passengers.

"*Feed me your sins.*"

He drained the sickness from the slum residents, turning it all into mana. His Sin Eater power meant that he could absorb it all, exceeding his normal mana limit, although it would leak away over time. He would use it well before that happened.

Returning to the shore, he conjured cloaks over the thirty Shades standing by, barely having enough mana for all of them, even after collecting extra. Immediately afterwards, the Shades merged to form five buses with shadowy, starlit exteriors.

"All yours, commander," Jason said. Shade had experience coordinating with Network forces from Broken Hill and knew what to do.

"We can get you to the aperture," the commander said. "Fair warning, though, establishing an arrival zone wasn't going well, last I heard."

"I'll make my own way," Jason said.

Jason's figure blurred as the air around him seemed to slowly bend. They felt him project his aura, which seemed to merge with the world around it, blending until it was once again undetectable. Then the warped space snapped back into place and he was gone. The commander and the other Network staff were left staring at the empty space Jason had just vacated.

"He can just go into dimensional spaces on his own?"

"Yes," Akari, said, distracted by the essence users she could still sense fighting to keep the waterfront evacuation zone free of monsters. "Where can you use me?"

"What's your specialisation?" the commander asked her.

"Killing things."

27

HUNTED

The proto-space version of Makassar was overrun with rainforest growth, the sky filled with volcanic ash. Four humanoid dinosaur hybrids were moving through the city, the gold-rank King in the lead. There were more of the silver-rank dino-men scattered through the proto-space as well.

King and his subordinate monsters moved away from the aperture and the horde of humans they anticipated being on the other side. They did not want to be dumped amongst them when the proto-space shifted them into the larger reality. Their powerful legs sent them thundering through the city at pace until King suddenly stopped.

"What is it?" asked Chesh. She was the only female of the group and the leader of King's silver-rank cohort, having proven her strength against Kowal and Silha.

"Something has changed," King said, tilting his head as if listening for something. The former anchor monster could still sense the condition of the proto-space. "There's something here that's slowing down the passage to the next world. The time between each of our brethren crossing over will be longer, making them vulnerable to those awaiting us on the other side."

"What is doing this?" Kowal asked.

"I don't know," King said. "I think some manner of unusual being has intruded upon this world. Spread out, find the others. Tell them to find this being and destroy it."

"Is there anything else we can do?" Chesh asked.

"As this realm breaks down, breaches will form. Tell the others that if they find a stable breach, send our brethren through. Make sure they know only to go if it is stable. If it is changing in shape or size, they must avoid it at all costs, for it will kill them."

When he appeared in the proto-space, Jason realised that it was a warped version of the equivalent space in normal reality. While this was uncommon, it was not so uncommon as to put him off, as he had encountered it before. This version of Paotere Harbour was post-apocalyptic, with the wooden boats smashed, rotted and half-submerged. The buildings he could see were in disrepair and overgrown, reminding him of the astral space in which he had spent half a year. These buildings were not ancient stone ruins, however, but the modern constructions of his own world.

The ambient magic was thick and rich, more than any place he had been before. The magical strength to sustain gold-rank entities would be useful to him, making his relatively low power level harder to sense. Like a quiet noise hidden by a louder one, the potent ambient magic would mask his presence.

The ambient magic that supported the gold-rank monster somewhere in the proto-space was not present on Earth. Once it crossed over, the monster would rapidly become starved for magic. The damage it could do until it did, especially in a densely populated area, meant that waiting it out would not be an acceptable approach for the Network forces. They would need to find a way to kill the monster without wiping out half the city themselves.

Jason had two goals in the astral space. One he completed just by arriving.

- You have entered a proto-space in the process of dissolution.
- As the physical space breaks down, dimensional apertures will appear, including stable apertures that allow monsters to escape

to the coterminous reality. Other apertures will be unstable, containing profoundly destructive dimensional forces.
- [Nirvanic Transfiguration] will slow the process of dissolution but cannot arrest it. Apertures from the proto-space will appear at a reduced rate.
- [Nirvanic Transfiguration] will allow you to actively stabilise or destabilise nearby apertures.

So long as Jason remained in the proto-space, the monsters from it would arrive in the real world as more of a drip-feed than a wave as their escape points appeared more slowly. Given the preponderance of silver-rank monsters, every moment he could stall their emergence would give the Network more breathing room to protect the civilians.

That would buy time for his second objective: to kill as many silver-rank monsters as he could before they reached the real Makassar. He had no illusions that he could match the Network's ability to sweep and clear but he would do his best. As for the gold-ranker, he would need to avoid it.

Even if he had been silver rank instead of at the peak of bronze, there was no way for him to overcome a gold-rank monster. The jump from bronze to silver he had learned to overcome, but silver to gold was on a whole different scale. If he was silver rank and the designated damage dealer in a whole team of silvers, it might be different. With others protecting and facilitating him, it might be possible, although at the early stages of silver, that would still be a sketchy proposition at best.

Jason knew full well that if the gold-ranker found him, he was dead. He had one chance to resurrect before silver rank, though, and if this was how he spent it, he could accept that.

All these thoughts passed through Jason's head in a moment. He could sense the monsters heading in his direction, probably attracted by the magical distortion of his arrival. He had emerged on the open ground of the docks and standing in the open was a quick path to being swarmed and killed. He looked around for the shadow of the closest building and then stepped into Shade and vanished.

A dino-man who had chosen the name Loth for himself watched rainbow smoke rise over a nearby rooftop. He had seen its like before, with monsters dissolving into the smoke sometime after death. What was new was the sheer amount, as if many monsters had died all at once.

He had been told of a being that was slowing their passage to the next world, so he was leading a group of the unthinking dino-monsters in search of a stable portal. All that rainbow smoke was likely to be related to the unknown being, however, and the priority was to hunt it down. If he destroyed it, he might get the chance to join King's cohort.

He had almost thirty dino-monsters under his control, although they were spread over a goodly area as they picked their way between the city buildings. The streets were broken and overgrown, some worse than others. The foliage ranged from almost intact with maybe some grass growing through a crack to full-blown trees rising through holes in shattered concrete.

Loth's control over the monsters kept their aggression in check, although if pushed too close together, their base instincts would take over. He had to spread them out, which the terrain made even harder. The outermost monsters of his group were at the very limits of his control range, where his dominion over them was weakest.

The bulk of Loth's forces were long-necked sauropods, the most common of the silver-rank monsters. He also had two triceratops-like, horn-faced chargers and one of the tyrannosaurus variants with the spike-projector forelimbs.

Loth marched confidently amongst his monster force. Although he mentally urged them to pick up speed, there was only so fast the hefty quadrupeds could go. The silver-rank monsters were fast for creatures of their size, though, imitating a small earthquake as they moved through the streets.

Suddenly, Loth regretted collecting only the strongest of the dino-monsters now that he needed information. The lower-rank creatures were smaller, quicker and would have made passable scouts.

His herd of monsters was powerful, but a sleeping person would feel its approach. He worried that the unknown being would flee, although if it was responsible for the rainbow smoke, perhaps not.

He could communicate with the dino-monsters, but they were not intelligent. The larger ones were little more than sacks of angry meat being driven by instinct and hunger. The pack hunters were cunning and at least smart enough to be acceptable for scouting.

Loth and his monsters were closing in on the area where he had seen the rainbow smoke when he heard one of his dino-monsters yell in pain and rage. Loth sent an admonishing jolt of mental force, thinking one of the monsters at the edge of his range had loosened from his control and become aggressive.

Wary of a chain reaction of fighting, Loth made his way quickly in the direction of his unruly monster. What he found was a sauropod thrashing its neck around angrily, seeking out an enemy it apparently couldn't find. Loth spotted the source of its rage: a black rot spreading from one of its rear legs to the rest of its body.

After realising it was not obstreperous monsters but an attack, Loth conjured a magical firearm. It was long, stylised with a dinosaur motif, and shot heavy, poisoned spikes. He went on the lookout for whatever was responsible, assuming it to be the unknown being. Some distance away, he heard another cry of rage and pain.

Loth found himself running back and forth as more of his monsters were afflicted, one after another without catching so much as a glimpse of the one responsible. Packed close together, the instincts of the monsters took over as Loth's control slipped further and further away.

The rage and pain of the afflicted creatures caused them to lash out and the others fought back, rapidly turning the monster-filled streets into a meat grinder. The critical point came when the tyrannosaur was afflicted and went berserk, annihilating what remained of Loth's hold on the monsters. Loth climbed the tallest nearby building to get out of the chaos.

As he looked down at the mess, he failed to see any trace of what was attacking his monsters, what had forced him to escape them. Then a jolt passed through him as he realised that he wasn't being attacked at all. He was being hunted.

The madness below accomplished the twin goals of depriving Loth of his minions and isolating him from support. His instincts told him to turn around and he saw a dark figure walking across the rooftop, silver eyes shining under an otherwise impenetrable hood. Loth raised his gun and fired, the spike passing through the figure as if it were an illusion. Then he realised it was not a dark figure, but a figure made of darkness, with no more substance than air.

As he made the discovery, Loth felt a blade slice between the armour plates covering his back. It was a shallow cut, barely breaking through his scales to strike flesh. He whirled but found no one. He turned back to the dark figure, but it too was gone.

Loth cast his gaze around, looking for any sign of his attacker. Normally, his senses were sharp, but he could detect nothing. Pain bit his ankle and he looked down to see a long, narrow line of darkness that ended in a hand gripping a dagger slick with Loth's own blood. He was barely able to spot it before it snaked off the edge of the roof.

He rushed to the side of the rooftop, but he wasn't foolish enough to stick his head over. He extended his gun instead, firing spikes from the muzzle into any lurking ambusher. Unfortunately for Loth, the spikes did little to the lurking ambusher in question.

The spikes easily pierced the bloody rags shrouding the figure perched on the lower ledge but did little to the leeches inside. Strips of wet, red cloth shot up, wrapping around the gun and Loth's arms, and he scrambled back. The gun was pulled from his hands as his retreat dragged the bloody rag entity up over the edge of the roof. It was half the size of Loth, whose silver-rank strength was easily up to the task.

Loth desperately yanked off the strips of cloth wrapping themselves around him but more and more kept shooting out from the entity. As fast as he worked, the strips grabbed his arms, legs and torso faster than he could get rid of them. They were not much of an impediment to his movement, because of his strength, but they were dragging the entity closer and closer to Loth, even as he continued to back across the roof. He didn't know what would happen if the entity reached him, but every instinct screamed at him not to let it.

Giving up on pulling the strips off by hand, Loth conjured a sword and raised it into the air, ready to swing down and sever the strips. Before he could, a set of vibrant energy beams struck the blade, spoiling his grip.

Turning to the new enemy, Loth saw that it was a floating cloak occupied not by a person but by an unnerving glowing eye. Four more eyes floated around it, the source of the beams still firing in his direction. In his moment of distraction, the rag-entity reached him and leeches started squeezing out between the cloth strips like the flesh of a soft fruit being squished in a fist. They swarmed over him and he collapsed, screaming. He never heard the spells being chanted at him.

Jason stood at the edge of the building, watching the monsters tear one another apart. Jumping off the roof, he dived in to accelerate the process. Since arriving in the proto-space with only one of Shade's bodies, the way he fought reminded him of his earliest days as an adventurer. His skills were greater, his abilities more advanced and his attributes well into the superhuman range, but there was an old-school feel of desperately walking on a knife-edge.

Only against the largest groups, organised by one of the intelligent monsters, did he hunt. Otherwise, he threw himself into the fray to get the most done in the least time. He paid the price, frequently pushing too hard and getting slapped down. His armour was hanging off him in ribbons, despite its self-repairing properties, and he was painted red in his own blood. Jason had been damaged enough to kill him a dozen times over, but his defensive measures and self-healing kept him going.

When the last of the large monster clutch was dead, Jason held out his hands to either side of him.

"*As your lives were mine to reap, so your deaths are mine to harvest.*"

The remnant life force of the monsters rose up and flooded into Jason, taking his health far beyond its ordinary limit and into the realm of role-playing game hit points. This had already proven key to surviving long enough to drain health when fighting against the gangs of silver-rank dino-monsters.

Without an army of Shades to play decoy and escape hatch, Jason found himself with less margin for error at the same time he was pushing the boundaries of what he could take on at once. As a result, he was relying on drain and recovery powers to get him through situations where he would normally rely on stealth and evasion.

Jason left the dead monsters behind, already on his way to the next fight. Shade lingered, flickering over the battlefield to touch each of the dead monsters.

- Would you like to loot [Tri-Horn Charger]?

As of his rank-up, Shade could use Jason's non-combat abilities, including the power to initiate looting. So often, when dealing with proto-spaces, Jason was faced with too many monsters and too little time. As he left fallen monsters behind to confront the next one, he left potential loot to literally go up in smoke. Now that Shade could trigger the looting for him, that was no longer the case.

Since Shade had ranked up, Jason had accumulated more than his inventory could store, most of which he shovelled onto the Network. Given the circumstances, the Network was hungrily devouring every resource it could get its hands on, making Jason a more critical asset than ever. He also stowed an amount in the storerooms of Asano Village, which had its own magical maintenance costs.

Jason did keep certain choice items and materials for himself, though. Colin's silver-rank vessel had two fairly straightforward requirements, which Jason had already collected. One was a wheelbarrow-load of silver-rank blood quintessence and the other, disturbingly, was a portion of Jason's own skin. The materials for Gordon's next vessel were less gruesome but more elusive, evading Jason despite all the looting.

Jason's looting ability could mercifully be used at range, helping him avoid mouthfuls of rainbow smoke. That range was limited but could be extended through Shade's presence, like Jason's other non-combat powers. After Shade queued up all the looting dialogue boxes, Jason accepted them all at once. Items appeared in his inventory as his currency counters ticked up.

Jason was well away by the time he triggered the looting. As rainbow smoke drifted up around him, Shade was about to leave, when he spotted a green blur shooting at him. He dashed for the nearest shadow but was too slow, the blur grabbing his head in a clawed and scaled hand. Shade struggled to escape using his incorporeal nature, but the claw was reinforced with magic that held him inescapably in place.

28
GAMBLE

King stood on a rooftop, clutching Shade's head in his hand.

"You can hear me through this vessel, can't you?" King asked.

"Yes," Jason's voice came from Shade.

"I am going to find you and kill you."

"Probably, yes."

"You do not fear death?"

"Strike me down and I shall become more powerful than you can possibly imagine."

"You are a fool," King snarled.

"Yes," Jason admitted. "I'm sorry for the circumstances in which you came into being. You were doomed to a short and tragic life from the very start."

"You don't know what my life will be."

"Yes, I do. This world has the magic to keep you alive, but the one you will soon find yourself in does not. You will rapidly grow weaker until it becomes bad enough that the humans can kill you. Hope that they do it quickly because they will study you if they can, in ways that strip away dignity and leave only pain. I'll do my best to stop them if I'm still alive, but I can make no promises. I fight for the humans, but I cannot speak for them."

"You talk as if you are not one of them."

"I was, once. Now I'm something else. Not to say that I'm better than they are, because I'm not. I just convince myself I am, sometimes. If it were up to me, I'd give your people a patch of land and leave them be. Let them see to one another when the time came. Do you understand how your kind end?"

"I do," King snarled.

"I'm sorry for that," Jason said. "I respect the desire to escape what others tell you is inevitable. My choice would be to give you a place for you to find your own way, but the humans would never tolerate that."

"I have known this from the beginning," King said. "Only by purging the humans from the world can we claim a place for ourselves."

"There is no place for you except here, and soon even that will be gone. Of your people, only you have the strength to withstand the humans on the other side, and that strength will leak from you like blood from a wound. The only questions are how ugly your demise becomes and how many humans you take with you."

"As many as I can."

"I thought as much," Jason said. "I imagine I'd feel the same in your situation. I can't even offer an alternative. When you appear on the other side, they will try to kill you, use you or both. I'll do my best to stop you and them, but we both know I can't."

"Then until this world ends, we will try to kill one another."

"Fighting you is a gamble I don't want to make," Jason said. "Come for me if you want, but I'm coming for everyone else. Do you have a name?"

"They call me King. You?"

"Jason Asano."

"Whatever my fate, Jason Asano, you will die before it plays out."

"That seems a likely order of events. I can't stop you, King. But you can't stop me either."

"I'll kill you."

"That won't be enough."

Still dangling from King's hand, Shade's body self-destructed, dissolving into nothing.

Jason still had a lot of mana from draining the monster corpses with Blood Harvest, so reconstituting one of Shade's bodies was not too draining. He had Shade self-destruct the one body in the proto-space with him, since if the monster could catch Shade, there was every chance he could track him back to Jason.

Not wasting time in getting back on the move, Jason started putting distance between himself and the gold-ranker. The broken and overgrown city offered shadows aplenty, and even across stretches of open ground, Jason was far from sluggish.

"If he knows that you are avoiding him and hunting the others, he may collect the other intelligent monsters together," Shade said. "From what we've seen, they seem to be small in number."

"If they all cross over together, I can live with that," Jason said. "Asya said that the Network is mobilising the magically enhanced heavy weapons and you've seen the details of that program, the same as me."

"The weapons are far from discriminatory," Shade said. "If they are targeting the gold-ranker, any silver-rankers will likely be caught up in the destruction."

"Exactly. If they're all in one spot, that's fewer missiles the Network has to throw around."

"King may be wary of an attack of this nature," Shade said. "This may be why the intelligent monsters are not gathered together."

"Or it could just be that they're trying to get as many monsters under their control as they can. I'm doing what I can here, but this whole space will last another few hours at best. I'll barely make a dent in the numbers in that time, so most of these monsters are going to cross over. If they're all gathered up for the Network to drop magic napalm or whatever on, all the better."

They had already seen signs of dimensional collapse in the form of blank, white void spaces that were the natural apertures forming as the proto-space collapsed. The voids were plain and empty to the eye, but Jason's magical senses warned him of dimensional forces within, of such wildly destructive might, only transcendent damage could surpass it. Jason and Shade had watched an entire building collapse when a large white void appeared over key structural points, instantly annihilating them.

Only some of the apertures were safe to pass through. Jason experimented with exerting influence over the voids; he had only used his ability to affect proto-spaces passively in the past. He could only actively affect a void when he was relatively close, within a few dozen metres. It was a useful range, but far less so than the passive effect that impacted the entire proto-space.

After a little practise, Jason could render the aperture safe or turn a safe one dangerous in a moment. Most of the voids he encountered were already dangerous and the ones that weren't, he made dangerous. He was not going to leave gateways out of the proto-space open behind him if he could avoid it.

Such apertures were the normal means by which monsters escaped a dissolving space. Jason was familiar with the process from his time shutting down proto-spaces for the Network, at which he was now an old hand. He knew that more and more apertures would appear, more and more of which would be stable. By the time the space was in the final stages of breakdown, safe apertures would be everywhere. Until that happened, Jason would buy what time he could.

After the talk with King, Jason skipped over the next two clusters of monsters he encountered. Moving past them undetected, he put them between himself and the gold-ranker hunting him. He and Shade then encountered another large group led by one of the intelligent dino-men. This one had discovered a stable and enormous aperture capable of taking in two of the giant monsters at a time. He was pushing his monsters through in a rush, like a drover sending cattle across a ford.

Jason moved as swiftly as he could undetected, suppressing his ability to affect the void. It meant a few more monsters crossing over, but if he got his timing right, that would be a cost worth paying.

The dino-man was caught up in herding his monsters through the aperture, pushing them faster and faster. He had packed them tighter than he really should, straining himself to push their aggressive instincts away from fighting each other in close confines and towards rushing the aperture.

When the two monsters currently moving through the aperture were torn to ribbons by the dimensional forces suddenly churning within, he was startled. About to urge his monsters to stop, he was instead sprayed with leeches from a figure moving out of the shadows and struck with beams from afar.

The animals he had pushed into rushing the aperture kept going as the dino-man's concentration was lost. They too were shredded by the aperture, even as the dino-man was shredded by Jason. Eventually, the monsters, as dim-witted as they were, grew wise and stopped charging forward but not until around a dozen had run in with results akin to a giant dimensional woodchipper.

The dino-man controlling them had fallen quickly to the combined onslaught of Jason's attack-oriented fighting style that rapidly loaded afflictions with a multitude of dagger strikes. Those were followed up with the powerful spell combination of his affliction, drain and finisher.

With Colin piling on, it went even faster. The ambush had been effective in cutting the dino-man off from using its abilities as it fell to panic under a pile of leeches and it lacked the physical fortitude of its larger, less intelligent brethren. At the peak of bronze, Jason had reached the stage where he could blitz physically weaker varieties of silver-rank monster.

With the one controlling them dead, the other monsters were freed to follow their instincts, which were aggressive at the best of times. With the danger of the aperture and the close proximity they had been pushed into, the monsters immediately attacked one another.

Jason joined in the chaos to clean up the remaining monsters. He went largely unnoticed as he made minor attacks on the giant beasts while they violently crashed into one another. Even so, he was hammered more than once, more by accident in the crush than by deliberate strike. The shield power of his amulet, his stacked-up health and his drain and recovery powers kept him fighting.

Once it was over, he drained the remaining life force from the monsters with Blood Harvest and left Shade to loot as he moved on. He took a fresh direction, knowing that the gold-ranker would likely find the battle site. He didn't want to leave a discernible path for him to follow.

Jason was feeling the mental strain as he continued his unrelenting battle through the proto-space. His nerves were frayed; the gold-ranker could find him at any moment and every monster he failed to kill likely meant lives lost once it crossed over. He was painted red with his own blood while his robe looked as bloody and torn as Colin's rags.

In the hours since he had spoken with King, the proto-space degradation had accelerated, leaving it an obstacle course of white void spaces. It was past the point where Jason had time to destabilise every safe aperture he found. He knew the effectiveness of his stalling was almost at an end. Monsters would already be pouring through myriad apertures across the proto-space.

Jason's presence continued to slow the dissolution, though, even this close to the end. Every minute there was no portal strong enough to allow a gold-ranker to cross was a small victory. It also brought Jason and King closer together as the proto-space shrank, the void devouring the proto-space from the edges in. The sky was no longer overcast with ash but a blank white as the sky literally came down on their heads.

King stepped back from the aperture, his simple proximity causing it to lose stability.

"It was the strongest portal we could find," Chesh said.

King's other two cohorts had already crossed over.

"I don't think any will be strong enough to let me leave until this world's final moments," King said.

"We never found the unknown being slowing it down."

"Jason Asano no longer matters," King said. "This world's end and our passage from it are inevitable. I can still sense the effect he has on this world, which will deliver him to me eventually unless he flees, which he will not."

"You seem certain."

"Like you, I came into this world with knowledge I do not understand the origins of. One of the things I know is arrogance. I felt it when I spoke with Jason Asano, enough to know that he will struggle to the bitter end."

"Do you think he truly can come back from death?"

"I was given just enough knowledge to understand how much more I do not know, so I cannot speak to what is or is not possible. If he truly can rise from the dead, I will kill him as many times as it takes."

Jason and King both had been pushed together as the void closed in. Soon they found themselves at either side of a rubble-strewn city block where patches of void had collapsed all the buildings. They stood, looking at one another, down a long street where rubble rested in grass grown through the cracked surface of the road. The world around them was silent. The void made no sound and King was the last remaining monster.

The others had flooded out of the apertures. Even the encroaching void became stable enough to serve as a giant aperture, closing in on them. It was almost stable enough for even King, which both Jason and King could sense.

"You cannot stop me," King said. "The void itself is already becoming the final gateway."

Jason and King walked towards one another as the void continued to close in on them. It was tight enough that Jason could exert his will to destabilise the entire void around them. He couldn't seal the passage, but he could trigger the lethal roil of uncontrolled dimensional forces, turning the giant aperture into a mouth full of gnashing teeth.

- The proto-space you are in has reached the final stage of dissolution. You are no longer able to directly transition out using [Nirvanic Transfiguration]. You will need to exit through an aperture.

- The final aperture of the proto-space is extremely stable. It will consume increasing amounts of mana to enforce an unstable state.

It didn't matter that he was locked into the space with King. Only by staying could he maintain the instability, which was the only weapon he had against the gold-rank monster. He only needed to hold on for moments as the void continued to encroach. King and Jason moved towards one another as the space went from the size of a city block to a warehouse to a cottage.

"I am faster than you can imagine," King said. "The moment you open a space for yourself to escape, I will go through before you've realised I moved."

"That's why I'm not going to," Jason said. "This space will close in on us and send us to the other side. After we pass through the dimensional forces, I doubt there will be enough of us left to spill onto the ground when we arrive."

"You seem certain you will come back from death," King said. "Are you just as certain that you won't be dragged off into the afterlife when you pass from this world to the other?"

"No," Jason said, "but stopping you is worth the gamble. If I die forever, there are others to take up my responsibilities. You may be the only hope for your people, but I am not the only hope for mine."

The two continued to walk forward as the void closed in, arriving face to face.

"My brethren are slaughtering the humans as we speak," King said.

"I guarantee they are paying the price," Jason said, his voice not aggressive but sad. "So much death, and for what? It accomplishes nothing."

"If we truly are as doomed as you say, then we shall write our story across the soul of the human race in blood."

"Death is a poor legacy."

"We shall see how you tolerate your own."

Jason didn't even feel the blow that killed him, clawed fingers burying themselves in his head. His body dissolved into darkness, taking the form of a large bird filled with sparks of stellar light.

- You have died.
- [Nirvanic Transfiguration] has protected you from the effects of death, transfiguring you to a new form of life.

- You have taken the form of a star phoenix. All equipment has been returned to your inventory.

- Your current form is impervious to non-transcendent damage. You have a short time to move to safety before returning to your normal form.

- This effect has been expended until you increase in rank.

Jason's starlight phoenix form hovered in front of King. Jason's aura and the instability of the space around them was undiminished.

"I'll kill you as many times as it takes!" King announced, then opened his mouth to give a magically empowered roar. Sonic forces that would have annihilated Jason's ordinary form passed harmlessly through his phoenix state.

The void closed in to the size of a large room, the dimensional forces starting to wash over them. King conjured a sword and started pouring the magic he had been reserving for the other side into it, causing it to glow with transcendent light. As he brought it down, Jason's aura turned the transcendent light blue, the same as Gordon's disruptive-force damage. Again, it would have killed Jason in an instant in his normal state but was harmless to the phoenix.

King howled as the void crashed in on them and the proto-space came to an end.

29

DYING OF THIRST IN THE DESERT

OUTSIDE OF THE COLLAPSING SECOND PROTO-SPACE, THE SKY GREW DARK over the real city of Makassar. A beautiful sunset contrasted the horror below, with large portions looking like the bombed-out capital of a failed state. When the sun had risen, it had been a thriving city, one of Indonesia's most secure safe zones—at least, publicly. The consequences of the Network and the Cabal waging war in the shadows had scarred the city with fire, destruction, and death.

The Network and their military allies had acted quickly and international support was swiftly mobilised but the damage was largely done. The first proto-space emptied itself of monsters and the belated response was not enough to stave off disaster in a city of so many. Moves were rapidly made to secure the populace and contain the threat, but the monsters were already loose.

Death and tragedy were everywhere, with too many civilians and not enough people to protect them. Mad panic clogged the streets before organised evacuations could be set up, leaving countless people out in the open. Only a tsunami of support from around Indonesia and its neighbouring countries prevented the city from becoming an abattoir.

The city was out of control, but there was at least a sense of progress against the bronze-rank monsters of the first proto-space. The few silver-rank monsters had been a key priority, found and eliminated with overwhelming force.

Then silver-rank monsters started manifesting out of the second proto-space. The first proto-space had appeared at the southeast of the city, while the second covered the west and the north. The Network knew it was coming but had to direct the bulk of their forces towards the immediate threat. The second wave of monsters would be greater, but people were dying from the first already. Even the minimal resources they dedicated to preparing for the second wave stretched them dangerously thin.

Despite the conflict between local Cabal and Network forces, they were forced to join hands against the danger. As international support started rolling in, the tension was somewhat alleviated as the reinforcements were a buffer between them.

Casualties amongst the Network teams ticked up, as monsters started emerging from the second proto-space. Silver-rank monsters, in ever-increasing numbers, were not something that any Network force was equipped to handle. It became a race between international support arriving and the monsters of the second proto-space appearing, both escalating as one hour became two became three.

It was the first time a category-four proto-space had reached the point of depositing its monsters, at least on dry land. The international response was likewise unprecedented as people and resources from around the globe descended on Makassar.

The head start the monsters had and the logistical problems of a densely populated city made things difficult for the Network forces. Lingering tension with their Cabal allies only added to already troubled communication as outposts were established around the city. Looming over all of it was the threat of the one or more gold-rank monsters the Network knew to be coming.

The decision was made to give up on trying to eradicate the monsters from the west and north until enough international support arrived to sweep the silver-rank monsters without disastrous casualties. A defensive line was set up and the Network focused on evacuating as many civilians as possible either across it to the relatively secure parts of the city, or out of the city entirely.

The silver-rank monsters did not make the task easy. Only so many people could be effectively evacuated. Despite rising casualties, the Network kept going with desperation. On top of the silver-rank monsters roaming around, they had no idea when a gold rank would appear. At that point, the section of the city it arrived in would be a full-blown war zone where any remaining civilians would be disregarded. Stopping any gold-rank monsters would be the priority, whatever the cost.

In the evacuation effort, the five Shade buses were present and active but far from the only magical vehicles. The fastest support to arrive from other parts of Indonesia and neighbouring countries were those with magical vehicles of their own. There were helicopters similar to Kaito's and buses like Shade. There were cars and vans, armoured personnel carriers, planes, tanks, and boats.

Shade was not even the only intelligent vehicle, although most were conjured and very much in need of drivers and pilots. They ranged in style from ordinary-looking vehicles to highly exotic. Some were sleek and futuristic while others looked like post-apocalyptic battle wagons. There were even plainly fantastical variations, such as a plane in the form of an iron eagle, complete with articulating wings.

Eventually, the horrifying decision was made to withdraw all forces from the zone around the second proto-space. Dinosaur monsters were pouring through sheets of rainbow light, the one-way apertures leading from the proto-space. All Network forces pulled back behind the established defence lines, with only drones being sent in to catalogue the threats and horrors beyond. The civilians left behind would have to find a place to hide, escape on their own or die.

At a command post, Asya's role as an International Committee member was convincing branches outside of Indonesia to send whatever resources they could. China had completely denied having a secret weapon, as expected, although revealing that she knew managed to shake loose some of the powerful nation's more public resources.

China had already sent a host of silver-rankers south, with more being prepped for departure. They were also sending a veritable arsenal of resources, from spirit coins to weapons to the results of their magical heavy weapons program. Missiles and vehicle-mounted weaponry designed to handle category-four threats had been loaded onto transport planes and were en route.

Australia sent other assets, including a freshly bronze-rank Kaito. He flew north with a helicopter-load of the strongest silver-rankers Australia had to offer, including Farrah. Over the last eight months, Kaito had been practically force-fed monster cores and his bronze-rank speed got resources on-site with haste. On arrival in Indonesia, he was immediately recruited into the evacuation units, while Farrah was moved to the defence front.

Above the restricted zone, one of the drones monitoring the situation was a cutting edge, magically enhanced, silver-rank surveillance model. It had even grounded some bronze-rank fliers by hitting their wings with its onboard weapon systems.

The early and timely arrival of several such drones was courtesy of the United States. What their operators were doing in the region with such advanced surveillance magitech had not been explained and, given the circumstances, no one asked.

The drone detected a category-four magic surge, sending an alarm to its operator at a Network control post. The operator sent word and his small tent was soon crowded with people. The outpost commander, the tactical commander and the International Committee liaison all came in to watch the monitor, as did Farrah, who no one was stupid enough to try and stop.

"So, this is it," outpost commander said in a voice full of trepidation. "A category four."

"Your friend Asano bought us valuable time," the tactical commander told Farrah. "In those extra hours, the heavy weapons from China arrived. I sent coordinates and they're being prepped for deployment."

"We need to know what we're dealing with," the outpost commander said. "One of the dinosaur monsters, but bigger? Are we going to have some kind of Godzilla turn up?"

"Could be, given the size of that aperture," the committee liaison said. On the screen in front of them, the rainbow light gold-rank aperture reached from the ground to the height of a four-storey building.

"I think one of the intelligent monsters is more likely," the tactical commander said. "Probably their leader."

The tactical commander had been focused on the intelligent monsters due to their organisation of the larger ones. Thus far, the smarter monsters had been consolidating rather than making large moves, as if waiting or preparing for something. This had led to a theory discussed amongst the tactical commanders of the defence-line outposts that the gold-rank monster would be their leader.

Farrah remained silent. Rather than the gold-rank monster, there was someone else she wanted to see emerge from the proto-space. She already had people keeping tabs on the Shade buses, which were connected to Jason. Shade couldn't communicate with him in the proto-space but could at least sense his general condition. Something very drastic had taken place in there and they weren't sure what it was. He had let Farrah know and she now anxiously awaited Jason's return.

Finally, something emerged from the rainbow aperture. It was diminutive compared to most of the dinosaurs, but at twice the height of a human, it was undoubtedly monstrous. It staggered from the light, slow and awkward. As it moved stumblingly forward, barely staying on its feet, it revealed a zombie-like appearance, with almost half of its flesh stripped away.

Its left arm was gone entirely and the flesh from the left side of its head was stripped to the bone. It was clad in the twisted remains of armour, most of which was missing, revealing wounds that even silver-rankers wouldn't live through. Its skeleton was on display in numerous places and its insides dangled out in front of it as it plodded one foot haltingly after the other.

"Undead?" the outpost commander postulated.

"The drone is detecting life force," the drone operator said. "That thing is somehow still alive. It's in a bad way, though."

"I think we can all see that," the committee liaison said.

"It's more than just what we can see," the operator said. "Whatever happened to that monster left it with a severe magical deficit. It's trying to absorb magic to fuel its recovery, but the ambient magic is too low. It's a man dying of thirst in the desert."

"You can tell all that?" the committee liaison asked. "How sophisticated is that drone?"

"I'm not at liberty to disclose that information."

"What was able to do that to a gold-rank monster?" Farrah wondered aloud.

"We have been getting reports of monsters arriving already dead," the tactical commander said. "The ritualists have been guessing that there's a problem with the apertures. If that's what happened to the gold-ranker, we may have just gotten very, very lucky."

The tent got a little more crowded as Akari burst in.

"Is he back?" she asked Farrah.

"It turns out the gold-rank monster arrived all messed up," Farrah told her. "The commander, here, thinks we got lucky."

"You think it was Asano?" the commander asked. "Even if he's the most powerful category two on Earth, he's still a category two. Doing that to a category four is impossible."

"Impossible is kind of his thing," Farrah said. "He does the impossible and then follows it up with either something idiotic or…"

She grinned as a dark shape emerged from the rainbow aperture.

"…an obnoxiously dramatic entrance."

They watched the drone footage as a large bird made of star-filled darkness flew slowly out of the rainbow light. It circled in the air over the gold-rank monster as the light inside collected into two points, close together. The darkness reshaped itself into a cloak, fully enveloping a humanoid figure. The two points of light inside the hood were its only feature, forming a pair of bright silver eyes.

"The fidelity on this drone camera is amazing," the committee liaison said.

"That's what you took away from what you just saw?" the outpost commander asked.

"I just think we could really use some of these," the liaison said. "Who do I talk to about getting some?"

"You would have to speak to my commanding officer," the operator said.

"And how do I contact them?"

"I'm not at liberty to disclose that information. The monster appears to be speaking, so I'm turning on the audio."

On the screen, they saw the monster talking. As the audio kicked in, they heard guttural words in a growling language, spoken in a voice filled with rage and pain.

"Does anyone understand that?" the tactical commander asked.

"It's hard to tell," Farrah said. "A lot of its mouth is gone, but I believe it said something about killing Jason over and over."

"I warned you," Jason told King. "Your demise would be ugly and killing me would accomplish nothing."

"I'm not done killing you!"

Despite his words, King was a spent force, barely able to take staggering steps in Jason's direction. He conjured up a sword not for a weapon but for a walking stick, which proved to be a mistake. Expending the mana only worsened his condition. His recovery attribute was the hardest hit by the weak ambient magic and the one he needed the most. It was also the one most reliant on ambient magic, however, which left King's path to recovery cut off.

"I CAN'T BE KILLED BY THE LIKES OF YOU," King screamed, as much plea as assertion. ·

"I sympathise with your fate, so I'll make it as quick and painless as I can."

Jason raised an arm, pointing it at a spot over King's head.

"*Mine is the judgement, and the judgement is death.*"

He brought his hand down like a gavel as a column of transcendent light shone down from the sky onto the almost helpless King.

The spell was not boosted by any of Jason's abilities, yet was the single most powerful casting of his execute Jason had ever done. Execute powers inflicted exponential damage based on the condition of the target and the gold-ranker had survived damage that would kill any silver-ranker, several times over. Half of King's flesh was already gone and he looked more like an unliving revenant than a living creature.

Even if Jason didn't have the ability to bypass rank suppression, the transcendent damage of his spell did. King was completely obscured in the radiant light of gold, silver and blue. When the light faded away, even the gold-rank monster had been unable to withstand it and was completely gone.

- You have defeated [King of the Dinosaurs].

- You have acquired a new title: [Giant Slayer].

- [King of the Dinosaurs] has been wholly annihilated. It has been looted automatically.
- [Armour of the Dinosaur King] has been added to your inventory.
- [Monster Core (Gold)] has been added to your inventory.

- 10 [Gold Spirit Coins] have been added to your inventory.
- 100 [Silver Spirit Coins] have been added to your inventory.
- 1000 [Bronze Spirit Coins] have been added to your inventory.
- 10000 [Iron Spirit Coins] have been added to your inventory.

- You have defeated a significantly more powerful enemy. Your [Defiant] ability has refined additional loot from [King of the Dinosaurs]:

- [Soul-Imprinting Triune] has been added to your inventory.

- 100 [Gold Spirit Coins] have been added to your inventory.
- 1000 [Silver Spirit Coins] have been added to your inventory.
- 10000 [Bronze Spirit Coins] have been added to your inventory.
- 100000 [Iron Spirit Coins] have been added to your inventory.

Jason had not needed to breathe for more than a year, but he took a long, deep breath and slowly let it out. In the wake of his transformation and return to physical form, his body felt like lightning was running through it.

A horrified scream rang out and he turned his head. The drone he sensed hovering in the air was not the only thing drawn to the gold-rank aperture and Jason turned to see one of the intelligent, silver-rank dino-men looking at him in aghast disbelief.

Jason conjured his dagger and went to work.

30
ENOUGH POWER

As Jason drained the life force from the dead monsters around him, the drone came down to hover in front of him.

"Jason," Farrah's voice came through it. "I can direct you back to the defence line."

"Shade has brought me up to speed," Jason said. "A lot of civilians were abandoned on this side of the line and a lot of them are still here, in hiding. Only the intelligent dinosaur-people have aura senses worth a damn, so there are a lot of survivors."

"You need to come in for a debrief," another voice said.

"Here's my debrief: the gold-ranker is dead and there aren't any more. There's a lot of scared people here, so I'm going to go get them. If you feel like helping at all, let me know and I'll be happy to coordinate with you."

"Bugger it, I'm in," Farrah said.

"Farrah," Asya's voice came through. "I think you might be going a little native. How are you, Jason?"

"There are people who need me in action more than I need rest."

"Akari will be in too," Farrah said. "Can you send some Shades our way?"

"He's sending bodies as the buses finish their current runs elsewhere. I'll have him divert some to you."

Asya's expression was dark as she left the drone operator's tent.

"He is not alright, whatever he might say."

"Of course he's not," Farrah agreed. "I bet that on the inside he's tangled up like a sack of loose yarn you found at the back of your grandmother's cupboard."

"He needs to stop and rest," Asya said.

"That's the thinking of someone who wants what's best for him," Farrah said. "We need to think about what's best for all the people in the restricted zone."

"We don't know what he's been through, Farrah. Whatever happened in there with him and that category-four monster, it turned him into a bird. That's not how his flying power works."

Farrah had a very good idea why Jason turned into a bird, but she was the only one Jason had told the true nature of his ability to, so she kept it to herself.

"He didn't come in because he knows that when he stops, he's staying stopped for a while," Farrah said. "He needs to keep holding down the lid before it boils over."

"Quite so," Shade said, appearing next to them. "Mr Asano is quite strained, but I have been with him long enough to know that he will not let himself rest until the job is done."

"Clearing this city of monsters will take days, at best," Asya said.

"Best not dally, then," Shade said. "I have already acquired Miss Akari."

Asya grimaced but gave a nod.

"They won't resume evacuation until sweeper teams start clearing out the restricted zone," she said. "I'll see if I can divert some resources to help in the meantime. I can probably get the Americans with their drones to look for survivor clusters."

"Now you're talking," Farrah said. "Shade, let's go."

While the Network held off on more evacuations, just as Asya said, they didn't waste time forming teams to clear out the restricted zone. That left

Jason, Akari, Farrah and five buses marauding around, collecting survivors. The strike teams coordinated with them whenever they came across civilian clusters, while Jason's mini-team directed strike teams towards monster herds.

Farrah rested on one of the buses more than fought, keeping herself fresh for when they needed maximum killing at maximum speed. Akari rested when she could, her endurance giving her a solid uptime. Jason never stopped at all and barely remained within the vicinity of the buses. He stayed in contact through his party interface while serving as scout and pathfinder.

Jason, Farrah and Akari fought only as necessary, but necessary turned out to be a lot. Active monster-slaying they left to the Network, yet they racked up no shortage of kills since the monsters were also going after the survivors. Fortunately, Jason had a new weapon against swarms of monsters.

New Title: [Giant Slayer]

- Overcoming a much stronger enemy has left a permanent mark on you that can be sensed by others. This may trigger a fear reaction from the unintelligent and the weak-willed if your aura is significantly stronger than theirs. Your actual rank being lower than theirs does not diminish the effect.

Jason was aura-blasting herds of unintelligent dinosaurs into leaving an area, giving them the breathing room to get survivors out of whatever hole they were hiding in and onto a bus. If there was an intelligent dino-monster controlling the herds, it didn't work, but that let Jason know that there was prey to hunt.

On the day after the gold-rank monster fell, enough strike teams made up of Network silver-rankers were combing the restricted areas that other evacuation measures were authorised. The Cabal had participated in monster clearing but not civilian evacuation, as they often seemed like monsters themselves. Some of the Cabal complained that they were less like monsters than Jason Asano but exceptions were not made.

Even before the official resumption of evacuation in the restricted zones, a handful of others had joined Jason in bucking the Network's direction and running evacuations early. These were mostly silver-rank teams with at least one vehicle power.

Farrah went off for sleep on the second day, rejoining after half a day of rest. Akari did the same on day three. Jason not only didn't rest, but he barely even paused, replenishing himself on enemies and pushing forward. By the fifth day, even Farrah looked at Jason with concern.

"Most of the survivors have been collected," she told him as he dropped off a busload of rescued people at one of the Network's evacuation camps. "Most of the monsters are gone."

"Guarantee me that if I stop, no one will die that would have lived if I hadn't," he said.

"You know I can't do that."

"Then you know I can't stop."

He offered no further explanation and stepped back onto the bus. Farrah and Akari shared a concerned look as they followed.

They had all seen piles of dead in the previous days that dwarfed Broken Hill. None of them came out mentally unscathed. Jason barely spoke, and as survivors became more scarce, he increasingly threw himself into eradicating every monster they encountered. Giant dinosaurs were wiped from existence with cold, brutal efficiency. Jason's intensity was starting to scare the survivors they found.

The Network forces had previously mapped out zones in the city, and as the work progressed, they started declaring them monster free. Holding teams were placed to make sure they stayed that way. A team of local Network officials came by, flanked by silver-rankers, to debrief Jason. He asked if they were the ones responsible for what happened and did not like their political answer about national sovereignty and passing off blame onto the Cabal. The silver-rankers overlapped their auras to shield the officials from Jason's aura pressure before Jason stormed back out into the city.

Adrien Barbou, now going by Mr East, looked at the paused image of a starlight bird and a zombie-like monster. Standing next to him was Mr North.

"Perhaps I was wrong in opposing the idea of killing him," Barbou said.

"Asano did not overpower the category-four monster," Mr North said. "He used environmental dangers, circumstance and opportunity."

"It could be argued that the ability to do so is more of a threat than raw power, in which he does not fall short anyway. He is strong for his level and his power continues to grow."

"Reports are that he will soon cross into category three, possibly even as a result of current events."

"Enough power trumps all," Mr North said, "and new power will not be enough for what comes next."

Barbou narrowed his eyes at Mr North before schooling his expression. A smile teased at Mr North's mouth.

"Speak your mind, Mr East."

"It's nothing."

"I said speak," Mr North demanded, his voice full of grave promise.

"It has occurred to me," Barbou said reluctantly, "that perhaps events have not slipped as far from their design as we all think. I have wondered, on occasion, if someone not only knew from the beginning what the ramifications would be but was also engineering those events to go exactly the way he wanted. If what seemed like plans going awry were actually masks in masks in masks. We are about to make what should be our endgame, but you are looking further to things that are, to the rest of us, obscured in the dark."

"I like you, Mr East. You see things that others overlook. You take fragments and recognise at least some of the whole."

"Are you going to kill me now?"

"No, Mr East. Good help is hard to find."

The aftermath of the Makassar disaster would affect the city for years to come, but Jason's part was done after eight days. The trip to Japan was postponed as he headed for home with Akari and Farrah in the back of Kaito's helicopter. Kaito had configured the main section of his conjured vehicle into a luxurious passenger compartment. Asya had remained behind as the requirements on the ground turned from the tactical to the logistical.

Jason had draped his heavily damaged combat robe over his chair and was standing, looking at it. The robe, custom made for him by Gilbert Bertinelli, had been a quiet champion for him, but the magic in it had died. Despite its considerable powers of self-repair, Jason had pushed it close to destruction many times, many of them during his desperate struggle in the latest proto-space.

Jason had a magic item that could increase the rank of a high-quality item and he had intended to use it on the robes once he reached silver rank. Now that was impossible and he carefully folded what was left of the garment and returned it to his inventory. He admonished himself for mourning the loss of a piece of clothing when tens of thousands were dead.

Farrah stood and moved next to where he was staring at a now-empty chair. Although she had not been with Jason as he fought alone in the proto-space, they had faced the horrors of Makassar together. Once they found a school where a class full of children had hidden in a courtyard. The monsters had found them first and now Jason and Farrah had seen things they could never unsee. They gently leaned into each other for comfort.

"I miss Gary," Farrah said. "I could use a big hairy ball of happiness right now."

"I hesitate to say it," Jason said, "since we could all use some comforting thoughts right now, but Gary didn't take losing you well. I doubt he took losing me much better."

"That's alright," Farrah said. "I can't wait to see the look on his face when he sees us again."

Jason turned his head to give her a sad smile.

"That's a nice thought," he said. "Now I have something to look forward to."

Jason stood under a dome in his cloud house, looking up at the water. From before Broken Hill and through a week in Makassar, he had only slept once, keeping himself fuelled on spirit coins, as well as the mana and stamina he drained. Now that he was back, he still hadn't slept.

In his time as an essence user, Jason had become completely

convinced that essences did something to the mind that helped it process trauma. There was a limit, however, that in the wake of Broken Hill and then Makassar he had slammed into like it was a solid wall.

He knew that compared to the people in both places who lost their lives or their entire families, he had nothing to complain about. He had the power and the resources to keep himself and his family safe, which was exactly what had been done with Asano Village. It made him feel all the more guilty that he had done that while thousands of other families died.

He sensed Dawn at the airlock and opened the cloud house to her with a thought. Moments later, she found him, standing in the same spot he had been in when she last left him.

"I'm sorry to come to you like this after what you've been through," she said.

"What I went through is nothing," Jason said. "The Makassar death toll officially crossed a hundred and fifty thousand today and they're still counting the dead in piles. Literal piles of bodies."

His voice cracked as he spoke, almost descending into sobs.

"I know," Dawn said softly. "It doesn't change the fact that you've seen horrors people never should. You need time to recover, which makes what I have to say hard."

"I need to go to Japan," he said.

"Yes. The grid could start going active in less than a week. Farrah estimates a little more, but time is short. We need that door before the world discovers it and its potential."

"Alright," Jason said.

"First you have to sleep," she said. "A lot. After that, you need some meditation. It will help you get back into balance, but you know that."

"I'll cross into silver. I can feel it."

"That's why you've been stalling," Dawn realised. "Silver rank feels like a reward you don't deserve."

"Everyone else got misery and death," Jason said. "I get strength and power? How is that fair?"

"You can be a fool of the highest order, Jason Asano, but even you're not fool enough to think the cosmos is fair."

"It should be."

"If you don't like the way of things, then change them. All you need is enough power."

31
SILVER

Jason was on the roof of the main residence in Asano Village. There was a helicopter pad and, as would soon become important, the facilities to clean a helicopter. He didn't use the cloud house to meditate because the supply of diluted crystal wash that was the fuel for its cleaning functions was a limited resource. Once he crossed the line to silver, there would be quite a mess.

Jason had fed everything from purgation quintessence to high-grade cleaning chemicals into the cloud flask, to lessen its reliance on crystal wash. There had been some measure of success, but it was ultimately stalling the inevitable. Jason had searched for a local substitute for crystal wash, but there was, in the end, nothing quite like the original.

For this reason, Jason chose not to cross over into silver rank in the cloud house where the finite supply of crystal wash would be tapped to clean some of the most intransigent filth it was possible to create. Instead, Jason chose the helicopter pad atop the main residence with its high-pressure cleaning systems. Farrah was watching over him, keeping her distance at the edge of the roof. She was not going to let anyone or anything interfere in one of the most important moments of Jason's life.

Standing at the edge of the roof, Farrah turned when she felt a surge of power behind her. Jason was in a cross-legged meditation pose, radiating silver light and floating an arm's length over the surface of the helipad. He unfolded his legs and dropped lightly to the rooftop.

Jason and Farrah shared a smile, but she didn't move closer, knowing the process had only just begun. Soon enough, Jason moved into the purge phase of his rank-up, his body excreting much of its mass right through the pores of his skin. Although it had already diverged quite a lot from a human's, there was still flesh, blood and bone in Jason's bronze-rank body. It was broken down and purged, oozing out of his skin until the skin was rendered down as well.

Jason's body was rendered down to a glowing entity of light, shining through the filth that stubbornly clung to it as it floated in the air. A tide of magic washed out of him, arresting the attention of everyone in Asano Village with magic or aura senses.

All around the village, those who had been given essences turned their head in Jason's direction. Some of the more distant ones set out to investigate, while the closer ones scrambled to get away from the crushingly oppressive strength of the aura projection. In the medical centre, the handful of Network personnel present felt like someone had walked over their grave.

Jason's aura continued to dominate the village as his body was remade within the silver light, growing from a kernel until a whole new body was in place, hidden under the muck. The light faded and he dropped to the rooftop, staggering but managing to keep his feet. Soon after, Farrah was washing him down with an industrial hose that would not have been out of place on a fire truck.

"How are you feeling?" she asked loudly.

"Like an inmate in a dystopian sci-fi prison movie," he called back as the powerful stream of water blasted him.

"You didn't pass out. That was good."

"I did get a bit woozy, but my energy is coming back fast."

"That's your silver-rank recovery attribute at work."

He had also consumed a silver-rank spirit coin.

"You should take down some proto-spaces to get a handle on your freshly advanced powers," Farrah suggested. "Especially since a good handful of your abilities ranked-up in a rush at the end."

"No time," Jason said. "I'm going to head for Japan today."

"Then I'm going with you. I've been cooped up with a bunch of ritualists for months, but now there's nothing more to do than wait for the grid to come back online. Now that you've hit silver rank, it's time for you and me to do some damage."

"It's a diplomatic trip," Jason said.

"Right up until it isn't," Farrah countered. "We should take my little apprentice, by the way."

As Farrah continued hosing him off, Jason thought about how adrift he had felt when he arrived in the other world. If Emi truly became an adventurer and joined his return to the other world, he wanted her as prepared as possible.

When Farrah was done, a thin film of hard-to-remove gunk still coated his new body. That much wouldn't be too taxing for a diluted crystal wash shower in the cloud house to remove. Jason opened a portal to the cloud house but paused before stepping through.

"You're right," he said. "We'll have to talk to her mother."

Jason felt like a live battery. He showered in the bathroom dome of the cloud house, still jittery from ranking up. Moving from bronze to silver was a significant jump in power and he could feel the magic moving through his body like an electrical current. He could feel the ambient magic in the world around him, in the air and the water splashing against his skin. Jason's ability to control his own physiology had reached a new level and he was able to regrow his hair simply by concentrating.

As he towelled himself off, he sensed Asya, Dawn and Farrah approach the cloud house through the underground tunnel. He also sensed something with them on the tram car. It appeared to be a large crate of magical materials. With his spirit attribute now silver rank, his perception no longer strained under the constant threat of sensory overload. He'd been working on managing it ever since his perception power ranked up, but now what had taken effort was a matter of ease.

Jason moved through a tunnel from the bathroom dome into a lounge dome, pouring a tray of drinks as he waited for Shade to show them in. Farrah arrived carrying the crate, which was more a challenge of awkwardness than weight, given her prodigious strength. Although they were both silver rank now, Jason's raw physical power was still no match for Farrah's.

"That's quintessence," Jason said, his magical senses recognising the contents of the crate. "It's all silver rank. That's a fortune."

"The international community wanted to show their appreciation for your efforts in Makassar," Asya said. "You saved a lot of lives, both in stalling out the second proto-space and dealing with the category four."

"I got lucky," Jason said. "It was a confluence of circumstances unlikely to be repeated."

"Not long after we met," Farrah said, "I mentioned to Rufus that you were lucky. You know what he told me?"

"Knowing Rufus, probably something he heard from his grandfather."

"Of course it was," Farrah chuckled. "He said that great adventurers are the ones that turn opportunity into fortune. Or something like that. The point is that when the same thing keeps happening, good or bad, eventually, you have to accept that it's not luck. It's you."

"You were not chosen by the World-Phoenix," Dawn said. "You were an opportunistic selection made available when you were drawn between worlds by happenstance, but we could have done far worse."

"Thank you," Jason said.

"We would have preferred Kaito, obviously," Dawn added, "but you can't have everything."

"That is ice cold," Asya said with a wincing chuckle as Jason looked at Dawn, slack-jawed.

"What kind of thing is that to say?" Jason asked.

"You punched my nose through my brain," Dawn said.

"What?" Asya asked.

"You're still complaining about that?" Jason asked.

"Coming from someone still angry they reused footage for the fourth season of *Airwolf*," Asya said. "I'm sorry, Jason, but that show was bad even before they cut the budget."

"I could swear this conversation started with thanking me for being great," Jason said. "It seems to have taken a turn."

"Nothing says thank you like a giant crate of quintessence," Farrah said.

"As I said," Asya explained, "the international community wanted to show their gratitude. The International Committee, the branches, everyone. China seemed especially grateful to avoid questions about a powerful secret weapon they didn't have to pull out."

"Asya had them dipping into their supplies for the good stuff," Farrah said.

"We know you've been trying to trade for certain hard-to-find materials for months," Asya said.

"What I've been after isn't enough to fill that crate," Jason said.

"I suggested we add in what you need to upgrade the cloud flask," Farrah said. "Dawn gave us the specific requirements."

"Farrah, that's a fortune in materials on your world," Jason said. "On this one, it's priceless."

"Jason," Asya said, "I'm not sure you understand how nervous the Network is about category-four threats. Every solution we have is expensive, untested and almost certainly going to have outrageous collateral damage. At category four, even a monster dumb and slow enough to stand in front of our heavy weapons is still an iffy proposition. One that's smart and fast? The Chinese sent us a magically enhanced nuclear device. It was our final contingency."

"Also, shut up and take the loot," Farrah said. "What kind of idiot complains about a huge pile of treasure?"

"Are you going to tell us you didn't pay a price in Makassar?" Asya asked.

"Of course I did," Jason said. "But so did thousands of others, starting with the citizens of Makassar. Are they all getting crates full of treasure shipped to them?"

"You were Rufus' student more than mine," Farrah said. "It seems you've picked up his habit of measuring himself by his failures. No matter how powerful he becomes, how skilled he is, he always focuses on the times he fell short. The people he couldn't help. I'm sure you saw it after I died."

"Yes," Jason acknowledged.

"It's the thing that makes him weak and holds him back," Farrah said. "You have your own flaws to be getting on with, so don't go taking his too."

"What flaws?"

"Are you serious? You believe in freedom but have the heart of a tyrant. You'll do what you think is right, regardless of what it costs or who gets in your way. That would be obnoxious enough if you were always right, but you have a nasty habit of getting confident first and informed second. Do you have any idea how much damage a self-righteous person with real power can do? Remember Anisa?"

Farrah shook her head.

"You have to recognise how much potential you have by now," she continued. "You're like Rufus in that so long as you get out of your own way, you're going to be one of the greats. More than me or Gary or even Emir. You just have to avoid destroying yourself along the way. Also, like Rufus, you're kind of a diva."

"A diva?"

"You were prone to melodrama long before you had magic," Asya said. "Also, your signature power is a sparkly cape."

"It's not a cape!"

"Look," Asya said. "The evacuees of Makassar are getting crates of food shipped to them because that's what they need. You got shipped a crate full of treasure because that's what you need. While you've been here ranking-up, Dawn and I have been briefing the Network on what happens after the grid comes back online. We need you as strong as you can be for that."

"Unless you think you're strong enough," Dawn added.

"There is no strong enough," Jason said.

"Which brings us back to you shutting up and taking the damn loot," Farrah said. "You can be such a pain to deal with sometimes. You turn the easiest thing in the world into a huge deal."

Jason looked around and saw three faces in agreement.

"Alright," Jason capitulated. "Give my thanks to whoever sent all this stuff."

"Oh, Terrance is going to have you record a bunch of thank-you videos," Asya said.

"That's what he thinks," Jason muttered, wandering over to the crate. He hefted it up and shoved it into his inventory before opening his spirit vault and walking in, leaving the three women behind.

"Where is he portalling to?" Asya asked.

"It's not a portal," Farrah said. "That leads to his spirit vault. It's the inside of his soul. Kind of. I think. I'm not entirely clear on the specifics."

"Jason's semi-spiritual nature had allowed one of his abilities to create an actual physical realm," Dawn explained. "You might consider him to be a living astral space."

Asya looked at the archway.

"His soul is through there?"

"It's more complicated than that," Dawn said, "but, broadly speaking, yes."

"Are we allowed to go in?" Asya asked. "He didn't say anything either way."

"You can only go in if you trust him," Farrah said. "And I mean really trust him, no reservations. He's the god of that world and has complete power over you in there. Unless you have complete faith in him, your own soul won't let you in. Jason's opinion is that anyone who can get in is allowed in."

Farrah turned her gaze on Dawn.

"Maybe she's powerful enough to not fall under his control."

"My true body, yes," Dawn said. "This avatar is incapable of entering Jason's vault. Or, more precisely, doing so would sever its link to my true self and it would die."

Asya moved hesitantly to the arch and raised a hand. It reached the darkness inside and stopped like it hit a wall.

"Complete trust isn't easy," Farrah reassured her. "It's okay to like him as much as you do and still have reservations."

"Can you get in?"

"When Jason and I were strangers and he was all but powerless, he threw himself into danger to save me and my companions. The kind of trust we're talking about comes from either a closeness you're still building to or from walking through fire together. Just because you aren't there yet doesn't mean you don't care about him."

"It means I have reservations."

"Of course you do," Farrah said. "Only Erika, Emi and I have been in there. If you had that kind of trust at this point in your relationship, that would not be healthy. You actually getting through that archway would probably scare him off."

"It would denote an inappropriate level of emotional investment," Dawn agreed. "Farrah does not want from him what you do. To trust as a friend and a companion is no small thing but does not require the same vulnerability as the kind of connection you want."

"I trust Jason with my life," Farrah said. "You probably would too, but the heart is a whole other thing. You're ready to start exploring that, but it's just that: the start. You are where you should be."

"Thank you," Asya said disconsolately.

"You should totally pin him down and knock one out, though," Farrah said. "He's stressed and you're so horny it's leaking out of your aura, even with that suppression bracelet."

While Asya looked scandalised, Farrah threw her the best impish Jason grin she could muster and ducked through the arch.

Jason's spirit vault had undergone another expansion and evolution with his ascension to silver rank. The first thing Jason noticed was that it was moving away from the stark black, white and red colours that had defined the previous iterations. Now the colours were more natural, and varied, less of a confronting assault on the senses.

The central pavilion was now a vast and elaborate series of interconnected, open-air buildings drawing on a mix of Asian and European styling. Jade, marble, bamboo and wood abounded, while at the centre there was still a four-sided pagoda.

The bottom floor of the pagoda held the four archways that were the centrepiece of the spirit vault. One archway was for Jason himself, through which he and Farrah emerged, while the others were for his familiars.

Even after dismissing their bronze-rank vessels, Jason could sense Colin and Gordon through the arches. Only if they decided to forgo being his familiars would that connection truly be lost as new astral beings took their places.

Materials started flying down from a hole in the ceiling, above which was the storage area higher in the pagoda. Blood quintessence flew down like a swarm of insects to dive into the archway that belonged to Colin. So long as he had the materials, Jason didn't need the ritual to summon new vessels for his familiars, but could use the archways instead. He had only used the ritual with Shade as a publicity exercise.

Colin's arch was the familiar obsidian, but instead of being filled with darkness like Jason's portals, there was a sheet of wet blood. In the past,

Colin's new vessels had emerged in a rapidly escalating stream of leeches that piled up. This time, something wholly different emerged.

It was a humanoid figure, wrapped in a hooded cloak over combat robes, all dark red leather in shades of dried blood. It stepped forward with none of the clumsy stumblings of Colin's bronze-rank form, striding confidently up to Jason. It raised hands with the red-purple hue of a bruise and pushed back the hood. The face underneath was identical to Jason's except for the skin, which was the same dark colouration as the hands, and the eyes, which were glistening red orbs.

"Aren't you fancy?" Jason said with a smile and held out a hand, palm up. "Would you like to show off a little?"

The Jason-clone exploded into a fountain of leeches, one of which landed on Jason's hand and he stroked it gently with his thumb.

"G'day, little mate."

The scattered leeches all shot out streamers of red leather, glistening wet, that converged on a central point and dragged the scattered leeches together, reforming the humanoid shape. The whole process happened in a flash, taking only a few seconds. Then Colin stepped forward and melted into Jason's body, vanishing in an instant.

Jason felt a connection to his familiar's biomass much greater than in the past. His new silver-rank body was akin to that of Colin's. Rather than it vanishing entirely, like a normal summoned familiar, Colin seemed to at least partially have merged with him. It didn't bulk him out, but his already heavy body grew heavier still.

He suspected that his growing symbiosis with Colin was not just a factor of Colin's growing strength but also Jason's nature, blending spiritual and physical elements. He anticipated that more so than Shade or Gordon, there would be additional effects that he would need to explore over time.

One effect that was a result of Colin's new rank he could already sense. His body became shrouded in dark mist. His clothes vanished into his inventory, which in his spirit vault meant whipping off his body and flying up through the hole in the ceiling. Then his body became covered in a slick coating of blood, seeping through the pores in his skin. That blood thickened and solidified into a leather combat robe. It looked much like the one worn by Colin's new humanoid form, minus the hood and with an even darker red colouration.

Item: [Sanguine Raiment] (silver rank, conjured)

Conjured robes with the power and resilience of an apocalypse beast (armour, cloth/leather).

- Effect: Increased resistance to damage. Highly effective against cutting and piercing damage, less effective against blunt damage.

- Effect: Heal over time effects have increased strength and duration. This effect scales with the amount of familiar biomass being shared with the summoner and amplifies the passive healing the familiar provides.

- Effect: Drain abilities have increased effect. This effect scales with the amount of familiar biomass being shared with the summoner.

- Effect: Resistance to blood effects is significantly increased.

- Effect: Can be used to make ranged grapple attacks. Health is continually drained from grappled enemies.

The mist faded and Farrah looked Jason up and down. He conjured his cloak to complete the ensemble, shadow draped over dark red.

"Nice to see you embrace the 'I'm coming to kill your children' look," Farrah said.

"It's not that bad, is it?"

"It's alright," Farrah said. "You're now the first person I'd think of if I woke up to find my livestock drained of blood, but it's fine."

"Wow. Alright, let's see what Gordon has got going on."

As with Colin, materials came flying down and into Gordon's arch, a dark void containing the familiar eye nebula. Gordon's new vessel floated out. It looked much the same as before, with a disembodied cloak containing the blue and orange nebula in the chest. The difference was that instead of four blue and orange eye-spheres orbiting him, there were now six. The orbs were also slightly different than before; instead of half being predominantly orange and the other half blue, all six were an even mix of the two.

Gordon drifted closer and Jason reached out to touch him, to get a sense of the familiar's new abilities. Unlike his other powers, the abilities of his familiars were not included with the description of the power that summoned them. When he touched Gordon, a list of the powers appeared and Jason raised his eyebrows as he read them.

"Bloody hell, Gordon."

"You look different," Erika said as Jason walked into the study of the main residence. She put down the computer tablet she was working on and studied Jason's face.

"I am different."

"You know, if this keeps up, you and Kaito will look like twins."

"That's not uncommon," Farrah said, following Jason through the door. "Siblings who are essence users often become quite similar, physically."

"Great," Jason said unhappily.

"I don't see why you're complaining," Farrah said. "You're the one who wins in that deal."

Erika and Farrah laughed at the affront on Jason's face, which then settled into a serious expression.

"What is it?" Erika asked.

"We need to talk about Emi," Jason said.

"What about her?"

"I'd like to start taking her with me more as I do things. If the day does come where we're in the other world, she needs as much experience under her belt as she can get."

"Jason, I look at how different you are from the brother I grew up with. How much death have you seen in the last week? If you tell me that it didn't mess you up, I'll call you a liar, and you want to drag my thirteen-year-old daughter closer to that?"

"I'm not talking about the violent stuff," Jason said. "My friend Humphrey was fifteen when he received his essences, but his mother wouldn't let him become an adventurer until he was seventeen. She spent years before and after he claimed his essences in training and preparation, not just fighting but taking him around the world. Letting him experience different cultures and see the aspects of being an adventurer that aren't about fighting and killing."

"That's easy to say," Erika said. "What happens when things go wrong?"

"Of course they're going to go wrong," Jason said. "Hiding her away just means that she won't be ready when they do. You said that I'm not the person I was before and that's true. I was thrown into this with no foundation under my feet and I've been tumbling ever since. I want to give her the grounding that I never had."

"We want to give her that," Farrah added. "Jason talked about his friend Humphrey and my friend Rufus experienced much the same. Your daughter isn't exactly a princess, Eri, but she isn't exactly not, either."

Erika rubbed a hand over her mouth thoughtfully.

"I don't like it," she said. "That being said, not liking something doesn't make it go away. When are you leaving?"

"This afternoon," Jason said.

"Then the answer is no," Erika said. "I'm not going to allow this without taking the time to think it through and discuss it properly with my husband."

"We can push it back to the morning," Farrah said. "Give you the night."

"We can?" Jason asked, looking at Farrah. "Alright, but I've delayed longer than I should already. We leave first thing, with Emi or without her."

A plane that looked more like a spaceship designed by ninjas hovered over the helipad of the Asano Village main residence. The air rushing down to keep it aloft tore at the clothes of the people gathered underneath and made it impossible to talk. There was a cluster of people present: Jason, Farrah, Dawn, Asya, Akari, Emi, Erika, her husband, Ian, and Jason and Erika's grandmother, Yumi.

Yumi was unrecognisable from her previous self, now that she had received a full set of essences. Concerned about the infirmity of age, she had chosen essences designed to work around it. After lengthy discussions with Farrah, she chose the blood, flesh and bone essences, giving her the avatar confluence. As a result, she had been able to remake her body into an idealised version of her younger self, and now looked no older than Jason.

A heavy platform descended from the bottom of the plane, attached by cable on each corner. Ian kissed his wife and daughter a silent goodbye and watched as the others rose into the body of the plane. The moment the platform sealed them inside, the rushing air died off, allowing them to speak.

"Let's go sit down so Shade can get some altitude without tipping us over," Jason said.

The Japan party had expanded; Erika was only allowing Emi to go with parental supervision. As Ian was busy with the medical centre, she decided to join the trip herself, passing the administrative tasks of the village over to her sister-in-law. Yumi had also gotten wind of the trip and added herself, which Jason had not resisted.

As they made their way from the room with the entry platform to the passenger compartment, the others looked around Shade's plane form. It was the size of a private jet, and with Jason now silver rank, there was no costly drain on his mana.

"I didn't realise there were this many shades of black," Yumi observed, looking around at the plane's décor.

They settled in to the flight and Yumi started probing Jason as to the actual purpose of the trip. Jason remained evasive. The magic door that was their objective was a secret restricted to himself, Dawn, Farrah and Akari. He was happy to run the others on the plane around in conversational circles as it kept his mind occupied. The bloody events of the past week continued to prey on his mind, and he found surrounding himself with friends and family to be a welcome distraction.

"Why isn't Mike with us this time?" Jason asked.

"Aram is still in Makassar," Asya explained. "There's going to a be a huge international contingent there for months, if not years. At least, there should be."

"Problems?" Jason asked.

"The Indonesian government has been making noise about the Network coming in and taking over," Asya explained. "They've been trying to seize control of Network assets, which has gone exactly as well as you'd expect. There's also the lingering hostility with the local Cabal. The next battle in Makassar will be a diplomatic one."

A few hours into the flight, one of Shade's bodies appeared next to Asya.

"Miss Karadeniz, Mr Aram wishes to contact you quite urgently. If you would please follow me to the communications compartment."

Asya followed Shade and came back a few minutes later as the plane shifted course. Jason frowned, remembering the news that caused a course-change on their last trip to Japan.

"Please tell me there isn't another gold-rank proto-space that got missed," he said to Asya.

"No," she said, her expression grave. "The next battle in Makassar won't be political after all."

On top of a semi-ruined building in Makassar, a portal arch rose up and Jason stepped through in his dark robes and starlight cloak. Jason had brought his full contingent of Shades, having left the rest of the passengers in Dili, which was just inside Jason's new maximum portal range for reaching Makassar. His portal was only strong enough to transport one silver-ranker, so he had Farrah stored in his spirit vault. Now that they were both silver-rankers, that no longer prevented his portal ability from working. He opened another archway to let her out and they moved to the edge of the building.

The news out of Makassar had been horrifying; seeing it for themselves was even worse. From their vantage on the rooftop, they could see two-storey monstrosities of dead flesh and ugly steel. Zombie giants of flesh augmented by iron implants shambled through the streets.

Around the giants, the multitudes of dead victims of Makassar yet to be extracted from the ruins rose to join them as shambling dead. Jason's fist clenched at his side as the bodies of the people he had failed to save the first time around were desecrated. He could sense the death magic emitted by the giants being invested into the corpses.

"For all that they're monstrous," Farrah said, "those things aren't actual monsters."

Jason pushed aside his fury, focusing on one of the giants. There was plenty of magic coursing through it, but as Farrah said, it was not the magic of a monster. It had the artificial feel of a living thing altered through magic, a feeling Jason was familiar with.

"This feels like the Builder's magic," he said, his voice carrying the hard chill of permafrost. "Someone made those things."

Extending his senses to the limit, he could sense the Network and Cabal presence already in conflict with the zombie giants and the army of the dead animated around them. He vaulted off the edge of the building, gliding with his cloak as he aimed for the closest zombie giant.

Jason could sense it was silver rank, as was the death magic it invested into the zombies rising up around it. That posed a potentially larger threat than the dinosaur monsters, through strength in numbers alone. The early death toll estimates were between one and two hundred thousand, which would be an ocean of silver-rank zombies. They knew the zombies would be far weaker than even the most meagre of silver-rank monsters, but a tsunami of them would be a terror to anyone without the power to deal with them.

Jason grimaced as he approached the ground, furious at being forced to take the fight to what had become victims in both life and death. Despite their unliving flesh, he did not draw his sword, having left it in his inventory. Instead, he conjured his dagger as he landed on the ground in front of the giant.

Gordon manifested next to Jason and immediately fired orange beams at the ordinary zombies slowly staggering in their direction. Each orb could now fire whichever of the two beam options was appropriate instead of being locked in, on top of the entirely new functions they had gained at silver rank.

With Gordon holding off the slow-moving horde, Jason chanted a spell at the giant.

"Bleed for me."

After Jason chanted his spell, blood flowed from the giant. Not the thick, black blood of the dead, but bright, red and fresh. Jason's Haemorrhage spell added a new affliction at silver rank.

- [Blood From a Stone] (affliction, magic): Negates immunity to blood and poison effects. This includes intrinsic immunities, such as from not having a biology or corporeal form. Entities without blood can bleed while under this effect. Cannot be cleansed while any blood or poison affliction is in effect.

Jason cast another spell.

"Carry the mark of your transgressions."

- [Mortality] (affliction, magic): Negates immunity to curses. This includes intrinsic immunities such as from not having a soul or not being alive. Cannot be cleansed while any curse affliction is in effect.

The giant slowly turned on Jason as his dagger shot out on the end of a shadow arm. His Hand of the Reaper power also added a new affliction to any attack made with his shadow arm.

- [Weakness of the Flesh] (affliction, magic): Negates immunities to disease and necrotic damage. This includes intrinsic immunities, such as from not having a biology or corporeal form. Cannot be cleansed while any disease affliction is in effect.

Jason went to work locking in the rest of his affliction suite, the sluggish monstrosity being strangely helpless for its rank. It had the resilience and strength of a silver-rank monster but the speed of an iron rank, and posed no threat to Jason.

"Gordon," Jason said.

The familiar floated into the air, halting its beam attacks. All six of

Gordon's orbs left his orbit and flew down to disappear into the dead flesh of the giant. Although it would take a minute for Gordon to conjure up new orbs, the new affliction they delivered was worth it.

Six black butterflies with blue and orange wing colouration in the familiar eye pattern were conjured on the body of the giant, immediately flying off to land on and disappear into nearby zombies. Shortly thereafter, butterflies manifested on them, finding more zombies as they spread and spread until butterflies were streaming out of the entire zombie horde and the sky was thick with the beautiful orange and blue creatures.

The effect on the zombies was significantly less appealing than the colourful display in the air above them. Like the giant, their bodies started flowing with red blood and their already rotting flesh underwent rapid decomposition.

- [Harbinger of Doom] (affliction, unholy, stacking): Continually drain mana from the victim to conjure a butterfly that seeks out nearby enemies. The butterflies are incorporeal and deal disruptive force damage in a small area when destroyed. Butterflies that contact enemies inflict one instance of each non-holy affliction present on the enemy it manifested from, including [Harbinger of Doom]. This effect cannot be cleansed while any other non-holy affliction is in effect. Additional instances can be accumulated. At the time of manifestation, one butterfly is generated for each instance of this affliction.

Jason's full suite of afflictions was carried by every butterfly, moving out like the tide. He didn't even bother to fight anymore, watching the giant in front of him with malevolence as its body rotted. Even the iron and steel components of its body were bleeding and rotting as if they were flesh.

As the monster crumbled in front of him, Farrah approached. She had used her own chaining area attacks, so the zombies were not just rapidly decomposing but on fire as well.

"We need to find who did this," Jason said.

"Yes," Farrah agreed darkly. "These people had it bad enough, without being turned into grotesque, undead puppets. How do we find them, though?"

"I only know one group with access to the Builder's magic," Jason said. "We let the Network dig into it while we go to Japan."

"You think this is an attempt to stall us?"

"It's possible. We've delayed too much, in any case. We can see what the Network has dug up by the time we're done in Japan. Two angry people can't match the investigative power of the entire Network, after all."

32
OLD AFFAIRS

The Four Cardinals of the EOA were sitting at the desk in their meeting chamber. On the wall, a news report was on the large screen.

"…Asano is believed to be responsible for what people are calling 'the Butterflies of Makassar,' which look so beautiful when filmed from high in the air, but once the colourful wave passed, only black-stained bones are left in their wake. Recently, in the wake of another humanitarian disaster, Asano was recorded warning the League of Heroes that his power was still growing. Many are speculating that we've seen exactly that as Asano joined top Global Defense Network members in putting a stop to the tide of wandering dead. GDN members from China and the US have made a big splash…"

Adrien Barbou silenced the report with a remote control. Although he was the new Mr East, he was already no longer the latest cardinal to join the ranks. The new Mrs South spoke up.

"The Network will try and pin this on us," she said.

"Was it us?" Barbou asked.

"Of course it wasn't," Mrs West barked. She was unhappy with the ally she had cultivated in Barbou being poached by Mr North but was not foolish enough to take it up with Mr North himself. Instead, she kept her ire for the new Mr East. "Why would we be insane enough to bring the world down on us when we're about to make our final move?"

"Actually," Mr North said, "I suspect we may bear a connection to this that could lead us to being liable if we don't get to the one responsible first."

"What connection?" Mrs West asked.

"We have not explored necromancy as a path to power in some years," Mr North explained. "There was a time, however, when we did conduct some experiments using some of the unique methods to which we have access. I believe what we witnessed in Makassar was an extension of those long-discarded experiments. I can only postulate that the person continuing that research saw hundreds of thousands of dead as an opportunity for field trials."

"You know who this is?" Mrs South asked.

"I have my suspicions. I believed the individual in question was long dead."

"He was part of the joint research program," Barbou guessed.

"Yes," Mr North said. "The previous Mrs South was meant to have scrubbed all traces of the project, but developments surrounding her defection have shown us that she was less thorough than she reported. Mrs South, I will be expecting you to root out any more remnants your predecessor left unchecked. Mr East, I will give you what I have and you can try and beat the Network to the punch and find our necromancer first."

"The Network has the old Mrs South," Barbou said. "I'm unlikely to find him first unless you know something to give me a head start."

"I do not," Mr North said. "I fully anticipate the task being impossible, but we might get lucky. Mrs South, your task will be to dig up anything you can that your predecessor left on the joint research project. If the Network attempts to paint us as the perpetrators of Makassar, I want ammunition that paints us all the same colour."

"And what about the final step in our plan?" Mrs West asked. "Will you be conducting that yourself?"

"I will leave the endgame in your capable hands," Mr North told her. "I am handing off full control of the final stage to you."

"You are?"

"I am aware that with the rapid changes in our leadership structure under the pressure of current events, you have not been entirely satisfied with the outcomes," Mr North said. "I can think of no better demonstration that you are valued and trusted than to give you complete control over the final stage of the plan. You are versed in all the particulars and familiar with all the players. I have been preparing you for this for a long time, Mrs West."

"Thank you," Mrs West said, visibly shaken. "But if I'm going to be in charge of the final stage, then what are you going to be doing?"

"Revisiting old affairs," Mr North said. "The time has come to make an acquaintance I have been anticipating for centuries before he was even born."

The Network's category-three tactical operatives once more poured into Makassar from around the world. This time, the focus was on those with powers to contain the specific threat at hand, although most silver-rankers had some answer to numerical danger. Most essence abilities were tactical in nature and affected a small handful of targets at best. It was at silver rank that most essence users found themselves better equipped to confront groups.

The undead were not a danger in the way the monsters had been. The city had been evacuated of the living and the risen dead had individual strength akin to a low-end bronze monster, and a mediocre one at that. They also were slow and completely lacking in exotic or even basic ranged attacks. This meant that bronze-rankers could be mobilised to add to the damage.

Unfortunately, the one area the zombies were at a silver-rank standard was in resilience. With silver-rank damage reduction and silver-rank durability, the ocean of animate dead was a difficult tide to push back. Rather than pour on less effective damage, the bronze-rankers were used to bait the unthinking undead, luring them into clusters to maximise the area attacks of the silver-rankers.

The undead were little threat to even bronze-rankers. The danger was not in confronting the hordes forming across the city but containing them. So long as they were kept from the evacuation points containing the city's surviving populace, the animate dead were a horrific but unimposing enemy.

After exhausting their mana and stamina, bronze and silver-rankers alike were pulled back to recover. The Network spared no expense in their use of spirit coins and potions to get them heading back out as quickly as possible. The biggest problem in dealing with the undead was their numbers and toughness, although, in certain corners of the city, the dead were being swept aside as if by a cleansing wind.

A healer from the United States with the life essence had an aura that infused the people around him with life energy. Normally, this increased the effectiveness of healing powers, which he could employ discriminately to affect only allies or everyone within the range of his aura. As one of the USA's elite, he fully explored the capability of his powers and found a potent interaction. When his life magic came into conflict with the death magic animating the zombies, the reaction was literally explosive, sending detonated gobbets of dead flesh scattering over the area. He could literally annihilate waves of undead, simply by walking amongst them as flying chunks of rot struck his force field and fell to the ground.

As the rest of his essences were magic, renewal and immortal, his abilities didn't just prevent him from becoming exhausted and needing to stop. He could also replenish other essence users, allowing him to keep them in the field for longer. He was one of a handful that, like Jason, combined a highly effective strategy with unflagging endurance.

The USA and China both finally demonstrated their power on the world stage, where Jason had so long been the focus of attention. Names that were already well known in their home countries were shown in their full power and glory since media were cleared to film from the air.

The US and Chinese silver-rankers were much more capable than the world standard. They demonstrated the fundamental truth that only in finding the synergies within their own power set would an essence user truly become capable. Even so, only a few floated to the top as the richest cream, demonstrating both power and endurance.

Even with an estimated two hundred thousand zombies, there was a constant influx of powerhouse individuals who could fully unleash against a sluggish enemy with no tricks beyond numbers and toughness. Within twenty-four hours, the operation went from desperate containment to a mop-up. The strange, undead giants were dead and the zombies they had animated were reduced to a handful of isolated pockets.

Jason left the clean-up to others, portalling back to Timor-Leste, where he had left the others while he portalled to Makassar with Farrah. Shortly thereafter, a sleek black jet was winging them in the direction of Japan once more. Also aboard with Jason and Farrah were Asya, Akari, Dawn, Erika and Emi. Joining them was Jason's grandmother, Yumi, whose essence combination had restored her youthful body.

"Do you think someone is trying to distract you from Japan?" Farrah asked Jason as they all sat together in a passenger cabin.

"No," Jason said. "I won't rule it out for the undead, given that someone was acting with deliberation, but I would count it as extremely unlikely. As for the original monster wave, not a chance."

"Agreed," Akari said. "No one is going to wipe out a city just to distract one person. With all the pieces that would have to be moved into place for a result that could only be counted as unreliable, it's simply not a feasible hypothesis."

"Good points," Farrah said. "If anything, it would have been an assassination attempt. Bait Jason out, have him burn through his mana and strike while he's exposed."

"That didn't happen, though," Emi said as her mother gave her a concerned glance. For the most part, Emi was staying quiet, listening and learning. She knew that her access to the adult conversations was predicated on not interrupting, however much she might *really* want to.

"Jason's new level of power meant that he was never pushed in terms of tactics or resources," Farrah said. "They may have given up without trying after seeing his new power level."

"It still seems like a stretch," Jason said. "The most likely scenario is that it had nothing to do with me. I'm not much more than a face on TV to most people. The real game is the EOA-Network-Cabal triangle. Makassar happened because, even now, they are jostling each other over petty power-grabs instead of what they should be doing. Outside of a PR perspective, they don't care about me that much."

"He's right," Asya said. "Jason matters a great deal to the Network internally, but because he's always refused to subject himself to it, he's immaterial to the political conflicts with the EOA and the Cabal. He's been a part of this for less than a year, compared to decades or even centuries of tension and contest. Although he provides the Network with a lot, it's not enough to tip those ancient scales."

"I am left wondering how someone even got all of those unliving giant things into Makassar," Akari said. "They are neither subtle nor small and there were so many of them."

"Questions the Network is better equipped to deal with than us," Jason said. "We should leave the investigation to them."

"I'm not sure they'd want you anyway, after what you told that reporter," Asya said. "Terrance was fuming when he called me after to give me an earful."

"Let him fume," Jason said.

"What did you say?" Yumi asked.

"That every magical faction bears some of the responsibility for Makassar," Jason said.

"What you said was 'blood is on every hand,' which is going to be hitting news reports right around now," Asya said.

"It's not untrue," Jason said. "The EOA caused the situation with the monsters while the Network and the Cabal were so busy scrabbling over petty territorial concerns that they let disaster through the gate they were meant to be guarding."

"I believe Terrance wanted to lay this at the EOA's feet."

"HE DOESN'T GET TO!" Jason roared, leaping out of his chair. "You tell Terrance that if he's more interested in looking like the good guys than being the good guys, the relationship between me and the Network is about to undergo a fundamental shift. If he wants me to spin the death and subsequent defilement of hundreds of thousands, then he is free to come find me and see how that proposal goes when he makes it in person!"

Jason stormed out of the cabin towards the private sleeping cabins in the rear.

"Is Uncle Jason alright?" Emi asked, her voice hesitant in the tense atmosphere.

"He's alright," Erika said, reaching out to give her daughter's hand a squeeze. "He just saw a lot of bad things lately. I'd be more worried if he wasn't upset."

"You can't witness what was done to those poor people without getting angry," Farrah said. "Unfortunately, we have nowhere to put that anger right now and we need to be cool-headed for when we arrive in Japan. I think your uncle is just trying to burn off some frustration, even if he doesn't realise that's what he's doing."

Farrah stood up.

"Speaking of which," she said, "I'm going to take some time for myself. I've only seen a zombie horde like that once before, when I was a new adventurer, and this was much worse. Your movies fail to capture the true horror of watching people reduced to grotesque marionettes."

She also headed for the sleeping cabins.

33
END RUN

As Shade, in his plane form, continued winging towards Japan, Jason was lying on the bed in a small sleeping cabin. Fresh from the land of the dead that Makassar had become, his mind was troubled. He looked at the door; there was no knock, but he felt Asya's presence on the other side.

"Come in," he said.

She entered hesitantly, unconsciously touching a hand to the aura-suppression bracelet that kept her from broadcasting her emotions. She had aura control training, but Jason's senses were strong enough that he would passively pick up on them anyway until she was stronger.

"I'm sorry to disturb you," Asya said. "Erika thought that maybe you need someone to talk to instead of brooding it out. She said that was your go-to move, but you don't have another six years to learn it isn't very effective."

Jason chuckled, despite himself, and sat up on the bed. He patted the spot next to him, even though there was a free chair.

"I'm trying to be healthier," he said.

She sat next to him.

"I don't want to complain," he continued. "Not when I've just been to a place where not only did so many die horribly, but they weren't even allowed to rest in peace."

"You're entitled to your feelings," Asya said. "Just because someone else is miserable doesn't mean you aren't allowed to be unhappy for yourself. You just have to keep it in perspective."

He gave her a sad smile, bumping his shoulder genially into hers.

"Thanks," he said. "I learned back in debate club that you were smarter than me. And better organised. It's why I always tried to throw you off with weirdness."

"You try and throw everyone off with weirdness."

"Yeah, but I eventually spotted the little streak of weird in you too. You hide it under all this well-groomed competence, but I remember when I was using the difference between vehicle Voltron and Lion Voltron as an analogy for the positive aspects of authoritarianism and you completely turned it around on me, without missing a beat."

"I remember that," she chuckled.

"I almost asked you out after that."

"Seriously?"

"Princess Asya was not meant to have even heard of Voltron, let alone know that much about vehicle Voltron, even though it's the crap one. Be still my heart."

"But you didn't ask me out."

"No," he said, shoulders slumping. "You know how it was."

"I do," she said sadly. "Can I be honest?"

"Always."

"I've always hated Amy's guts."

Jason burst out laughing.

"I think we can add character judgement to the list of things you're better at than I am. Although I'm pretty sure, at this point, the list is just most of the things."

"Don't sell yourself short, Jason. Do you have any idea how intimidating you are?"

"Of course I am. I have spooky magic powers."

"Not like that," she said. "Not to strangers. I'm talking about to people who know you. I was born with every advantage. My family had money and influence. My education was the best, not just the academy but private tutors, international study trips just for me and my brothers. I had so much going for me and I worked so hard to make the most of it. I had this life plan. Federal police. Federal bureaucrat. Federal office. I was going to be Prime Minister one day."

"I believe you," Jason said sincerely. "If that still happens, please do something about media monopolisation."

"I'll see what I can do," she laughed, "but don't get your hopes up. When the Network recruited me, I discovered a whole new world where I could not just do but become things I never imagined."

"When I discovered magic, I found out I could get hit with a shovel a lot and then sacrificed."

"My introduction was more measured," she said, "but it was also more shackled. You were thrown in a world full of wildness and danger and you didn't just survive, but thrived."

"Technically, I didn't survive."

"Life threw you in the fire and you came out reforged. You came back, striding across the world like you owned it. You were always confident, Jason, but there was a hollowness to it. After getting to know you, I realised that a lot of it was façade. Not anymore."

"I was a teenager. Of course it was empty confidence."

"When the Network recruited me, I was so impressed with myself for becoming a person worthy of being drawn into a world of magic. But you were literally drawn into a world of magic, facing dangers and having experiences I can't imagine, even now. Being a functionary for the Network seemed so amazing until you let me see your recordings. The things you saw. The things you did."

Jason bowed his head.

"There's so much those recordings don't show," he said. "I was so scared. And when I thought about coming home, I was thinking of Erika cooking barbecue by the beach while I played with Emi. Not wading through an army of the dead that I failed to save in the first place."

He bowed his head.

"I don't think I'm built for this," he whispered. "I'm not the guy who saves the world. I'm the comic relief sidekick."

"No one is asking you to save the world."

"We haven't told you the real reason we're so adamant about getting to Japan, have we? I'm sure you've realised it's more than just visiting the Asano clan."

"I assumed you'd tell me when you are ready. My being part of the Network complicates things, I know."

He turned to look directly at her.

"I've always found that trusting in people, rather than the groups they belong to, has always steered me right. I don't trust the Network to do what's right or best, but I trust you to at least try."

She smiled. "You're not a comic relief sidekick, Jason. You're a bunny-ears lawyer."

"You think so?"

"No one is ambivalent to you, Jason. I hate to break it to you, but as long as I've known you, everyone has either really liked you or *really* didn't but put up with you for one reason or another. Anna would put you in a rocket and fire you into the sun if not for the loot hose you've been spraying into her branch."

"I got that impression."

"I've been on both sides of that coin. When you first swaggered into debate club, spewing nonsense at a hundred kilometres an hour, I wanted you gone so badly. Your actual debate skills were never great, but you always had that way of pulling people into your pace. So I tolerated you until I realised I wasn't just tolerating you anymore. You'd dug under my skin, like a tick."

"Like a tick? Any chance of getting a better simile?"

"Nope," she said with a grin. "You are everything I should hate. I prepare, you improvise. I'm professional; you're casual to the point of self-destructiveness. I always take the best path while you blow up the path, use it to make a new path that's all wonky and doesn't go the right way, yet somehow you get where you're going. Mostly."

"The trick is to not worry about the destination."

"I always worry about the destination. You take the risks I never would, with the courage to accept the consequences I never could."

"You make me sound kind of awesome."

"This would be the part where you tell me the things you like about me."

"Oh, I hated you too. So stuck up, as if meeting people's expectations was some kind of higher calling. Obviously, I was attracted anyway. I was sixteen and you were so smart and sharp, like an evil lady torturer. Plus, you already looked like the winning entry in a design-an-absurdly-gorgeous-woman contest."

"I'm not sure you understand how compliments work."

"I told you that I hated you at the start. I thought you were just another rich-prick automaton, built from your parents' money. Then I started catching glimpses behind the curtain. Why did a rich girl in 2010 know anything about Tom Selleck's moustache? Then there's the way you throw yourself so hard into everything. You put on this reserved face, but you show your passion with how much you invest in everything you do. That was kind of annoying in debate club, but watching you kite surf was one of the sexiest things I have ever seen. How were you that good?"

"I took lessons."

"Of course you did. It makes total sense that you tried to join the Federal Police, overshot and wound up in the magic police. I bet you overdid it there too."

"I originally signed up for tactical," she admitted. "I wanted to learn how to use my powers properly. They let me do the training because they let anyone with a full essence set, but they pushed me into a management track. It turned out to be a blessing in disguise since I never ended up using cores."

Jason chuckled.

"That drive you have is still very sexy."

"Most men I meet don't like that about me," she whispered. "They want to slow me down, bring me to heel. They look at everything I've done for my own ambition like I'm filling out my wife resume and expect me to give it up and settle down."

"You must know a lot of really dumb guys."

"Every woman knows a lot of really dumb guys, Jason. My mother likes to set me up. I never really got over this weirdo I knew in high school, though."

"He must have been really good-looking."

"He had a chin that could cut glass, but he's had a lot of work done."

"I have not had any work do—"

His indignation was cut off by a pair of soft lips pressing into his.

When Jason and Asya returned to the main cabin, all eyes turned to them.

"What?" Jason asked.

Erika shook her head, although a smile played at the corners of her mouth.

"You could at least be a little discreet," Yumi told him.

"Shade," Jason whispered. "Did you soundproof the cabin like I told you?"

"You can't soundproof social cues, Mr Asano."

"Yeah, that's fair. Where's Emi?"

"In the cockpit," Shade said. "I'm teaching her to fly a plane."

"Oh, nice."

Jason and Erika were sitting in the cockpit together while Emi was back telling her great-grandmother all about what she'd learned. They relaxed with glasses of iced tea and looked out at the open sky.

"So, Asya," Erika said.

"Uh, yeah. I know it doesn't seem like the time."

"It's exactly the time," Erika said. "I've been watching you pull deeper and deeper into yourself, Jason, and I've seen where that leads when the only ones relying on you are me and Emi. I don't want to see that when the stakes are so much higher. In times like these, you should take the joys you can find."

"Thanks."

"Maybe next time don't take them in a confined space with my daughter nearby."

"Sorry. It wasn't really planned."

"So, is this a thing, now, or were you just blowing off steam?"

"We haven't talked about it, but it's a thing. I'd be lying if I said I didn't have concerns, though."

"Like your plans to traipse off to another universe?"

"Yeah."

"Are you worried that she'll want to go with you, or that she won't?"

"I don't know. Both, somehow, if that makes any sense. My biggest worry is that she's more invested than I am, emotionally. I'm not saying I don't feel anything, but she's further down that road than I am."

"Baby brother, it doesn't matter where you are now. It matters where you're going. If you both end up in the same place, then great. If not, then you have bigger concerns than a relationship that didn't work. Try and figure it out before you drag her off to another universe, though, yeah?"

"I'll do my best."

"She had a thing for you back in school, right?"

"It wasn't wholly unreciprocated," Jason said. "But then Amy..."

"Did it never occur to you that Amy finally taking you off the shelf right as you took a healthy interest in someone else wasn't a coincidence?"

"I'm not a complete idiot."

Erika looked at him from under raised eyebrows.

"I'm not!"

Emi was back in the cockpit while Jason watched her listen to Shade's flight instructions with an adorable look of concentration on her face. Asya opened the door, calling Jason back into the main cabin with the other passengers.

"I was just contacted by the Network," Asya explained. "Details are still sketchy, but it's looking like as many as nineteen countries are about to divest themselves from the Network."

"Divest themselves how?" Farrah asked.

"The information I have suggests it will vary by country," Asya explained. "We don't have anything solid yet, but none of it is good. Reports are ranging from expelling Network personnel to forcibly seizing Network infrastructure."

"Doing that now is madness," Akari said.

"No," Jason said. "The grid is about to come back online. Assuming you knew that, it would be the perfect time to swoop in."

"He's right," Asya said. "The EOA are making their end run. All the countries in question are having them take on the Network's responsibilities."

"The EOA doesn't have the people or the resources," Farrah said. "Or access to the grid."

"Which is about to put the Network in an awkward position," Asya said. "Does the Network fight the local government and stay present anyway? If we do, suddenly, we look like a despotic force and support for us around the world dries up. If we accept being tossed out, suddenly, we have a nasty choice. Either leave those nations to be overrun by monster waves, or give the EOA the tools, knowledge and access to the grid to stop them."

"Giving the EOA the legitimacy and power it has always been after," Jason said. "Which countries?"

"Indonesia is the lynchpin," Asya said. "They aren't happy about magical factions either ignoring or running roughshod over them. The EOA swooped in and made similar approaches to other nations. Venezuela, Myanmar, North Korea, Iran, Turkey, the Philippines, Taiwan."

"Taiwan?" Jason asked.

"The Network is very established in China."

"Ah."

"What is the Network's response?" Farrah asked.

"I don't know," Asya said.

"It doesn't change what we have to do," Jason said. "Not unless Japan is on that list."

"It's not," Asya said.

"Alright, then," Jason said. "It's not like we could do anything about it anyway. We do what we can do and leave diplomacy to the diplomats."

34
GIVING FACE

"Are we landing at Kansai International Airport?" Emi asked as she emerged from the cockpit. "It's on an artificial island."

Jason looked up from the book of astral magic theory he was reading.

"Sorry, Moppet," Jason told her. "I'd love to do some exploring with you, but we've already had too many delays. Dropping right out of the sky should be fun, though, right?"

"What do you mean, right out the sky?" Erika asked.

"We're going to fly right over Ashiya and jet suit down," Jason explained.

"Oh, I'm sorry," Erika said. "I must have totally forgotten when you explained that YOU'RE GOING TO THROW US ALL OUT OF AN AEROPLANE!"

"Totally understandable," Jason genially acknowledged. "It's a busy time for everyone, so slips of the mind are only to be expected. Do we have an ETA, Shade?"

"I will be starting the descent to drop height in approximately nine minutes," Shade said.

"You've told them we're about to arrive, right?" Jason asked Akari.

"Yes, I already got the estimated time from Shade and notified my father," Akari said. "He was a little thrown when I told him how we'd be arriving, but we're part of the Network, so very little is truly extraordinary."

"Oh, so you told her about the jumping out a plane thing," Erika said.

"We can't go keeping things from her, Eri," Jason said. "It may be distant, but she's family."

"I'm your sister!"

"Exactly. Family is important," Jason said.

"Shade," Erika said. "Is there any chance you could drop Jason out of the plane now?"

"I'm sorry, Mrs Asano, but I believe Mr Asano is a necessary presence when we meet the Asano clan."

"Fine," she grumbled.

In a smaller cabin at the rear of the plane, Jason and Akari went over some last-minute details in preparation for meeting the Asano clan. It wasn't anything they hadn't already gone over, but Jason wanted to be fresh when they hit the ground. When they were done, they stood to join the others in the main cabin.

"Before we go," Akari said, "are you sure that you're up to this?"

"I'll try not to take offence at that."

"I'm just saying that you've been through a lot recently. Broken Hill and then Makassar, twice."

"It's bad, yeah," Jason said. "But that's the job."

"Is it your job? You never actually joined the Network."

"No, I joined the Adventure Society, which means putting myself between the bad things and the people who aren't equipped to face them. Jumping worlds doesn't change that."

"And this Adventure Society is some bastion of virtue, compared to the Network?"

"Of course not, but they let you make your own choices. You just have to be willing to live with the consequences. My friend Rufus taught me that."

"He also picked up some of Rufus's bad habits," Farrah said, opening the door. "Get in here; we're about to jump out of a plane."

Jason and Akari went in to find the rest of the passengers waiting for them.

"You know, it's a lot easier to deflate Rufus's sense of self-importance," Farrah said. "He's not actually responsible for saving the world."

"What exactly are you saving the world from?" Asya asked. "The monster waves?"

"That's a symptom," Jason said. "I can leave that to the Network, ultimately. My concern is that they're going to make the disease worse."

"How?" Asya asked.

"Imagine a house on stilts," Jason said. "There are so many stilts that the house is nice and stable until someone comes along and starts messing with the stilts and introduces a decaying factor. Magic termites or something. Things get wonky and people start taking a look at the stilts. They figure out how to slow down the decay, but then they realise that the stilts are made of solid gold. Do you trust them to leave the gold where it is because it's keeping the house from collapsing?"

"What are you saying?" Asya asked.

"He's saying," Farrah said, "that after the grid comes back up, there's going to be a magical gold rush. Unfortunately, every lump of gold that's dug up brings your world a little closer to collapsing. There's a lot of gold down there, so it won't seem like anything is happening at first. By the time you start noticing the effects, it will be too late."

"That's why you didn't tell me before. You don't trust the Network."

"No," Jason said. "I trust people, not institutions. I'll trust the people in the Network or the Adventure Society, but as a whole, you have to be careful."

"The Network won't do something destructive to the world," Asya said. "They wouldn't."

"I hope that's true," Jason said. "But when they see the Cabal and the EOA reaping the benefits, will the Network really stand still? Every branch?"

Asya looked uneasy, not answering. Jason put comforting hands on her shoulders.

"I'll give you a proper, thorough explanation once we're on the ground and settled. I just need to get my hands on something before anyone else finds out about it."

"Mr Asano," Shade said. "We are approaching the drop zone."

"Alright," Jason said. "Everyone hold still while Shade suits us up."

Jason and Farrah could both fly but were put in jet suits anyway, for better flight uniformity.

"This is awesome," Emi said.

"It's reckless," Erika said. "Planes are meant for landing."

"Technically, he's not a plane," Jason said. "He's the living shadow of death itself. Actually, that doesn't make it sound safer, does it?"

"No," Erika said, drilling a glare into him. "No, it doesn't."

"I anticipate it being a novel experience," Yumi confided in Emi. "I've been back to Japan several times since I was young, but this promises to be a rather unique visit from the outset."

"See?" Jason asked. "Even Nanna is keen."

Yumi's glare joined Erika's in latching on to Jason.

"See?" Jason asked. "Even Grandmother is keen. It feels weird calling you Grandmother when we look the same age. Can I just call you Yumi?"

"No," Yumi said definitively.

"Are we okay to use these from all the way up here?" Emi asked. "All the videos I've seen of suits like this are really low altitude and usually over water."

"That's just a safety precaution," Jason said. "They can go way higher, so we can ignore that restriction."

"That really seems like something we shouldn't ignore," Erika said.

"Shade is very reliable," Jason assured her.

"Mrs Asano," Shade said. "Be confident that I will not let anything happen to Miss Emi. As with the plane form which you currently occupy, these jet suit designs incorporate magic along with design aspects from a reality more technologically advanced than your own."

"How do we get out of the plane?" Emi asked. "Do we use that platform we boarded with, under the plane?"

Erika spotted Jason's grin and a look of horror crossed her face.

"Don't you dare," she warned him.

"It's just efficient, Eri," Jason said. "Shade, if you would?"

The plane around them exploded into a cloud of darkness, dumping the passengers into the sky.

In the city of Ashiya, near Kobe, the Asano clan compound had been constructed across hills overlooking Osaka Bay. In a place where space was at a premium, the land value alone was astronomical, let alone the buildings that occupied it. Designed by Frank Lloyd Wright and built twenty years before World War Two began, the famous American architect's mastery of spatial composition incorporated the hills into the design of the buildings. The compound had four levels, yet no individual location was greater than two storeys.

With Shade controlling the flight suits, eight figures dropped out of the sky. Jason, Akari, Asya, Dawn, Farrah, Yumi, Erika and Emi, all flying in a V-formation as they swooped over the landscape to touch down in a courtyard in front of a waiting group, also of eight. The jet suits landed in front of the group in a line, keeping their distance so as not to blast too much air over the people awaiting them.

The jet suits turned into shadows, all zipping into Jason's shadow like they were being sucked into a void. This left Jason flanked by friends and family, all dressed formally. Jason wore one of his remaining suits from the other world, a dark and dignified outfit designed specifically for such meetings. Jason's general lack of formality had left him little reason to pull it out until now.

Both groups stepped forward and Jason noticed that the other group had been matched to his own, including a female elder and a girl in her early teens. They even matched up in rank, except for Dawn's counterpart. Despite Dawn being, by any detectable measure, normal rank, her counterpart was a woman who looked to be in her mid-thirties but whose rank was near the peak of silver. Outside of Dawn's true rank, the woman was the most powerful member of either group. She also bore a solid resemblance to Akari.

All of the Asano clan wore western-style business attire. The man in the middle, Jason's counterpart, was Akari's silver-rank father and patriarch of the Asano clan. Like Jason's eldest paternal uncle, Ken and Hiro's older brother, the patriarch was named Shiro.

"Mr Asano," Shiro greeted with a polite bow.

"Mr Asano," Jason greeted back, reciprocating the bow. "First, allow me to apologise in advance. In spite of my heritage, I do not know your culture well and am certain to make blunders in my decorum. Please know that any slight is unintended and is a result of my ignorance alone and not any absence of respect."

"Thank you, Mr Asano. I too would like to apologise for the pretence under which I sent my daughter to you. We presumed to judge your worthiness to the Asano name, only for you to make that name echo across the world."

"These are difficult and dangerous times, Patriarch. I understand your position and the need to act delicately. I took no offence at all."

Jason took an elaborate wooden box from his inventory, almost a treasure chest in design. It was unremarkable magically, being only a mildly reinforced iron-rank container. It looked well-made but otherwise ordinary. What made it special was twofold: that it had come from the other world, and the gold-rank magic detectable on the object within.

"I offer a gift as a gesture of respect to the Asano clan," Jason said, gently setting the box down between them. "This container comes from another universe. It was the packaging for a suit of armour that was made for me there and I have long used it to organise many magical items from the other world. The armour that came with it was ultimately destroyed in the category-four astral space in Makassar, so it seemed appropriate that I use it to store a new set of armour I obtained there."

Jason opened the box, revealing the folded set of armour mixing cloth, leather, and hard chitin plates. It had been worn by the dinosaur man, King, and almost destroyed passing out of the astral space. A gold-rank item was a gold-rank item, however, and over time, it repaired itself and was now fully restored.

"It is called the Armour of the Dinosaur King. I hope that should any member of your clan reach category four, this armour can help vouchsafe their life."

Jason felt tremors run through the auras of the Asano clan members at being presented a set of gold-rank armour, although their demeanour did not shift, aside from the briefest glare Shiro flashed his daughter, who stood next to Jason. The patriarch took out a box of his own, this one a plastic container with an image Jason recognised on the side. The patriarch looked embarrassed as he placed it next to Jason's box.

"Next to your gift," Shiro said, "I can only make a paltry offering in reciprocation. This is a framed set of animation cels from *Beast King GoLion*."

Jason's face lit up in a grin.

"Seriously? That's awesome."

"You need not be polite, Mr Asano. Our gift pales in comparison to the treasure you have given."

Jason gave Shiro a smile.

"I disagree, Patriarch. The true worth of a gift is not in the value but the sentiment. Does not a mother value a handmade card from their child over an expensive one bought from a store? My gift is simply something that I came across in my travels, while your gift demonstrates thoughtfulness, care, and effort. My father will be truly delighted when I show him what you have given me."

Jason picked up the box containing the Asano clan's gift and placed it in his inventory. The woman standing next to Shiro conjured a silver cabinet and placed Jason's gift inside, after which the cabinet vanished.

Jason gave another respectful bow.

"Your consideration humbles me, Patriarch."

"As your generosity does me, Mr Asano."

Shiro turned to the woman who had conjured the cabinet, a silver-ranker standing across from Farrah. She bore quite a resemblance to Akari.

"This is my younger daughter, Asano Mei," Shiro introduced. "Please allow her to escort you to your accommodations while I take the chance to catch up with my long-absent elder daughter. You can rest after your journey and I will have refreshments sent to you. Later, if you are amenable, I will give you a tour of our home."

"We thank you for your hospitality," Jason said, allowing himself and the rest of his group, barring Akari, to be led away.

Most of Shiro's party left as well, once Jason and his group were out of sight. That left Akari, Shiro, and the powerful silver-ranker that was Akari's grandmother. Shiro cracked a huge smile and gathered his daughter in a huge hug.

"I missed you, child."

"And I, you, father."

"This man you have brought back. He is not what I expected."

"He never is," Akari said.

"He may not know our ways, but he does know how to give face."

"I will admit that surprised me," Akari said. "I half expected him to arrive in a floral-print shirt, board shorts and sandals. I even suspect he's putting on a more formal display just to mess with me, if he guessed what I reported back to you. I am sorry about my judgement on the gift. I don't know what he originally intended to offer, but I doubt it could be as grand as a treasure taken from the first category-four monster to arrive on Earth. He didn't tell me that he even had it, let alone that he would gift it to us."

"He put on quite the display," Akari's grandmother said, claiming her granddaughter for a hug of her own. "It makes me wonder what he wants from us."

"It's about the Tiwari clan," Akari said. "He knows more than I was willing to communicate until I saw you in person."

"Because of this Dawn person?" Shiro asked.

"Yes."

"You were very vague, only stating that we must show her the utmost respect of an elder. Are you ready to tell us more?"

"Of course," Akari said. "Let us go inside and I will explain everything."

35

NOT IN A POSITION TO CRITICISE

In a quiet dojo, Akari and her father faced off. They each wore a gi and a suppression collar and were wielding wooden swords. The swords and the room were both parts of an integrated magical system where the swords would not deal damage but inflict numbing pain that would briefly paralyse, in accordance with both the location struck and the force of the strike.

At the side of the room, Jason was in a relaxed kneel, also wearing a gi and suppression collar. Kneeling to one side of him was his grandmother, Yumi, with Emi on the other.

"I have always held, Mr Asano," Shiro said, "that to truly know a person, you must cross swords with them. To master the blade, you must put yourself into it, mind and spirit in alignment. To a blade master, your sword is who you are."

"That would mean that you can only really know someone if they happen to be really good with a sword," Jason said. "That's a pretty small sample size."

Shiro chuckled.

"Sadly true."

"What if I got one of those bendy swords you hide in a belt?"

Shiro laughed again.

"Simply suggesting it tells me a great deal about you, Mr Asano. If you actually did it, that would tell me something more. Should you then wield it against me, I would truly have your measure. This method is more flexible than you may think. For example, my daughter has been away for some time. If and how her sword has progressed in that time will enlighten me both on her and on you, who has been her sparring partner in that time."

Jason took the cue to fall silent as Shiro refocused on his daughter. They started circling one another with careful footsteps.

"Where has my aggressive daughter gone?" Shiro provoked. "Has your time away filled your heart with doubt?"

"You are the teacher and I the student, father," Akari responded calmly. "It is not for me to instruct you on the difference between hesitation and consideration."

"Interesting," Shiro said. "Are you a man whose sharpest blade is his tongue, Mr Asano?"

"Yes," Yumi said, answering for her grandson.

Emi smothered a little laugh.

"Have you lost your boldness, Daughter?"

"Perhaps I have merely learned to spot the difference between boldness and reckl—"

Without warning, Akari shot into action mid-sentence, launching into a barrage of strikes that had her father moving back in measured steps as he fended off attacks. It was spectacular to behold, as the speed and agility of silver-rankers made a swordfight more akin to film choreography than a fight between normal humans. Not only were reaction times, balance and spatial awareness vastly heightened, but even if the swords were real, no single blow would land a debilitating strike. Silver-rankers were just too hard to put down.

The factors affecting the combatants led to longer exchanges, with greater risks taken and the action-movie clashing of blades in rapid succession. Akari's father calmly withstood his daughter's barrage, slowly clawing back control of the lengthy exchange. He had been on the end of such turnarounds many times while sparring with Akari during her residence at Asano Village. Shiro launched into a counterattack, making his own sequence of unrelenting attacks until Akari deftly disengaged, dancing lightly back.

"You have sharpened your aggression from a blunt stick to a sharpened one," Shiro told his daughter. "It is not a sword yet, but you have made impressive progress. It seems that broadening your experience has had a positive influence. Let us see which other flaws you have managed to work on."

Moving to attack Akari, Shiro incorporated quick footwork; small but critical shifts in position as he threw attacks based less around speed and more around unexpected angles and nuanced variations. Akari countered by defending with efficiency, exploiting the lack of the same in her father's approach until he backed away.

"Adequate, Daughter."

Shiro continued to spar with his daughter until he finally nodded with satisfaction.

"In a very short time, you have made progress in tempering your aggression, responding to unusual attacks and utilising your physicality. I see that you have been diligent, Daughter, and I am curious about your recent sparring partner."

Shiro turned to Jason.

"Are you stronger than my daughter, Mr Asano?"

"When your daughter came to visit my family, the flaws in her mindset were obvious. Too reckless, the under-use of her superhuman physicality. A lack of experience against people using anything other than clean, efficient fighting styles. The technique you drilled into her over the years was carrying her, which had allowed her to avoid her shortcomings. You might say that she was an excellent sword being poorly wielded. Fortunately, my own approach was very suitable for exploiting those flaws. Once I started hammering on them, she adapted and my early victories became a cavalcade of defeats. Akari is far more formidable than I am."

"You use her first name?"

"Impolitic, I know, but when everyone is named Asano, a logistic necessity."

Shiro turned back to Akari.

"And you, Daughter, how would you assess Mr Asano's ability as a swordsman?"

"You and I live our lives around the sword, Father," Akari said. "Jason does not. He accepts that he will never be a swordmaster the equal of you and I, and embraces the limitation. He trains his swordsmanship for practical purposes rather than as a way of life, and his practical purposes are not to be found in an empty dojo."

"Meaning?" Shiro asked.

"If you ever fight him for real, Father, do it where you can see him."

Shiro let out a chortle, taking the training sword from Akari and holding the hilt in Jason's direction. Jason stood, bowed and stepped onto the tatami mats, claiming the sword.

"Tell me, Mr Asano," he said. "Is my daughter saving you face or are you truly more at home in a more real-world environment?"

"Definitely saving face," Jason said. "I'm quite rubbish."

"He also lies," Akari said. "He always keeps a trick in reserve and employs shameful tactics."

"Yep," Jason agreed merrily. "I'm very pro-cheating."

"Do not bother trying to unbalance my father with words, Jason," Akari said. "His will is as sharp as his blade."

"He's holding a blunt training sword," Jason pointed out. "Also, how do you know I'm not just stalling for time while Farrah uses earth magic to dig a tunnel under us and draw a ritual circle on the underside of the floor?"

"What?" Shiro asked as Jason let out a chuckle. "Mr Asano, you seem like a different person from the one who arrived at my home yesterday."

"I'm in favour of letting people know what they're going to get with me, Patriarch, and letting them take it or leave it. However, I wanted to demonstrate the esteem in which I hold your clan and make my arrival as respectful as I was able."

"I see. You hold my clan in high regard?"

"You've had your daughter observing me, but I've done my homework on you in turn. Your clan has spared nothing in dedicating their time, resources, and people to combat the troubles the world faces now. I have also seen Akari working with the Network in Australia. She fights with dedication, and not for pride or reputation but to help people as best she can. She's a credit to herself, your clan and to you, her father."

"Your sharpest blade truly is the one in your mouth, Mr Asano. Let us see how you do with the one in your hand."

Shiro and Jason walked through the grounds of the Asano compound, Jason still rather woozy.

"I apologise for striking you so many times in the head, Mr Asano."

"No worries," Jason said. "The tingle of those training swords gives you a bit of a buzz, once you get used to them. You know, you're a lot more relaxed than I was expecting. Akari took weeks to loosen up even a little."

"As you have placed effort into accommodating our sensibilities, I try to accommodate yours in turn. I was unsure what to expect, to be honest. Your media appearances, reports from the Network, what my daughter told me, and the footage I have seen of you in battle all paint pictures that don't quite line up. I was hoping that, in person, I might find the connective tissue."

"Sometimes I'm not sure how it all comes together either," Jason admitted. "In the other world, I resolved to remake myself, only to come home and find myself falling into old patterns. Before the current crisis, I went walkabout, to try and settle myself."

"Walkabout?"

"The term comes from an Indigenous Australian term, although the way it gets used by everyone else comes more from *Crocodile Dundee* than Aboriginal culture. It's a solitary journey, usually a rite of passage into manhood. I'm still pretty much a man-child, so manhood never quite seems to take with me. But the walkabout helped me find some balance that I seem to be rapidly losing again. But that's life."

"You are new to magic, yet in just a few years have seen more than most," Shiro said. "It is easy to forget that, given that your name has become so synonymous with magic."

"Our name," Jason corrected.

"Just so."

Jason looked around at the western-style home.

"I was surprised to find your home is built in the western style. By one of the most famous architects in the world, no less."

"Frank Lloyd Wright spent several years in Japan, in the early twenties," Shiro explained. "Less well-known than his role as an architect, he was also a rather prolific dealer in Japanese art. A number of his building designs remain here, although ours is the only extant residential building.

My mother assisted him with some trouble he was having with the Cabal, who were much less reclusive a century ago."

"The Cabal?"

"I'll spare you the details for the sake of dignity. Suffice to say it involved a kitsune and a significant quantity of lard."

"Kitsune are real?"

"Oh, yes. Have you had many dealings with the Cabal?"

"No," Jason said. "My friend, Craig, is a vampire, but that's about it."

"They are a strange and eclectic group, taken as a whole. My understanding is they were the magical factions of ancient times, only coming together in the face of external threats. Their internal politics are fractious and uneasy, but they are the object of romance and legend. I admit that they have always fascinated me."

"It's time our discussion turned to my reason for coming to Japan," Jason said. "I take it that Akari has apprised you of everything."

"Yes. You have surprisingly won my daughter over, Mr Asano."

"Alright, this is getting silly," Jason said. "Almost everyone here is an Asano. Although I realise it denotes a level of intimacy, is there any chance I can convince you to take a cue from my culture?"

"First names? I suppose we can be considered family, of a kind. I propose that you and I take that step and see how others react."

"That works for me. Shiro."

"Then let us return to the topic at hand, Jason. The truth is, our intention was always to bring you here, to settle an old debt to the Tiwari clan. We had no idea that the stakes would turn out to be so high. You truly believe that the world is in peril?"

"I've seen a being with power beyond the gods trying to strip an entire planet for parts. I fought him, hand to hand."

"How did that go?"

"Very badly. All my attacks bounced off and he easily killed me."

"Killed you?"

"I've died three times, so far. That was number two."

"That's an extraordinary claim."

"Extraordinary claims and fields of death are my life now. Even though it wasn't so long ago, and didn't last very long, I miss the life of light-hearted adventure and quips. I want to see this world safe and go back to exploring the other one."

"You have a means to go back?"

"I'm assured that it's inevitable, assuming someone doesn't kill me in a way that sticks. But first, I need that magic door the Tiwari have been looking after."

"Arrangements are being finalised as we speak," Shiro said. "I will take you to meet them after lunch. In the meantime, I would like to discuss what happens after the grid comes back online."

"We're not sure exactly what will happen," Jason said. "What we do know is that certain elements that make up the fundamental building blocks of our world will be rendered physical. This should be something that only the Tiwari door can accomplish, but our world has gone rather awry."

"What exactly is the danger?"

"There will be objects that manifest in affected areas. It's a component of the dimensional makeup of our world, affecting the dimensional membrane that separates our physical reality from the astral."

"I confess that I am not well-versed on these concepts," Shiro said.

"Basically, the dimensional membrane is like the skin of our universe, keeping the insides in and the outsides out. These objects I'm talking about also make up the link between this reality and the other one to which we are connected. That link had been stable for billions of years before someone came along and interfered with it. Now, centuries later, it's reached the point of continuous dimensional spaces and monster waves."

"And these objects represent some kind of new threat?"

"Not exactly. The objects represent a source of unparalleled power. They're like a diamond spirit coin combined with a category-five monster core, in a form that can be used at need and the rest kept for later."

Jason had an increased understanding of the astral magic involved, since he had been studying with Dawn's assistance. His knowledge was still shallow but was quickly accelerating.

"That kind of power would be world-changing," Shiro said. "It would let us move past the category-three threshold we've been stuck behind."

"Yep, and they're going to start popping up in the middle of these events that we don't yet understand. Every faction will be scrambling for them, even though each one they take will make the world a little less stable."

"How many of these objects are out there waiting to be exposed?"

"I don't know," Jason said. "Millions. Billions, maybe. But that will just give people an excuse to take them and say it doesn't matter because so many are left."

"The Network won't be any different," Shiro said. "They will scramble after them like the other factions, if only to avoid being overtaken."

"I agree. Unfortunately, I am not in a position to criticise—not that it's ever stopped me before. I also need to collect them, to realign the link between worlds. My understanding is that the door can be used to accelerate the process, meaning I need to take it off the board before the other factions become aware of that fact."

"Yet you trust me with this information."

"Honour may not be for me, but it is for Akari. I'm betting it is for the man who raised her as well."

"The temptation you describe is great," Shiro said. "I am not sure how well my integrity will hold up."

36
HONOUR

"Where are our guests now?" Noriko asked. She was the strongest member of the Asano clan and the patriarch's mother. Noriko and Shiro were in a room with the rest of the clan leadership, eight elders kneeling around a low table.

"Lunch is being prepared, hosted by my daughters," Shiro said. "Jason is taking a call from the Network."

"We're monitoring it?" Noriko asked.

"We are," Shiro said, "although that does not make me comfortable. We are hosts."

"You will need to swallow much more than that before we are done," Noriko said. "Akari told us the basics of what is to come, but if the power on offer is as formidable as what Jason described to you, then we have no choice but to pursue it."

"Akari will not like going against him."

"If this far-flung relative speaks the truth at all," one of the elders said, "it could be some elaborate ruse at our expense."

"I'm not sure that's a risk we can afford to take," said another. "If the power is truly as Shiro has described, we cannot afford to step back from it."

"Exactly," Noriko said. "Not only must we fully pursue the opportunities that will be available to all, but we must seize the one that only we have a chance at. It will allow us to not just keep up with those standing at the peak but potentially raise our entire clan to stand at the absolute pinnacle."

"You don't just wish to go after the magic that is coming," Shiro realised. "You are suggesting that we seize the object that Jason has come for?"

"Yes," Noriko said.

Shiro frowned unhappily.

"You wish to repay a debt with betrayal?" he asked. "This, on top of betraying those we entertain as hosts."

"To do any less would be a betrayal of our own people," Noriko said. "There is only shame in weakness, and in the chaos to come, only the strongest shall rise. The rest will be lucky to survive and I refuse to abandon the fate of the clan to luck."

"What about Network repercussion?" an elder asked.

"You think the Network will stand by Jason and his intentions when they see the EOA and the Cabal grabbing the power to push themselves to category four?" Noriko asked. "As much power and knowledge as he apparently represents, he is not worth giving up category-four power. Jason will either be forced to accept the Network's intentions or stand aside."

"He will not stand for it," Shiro said. "I can be certain of that much from Akari. She will react poorly to this as well."

"You are her father and will take her in hand," Noriko said. "One of your roles as her parent is to guide her through the hard but necessary choices."

"I guided her onto a path of respect for others and for herself. Turning her from it is not so simple as you make out."

"Yes, it is," Noriko said. "Do not confuse your own reluctance with difficulty. Mei and Akari are obedient girls."

"How will Asano react?" an elder asked. "We have all read Akari's reports from Australia. It does not seem out of character for Jason to do something rash."

"Then he will reap the consequences," Noriko said. "He will be cautious while he has family here."

"Hostages?" Shiro asked. "That goes beyond slapping our own faces. Do you intend to burn our name in effigy?"

"One of my roles as your parent is to guide you through the hard but necessary choices, Shiro. This is not a time for hesitation or half-measures. The world is changing and we must be ruthless if we do not wish to be cast aside by those with the will to rise to the top."

"Are we not being pre-emptive?" Shiro argued. "All we have is one conversation with Jason to go on. He could be exaggerating or blowing things out of proportion."

"Agreed," an elder said. "We should learn more before acting."

"Those are the words that will doom our clan!" Noriko pronounced. "All across the world, people are readying to act with boldness. If we hesitate when faced with an opportunity like this, then we are truly without hope."

Shiro hung his head, seeing that he would not be able to turn events.

"Jason's senses are sharp," he said. "Our preparations must be carefully conducted."

"Do not tell Mei and Akari anything," Noriko said. "So long as they believe we are going along with Jason's intentions, they will be a mask for our own."

Jason was on a video conference call, Asya standing beside him. There were a half-dozen people on a screen in front of him, including Terrance, Anna and Ketevan from the Sydney branch of the Network. The other three were all from the International Committee's offices, each one much higher up in the organisation than Asya.

"You messed up really badly with those comments about sharing the blame, Jason," Terrance said. "Coming right in front of the announcements about the EOA cutting deals with all those countries, you as good as legitimised them."

"Yes, because my influence is so all-encompassing that one remark from me can change the fate of twenty countries," Jason said. "That's hot nonsense. I may have spoken in anger, but I didn't lie, Terrance. The EOA might have dropped the grid, but Makassar is on the Network and the Cabal."

"It doesn't matter who is responsible, Jason," Anna said. "The important thing right now is undercutting the EOA's influence, and you gave them a boost instead, right when they needed it most. Because, no, you can't sway the fate of twenty countries alone, but you are a voice that people listen to."

"Then I'm going to try and give that voice some integrity," Jason said. "Yes, pushing it all onto the EOA right now would help the Network, but if you keep compromising your principles to meet the needs of the moment, eventually, you don't have any principles left. You wake up one day with blood on your hands, not recognising the person in the mirror."

"It's all well and good to talk about ethics," Anna said, "but we have to deal with the reality right now. And right now, the reality is that this move by the EOA has them gaining massive amounts of ground on the Network and you helped with that."

"I'm not part of the Network," Jason said. "I quite specifically didn't join because I didn't want to be making a choice between the right thing to do and what I was told to do."

"That is actually our reason for contacting you," said one of the International Committee members. It was a stern-looking woman, the first member of the IC to speak since the initial introductions.

"The agreement you reached with the Sydney branch has been deemed to be no longer feasible," she explained. "The time has come for you to truly come under the Network's umbrella. To become a member with all attendant responsibilities and privileges."

"You know that isn't happening," Jason said.

"Either way, our agreement with you is annulled, as of now," the IC member stated.

"Fine," Jason said and ended the call without further discussion. Then his face contorted in anger.

"Jason?" Asya asked. She had remained silent through the process.

"They know," Jason said. "I'm not sure how, but they know what's up for grabs once the grid comes back up. They know I won't stand for it, so they're cutting ties now. The next step will be to undermine my influence. They're going to start portraying me as a fringe rogue element. Probably some kind of extremist."

"You can't be sure of that."

"I am. I understand that this puts you in an awkward position."

"You know I wasn't the one to tell them, right?" Asya asked, uncertainty and anxiousness on her face.

He stepped forward, catching her in an embrace.

"Of course I know that," he said, comforting her with a firm but delicate hug, their bodies fitting into one another. "I told you that I trust people over the organisations they belong to. What just happened is the reason why. I trust you."

"So what now?"

"Now it's time for you and the others to go," Jason said. "Things are about to get very ugly."

Akari and Mei approached the rooms where Jason and his companions had been staying and Jason let her in.

"Where are the others?" Akari asked upon finding only Jason inside.

"They decided to go play tourist while I take care of business," Jason explained. "Any danger that finds them with Farrah there will soon wish it hadn't."

"Security didn't notify us of their leaving the premises," Mei said.

"They went with my shadow friend, Shade," Jason said. "He's very stealthy. He could be right there in the room with you and you wouldn't even know."

Akari narrowed her eyes at Jason.

"Jason, what are you doing?"

"If it's any consolation, later," Jason said, "your father was heavily against your family's decision."

Akari frowned, confusion and worry passing across her face.

"It hardly takes two of us, now that you are the only one travelling to the Tiwari clan," Akari said. "Mei, you escort Mr Asano while I inform Father of the change."

Mei looked from Jason to Akari with concern, having no idea what was causing the tension between them.

"Very well," she said.

"Father, he knows," Akari said, striding into the patriarch's study without knocking or preamble. Shiro leaned against the desk, wiping a cloth carefully down the length of an unsheathed sword.

"Who knows what?" Shiro asked, not looking up from his task.

"Jason knows what you are going to do."

Shiro slowly raised his head to look at his daughter.

"And what makes you think I'm going to do anything?"

"He sent all his people away in secret and made some barely veiled implications."

"What did he say?"

"He made the point of saying that his familiar can be in a room and you wouldn't even know it was there."

Shiro let out a laugh.

"He sent you on a fishing expedition, Daughter. His task is an important one and he is being appropriately cautious. He's doing the right thing. Return to your task."

"Are you sure, Father?"

"Quite certain, Akari. Attend your duties."

She gave a slight bow, then left again. Shiro put down the blade, walked to the door and closed it, before pulling out his phone to call Noriko.

"Yes?" Noriko answered brusquely.

"Asano knows."

"How certain are you?"

"He most likely had his familiar watching our meeting."

"That shouldn't be possible," Noriko said. "We have embedded protections in place."

"It occurs to me that Jason's companion, Farrah Hurin, is the foremost expert in array magic on the planet. Are you willing to bet that she couldn't have circumvented our magical defences?"

"Do you know if he's warned the Tiwari?"

"I do not."

There was a period of silence as Noriko processed the new information.

"It's not too late to turn back to the honourable path," Shiro said.

"Honour," Noriko said with disdain. "You sound like your new white friend, Asano."

"He is not white."

"Not in the skin, but there is no Japanese in him."

"That doesn't matter," Shiro said. "Choosing the path of power makes sense when there is power to be had, but if not, why throw away our face for nothing?"

"The fact that this is an opportunity we cannot afford to miss has not changed," Noriko said. "It will just cost us a little more blood. And those who win always have face."

"I hope you do not truly believe that. You want to move forward, whatever the cost? Whatever the risk?"

"The cost of not seizing this chance is worth any risk."

"I disagree," Shiro said. "I'm putting a stop to this before it begins. It's not too late to do nothing."

"You'll do no such thing," Noriko hissed.

"I have always valued your guidance, Mother, but I am the patriarch of this clan, not you."

"If the puppet cuts its own strings, Shiro, it falls down, helpless. Do as you're told."

"You are that unwilling to compromise?" Shiro asked, voice heavy with resignation.

"My will is unbending, son. This is not news to you. Your choices are either to work for the betterment of the clan or throw it into chaos for some Australian you met yesterday."

Mei was driving a black town car into Kobe. Shiro and Akari sat together in the back, with Jason across from them.

"You look conflicted, Shiro," Jason said.

"Do I?" Shiro asked. "Is that why you sent my daughter to see me?"

"Yes. I think the man who raised Akari will want to be able to look her in the eye tomorrow. There is still a window to stop this before it starts."

Akari watched the two men warily but did not interrupt, despite her burning curiosity.

"I can't stop this, Jason," Shiro said. "I tried."

"Unfortunate, but unsurprising."

Shiro sighed, turning to look at his daughter. Jason said nothing, sitting casually.

"I can speak for most of the clan," Shiro said with the weariness of a tired old man. "Most of our oldest and strongest warriors will remain loyal to my mother, however, and I'm sure you know that, with essence users, it is a power game, not a numbers one."

"The tyranny of rank," Jason said. "I'm quite intimate with the concept."

"So those are my options," Shiro said. "Keep the clan together and throw away our face, along with who-knows-how-many lives of an ally clan to whom we are in debt. Or, we split the clan. Tiwari blood will be spilled either way, and our clan could very easily meet its end."

"Father, what are you talking about?" Akari asked.

"Your grandmother wants to take the magic door by force," Jason explained. "She will not be dissuaded, it would seem, despite your father's attempts to maintain the clan's honour."

"Father, is that true?"

"I'm sorry, Akari."

"It won't even do any good," Jason said. "According to the Tiwari, I'm the only one who can use the door."

"You did contact them, then?" Shiro asked.

"Yes," Jason said. "Their patriarch was hard to convince that you would throw away your honour, Shiro."

"Why can only you use it?" Shiro asked. "The prophecy about a man who walks between worlds?"

"After your meeting," Jason said, "I spoke at length with the Tiwari patriarch through an intermediary. The prophecy is a poetic way of describing a very real magical restriction."

"Was it left here for you?" Akari asked.

"Partly, I suspect," Jason said. "I imagine the first choice was that the Network founder would return for it, using the restriction as a security system. Another outworlder being sent here was probably a less-than-reliable backup plan."

"How do you see this going?" Shiro asked. "My mother will not be inclined to accept the Tiwari's claim. Even if she does, that just means she'll try and capture you as well, Jason."

"It will take a lot to make her back down," Jason said. "I'm hoping that the combination of the Tiwari being ready, the fact that she can't even use the door and the threat of a schism in the clan will be enough to get her to withdraw. I've convinced the Tiwari to let your clan leave in peace so long as your clan is willing to do so. The friendship between your clans is dead either way, however."

"You think I'll turn on my mother and start a civil war inside my clan?"

"I'm hoping that you'll save your clan's soul, Shiro, as well as its people. Once the fighting starts, I won't stop until the job is done."

"My daughter told me not to fight you unless I can see you," Shiro said.

"You won't see me," Jason said. "You'll see your clan staggering out of the dark, dead on their feet."

"You're very confident."

"Yes. I'm either right to be or I'm not. Do you really want to find out, Patriarch?"

Shiro looked into Jason's cold, silver eyes. He had never sensed so much as an echo of Jason's aura, but suddenly, he felt something his senses could barely touch, like an object just beyond the reach of his fingers. It was deep, like a dark abyss, with the promise of power and danger.

"Are you still human, Jason?"

"No," Jason said. "Not anymore."

37
THEY GET TO SEE WHAT I'M LIKE

The Tiwari clan seat was located in Arima Onsen Town, nestled in beauteous nature amongst thickly forested hills. They made their way north towards Kobe's Kita-ku ward. The car taking Jason to meet the clan also contained the Asano clan patriarch, Shiro, and his two daughters. The elder, Akari, sat next to her father, unsettled at the discussion between Shiro and Jason. The younger sister, Mei, drove the town car, with Shiro and Akari facing Jason in the back.

"So, what exactly was the plan?" Jason asked.

"Use stealth specialists to follow us to where the Tiwari clan is hiding the door," Shiro said. "Two of them, each category three."

"It seems that either your mother doesn't trust you, or someone else is trying to horn in," Jason said. "Or both. There are currently four silver-rankers following us. That I've noticed, at least."

"I can't sense them," Shiro said. "Are you sure?"

"They are all in cars," Jason said. "It could be that a bunch of silver-rankers all wanted to visit the same hot springs town at the same time and are driving there individually," Jason said. "Shade, go take a look. If they are here for us, go with plan C. Variant three, please."

"Are you sure you want to make that level of commotion?" Shade asked.

"If the Network wants to tear up our arrangement, they get to see what I'm like operating without shackles."

"Not having access to military supplies will make replenishing supplies for plan C harder."

"No, it'll just make it less legal," Jason said. "It won't be hard."

"Very well," Shade said.

"What's plan C?" Akari asked.

"Plan C is all about Shade," Jason said. "He can turn intangible, store objects in his own dimensional space and is very, very hard to detect. We loaded Shade up with a bunch of useful items and came up with a series of plans where Shade plants objects near targets."

"Like cameras?" Akari asked. "That would be useful. Is that what the C stands for?"

"No," Jason said, pulling out a palm-sized black box with a small antenna. It had a switch and a button under a plastic flip cover, as well as a green indicator light.

"Everything is in place," Shade said.

"That was quick," Shiro said.

"I was already moving when the discussion began," Shade said.

"Plan C does not stand for plan camera," Jason said, flipping the switch on the device, and causing the light to go from green to red. "It stands for C4. Give me the timing, Shade."

He lifted the cover over the button.

"Now," Shade said.

Jason pressed the button and a trio of simultaneous explosions rang out behind them.

Shiro and Akari both craned their necks to look out the back.

"I'd make sure we get out of the area before the authorities get involved," Jason told Mei, who was in the driver's seat. "It'll be quite the commotion."

"Commotion?" Shiro said, looking aghast at Jason. "Do you know what you've done?"

"Don't worry," Jason said with a friendly smile. "I made sure they were shaped charges, so the silver-rank shrapnel I made will have passed right up through the cars where Shade attached the charges. It'll hit anyone inside like a, well, bomb, while not impacting nearby civilians. Too much."

Any shrapnel that makes it above a certain height will break down into metal powder, too light to fall down and hurt anyone."

"Silver-rank shrapnel?"

"Yes. My artifice abilities are very basic, but investing some caltrops with a few simple properties is within my capabilities."

"How can you set off bombs in Japan?" Shiro asked.

Jason looked Shiro square in the eye, the friendly, casual expression vanishing into an icy glare.

"I need something to save the world and you want to take it for your own power? The Network wants to drop me to scrabble over magical scraps, disregarding their very purpose? I can handle that kind of greed, but this is what handling it looks like. The gloves are off, Shiro. I don't want to kill anyone, but if saving this world from people like you means wading through a river of their blood, I will. Speaking of which, any lethal casualties, Shade?"

"No. The silver-rankers were each travelling alone, presumably to avoid low-rankers being detected. The blast itself had minimal impact on them, but the magical shrapnel was much more effective. Their lives are not endangered, but their ability to continue is certainly impacted, and they are no longer following."

"Good," Jason said. "Collateral?"

"I selected a moment to avoid collateral damage, although there was some cosmetic damage to surrounding vehicles."

"The concussive redistribution magic on the container for the shaped charge directed the sound and force up," Jason explained. "Even more focused than a regular-shaped charge. More power where you want it and less collateral damage. A little simple magic goes a long way when you use it right."

"There was also some minimal property damage. Nearby civilians are unsettled, with a few minor injuries from low-speed traffic collisions in the ensuing chaos. One elderly man was having heart problems, so I fed him a potion. Civic authorities have begun to arrive."

"Thank you, Shade," Jason said. "Excellent work, as always."

As their car left the area quickly, Akari and Shiro continued to look at Jason with horror. His hard expression returned to the friendly one from before, as if nothing had happened. He pulled out a sandwich, took a bite, and then looked at them apologetically.

"Sorry, did you want one?" he asked with his mouth full. "I have more. Salad, ham. One with three different kinds of salami."

They both shook their heads. Jason took another bite and then looked at Shiro.

"So what now?" Jason asked. "What's your mother's contingency for her scouts getting taken out?"

"Contingency?" Shiro asked. "This is not our area of expertise. We're monster-hunters, not special-forces soldiers. If the scalpel doesn't work, my mother will use the hammer. If she can't follow us to where the Tiwari are storing the door, she will likely use our silver-rank forces, most of which are loyal to her, to attack the Tiwari directly, capture the patriarch and force him to reveal the location."

Jason nodded.

"Call your mother and give me the phone."

"You want me to call her?"

"If we have any chance of ending this peacefully, we need to talk without being able to stab each other."

Shiro nodded. "She wouldn't hesitate to try and solve you out of the equation, given the chance."

He dialled and handed Jason the phone.

"You shouldn't be calling me," Noriko's voice came through by way of a greeting.

"I shouldn't be blowing up cars on the streets of Kobe either, yet here we are."

"Jason Asano," she hissed. "You aren't one of us. You don't deserve that name."

"I have zero interest in joining your clan, Noriko. The question is whether you are going to destroy that clan."

"I'm doing this for the clan. My son is weak, which is how you managed to turn him against me."

"Shiro didn't turn against you, Noriko. He wants to save the soul of your clan. If you attack the Tiwari, even if you win, the Asano clan will never be what they were."

"I'm a century older than you, boy, and you seek to lecture me on the soul of my clan?"

"You do have a wealth of experience over me," Jason acknowledged. "If I can see that your clan teeters on a precipice, then surely you can too.

If you attack the Tiwari, then you create a schism in your clan at the same moment you create a dangerous enemy, and for what? A magic door you can't use."

"So you say."

"The Tiwari have had this object for centuries," Jason said. "You think they haven't tried to access its power? If they had succeeded, they would be ruling the world with their gold-rankers, not calling in favours to have your clan bring me to Japan."

"Even if the Tiwari do not lie and the item is locked," Noriko said, "we will find a way."

"Will you?" Jason asked. "After the infighting and the retaliation from the Tiwari clan? After I tell the world about the door and the fact that you have it?"

"We will do what we must."

"And is what you must do push through past every omen that you should stop? Your plan was already sketchy. Now your scouts are gone, your clan's support has evaporated and the Tiwari know you're coming."

"My clan must seize this opportunity, whatever the cost."

"The opportunity isn't what you think, Noriko. The opportunity you have is to step back and keep your clan whole. You already know more about what's coming than almost any faction on Earth. Take the time to prepare and get a head start when the time comes to start racing after resources, with the full strength of your clan. Shiro might be against attacking and stealing from the Tiwari, but he won't stand by while everyone else grabs for power. You aren't choosing between having the door or not, Noriko. You're choosing between facing what's to come with a full and ready clan, and scrabbling after leftovers with your handful of silver-rankers while dodging Tiwari vengeance."

"I thought you didn't want people going after these objects of power."

"I don't," Jason said. "I'm not stupid enough to think I can stop them, though. Your clan included. I have also secured the assurance that the Tiwari will not seek retribution so long as you do not attack them."

"I have only your word on these things."

"You have little more than my word on almost any of this," Jason said. "The power you seek: my word. The danger it poses: my word again. You chose boldness because you didn't have time to verify and now you're mired in a bog of my design. Will you be sucked under and drown if you move ahead or am I lying and solid ground awaits you?"

"You like to hear yourself talk."

"Yes. Especially when I'm right. Go home and take all the advantages or fight and give them up. I'll be waiting for your decision with the Tiwari clan."

Jason hung up the phone and handed it back to Shiro, before turning to Akari.

"I never wanted to back your grandmother into a corner. All I wanted to do was show her that backing off isn't the weak, short-sighted move but the smart, forward-thinking one."

He then turned to Shiro.

"This is where we part. Go home. I hope this is the last time I have to deal with your clan, Shiro, because next time, there will likely be blood. I'm sorry it ended like this, Akari." A Shade body emerged from Jason's shadow and Jason vanished into it.

Jason rode in a Shade car towards the Tiwari clan seat, the palatial Arima Grand Resort.

"How did I do?"

"You were somewhat unfocused," Shade critiqued. "Your strengths are playing to emotion and controlling pace, which lends itself to a more rambling style of argumentation. Presenting the facts to demonstrate that one choice is objectively better is not your strongest approach. That being said, it was an adequate performance."

"We'll only know how adequate it was once the decision is made," Jason said. "Is she taking precautions in case you're watching?"

"None that I have noticed."

"I might take a peek, then."

Jason closed his eyes and saw through Shade's eyes.

Noriko stood beside a parked van, arguing with the silver-rank clan elders, their strongest combatants. The general consensus was to withdraw, though she tried to convince them to push on.

"It is probably all bluff," she said.

"Perhaps," an elder said. "I am unwilling to risk the clan on 'perhaps.' Unless everything goes perfectly and the boy is lying *and* this magic door gives us vast power, this act will split the clan and throw away our face forever."

"Agreed," another said. "We can struggle for power with everyone else without destroying who and what we are in the process. We even have a lead on everyone else. We should be dedicating ourselves to making the most of it."

The arguing continued, but ultimately, the choice was made to abort the attack.

"I will contact Shiro and that obnoxious brat," Noriko said.

"Oh, don't bother with me," Jason's voice said as a dark figure with silver eyes stepped out of the dark.

"You can watch us through your shadow beings," Noriko said.

"Yes. Your strategic situation was rather untenable, should you have decided to go through with the attack. I am not here to crow, however. My Asano family and your Asano clan henceforth have no connections, Noriko."

"If we meet again, it will be as enemies."

"I hope that day never comes," Jason said. "You should hope for it more."

38
FANBOY

The Arima Grand Resort was a palace hidden in a forest, the most opulent of the many accommodations in Arima Onsen Town. With magic now out in the open, Jason didn't have to bother hiding it as he approached the resort. Shade transformed from car to a cloud of shadow right outside the lobby, then Jason strode out of the cloud as the dark miasma was sucked into his shadow.

Ignoring the resulting stares, Jason made his way across an atrium larger than most homes. A young man of maybe twenty, with an earnest, nervous aura, hurried through the lobby to intercept him. Anxiety was plain on his face, but his aura was solidly controlled. If Jason's senses weren't so much more powerful than the freshly bronze-rank young man's, he wouldn't have been able to read his emotions at all. Most interestingly, his aura contained no trace of monster cores.

"Mr Asano," the young man greeted with a respectful bow. "My name is Tiwari Itsuki."

Jason returned the bow, a smile playing on his lips. The young man's aura shuddered with anxiety.

"I apologise for being the one to meet you, but preparations are being made should events go unfortunately. Would you please follow me?"

"Of course," Jason said, following the young man, who did a mostly adequate job of hiding his nervous energy. "I wouldn't be too worried, Mr

Tiwari. I'm confident that the Asano clan has reconsidered their path going forward."

"Truly?" Itsuki asked as he led Jason across a lobby full of people staring at them.

"I just came from a chat with Asano Noriko. It could have been a bluff, but I believe the Asano clan will be packing up and going home without paying you that visit."

"I knew you would do something," Itsuki said.

"Don't go crediting me too much."

Itsuki guided Jason out of the lobby and into the internal halls.

"There's no reason to be modest, Mr Asano. I've been following your exploits through the news, obviously, and all the Network reports I could find. I actually asked my father if I could be the one to meet you. I'm taking you to the family's private residence at the rear of the resort grounds."

"I'll have to disagree about modesty," Jason said. "Always either be modest or wildly self-aggrandising. Avoid anything in between, for there lies mediocrity."

"That's... an unusual perspective."

"If it comes up," Jason said, "tell them to put that on my tombstone."

"Uh..."

"I'm not what you expected?"

"Not quite. I'd heard some things from Asano Akari, but they seemed a little outlandish. I'd thought she was joking."

"You know Akari?"

"I haven't seen her in person since she left. I suppose I won't be able to at all now."

"It might be a bit awkward, yes," Jason said, sensing the regret and loss in the young man's aura.

"I see you didn't use cores to reach bronze rank," Jason said, changing the subject. "Sorry, category two."

"Bronze rank is fine. We have been using the otherworld terminology since we started training our people with the Hurin techniques."

"The Hurin techniques? They named them after Farrah?"

"Yes, Mr Asano. I had long considered myself unlucky, being unable to absorb essences until I was nineteen. The timing was perfect for the new techniques, however, and I was sent to Sydney with the first international representatives for training. I was in the same training group as Taika Williams."

"You know Taika? Have you and I met before?"

"I attended some lectures you gave on aura control at the Sydney branch, but this is our first time actually meeting."

"Sorry I didn't recognise you. I've been rude."

"There were over a hundred people in attendance and I was just a fresh iron-ranker. There is no need to apologise."

"I did mostly leave training people to Farrah. I'm a bit rambling and unfocused to be a good instructor. Getting Farrah worked out better for you. I taught some people aura control in the other world for a while and they paired me with someone to keep me on track. That turned out to be a good idea."

"Miss Asano told me that you are difficult to keep on any track you don't want to be on, Mr Asano."

Jason laughed.

"That sounds about what Akari's assessment would be. That's why they had my friend Humphrey riding herd on me."

Jason's face took on a sad, reminiscing smile.

"The way things are going here," he said, "I can't wait to go home."

"To Australia?"

"No."

Itsuki looked at the expression on Jason's face and didn't probe further. They left the main resort building through a side door and Itsuki took the driver's seat of a waiting golf cart. The resort was a sprawling complex made up of multiple huge buildings set into the forested surrounds, rising up the side of a large hill.

"You must have been quite active to reach bronze rank in what? Five months?" Jason asked.

"I've done my duty as a member of the Network as best I can," Itsuki said.

Five months was basically unheard of, even in the other world. Jason knew that ranking up in five months was only possible with a vast number of monsters. Even then, the boy would need an impressive level of talent and, more importantly, dedication. Only the kind of consistent conflict Jason himself faced living in an astral space could grant that kind of advancement. The boy had to be all but living in proto-spaces.

That kind of drive suggested an implacability rather at odds with the nervous young man driving the golf cart. Either he had unexpected depths or the off-kilter predilections of a serial-killer, redirected into monster hunting. Either way, he was someone worth paying attention to.

"If you don't mind," Jason said, "would you be willing to share your essence combination?"

Itsuki's aura shuddered and his nervousness was made plain on his face.

"It's alright to say no," Jason chuckled.

"No, it's just a little embarrassing."

"Oh, I wouldn't worry about that," Jason said. "I have a friend, one of the most skilled essence users I ever met. Someone who taught me, in fact. He has a story about a lesson he learned getting showed up by a man with the duck essence."

"It's not like that," Itsuki said. "It's just… my essences are dark, blood and omen, with a doom confluence."

"Oh," Jason said. "You really have been following my exploits, haven't you?"

Itsuki's face went red.

"I've never met a fan before. Do you have any of my merch? The proceeds go to charity, which is the only reason I went along with Terrance and his nonsense."

"Terrance?"

"Never mind. You didn't get the knockoff stuff from China, did you? I'm sure the Network there is behind it, not that they'll admit it."

"Mr Asano, please."

Jason laughed, slapping Itsuki on the shoulder.

"I'm just messing with you, bloke. Are you an affliction specialist?"

"Yes."

"Nice. We should find some time to swap notes, maybe clear out a proto-space together."

"Really?"

"If events don't overtake us, sure. No promises, though. Events overtake me quite a lot. Just earlier, I was setting off a bunch of car bombs."

"That was you?"

"Yep. Only had to use three, because two of them were in the same car. They definitely weren't just some couple going on holiday, right, Shade?"

"I am quite certain of their sinister intentions," Shade said. "Unfortunately for them, it takes a lot to catch up to you in sinister intentions."

"Oh!" Itsuki exclaimed, almost driving the cart off the path. "You're Shade, the shadow familiar."

"I know," Shade said. "I am starting to see why people telling you your name all the time is annoying, Mr Asano."

Jason laughed as Itsuki went pale.

"Don't worry about it," Jason told him. "Do you have a familiar? They're pretty rare on this side."

"Yes, Mr Asano, I do. My father made sure I had the ritual training to make it possible. I only have the one, though, and it does not communicate. I don't exactly know what it is."

"We can take a look later," Jason said. "See if we can't figure it out."

"I apologise, Mr Shade," Itsuki said. "I've watched the ritual of your summoning many times."

"Because that's not creepy at all," Jason said.

The golf cart rode up the hill through the complex that was oddly like a small town, if there was a small town occupied exclusively by billionaires. They arrived at the rear of the complex, which was the highest point on the hill. Compared to palatial buildings elsewhere, the Tiwari residence was smaller, more modest and had more traditional Japanese influence in the architecture than western. More modest meaning that it was a giant mansion, rather than a hotel for people who thought the Palace of Versailles was an adequate start.

Jason could sense the protections embedded into it. They were not so intricate and formidable as a Network branch office, but he would still have to be careful should he attempt to intrude, unnoticed or otherwise. The protections had not been enough to prevent Shade entering to approach the clan patriarch, so that Jason could clandestinely warn him of the Asano clan's intentions.

The defences seemed to be in an active state, which probably meant they were burning through spirit coins. As he watched, the defences started spooling down.

"They must have heard the Asano clan isn't coming," Jason said.

"What makes you say that?" Itsuki asked.

"The magical protections are being wound down."

"You can read our magical defences just from looking?"

"The benefits of a grounding in magical theory were explained to me many times," Jason said. "It turned out to be very true. I take it that you were only taught the practical basics of rituals?"

"Yes, Mr Asano."

"Try studying up on the theory. It'll be worth it, I promise."

"I'll do my best," Itsuki said. "There is only so much material I can get my hands on."

They stopped outside the building and went to the doors on foot, where two men were standing guard in black suits. They bowed as Itsuki and Jason approached.

"Lord Itsuki. The defences are being stood down to readiness condition two. Your father wishes you to bring Mr Asano to the patriarch's office."

"Thank you, Ryuhei."

Itsuki was like a different person in front of the doormen. All trace of nervousness was gone from his face and his aura was brought under control. If Jason's senses weren't so powerful, he wouldn't have been able to read him at all.

"That is some impressive aura control," Jason said. "You learned Farrah's lessons well."

"And yours, Mr Asano. The compliment is great, coming from you. Miss Hurin once told me that your aura has strength and power enough to be used as a weapon itself."

"I prefer not to," Jason said. "Some weapons are best left in their sheath."

The inside of the Tiwari residence was busy, although the people hurrying about frequently looked at Jason and Itsuki as they passed. The building seemed deeply modernised, under a façade of old-world dignity. Jason's silver-rank perception picked out surveillance systems and communication signals imperceptible to a normal human, all hidden under traditional Japanese décor. Itsuki led Jason to an elevator, where a man with an expensive suit and a discreet earbud stopped them. Jason could sense that he was silver rank.

"Uncle Souta," Itsuki greeted.

"Itsuki," the man said, then bowed respectfully to Jason, who reciprocated.

"Mr Asano," Souta said. "My name is Tiwari Souta. I am afraid that you will need to disable whatever means you are using to obfuscate our security before moving forward. I apologise, but given the circumstances, we are wary of allowing anyone with the name Asano access to our clan leadership."

"Uncle Souta! Mr Asano was the one who warned us!"

"Decorum, Itsuki," Souta scolded.

"Apologies, Uncle."

"It's perfectly understandable," Jason said. "Dial it back, please, Shade. In fact, you may as well pop out."

A Shade body emerged from Jason's shadow.

"It wouldn't do to go smuggling people in, so let's get out in the open, yes? Front and centre, gents."

Gordon manifested next to Shade, while Jason pointed an arm down the hallway, palm out. Glistening blood seeped through the skin of his palm and then sprayed out in a stream, unsettling Itsuki and Souta. The blood congealed into a robed figure that looked identical to Jason, except for the red-purple colour of its skin.

"Gentlemen, meet Shade, Gordon and Colin. My closest companions."

Jason and his familiars all lined up together, looking like a blood clone, a shadow clone and an alien void monster.

"I'm not so sure about this," Souta said.

"If you accept me, you accept them," Jason said. "Literally, since they are my familiars. If you don't accept them, then you might as well tell me where the door is and I'll make my own way."

Souta looked over the four of them, lingering on Gordon, who looked like a floating violation of the laws of physics.

"If you had not revealed them, would we have any means of detecting them?"

"No, but your patriarch certainly knew about Shade. I'm pretty certain that Itsuki, here, could have told you about the others, if you didn't know already. Don't go crediting me with too much honesty."

Itsuki had been looking at the familiars with distracted amazement, only looking up when his name was said.

Souta looked at Itsuki sternly, but Jason could sense the man's mix of exasperation and affection. He tapped his earbud, then nodded.

"Very well. Please come along."

Jason's familiars unmanifested. Shade returned to Jason's shadow,

Gordon vanished and Colin was reabsorbed, then Souta, Itsuki and Jason entered the elevator.

"Do you get heavier when Colin is inside you?" Itsuki asked.

"I think so," Jason said. "I didn't used to, when he would just disappear, as much as it seemed like he was entering my body. Now we seem to merge more physically than before. I'm not sure if it's him or me that changed, or a little of both."

The elevator ride was short and they walked down another hall towards a set of double doors.

"Is your father the patriarch?" Jason asked Itsuki.

"No, my uncle is. Father is the youngest brother, Uncle Souta is in the middle and Uncle Denji is the patriarch."

"Your father has two older brothers as well?" Jason asked. "Itsuki, are you trying to steal my identity?"

"What?"

"Mr Tiwari," Jason asked Souta. "Does Itsuki have a poster of me on his wall?"

"I don't," Itsuki said unconvincingly.

"It's the one where I'm on the roof of a building like Batman, isn't it? I always thought that one was over the top."

"That one was your idea," Shade said.

"Quiet, you."

They reached the doors where a pair of men in black suits stood guard.

"I love the men-in-black look your security people have going on," Jason said. "Very intimidating."

The men opened the doors to allow them into a large office where the back wall was made entirely of glass, looking out over the resort as it sprawled down the hillside. Two men were waiting for them, both silver-rankers, bearing no small resemblance to Souta.

"Mr Asano," the patriarch, Denji greeted. He moved forward to shake hands rather than offer a Japanese bow. "It is good to meet you in person, although your shadowy go-between was quite remarkable. And stealthy."

"I have a friend who could recommend ways to keep him out," Jason said. "You'll have to forgive me for asking her not to."

"You speak of Miss Hurin," Denji said. "My nephew holds you both in high regard. I understand she is also in Japan?"

"She is making sure that my friends and family don't suffer the undue attention of the Asano clan. Given our shared ancestry, our meeting was rather disappointing."

"Disappointment is the order of the day," Denji agreed. "I have just gotten off the phone with Asano Shiro, who I have known since we were boys. It is sad to lose a friend and an ally, but their intentions today are beyond forgiveness."

"Shiro was against the move from the beginning," Jason said.

"Oh, I don't doubt it," Denji said. "It's his mother. I do not know how you convinced that woman to back off."

"I didn't do anything. She merely came to see the consequences clearly."

"That seems suspiciously easy, given the woman in question."

"I was thinking much the same thing. I imagine that she'll come for me again, once I have the door."

"That would not surprise me, although perhaps the fear of Network retribution will stay her hand."

"I doubt it. The Network and I will be increasingly at odds from now on. Which puts you in something of an awkward position. Sorry."

"Not at all," Denji said. "Our clan's first duty is to the Network's founder and the task left to us, not the Network's modern incarnation."

"And that task is protecting the door?"

"Yes," Denji said. "Until the person that can use it arrives."

39
A VERY BAD MISTAKE

ITSUKI LEFT JASON WITH THE THREE ELDERS: THE TIWARI CLAN PATRIARCH and his two younger brothers. The patriarch was Denji, the middle brother Souta and the youngest, Itsuki's father, was Koya. The office of the patriarch was a large room with a desk to one side and a lounge area on the other, with armchairs in a semi-circle around a coffee table, looking out through the window wall.

Denji invited Jason to sit. They all took lounge chairs as a security guard in an expensive black suit came in with a tray of tea. Jason nodded his gratitude and took a sip, then murmured something too softly for even silver-rank perception to make out.

"I'm not sure if you are aware of how monumental your arrival is for our clan," Denji said. "Since we learned of your existence and that you met the conditions of our long-held purpose, there has been much discussion within the clan. Not everyone is happy or even accepting of your arrival. You represent the destiny of the clan, which is a concept that not everyone has come to terms with."

"Some of your members don't want me to take the door?"

"In practical terms," Denji said, "we are no different from any of the other Network clans. The door remains hidden and untouched, with very few clan members even knowing its location, let alone having seen it. Even so, being keepers of the door gives us a sense of purpose. Many of our members are fearful of what it means should that purpose come to an end. When who and what you are came to light, many sought to discredit you and claim you were not the object of prophecy."

"And you put stock in this prophecy?" Jason asked.

"In honesty, Mr Asano, the prophecy is a simple concept to placate the clan. The elders have passed down the records from the founder, which give a more comprehensive explanation. This is not something shared with the clan at large, which has unfortunately led to duty sometimes drifting in the direction of faith. Some of our members may even intend you harm."

"I learned that as soon as I tasted the tea," Jason said with a smile.

"The tea?"

"I don't know about yours," Jason said, "but mine has rather a lot of poison in it."

"What?" Denji asked, leaping to his feet.

"It's actually not bad," Jason said, taking another sip.

- You have been afflicted with poison [Serpent Nettle Extract].
- You have resisted [Serpent Nettle Extract].
- [Food Poisoning] does not take effect.
- You have gained an instance of [Resistant].

"Serpent nettle extract," Jason said. "I assume I'm respected enough that it's a category-three poison they used on me."

The faces of all three Tiwari elders darkened with rage.

"Serpent nettle extract is a poison our alchemists harvest from plants in some of the more common proto-space environments in this area," Souta said. "You might call it a Tiwari clan specialty. This definitely came from within the clan."

"I think that's jumping to conclusions," Jason said. "Someone could easily obtain some and use it to sow discontent. That's what I'd do."

He took another sip.

"Why are you still drinking it?" an aghast Koya asked Jason. "Serpent nettle extract is the most potent venom we've ever encountered!"

"Actually," Jason said, setting the cup down with distaste, "the flavour profile starts out well, but that aftertaste leaves something to be desired. If there's any poison in yours, I'd give it a miss. I don't want to be rude, being your guest, but is there any chance of a palate cleanser?"

Souta stepped up, took an eyedropper from his pocket and squirted clear liquid into Jason's cup. A sickly green mist rose, letting off an unpleasant stench.

"Yep," Jason said, holding his nose. "That's the aftertaste."

"The smell is unpleasant but harmless," Souta said. "That was definitely serpent nettle extract."

Souta squirted liquid into the other cups, but only Jason's evidenced a reaction.

"It was Noguchi," Souta said. "He served the drinks, so he had to know which cup to give Mr Asano."

Souta said no more, striding towards the door.

"Mr Tiwari," Jason called after him and he stopped.

"I had my friend go after the server as soon as I tried the tea," Jason continued. "Please allow him to guide you."

"Your friend?" Souta asked.

One of Shade's bodies emerged from Souta's shadow.

"This way, Mr Tiwari," Shade said and started gliding down the corridor. After a wide-eyed glance at Jason, Souta followed. Koya and Denji, in the meantime, were giving their own shadow wary looks.

"I'm beginning to be very glad that I'm not Noriko Asano," Koya said.

"You seem oddly relaxed, given the attempt to murder you," Denji said to Jason.

"Oh, I'm sure you'll tell me if it's anything beyond internal clan politics," Jason said. "I respect anyone with the decency to try and kill me directly, rather than go after my family. I'll try and kill them right back, if it's appropriate, but I won't hold it against them. Noriko Asano was all for going after my family, so she's going to cop it when she inevitably comes after me again."

The two brothers looked at Jason's friendly smile much differently than when he first arrived. They had the expressions of people who suddenly found themselves holding a snake by the tail.

"We are truly sorry, Mr Asano," Koya said. "You gave us a warning when the Asano clan were going to come after us and we repaid you with enmity. I'd like to assure you that this was not the clan leadership."

"That being said, while the clan elders may not be to blame," Denji said, "we are responsible. Such is the nature of leadership."

"I appreciate that," Jason said. "The simple fact is that I'm not interested in what my taking the door means for your clan, as callous as that sounds. Do you know why I need it?"

"According to the clan records," Denji said, "the magic of our world would become imbalanced and require intervention. Someone would appear to make that intervention and the founder intended it to be himself. He believed that if something happened to him, someone else would appear, however."

"And something did."

"We do not know what, however. There have long been rumours of betrayal by aspects of the Network, but this was the mid-sixteenth century. The Network was still a collection of unaffiliated secret societies, without a fragment of the power required to take down the founder."

The office door burst open as Itsuki rushed in.

"Mr Asano!"

"Itsuki!" Koya scolded. "What are you doing, coming into the patriarch's office like that?"

"Uncle Souta said that Mr Asano had been poisoned," Itsuki said.

"I'm quite fine," Jason assured him. "Thank you for your concern."

"Souta told you that?" Koya asked his son.

"He didn't tell me, as such," Itsuki admitted. "I might have just overheard."

"And he didn't sense you listening in?" Jason asked. "Not bad. Patriarch, given the circumstances, I think it might be best to cut through the niceties and go directly to the door right now."

"Of course," Denji said, then shook his head. "After all this time, it's not how this moment was meant to go."

"I wouldn't worry about it," Jason said. "*Star Wars* fans feel like this every time a new movie comes out."

Jason's companions emerged from Jason's portal onto one of the Arima Grand Resort's helipads, the one reserved for the Tiwari clan's private use in the middle of a wide lawn. Waiting with Jason were Itsuki, Koya and Denji. Only Farrah didn't come through, as she would need her own portal. While Jason waited out the cooldown on his portal power, he introduced the others to the Tiwari family.

"I cannot express enough our dismay at the attempt on Mr Asano's life," Denji said.

"The what?" Erika asked.

"It was just poison," Jason said.

"Oh, that's fine," Erika said with relief. "I once saw him drink bleach to make a point, and I'm not sure that even counts as poison. I'd have said it was more caustic than poisonous."

"Bleach is corrosive," Emi said. "I'm pretty sure it's poison if you drink it, though."

"Why exactly are people trying to kill you?" Yumi asked.

"They probably met him," Dawn said.

"Rude," Jason said.

"You punched my nose into my brain."

"That again?" Jason asked. "I've died three times so far, and you don't see me complaining."

"Really?" Asya asked. "You kind of bring it up a lot."

"That's because if people realise I just keep coming back, they'll realise there's no point killing me in the first place."

Denji and Koya shared an uncertain look as they witnessed the exchange, while Itsuki had a wide grin on his face. Jason used his portal again and Farrah stepped through.

"Any issues?" Jason asked her.

"I told you over the phone," Erika said. "Nothing happened."

"One of the Asano clan came sniffing around," Farrah contradicted. "Just a bronze-ranker."

"When was this?" Erika asked.

"I didn't want to worry you," Farrah told her. "Don't worry; he didn't get any messages back and I was thorough. No one will realise it's a corpse; they'll just think someone burned some rubbish."

"You killed someone?" Erika asked her.

"I'm fair game," Jason said, then his voice turned cold. "You are not."

"He has to be decisive when protecting the family," Yumi approved. "If we show weakness, we'll be treated as weak."

Jason introduced Farrah to the Tiwari clan.

"You know, Miss Hurin technically meets the requirements for the prophecy as well," Itsuki pointed out. "Depending on how important you consider the 'man' part of 'a man who walks between worlds.' Given that I don't think they technically walked, it means there is leeway for interpretation."

"Actually, there is more to the requirements than that," Denji said. "You have never been to see the door, Itsuki, but you will soon learn."

"I get to go?"

"You will, in fact, be the last Tiwari to see the door, if things otherwise go as planned."

"Because that's the way it always goes," Jason muttered. "Alright, everyone back off so we can get this show on the road."

Everyone backed away onto the surrounding lawn and darkness came storming from Jason's shadow, Shade taking his sleek plane form.

"The door isn't here?" Farrah asked.

"Yeah, I thought they'd have it in a basement or something," Jason said.

"The greatest security is secrecy," Denji explained. "From the beginning, the door has been hidden on an uninhabited island in the Pacific Ocean."

Jason and the others descended towards the water in jet suits, hovering over the water as Shade took the form of a large, twin-level motorboat. They settled onto the large upper deck.

"This is rather convenient," Koya said as the jet suit evaporated around him.

"That was amazing!" Itsuki said. "Will my familiar be able to do things like that?"

"I don't know," Jason said. "Shade's ability to take different transportation forms actually comes from one of my abilities. It was a gift from Shade's dad."

"Your familiar has a father?" Denji asked.

"Yeah, his old man is Death."

"What do you mean, Death?" Koya asked.

"You, know, Death," Jason said. "Scythe, robes, that Ingmar Bergman film. No wealth, no land, no silver, no gold; nothing satisfies me but your soul. Death."

"As usual," Shade said, "what Mr Asano is describing is only true from a very specific point of view."

"I'm like Obi-Wan Kenobi," Jason said cheerfully. "Let's get this boat moving!"

Soon the boat was roaring over bright, clear water, between towering islets of stone. They passed by small, uninhabited islands covered in lush greenery. Denji directed Shade where to go as Erika spoke to Jason.

"We had a plane and those jet suits," she said. "Why do we need to go anywhere by boat?"

"Look around us, Eri. How can we not go by boat?"

"I thought you were in a hurry."

"I am, Eri. But I also want to have a nice, fun day before I find myself annihilating monster victims animated as walking corpses again. Let me have this one."

She pulled him into a hug.

"Of course, little brother."

Jason moved over to the railing, joining Farrah in leaning against it and looking out.

"This is what adventuring in my world is meant to be," he told her. "Exotic locales and ancient treasure in hidden ruins. Looking at all this tropic beauty, the horrible things we saw just a few days ago seem so far away."

"It's a nice change from the dark days behind us," Farrah agreed, "but I fear there are more to come. For now, though, let us take our joys where we can find them."

"Deal."

He turned to look at Asya and flashed her a grin. She was sitting on a bench that ran along the side of the motorboat's upper deck and he sauntered over to join her, their bodies leaning into one another.

"How glad are you right now that you never joined the Federal Police?"

"I'm not sure how much the Network is for me either," she said. "I don't like the direction they're taking. You need to explain to them why this is so important."

"I told them I have to save the world," he said. "I'm not sure how to raise the stakes from there. I mean, yes, I might be saving the universe, but probably not. Dawn thinks it should be able to endure Earth's destruction."

"You were very vague about the details."

"Because I didn't want an army of Network goons racing me to this door."

"They're an army of goons now?"

"You'd prefer the term faceless henchmen?"

"How about faceless henchpeople?"

"I can work with that."

"Jason!" Itsuki exclaimed, arriving above deck after exploring the boat. "Your familiar is incredible!"

"Mate, you seriously need to learn to how to read body language," Jason said, disentangling himself from Asya.

"What?" Itsuki asked with an oblivious expression.

"Never mind," Jason said. "You know, I actually met Shade before he became my familiar, even though I summoned him. I had recently met this new friend, Emir, who was holding a competition. I originally met Farrah and her companions because they were working for him, as it happens, but they were out of town when he arrived and he came looking for me…"

The boat was anchored in a lagoon at an uninhabited island, waiting for low tide. Jason had suggested Shade take a submersible form, but Denji explained that there were magic protections they would need to move past. While they waited, Jason, Erika, Emi, Asya, Farrah and Itsuki were swimming in the turquoise waters.

Yumi and Dawn chatted with Denji and Koya, who were startled at the revelation of Dawn's true identity, much of which she had to explain to them. She was a treasure trove of knowledge about the very concepts around which their clan had been built and they found her company a revelation.

Sunset colours worked their way into the sky as the tide dropped low enough to reveal the sea cave into which they would be heading. The swimmers reboarded and they beached the boat, which then vanished into Jason's shadow, depositing the passengers onto the soft sand. When they sorted out who would and wouldn't go into the cave, Emi protested when told she wouldn't be going in.

"I've been hidden away this whole time! What was the point of bringing me?"

"I know, Moppet, and I'm sorry," Jason said. "I knew that people would probably try to kill me, because they usually do, but I didn't expect the whole Asano clan to turn on us. Akari's nan really buggered up the trip. But this is a sacred place for the Tiwari clan, not a tourist spot."

Koya and Denji shared a glance, both nodding.

"Since she is your niece, Mr Asano," Koya said, "we are willing to bring her along, given your status in this. She can bear witness, alongside my son."

"Alright," Jason said. "But I want quiet, and I want respectful, young lady. Is that understood?"

Emi nodded eagerly, a huge grin on her face.

"I also need your mother's permission," he added, upon which Emi turned a weaponised expression of longing on her mother.

"Is it safe?" Erika asked.

"For her, yes," Denji said. "Only Jason will face any challenges within."

"Wait," Jason said with exaggerated panic. "Is it safe for me?"

"I believe so," Denji said.

"You believe so? I'm not feeling the confidence."

"Stop being a coward," Farrah said.

"Cowards live!"

"Well, you keep dying, so clearly that's not you."

"Why am I always the one who has to save the world," he muttered petulantly. "No one tells Kaito he has to save the world."

"Seriously?" Erika asked.

"For him, it's all, 'Kaito, fly around in your helicopter with your wavy hair,' and 'Kaito, team up with this hard-edged, implausibly attractive detective and solve crimes.'"

Watching the exchange with increasing misgivings, Denji leaned towards his brother.

"Have we made a very bad mistake here?" he whispered.

"It's probably fine," Koya said. "I was having Itsuki tell me about anything he learned from the Asano girl while she was living with them in Australia. Some of the things she told him are starting to make a lot more sense."

"I hope you're right."

40
AN UNEXPECTED DIRECTION

Inside a partially submerged sea cave, Jason walked over the surface of the water. His cloak was wrapped around himself and Emi, keeping their bodies light. The Tiwari patriarch also walked over the water, while Itsuki and his father rode in an inflatable dinghy. As they moved deeper into the cave, motes of light emerged from Jason's cloak, spreading out to illuminate the cave in soft starlight.

"It's pretty," Emi said.

"I've always thought so," Jason said. "So much of what I do is ugly, so I quite like this."

Some distance into the cave, the floor rose above the water level and all five people stood on the wet sand from which the water had receded.

At the back of the cave was a hewn wall carved from the solid stone, with metal rungs set into it. Jason spotted the pockmarks where the rungs had corroded away and been replaced several times over the centuries.

"There's no magic here," Jason said, tilting his head. "It's deeper. Much, much deeper."

"You can sense that?" Koya asked.

"Barely, and only because I was looking for it. The logistical problems involved in sinking a mineshaft on a tropical island are formidable. Without magic to keep the shaft sealed and reinforced, maintenance must be an issue."

"The founder didn't want anyone to notice a patch of magic in the middle of nowhere by happenstance," Denji explained. "The wall holds back the high tide and there's a shaft on the other side, going deep enough that the magic down there is undetectable from the outside. Unless your magical senses are absurdly powerful, anyway."

"How are your senses so strong?" Itsuki asked Jason.

"Supernatural senses—that's your magic and aura detection—are a function of your aura, like a radar tower sending out signals," Jason explained. "Except not, but for the purposes of this analogy, it's close enough. A stronger aura is like a stronger radar emitter, giving you a more powerful sense of your surroundings."

"I'd love to have senses that strong," Itsuki said.

"Be careful what you wish for," Jason told him. "Not every power is worth the price."

Jason leapt lightly up to the top of the wall and used an extending shadow arm to pull Emi up after him. He opened his inventory and took out a necklace with a blue jewel.

"This will let you breathe if the air gets a bit sketchy down there," Jason said as he affixed it around her neck. "Ready?"

Emi flashed him a grin and they jumped off, Jason's cloak allowing them to float down. Motes of light from Jason's cloak trailed them like fairy dust as they descended for what felt like an eternity until they finally emerged from the shaft into a large chamber and set down on the floor.

Jason's starlight motes spread out to reveal a five-sided room. Each wall was made up of liquid-smooth marble whose colouration reminded Jason of the light generated by transcendent damage. The marble was white with streaks of blue, silver, and gold, with an aperture in each wall the size of a human head. There was a soft white light shining from each of the five apertures.

This far down, the magic was not just detectable but intimidating. Between gods and the Builder, Jason had experienced enough transcendent-rank power to recognise it when he experienced it. Fortunately, he could also sense that it was at a remove, preventing it from overwhelming him. He glanced at Emi, who didn't even seem to notice it due to her lack of aura senses. She eagerly looked around the room.

"Where's the door?" she asked. "Has the door been a metaphor this whole time?"

"We'll have to wait until the others get down here," Jason said. He could sense the three clansmen slowly descending the shaft.

"If they tell us the door was inside us all along," Emi said, "I'm going to need you to beat them up."

Jason laughed, tousling his niece's hair.

"Uncle Jason," she complained, pushing his hand away.

The three Tiwari men dropped through the ceiling on the end of magical ropes, their feet slipped into loops at the end.

"How does this work?" Jason asked.

"It's quite simple," Denji explained. "You can sense the power of it, yes? How it's sealed away?"

"Yes."

"You stand in the middle of the room and concentrate—after the rest of us are out of the way."

Jason looked around the clean pentagon that made up the room.

"Out of the way where?"

"We can stand in the corners, where the walls meet," Koya said. "So long as we're clear of the apertures in the middle of the walls, we'll be unaffected."

"You'll find the power quite easy to access," Denji said. "Enduring it is up to you."

"So I just want the door to open and it does?" Jason asked. "That sounds suspiciously like the door was inside me all along."

Emi snorted a laugh.

"That's not how it works at all," Denji said. "Be aware that the power you will be exposed to is vast. None of our people have ever been able to endure it and enter the door. Only upon hearing about your powerful aura did we seriously consider that you might be the person we were waiting for. That will hopefully allow you to resist the power long enough to gain passage."

The others moved to the perimeter of the room, to the points where two of the pentagonal chamber's five walls met.

"You are responsible for the safety of my niece while I'm otherwise indisposed," Jason told the Tiwari men. "I recommend you take that responsibility very seriously."

"Of course," Koya said.

"No," Jason said. "This is not a matter of course. You keep her safe or you'll wish your clan had used a better poison on me."

"Uncle Jason, don't be a dick. They know you'll wipe out their whole clan if anything happens to me. You don't have to rub their noses in it."

"Sorry, Moppet."

The Tiwari men looked from Jason to his niece with pale expressions.

"Okay," Jason said, rubbing his hands eagerly as he made his way into the centre of the room. "Let's give this a try."

Jason moved into the middle of the room and extended his senses. The power in the room answered immediately, transcendent light beaming out from the apertures in each wall, meeting in the middle to shine directly on him. The power crashed over him in a tsunami of pure, clean magic, drowning him in it like the aura suppression of a god. Even Jason's powerful aura was like a paper boat in a hurricane, blasted away in an instant.

Jason forced his eyes open to check on the others, who were unaffected as promised. He paid them no more mind, gritting his teeth as he stood against the storm of magic. It was not Jason's first transcendent-rank rodeo, however, nor his first time having his aura pounded down to nothing. It felt like he was being squeezed in a giant fist, but he endured with little more than a grim expression. Suddenly, the light vanished and Jason vanished with it.

Jason felt like something was trying to pull his body apart, but the sensation passed after just a moment. His vision swam into focus and he found himself in an alien landscape filled with amber light. A pair of windows popped up to obscure his view.

- You have entered a space of combined physical and astral nature, the [Fundamental Realm]. You have gained an instance of [Dimensional Discorporation] and will periodically gain additional instances until you leave this space.

- You are a gestalt entity combining physical and astral nature; [Dimensional Discorporation] has no effect.

- You have resisted [Dimensional Discorporation].
- You have gained an instance of [Resistant].
- You have gained an instance of [Integrity].

Jason dismissed the first window, reflecting on the foresight in the ability the World-Phoenix had designed for him. It irked him to be dancing to someone else's tune, but he was forced to admit that, as much as he mistrusted anyone or anything with that much power, the World-Phoenix had given him much. From coming back from the dead to bringing him home, she had asked no more in return thus far than things he would have done anyway.

Closing the first window cleared his vision a bit and he glanced around. The place he found himself in was not the subterranean chamber he had just come from. The first thing he'd noticed was amber light, thick to the point of rendering the world around him monochromatic. Just as thick as the light was the aura suffusing everything, so powerful, it seemed almost solid. He was on a small rise under an open sky, the terrain around him generally flat but uneven. It was covered in grass, with fragmentary ruins sticking out of the turf.

Seeing no immediate threats, or much of anything at all, he took a look at the second window.

- You have entered a domain of the Builder.
- By entering this domain, you have subjected your soul to the influence and authority of the Builder. You have gained an instance of [Builder's Dominion].
- Your soul has learned to reject the influence and authority of the Builder; [Builder's Dominion] has no effect.
- You have resisted [Builder's Dominion].
- You have gained an instance of [Resistant].
- You have gained an instance of [Integrity].

"Dawn didn't warn me about that," Jason snarled. "I think we need to have a little conversation."

"As do you and I," said a voice.

Jason looked to see a man emerge from behind the shattered remnant of a vaguely Greek column. The man had a sharp suit, an expensive haircut, dark eyes and a predator's smile.

"It's about time you showed up," the man said. "I'm a busy man, Mr Asano, but I knew you'd get here eventually. I was confident that whoever sent you back to this world would make sure you were up to the task, which is why I never bothered to stop my people from trying to kill you. If they succeeded, you weren't good enough for what needs to be done anyway."

"You have me at a disadvantage," Jason said.

"Oh, you have no idea," the man said, grinning like a snake who found a nest full of baby mice. "I have many names, but the one you are most likely to know is Mr North."

"The leader I was told the EOA didn't have," Jason said. "You have a lot to answer for."

"But now is not the time," Mr North said.

"Are you sure that's your choice to make?"

"No, it's yours, but you're a smart man, Mr Asano. More or less."

Jason paused to take stock, pushing his senses to their limits. Detecting anything through the oppressive aura suffusing the space around them was like pushing through treacle, but he managed to get a read on Mr North.

"You're gold rank."

Mr North's only response was another Cheshire grin.

"What are you?" Jason asked. "You're not an essence user. Some kind of native magical creature? But Earth doesn't have those. And there's something else…"

Jason's eyes went wide.

"You're a familiar. A bonded familiar, but your bond has been severed."

"Your senses are as sharp as advertised, noticing that much in this place. I was a rune spider, originally, although I've come so very far from those days. Becoming a familiar offers a creature like me many opportunities if you look at things in the long term. You do have to pick your essence user with care. Someone who will rank up well, obviously, but there are other pitfalls. As I came to discover."

"Your essence user died?"

Jason's first encounter with a native magical creature had been the familiar of Landemere Vane, both the first person he met from another world and the first person he killed. Vane's familiar had tried to take revenge, only to fall victim to aging masonry.

"My essence user did die," Mr North said. "That was not until after our bond was severed, however. You've heard of bonded familiars parting ways with their essence users, yes?"

"I have. The connection is intimate, so when the familiar and the essence user become irrevocably at odds, the bond breaks."

"My essence user was blinded by faith. Sacrifice after sacrifice, giving up power and prestige to lift up a bunch of savages."

"The Network founder was your essence user," Jason realised. "That's how you knew about this place."

"Just so," Mr North said. "It's so nice to talk to someone quick on the uptake. My own minions were quite disappointing before Adrien Barbou came along. Thank you for putting him in a position to come my way. If the Lyon branch's plans had worked out better, I'd have missed out on a quality subordinate."

Jason narrowed his eyes.

"You're what happened to the Network founder, aren't you?"

"I am," Mr North said. "Trussed him up and handed him off to some gentlemen in Philadelphia. This was back in the colonial days, long before the Network proper. They didn't have the power to take him down, of course, leaving me to do all the work. I felt bad, later, about the unpleasant end my bond-mate came to. We were so close, once, after all. I was quite angry at the time, though, and I've been reaping the benefits of that deal ever since. It gave the US Network branches quite the head start, once the magic started ticking up."

"The US Network branches are feeding the EOA resources and information?"

"Only a few critical members," Mr North said. "For the most part, their animosity to my little organisation is quite genuine. Feel free to tell them; they're a little too unified at the moment. A little internal strife would serve me well."

"Why are you here and what do you want?"

"For you, obviously. This world needs saving and I've put a lot of work into it. I need to make sure you do it right."

41

PARADE OF DELIGHTS

"Saving the world the right way requires your guidance, does it?" Jason asked Mr North. "You'll forgive me for not taking you at your word."

"Repairing the link between worlds is just the beginning," Mr North said. "If you make a mistake now, we'll all pay for it later."

"Oh, so you're an altruist."

"It's not inconsistent with selfishness to save the planet you're standing on, Mr Asano."

"What is this subsequent threat I need to be wary of?"

"While I recognise that being more forthcoming would help establish trust," Mr North said, "that isn't a feasible approach at this time. If you learn too much now, things won't go the way they need to. Suffice to say that you will learn, in time, and you won't be happy about it."

"You're not exactly selling it here."

"I know having things kept from you isn't what you want, Mr Asano, but it's what you need. It won't feel like it, but I'm helping you right now. Even telling you this much may be too great a compromise."

"Then why are you here?" Jason asked. "If you wanted to not tell me things, you could have done that from home."

"I need to set you on the path. The day will come, Mr Asano, when you and I become allies."

"You're responsible for hundreds of thousands of deaths."

"I don't deny it. Not to you, anyway. That doesn't change the reality."

"I could just kill you here," Jason said.

"You could try," Mr North said. "I'm gold rank but not an essence user. The odds would be in my favour, but you've beaten long odds before. You have a way of coming through in the critical moments I won't underestimate. It would be a risk, though. You have responsibilities. Will you put your ability to meet them in jeopardy just to punish me for past injustices?"

"I think you've got plenty of injustice left in you," Jason said. "How much death and misery are prevented if you die in this hole?"

"It's just the opposite, Mr Asano. You're here to save the world this time, but I'm the only one getting ready for next time."

"Which you aren't going to tell me about."

"Correct."

At his side, Jason's fingers twitched, eager to conjure his dagger and lunge at the man in front of him.

"How do you see this going?" Jason asked.

"You're here for the door," Mr North said. "I'm here to make sure you don't just claim it but absorb it."

"Absorb it?"

"It's critical that the door cannot be taken from you by anyone. It has to become a part of you."

"How does a door become part of me?"

"It's not a literal door, Mr Asano, although it often appears as such. It's an astral construct with the power to manifest in physical reality in the form of a portal. Much the same principle as your portal archways."

"This door is an object of the Builder."

"Yes."

"The Builder has tried to worm his way into my soul before. I'm not giving him another shot."

"It has?"

"Someone tried to shove a star seed up in me."

"And it didn't work?" Mr North laughed. "Mr Asano, you are a parade of delights. It seems that I couldn't have asked for anyone better. You need to take this particular object off the Builder's hands."

"So say you. You could easily be his lackey, setting me up for a fall. You don't seem to be bothered by the Builder's influence in this place."

"My bond-mate's deity and the Builder long ago came to an accord regarding your world and the other. While my bond-mate is long dead, I still enjoy an amnesty from the Builder's incidental attentions."

"Again, I have nothing to go on but the word of a man who should be on trial in The Hague."

"Let me show you, and you can decide for yourself. I've made no small preparations for this."

"I'll go along with this. For now."

Mr North grinned.

"If you were near the end of silver, instead of just the beginning, this would be a very different conversation, wouldn't it?"

"It wouldn't be a conversation."

"So intimidating."

"Just get on with it."

"Of course. Follow me, Mr Asano. We need to go to the heart of this little realm."

The amber-lit terrain was uneven but mostly flat grassland, dotted with fragmentary ruins. As he followed Mr North, Jason's eyes picked out chunks of ruin sticking out of the ground that looked Greek, Cambodian, and Mayan, along with more alien elements that would not have looked out of place on the cover of some Lovecraftian fiction.

"You are not what I expected, Mr North."

"You're the only person I've seen in centuries who has been to my home world, Mr Asano. I feel like I can be myself around you. With the EOA, I have this need to be the stern and sinister authoritarian figure, which can be fun, but it gets tiring after a while. That being said, I've heard you're not above playing the sinister authoritarian yourself. You should consider joining us, now that you're no longer affiliated with the Network. I know that might seem like an outrageous proposition, but have you considered that if you were part of the leadership, you could take the organisation in a more positive direction? You wouldn't even have to take orders from me. We could be partners. Maybe even friends."

"Do you know what a nightmare hag is, Mr North?"

"It's some kind of fear monster, right?"

"It's an astral being, not a monster, but yes. It takes things from your deepest fears and makes them manifest. Would you like to know what it showed me?"

"I'm not sure I grasp the purpose of this conversational segue, but do tell."

"It showed me a version of myself that could be friends with you."

"You do realise how self-centred it is that your greatest fear is some version of yourself, right?"

Mr North led Jason to a small dell that had been hard to notice with the light washing out the geographical features. At the bottom was a series of large standing stones, arranged in a circle. The stones were the same marble as the walls of the pentagon room through which Jason had entered the realm: white with veins of blue, silver, and gold. The stones hadn't been polished slippery smooth, however, looking rough-hewn and weathered.

Mr North made his way down the slope of the dell, with Jason following. Mr North pointed out a series of wooden crates on the grass inside the stone circle.

"Prying this place out of the Builder's control and into yours will be an intricate and elaborate process," Mr North said. "I've been gathering the materials we need for longer than you've been alive. I'll talk you through the process as we unpack it all."

As they reached the circle of stones, Jason reached out and touched one.

Item: [Fundamental Gate] (transcendent rank, legendary)

???. (???, ???).

- Effect: ???.
- Effect: ???.

- Your soul's ability to resist the Builder's influence and your [Spirit Vault] ability allow you to incorporate this item into your spirit vault. Doing so will purge the Builder's influence and the item's effects, instead altering your abilities.

- This item's impact on your abilities will be diminished due to your rank being lower than that of the item. The effect will further increase as your rank increases.

- Once incorporated, this object cannot be removed or made use of by anyone else. Incorporating this item into your spirit vault will affect the following abilities:

- [Spirit Vault]: Your ability to sense Builder-related items and resist their effects will be significantly increased. You will be able to directly influence Builder-influenced energy using aura manipulation.

- [Path of Shadows]: This ability will gain an additional effect. If you can comprehend the fundamental aspects of an area of physical reality, you can open a portal to the [Fundamental Realm].

To Mr North, Jason appeared to be staring blankly as he read the screen.

"What are you spacing out about?" Mr North asked. "We have hours of work ahead of us. I just hope your astral magic is up to scratch or this will take even longer."

Jason ignored him, still staring into space.

"Asano?"

Jason reached out and touched the stone again and darkness spread over it like a shadow was passing over. White stone became opaque, like smoked glass, with the blue, silver and gold veins becoming twinkling lights within the darkness. The stone had turned completely dark and the other stones started following suit.

Mr North turned his head wildly, watching the stones change.

"What did you do?"

"I hate to break it to you, Mr North, but smugly thinking you know what the enemy you're trying to turn into an ally will do is a good way to get slapped down. I learned that the hard way myself."

Jason waved his arm and an obsidian portal arch rose up in the middle of the circle. The stones started to break down, dissolving into dust. The dust was drawn through the air, as if by a vacuum, getting sucked into the dark portal.

"WHAT DID YOU DO?"

"Since we won't be needing them anymore," Jason said as he picked up one of the wooden crates, "I'm just going pop these into the old dimensional space. Waste not, want not, yeah?"

Mr North looked on in horror as the stones crumbled away, while Jason started shoving crates into his inventory.

"You've ruined everything."

"Oh, calm down. You wanted me to absorb the magic door, right? I'm absorbing the magic door."

"You can't just absorb it because you want to!"

"No, *you* can't just absorb it because you want to. I'm a man of many talents. Cooking, absorbing magic doors..."

Jason frowned, pausing with another crate in his arms.

"Alright," he acknowledged. "Two talents. And my sister is better at one of them, but still. I hope Kaito isn't any good at absorbing magic doors. Probably not; that would be weird."

The obsidian arch of the portal was slowly transmuting as it absorbed the dust from the stones, turning from pure black to a smoky crystal with blue, silver and gold shimmers within.

"Why are you talking nonsense?" Mr North asked. "This space is going to break down, and us with it!"

"Yeah? Hang on a bit." Jason quickly stowed the last two crates, the last of the stones crumbling to nothing as he did. He then looked around.

"Seems fine to me."

The ground lurched and the amber light took on streaks of red tint.

"Oh, there it is," Jason said. "Come on; out we pop."

He then stepped through the arch into which all the stones had vanished. Mr North looked around at the space unravelling around them and scrambled after him.

In the pentagonal room at the bottom of the shaft, Emi was running her fingers over the smooth marble, marvelling at the slick smoothness, almost devoid of friction.

"The wall is getting warmer," she said.

"Oh?" Koya asked and the three Tiwari men put their hands to the wall.

"You're right," Denji said.

"Does that mean Mr Asano did something?" Itsuki asked.

"That's what we came here for," Denji said. "Let's hope he did it right."

"The wall is changing colour," Emi said, stepping back from it warily.

The others joined her.

They watched as the white marble walls turned grey, as if the vital essence were being leeched from them. The apertures in the middle of each, still emitting a soft glow, started to dim. Once the light of the apertures had completely gone out and all the colour was gone from the walls, the walls crumbled like sand, spilling onto the floor. Behind them was the plain stone from which the shaft had been dug, identical to the stone under their feet.

In the middle of the room, a line of dark appeared on the floor, from which rose a portal arch. Instead of the familiar obsidian, the arch was murky crystal with lights shining dimly within. The dark void filling the portal was the same, from which Jason stepped out to be caught in a limpet hug by his niece.

"Look out, Moppet," Jason said, lifting her up, still attached to him, and moving her out of the way. Another person stumbled out, after which the portal disappeared into the floor.

Mr North's expression became stern as he stood up straight, panning the room with a stern glare as he adjusted his tie and cuffs. The grinning, languid man Jason had met was nowhere to be seen. Mr North's sharp eyes took in the scene before settling on Jason.

"For all our sakes, Mr Asano," he said, his voice gravel hard, "I hope you haven't made a terrible mistake."

"Caution has its place," Jason said, "but the first step of doing the impossible is having the nuggets to try."

"I will take my leave."

"It won't be today, Mr North," Jason said, "but the day will come when you and I have a reckoning."

"I know you like to be dramatic, Mr Asano, but you'll find yourself with much bigger problems than me to deal with. Assuming you didn't just ruin everything."

Mr North directed his arms at the ground and threads of web shot from his sleeves. He used it to draw a complex sigil on the ground, which lit with pale blue light when it was completed. He stepped onto the sigil and it rose into the air, swiftly carrying Mr North up and into the shaft.

"Who was that?" Denji asked. "Where did he come from?"

"Magic Spider-Man?" Emi suggested.

"That was Mr North, the head of the EOA," Jason explained.

"And you let him go?"

"He's category four, Patriarch," Jason said. "He let us go."

"How can he be category four?" Koya asked. "How would he sustain himself?"

"He's had access to the door for centuries. I imagine he has a stockpile of the objects the magical world will soon be fighting over."

42
COLLATERAL DAMAGE

Dawn, Erika, Yumi and Asya waited on the sandy beach of the lagoon for the others to emerge from the sea cave. Jason and the others appeared on black jet skis that dissolved into darkness as they beached themselves on the sand. Erika snatched her daughter into a worried hug and Farrah slapped Jason on the arm.

"Got it done?" she asked.

"Yeah," Jason said.

Dawn had been staring at Jason even before they left the cave, her gaze unerringly locked onto his aura through the stone.

"What did you do?" Dawn asked him. "The transcendent strain in your aura has been strengthened. It may only offer flavour, rather than power, but it is a startling thing to detect in an aura at your rank. It might be intimidating, but it will also draw attention."

"Probably for the best that he can hide his aura so well, then," Farrah said.

"Yes, it is," Dawn said. "What does have power is the force inside your aura antithetical to the Builder. Most people wouldn't recognise it, but I'm familiar enough with the Builder to know what it is. It was there the first time we met, but now the glowing ember is a burning flame."

"The Builder and his freaky cyborg army killed a lot of people in the other world, including both Farrah and me," Jason said. "I am antithetical to the Builder."

"You'll be lucky if any of the Builder's adherents don't attack you on sight after sensing that aura," Dawn said.

"I'll consider myself lucky if they do," Jason said. "Rooting out those infiltrating pricks is something I've done before and I'll be more than happy to do again."

"So, this is it," said Denji. "Our clan has fulfilled its purpose. Now I am unsure of what course to chart."

As Tiwari clan patriarch, it was Denji's duty to lead a clan now riddled with fissures. Large portions of the clan had treated their long-held purpose as mythological, so Jason's arrival had left many uncertain or angry. Denji would be required to lead his clan to a new purpose.

"The first thing is to consolidate the clan in the wake of our new reality," Denji's brother, Koya, said. "Things will be uncertain as we choose our own destiny, but we must move forward together."

"Father is right, Uncle Denji," Itsuki said. "We will all be together."

"We are far from a unified force, son," Koya said. "I think it might be a good time to broaden your horizons. Mr Asano, I was hoping that you might take Itsuki under your wing for a time."

Itsuki's eyes went wide at the idea.

"You might not want to do that," Emi said. "He may learn more about the A-Team than magic powers."

"The old Liam Neeson movie?" Itsuki asked.

"Oh, holy crap," Jason said. "What have you been teaching this boy? He definitely needs to have his education expanded upon."

"Did I miss something?" Koya asked.

"Clearly," Erika said. "Does your son even know who George Peppard is?"

"The male lead from *Breakfast at Tiffany's*?" Koya asked. "What is going on?"

"You can just ignore them," Yumi said. "My grandchildren have skewed views on certain cultural properties. You should also ignore *Breakfast at Tiffany's*. Mickey Rooney as a Japanese man? Excruciating."

"You know what's worse?" Jason asked. "That movie where Obi-Wan Kenobi plays a man named Koichi Asano."

"That movie," Denji growled. "I can only imagine how aggravating it must be to have your name being used like that."

Asya wrapped her arm inside Jason's.

"If I had a bingo card for you," she told him, "I'd have just crossed off 'get the patriarch of an ancient Japanese clan to complain about old movies during a treasure hunt on a deserted tropical island.'"

"That's a very specific bingo card."

"Yours would be," she said. "There really is no one quite like you."

"Yeah, I'm not like the other girls," Jason said.

"If you two are going to make out," Emi said, "could you save it for the plane? Also, can we get a plane?"

"Shade is my familiar, Moppet. You can't just tell him to…"

Darkness streamed out of Jason's shadow to take the form of a plane, blasting down air as it hovered in place. One of Shade's bodies emerged from Jason and stood next to Emi.

"Would you like to come aboard, Miss Emi?" Shade said loudly, over the rush of air.

"Traitor," Jason accused.

The Tiwari men were returned to Japan and Itsuki went with his father to pack his things. Souta Tiwari, who had been looking into Jason's poisoning, met them on arrival. He offered to report to Jason, but he said that he was uninterested in Tiwari clan affairs. Jason already knew everything from the Shade dwelling in Souta's shadow and it truly was internal Tiwari affairs. Jason had bigger things to deal with than some disgruntled clansmen, although if they'd gone after his family, instead, it would be a different story.

"Mr Asano," Souta said as they waited for Itsuki to return. "The Japanese authorities came to find you during your absence. We truthfully told them that you had already departed, but it might be time for you to bring this trip to Japan to an end."

"Well, I did set off a bunch of car bombs, so I can hardly blame them. Good thing you tried to murder me or I'd feel bad about bringing that to your door."

Souta gave Jason an awkward smile.

"Don't worry, mate. We'll be off and away promptly."

Koya looked at his son, madly shoving things into the dark, floating orb that was the aperture to Itsuki's storage space.

"This is an important opportunity, son, but while I know you admire Mr Asano, do not lose sight of how dangerous he is."

"We are all dangerous, Father. We have all slain many monsters."

"That's not what I mean. You need not fear the man who kills, for all you need to do is be better. Fear the man who kills, then smiles and laughs like it is any other day. There is no line such a man will not cross, whatever he might tell you. Or tell himself."

"I don't think he's like that," Itsuki said. "Look at the things he's done. It's clear how hard he's trying to be a good man."

"Exactly," Koya said. "Good men don't have to try."

On the way back to Australia, Jason, Farrah and Dawn sequestered themselves in a cabin to discuss the next move.

"If you absorbed the door, you should have some idea of how it operates," Dawn said to Jason.

"Yes," he agreed, "although how to operate it properly is another matter. I'm going to need to advance my knowledge of astral magic or I'll just fumble around, accomplishing nothing."

"I can continue to help you with that," Dawn said. "In the meantime, Miss Hurin can work on our own system to tap into the grid, now that you have lost access to Network resources."

"We're going to need access?" Farrah asked.

"As best I can understand," Jason said, "the underlying makeup of reality is made of nodes, of which just this planet has an incalculable number. Fuelling those nodes are what you might call reality cores. Batteries for the universe. These are the things that everyone is going to be fighting over."

"These events you described taking place after the grid goes back up," Farrah said to Dawn. "They're going to reveal these reality cores?"

"Yes," Dawn said. "As best as I can determine, each event will reveal one, which you can expect the magical factions to be fighting over."

"What about the proto-spaces?" Farrah asked.

"They will continue, and we need to use them," Dawn said. "They represent the points at which the dimensional membrane around this reality is most strained. There, rituals to find the altered nodes will be more effective, allowing us to detect them over a wider area."

"As best we can tell, the Network founder used the door to create the imbalance in the link and then founded the Network to slow down the damage once it escalated," Jason explained. "The whole reason the link between worlds is out of whack is that the door was used to modify specific nodes. That's what we need to track down: the nodes the founder modified, so we can restore them to what amounts to factory default."

"It will be quite hit and miss at first," Dawn said. "As more of the link is normalised, the rest will start to stand out and our successes will accelerate at the end."

"Which will stop it siphoning magic from my world," Farrah said. "That will finally trigger the oversized monster surge, giving the Builder's forces a chance to invade."

"Yes," Jason said. "This world is just collateral damage. Unfortunately, the only way out is through. Someone like me coming along to fix the link was part of the plan. I'm going to be the trigger that starts the invasion."

"There is no other option," Dawn said.

"I know," Jason said. "We need to identify the nodes and fix the link, hopefully before the magical factions plunder too many of the nodes and the whole system is thrown off."

"What if one of the nodes we need is affected by these events?" Farrah asked.

"I don't know," Jason said.

"We will need to figure that out as we go," Dawn said. "Even I can't know that until I see it for myself. I suspect, though, that we will have an amount of leeway."

"Meaning we don't have to hit every node?" Jason asked. "That's welcome breathing room."

"These are just educated guesses," Dawn said. "It could well be that I am wrong and every affected node must be restored."

"I guess we have a plan, then," Farrah said. "If we're going to be running around in proto-spaces, though, won't the Network get grouchy?"

"Let them," Jason said.

"A support team might be useful," Farrah said. "Silvers would be best, but we have bronze-rankers we can trust. They can help keep the monsters and the Network off our backs while we're operating in proto-spaces."

"We can talk about it after we get back to Australia and take stock," Jason said. "There are a lot of things up in the air right now."

Jason sat alone in his cloud house, in a dome beneath the water offshore of Asano Village. Emi was giving Itsuki a tour of the village while Jason meditated, feeling completely safe for the first time since his second battle in Makassar. Some of his abilities even ranked up, although he knew that speed to be an illusion.

Early in a rank, abilities always went up faster, but with every rank, the later thresholds became harder and harder to pass. His powers might go up two or three ranks quickly now, but it could be a decade or more before they started reaching gold. He could only hope that the challenges ahead were enough to accelerate the timeline a little.

He had a monitor manifest out of a cloud wall so he could watch the news. It was story after story on the changes currently rocking the world as everyday life and magic continued to collide.

"…it has been almost twenty-four hours since the last new monster wave, with waves that appeared before that point being dealt with across the globe. A Global Defense Network spokesperson claimed that under normal conditions, monster waves would no longer appear, although she did stress that regions that have ejected the GDN presence are not operating under normal conditions."

The League of Heroes logo appeared on the screen.

"Questions continue to be asked about the League of Heroes that have taken over in the wake of GDN departures, specifically about the organisation behind them, the Engineers of Ascension. There is also the enigmatic and reclusive Cabal, although they are yet to make any visible attempts to seize political power. The EOA, as they are commonly known, was first revealed by Jason Asano, who himself is coming under fire amid accusations of a series of car bombings in Japan…"

Jason flicked off the screen with a mental command and it sank into the cloud wall. He got up, walked through the cloud house, following the tunnel linked to the central underwater dome. He then took the tunnel to the airlock, leaving the cloud house for the tunnel system running under Asano Village. He took out the cloud flask, removed the stopper and placed the end into the physical aperture next to the airlock. The cloud house started breaking down and flowing into the flask.

Jason hadn't yet used the new form of his cloud flask, the palace, which became available when he had raised the flask to silver rank. He didn't expect the palace form to be as grand as Emir's, since Emir had already taken his flask to gold rank. The cloud house form had become more impressive at bronze rank and Jason imagined the palace form would operate on the same principle. Even so, he did not anticipate being disappointed to only get a small palace.

He did not test the palace form after the cloud house had returned to the flask. Instead, he placed the flask in his inventory and sat in the small, underground tram cart that would carry him through the tunnels to Asano Village.

As he neared the village, he sensed Annabeth Tilden arrive at the main gate. The serene bushland of Asano Village allowed Jason's senses to be quite alert to distant events, compared to a crowded city where the stimuli was so much heavier. His silver-rank spirit attribute helped him filter it all, but only at higher rank would he be able to actively monitor a whole city when he blanketed it with his senses.

Leaving the secret tunnels in the basement of the main residence, Jason hunted up Farrah and they went outside. Shade took the form of a car and drove them out to the main gate, where Annabeth was waiting in her own car. The Network Sydney branch committeewoman was accompanied by Nigel, the man in charge of the branch's tactical training, along with a pair of other silver-rankers.

Nigel had worked closely with Farrah as they revamped the Network's training program, with Nigel himself, a rare non-core user, soaring up to silver rank after using Farrah's training methods. Nigel had reached his rank in almost as little time as Jason.

Jason and Farrah stepped out of the cloud of darkness that had been their car, while Anna and Nigel got out of their own car. Nigel conspicuously placed himself in a position to intervene if Jason or Farrah made a move on Anna. The other silver-rankers stayed close to her person. Looking on were some lingering fringe types, religious zealots and conspiracy theorists still camped outside the main gate, although most had moved on.

"Really, Nige?" Jason asked, looking at Nigel in between himself and Anna.

"I hate it when people call me Nige."

"I hate it when people betray me, so I guess we're both out of luck. Hello, Anna."

43

I INTEND TO DO DAMAGE

Annabeth Tilden and three silver-rankers were standing outside the main gate of Asano Village, facing Jason and Farrah.

"We didn't betray you, Mr Asano," Anna said.

"No?" Jason asked. "Then I guess the GDN spokesperson on the news stating that our association had been ended due to my increasingly dangerous and radicalised behaviour was a terrible mix-up. I'm surprised Terrance made that kind of slip."

"You set off car bombs in traffic," Anna said.

"I'll do worse before I'm done," Jason said. "The thing is, Anna, I am dangerous and radicalised. I have been from the beginning. Remember when I first came back? Faith-healing my way through a hospital and a rolling gunfight in the streets? Since I started working with the Network, I've been holding back, but now you've cut those fetters. You opened the floodgates, Anna. You don't get to complain when the water comes through."

"It doesn't have to be like this, Asano."

"As long as I eat the fact that you're attacking me in the news, stay quiet and do as I'm told? Why are you here, Anna?"

"Can we talk where there aren't a bunch of hungry loons filming us on camera phones?" she asked. Just as she said, the fringe elements camping outside Asano Village had no shortage of people filming them as they spoke.

"The village is for guests, friends and allies, Anna. I'm not saying the village's defences are impregnable, but if you want in, it'll take more than the four of you."

"We aren't your enemy, Jason. I'm here to try and stop us from reaching that point. There are forces larger than either of us who see you as an antagonistic force, but if you're willing to make some concessions, we can stop this from escalating into conflict."

"Concessions?" he growled.

He took a step that prompted her bodyguard, Nigel, to move between them. Jason stopped, closed his eyes, and after a moment, the tense rage passed from his shoulders.

"This is you, genuinely trying to help me," Jason said softly. "You want to mend fences; I understand that. I respect it. I'm sorry, Anna, but they haven't told you why they turned on me in the first place, have they? It wasn't about car bombs."

"Then what?"

"I'm not sure how much they know, yet, but it's only a matter of time before your bosses realise that I have something they want. Something everyone will want. People are going to make some bad choices trying to get it and they will reap the consequences."

"Is that a threat?" Anna asked.

Jason smiled.

"Since I came to this world," he said, "I've been playing the essence user. It made sense to affiliate myself with the Network, given that their first priority was protecting the world from magic. That's already changing. What's coming will be a gold rush and an arms race, all in one. The old priorities will be gone."

"So you say," Anna said.

"Believe me or not, I don't care," Jason said. "I don't need the Network or anyone but the people already standing with me. I'm done playing essence user and following the rules of this world. I'm an adventurer again."

"What does that mean?"

"Adventurers get the job done," Farrah said, stepping up next to Jason. "We don't have oversight or chains of command or public relations departments. We do what it takes, whoever or whatever gets in our way. The Adventure Society sees the job that needs doing and finds the people to do it. Right here, right now, the Adventure Society is us, and we're the people for the job. We're going to do what needs to be done and we'll go through anyone or anything in our path, without hesitation, remorse, or mercy. I like you, Anna, so I'm hoping that's not you."

"That's what a threat sounds like, Anna," Jason said. "This world needs saving. I don't know if the people behind you understand the true threat or not and I don't care anymore. Just don't get in our way."

"And what exactly does the world need saving from?" Anna asked.

"The dimensional incursions are getting worse," Farrah said, "and the rate at which they're getting worse is increasing. When we first arrived here, category-three incursions were moving from the exception to the norm. Now we're starting to see category-four incursions. They're not just getting worse but getting worse faster than ever before."

"Are you claiming you're going to stop the monsters from coming at all?"

"I don't know," Jason said. "It could just be that we stop them from getting worse."

"Then why not work with us?"

"You broke those ties, not us. Anna, I've worked with a lot of good people at the Network. You're one of them. But not a lot of the good ones end up in charge. Think about the other members on the Steering Committee. Do you trust them to do the right thing? Someone knows that when I do what I have to do, the power you're about to start fighting over will no longer appear. Anna, tell me that the people in charge will choose to address a looming threat over immediate gain."

"You know I can't."

"Then you need to look at your own loyalties and priorities. When you go home to Susan and look her in the eye, I bet you feel proud at the work you've done each day. You should. If you want to keep feeling that way, maybe start thinking about how much you let the International Committee dictate your choices."

"You're not my conscience, Jason. I make my own choices."

"Yet you came here to convince me to let you make mine?"

"There are people following you who will be caught up in your mess.

Asya Karadeniz is throwing away her future by quitting the Network. Don't take her down with you."

"I actually hope you're right, Anna. I hope the Network doesn't lose its way. But the fact is, the Network and the monsters they fight were both incepted by the same person. Your house was always built on sand."

"What are you talking about?"

"The Network was never intended to protect the world from monsters. It was a regulatory measure so the dimensional incursions didn't destroy the world too quickly. A stop-gap until either someone like me came along to turn things back or the world was destroyed. Either result gets what the founder wanted, which is to open the gates of an entirely different world to invasion."

"Even if all that were true, and I'm not acknowledging that it is, it doesn't matter. It doesn't matter what someone centuries ago intended when it's the people of today that control the Network's destiny."

Jason smiled.

"I like that," he said. "I hope you have ambition, Anna. With people like you at the helm, the Network really could be what I think we both want it to be."

"Then instead of moving away from it, move closer. With what you have to offer, you could be a positive influence. Help me make the Network everything it should be."

"That's not going to work, Anna. I'm self-aware enough to know that I'm more trouble than I'm worth in an organisation. As soon as the group's ideals and mine come into conflict, we both know what I'll do. Call it independence or arrogance, but I work better from the outside."

"It's arrogance," Farrah said.

"Whose side are you on?" Jason asked her.

"Justice."

Jason chuckled and stepped towards Anna, only for her silver-rank bodyguard, Nigel, to move into his way.

"If I wanted her dead, Nigel," Jason said, "you wouldn't see it coming, let alone have a chance to stop me."

"It's fine, Nigel," Anna said, and he begrudgingly let Jason past.

Jason held out his hand and Anna shook it.

"I hope that we can work together again, someday, Anna. You'll soon learn why it can't be today, though."

"If you really do need to save the world, you can't do it alone."

"He's not alone," Farrah said.

"I suppose not," Anna said. "But I know you feel isolated right now, Asano, and perhaps inclined to lash out. Just give your actions some consideration before you do anything drastic…"

She looked around at the people filming them with their phones.

"…like having a conversation like this in front of people who are probably live-streaming it. But I guess that was the point of having it here, wasn't it?"

"If you play by your opponent's rules, Anna, they get to decide who wins."

"The idea is for all of us to win, Jason. There doesn't have to be sides. I know you like playing chaos-bringer, but that will lash back on you. And the people around you."

Jason nodded.

"A lesson I never seem to learn properly," he acknowledged. "I'm not your enemy, Anna. But if your organisation comes for me, they will be, and this is not the time for half-measures."

Anna frowned.

"I hope things go well for both of us," she said.

"So do I."

"Why are you so certain the Network will be at odds with you?"

"Dawn briefed you on the events about to take place. There's no preventing them, only managing them, at least until I put a stop to them for good. What she didn't tell you is that each event will contain a treasure that offers a path forward to those bottlenecked at the upper reaches of power. We've started calling them reality cores."

"You're saying that there's a way beyond category three?"

"I'm sure you understand the ramifications," Jason said. "The Network will be fighting the Cabal, the EOA and each other over the reality cores, but they also won't want me turning off the power spigot. Saving the world will stop it from getting fresh wounds they can dig through for nuggets of power."

Anna looked around at the people filming them.

"Jason, do you have any idea what you've done by releasing this information? Even if you're lying, you've done incredible damage."

"The Network, the Cabal and the EOA are about to start strip mining this planet for the very things holding it together, even as forces threaten to tear it apart. I intend to do damage."

"It's time for me to leave," Anna said. "After this conversation, I have to go get demoted."

"I hope that isn't true," Jason said. "We need people like you."

Jason had called a family meeting in the sitting room of the main residence, with Erika, her husband, Ian, Emi, Jason and Erika's father, Ken, their uncle, Hiro and grandmother, Yumi. They were all sat in armchairs and on couches while Jason and Farrah stood before them.

"I have something to tell you about how you're going to spend the next few months," Jason said, "and I don't think you're going to like it."

"You're going to stash us away somewhere," Yumi said.

"Yes," Jason said.

"What if we say no?" Erika asked.

"Then things will be awkward when I do it anyway."

"Why?" Ken asked.

"Because I have something that people will want me to give them. Once they realise I can't, they'll want me to use it for them. If they take hostages to try and make me, I have to be able to say no. If you all are the hostages, I don't trust that I can."

"We built Asano Village to keep us safe," Hiro said.

"And when the Network was at our backs, that was enough," Farrah said. "Now that they're at our gates, it isn't."

"Where is this deep, dark hole you want to throw us in?" Erika asked.

"The safest place I have access to. You can spend the time preparing for what comes after, if you still intend to travel with us to the other world. Emi can prepare for her chosen essences, since the ones I picked out were apparently not good enough."

"Uncle Jason, you only picked those out to keep me safe," Emi said.

"Good," Erika said. "Emi, you're taking those."

Ian placed a hand on his wife's shoulder.

"Eri, we need to let her be what she wants to be, not what we want her to be."

"You'll have plenty of time for discussion on that topic," Jason said.

"Emi won't be ready for essences for about another year. As for you, Ian, I suggest you get ready to introduce some medical knowledge to a population that relies largely on magic and faith."

"I don't think that matters," Ian said. "Working with essence users, I've learned that their bodies defy my medical understanding."

"Do you remember my friend Jory, from my recordings of the other world?" Jason asked. "He is all about helping regular people, who do fall under your expertise. I think you'll be the most exciting person he's ever met in his life."

"Really?"

"Oh, yes. Just before I last saw him, the Church of the Healer gave him a mandate and funding to spread his methods around the world. You're going to be a busy man. What all of you need to do is learn some languages. Fortunately, you're all essence users, except for Emi, who's already been learning for months. I'm not sure I ever explained what a spirit attribute is, but you have one, and it will positively affect your memory. You've probably already noticed."

"So that's it?" Erika asked. "You're locking us away and we don't get a say in it?"

"Yep."

"And what if something happens to you?" she asked.

"Actually, I'm pretty safe," Jason said. "Word will soon get around about the magic door I have inside me. Not only will people want me alive to use it, but they will, eventually, want me to save the world with it. They'll just want me to hold off until they've harvested as many reality cores as they can."

"So they'll lock you up in a deep, dark hole, too," Erika said.

"Probably, yeah. That's why I need you safe."

"What about Mum? Kaito?"

"They'll be safe here," Jason said. "It won't be long before anyone who would go after my family realises that the people I would potentially compromise myself over aren't here anymore."

"And until they figure that out?"

"We'll be operating a team out of the village in the short term," Farrah said. "By the time we move on, anyone who would try will have investigated enough to know."

"And what if they decide to try anyway?"

"Then things will get ugly," Jason said.

"Why can't you take everyone?" Emi asked. "You're putting us in the cloud palace, right? Won't there be room?"

"I'm not putting you in the cloud palace," Jason said. "I considered it. Taking the whole family and stashing you at the bottom of the sea. But if the whole family vanishes, people are going to wonder why and go looking. If they find you while I'm on the other side of the planet, I can't protect you."

"Where do you want to put us, then?" Erika asked.

"There's another reason I chose all of you and not any of the others," Jason said. "All of you have been able to enter my spirit vault."

44
A CHANCE TO CONTROL THE NARRATIVE

Amy and Kaito had taken over the main residence of Asano Village when Erika's family was stashed away, cementing Amy's position as de facto mayor. Jason had claimed the bushland house previously occupied by his grandmother, where he dove into the study of astral magic. He wanted to be closer than where he had kept the cloud house underwater, so he could respond to threats rapidly without using his portal. He missed the cloud bed but had hung a hammock as a makeshift replacement.

Jason put one of his many theory texts back into his inventory with the others. It was an evolving collection, starting with what Knowledge gave him and then adding in notes first from Clive and then Dawn. After studying for most of the day, he was mentally exhausted enough that he felt low on mana. A glance at the mana bar at the periphery of his vision told him otherwise.

He contemplated the interface elements that were so familiar now that he would only really notice their absence. The mana bar, the stamina bar and the little human shape that indicated his bodily health. He had come so far from when those elements had first appeared in his view. Jason was still human-shaped, just like the health indicator, but he was far from human anymore.

Dawn walked in and saw that he wasn't reading. She had also been staying in the house, to the slight chagrin of Asya. Asya had left her position with the Network, but Jason did not want her living with him. Not only was it far too early in the relationship, but Jason didn't want the distraction. He considered himself a disciplined man, but given the choice between dry magical theory and the soft lips of a beautiful woman, he knew he wasn't that disciplined.

"Need a break?" Dawn asked.

"Yeah."

"Your ability to concentrate at your rank is much improved over baseline, but even if you don't really have a brain anymore, keeping the mind fresh is important for learning. Taking regular breaks is sensible."

Jason nodded wearily and stumbled out onto the balcony to take in the scent of the bush. Dawn had been living with him for weeks, forcibly dragging his understanding of astral magic upward. Before they could use the magic door to start modifying nodes, they had to find the right nodes by conducting astral magic rituals in proto-spaces, where the dimensional walls were stretched thin.

Sending Dawn's avatar through proto-space apertures would be a questionable proposition, so Jason would be required to carry out the necessary rituals. Farrah would obviously assist, being the superior ritualist, but astral magic was Jason's field, not hers, and his understanding of it had surpassed her basic knowledge.

Jason appreciated the education, knowing exactly how valuable Dawn's tutelage was. Jason chuckled to himself in anticipation of telling Clive about it. That did not make it any easier to slog through text after text as his understanding of astral magic grew.

It had been weeks since Jason had entered a proto-space to fight a monster while he awaited Farrah devising their own means of monitoring the grid. She knew the system the Network used well enough to replicate it easily; she used her own time on Earth to explore magitech. The delay came from the need for additional functionality, over and above the Network's base system.

The most important additional feature was the ability to differentiate proto-spaces, not just by rank but by certain requirements determined by Dawn. Only some spaces would help them find the reality nodes Jason needed to modify using the magic door.

Another source of delay, but one both Jason and Dawn approved of, was an idea Farrah came up with while working on the grid detection system. The original plan was to turn the former Network liaison office in the village into a tracking station, until Farrah struck on the idea of incorporating the system into the cloud flask. Once she had a viable design, they needed to find the right components and feed them into the cloud flask. The incredibly sophisticated item would then be able to reproduce the functionality.

Jason was uncertain of the idea at first, but Farrah told him about the many times that Emir had done similar things with his own cloud flask. This gave Jason assurance. If his cloud constructs were able to track events on the grid, they would have the flexibility to operate from the road.

While Jason and Farrah were engaged in their various tasks, a combat team was being put together. Asya, Jason's old friend Greg and Kaito had all worked together while in the Network. Now they had left, they formed the core of the new team. To their number was added Itsuki and Taika. The team had a lot of versatile attack options but lacked defensive and healing specialists.

The healing was resolved with an arrival from Japan. In the wake of Jason's visit, Shiro and his mother had entered a leadership battle for control of the clan and Shiro was concerned for the safety of his daughters, despite their silver-rank strength. He had contacted Jason, asking him to take in his daughter Akari once again, this time accompanied by her sister, Mei. Not only were the sisters both silver-rank, but Mei was a healer.

Jason had warned Shiro, in no uncertain terms, that placing his daughters in Jason's company could be placing them in even greater danger. Shiro requested that Jason accept them anyway, sparking suspicion that Shiro was attempting to plant spies in Jason's camp. After the two women arrived, Jason rudely and forcibly scrutinised their auras as he questioned them. Only after this interrogation was he finally satisfied they were not spies for their grandmother.

The arrival of Akari made the depth of Itsuki's crush on her painfully apparent, but Jason noted that for all of Akari's eye-rolling, he frequently spotted the pair together. Jason discussed the inclusion of Itsuki, Akari and Mei at length, both with the people themselves and their fathers, who had placed them all in his care. All three had lost their mothers young and were subsequently raised by stern warrior men.

To Jason's surprise, both Shiro and Koya strongly advocated their children's inclusion in Jason's team. Jason discovered that Network families shared the trait with adventurer families of pushing their little birds out of the nest.

Itsuki was becoming antsy as days and weeks passed without his entering a proto-space. He had been used to plunging into one after the other, which was how he had reached bronze rank at an almost unheard-of pace. For this reason, Jason had Itsuki work extensively on meditation, consolidating the powers he had rushed to rank up.

"Something is troubling you," Jason said to Itsuki one day as they sat on the balcony of Jason's house. He had invited Itsuki over to discuss affliction specialist tactics but decided to ask the young man about the strain of uncertainty in his aura.

"It's more than just Akari being here or it being so long since you did any monster hunting," Jason clarified, and Itsuki nodded.

"It's something my father said before I left Japan."

"Oh?"

"He said that I should be careful of you."

"Sound advice," Jason said with a chuckle.

"I told him that you obviously work hard to be a good person."

"Thank you for noticing," Jason said. "I have my slip-ups, but I do make a conscious effort."

"He told me that a good person doesn't have to try to be good."

"I see," Jason said with a frown. "I'll have to respectfully disagree with your father on that; what you just described tells me a lot about your father's life. He was born into money and influence. When everything comes easy, it's easy to be good. It costs you nothing, or so little as not to matter. I learned this for myself in the other world."

Jason gave Itsuki a smile tinged with sadness.

"I would probably have said something similar a few years ago. It was only when things got hard and I was truly put to the test that I discovered how fragile what I thought of as my bedrock principles really were. It was profoundly disappointing. Do you know what the opposite of good is, Itsuki?"

"Evil would be the obvious answer, but that's not the answer you're looking for."

"You're right. The opposite of good is easy. That may have been the moral of the last Harry Potter book, now that I think about it. Anyway, people don't do bad things because there is some antagonistic force driving them to sin. They do them because when the right thing is hard, making little compromises doesn't seem so bad. A shortcut here, a little selfishness when no one will ever know. Every step makes the next one a little easier."

"That happened to you?"

"Yes, which is why I try hard to be diligent now. I've learned enough about myself to know that I'm better off avoiding slippery slopes. I have arrogance and pride enough I could slide very low. I don't want to speak poorly of your father, but claiming that there is some inherently good person out there who never has trouble making the right choice is naïve. But don't take my word for it either. If you want to do things that are truly important, you'll learn for yourself when the time comes and you have to make the hard choices."

Itsuki looked conflicted.

"I'm not sure I feel better."

"Good," Jason said. "Be wary of anyone who is completely certain of the right path. I have been, from time to time, which has done damage along the way."

Erika, her family, and the others remained sequestered away in Jason's spirit vault. Jason wanted to give the impression to the world that they had been stashed in some quiet corner of the Earth, rather than being carried with him. He did not doubt that there were people acting as eyes for external powers amongst the residents of Asano Village.

Jason and Farrah regularly visited them in the spirit vault, both to help with the sense of isolation and to bring supplies. Jason's silver-rank soul garden, inside his spirit vault, was larger and more elaborate than previous iterations. He had even found that he could manipulate it to a degree, adding living quarters to the multi-level central pavilion.

Jason's spirit vault could only be entered by those who trusted him completely. Erika and Emi had been able to enter from the beginning, as had Jason's father, Ken. Ken's brother Hiro turned out to be able to as well. He had come to trust Jason, who had taken him from his old life and helped restore him to the bosom of his family. Jason had hidden his secret delight when his grandmother, Yumi, had been able to enter.

Only three people not amongst Jason's blood relatives had managed to make their way into the spirit vault. Farrah was one and Asya was another, having finally made her way inside as her relationship with Jason deepened. The third person was Ian, Erika's husband. Farrah had been surprised at how easily Ian had entered the vault and asked him about it.

"I've known Jason since he was twelve years old," Ian had told her. "I've seen him at his highest and his lowest points. At the end of the day, what matters is that I know he would do anything for my little girl. We're here right now because Jason doesn't trust himself to choose the entire world over my wife and daughter. What matters next to that?"

Even Dawn was uncertain exactly what form the next magical events would take. All she knew was that the underlying patterns on which the world was built, taken from other, older realities, would start to make themselves known. As weeks passed since the last monster waves were suppressed, some started to believe that the promised events would not come to pass.

That hope was first dashed in the historic Russian city of Kostroma. In a single moment, late in the morning, the entire city was sealed off in a dome. Investigation over the subsequent hours revealed that the dome was actually a sphere, extending underground and completely encapsulating the city. Forty-three hours after the sphere moved into place, it vanished, revealing a city vastly changed. Buildings had been remade, similar to their original forms but with new architectural styles and entirely new materials, rendering them alien in nature.

Like the Network, Cabal and EOA, Jason, Farrah and Dawn had travelled to Kostroma to investigate while the sphere was in place, keeping themselves low-profile. When the sphere dropped, they made their way inside.

"I've seen this kind of construction before," Farrah said as they rode into the affected area on black motorcycles, using Jason's party interface to communicate. "Not the architecture, but magical construction methods were used to create these buildings."

"They don't look new," Jason observed. "There's weathering. Years of it."

"That would appear to be the nature of the events," Dawn said. "They remake the affected area in the image of worlds used as patterns when the original Builder created this universe."

"What about the people?" Jason asked.

It didn't take long to find out. Russian authorities had sealed off the area around the sphere but had chosen not to obstruct any of the magical factions. As for Jason and his companions, they had no trouble circumventing the restrictions. What they found as they encountered people was that the residents were no longer human. People were getting up from where they had apparently fallen unconscious, out on the street or in their cars. It had apparently happened quickly enough to cause traffic accidents.

"Is that a leonid?" Jason asked, looking at a huge, hairy, lion-like woman.

As they saw more and more people, Jason realised almost all of them had been transformed from human to entirely different humanoid species. Only a scattered few had retained their original state. Jason, Farrah and Dawn spotted elves and the dark-skinned runic people, with their tattoo-like rune markings that faintly glowed. They saw most of the species from Farrah's world and more besides, although most of the people had turned into leonids. As the recovering residents realised what had happened to them, they started to panic.

"I had been uncertain as to what would happen to the people," Dawn said. "I had feared they would die if caught up in the changes. This is drastic but better than death."

"Is there any way to undo this?" Jason asked. "Maybe with the magic door?"

"I'm sorry," Dawn said. "You could no more undo this than unscramble an egg."

"Then it's time to go," Jason said. "If we run into anyone from the magic factions, it will just cause problems. If we can't help these people, we can at least avoid making it worse."

Flying back to Australia, Jason rubbed his forehead, his expression dark.

"This is a disaster," he said. "I can't even begin to parse the ramifications. We already treat other ethnicities so poorly and now this? It's going to be a horror show."

"They were all essence-capable species, like humans," Dawn said. "None have high levels of inherent magic. I suspect any magical entities in the city were unaffected, be they essence users, Cabal or modified EOA members. They were likely rendered unconscious with the rest, though."

"I recognised some of those races from my world," Farrah said. "Not all of them, though."

"It looked like the pattern expressed by the event was taken from a leonid-dominant area," Dawn said.

"What about animals?" Jason asked. "I didn't spot any, but there has to have been cats and dogs and birds. How many rats are in a city?"

"It is likely that some, if not all, of the animals were also affected," Dawn said. "They will be unlikely to pose a threat, however. They will likely be transmogrified into creatures of similar ecological niche and magical power."

"I even saw draconians," Farrah said. "They're pretty rare on my world. I didn't see any celestines, though."

"Probably due to the unusual origin of the celestine species," Dawn said.

"Unusual origin?" Jason asked. "I've never heard of that."

"Me either," Farrah said.

"A little ironic, given that if the two of you were to breed, a celestine would be the result. An outworlder breeding with another species will produce offspring of that species. Should two outworlders have a child, the result is a celestine. Of course, celestines can have more children with their own kind, which is how celestines propagate. I myself am a product of two outworlder parents."

"It's kind of a shame people aren't turning into celestines," Jason said. "If everyone was turning into elves and celestines, there'd be a lot less trouble. Not none, but people would be less prejudicial to a bunch of attractive people."

"It will make an interesting change to the magical landscape if they start getting essences," Farrah said. "Other races mean other abilities."

Jason lifted his head, wide-eyed.

"Shade," he said, "can you please make a video call to Anna Tilden?"

Moments later, Jason was looking at Anna's face on a wall monitor.

"I didn't expect to hear from you anytime soon, Mr Asano."

"I know you're a long way from Russia, Anna," Jason said, "but I assume you're being kept in the loop."

"People turning into some kind of monsters," Anna said. "Information is sporadic, this early. Are you there?"

"We were. They aren't turning into monsters, Anna. They're turning into other species. Species that can use essences to awaken powers that are usually different from the ones that humans get."

Anna sat up straight behind her desk.

"I thought that might get your attention," Jason said. "Those people will be incredibly valuable to the Network."

"Why would you tell me this?"

"So you have a chance to control the narrative. If the Network sees their value, those people are less likely to be rounded up into camps. If the Network gives enough of them power, it'll be harder to persecute the rest."

"I don't have the influence to make that kind of thing happen."

"But you have the voice to make yourself heard. If it works out, maybe that influence will come."

Anna nodded.

"I can try. Thank you, Asano."

45
YOU SHOULDN'T LIE TO YOUR WIFE

With the monster waves gone, recovery efforts were underway. The death toll continued to grow as the full depth of the monster wave catastrophe was assessed. It blew past early estimates to cross the two-million mark as abandoned rural areas were once more made accessible.

Stalled distribution lines for food and other necessities were opening up again, complicated by a global economy more ravaged than the global populace. Calls for unprecedented social welfare programs were enacted immediately in some areas and determinedly opposed in others. In the United States, such proposals were the latest battle line in a growing culture war, with claims of socialist takeovers driving massive protests against proposed aid programs.

There was no shortage of people calling for such programs to be enacted, though, leading to open clashes between protesters. While the cities had been relatively safe, they had all suffered some level of overcrowding and food shortage.

Amid recovering from an unprecedented global disaster came the events in Kostroma, with more locations following after. Although the magical factions between them did a solid job of controlling the media, once footage spilled onto the internet, the media companies jumped in with both feet, airing constant footage of people and places transformed.

In the weeks following Kostroma, there was a handful of subsequently affected sites around the world, though none were as large. A small town in the United States. An almost uninhabited stretch of land in Africa. A section of Alaska that was populated only with wildlife. These places were much easier to contain; the magical factions did a much better job of keeping the media out and their response hidden.

There was no warning of a transformation event and no escape once the sphere locked in. Once people realised that there was no way to protect themselves from the transformation, new waves of unrest began. Reactions to the transformed, as they quickly became known, varied widely, from the accepting to the violent. A staging site outside of Kostroma processing the affected residents was attacked by a violent mob. The Russian government denied involvement, despite a failure to crack down on the activity.

In the midst of this came the first footage of the magical factions in open conflict. As Dawn had predicted, a single reality core appeared in each of the affected zones and the factions immediately scrambled after it.

Part of this was Jason's doing. His conversation with Anna, as predicted, had proliferated wildly. What had been a closely held secret about the spoils of the transformation events became open knowledge to every EOA cell, Network branch and Cabal group. With category-four power on the table and the competition fierce, all pretence was dropped in pursuit of the new source of power.

Reality cores were roughly the size and shape of an ostrich egg, but were made of dark crystal that glowed with an internal transcendent light. The Cabal claimed the ones in Kostroma and Africa, the Network the one in the USA.

As fifth, sixth and seventh locations became affected, it was harder to keep track of who was claiming what from the outside. Despite Jason and his companions never participating, they followed events closely. Itsuki, arriving at Jason's house in the village, found him and Asya watching yet another news report.

"If we aren't getting involved," Itsuki asked them, "then why is all this so important?"

"It's about the balance of power," Asya explained. "One faction gaining too much strength could easily lead to it either dominating or being allied against by the others. Skirmishes over specific objectives could deteriorate into outright magical war."

The second major population centre to be affected was Pudong, China. When the sphere dropped, it was transformed into a crystal city filled with people who mostly turned into an earth-affinity species with gemstone-like scales covering their bodies. Neither Jason nor Farrah had seen the species before, although Dawn was familiar with them. Millions of people were affected in Pudong. International groups were already voicing concerns about the Chinese response.

While the Network leadership got caught up in competing for reality cores, the rank and file were refocused on their long-held duty of intercepting dimensional incursions before they became monster waves. This duty, however, came with some unexpected changes.

Rebooting the dimensional detection grid had apparently activated previously unknown elements—grid coverage of the oceans. As if the systems had been there, waiting and dormant all along, suddenly, underwater dimensional incursions were detectable.

Given the surface area of the Earth, the Network had always estimated that two-thirds of dimensional incursions went unchecked, with monster waves appearing in the unseen depths. When the monsters had been category two, living and dying in the ocean depths, the Network had only ever dealt with the occasional category three that lasted much longer and sometimes became a threat to shipping. Now that category-three monsters were emerging more frequently as category-four incursions increasingly took place, the Network was forced to respond.

In the short term, monster surges were often being allowed to take place. This was the same policy as before the underwater grid activated and getting the resources to fight category-four monsters underwater was tricky. When it wasn't possible, the monsters were allowed to emerge so the low magic would choke the category fours and the rest could be cleaned up by difficult but manageable operations.

Stockpiled essences that offered any help were broken out and assigned to new trainees in a recruitment storm made possible by the Network's now public operations. Water essences had always been useful and were in short supply, but there was a large stock of aquatic essences that were previously unvalued. Promising recruits were given more desirable essences like shark, turtle and octopus, while less appealing ones like coral and manatee went to those volunteers filling out the numbers in a crisis.

New recruits could only help down the line, though, even being rushed through accelerated training programs. The Network needed new infrastructure, logistics and protocols, but most of all, more warm bodies to cover what was suddenly a tripled number of incidents. Part of this was supplied by Network personnel ousted from countries like Iran and Venezuela.

Thus far, the EOA had managed to keep up with the challenge, now that they had claimed the Network's role in those regions, although how long that would last was an open question. Surprisingly, they were much more prepared than the Network for underwater operations, as if somehow they had known what was coming beforehand.

The open nature of the magical threat and the fresh memory of the monster waves also made it much easier for nations to fund and mobilise support, be it for the Network, the EOA or the Cabal, who were still working with the Network in many areas. In Africa, especially, the Network and the Cabal were in defiance of the conflict between their organisations as they continued to work together in relative harmony. Only the appearance of reality cores brought about any discord, although, for the moment, the cooperation was holding.

Although it required more tweaking than Farrah had wanted, she finally completed a design for a grid detection system that Jason's cloud constructs were able to replicate. Jason decided that was a good time to leave Asano Village behind, protecting it by having no high-value targets present.

He considered taking his mother, concerned someone might see her as a potential hostage, but anyone who went to the trouble would certainly know beforehand of their estrangement. There were definitely spies amongst the village residents, including Kaito and Amy. Both had been approached to spy on Jason by people who understood their fraught history. Both had the presence of mind to accept the generous offers, while immediately telling Jason so he could feed disinformation.

Kaito was coming with Jason as part of his support team, while Amy remained behind to administer the village and watch over their children. They said their goodbyes to one another away from Jason, although they knew that his senses picked up everything in the village.

"It's creepy knowing that he's kind of watching us right now," Amy said to her husband as they embraced outside their eldest daughter's bedroom. "He told me that he wasn't the person I knew anymore and he was right. He's almost alien."

"He can only sense our auras, and only if he's paying attention," Kaito assured her.

"So he says," Amy countered. "The truth is that we don't know what he's capable of. You and I both have magic now, but can you do anything like the things he does? He turned into a bird made of outer space. He used those butterflies to wipe out whole sections of a city. Yes, they were those awful undead things, but what if they weren't? What if he starts doing that to regular people?"

"People have had power like that long before Jason came along. The whole Cold War was a bunch of people playing chicken with nuclear annihilation."

"But it's Jason, Kai. I still know him well enough to realise how wrong it could go. He's rash and impulsive. He gets caught up in ideas and stops looking at the consequences, without generals or launch codes or anything else to stop him."

"We have to trust him, Ames."

"Do we?"

"I've learned enough about all this to know that yes, we do."

"There was a time I relied on him more than anyone," Amy said. "I don't think I can go back to that."

"Let me do that. You just concentrate on looking after the people here."

"You just make sure you come back to me. You have two little princesses that will be waiting for you."

In the city of Bregenz, Austria, a Network team had sealed off the road running up past Sacred Heart Church, along with the church itself and the surrounding area. The Commander of Tactical Operations was named Franz. He watched as the ritualist team worked on opening the aperture that had appeared. The tactical teams were ready to move in—one nine-person section of category threes and two sections of category twos, each led by a category three. There was also a military contingent, armed with magical firearms.

Franz was glad he had not been assigned to the response teams put together for the transformation events. Working for the Network gave him a sense of purpose and he was much more interested in protecting people by fighting monsters than chasing after power by fighting people. Despite having plateaued at category three, he had no ambitions to rise higher.

Few people could even dream of the lifespan and power that Franz already enjoyed. Since magic had come out in the open and his status was no longer a secret, even his mother-in-law had stopped telling his wife she could do better.

Franz knew that many of the Network's tactical members were annoyed at being left out of the hot new action, but he knew them to be fools. It wasn't like participating meant anyone involved would get a taste of whatever power the higher-ups deigned to let trickle down. More likely was that even if one of the events did take place in Austria, what waited for them was death.

It wasn't monsters they would be facing as they fought over reality cores. The so-called superheroes of the EOA weren't a grave threat, but he had heard strange stories about the Cabal. Even worse, he'd heard about Network branches fighting one another, although any talk like that was quickly hushed up.

Franz was leading a team about to enter a dimensional incursion space, work he was more than happy to get back to after being sent to a series of little mountain towns littered with dead. One of his people pointed up. Franz used the telescopic vision of his perception power to spot a helicopter, high in the air. It rapidly descended but made oddly little noise. Franz's magical senses told him it was a category-two conjured object.

The helicopter was large but sleek, with tinted glass making up a large portion of the fuselage. It dropped down to hover above the street, where more than two dozen guns were pointed at it. A side door opened, revealing a figure they all recognised.

With his blood-red robes and dark cloak, Jason Asano was a red lightsaber away from being the next disappointing *Star Wars* villain. He dropped lightly from the helicopter and walked to Franz, somehow knowing that he was in charge.

Franz looked at the bright silver eyes in the otherwise impenetrable darkness of the hood. Jason then pushed the hood back off his head to reveal a face with sleek black hair and the too-polished handsomeness of a category three. The man gave him a friendly smile.

"Hello, Franz. Can I call you Franz? I know there are standing orders not to let me into any dimensional spaces, but you know that's just the Network wanting me to haul off on one of their teams so I look bad in the press."

"Is that what I know?" Franz asked. "You don't know what I think, Mr Asano."

"I don't? It's what you told Maria. You shouldn't lie to your wife, Franz."

Franz went stiff.

"Are you threatening my family?"

"No. I just want you to understand that I came here knowing exactly what I was walking into. If I have to go through someone, it'll be you. Your family is safe, however this goes."

"I appreciate that."

Franz looked at the others leaving the helicopter.

"We know who you have. You have four category threes, including yourself. I have twelve, including me. Are you confident with three-to-one odds, Mr Asano?"

"Actually, it'll just be me, so twelve-to-one odds. Also, yes, I'm confident. And call me Jason."

Franz looked at Jason, whose expression and body language was completely relaxed, except for the silver eyes locked on to Franz like sharp, pointed icicles. Franz relied on his aura senses to guide him in uncertain situations, but he couldn't sense Jason at all. He couldn't read the other category threes behind Asano either; the one he guessed was Farrah Hurin was even using her aura to prevent him from reading the category twos. It was a skilful demonstration of aura control.

Asano wasn't just hard to detect but a ghost to his magical senses. He remained invisible to all but his eyes.

"Mr Asano, how do you see this going if I tell you no?"

"Franz, I'm asserting right now that I'm going to go through that aperture and that you can't stop me. Either you assume that I'm right and let me through, or don't and you'll find out for certain."

Franz looked into Jason's unflinching eyes again and slowly nodded.

"Alright, let them through," he announced.

"Boss, the standing orders are—"

"I know what the standing orders are. If this guy wants to clear some of the monsters for us, I'm going to let him. You don't like that, Baumgartner, feel free to try and stop him."

The hood crawled back over Jason's head on its own and he slowly turned to look at Baumgartner, his silver eyes seemingly disembodied in the darkness of the hood. Baumgartner looked back nervously, frozen on the spot.

"I'd say that's a no," Franz said. "Any chance you could leave a guy some loot in there?"

"I think I can manage that," Jason said. "You made a wise choice, Franz."

Shade's bodies emerged from the shadows of every one of Franz's silver-rankers, including Franz himself. As Jason strode to the aperture, the bodies returned to his own shadow in a swarm.

46

THE DECISION HAS BEEN MADE

At Jason's request, Kaito didn't conjure a new helicopter upon entering the proto-space. Farrah carried a device that she and Jason had built together to find the optimal spot within the proto-space for Jason to conduct his ritual. They would inevitably encounter monsters along the way to that spot. They viewed it as a chance to put the bronze-rankers on the team through their paces.

The extradimensional realm diverged heavily from the physical reality outside. The Austrian city was replaced with a primordial jungle in which ancient ziggurats poked out of the canopy. The environment was sweltering with both heat and humidity.

"This air is hard to breathe," Kaito said. "It's heavy."

"My clothes are getting sticky," Itsuki said. "It may impair my mobility."

"You still sweat because you ranked up so quickly," Farrah told him. "You focused strictly on advancing your essence abilities. You need to take the time for exercises that will help your body become more magical. I gave you the basics in training, but you've clearly neglected them."

"Sorry, Miss Hurin," Itsuki said, looking every inch the chastised schoolboy. The Asano sisters, Akari and Mei, watched him with amusement.

It was a silver-rank proto-space, so only the anchor monsters holding the space together, and possibly a few others, would be silver rank. For this reason, Jason and the other silvers didn't engage, letting Kaito, Asya, Greg and Itsuki do the sweeping.

They each had their own motifs in their abilities, but Itsuki was the odd man out in more ways than one. The others heavily featured conjured tech in their power sets, which was common for earth essence users even without the technology essence. Itsuki's powers were more fantastical in nature. Add the fact that the others had worked together before and were already comfortable with one another, Itsuki literally and figuratively stood apart.

Of the four bronze-rankers, Kaito was the least comfortable due to operating outside of his helicopter. His abilities were very much in the support vein, but Jason and Farrah wanted him to experience less than ideal conditions. His vehicle essence powers were not useless without it, however, allowing him to conjure surveillance drones to scout for threats and gun drones to handle them.

Although she was a sniping specialist who favoured strong, singular long shots, Asya conjured a carbine rifle more suited to the closer confines of the jungle. It was a futuristic weapon with glowing blue bits, which Jason strongly approved of.

The person with the actual technology essence, Greg, was ironically the one calling up the most outmoded technology. He conjured an entire outfit from a version of the nineteenth century that only ever existed in pulp novels and old film serials. He had a long brown coat, vest, and bowler hat with a pair of goggles slung around the brim. He had a backpack covered in loose flaps and the whole ensemble had enough pouches and pockets that it looked hard to walk in.

Greg also conjured a gun that looked like a replica from a fifties sci-fi movie but was made of brass. He reached back to rummage through his backpack, pulling out a cable and plugging it onto the base of the strange gun's grip, causing it to hum with power.

Itsuki's powers were more classically magical. Although they shared the dark essence, Itsuki didn't have a cloak like Jason. Instead, he transformed himself into a semi-translucent figure, like a statue made of smoked glass. It made him much harder to sense, allowed him to blend into shadows and, as of bronze rank, made him semi-tangible. This reduced the effect of many attacks on him while also allowing him to go places he otherwise couldn't. So long as he moved slowly, he could pass right through barriers like cages or thorny bushes.

Itsuki was used to playing stealthy scout, much like Jason, which was a poor fit with the others. They already had Asya's enhanced perception from her master confluence and Kaito's drones, making Itsuki's potential contribution limited.

Itsuki had been startled and delighted to experience Jason's party interface, which had given him a whole new perspective on his own abilities. Shade had identified Itsuki's summoned familiar as a darklight ogre, which was a defensive combat familiar whose abilities compelled enemies to attack it while inflicting debuffs on any that did.

Using Magic Society records, Jason had identified the ability that summoned Itsuki's familiar and discovered that the familiar would gain new forms as Itsuki ranked up, eventually becoming something called an eclipse titan.

Once they started encountering monsters, Greg's gun was revealed to fire arcs of electricity that chained from one monster to the next. It did minimal damage but delivered a paralysing jolt, setting up monsters for follow-up attacks. A well-aimed burst of gunfire from Asya or a stream of heavy bullets from Kaito's gun drones finished the job, their smooth teamwork showing off their experience working together.

Jason and Farrah assessed the bronze-rankers as the team progressed towards the location for the ritual.

"Itsuki will have to work a little to find his path," Jason assessed. "This isn't a great team composition for him."

"That's good," Farrah said. "His family has clearly been feeding him ideal scenarios to rank him up quickly. A little hardship will knock some unwanted sensibilities out of him."

Itsuki slowly learned to adapt to his teammates, using stealth to approach monsters detected by the others and lay on afflictions. He was more of a team player than Jason, whose afflictions were damage-focused. Itsuki softened the enemies up with more debilitation effects than damage, luring enemies into kill boxes for the others before he vanished as the damage poured in.

Once the team reached the site for the ritual, they needed to clear the space for the largest magic diagram Jason had ever worked with. Kaito and Greg's experience setting up landing zones came into play. Kaito used an ability from his soaring essence to launch himself into the air, at which point he conjured his helicopter around him. He then flipped it, the blades reconfiguring to maintain its hovering while upside down, and descended the helicopter into the jungle canopy. As the rotor blades dropped into the trees, they worked as a giant saw, rapidly clearing the area. Kaito even moved the helicopter around, still upside down, to clear a wider area.

"I was once shot off the side of a mountain by a waterfall experiencing intermittent service failure," Jason said, watching the upside-down-helicopter-turned-power-saw. "I've come back from the dead, fought interdimensional dinosaurs and met my evil magic clone. Somehow, this is still the most ridiculous thing I've ever seen."

"He's very precise," Akari's sister, Mei, said. "You don't see a lot of that in upside-down helicopters."

Rather than dismiss his helicopter, Kaito cleared a second space in which to land it. While he was doing that, Greg swapped out the cable running from his backpack to his gun for a hose, turning it into a flamethrower. A stream of fire erupted from the weapon, clearing the ground now littered in shredded trees until all that remained was charcoal and ash.

Kaito brought his helicopter back to blow away the burnt debris, while Greg moved on to the second cleared space. In short order, the pair had cleared out two spaces, one for the ritual and one for the helicopter.

"You've got the logistics down," Jason told Greg.

Farrah used an earth-shaping power to flatten out the cleared ground, ready for the ritual.

"This is what we were doing while you were bludging, taking a gap year despite only having completed one semester of university a half-dozen years ago," Greg told him.

"That does sound pretty slack," Kaito agreed.

"I was helping earthquake victims and healing people with Ebola," Jason said. "And it was only half a year."

"That's what you told us you were doing," Greg said. "I bet you actually spent most of the time in a resort in Bermuda."

"What I told you? It was on the news."

"Because the EOA put it there," Farrah contributed, continuing to flatten out the ground. "There's no reason to suspect anything they're behind, right?"

The three Japanese members of the team, Akari, Mei and Itsuki, looked on as the others continued to rib Jason.

"Are they always like this?" Mei asked her sister. "It seems very disrespectful."

"I believe it's an Australian cultural practice," Akari said. "You get used to it."

"Do you really?" Itsuki asked.

"Not really," Akari admitted. "They're all very strange."

"I thought Miss Hurin was from another universe, not Australia."

"She seems quite proficient at assimilating."

Carrying out the ritual went smoothly. While Jason did so, with Farrah's assistance, the rest of the team patrolled a wide perimeter to keep any wandering monsters away. If the ambient magic was too badly stirred up, they would need to start over.

Greg's abilities were especially useful, as his power set focused on control and area denial. As such, he was given the largest area of ground to cover. Given time to set up, he conjured iron rods that ended in spheres, which he planted at regular intervals. They would make paralysing electricity attacks, while automated turrets he placed behind them would follow up. Looking like gatling coil guns from the nineteenth century, the turrets could rapidly shoot electrified nails.

When a large pack of iron-rank monsters appeared in his patrol area, Greg deployed a shaft from the top of his backpack. It sprouted helicopter blades, allowing him to swoop over the pack and strafe them with his flamethrower. Only a trio of the toughest monsters survived. Greg landed and the rotor blades were flung from the shaft. Two of the monsters were killed while the third was outright decapitated.

After the ritual was complete, the team climbed into the helicopter and headed back for the aperture.

"A couple more rituals and we should be able to triangulate the first node I need to modify," Jason said. "As for how many nodes it will take in total, I have no idea. That means a lot of proto-spaces."

"Are people just going to let us in, the way they did here?" Itsuki asked.

"No," Jason said. "We went to the extra effort here to make a point that we will be peaceful in our operations. Sooner or later, though, someone is going to take a hard stance."

"What happens then?" Itsuki asked.

"We hurt as few people as we can, but we don't stop. The Network rank and file are just doing their jobs and don't seem interested in impeding us, at least until the people at the top pay attention to anything but the transformation events."

"You think they'll eventually try and stop us?"

"Yes. Even if they don't realise it now, what we are doing will turn off the reality core spigot. If we're lucky, they won't twig until we're close to the end and the transformation events start slowing down. At that point, someone will definitely put it together. My concern is that someone clearly knew more about what's going on than is good for us. We may start meeting real opposition much earlier."

"And then we fight?" Itsuki asked.

"Not if we can avoid it," Jason said. "We can't fight the whole Network."

Itsuki nodded.

"That task force we met outside the aperture," he said. "Are you really strong enough to take on twelve category threes alone?"

"Of course not; it was all bluff. Well, mostly bluff. I mean, I'd have to cheat, certainly. Probably."

"It's a matter of training," Farrah interjected. "Those men were traditional essence users from this world. Their training is all about group tactics for monster elimination, not intelligent, singular enemies with a wide variety of powers. They aren't ready for someone who fights like Jason."

"Basically, they're specced for PvE, not PvP," Jason said. "Once Farrah and I return to her world, I won't be able to swagger around like that. I'm making hay while the sun shines."

"I imagine he'll swagger about anyway," Farrah said. "He's just going to get slapped down when he does."

Things were tense when Jason and his companions returned to the aperture, but they were allowed to depart unchallenged. Soon after, Kaito's helicopter landed next to a tour bus on an isolated stretch of road near the Czech border. Kaito dismissed the helicopter and they piled into the tour bus, which was a luxurious, twin-level cloud coach on the inside.

"Were there problems with the Network?" Dawn asked by way of greeting as they arrived.

"No," Jason said, falling into a soft cloud chair. "The extra legwork seems to have done the trick. This time."

"Now that we are in the right region," Dawn said, "you can ideally utilise Kaito to beat the local branches to new apertures. Did you take notes?"

"I did," Jason said.

"Good. Hopefully, the results of these rituals help us refine exactly which nodes we are looking for. Until we get more data, we can't even be certain we're after the right nodes."

An attention-getting supercar drove through the town of Conrad, Montana, making its way to an oilseed refinery on the outskirts. It parked in front of the administration building and a man in a sharp suit named Emerson Cleary stepped out, bringing a briefcase from the passenger seat with him. From the vehicle's meagre trunk space, he took a small box that barely fit and carried it into the building, holding it by the handle on top.

The office was a cheap but functional prefab affair, with a middle-aged receptionist talking on the phone. Cleary sat the box on the desk and pressed his finger on the phone cradle, hanging up the call.

"Excuse me?" the receptionist asked indignantly. She gave him an unfriendly look up and down, before looking out the window at his car. "Who exactly do you think you are?"

"Where can I find Mr Tallman?" Cleary asked.

"I'd asked if you checked the shop where they sell manners, but clearly not," she said.

The office manager hurried in from the back, his body language obsequious.

"I'm sorry, sir, I'll take you to the special projects building at once."

"I haven't logged him in as a visitor yet," the receptionist said and the manager turned on her.

"I swear to God, Janet, if I find a single record of this man ever having been here, you will be unemployed by the end of the day. You are not to so much as breathe a word of this to anyone."

"If you look in the parking lot, Darren," she said, "you'll see thirty or so dusty trucks and one shiny, red mid-life crisis. I think people might notice."

"Shut up, Janet! Can I take your briefcase or your box, sir?"

"Reach for that box, Darren," Cleary said, "and you and Janet will both be dead before your hand gets there."

Darren went pale.

"This way, please, sir. May I ask your name?"

"Probably best that you didn't."

None of the employees ever went into the special projects building, which was a small brick hut with no signage in a corner of the industrial lot. Darren hovered curiously as Cleary stood at the door until Cleary glared at him. He skittered away. Cleary went inside, where he stepped into the silent elevator and descended deep into the Earth.

When the elevator reached the bottom floor, Cleary walked down a corridor with lights that lit up at his approach and dimmed once more behind him. Eventually, he reached a circular room with several doors. One of them opened and a pasty-faced man appeared.

"Deputy Director Cleary," he greeted, although his eyes were locked on the box. "That's it?"

"This is it," Cleary confirmed.

"I would have thought they would send more security."

"They did," Cleary said. "You just haven't seen them."

"I see. This way, please."

The man opened a door and led Cleary through. After walking down another hallway, they reached a second door, beyond which was a large room, mostly empty. There was a table and chair, but what drew the eye was a pair of large cylinders, situated in the middle of elaborate magical circles. The cylinders were filled with milky liquid and what appeared to be human forms could just be made out through the white murk.

"So this is them," Cleary said.

"Yes. I need written confirmation of the orders before we can move forward."

Cleary set the box and his briefcase on the table and opened the briefcase. He took out a folder and handed it to the other man, who looked through it. As he did, Cleary opened the box, revealing an object the size of an ostrich egg, shining with transcendent light.

"Are we waking up both?" the pasty man asked.

"Just one, until we secure a larger supply."

"Very well. When do we start?"

"Immediately," Cleary said. "The decision has been made to bring Jason Asano's project under our control."

47
FIRST PRIORITY

IN SWITZERLAND, THE RESORT TOWN OF INTERLAKEN AND THE LAKESHORE villages around Lake Brienz had been evacuated during the monster waves. Determined an insufficiently populous area to warrant its own safe zone, the locals had been sent to the closest established safe zone, in the city of Thun.

A month after the last monster wave, people were cleared to return to their homes. Buses shipped residents back to their villages, where they would be left to assess the damages. There was a lot of destruction. The evacuations had been done promptly, but the scent of people had been left behind. Monsters denied their prey had taken their frustrations out on the buildings.

The act of god claim made by insurance companies was currently under attack around the world, on multiple fronts. In the wake of the monster waves and now the transformation events, many countries were already ramrodding legislation to render the claim invalid, along with a barrage of lawsuits. No few of them were attacking the act of god claim on the grounds that with magic at large in the world, making assertions about gods was a much less nebulous affair than in the past. Such grounds were not considered to have a high chance of success, but it took more than a few global disasters to put a stop to litigation.

For the moment, none of these events helped the people on the buses moving around Lake Brienz. In one of them, a passenger pointed out an isolated building by the lakeshore that seemed untouched.

"Was that large chalet there before?" she asked her husband.

"Of course it was," he said. "You think someone came here and built a chalet with monsters running around everywhere?"

Inside what looked like a chalet in the Swiss Alps, Jason languidly stretched out in a cloud bed. Asya moulded herself to his body almost as well as the cloud-stuff the bed was made of.

"If I didn't have to go fight evil," he said contentedly, "I could stay like this for a long, long time."

"Lazy," Asya teased, kissing his neck. "Since we will, eventually, have to get out of this bed, there's something I'd like to talk to you about. Something important."

"Is it the hot chocolate?" Jason asked. "Shade promised to stop letting Colin help anymore. He means well but doesn't understand that not everyone needs that much protein in their diet."

"No." She giggled, a tinkling water sound. "I'm talking about when you leave. For the other world."

"Oh?"

"I know you're taking your sister and her family by stashing them in your spirit vault. I want to go with you."

"Ah," he said. "Please tell me I'm not the reason you're asking."

"I like you quite a lot, Asano, but not enough to leave my family and everything I've ever known. I want to go to the other world because it's another world. A whole new universe, full of magic and miracles. Literal miracles."

"That's true," Jason said thoughtfully. "You can just hang around in the local worship square for a bit and some god will show up and do something flashy."

"I want to see things that aren't possible here. To do things that almost no one from our world has ever done."

"I see," Jason said with a grin. "Magic and wonders. That is a good reason."

"So you'll take me with you?"

Jason could feel her anxiousness in both her body and aura as she waited for his reply.

"I'll tell you what I told Erika," he said. "There's still time until I go back. Think it over. Ask me any questions that come up. We can talk about it again when the time comes and as many times as you like before that."

"Is that a provisional yes?"

"It's provisional yes," he confirmed with a chuckle. He felt her body move next to his as her tension melted away and he pressed his lips to hers.

The Los Angeles Network branch's plane was no small private jet but a full-sized plane as big as a passenger jet. Based off a corporate jet variant of a passenger liner, it was built to include magic from the frame out and could serve as a mobile command post for Network operations. Amenities included the shower facility from which Jack Gerling emerged, rubbing his bushy beard unhappily.

"That gunk doesn't come out easily," he growled like a bear. With his towering bulk and hirsute body, he didn't just sound like a bear but also looked like one.

The other Network members on the plane looked at the brutish man with trepidation. Even disregarding magic, he looked like he had shambled out of the woods in search of food. Once magic was taken into account, it became even worse.

The US branches of the Network had been pooling resources for years, giving up enough monster cores to raise countless essence users to category three. Finally, they managed to get two people across the threshold of category four. Jack Gerling was one of those chosen, due to his rare and powerful essences.

His might essence was common, but no one would complain at its inclusion. His potent essence was extremely rare and the vast essence was so unheard of that they had to go through records hundreds of years old to identify it. The result was the onslaught essence. Gerling's powers turned him into a walking bomb. Now that he was category four, he could down the plane he was on and everyone in it with no more effort than it took to snap his fingers. This fact was not lost on the Network staffers currently onboard.

One of the Network staffers approached Gerling.

"Sir, Deputy Director Cleary has asked that you join him for a meal."

Gerling scowled.

"What kind of meal?"

"His exact words were 'an ass-load of fried chicken and hot sauce,' sir."

"Yeah? I like the sound of that."

Greg stepped onto the upper-floor balcony of the chalet. His hands were wrapped around a mug of hot chocolate, warming them against the crisp morning air. His bronze-rank body could easily endure the cold, but he still enjoyed the comfort of its warmth. He moved next to Jason, standing at the balcony to take in the view of the lake.

"See the village across the lake?" Jason asked. "It's empty."

"Evacuated?" Greg asked.

"Yeah. They're coming back, though, even as we speak."

"Maybe that means the world has turned a corner from the monster waves."

"I hope so," Jason agreed. "If we can shut down these transformation events, it really will have. I'm so tired of dark days, but at least we have the power to do something about it. Most people are stuck hoping that people like us will get it done."

"Not a good time to feel powerless."

"No," Jason said. "My first night in the other world, my friend Rufus told me that I had a choice. I could let other people protect me or take the power to control my own fate."

"Meaning essences."

"Yes. There's a responsibility that comes with that, though. When the bad things happen, we have to stand between them and everyone else."

"I'm not sure everyone sees it that way."

"Rufus does," Jason said. "He carries it around like a weight. I try to follow that example."

"I know. Farrah says you shouldn't."

"Farrah doesn't lead," Jason said. "She's smarter than anyone on her own team and she's smarter than me, but she doesn't lead. I'm responsible for all of you and she's smart enough to avoid carrying that. She might tell us to let go of that burden, but she knows we won't. She just wants us to not carry so much of it that we break."

They stood in silence for a long time, looking out through the pristine air. Greg didn't drink from his mug, but let it sit on the railing, nestled warmly between his hands.

"Was it on the news?" he asked Jason.

"Was what on the news?"

"That people are bussing back into the local villages."

"I can feel them. Buses full of people, working their way around the lake. Auras full of hope and trepidation. Uncertain of what they'll find but yearning for home."

Greg panned his gaze around the lake, not spotting any movement. If there were busloads of people out there, he couldn't see them.

"You can sense them from here?"

"Yes."

Greg looked at Jason, frowning.

"You're worried about me," Jason said, smiling as he continued to look out over the lake.

"Sometimes I wonder if you're getting a little too far from human, Jason."

"I'm not human."

"I don't mean human as a species," Greg said. "I mean the experience of being a human."

"Same answer. I'm not a human. If I keep looking at the world as if I were, I'm not sure I can do the things I need to. I hope Makassar is the worst thing I ever experience, but I have to assume it won't be. I need to be able to handle the next thing, and the thing after that."

"So you just become detached from everything?"

"No," Jason said, turning to his friend with a smile. "I just pick my attachments carefully. I've seen what I'll become if I don't have them. As time goes by, I've been missing my friends in the other world more and more. I'm starting to realise that monsters aren't the only things we're meant to protect each other from."

Greg looked down into his steaming mug.

"Stopping you from turning into a spooky murder machine is a lot of responsibility," he said.

"You should try needing to save the world."

"Oh, please," Greg scoffed. "A drama queen like you? You're loving it."

Jason let out an affronted laugh. "Is that how it is?"

"You know it is," Greg said with a grin. He sipped at his hot chocolate, then spit it over the balcony and peered into his mug.

"What is in this? Is that beef stock?"

"I apologise," Shade said, emerging from Jason's shadow. "It seems I had not excised all the cocoa that Colin supplemented after all. I shall fetch you a fresh cup."

"Thank you," Greg said, still making a face as Shade floated away with the cup. "Am I imagining things, or is Shade getting quite butlery?"

"He's become fascinated by the profession," Jason said. "He likes the quiet, dignified competence of duty. It hasn't made trying to get him to be more relaxed any easier."

"You always try and turn everyone into you," Greg said. "Maybe instead of trying to pull everyone to your pace, you should appreciate them for what they have to offer the way they are. If Shade wants to be Alfred to your Batman, let him."

"I wish I had a secret cave lair. Behind a waterfall."

"We're standing in your magical, shape-changing chalet that turns into a hovercraft tour bus. There was also mention of turning it into a palace?"

"Haven't tried that, yet. I've never actually needed a palace for anything."

"No one has ever needed a palace, Jason. They just wanted a lot of golden sconces more than they wanted poor people to have food."

"Still a dirty socialist, then?"

"Aren't you?"

"I'm not sure how many princes and wealthy aristocrats you can make friends with before it becomes hypocritical. It's not really a hovercraft, by the way."

"What?"

"The tour bus form the cloud flask makes. It's not really a hovercraft. Now that it's silver-rank, it could actually fly if the magic here wasn't so thin. It'll have to wait until I go back to Farrah's world."

Jason felt a nervous tremulation in Greg's aura and waited for his friend to speak.

"So, ah, has Asya talked to you yet?" Greg asked.

"About going to the other world?"

"Yeah."

"She has. Have you both been working up to ask me?"

"We figured one of us should soften you up by sleeping with you first," Greg said. "I won't lie: I'm glad she volunteered."

Jason burst out laughing.

"And he's president?" Gerling asked as he tossed the bone from a drumstick into the large bin Cleary had made sure was on hand.

"Yes," Cleary said, then bit into a chicken wing. Cleary had replaced his suit with a more casual shirt and pants before joining Gerling in a fried chicken dinner, although Gerling was consuming the bulk of the piled tray.

"The TV guy?" Gerling asked, grabbing another piece.

"Yes."

"That's our country you're talking about?"

"Yes."

"And he beat Bill Clinton? I bet Hillary would find it weird being back in the White House without being president. I thought they'd get divorced after she was impeached over the intern sex thing."

"The nineties were a simpler time," Cleary said.

"You're alright, Cleary," Gerling said as Cleary tossed his own chicken bone into the bin. "I appreciate you sitting down and eating with me. My last handler would have thrown me the chicken like I was a monster in a pit. Most people are scared of me."

"Oh, I'm definitely scared of you," Cleary said. "I won't lie to you, Mr Gerling: my job is to make you as amenable as possible to the requests of my superiors. If you want something, my job is to get it for you, as close to the way you want it as is practically possible. I think keeping things friendly between you and me will make it a better experience for both of us, and if that means eating some delicious fried chicken, I'm willing to take that hit."

"Good to hear," Gerling said with a bellowing laugh. "The last guy was a little too much stick and not enough carrot."

After years of working to get a pair of category-four essence users, the US Network branches discovered an unhappy reality: without a supply of gold spirit coins, they would be power-starved, rapidly weaken and possibly die. The Network researchers managed to place both men in magical stasis, itself quite resource hungry, forestalling their demise.

The supply of gold spirit coins was exceptionally small. The category fours could only be temporarily revived for critical missions where overwhelming force was required. It also meant that, despite their world-beating power, the category fours were beholden to whoever could provide the coins to keep them alive. Gerling's previous handler had enthusiastically waved that sword of Damocles, forgetting that it was a lot easier to replace a handler than a category-four essence user.

"Things are different now," Cleary said. "These new reality cores not only mean that we can keep you out of stasis but that we should be able to add more category fours to the roster."

"And you pulled me out to fight for them?"

"Yes. The Cabal is slowly-but-surely gaining an advantage in these transformation spaces. They seem to have some kind of connection to them, which our researchers suspect is related to the origins of the Cabal's various factions."

"Bunch of creepy weirdos," Gerling said. "I don't mind kicking their asses back and forth a little."

"We aren't actually certain how effective the reality cores will be in enhancing their power," Cleary said. "We have people looking into it, obviously. We estimate that our essence users will get stronger using cores faster than they will. Reality core power can be directly consumed with a simple ritual, like a supercharged monster core gobstopper. If the Cabal can leverage them effectively, though, we may need to initiate large-scale interdiction before they become too powerful."

"Large-scale interdiction?"

"War, Mr Gerling."

"Well, damn; count me in. I'm the most powerful thing on this whole goddamn planet, so let me loose."

"That's far from our ideal scenario and, for now, we aren't even pitting you against the Cabal."

"That's not the first priority?" Gerling asked. "If they're sending me, that usually means it's the first priority."

"There is, potentially, an additional source for the reality cores. One that will produce them faster, more reliably and, best of all, exclusively. It might even be possible to shut down the transformation events and leave us with the sole means to reach the highest levels of power in the world."

"That sounds just dandy," Gerling said.

"Yes, it does," Cleary agreed. "We can stop pretending the International Committee has any purpose other than doing what we say, that the governments of the world work with us instead of for us and that the other magical factions have any reason to exist at all."

"Well, damn," Gerling said. "We're looking to take over the damn planet?"

"We already have, Mr Gerling. The goal is to reach the point where we can stop pretending we haven't."

48
NODE SPACE

THE NETWORK TEAM FROM THE POTSDAM BRANCH REACHED THE APERTURE on Babelsberg Park and found it already open. The residue of the ritual used to open it was on the ground and in front of it was a Japanese woman with a category three aura, meditating with her eyes closed.

As trucks and helicopters arrived she gave no reaction, remaining cross-legged on the grass until the operations commander approached her. She opened her eyes, dexterously rising to her feet by uncrossing her legs.

"Who are you?" the commander asked.

"Asano Akari."

"Asano? As in…?"

"Yes. He asked me to stay here to prevent children from wandering in. I'm sure you can take care of that now."

She turned to enter the aperture, but the commander called out to her.

"Miss Asano."

She turned back.

"Our people are tracking you by the proto-spaces you're visiting. There are a lot of Americans and International Committee people around, talking to our high-ups. I don't know what they have planned, but tell him."

"Why would you warn us?"

"There are people that don't like the way the Network has treated him.

A lot of people. I was sent to Makassar, both times. I saw him going places no one else could go, saving people we had all written off. Days of it; never stopping, never resting. He drives himself like a workhorse and then we turn on him? That isn't right."

Akari stared at the man and then gave a slight nod.

"I will relay your words to him. I know they will mean a great deal."

Akari moved to the aperture and stepped through.

Cleary and Jack Gerling were in a hospitality suite at the Network's Berlin branch.

"You've reviewed the briefing materials on what we know of Asano's abilities?" Cleary asked.

"Such as they are," Gerling said. "Too many holes, damn stealth types. He's got a lot of escape options."

"We anticipate that you will be able to handle most of his methods through simple power disparity."

"His aura is really as strong as all that?"

"We estimate its strength to be somewhere in the range of what would normally be the zenith of category three. Added to his superior control, we strongly recommend against aura conflict. You should focus on areas in which your superiority is clear. Power, speed, strength. Direct confrontation. The two largest threats to that are if he escapes through ordinary evasion or his portal ability."

"You have countermeasures?"

"We do, and we plan to catch him coming out of a dimensional space. We've been tracking his patterns. He's been going into a series of incursion spaces, using his team to keep monsters clear of his location while he conducts a large ritual in each."

"What's he doing?"

"We think he is trying to stop the transformation events."

"I want to see one," Gerling said. "People turning into elves and rock people and whatever. Can you get me an elf?"

"Yes," Cleary said. "Just one?"

Gerling laughed.

"One will do for now. Can't get too distracted on the job."

"I appreciate that. Asano's pattern is to enter the incursion spaces, perform his ritual and then move on. First Austria, then Switzerland and now Germany. He's been responding quickly, entering spaces before our people get there, in most cases."

"Why don't our people stop him?"

"He and his companion, Farrah Hurin, have a lot of goodwill amongst the rank and file. They're role models to our younger people. Asano has used interviews to characterise himself as a symbol and credit our personnel as the true protectors of the planet. Given the way that the upper echelons of the Network have been pushing the lower over the last year, it inclines them to give Asano leeway."

"Meaning they won't stop him unless we ride them."

"There have been some who diligently attempted to stop him. After a series of brief altercations with Farrah Hurin, no one else made the attempt."

"Not Asano himself?"

"Asano claims that he is unable to stop his powers once they affect a person. It could be a lie and he doesn't attack our people to maintain it. It could be genuinely true and he wants to avoid killing our people to maintain their goodwill."

"I have trouble believing that one woman could beat a whole section of category threes."

"I believe it was more that she made some quick examples and the rest were reluctant, given that she was just one of four category threes in their group. The Japanese sisters are largely unknown but all our people have seen what Jason Asano does to the things he fights. The news played the footage of him killing that category four monster in Makassar on a loop. The most powerful monster ever to set foot on Earth and it looked like he tossed it through a wood-chipper. No one wants to end up like that."

"That was when Asano used that power to turn into some kind of magic bird," Gerling said. "The briefing notes had nothing about what that power was."

"We don't know," Cleary said. "There are too many unknowns about him, which is why we brought you here. Nothing solves a problem as well as true power."

Having finally isolated what they hoped was the first node Jason needed to modify to repair the link, the team returned to Austria. Kaito's helicopter set down in the Ziller Valley, in an isolated and open space close to the river close to the point where Jason could access the area of node space he needed. Accompanying Jason was the whole group: Dawn, Farrah, the Asano sisters, Greg, Asya, Itsuki and Kaito.

Kaito left his helicopter parked on the grass, ready for everyone to jump in at need. The others would remain while Jason entered alone; only he could enter the space where the node could be modified. He had experimented with node spaces in preparation, opening the door to acclimatise to the conditions without making any changes.

The experiments revealed only Jason and Farrah were able to enter a node space once Jason opened the door. This was a result of their astral affinity, the mechanism preventing non-outworlders from using the door. Farrah could only withstand conditions within the node space for a limited time due to the corrosive aura it contained. Jason was able to withstand it, but Farrah's aura was ground down, after which the space started to have a deleterious effect on her body. For this reason, only Jason was going to go in, while the others would wait outside.

"It will take you time to understand what you are seeing in there," Dawn advised Jason. "I have pushed as much theory into your head as I can, but knowing the theory is not the same as applying it. Take as long as you need to be certain of every change you make. What you are about to do is outside even my experience."

Jason solemnly nodded and opened the portal. He ran a hand over the ground and a line of silver light appeared running along it. From the line rose an arch of smoky glass with blue, silver, and gold light twinkling within, the new material from which his portal arches were made. Instead of filling with the familiar dark void, though, it filled with a sheet of silver light. A powerful aura spilled from it and Jason's companions, except for Dawn and Farrah, all took an involuntary step back.

"See you soon," Jason said and then stepped through the door.

"What kind of anomaly?" Cleary asked.

He was in the Berlin branch's grid monitoring station, hovering over the chair of an operator.

"At first, I thought it was the start of a transformation event," the operator explained nervously. "Then I realised it was too small. Much too small, as in, not much bigger than a person."

"Where a normal transformation event is the size of a city," Cleary said and patted the operator on the shoulder. "You did well to bring this to my attention quickly."

Cleary left the monitoring centre, just one small part of the Berlin branch's extensive complex. Waiting outside were Cleary's functionaries, who trailed him as he strode away.

"Prep helicopters and a full operations team," Cleary instructed.

"We'll have to use the locals," Cleary's assistant said. "Our own forces are still being cleared."

"They haven't been cleared yet?"

"They're a heavily armed contingent of non-governmental soldiers with magical abilities, sir. The German government, the Berlin Steering Committee and the International Committee are dragging their feet. They're trying to dig up our objective and you said secrecy is paramount, so I chose discretion over applying pressure."

Cleary nodded.

"It was the right choice, but now we have a window of unknown duration. Use the local teams and prep them for departure."

"Destination?"

"The Ziller Valley."

"Austria?" the assistant asked. "That will add complications."

"Handle them. Speed over everything."

"I'll make sure any complications are dealt with by the time you're in the air, sir."

"Where is Gerling?"

"The spa facility, sir. Would you like me to send someone?"

"I'll go," Cleary said. "Get going; I want wheels up in ten."

The landscape Jason found himself in was an alien reimagining of the space by the river he had just left. Like the space in which he claimed the door, it was washed into monochrome by the light that shone with no apparent source. In this case, the light was silver instead of amber, giving everything a blank metallic sheen.

The surroundings looked vaguely natural at a distance, but up close, it was clear that everything was composed of tiny cubes, as if the entire landscape had been built from tiny, silver building blocks.

Jason felt the aura of the place trying to suppress his own, giving him the unusual sensation of feeling feeble before an overwhelming power. It had only been a couple of years since Jason was freshly arrived in the other world, feeling vulnerable and exposed every day. In this place, that feeling came back. It was as if he were standing before the full vastness of the cosmos and being shown his tiny, irrelevant place in it.

Shaking off the sensation, Jason extended his aura out, pushing back against the oppressive force to expand his senses. The first thing he detected was points of power, buried everywhere under the landscape. Unlike the transformation events that revealed only a single reality core with each event, the doorway gave Jason ready access to a treasure trove. He left them where they were as he started to move.

Exploring the space with his senses, he walked slowly, trying to understand the complexities of the world around him. He slowly began to marry what he perceived with the theory he had learned, but it was slow going. He took his time, examining tiny aspects of the magic flowing through the place like duelling orchestras.

When he finally managed to truly grasp the nature of just one tiny aspect, fitting it to the theory Dawn had been stuffing into his head, it felt like a triumph. It was a first step, allowing him to move onto the next.

Kaito's drones were the first to detect the approaching helicopters and he warned the others. Farrah looked unhappily at the door standing out in the open. Jason's party interface had terminated the moment he entered, leaving no way to communicate with him.

"We can't let him walk out of there not knowing," Farrah said.

"His freedom is paramount," Dawn agreed. "The question is how powerful the forces approaching are. If they aren't too…"

Farrah looked at Dawn, who had trailed off, wide-eyed.

"What is it?" Farrah asked.

"Gold-ranker," Dawn whispered.

Farrah froze for a moment and then turned to the others.

"Everyone into the helicopter!" she yelled, shoving Dawn in the direction of the vehicle. "Get in it and go, all of you! As quick as you can!"

"What about you?" Kaito asked.

"I'll get Jason and we'll portal back to the cloud house," Farrah said. "Rendezvous there, no more questions. As fast as you can go, gods dammit!"

Without another word, Farrah plunged into the portal. Dawn hurried to the helicopter.

"Move!" she ordered. "We may already be moving too late!"

They clambered into the side door of the helicopter and it lifted into the air, even before Kaito slid into the pilot seat. Using every power at his disposal, Kaito accelerated the vehicle, sending it firing through the air faster than any ordinary helicopter could match.

"What is happening?" Akari asked.

"There's a gold-rank essence user on one of those helicopters," Dawn said.

"A category four?" Akari asked, turning pale. "Since when do they even exist?"

"China and the United States both had people reach gold rank several years ago," Dawn explained. "They have been keeping them in magical stasis since then."

"It's true, then," Asya said. "They really do have them."

"Yes," Dawn said. "Now that they are operating openly, I am more free to speak on it."

"Why weren't you before?" Greg asked.

"There are rules by which I am required to operate," Dawn explained. "They are a frustrating but necessary restriction for someone like me to intervene in the affairs of your world."

"They must be using reality cores to sustain the category four," Asya reasoned.

"It seems likely," Dawn said.

"How many are we dealing with?" Itsuki asked.

"One," Dawn said. "One is all it takes."

She bowed her head, crestfallen.

"I'm sorry," she said.

"For not telling us earlier?" Asya asked. "You told us what you could on the way to Makassar."

"No," Dawn said. "I'm sorry for what is about to happen. The gold-ranker has left his helicopter. Everyone get out the gold spirit coins that Jason gave you and eat them when I say."

Gerling hurtled through the air, periodic explosions throwing him onward, faster and faster. For all its speed, Kaito's bronze-rank helicopter, even with Kaito using every power at his disposal, could not match the crude explosion-flight of the gold-ranker. The helicopter opened up with weapons and deployed drones to intercept, but Gerling went through them as if they were a light pattering of rain. When Gerling struck the helicopter, it exploded in a burst of force and fire, tiny pieces scattering across the sky.

49
LOADED FOR BATTLE

The alien landscape of the node space was an uncanny mix of familiar features washed out in metallic silver light. A close examination of the ground, rocks and plants did not help. Being made up of tiny blocks gave it the feel of a low-resolution image. Jason wandered over to the river, which he found looked like mercury under the monochrome light.

Jason was uncomfortably uncertain about how to identify if he had the right node, figure out how to alter it and finally repair it without making things worse. Even the terrifyingly knowledgeable Dawn had limited advice. She told him to trust his senses over his eyes and to take his time, matching the theory he had been taught to the reality he encountered. Once he understood one in terms of the other, he would be ready to intervene. To Jason, that sounded a lot like 'get in there and figure it out, idiot.'

He wandered in search of some core area—a big magical-looking thing he could interact with. Eventually, as his aura adapted to the harsh conditions of the space's own corrosive aura, he realised that the entire space was the core he was seeking out.

Despite all the magical theory he had studied, he was unprepared for the discovery that the very land he was walking through was the mechanism he had been searching for. The work of the original Builder was so vast and more nuanced than Jason could even begin to comprehend. For a moment, he despaired of ever understanding enough to begin his task, let alone complete it.

Schooling his negative thoughts, he renewed his determination, once more probing the space around him with his magical and aura senses. He stopped looking for individual elements and started looking at everything as a collective whole. His more holistic approach swiftly revealed incongruities in the otherwise exquisite design.

The original artistry of the place, expanded over billions of years from the reality seed from which his universe had been created, was far too sophisticated for Jason to interfere with in any way beyond crude bumbling. Fortunately, this had also been true for whoever had made the changes Jason had come to correct.

The design of the space was so magnificent in its sophistication that it blurred the lines of what constituted the natural world.

"I hope the intelligent design people don't find out about this."

Jason was looking at the blueprints of reality. The underpinnings of matter and energy. The book in which the laws of physics were written. Incepted as a seed from which the entire universe sprouted, it was like looking at the results of a self-learning program that had been running for eons. Jason was staggered at a mind that could accomplish all that, if such a thing could even be called a mind. Jason was filled with awe and—for the first time since learning of its existence—respect for what the Builder was.

Seeing the result of the Builder's core purpose, creating universes, it brought home to Jason the vast alien consciousness that even the newer, once-mortal Builder must possess. It reinforced what Dawn had told him about great astral beings needing mortal vessels not just to interact with physical reality but even to think on a mortal scale. Jason had thought that the Builder he encountered had been using the bodies he inhabited as interchangeable puppets. Now he realised that Thadwick and the other body he used may have had much more of an effect on the Builder than he previously imagined.

"You picked a dud vessel there, mate," Jason muttered to himself.

He had to wonder how much the cultists who prepared Thadwick to serve as a vessel understood the process. Then he remembered that this was done right after Rufus had wiped out the local leadership. It was likely that they had managed to dig out the mechanisms for creating vessels without grasping the ramifications of who they selected to be the raw material. Choosing the most expendable person had consequences that were unfortunate for the Builder's cult but a blessing for Jason himself.

The inexpert alterations Jason sensed in the node space were marring the sublime intricacy of the original work. This made the crude flaws in what was otherwise a perfect system easy to pick out. Like a scratch in a record, they threw off the harmony of the pattern with a jolt.

Jason and his team had been unsure of how reliable their method of identifying the correct node was. They had been successful the first time out, but whether this would continue or if they just got lucky, he didn't yet know.

Dawn had advised Jason to take his time to comprehend the space properly, and that was exactly what he did. The more he examined the perfection of the design, the more the changes he spotted seemed blasphemous. The door Jason had used to access this space was created by the second Builder, which made sense to Jason. He could not imagine the person who created the magnificence around him giving some idiot the tools to vandalise it.

Jason wasn't sure how long he spent working to understand the node space with what amounted to meditative examination. He had an eerie feeling that time flowed differently within it, although that was more likely to be his imagination than the reality. Sensing the space around him and trying to transpose that with his understanding of astral magic theory was challenging. It was the difference between having an anatomy textbook open in front of him and a surgery patient open in front of him. Fortunately, his goal was not to make changes but undo the damage that had already been done.

Jason's examination finally helped him understand that if he could delicately undermine the changes that had been made, the space would heal itself. Rather than relying on Jason's ham-fisted fumbling, it would be more like plucking a splinter than stitching up a wound. The actual mechanism for making changes was ostensibly easy, just a little well-placed aura pressure, but Jason did not rush. Measure twice, cut once was good advice for the building blocks of a house, let alone the building blocks of the universe.

Finally, Jason made his first adjustment, a tiny, delicate, and oh-so-careful change. He then watched and waited, hoping he hadn't made things worse. Straining his perception to the limit, he finally sensed signs that the affected area was returning to its natural state as the garish wound settled back into its pristine surroundings. He continued observing until he was certain that he wasn't just imagining the gradual shift change before moving on to do it again.

In the space between Jason's magical archway and the operations camp rapidly established by the Network tactical support team, Gerling dropped the ragged, unconscious Asano sisters on the ground. Network personnel moved to clamp category-three suppression collars onto their necks, while someone brought Gerling a folding chair and a can of beer. Cleary came out of the command tent and walked over as Gerling sat down, unconcerned as he waited for Jason to emerge.

"We're looking at using reality cores to potentially develop category-four suppression collars," Cleary said, looking at the unconscious sisters. "More category-four essence users is obviously the priority, but we're sure the Chinese have their own category fours already, which are most likely being woken up like you."

"You want to lock them down if we can, instead of killing them?" Gerling asked. "Seems like an unnecessary risk."

"Not my call," Cleary said. "A category-three collar is all we need for Asano, in any case. We didn't find any trace of Farrah Hurin, so we suspect she went in to warn him and he'll know what he's walking into. He could emerge at any moment."

"What about the others?" Gerling asked.

"The unknown entity, Dawn, appears to have been killed by the explosion. We're taking samples from what's left of her, but it's not much. The category twos survived the explosion, probably by consuming high-rank spirit coins, according to early examination of the bodies. Between the explosion and the subsequent weakening effect, though, only one survived the fall. It was the Tiwari boy, using a teleport power to escape the helicopter right before you hit it."

"He got away?"

"No. He's stealthy, but our category threes tracked him down. He's under interrogation now."

"Bring him out," Gerling said. "The bodies too. You said you wanted Asano humbled, right? Let's show him the extent of his failure."

Farrah was increasingly suffering as she forced herself onward through the alien silver landscape. Her excellent control over her aura prevented it from collapsing suddenly, eking out every scrap of strength before it finally gave way. She continued searching for Jason regardless, even as the mystical corrosion started impacting her body. She finally found Jason returning to the door, having rectified the node as best he could.

"What are you doing?" he asked, moving close and pushing his own aura out to protect her. The overextension meant that his own aura was being chewed away, but he ignored it, leading Farrah back in the direction of the door.

"The Network will be waiting outside," Farrah said. "They have a gold-ranker with them."

"China?"

"I don't know."

"What about the others?"

"They fled in Kaito's helicopter. I don't know if they got away."

"If they got caught, I'll open a portal for you to get them out through while I distract the gold-ranker. I'm what he's here for. If they got away, I'll open a portal for us to get out through."

"Don't risk yourself. You're the one who can fix the world now."

"They won't kill me. They need me alive."

"Do they need your arms and legs?"

"I've been through worse than anything they can do, and I still have tricks up my sleeve."

Jason and Farrah stepped out of the magic door, which descended into the ground and vanished. Farrah had her obsidian armour and sword already conjured, while Jason had his blood robes, cloak, and his dagger. He also had two orange and blue orbs with an eye pattern floating around him. Jason's familiar, Gordon, could surround himself with six orbs, three primarily blue with some orange and three primarily orange with some blue.

As of silver rank, and while Gordon was subsumed into Jason, Jason was now able to call up one of each orb for his own use. Just like Gordon, he could make attacks with them or use the new functions available with the rank-up. One orb could trigger the butterfly effect that spread Jason's afflictions, while the other could turn into a floating shield.

There was a Network operations camp set up nearby, the layout familiar to Farrah and Jason both. It was some distance away, as the magic door had been given a lot of space. The only things nearby were the folding chair containing Gerling and the people around him, living and dead.

The Asano sisters were alive but much worse for wear, collared and sprawled on the ground. Itsuki was also collared and unconscious, his wound suggesting he went down fighting. Jason could sense their auras, suppressed though they were. He could not sense Kaito, Asya, Greg or Dawn. There were three corpses on the ground, too damaged to recognise, but he knew.

In the folding chair was a man sitting amongst Jason's beaten and killed companions with a can of beer in his hand, as if he were at a casual barbecue. He was a hairy behemoth in plain fatigues, who tossed aside the can as he rose slowly from the chair. The can landed on a body whose long dark hair hadn't all been burned away.

Inside Jason's spirit vault, Jason's family looked up at a sky filling with angry red clouds as thunder pealed. The floral scent of the gardens turned coppery as the flowers faded and the plants grew savage barbs.

A scared Emi hugged her father tightly. They all knew they were in Jason's soul.

"Daddy, what's happening to Uncle Jason?"

"I don't know, sweetie," Ian said, placing a comforting hand on his daughter's head. "I don't know."

Gerling was around ten metres away from Jason and Farrah and took a few steps forward.

"Look at you two, all loaded for battle. You think you can beat me?"

"Let the others go," Jason said. "I have what you want. They get you nothing now."

"If it were up to me, I'd go for it," Gerling said. "Personally, I'd like for you and me to rumble. I want to see for myself all this power you're meant to have. But the big boys back home don't want you beaten. They want you broken. Humbled. You've been walking around, doing whatever you want for far too long. It's time for you to learn that you don't run this world, Asano. We do."

"You don't have to kill anyone else," Jason said.

"Yeah," Gerling acknowledged. "It's not exactly out of my way, though."

"Get them out," Jason told Farrah silently through the voice chat of his party interface.

Then he burst into action, charging directly at Gerling as Shade bodies spread out beside him.

A wild grin erupted on Gerling's face and he threw a fist at Jason from which a bolt of force shot out. Jason moved to step into a Shade body and shadow-jump away, only to fail. He felt some oppressive magic shut him down the moment he tried, and the force bolt exploded as it struck him, throwing him through the air.

Jason used his silver-rank agility to acrobatically adjust his trajectory, flipping in the air to land on his feet. The simple attack was not a high damage one, but coming from a gold-ranker, it still felt like being hit with a hammer. He resumed his charge, not dodging a second bolt, but instead of striking Jason, it passed right through.

At silver rank, one of the effects of Jason's cloak was to give him some limited ability to manipulate space. It had taken him some time to get a handle on it, but now Jason could dodge attacks in such a way as they seemed to hit. It was an ability with limitations and restrictions that Jason expertly hid, making what was little more than a magically enhanced dodge appear as a mysterious defensive power.

Missing his attack didn't dismay Gerling. Instead, he was delighted as he launched himself forward to meet Jason in a rush. He tried to crash-tackle the smaller man, but Jason managed to evade. Some strange magic prevented his shadow jumps, but that was not the extent of his evasive skills. Using Shade's bodies for pure obfuscation, Jason stepped through them, one of many dark figures for Gerling to pin down.

The gold-ranker's first approach was to swing with his fists as they shimmered with force. Jason had more skill, more combat experience and was devilishly elusive. It still wasn't enough in the face of the gold-ranker's raw speed. A fist soon landed in Jason's gut, sending him tumbling across the grass.

Gerling followed up quickly, punting Jason before he had a chance to get up. Once more, Jason rolled across the ground after suffering a savage blow. Gerling leapt into the air and used a special attack that drove him down like a hammer, Jason barely rolling away as Gerling's boots hit the ground. The attack still caused a small crater, the secondary force shattering the shield Jason managed to interpose using one of the orbs floating around him. Jason was showered in earth and once more sent tumbling away.

Lying where he fell, Jason raised an arm in Gerling's direction but it wasn't aimed at the gold-ranker. While Gerling had been kicking Jason along the ground like a ball, Jason had been taking the blows, letting them knock him further and further from Itsuki and the Asano sisters. Farrah had made her way to the prisoners and Jason raised a portal arch right next to them.

Gerling turned and looked, not rushing after Jason or the portal as he stood and laughed. The arch rose up like normal, but instead of filling with a dark portal, it remained empty and inert.

"You didn't seriously think we'd try this without doing something about those portals, right?" Gerling mocked.

50

GOING FOR GOLD

JASON AND FARRAH BOTH EXTENDED THEIR SENSES WHEN THE ARCH remained empty and the portal failed to open. If they hadn't been so shocked by their captured and dead companions, they might have paid more attention to their surroundings, but it was only now that they detected the magical devices set up in a wide circle around them. Farrah was familiar with the magic and knew it would be made up of a series of magic rods hammered into the ground, just out of sight.

"It's a dimensional condensation net," she told Jason through their party chat. "Keep him distracted while I take it out."

Jason cast a spell at Gerling.

"*Your fate is to suffer.*"

Gerling glared at him.

"A category three actually affecting me with his crap?" Gerling said.

He looked down at his arm. While kicking Jason across the ground, he hadn't even noticed Jason getting in the two shallow cuts. Wounds that shallow should have already healed. That they hadn't demonstrated the noxiousness of Jason's abilities, something Gerling had been thoroughly warned about. Gerling looked back up at Jason even as he rapidly chanted more spells.

"*Bleed for me.*"

"*Bear the mark of your transgressions.*"

Fresh blood leaked from the two cuts and a symbol was branded onto the back of his hand by a small flash of transcendent damage.

Despite knowing full well the nature of Jason's power, Gerling didn't rush, staring down Jason.

"I don't like your aura," Gerling said. "I can feel it. Judging me. I'm not yours to judge, Asano."

Gerling projected his aura to suppress Jason's and was startled at the result. He had heard that Jason's aura was strong, but he wasn't prepared for the degree to which that was true. Gerling's gold rank aura was stronger but far from overwhelming, despite the full rank of difference. Even that gap was made up by the difference in aura control. Gerling's aura control skills were adequate, but Jason's were immaculate. Trying to suppress Jason's aura was like trying to grip a wet, frictionless ball that kept slipping through his fingers.

Jason gave no reaction to Gerling's attack, as if he hadn't even noticed. Instead, he looked at the conjured dagger in his hand as it started to transform. The sinister blade grew longer as it extended into a sword shape, also changing colour. It turned from obsidian black and blood red to pristine silver. The red embellishment remained, but the barbed motif was smoothed into clean lines, with bright red runes set into the blade.

Ability: [Blade of Doom] (Doom)

- Conjuration (holy, unholy, curse, disease, poison).
- Cost: Moderate mana.
- Cooldown: None.

- Current rank: Silver 1 (19%).

- Effect (iron): Conjures [Ruin, the Blade of Tribulation]. Attacks made with Ruin will inflict an instance of [Vulnerable] and refresh any wounding effects on the target. Wounding effects refreshed by Ruin require more healing than normal to negate. Ruin is an unholy object.

- Effect (bronze): Ruin inflicts one instance each of [Ruination of the Blood], [Ruination of the Flesh] and [Ruination of the Spirit].

- Effect (silver): Blade gains a second form: [Penitent, the Blade of Sacrifice]. Attacks made with Penitent will inflict an instance of [Price in Blood] and refresh any wounding effects on the target. Wounding effects refreshed by Penitent require more healing than normal to negate. Penitent is a holy object.

- [Vulnerable] (affliction, unholy, stacking): All resistances are reduced. Additional instances have a cumulative effect. Consumed to cleanse instances of [Resistant] on a 1:1 basis.

- [Ruination of the Blood] (damage-over-time, poison, stacking): Inflicts ongoing necrotic damage until the poison is cleansed. Additional instances have a cumulative effect.

- [Ruination of the Flesh] (damage-over-time, disease, stacking): Inflicts ongoing necrotic damage until the disease is cleansed. Additional instances have a cumulative effect.

- [Ruination of the Spirit] (damage-over-time, curse, stacking): Inflicts ongoing necrotic damage until the curse is cleansed. Additional instances have a cumulative effect.

- [Price in Blood] (affliction, holy, blood, stacking): This affliction is applied equally to the person it is inflicted upon and the person who inflicts it. This affliction cannot be cleansed while a person who shares it is alive and is immediately negated if the person who shares it dies. Damage between people who share the affliction is increased, including damage sources in place prior to this effect. Damage from holy sources is further increased. Only damage actually inflicted is increased; damage negated by damage reduction and protection abilities is not. Additional instances have a cumulative effect.

The second form of the Blade of Doom power was a double-edge sword with a double-edged power. The Price in Blood affliction caused both the deliverer and the recipient to hurt each other all the more, making avoiding damage a critical objective. It was a massive gamble against a gold-rank enemy, but silver-rank attacks against such a foe were like digging through a brick wall with a spoon and Jason needed to hold Gerling's attention.

Jason stilled the storm of fury in his soul, tapping into his meditative techniques to push the rage and pain from his mind and let a calm settle over him. He knew that control was what he needed, while the illusory strength of passion would only hurt him. If he were alone, he might have been consumed by it, but he still had people he needed to get out alive and couldn't allow himself the indulgence. A calm came over him as his silver eyes locked on to Gerling. He started walking slowly forward. Gerling grinned, rushing at Jason to swing a fist at lightning speed.

Gold-rankers were absurdly fast. Jason had seen Emir move at full speed a few times and, to iron-rank Jason, it had been indistinguishable from Sophie's movement powers. The speed attribute alone of a gold-ranker was almost a teleportation power. Even at bronze rank, the speed of a gold-ranker would be little more than a blur. Only at silver could Jason's reflexes keep up at all, and even then, it was like moving through molasses.

Jason had every other advantage. His skill, both in terms of fighting technique and the use of his abilities, was as far above Gerling's as Gerling's raw power was above Jason's. Jason's powers were also better suited to a close-quarters fight. His cloak hid his movements and manipulated space, while his weapon gave him the reach on the unarmed Gerling.

Gerling's powers, on the other hand, made him more of a siege weapon than a duellist. His explosive powers were better suited to assaulting an army than a person. Even so, he was simply so fast, so strong and so tough that it didn't matter. Jason landed half a dozen hits with his sword, massively accelerating his already locked-in suite of powers and Gerling was barely impaired.

It took Gerling time to hit Jason, whose skill and abilities made him frustratingly evasive. When the hit landed, however, the result was devastating. Gerling's strength, enhanced by an explosive fist power and Jason's own damage-accelerating power left Jason as little more than a bloody mess, bouncing along the ground like a skipping stone.

Instead of following up, Gerling dashed off to Farrah. She had been making her way to one of the buried rods restricting Jason's portal, using her lava cannon power to devastate the team of silver-rankers that moved to intercept her.

"Hello, hot stuff," Gerling said and swung his fist.

Farrah did not fight like Jason, as reflected by her equipment. Where Jason conjured sleek robes and a wispy cloak, she conjured heavy obsidian armour. Instead of a dagger, she conjured a huge sword that could extend out into a barbed lava whip. She had orbs floating around her, but instead of glowing eyes, they were searing flames.

Jason's style was elusive, deceptive, and mobile. Farrah, by contrast, was all about power, not just using it but also dealing with it. For all the power at her command, she had won it fighting monsters that were stronger and tougher than she was, just like Gerling.

Gerling was surprised at his inability to land a solid hit. Farrah's slight but efficient movement always managed to deflect his hits or shift her angle just the right way to negate the bulk of the damage. Only the explosive power shrouding his fists had a major effect, blasting off chunks of her armour.

Farrah drew on her vast combat experience and moved with the hits, letting it lead her into counterattacks. Like Jason, Farrah was much more adept with her powers than Gerling. Her whip sword made of lava and obsidian danced like a monstrous snake as it drew blood, while the burning orbs floating around her lunged in to burn his face, distracting him. The attacks had full effect as well; the damage reduction from his superior rank was not a factor.

Ability: [Limit Breaker] (Potent)

- Special ability.
- Cost: None.
- Cooldown: None.

- Current rank: Silver 2 (07%).

- Effect (iron): Ignore rank disparity in resistances and damage reduction.

- Effect (bronze): Increase the effect of abilities by increasing their cost.

- Effect (silver): The enhanced state from consuming a spirit coin lasts for significantly longer and the after-effects are reduced.

Farrah's attacks also left Gerling covered in burning flames. Momentarily being on the back foot enraged him and he clapped his hands together to create an explosion that swept out in front of him. At the same time, though, a wall of obsidian rose up between him and Farrah. He sneered as the explosion blasted the wall to fragments, only to be startled when the fragments flew the wrong way. Even as the force of the explosion passed through the shattered wall and knocked Farrah off her feet, the fragments of wall blasted back into Gerling, digging into his flesh. Lying on the ground, Farrah quickly chanted a spell.

"*Children of the volcano, be reborn in fire.*"

The shards of obsidian buried in Gerling's flesh melted into magma, inflicting a pain even the gold-ranker couldn't ignore. Farrah got to her feet as Gerling yelled in rage and pain, stumbling back, and not hearing the quiet chant behind him.

"*Your blood is not yours to keep but mine on which to feast.*"

At silver rank, Jason's recovery powers were terrifying to behold. Far from appearing near death, he now looked completely fresh, his conjured robes and cloak covering the blood coating his body underneath. The life force he drained from the gold-ranker brought his health back up to full and beyond, with his Sin Eater ability allowing his health to surpass its normal maximum.

Jason didn't launch Colin into the fray, and not just because Gerling was covered in flames. Area attacks were a critical weakness for swarm-type enemies and Gerling seemed to be all about explosions. More importantly, Jason was going to need the healing his familiar provided by remaining subsumed. Knowing he would need to rely on himself, he used a damage spell that took advantage of the afflictions still accumulating on Gerling.

Ability: [Punition] (Doom)

- Spell.
- Cost: Moderate mana.
- Cooldown: 30 seconds.

- Current rank: Silver 1 (09%).

- Effect (iron): Inflicts necrotic damage for each curse, disease, poison and unholy affliction the target is suffering.

- Effect (bronze): Inflicts or refreshes the duration of [Penitence].

- Effect (silver): Damage per affliction can be increased by increasing the mana cost to high, very high, or extreme. This reduces the cooldown to 20 seconds, 10 seconds or none. Consecutive, extreme-cost uses have a shorter incantation.

- [Penitence] (affliction, holy): Gain an instance of [Penance] for each curse, disease, poison or unholy effect that is cleansed from you. This is a holy effect.

- [Penance] (affliction, holy, damage-over-time, stacking): Deals ongoing transcendent damage. Additional instances have a cumulative effect, dropping off as damage is dealt.

"*Suffer the cost of your transgressions.*"

Jason's abilities were largely mana-efficient, a trait shared by most affliction specialists. Punition stood out as his big, instantaneous damage spell, although it required set up to be effective. As of silver rank, it became a mana sink, giving him a large hammer to swing when he needed to go all out.

Against a silver-rank opponent, even a moderate time under Jason's afflictions would have placed them in a bad position. Gerling, however, demonstrated the near-indestructibility of a gold-ranker, showing the marks of both Jason and Farrah's attacks without yet being impeded by them. Even Jason's newly enhanced Punition spell failed to make a sizeable dent in the gold-ranker's condition, although it was enough to surprise their powerful enemy.

Gerling was frustrated at how much he was being shown up by the two silver-rankers. They should have been so overwhelmed by his power that he hadn't treated them as real opponents. As he was filled with anger, that changed. He hammered his fists together and a powerful blast exploded out, sending Farrah and Jason flying.

The two silver-rankers scrambled to their feet as Gerling strode from the cloud of earth and dust thrown up by his power. He was still wreathed in fire from Farrah's abilities, but his disregard and iron glare made the flames seem more like his power than hers. He stomped his foot and the ground in a wide area around her exploded up, throwing her into the air and battering her with both force and magically empowered rocks that exploded as they came near her.

At the same time, Gerling threw a fist in Jason's direction and he was blasted with a broad wave of force. If he had not been denied shadow-jumping, he could have avoided it, but was instead battered and blasted back.

This was the signal of a change in the tenor of the fight as Gerling unleashed one area attack after another in an unrelenting assault that gave neither Jason nor Farrah time to recover and rally. It was a terrible strategy against enemies of a similar rank. Such abilities were high cost and relatively low damage, which was how the silver-rankers survived the barrage. Jason's stacked rapid healing effects kept him healing through the damage while Farrah's armour and magically enhanced toughness allowed her to endure.

Network personnel were watching from the nearby camp. The second in command of the Berlin forces threw an unhappy glance at Cleary, on the other side of the camp.

"Boss," she told her commander, "this isn't right. I'm pretty sure we're working for the bad guys here."

"Tell me something I don't know," he growled.

"Maybe we don't have to?"

"What are you suggesting? That's a category four over there and I have zero interest in having my head crushed in his fist like a soft fruit."

"Those things stopping them from escaping. Maybe we could take one out."

"How? By taking out our own people guarding them? Look, I'm not opposed to doing something. Just come up with an idea better than that."

"Maybe we just need the right opportunity, boss. If it doesn't come, it doesn't come, but if we're ready and it does…"

"Alright," the commander said. "Spread the word. Careful and quiet."

Jason and Farrah's superior skills were overwhelmed by the combination of power disparity and cheap tactics. Gerling had enough area abilities to almost stun-lock them both. Their attempts to push back fell short. Jason barely managed to stay alive, throwing out Punition and his health drain spell every chance he could. He called out Gordon, who chained his shield orbs to protect himself and Jason, as well as inflict his butterfly effect on Gerling. After three attacks, each one destroying a shield orb, a disruptive force blast from the gold-ranker left the incorporeal familiar ragged. Since it took a full minute to recover a destroyed orb, Jason called Gordon back into himself before the familiar's vessel was destroyed.

The butterflies manifesting on Gerling did not impair the gold-ranker; instead, they flew off in every direction. The Network forces had staged teams near the buried rods preventing Jason's portal from working and the butterflies went in their direction. Some of the butterflies were caught up in Gerling's area attacks and others were shot down by the Network troops using disruptive force attacks that caused the butterflies to detonate. As Jason's powers kept multiplying the butterfly affliction, though, more and more butterflies went out, increasing the pressure.

Farrah burned through her mana, re-conjuring armour over and over as the explosive attacks broke it apart. The area attacks drew close to the Asano sisters and Itsuki, who had made their way to the inactive portal as they watched the conflict. Farrah knew she had to push back before their collared companions were caught up and killed. After withstanding another attack, Farrah took out a gold spirit coin and slipped it into her mouth.

Farrah's body was immediately flooded with power, her Limit Breaker ability handling the gold-rank energy in a smooth flow, compared to the brutish force other essence users experienced when using a coin. She leapt through the air using a special attack, her sword lighting up with white-hot flames as Gerling's latest area attack failed to knock back the momentum of her enhanced attack. He was forced to take it head-on.

Unfortunately, he could. Even with her attributes raised to gold, Farrah was not a match for a true gold-ranker, although the boost was enough to push him with her greater mastery of both fighting technique and ability use. In the break, Jason made his way for the closest buried rod, hoping to disrupt the effect.

Gerling was not unaware of Jason's actions and used one of the long cooldown abilities from his vast essence. A void sphere appeared in the middle of the area they were fighting, creating a massive gravitational pull towards it. Gerling and Farrah both resisted, Gerling only partially affected by his own ability while Farrah dug her sword into the ground as an anchor. Itsuki and the Asano sisters braced themselves against Jason's inactive portal arch.

Jason and the Network troops around the perimeter of the battle zone suffered the full brunt, all being dragged to the sphere, which then exploded. Jason and the other silver-rankers survived, although they were savaged by the raw power of the blast that scattered them back around the battlefield. All the bronze-rankers from the Network teams that had been sucked in were dead.

At the camp, Cleary ordered new teams in to replace the one that had been guarding the buried rods. The commander stormed up to him, furious.

"Are you joking? Your guy just took out half my entire contingent, a lot of them dead. Now you want me to send more in there?"

"Unless you want to be the next on the list when my category-four friend comes back, yes."

The commander bared his teeth but finally turned away.

"Alright," he announced to his sections. "Everyone head to your assigned back-up points."

The commander glanced back at Cleary.

"And remember what you were just told," the commander said to his personnel. "Move out."

Cleary frowned, uncertain of what the commander had been referencing, but put it to the back of his mind as he returned his attention to the fight. The fact that there was a fight at all, rather than a one-sided hammering was not a part of his plans.

Jason managed another draining spell on Gerling, instantaneously flooding Jason with healing. Despite the massive health drain, it barely seemed to affect Gerling. Despite Farrah's flames and Jason's afflictions, Gerling was still going strong, the absurd resilience of a gold-ranker proving dominant. If Jason had a whole team of silver-rankers to hold up Gerling, he could probably do the damage required to take him down but just he and Farrah were not enough. Even with his afflictions running rampant, Gerling was still going strong.

Butterflies were landing on the silver-rankers lying hurt on the ground, even as the freshly healed Jason stood up, delivering affliction packages that would most likely kill them before they got help. Jason used his Feast of Absolution power, replenishing his mana and stamina as he drained the afflictions from them. He was careful not to include Gerling. Gerling was not hurt to the point that switching from the sinister afflictions to holy ones would be effective.

Farrah was winding down, her gold-rank power fading away. Soon it would be gone and she would be weaker than before. Jason made another run at the buried rods, even as reinforcements from the camp moved around the outside of the battlefield to guard them.

Farrah was sent hurtling off as her power faded and Gerling hit her square in the chest with a potent ability. Gerling then zipped to intercept Jason, grabbing his neck from behind and tossing him back, far from the buried rods. Gerling moved over Jason and planted a foot on his chest.

"You're done, Asano. You put up a good fight. If we were the same rank, you'd have won. But we're not. Power is always king."

"In the other world, they call it the tyranny of rank," Jason said.

"Tyranny of rank? I like that."

"I hope you like your flesh melting off. Good luck clearing those afflictions."

"What did I just tell you? Luck doesn't matter. Skill doesn't matter. Only power matters."

Jason's face filled with anguish as he felt a familiar surge of power from within Gerling, the reason that Gerling had been chosen as the gold-ranker they awoke. Gerling, it turned out, shared a power with Humphrey, also gaining it from the might essence. That power was called Immortality, and it instigated an incredibly powerful healing effect. It was a power known by the Magic Society, so after Humphrey had looked it up, Jason learned that, at silver-rank, it gained the ability to purge all afflictions, ignoring any and all effects that prevented cleansing. Jason had encountered a similar effect used by the archbishop of the church of Purity.

"That power," Jason said. "A friend of mine has it. I know that it can bring you back from the dead at gold rank."

"Now you know that killing me wouldn't have helped you."

"That's alright," Jason said. "Now I get to kill you twice."

Gerling chuckled as he took a battered and singed but still functioning suppression collar from a belt satchel. As he bent down to put it on his prisoner, explosions erupted around the edge of the battlefield.

Moments earlier, Cleary had been watching with satisfaction as Gerling ended the fight. Farrah was badly hurt, her collared companions rushing to check on her. Asano was seemingly immortal, but Gerling now had him literally underfoot. Too late, Cleary spotted the new teams at the buried rods digging into the ground before they all started running.

"What are they…?"

Grenades the teams had just dropped into holes alongside the rods started going off. The empty space in Jason's inactive portal was suddenly filled with darkness. The Asano sisters dragged Farrah through, Itsuki following. Cleary watched in horror as Jason slipped out from under Gerling's foot and flung himself at the portal.

Gerling was only startled for a moment and he still had gold-rank reflexes. He threw out a hand in Jason's direction and fired a force bolt. It flew past Jason, exploding between Jason and the portal. Jason was flung back even as Gerling moved forward. Gerling grabbed Jason's head in a huge, meaty hand, clamping the suppression collar into place with the other.

As soon as Jason's powers were cut off, the portal descended into the ground and vanished. Furious, Gerling hammered his fist into Jason's head until Jason fell unconscious, and then hammered it some more.

Jason woke up in a transport container, reinforced with what looked like a roll-cage, to which Jason had been very thoroughly chained, hands and feet. Jason waited to recover more before acting. His portal was still a couple of minutes from being usable again and he would need to move fast. His powers were suppressed, but Colin, inside him, was healing him at a formidable rate.

The container was on the move, on a transport helicopter Jason guessed from the motion. Gerling was likely to be close by, but Jason wasn't going to risk extending his senses until he was prepared to act.

It was hard to sense if his powers were off cooldown while they were suppressed, but Jason was used to this, having long used suppression collars in his aura training. That was how he could be sure when his portal was ready and he could begin to act.

Jason plotted through his series of rapid actions, ready to execute them as quickly as possible. He pushed off the silver-rank suppression effect with his aura, then conjured his cloak and used the space distortion ability to slip out of the manacles and leg chains, even as he called up a portal. He dove through it just in time as the container was ripped apart to reveal Gerling, who had sensed Jason's aura when he overcame the collar. All Gerling found was Jason's portal, descending into the floor.

"What the fu—"

51

PREPARE FOR THE REMATCH

THE CLOUD HOUSE WAS IN A VACANT LOT OF AN ABANDONED AUSTRIAN town. Inside, Farrah, Itsuki and the Asano sisters waited anxiously. The portal had closed right behind them and Jason's fate was unknown. Farrah had taken out suppression collar skeleton keys she made herself after seeing the crude ones Jason had made. She unlocked the collars around the necks of the others, then magically examined them for tracking magic. The cloud house should be more than capable of blocking it, but she wanted to be careful.

Ten minutes after they arrived, the portal reappeared and Jason stumbled through, the portal sinking into the floor immediately after. Farrah wrapped him in a fierce hug. Once she let him go, Jason opened his spirit vault, concerned about whether his mental state, the suppression collar, or both had affected his family within.

Heading into the vault, he immediately spotted the differences. The colour seemed washed out of everything, from the drab flowers to the grey sky. Rain was falling, which he had not seen before in his spirit vault. As soon as he emerged from the portal in the central pavilion, his family rushed up to him from where they had been clustered together in a small sitting area, under the pavilion.

"Jason, what happened?" Erika asked.

"Come out into the cloud house," he said. "We need to talk."

"What in the god damn hell?" Cleary asked angrily, sitting in the transport helicopter as it approached the Berlin Network headquarters. "Our own people betrayed us and let Asano get away."

"No, they didn't," Gerling said. "They let his companions get away, but we got Asano. Him getting loose was on us. He clearly had some means to disable a suppression collar."

"He was searched," Cleary said. "Thoroughly. If he had a magic key jammed up his ass, our sensors would have found it when we checked him."

"Lack of intel, then," Gerling said. "It must be some ability."

"To ignore a suppression collar?"

"Who knows what abilities he learned in the other world? His aura was like nothing I've ever seen, both in power and control. Based on the aura surge I felt when he was escaping, it's probably related to that."

"How can you be calm?" Cleary asked. "He got away."

"My job was to catch him and I caught him," Gerling said. "Containment was your area. I'm the talent, which means your head is the one on the block."

"I'm going to kill those traitorous bastards," Cleary spat.

"No, you're not," Gerling said.

"Excuse me?"

"You shanghaied a bunch of the Berlin branch's tac-teams, got half of them killed and sent the other half to die. Are you that surprised they screwed you? I would have. Now you want to what? Take them back to their branch and execute them in front of the rest? They will string you up."

"Not with you there."

"If you want to go after them, that's all you," Gerling said. "They've already demonstrated what they'll do when you push them hard enough, even when I'm right there. Frankly, I admire them for having the sack to go for it."

Cleary scowled unhappily but fell silent, calming himself with deep breaths. Only once the helicopter was about to land did he speak again, the tense rage in his voice replaced with weariness.

"Did I hear you call yourself the talent?"

"I regretted it immediately," Gerling admitted.

In the cloud house, Jason's family and other companions sat in morose silence. Emi was curled up against her uncle, clutching him.

"What about the bodies?" Ian asked.

"I'll make sure they're sent home, with respect," Jason said.

In the frenzy of the moment, Jason had been moving too fast for the horror of what had happened to catch him. Now that he'd stopped, it came on in force. The image of the dead bodies at the man's feet was seared into his brain. He lost track of them in the fight, unsure even how intact they were after all the area attacks being thrown around.

"What about Dawn?" Akari asked.

"What was with us wasn't really her," Farrah said. "I don't know how long it will take, but she will be back."

"Isn't there something you can do?" Erika asked. "You came back from…"

She struggled to say the words.

"…Farrah came back. Isn't there some way for Kai to come back too?"

"I'm sorry, Eri," Jason said.

"The circumstances were very specific," Farrah added, and the group fell silent again.

"What do we do now?" Akari asked.

"First thing is we lay low," Jason said. "That gold-ranker is still out there and the resources the Americans have at their disposal are not to be underestimated. We have to be extremely careful."

He winced, his expression filled with sorrow and self-recrimination.

"The way we should have been already," he added. "I should never have let you all participate."

"It was our choice," Akari said. "You think you are the only one with the right to fight for their world? That only you are doing this for the right reasons? Kaito, Asya and Greg weren't just doing this to help you with a personal project, Asano. We all came into this understanding what was at stake and the price we might have to pay."

Jason stared at her with a deer-in-headlights stare, then gave the faintest of acknowledging nods.

Things had not gone well at the Berlin branch. The American contingent was forced to hurriedly board their transport plane and decamp for the Ramstein Air Base in Germany's south-west. Despite Gerling's warning, Cleary had been startled at the Berlin branch's fury. If not for the presence of the gold-ranker, he realised that they may not have been allowed to leave at all.

"It's time to regroup anyway," Gerling told him. "Asano is not going to continue his current approach. We need to consolidate our resources here in Europe before we get the whole continent up in arms because of how we're riding roughshod over their branches."

"They'll do what they're told," Cleary said.

"I think that you're overestimating how much crap people are willing to eat," Gerling said. "You think most of the Network cares about reality cores that the vast majority of them will never so much as lay eyes on? That's the obsession of the few who will actually get to reap that power. Maybe you can't see it because you've been living through it, but those monster waves and these transformation events are terrifying to the people who don't have the power to fight against them. That's what the actual people who make up the Network care about, not which branch has the most category fours for some pissing match."

"Are you questioning our purpose here?" Cleary asked him.

"No," Gerling said. "I'm just pointing out that it's *our* purpose. I hate to break it to you, Cleary, but however we end up spinning it, we're the bad guys. I'm on board with that and you need to be as well."

In Sydney, the Steering Committee of the local Network branch ended their meeting. All but one of the members shuffled out of the conference room, leaving Annabeth Tilden alone to exhaustedly rub her temples. Her brother, Terrance, came in after the committee members had left.

"Well?" he asked.

"We confirmed Asano escaped," Anna said. "He's probably going to go on some kind of rampage."

"I hope not. He'll die, and if what he's doing is as important as he claims…"

"Yeah," Anna said. "Ketevan has already made a formal request to Berlin for the return of the bodies to Australia. The bastards killed Asya."

"What is our stance going to be?"

"Our Steering Committee is adopting a wait-and-see approach."

"Meaning they're going to chicken out until they find a bandwagon to jump on," Terrance said. "Our people aren't going to like that. Do you know how many of them have fought alongside Jason? Worked with Farrah on restoring the grid? Flew with Kaito or got a medivac to the Asano compound? If we lie down on this, we may have a rebellion on our hands."

"You think I don't know this?" Anna asked. "What do you think I've been trying to hammer into the heads of the Steering Committee?"

"Maybe you shouldn't bother."

"What are you saying?"

"The Network is fracturing, Anna. Maybe it's time for a management restructure."

"I'm hearing similar talk out of Europe," Anna said. "The Berlin branch is furious about the International Committee forcing them to help the Americans and getting a bunch of their people killed. A lot of other branches are up in arms over the allocation of resources to fighting over reality cores instead of monster wave recovery. Now that we can monitor the oceans with the grid, there's a lot of call for shifting priorities back to our traditional role."

"That's not going to happen. We're out in the open now. The leadership has been hiding their power and now they're looking to flex in front of the whole world. They don't care about stopping monsters as much as accruing political power."

"That's what worries me," Anna said. "There's talk of pressuring the International Committee to censure the US and China and force them to go back to the old priorities. That would be great except that neither one is going to roll over and show their stomach."

"No, they won't. From their perspective, the International Committee serves them, not the other way around. It's just always been easier for them not to make a point of it. If the IC actually pushes it, the Network will fracture into factions."

"That may be inevitable. There has always been a disconnect between the leadership and the bulk of the Network's personnel, but now the leadership is throwing its authority around like never before. This couldn't have come at a worse possible time."

There was a hard knock on the door. Michael Aram opened it and came in before waiting for a response.

"Anna, I've been contacted by Craig Vermillion."

"We aren't exactly on the best terms with the Cabal right now," Terrance said.

"He knows," Aram said. "He knew you would trust me and asked me to set up a discreet meeting. I think you'll want to hear what he has to say."

Gerling had been assigned a pair of assistants to see to his needs. They were both young Network functionaries, iron-rank admin staff with no tactical training. One was David, a man who Gerling disliked for his annoyingly transparent ambition, but he was enthusiastic about meeting Gerling's requests. Fiona was a plain but highly competent woman that Gerling appreciated for her ability to know when to be around and when not to be, compared to the stifling David.

Gerling was walking through an aircraft hangar to meet Cleary, when his assistants approached him.

"We've found an elf for you, sir," Fiona told Gerling.

"We have?" David asked.

"It turns out that one of the early reactions to people transforming into strange new species is—"

"Rich people paying to have sex with them," Gerling realised.

"Precisely," Fiona said. "Brothels are opening up like mushrooms after rain in the transformation zones and we have contracted someone who has quickly come into high demand, despite her considerable rates."

"Excellent work."

"Contracted?" David asked. "I thought we were just going to grab some elf."

Gerling and Fiona both turned on him with disdain.

"Do you think I'm a rapist?" Gerling asked.

"You kill a lot of people," David said uncertainly. "I thought you did what you wanted. Isn't that what power is for?"

"And you think what I want is to rape people? Fiona, get this guy replaced."

"Yes, sir."

"You just said that you wanted us to get you an elf!" David whined.

"I assumed not raping people went without saying," Gerling said. "Fiona, make sure the next guy understands that."

"Yes, sir."

"Oh, and how did you go with getting the people I asked to have sent from the States?"

Fiona checked her watch.

"They should be wheels down in about seven hours, sir."

"Thank you."

"Sir…" David said.

"Make sure the next person isn't like this idiot," Gerling said to Fiona, gesturing at David. "Is he someone's nephew or something?"

"His father is the Director of Tactical Operations in New York."

"Ah. Probably just fire him, then, rather than fire him out of a cannon."

"We don't have a cannon, sir," Fiona said. "I can probably find someone who can conjure one."

"What?" David asked as Gerling chuckled.

"That's fine," Gerling said. "Just reassign him to someone who'll appreciate a sycophant."

"Very well, sir," Fiona said. "Is there anything else?"

"Not unless you have anything else for me," Gerling said.

Fiona waved her hand and a portal appeared. She reached in and pulled out a can of beer. Gerling laughed as he took it.

"You want to come work for me permanently, Fiona?"

"I would very much like that, sir."

"Oh, come on," David complained.

Gerling left his assistant and former assistant behind as he made his way to the office that Cleary had appropriated in the hangar. Cleary stood over a desk with a monitor set into it, poring over a map on which transformation zones were marked. He looked up as Gerling came in without bothering to knock.

"You requested a training team be sent here from the US?" Cleary asked.

"That's right."

"You asked specifically for people that trained with Asano and Hurin in Australia. You want to learn more about them from people who know them?"

"No," Gerling said. "Those people learned the techniques taught by Hurin and Asano and then brought them home. I want to learn about how they fight and how to fight like them."

"You beat them both."

"I should have annihilated them both. You don't understand how much more powerful than them I am. My old instructor always said that I was coasting on the power of my attacks, but I never listened and now Asano and Hurin made me look like a fool. Feel like a fool. You concentrate on finding them; you don't need my help for that. I need to prepare for the rematch."

"Interesting choice of venue," Anna said. She was in the townhouse that was previously the home of Jason's Uncle Hiro, now apparently owned by the vampire, Craig Vermillion.

"After the EOA purchased all of Hiro's assets, I quietly picked this up off them through an appropriate series of cut-outs," Craig said. "I like to have an off-the-books spot with the little comforts."

They sat down in the lounge.

"Before we begin," Craig asked, "is it true about Asya?"

"Yes."

Craig bowed his head.

"These are dark times, Anna."

"What do you want, Craig? I have enough on my plate to be going on with."

"Oh, it's worse than you think. You are aware that the Cabal has been coming out on top in the contest for the reality cores."

"I genuinely don't care."

"You should. The Network is not the only one threatening to fracture over the behaviour of its most powerful members."

"Oh?"

"Do you know how vampires grow more powerful, Anna?"

"Time, right? But then you get too powerful and the ambient magic can't sustain you."

"Yes," Craig said. "The old ones have all been slumbering since they reached what you call category four."

Anna's eyes went wide.

"Reality cores," she whispered in horrified realisation.

"Exactly," Craig said. "It's not as simple as handing over a core, but some of the Cabal's upper echelons are working on imbuing blood with that power, which should be able to start waking them up. I've heard the rumours of the Chinese and Americans having people of that level and they're probably stronger than an equivalent vampire. How many do they have, though? Two? Three? Five? I promise you that we have more."

"How many more?"

"I'm not sure any one person knows," Craig said. "The Cabal is a nest of secrets."

"Why are you telling me this?" Anna asked. "You're Cabal. You're a vampire."

"And I like the world the way it is. Was, before the damn EOA messed everything up. Even as bad as things have gotten, do you think I want the planet ruled by people with eight-century-old social values and a thirst for human blood?"

52
FINISH THE JOB

No one paid attention to one more man in a dark suit and dark glasses. There was no shortage of them as the funeral was conducted under a bright, clear sky, despite the winter. Jason's use of aura control had progressed to the point that in a crowd with that many essence users, he could manipulate their perception to go unnoticed, even when standing right amongst them.

It helped that all the essence users were lower rank than Jason. The Network leadership would never allow precious silver-rankers to take time away when there could be a transformation zone to fight over at any moment. The Network members were mostly from the ranks, crowding the grassy, outdoor venue for Kaito's service. In the months he had been one of them, Kaito had flown them into hot zones, evacuated them when injured and delivered critical supplies in the midst of danger.

Jason watched Amy, standing stony-faced at the front. Someone had given her an aura suppression bracelet so her emotions weren't on open display in front of all the essence users present.

Publicly, Jason was an internationally wanted criminal. A rogue element, responsible for bombings in Japan and killing Global Defense Network personnel in Austria. The Network leadership knew that with the failed capture attempt and the death of Jason's brother, lover and friend, they had declared war. Accordingly, they sought to sever Jason's influence and connections inside the Network.

Ostensibly, this meant that the Network was on the lookout for Jason at events like his brother's funeral. In reality, they knew that even a gold-ranker had failed to pin him down, and no shortage of people had died in the attempt. Most Network members didn't even agree with what the Americans had done, especially those from the Australian branches that had worked alongside Jason and his brother. The last thing the people looking for Jason wanted was to find him.

After the service, many people came up to Amy, offering their condolences. Her eyes went wide when she found Jason standing in front of her. She glanced at the people around them.

"How are you here?" she asked in a conspiratorial whisper. "Why aren't people jumping all over you?"

"A trick of perception. So long as no one draws too much attention to me, they won't notice that it's me."

"So I could yell out and people would try and grab you?"

"Yes."

"Why shouldn't I, then? You were meant to bring the father of my children back home."

"I know," Jason said, his voice cracking.

She scowled as they continued to converse in hushed tones.

"What are you going to do about the people that killed him?"

"The man in question is powerful. Far more than me, but his time will come. First, I have to finish the job that Kaito and I started."

"Is it worth it?"

Jason nodded.

"Things are going to get worse before they get better," he said, "but Kaito played his part in getting us all past this. I know it isn't a comfort, but he died for something that truly matters. To give his children a future."

"I know it was his choice to go," she said. "Even so, I can't help but hate you for taking him."

Jason nodded but said nothing else. If his words couldn't make things better, he kept his mouth shut.

Michael Aram discreetly approached Annabeth Tilden after the service, as she was walking back to the car with her wife. He was in charge of security and media management for the event.

"Committeewoman," he greeted her, with a respectful nod.

"What is it, Aram? Shouldn't you be answering to Ketevan?"

"She asked me to keep you in the loop. Some of our security personnel have glimpsed a blurred artefact on the camera feeds."

"He's here, then," Anna said. "What did Keti tell you to do if he was here?"

"Pretend he wasn't."

"Good. If he didn't want us to know, we wouldn't."

"Is he provoking us?"

"Not at his brother's funeral. He's probably going to pay me one of his trademark unexpected visits. Thank you, Aram."

Aram left them and they reached their car, the driver opening the rear door to admit Anna and her wife. As they sat, a shadow emerged from Anna's shadow to sit opposite them. Jason appeared from within it.

"Anna," he greeted, then turned to Anna's wife. "Susan. We haven't met since I obtained those paintings from your gallery."

"The paintings by Dawn," Susan said.

"Have you actually met the artist?" Jason asked.

"No," Susan said. "She always worked through an intermediary."

"I'll introduce you if I get the chance. She was killed alongside my brother, but she'll be back, sooner or later."

Susan frowned, but Anna forestalled questions with a shake of her head.

"Are you here to kill us?" Anna asked.

"I'm here to thank you for getting the bodies sent home," he said. "It would have been awkward to make arrangements myself, given the circumstances."

"Asya was a friend," Anna said. "Were you and her…?"

"Yes."

"Then I'm doubly sorry. There was talk of using the bodies or this funeral as bait," Anna said.

"I know," Jason said. "Thank you for putting a stop to that particular idea. My sister-in-law and I have our issues, but she deserves to say goodbye to her husband in peace."

"You should know that the Americans may soon be too busy to direct more attention your way."

"I'm aware," Jason said. "The Cabal leadership are looking at waking up old vampires, and both the Network and the Cabal are seeing dangerous splits between the leadership and the bulk of their membership. Medieval bloodsuckers and a potential magic civil war, all while the world is slowly being transformed."

"You know a lot. Have you been talking to Craig Vermillion?"

"No, Anna. I've been spying on you."

"Oh. Then you know about the gift I got for you?"

"I do. And thank you, even if it does play into your agenda."

"Be careful with it," Anna said. "I'm not entirely convinced it isn't a trap."

"The same has occurred to me. I'll be cautious."

"Mr Asano, the days ahead are going to be dark and full of chaos. Probably worse than what we've seen, if Vermillion's estimate of the number of ancient vampires is even close to accurate. Is what you're doing going to stop it?"

"I can stop the transformation events and cut off the reality core supply. Eventually. It just got harder now that I have to change up my methodology to avoid being hunted down. People want what I have and it doesn't stop with the Americans. Being distracted by wider events isn't the same as giving up."

Anna nodded. "There was some concern that you would lash out in revenge."

"I'm not strong enough to go after the gold-ranker."

"I meant against the Network at large."

"Without the Network's tactical team having the courage to defy the gold-ranker, I would have lost even more people. I know that they were acting against the Americans rather than for me, but I'm grateful, nonetheless. I won't repay that with ill-placed vengeance."

"A lot of people will be glad to hear that."

"I won't deny I felt a powerful urge to start clearing out Network branches one by one," Jason confessed. "It was a closer thing than I'd like to admit, but there would be no coming back from that. Having power gives me a chance to do the things I need to, even when others say I shouldn't. Unfortunately, it also gives me the power to do things I want to, even when people are right that I shouldn't. It's a path to making costly mistakes."

"It was the Americans who did this, Mr Asano, not you."

"I could have done it differently. More carefully. I have to now, but I could have from the start and kept others out of it. Not considering the consequences of my actions to the people around me is a lesson I've failed to learn before, and this time, it wasn't just a close call. The people around me paid the price for my arrogance and short-sightedness. Perhaps this time I will finally learn."

"What will you do now?"

"I'll make use of your gift. Force the Americans to refocus their gold-rank assets on the transformation zones instead of me. Then I'll get back to the job that my brother, Asya and my friend died for."

"Good luck, Mr Asano."

"And to you, Mrs Tilden."

Jason's shadow rose up to engulf him and he was gone.

A contingent of people from two Japanese clans had arrived in Australia and settled in Asano Village. First were members of the Asano clan forced out by Noriko Asano as she wrested control of the clan from her son. There were only a handful of them—the former clan head, Shiro, and his closest family.

Shiro's daughters, Akari and Mei, had been travelling with Jason since his trip to Japan. Their father had sent them to Asano Village due to the clan turmoil and now had followed with the rest of their family. Jason met with Shiro, without anyone in the village being aware that he had returned.

"Thank you for seeing my daughters safe in the most trying of circumstances," Shiro said as they met in the house Shiro and his family had been assigned. It was a large home out in the bushland, surrounded by trees. "I know you lost people of your own."

"It was fortune, rather than any capability of mine," Jason said. "You should thank the Network tactical team that unravelled the trap."

"You are modest. My daughters have told me of how powerful that category four was and you fought him, face to face."

"Did they tell you I lost? It was an escape, not a victory."

"Escape in the face of that kind of power is a victory. Akari wants to keep helping you. She knows how important what you are doing is."

Jason shook his head.

"I've already made that mistake before. The way we will be operating now, Akari can't participate. It will just be Farrah and myself."

Shiro nodded.

"I am glad, to be honest. I know I should let my daughter make her own choices, but I would rather have her close and safe. Thank you for giving us sanctuary in hard times."

"I'm honestly not so sure how secure this sanctuary is," Jason said. "Farrah is working on activating some of the stronger defences as we speak, but forces are emerging that are stronger than any of us. I'm afraid of this village becoming a target."

"We will do our best to defend it, if it comes to that," Shiro said.

"I appreciate that," Jason said. "Having more silver-rankers here gives me some peace of mind."

The second contingent from Japan had arrived with the Asano clan, despite their recent conflict. The Tiwari clan's core leadership had tried to dig out those who had acted against Jason, only to find much of the clan turning against them. Playing on the unrest stirred up by Jason's interaction with the Tiwari leadership, the leadership of the Network's Kobe branch had taken advantage.

The Network supported a coup by a hidden faction of the Tiwari clan, in return for information about the magic door they had been guarding for centuries. Handing the door over to an outsider had been more contentious to the clan than the patriarch had realised and he found his entire family expelled. The two former patriarchs, Asano and Tiwari, realised they were in similar circumstances and both turned to Jason.

"They call fulfilling our ancient purpose a betrayal, even as they were selling out everything we are to the Network," the ousted patriarch explained to Jason. There were more exiled Tiwari than Asano clan members and they had been assigned to a cluster of houses in the village's beachfront area.

Koya Tiwari, Itsuki's father, also thanked Jason for bringing his son alive through such a dangerous trial.

"He is not happy that you are leaving him behind," Koya said. "I confess that I am."

While Jason had quietly met with the exiled patriarchs, Farrah had been activating additional defences around the village. These were protections that she had put in place from the beginning but never activated due to the cost. Afterwards, as she and Jason flew away from Asano Village in Shade's plane form, she discussed an issue with Jason that had come up during the activation.

"Is there a problem with the defences?" Jason asked, seeing Farrah's troubled expression.

"Just the opposite," Farrah said. "It worked too well. I was able to put the stronger defences in a semi-dormant state that consumes minimal resources, only becoming active and power-hungry as needed."

"That's great. Which makes me wonder why we didn't do it that way in the first place."

"Because we couldn't. The ambient magic was too low, even with the magic-collecting systems built into the village's infrastructure."

"You're saying that the ambient magic is rising?"

"We built those defences a year ago, and since then, we've had the monster waves and the transformation events. I think they are causing a more precipitous rise in the magical density than any of us realised, even Dawn."

Rainbow light burst into place in the middle of the plane, fading after an instant to reveal Dawn. Her new avatar projected a silver-rank aura.

"Miss Hurin is quite right," she said.

53
INEVITABILITY

As Jason and Farrah flew through the air in Shade's plane form, the sudden manifestation of Dawn's new silver-rank avatar took them aback. They shot out of their chairs.

"I have some questions," Jason said to Dawn. "They can wait until you get some clothes, though."

"I apologise for the impropriety," Dawn said. Jason turned around and pulled some of Farrah's spare clothes from his inventory, handing them backwards.

"No worries," Jason said. "I know what that's all about. Waking up naked in other universes is kind of my thing. Welcome back, by the way."

"I made some enquires while I was using my true body again," Dawn said as she quickly slipped on jeans and a t-shirt. "I have something for you, next time you return to Australia."

"We've just come from there," Jason said. "We probably won't be back for a little while."

"It isn't urgent," Dawn said. "It's personal, rather than a part of our task."

"You told us you couldn't create an avatar above normal rank," Farrah said to Dawn. "I take it this new one being silver has an unfortunate connection to the rise in Earth's magical density."

"Yes," Dawn said. "Each proto-space that becomes a monster wave pushes more energy from the astral through the dimensional membrane of this world, degrading the membrane as it does. The inactivity of the grid only saw an increase in monster waves by a third, given how many go unnoticed in the depths of the oceans, but that increased activity appears to have crossed a threshold, accelerating the degradation."

"Which is triggering the transformation events," Jason said.

"Yes," Dawn confirmed. "They are an unintended consequence of the original Builder's designs for this universe being affected by the rising magical density and the influx of magic through the link to the other world. It also means that I can project a more powerful avatar into your world without causing further damage."

"Does the damage already done mean that the transformation events will continue, even after we normalise the link?" Jason asked.

"It's possible," Dawn said, "but unlikely. The most probable case is that the transformation events will end once any one of the three factors is removed. Since the intrinsic makeup of your reality and the magical density can't be undone, that leaves restoring the link to its original state, or as close as we can manage. Without surges of magic coming from your world, Miss Hurin, it should stop triggering the events."

"Does this accelerate the timeline for the destruction of Jason's world?" Farrah asked.

"Yes," Dawn said. "It will still be decades before the planet becomes uninhabitable, but even if the link is repaired on the most optimistic schedule, Earth's dimensional landscape will forever be altered. Dimensional instability. There is little chance of completing the work before Earth's magical density crosses the iron-rank threshold."

"Does that mean what I think it does?" Jason asked. "Direct magical manifestation?"

"Yes," Dawn confirmed. "No more proto-spaces. Monsters, as well as essences and awakening stones, will start directly manifesting. Once that happens, repairing the link on this end will be critical to prevent even more accelerated degradation of the dimensional membrane. Additionally, once the changes to the link on this end are completed, you will have slowed things down enough that you will have years in the other world to fix the link on that side."

"Won't directly manifesting monsters be good from a safety perspective?" Farrah asked. "Instead of silver and gold-rank proto-spaces, they'll be dealing with iron-rank monsters, maybe the occasional bronze."

"I mentioned dimensional instability," Dawn said. "By that stage, the dimensional membrane of this world will be poked full of holes. There will be isolated zones of bronze, silver and possibly even gold-ranked magical density that remain permanently in place."

"Like my world," Farrah said.

"It will lean more towards the lower ranks overall than yours, but yes," Dawn said.

"My world can't handle that," Jason said.

"Yet it must," Dawn said. "What I am describing is, at this point, an inevitability."

"If gold-rank monsters just start showing up," Jason said, "we don't have the people to deal with them. They'll render whole sections of the world uninhabitable."

"Yes," Dawn said.

Jason let out a groan as he slumped back into one of the plane's luxurious black chairs.

"This is getting further and further out of hand. I was meant to save the world, but it just keeps getting worse, and all I've accomplished is leading people I care about to their deaths."

Dawn frowned. "Where are we going?"

"The USA," Farrah said. "The Network is currently splitting down the middle over its role in everything that's going on. New alliances are being formed across old branch and geographical boundaries. The rank and file versus leadership are the new fault lines. Someone we worked with in Australia got her hands on the location of the US Network's reality core secure storage and gave it to us. That's every reality core from every US branch, aside from the ones being experimented on or used to wake up however many gold-rankers they have."

"We're going to steal them," Jason said. "The hope is that will force the Americans to go all out collecting more."

"Meaning using their gold-rankers to fight for cores in transformation zones to replenish their stocks," Farrah clarified. "Which would give them less time to get in our way."

"We know the information is unreliable," Jason said. "The information made it to Australia, so there's a good chance it was planted as a trap or the leak was discovered and the cores have already been relocated. Even so, we think it's worth the risk for the pressure it would put on the Americans and take off us."

"Do you?" Dawn asked. "You admitted yourself that the information is questionable at best. It also distracts you from your purpose. You need to examine your own motives, both of you. Is this truly the best option or is it simply the revenge you have the strength to take since you can't go after a gold-rank enemy?"

Jason looked like he'd been slapped and was about to shoot back invective before stopping himself.

"Bloody hell," he muttered unhappily.

"No, the objective is worthwhile," Farrah insisted.

"Yeah," Jason said, "but is it a plausible outcome? Honestly? Dawn's right that we aren't thinking straight. There are too many variables."

"I can crack any magic protection the ritualists of this world can throw out," Farrah said.

"But can you do it while dodging all the non-magic protection?" Jason asked. "Drones, motion sensors, biometric locks. What if it's an underground bunker with one way in and forty silver-rankers around it? What if we carve our way through all of that—which we can't—and the cores are already gone? The American silver-rankers may not be Adventure Society elite standard, but they're a lot better than anyone else we've seen here."

"We can scout it out. Formulate a plan."

"And how long do you spend on this operation?" Dawn asked. "Time is more critical than ever."

"I just..."

Farrah clenched her fists in front of her.

"...I just really want to kill someone for what they did."

"I know."

"Do you?" Farrah asked testily, rousing an angry expression from Jason.

"Yes, Farrah, I do. It was my brother. My girlfriend. My childhood friend. You think every fibre of my being isn't baying for blood? My family are still living inside my soul and they're scared because the sky is red and every single thing in there is razor-sharp."

Jason's aura came pouring out in an angry wave, crashing over Farrah before he forcibly reined it in.

"I'm sorry," Farrah said faintly. "I shouldn't have said that."

Jason nodded.

"We're both on edge. I say some stupid things at the best of times."

"You should redirect your destination," Dawn said. "Start looking for the next node."

"No need," Jason said wearily. "We're already on course. The next place we need to look is in a sandwich."

"What?" Dawn asked.

"You're an idiot," Dawn said.

She, Jason and Farrah emerged from a shop called The Brown Jug in Sandwich, Massachusetts, with a large bag of sandwiches.

"These sandwiches look pretty nice," Jason said.

"They do look quite good," Farrah agreed.

"And how often do you get to eat a sandwich in Sandwich?" Jason asked. "Pretty often, if you live in Sandwich, obviously. The concept itself is like a sandwich. A conceptual sandwich."

"Please stop saying sandwich," Dawn said.

"You have a lot of power, Dawn," Farrah said, "but I don't think you could stop him if your real body was here."

In the time it had taken them to reach Cape Cod, the Network had already set up operations and breached the aperture that Jason and Farrah were targeting. For this reason, they had decided to wait for them to wind down after killing the anchor monster.

With how thin the Network was stretched at the current time, they would not be as thorough about sweeping proto-spaces for loot and Jason was going to wait for them to go in and out before making his own intrusion. Even if there was little time left, Jason's ability would extend the stability of the space.

That left the trio meandering down the streets of Sandwich, eating what Dawn was forced to acknowledge was a pretty good sandwich. Food rationing wasn't easing up everywhere, but the United States was doing better than most places, which Jason and his companions took advantage of.

Wandering by the town pond, Jason found an unobserved spot to let his family out of the spirit vault where they had spent weeks in isolation with very few reprieves. He hadn't even risked letting them out for Kaito's funeral service and their time in his spirit vault had grown less pleasant in the time since Kaito's death. Jason might be able to hide it on the outside, but his rage and shame were made manifest for the people living inside his soul to see. A summer outing in Cape Cod was a blessed relief.

"How many awful sandwich jokes has Jason made?" Erika asked as Jason handed out food from the bag.

"All of them, as far as I can tell," Farrah complained.

"I'm eating a sandwich in Sandwich," Jason said. "How can I not make a meal out of that?"

"I stand corrected," Farrah complained.

Erika watched her brother—his eyes that weren't really laughing and the smiles that didn't turn the corners of his mouth quite the way they should. She had seen him at his lowest and knew that for all he had changed, for all his power, there were still dark holes into which he could descend. She wasn't sure if the façade he was putting up was healthy but at least he was trying. She remembered the times when he hadn't been.

As they had an impromptu picnic on the grass, Erika pointed a nervous Emi towards her uncle, standing alone as he stared out over the water.

"You need to tell him," Erika said.

"Can't you do it?"

"No," Erika told her daughter. "You have to take responsibility for your own choices."

Emi made a hesitant path to Jason, slipping her hand into his. He smiled sadly as he continued to stare out at nothing.

"Uncle Jason?"

"Yes, Moppet."

"I... don't think I want to fight like you do. I don't want to be an adventurer."

Jason turned to his niece, looking back with fearful eyes. Jason crouched down, gave her his first unabashedly happy grin in a long time and swept her up in a hug.

"After Uncle Kai," she explained as Jason continued to hold her tight, "I don't think I want to kill things."

"Good," he said.

"You're not disappointed?"

"Not even a little bit," he said. "You have to do what you want to do, Moppet. Not what you think I want you to do."

"But you spent so much time training me. You even took me out of school."

Jason let go of the hug and held her by the shoulders, locking eyes with her to convey his sincerity.

"You think that was a waste? You got lots of exercise, learned self-discipline and magic. What's wrong with that?"

"Does this mean I have to stop learning magic?"

"Don't be silly," Jason said, tousling her hair. "The other world has a whole Magic Society, you know that. Farrah's already a member. They'll be ecstatic to get a brilliant young lady like you on the books."

"I can still go to the other world?"

"I need you where I can keep you safe, Moppet. I have friends I can trust there."

Jason felt lighter as he let his niece walk him back to the group. He knew there was a lot of himself in her. He was happy that she wouldn't insist on following his path and paying the price it cost to walk it. Even so, he would see her trained properly. He likely had a little Clive on his hands and she would inevitably want to explore a world full of mystery and magic. He would make sure she was ready.

Jason's family were only out a short time, for the sake of caution, before returning to the spirit vault. Farrah went with them, so she could be carried into the proto-space with Jason. When he entered a proto-space alone, he didn't even need an aperture. They had only used apertures in the past to let in the rest of the team, but Jason was not going to do that again.

He hadn't directly entered proto-spaces in the past because he needed space and uninterrupted time to conduct the rituals that would help him find the next node. This had been the main role of the team and their absence would make things harder, especially without Greg and his excellent zoning abilities. Now, half the team was dead and Jason would no longer risk anyone else. That left no reason to use apertures and deal with the Network.

Shade had been keeping an eye on the Network's operation, notifying Jason as it wound down and they withdrew. They even sealed the aperture back up to avoid mishaps, leaving only a pair of guards behind at the aperture site.

Jason took that as his opportunity to enter, picking a spot well away from any essence users he could sense, as he couldn't hide his aura while transitioning through the dimensional boundary.

Jason let his aura blend into the ambient magic until he felt almost indistinguishable from the world around him. As he reached what felt like a oneness with the universe, his body blurred and vanished and he slipped through the membrane of reality. He let Farrah out of the spirit vault immediately upon arriving in the otherworldly space. It was a primordial realm of rocky terrain, turgid water, stunted plants, and hot, heavy air.

"That was weird from the inside," she told him. "It was like your whole soul garden suddenly expanded off into the horizon for a moment. There was this strange sense of being connected to the whole of reality. Is that what it's like for you?"

"I'd more describe it as tingly," Jason said.

"Tingly?"

"Yep."

"You have the soul of a poet."

"Didn't you just say I had the soul of a connectedness to all things?"

"Just shut up and get on with saving the world."

Jason and Farrah had been forced to devise new approaches to making sure the ritual was not interfered with by wandering monsters. They came up with a trio of solutions, the use of each predicated on the strength of the proto-space. The first option was for low-ranking proto-spaces where the monsters were weak. In such cases, Jason would just blast out his aura at full strength and range, which would scare off any low-ranked monsters. Farrah would mop up the monsters that still approached.

The next approach was for more powerful proto-spaces where the monsters could pose a potential threat. In this case, Jason would still project his aura, but modulated to seem weak and vulnerable. Then he would open up a can of afflictions on the would-be predators and let butterflies of doom deal with them, clearing out a large enough space for Jason to work.

The final approach was for the strongest, gold-rank proto-spaces, should they run into one. If possible, they would avoid these spaces altogether. Alternate avenues were worth more than the risk of being eaten.

Whatever the approach, Farrah's role was playing clean-up and intercepting any monsters that still wandered by. It wasn't as reliable as having a team patrol the zone, but even if there were some interruptions, they were confident they could make it work. In this particular instance, they were lucky in that the Network had abandoned it and the monsters were low-ranked. It was only the first of many times they would go through the process, but this time, at least, it went off without a hitch.

54

THE EDGE OF MADNESS

Jason, Farrah and Dawn travelled from place to place, in search of nodes to repair. They used the grid interface in the cloud house to choose their next destinations, refining their accuracy as they learned more from each proto-space and node they explored. After the USA was Canada, Tanzania, Myanmar and more.

They lived an isolated life, with Jason's family. Other people meant nothing but danger. Seeking help from others exposed vulnerabilities, while those who were genuinely willing to help would themselves be in danger by association.

Their methodology would use the cloud house's grid interface to detect a suitable target area, then travel there and set up the cloud house as a home base. This allowed Jason's family to safely live outside of Jason's spirit vault, which was slowly becoming less inhospitable but was still far from welcoming.

Once they arrived in a region, Jason and Farrah would wait for proto-spaces to form, in order to go in and identify the right node. They became increasingly proficient at the sequence of entering a space, performing the ritual and getting out before the Network was any the wiser. When possible, they covered any trace of the rituals, hoping to keep the Network unaware of their patterns.

The current lifestyle of Jason and the others afforded a lot of downtime as they travelled or waited on proto-spaces to manifest. Jason and Farrah took the time to maintain a regimented training schedule, which was not always possible when things were busy. Farrah had constructed a new set of exercise equipment for their heightened attributes; any non-magical weights heavy enough to be valuable were too heavy to be practical.

Other time was spent on magical theory. Dawn continued to teach Jason while Emi learned from Farrah. After deciding not to follow her uncle, Emi had been reinvigorated, going as far as choosing a magical specialty. Farrah advised against making the choice too quickly, wanting her to see the breadth of options the other world had to offer.

"Fortunately, thirteen-year-olds are famous for taking good advice when presented with it," an exasperated Farrah told Jason while they were doing their physical training, which made him laugh.

"What is it that she wants to learn?" he asked.

"It's a very niche field related to mine," Farrah explained. "I'm a specialist in formation magic and arrays. Permanent and semi-permanent versions of ritual magic, which is one of the core magical fields. It's less specialised than, say, astral magic, which is why I have a broader knowledge base than you're developing, and can tap into a lot of areas."

"Okay."

"What Emi is looking at is a specialised version of my field called formation interactivity. You understand that putting magical formations close together is tricky because they interfere with each other, right?"

"Yeah."

"Formation interactivity is the study of the effects of having formations close to one another. At a basic level, it's about reducing the effects so that formations can be used in closer proximity. Advanced applications involve generating positive interactions, but that is not a developed area of study. It's also notorious for being one of the most impenetrable branches of magic, which is why it's underdeveloped."

"And my niece has got it into her head to be a groundbreaker," Jason said.

"She's implausibly smart, I'll admit," Farrah said. "Even so, that field is a career. If that's the way she wants to go, she wouldn't have time to be an adventurer. That's locking-yourself-in-a-room-and-never-coming-out research."

"I assume your intention is to keep working on her foundational skills until you get her into a Magic Society branch and broaden her horizons?"

"That's exactly my intention. My concern is that she's as stubborn and unpredictable as you and your sister."

"I'm sure it'll be fine," Jason said.

While the cloud house life was largely isolated from the world, the internet was a window into what they were missing. There was always at least one online news feed running somewhere, and as weeks passed, they became increasingly happy to be missing it all. As they hid away, quietly completing their tasks, the world was ever more precipitously teetering on the edge of madness.

"Is that a centaur?" Jason asked, glancing at a wall monitor after emerging from the showers post-workout.

"No," Farrah said, likewise emerging. "It's a lot of centaurs."

"I know Salzburg has an old-world charm," Jason said, "but there weren't centaurs around when we were in Austria, right?"

"There were," Dawn said. "Like other members of the Cabal, they have become experts at hiding their presence over the centuries."

"They'd have to," Jason said. "You can't hide being half-horse with a pair of extra-loose slacks. My friend Craig once told me that all Cabal members can pass as human, shape-change into humans or otherwise have the means to remain hidden from the world. Usually a combination of illusion powers and isolation. Hillfolk, haunted houses, mysterious things in the woods and so on."

"That's an incomplete but sufficient description," Dawn said.

"Where do creatures like that come from?" Farrah asked. "The Cabal has always struck me as odd. How does a low-magic world have such overtly magical creatures? It hasn't even developed non-human essence-using species."

"Like so many of this world's issues," Dawn said, "it stems from the same original sin."

"Original sin?" Jason asked. "Are you going native on me, Dawn?"

"The connotations of the term are usefully descriptive," Dawn said. "It goes back to the way the original Builder constructed the seed of this universe using the patterns of existing worlds. There is a reason the other great astral beings intervened. This world is now ravaged by the ramifications of that choice, while yours, Miss Hurin, is also being affected. Soon, it will also experience the consequences of the Builder's experiment in full force."

"Which we're going to unleash," Farrah said unhappily.

"You have to cut someone to perform surgery," Jason said. "If there's a better option, you take it, but sometimes there just isn't."

"Just so," Dawn agreed.

"So the Cabal members are echoes of the worlds the original Builder based this on," Jason said.

"Yes," Dawn confirmed. "Even before the magic level started to rise, beings arose from the incongruities of the unconventional means by which your universe was established. It was rare, but over hundreds, thousands, millions of years, they slowly emerged. And like other living things, they evolved. From simple magical entities to complex beings, they adapted to their environments over countless generations while still being shaped by their origins. Because they were rare, even with the power they possessed, those that adapted to remain hidden are the ones that survived."

"So they really are connected to the transformation spaces," Farrah said.

"After a fact, yes," Dawn said. "All magical things will grow stronger over time as the ambient magic rises. Part of the reason that Earth's essence users are mediocre is that they spend most of their time suffering low-level magical starvation. These transformation zones seem to affect Cabal members even more than the rising ambient magic."

"Which is why they're winning out in the competition for reality cores," Jason said. "The transformation zones they're fighting in make them stronger."

"If the Cabal is looking to revive a bunch of ancient vampires, isn't that bad?" Farrah asked.

"I'm pretty sure it is, yeah," Jason said. "There's nothing we can do about it, though, except to keep doing what we're doing. We're two people, not an army that can run around competing for cores all over the world."

"Exactly," Dawn said. "It is wise to focus on what you can do and not concern yourself with what you cannot."

The first node Jason successfully identified and repaired, right before fighting the gold-ranker, turned out to be one of the ones they needed to find. The process wasn't always reliable. The nodes in the USA and Myanmar were false positives that didn't need repairing. The only gains were that with each failed node, they would be better at eliminating further false positives as they refined the process. The nodes in Canada and Tanzania had been modified, and Jason managed to rectify both.

As they worked, the descent into chaos that began with monster waves and transformation events escalated. In just a few weeks, things had grown increasingly worse as sections of major cities started to be caught up in transformation zones.

The Bankstown area of Sydney was turned into a city of low-level volcanic activity and stone buildings. The people there were primarily turned into members of the smoulder race, with onyx skin and glowing, fiery eyes. The area affected included Bankstown Airport, which was the Sydney Network branch's major transport and logistics hub. Not only did the Network's non-essence user staff get transformed, but their planes were turned into bird-like magical constructs. This rendered them inoperable without an essence user with the ability to use specialised magical tools, an ability that rarely appeared on Earth.

Earth had taken a magitech route, combining technology with magic. In terms of accessibility, convenience and cost, this was objectively better than relying on purely magical devices. Magitech communication was much more practical and vehicles didn't require someone like Clive with a special power to operate.

Pallimustus also had vehicles that could be driven by anyone but only operable in zones of high magical density. Only something like the vortex accumulator in Jason's cloud constructs could circumvent this problem, but it was a level of magic engineering undeveloped on Earth. Magitech was much more suited to Earth's conditions and advanced in different directions.

Bankstown Airport was now covered in stone buildings, with lava pooling in random areas and a bunch of giant metal birds that couldn't move. This greatly impaired the Sydney Network branch, especially as they joined a growing movement actively working against the Network's global leadership.

Three factions quickly emerged: The Chinese branches and those who allied with them, forcibly or not; the USA, who did not accept allies; and most of what was left. This third faction was the largest, but also the most scattered and least stable. The people attached to the International Committee split rather evenly between the three factions.

The first two factions were focused heavily on claiming reality cores and, accordingly, became open rivals. The third faction took the name the Network had publicly been using, the Global Defense Network, and continued to intercept proto-spaces. What they did do was take the American spelling of defense with an 's' and change it to the international defence, with a 'c.' Most government bodies continued to work with this faction, providing much-needed legitimacy and support.

Sometimes the transformation events were relatively peaceful, although this was rare. Coconut Grove in Miami, Florida, was transformed into an elven utopia, with beautiful architecture interwoven with rich, sprawling gardens. The residents were transformed into beautiful elves, which, while still traumatic, could have been far worse.

More common were cases like West Canfield, Detroit. The people were turned into goblins and their homes into underground warrens, which rapidly devolved into a lawless combat zone into which the National Guard was sent to restore order. After the first hideous former humans were gunned down, things devolved quickly.

Transformation zones fluctuated in area, from one or two kilometres across to engulfing entire large towns. Less-developed areas, like farms and countryside, tended to have larger areas affected, while events in cities were more contained. Despite the smaller scale, though, once major cities were impacted, it was as if an invisible line between stability and chaos had been crossed.

Conflict between the magical factions became more heated and harder to hide from the population at large. As open battle spilled out of the transformation zones, the people of the world realised that a war was being fought and that their only options were to be innocent bystander or collateral damage. EOA superheroes fought the essence users of the Network, who themselves were caught up in infighting.

Driving the escalation was the knowledge that with each passing day, the mythological beings of the Cabal were growing in power as they operated more and more in the open. Centaurs, ogres, fairies, and more variously delighted and horrified when they were spotted by the media and revealed to the world.

The Cabal would have been dominating already, except that, like the Network, current events had revealed old fault lines in their organisation. Factional infighting abounded as conflicts older than any living civilisation were taken up once more.

Government forces stepped in as best they were able as cities rapidly turned into battlegrounds. Government-Network alliances were strained or broken, which was often the best-case scenario. In China and the US, Network deep state actors rapidly seized control.

The Global Defence Network faction did their best to hold everything together. The other Network factions were focused on their conflicts with each other, the EOA and the Cabal as they fought over reality cores, allowing the GDN to claim the grid infrastructure and continue to intercept proto-spaces. Rapidly forming new agreements with world governments, they avoided the reality core war. The biggest problem was that many of their silver-rank personnel had been pulled into other factions, making higher-rank dimensional incursions difficult and dangerous to handle.

Emergency powers were enacted and martial law was put into place. The cities, which had been largely shielded from the monster waves, were now battlegrounds. People were fleeing into rural areas to escape the fighting. Jason, meanwhile, continued his work as weeks turned into months. At the same time he arrived in his latest location, Venezuela, the ancient vampires the non-Cabal factions had been worrying about made their presence known in the city of Venice.

55
TRYING TO BE MERCIFUL

In Venezuela, Jason identified and repaired another node. He was starting to get used to the process and had gotten the time required down to under an hour. After leaving the node space, he opened a portal back to the cloud house, currently disguised as a complex of hastily erected prefab buildings in the mountain town of Galipan.

Close to Caracas, Galipan had long been a tourist staple but was rapidly turning into a refuge for mid-level government and military officials from Caracas and La Guaira. After a transformation event triggered open battle between the magical factions, many low-to-mid-level authority figures had immediately looked to escape.

Galipan had been overlooked by the upper-level officials, allowing the middling people to move in and force the locals out, claiming the inns and residences for themselves. The new prefab buildings were assembled for their support staff, not the displaced locals.

Jason's family had been laying low in the cloud house as Jason and Farrah once more went through a series of proto-spaces to pinpoint the right node. Dawn remained with the cloud house to intercept any danger, now that she possessed a silver-rank avatar.

No one left the cloud house other than Jason and Farrah. A bunch of foreigners would not be out of place back when it was a tourist village, but now they would stick out like a sore thumb. They were all caught up watching the news from around the world as order deteriorated.

Cities fell under martial law or became outright battle zones with soldiers fighting essence users fighting superheroes fighting all manner of strange creatures. Channel after channel, news site after news site showed the world descending into disaster and unrest.

"…the 'puppet presidency' riots continue in many major US cities, with the new administration's attempts to mobilise the National Guard in response meeting resistance from some state governors…"

"…spokesperson stated that there was no internal strife in the CCP after the recent leadership changes, but with China's media blackout continuing, there is no way to know the true state of…"

"…infighting within the Global Defence Network has been blamed for the new monster surge in the small island nation…"

The family all sat together in the lounge room, watching as the world fell apart.

"It's like watching the end of the world," Erika's husband Ian said as Jason, Farrah and Dawn returned to the cloud house.

"That's what we're trying to avoid," Jason said.

His family turned to look at the returning trio.

"How did it go?" Jason's father Ken asked.

"Another one down," Jason said. "Time to pack up and move on."

"Not quite," Dawn said. "There is still one more thing to deal with."

"What's that?" Jason asked, then tilted his head as if trying to hear something in the distance.

"Oh," he said as something entered the range of his aura senses, moving fast. "I'll take care of it."

"What is it?" Farrah asked.

"Some EOA lackeys," Jason said. "We've had a good run, but someone was bound to find us eventually, and the EOA is working with the government here."

"Why would the EOA go after you?" Farrah asked. "I thought North wanted you to do what you're doing."

"So he said," Jason told her. "Could be he was lying. Could be that he wants to test my ability to affect Builder magic after absorbing the door. Most likely is that he just hasn't told his organisation anything about it."

"What if his organisation ends up stopping you?" Farrah asked.

"Then Jason was never strong enough to get the job done anyway," Dawn said, then turned to Jason. "Deal with them and then we can depart."

A full twenty superheroes in matching pseudo-military outfits flew through the air, soaring up the mountain. As they closed in on the town of Galipan, they slowed down and released a camera drone, in accordance with League of Heroes media protocols. They made their approach to the town low and slow, making sure the people there had the chance to notice them and to pull out their phones. The flying superhumans paused, hovering over the town and the new expanse of prefab constructions.

"Which one is it?" one of them asked their leader. "Should we start searching them?"

"No need," the leader said, nodding at a figure rising up from amongst the buildings.

He flew slowly towards them, a cloak spread out behind like void-black wings. Under the cloak was a robe the colour of dark, dried blood. From within the cloak's hood was a pair of silver eyes that shone like starlight, while two large blue and orange orb-eyes floated around him.

"Jason Asano," the leader announced loudly, making sure his voice would be picked up on phone cameras. He spoke in English, which told Jason that this was all for the publicity.

"I am Autoridad," the leader announced. "We are taking you and your associates into custody."

Hovering in the air, the heroes spread out in a semi-circle around Jason. Jason's wing cloak held him up and he looked almost like he was underwater as his cloak floated around him. The heroes had more sober and sensible outfits than their US counterparts, with their costumes bearing a militaristic and authoritarian style. The Venezuelan flag was prominently on display. Venezuela had ousted the Network in favour of the EOA and their superheroes, an arrangement that was holding even through the current chaos.

"How much do you know about the process that gave you your extraordinary abilities?" Jason asked. "Did you know that the earlier, weaker versions of the process had a habit of turning people insane? The reason your generation doesn't meet that end is that there is something inside you called a clockwork cor—"

"We aren't here to listen to you, Asano," Autoridad cut him off. "Surrender or don't."

"I'm trying to explain why coming after me is a bad idea," Jason said. "I'm trying to be merciful. I don't know what will happen when—"

Jason was cut off again as eyebeams blasted from Autoridad in his direction. One of the orbs around Jason became a shield of force, rippling like water as it intercepted the blast.

"Look, banana republic General Zod," Jason said. "This is your chance to walk away. Fly away, whatever. Please take it."

"You essence magicians all think yourselves so powerful. You mentioned the weaker versions of us that came before. You know that they can boost their strength, yes? You may be arrogant enough to think that you're stronger than all of us, but we now have a boost strong enough to work on us. Using the power of reality cores, we can become far more powerful than you."

"Why are you the only one who gets to monologue? I thought I was the villain here, superhero."

Autoridad reached for an injector pen in a sheath on his belt.

"Don't do it," Jason warned.

Autoridad ignored Jason and grabbed the injector pen. Then he dropped it as he and his fellow superheroes simultaneously started having seizures and fell from the sky. They landed hard on the street below as the people filming with their phones scattered out of the way. Jason floated down into the midst of the fallen heroes who continued to twitch on the ground.

Jason's cloak vanished as he alighted upon the ground, revealing an unconcerned face as he panned his gaze over the heroes. Silver liquid seeped out of their tear ducts as their twitching seizures came to a stop, along with their lives.

"So that's what happens," Jason muttered absently. Leveraging his soul attack was apparently quite effective against clockwork cores. Absorbing the door had enhanced his ability to affect the Builder's magic, although how it would fare against star seeds he didn't know. He was looking forward to finding out.

The town was silent, people moving out of his way as he ignored them, walking over to one of the buildings. His family stepped out of it and he absorbed the building into his cloud flask.

Once more flying over the ocean in Shade's plane form, Jason, Farrah, and Dawn were in a small conference cabin, discussing their next destination.

"After refining the search parameters with the details from the last node," Farrah said, "we've got two viable target regions to search for the next. One is in Australia, the other in Europe."

"I'd like to go home," Jason said. "I know the village has been kept out of everything we've seen on the news, but I'd still like to check on it. There's also whatever mysterious thing Dawn arranged for us while she was between avatars."

"The question is Europe," Farrah said. "Venice had been entirely taken over by vampires. Are they looking to establish a safe haven for themselves and that's the end of it, or is this just the beginning? Should we go now, before things get worse, or give it time and wait for things to settle?"

Jason absently tapped a finger to his lips as he considered.

"Craig Vermillion suggested there's a lot more of these old vampires than we've seen," he said. "Especially in Europe. I think I'd prefer to know what we're walking into, even if it's bad, rather than be caught up in some kind of vampiric uprising."

"If we were," Farrah said, "maybe we could make a difference."

"We are making a difference," Jason said. "The sooner we cut off the reality core supply, the sooner the vampires go back in their box."

"Those cores aren't like spirit coins," Dawn said. "It will take time before they are consumed. Once the Cabal rouses their vampires, it will be some time before they return to slumber."

"All the more reason to get this done," Jason said.

"We have had distraction enough," Dawn agreed. "We are trying to help this entire world, not just some of the people on it."

"Australia it is, then," Farrah said. "Maybe it's time to explain what you arranged for us. You said it was personal."

"I'll explain after Mr Asano's sister is done with him," Dawn said. "You and I should give them some privacy."

There was an angry hammering on the cabin door and they could all sense Erika's aura on the other side of it. Dawn and Farrah left the cabin, letting Erika in. Erika marched in and tossed a computer tablet on the table, paused on a video.

Jason didn't ask, instead reaching out to unpause the video.

"…disturbing footage and viewer discretion is advised. It would appear that the world's first superhero has gone full villain, killing an entire team of Venezuela's superheroes. The Venezuelan government have released a statement saying that this will impact their ability to prevent monster waves…"

Jason paused the video again and met his sister's glare with a blank expression.

"What is it, Erika?" he asked softly.

"You're just killing people on the news now?"

"Yes."

"What is my daughter meant to make of that, Jason? You know how much she looks up to you. She was scared of telling you that she didn't want to go fight monsters with you and now she sees you slaughtering people on television?"

"Did they have the audio of that footage? They weren't just coming for me, Erika. They were coming for all of us. I won't let that happen. Not again."

"And what? You'll kill whoever it takes to make that happen?"

"Yes."

Erika had been turned from angry to unsettled at the quiet determination with which Jason answered her questions.

"You were worried about the things you've done changing you," she said.

"Yes."

"You were right to be."

With a worried look at her brother, Erika left the cabin.

"I know," Jason whispered to the empty room.

Craig Vermillion drove a small powerboat over Sydney Harbour, approaching a larger vessel and pulling up alongside. He tied off his own boat and hopped lightly from one to the other.

The larger boat was a modified fishing boat, to which a powerful chain winch had been affixed for dragging heavy objects up from the depths. Craig made his way past the crew, human minions of the Cabal, and into the captain's cabin.

"Craig," the man inside greeted, getting up to shake Vermillion's hand.

"Franklin."

Craig looked at a large crystal bottle on the table, held securely in a foam-lined box. Inside the bottle was a purplish liquid.

"Is that it?" Craig asked.

"It is," Franklin said.

"Literal blue blood."

"I don't know how they make it," Franklin said. "I got a glimpse of one of their magic rocks. I'd rather be well out of all this, to be frank. Which I am."

"Still with that joke, Frank? You've been telling it for, what? Forty, fifty years? Has anyone ever laughed?"

"It's not really the time for laughter, is it?"

"Not an excuse, Frank," Craig said, then his shoulders slumped. "You know, you don't have to go back to the Cabal. If you don't want to be part of this, you don't have to be."

"I'm not one for rebellion, Craig."

"It doesn't have to be rebellion. You can just lie low somewhere and wait for it to all blow over."

"Do you really think that's going to happen?"

"The reality cores will only last so long," Craig said, gesturing at the bottle of modified blood. "Once they can't make any more of this, the old ones will go back to sleep."

"Assuming that your boy Asano somehow manages to undo all this mess."

"He will."

"He's one man. He's powerful, but compared to the old ones? We already know he lost to his own group's essence magician. This is the way things are now, Craig. We need to compete."

"It doesn't have to be an arms race."

"Yeah, Craig. It does."

Vermillion sighed.

"I'm going," he said. "If I can't stop it, at least I won't be a party to it."

"You may come to regret that, Craig."

"When you're as old as us, Frank, regret is an inevitability."

"Ain't that the truth."

Franklin withdrew a memory stick and held it out for Craig.

"A list of safe houses and supply caches I don't think are on the books," he explained. "No guarantees, though, so keep your eyes sharp. Security codes and protocols are all in there."

"They won't be happy if they know you gave me this."

"Then don't tell them."

Craig took the stick with a laugh and shook his friend's hand again.

"Good luck, Frank."

"You too."

"Are you sure you won't come with me?"

"Get going, Craig. You want to be long gone when we wake this guy up."

Craig went back to his boat and took off. He took the battery out of his phone and threw them both into the harbour. Behind him, the huge chain winch on the boat stirred into rumbling, diesel-powered action. Craig and his boat were nowhere to be seen by the time it hoisted what looked like a stone sarcophagus from the water.

56
APPRECIATION

IN ASANO VILLAGE, A PORTAL ARCH QUIETLY ROSE UP INSIDE A HOUSE. Cheryl Asano, Jason's mother, froze as if time had stopped. She had seen little of her youngest son since his return from apparent death, except on the news. She hadn't seen him at all since her eldest son followed him out into an increasingly mad world, only to return as a corpse. She had only seen his famous portal a handful of times in person. Like most people in Australia, she had seen it on the news as thousands of Broken Hill residents escaped through it to safety. She had watched everything she could find online about her son over and over again.

She gulped as her son stepped through the portal, his expression slightly surprised to find his mother standing right in front of him.

"Hello, Mother."

"Jason, I…" She trailed off, not knowing how to begin.

"Hold that thought," he said as Erika and Emi emerged from the portal. Neither had seen her since Kaito's death and, unlike Jason, immediately moved to hug her.

"I'm going to quietly go round people up," Jason said. "Mother, we're using your place as a gathering point because it's more discreet. I don't know how many people are the eyes and ears of outsiders."

"Jason…" she began, but his shadow rose up. He stepped into it and was gone.

Jason found Taika in the village's main security office and happily grabbed the big man in a huge hug.

"I'm sorry about your bro, bro."

"Thanks, mate."

Jason had originally intended to take Taika as part of the team travelling with him, only to change his mind. He had not wanted to entirely deprive the village of people he could trust and rely on. Given that Taika would likely be dead otherwise, he was relieved at how it worked out.

"Bro, I saw you killing those superhero guys with your mind. They say you're a proper supervillain now, but if the other guys are all dressed like tin-pot dictators, and flying around like M. Bison, that makes you the good guy, as far as I'm concerned."

"You don't think I'm bad for killing all those people?"

"They came for you and yours, bro. Put 'em down hard and don't look back."

Jason knew that for all his jovial personality, Taika had already seen dark days before Jason came along, having left New Zealand as a teenager to escape dangerous circumstances. Taika had become familiar with the cruelty and fickleness of death long before Jason.

"Taika, I need you to round up some people in the village and take them to my mother's place."

"What do I tell them when they ask why?"

"That it's mandatory and you don't know. Don't mention me at all. Some of them will probably react poorly."

"No worries, mate," Taika assured him. "I got you."

Jason was very good at hiding any kind of nervousness or uncertainty, both in his body language and his aura. He was visibly anxious as he sensed a group of people approach his mother's front door.

They were the last to arrive by design; Jason had asked Taika to bring them last. There was no shortage of people present already, crowding even the generous, open-plan space of his mother's house. Already arrived were Amy and her daughters, too young to understand what was going on. The

Japanese Asano sisters and Itsuki were both present, as were the family of Jason's deceased friend Greg. They had known Jason since he was a young teenager but now looked at him like a stranger. Between who and what Jason had become and the death of their son, Jason could feel the distrust and hostility in their auras plain and clear.

Jason was anticipating worse from the people Taika was leading to the door. The Karadeniz family, Asya's parents and siblings, were taken aback when they saw all the people. When they spotted Jason amongst them, their expressions went dark.

"Mr and Mrs Karadeniz—"

The long legs of Asya's mother let her stride across the room in just a few steps, where she loudly slapped Jason across the face. Jason had nothing to say, bowing his head the way he had before Greg's family. He felt that his eyes should be welling with tears, but that was not something his body did anymore. It had been years since Jason had been a human, but he had never felt as inhuman as at that moment.

"Why are we here?" Asya's father asked in a hostile voice.

Jason nodded absently, more to himself than anyone else.

"I have some friends who have afforded us a unique opportunity," Jason said. "One that has, to my knowledge, never been afforded to anyone else on Earth."

"What kind of opportunity?" Greg's father asked.

"One for comfort, I hope," Jason said as he raised a portal. "Please all go through."

"You seriously expect us to go through that?" Asya's mother asked.

"If you choose not to, I understand," Jason said. "If that is your decision, I won't tell you what you missed. I don't want you carrying that regret for the rest of your life."

"Why not just tell us what's through there right now?" Asya's father asked.

"Because I don't think you'll believe me," Jason said. "Even if you do, I'm worried about misunderstandings if you don't see it for yourself."

"Don't play games," Greg's father said. "You've always liked playing games, Jason, but I won't stand for it."

"That's right," Asya's father said. "What is on the other side of your magic door, Asano?"

Jason stared at him, hollow-eyed, for a long time.

"Your daughter," he said finally. "Go through or not. All I'm offering you is the choice."

"What are you—"

Shade rose out of Jason's shadow. Jason stepped into him and was gone.

"Mum, are you crazy?" Asya's brother asked. "He killed a bunch of people with his brain. That was two days ago."

Jason used his ability to shadow jump between Shade's bodies to avoid using up the energy of his portal. He appeared next to the other side of the portal, which was some twenty kilometres offshore from Asano Village, atop a tower at the centre of his cloud palace.

Jason had finally used the palace configuration of his cloud flask. It produced a sprawling construct, floating on the surface of the Pacific as ocean waves failed to so much as make it shudder. It was solid as an island but smaller than the palace form Emir preferred as Jason usually deployed his cloud constructs in their adaptive forms.

The adaptive form offered both protection against search magic and camouflaged against direct observation. The palace was made up entirely in shades of blue and white that, from a satellite, would be indistinguishable from the water around it.

Even in the adaptive form, the palace was still sprawling and huge. A series of concentric rings made up the four-storey buildings, connected by covered, open-air walkways like the spokes of a wheel. At the hub of the wheel was an eight-storey tower with a flat rooftop designed as a lookout. This was where the portal emerged, the salty ocean wind blowing over it in spite of the elevation.

Jason waited, knowing that a discussion was taking place in his absence. Having finally admitted to himself that he was not as capable of moving people to act as he had once thought himself, he had left Erika and Emi to be his ambassadors. Even his short display with Greg and Asya's families showed him that he would only make things worse. To Jason's surprise, when someone finally came through the portal, it was Asya's father.

"Asano, what do you mean by saying my daughter is…"

His words dropped away as he noticed the floating palace around him, the beautiful building made of clouds spread out before him. More people came through, spreading out along the balustrade that circled the tower roof and goggling at the palace. Erika moved to stand beside her brother, hooking her arm into his elbow as they looked out at the palace below and the ocean beyond.

"You once told me that you came back to show me wonders," she said. "With all the horrors that magic has brought, it's easy to forget the marvels."

"I thought I would be the only magical thing in this world," Jason said. "I wish I'd been right."

There was a huge elevating platform in the centre of the flat tower rooftop and Jason directed everyone onto it. He could have opened the portal directly to their destination, but he had wanted to prime them to witness the extraordinary. For that reason, he led them on a meandering path through the palace, picking up Ken, Hiro and Yumi along the way.

The interior of the palace was more colourful than the disguised exterior, with the glorious sunset colours that were cloud construct default. It was also filled with the plants Jason had harvested during his long stay in the jungle astral space of the Order of the Reaper, with lush green leaves and vibrant flowers. Since they were all non-magical plants, feeding plant, earth and water quintessence to the cloud flask was enough to maintain them. The jungle plants gave the palace a lush, tropical feel, complete with rich, fresh aromas.

The group had lost any notion of interrogating Jason for the moment. They toured the wondrous space until Jason brought them to a vast and empty chamber. It was circular in shape, with a ceiling high above them. The only things in the room were Dawn, Farrah, and three of Shade's bodies. Each instance of Shade was standing in the middle of a hellishly complex ritual circle, all in a row. There was a fourth, empty ritual circle, positioned behind the line of three that Shade occupied. All four circles were piled high with spirit coins of all ranks, with even a diamond coin in each one.

"I'm sure you have all seen my companion, Shade," Jason said. Shade was, indeed, a well-known figure, even having been interviewed once when Jason allowed a media junket in Asano Village.

"What you may not know that that Shade's progenitor—his father, if you will—is an entity that governs the souls of the dead."

This caused a stir in the group. Jason sensed grief, anger, and disbelief in their auras.

"This," Jason said, gesturing, "is Dawn. She is a deeply remarkable person, not just for her origins and power but for her kindness. Recently, she took the time to contact Shade's father in order to give us all a gift. I don't even know what price she paid for this gift. She refuses to tell us. Suffice to say, I am quite certain it was great."

"What are you talking about, Asano?" Asya's father asked. His shock at their surroundings was wearing off and his patience with it. "If this is some kind of nonsensical séance…"

"That's exactly what it is," Jason said. "What we have for you here is an opportunity that so many lost in grief can only helplessly wish for: a final chance to say goodbye."

As he sensed the sceptical affront rising from the group, Jason marched to the middle of the empty ritual circle and opened a portal. This was not a normal portal, despite the identical look, but a medium for the ritual magic Dawn had put in place. It was an intricate work of magic far beyond Jason and Farrah's capabilities. He had been very careful crossing the sophisticated magic diagram, so as not to disturb it.

Dark streams of power flowed from Jason's portal into the shadowy forms at the centre of the other ritual circles, which immediately started to undulate. The group looked on in trepidatious anticipation, disbelief mixed with hope, fear, and confusion.

Over the course of around a minute, the three dark shapes took on the forms of Asya, Greg and Kaito, but dark and semi-translucent, like ghosts. At first, they were unmoving, their expressions blank like dummies. Then they suddenly animated, roused from torpor.

"For the next nine hours," Jason said, "they will be here for you to say the things you need to say. This will never happen again, so don't leave anything unsaid."

At first, nothing happened. The three souls projecting into Shade's bodies as vessels were disoriented by the process and their loved ones were all in shock.

Then Greg waved.

"G'day, Mum."

Like a dam had broken, Jason felt a maelstrom of emotion bombard the room as the group swarmed the three souls. Projecting through Shade, the ghost-like figures were oddly soft to the touch, as if they were made from the same cloud-stuff as the palace. Dawn could have arranged a more realistic depiction but felt being too lifelike could be dangerous. Jason wholeheartedly agreed, wanting to avoid the desperate hope of resurrection.

Dawn was the leader of the Cult of the World-Phoenix, albeit on a working sabbatical. Before creating her current avatar and returning to Earth, she had contacted her counterpart in the Cult of the Reaper, convincing him to allow Shade, a shadow of the Reaper, to act as a vessel to project the souls of Jason's fallen companions.

It was not a new or unique event; contacting the dead had a long history. There were very strict rules, however, the most important being no discussion could be made on the nature of the afterlife. Other rules included the fact that each soul could only be contacted one time.

Jason watched as the group converged on their dead loved ones, wandering over to stand next to Dawn.

"I don't think I can express the graciousness of what you've done here," he told her. "All I can do is thank you."

"When I came to you to save the world, you didn't negotiate or ask for payment. You didn't try and pass it off. You got to work. Call this my appreciation for that."

57
BROODING LONER

Vampires were neither strictly living nor strictly dead. Most of the undead were quite explicitly deceased, rendered animate by one force or another. In the case of vampires, however, that force was life energy, rendering them, to almost any test, alive. Some even considered themselves more alive than ordinary humans and treated their induction into the ranks of undead as being as born again, much like an Evangelical Christian.

Many such vampires counted their age from the moment they were turned, although Franklin was not one of them. He was not dismissive of the life he had lived and did not disdain his long-dead family. His last relative had been a vampire, like him—a nephew turned by Franklin himself to save the young man from an illness long-since cured by humanity.

In more than a century of life, Franklin had learned that regrets were inevitable. He regretted not turning more of his family and he regretted that the one he did turn was such a disappointment. It was Franklin himself who had turned his nephew over to the Network to keep the peace after the latest in a long line of mistakes was too grave for the Cabal to ignore.

That had been before the world changed and the Cabal grew ambitious. Magic was not just exposed to the world but was growing in strength. A land of stone and fire had arisen right in the city, Bankstown, turning into a place of pooling lava and dark stone. The people caught up in the change transformed into a species with dark skin and eyes of fire.

Different forces, magical and otherwise, took different attitudes to the transformed zones once fighting over the reality core each held was settled. Most governments declared them disaster sites, off-limits to civilians, then worked with the Network to recover the transformed people and salvage whatever magical materials were found within. The EOA was generally the weakest competitor in the fight for reality cores and left once it was decided.

The Cabal would usually wait until the fighting was settled and then occupy the zones. For reasons unknown to them, the transformed zones made members of the Cabal grow stronger. Many of the Cabal's members had hit a ceiling in terms of power growth, as if the world were not magical enough for them to get stronger. In the transformation zones, this was no longer the case. There, previously stagnant power once more flowed through the Cabal's members. As more and more transformed zones appeared, the Cabal started moving towards overall parity with the Network that had been dominating for the last century.

Within the Cabal, the boost in power meant the least to the vampires, who suffered from a different kind of ceiling. Although their powers never stopped growing, once they crossed a certain threshold, the world's magic was no longer enough to sustain them. As their might reached the invisible barriers imposed by reality, they fell into torpor. This had placed the vampires in an awkward position within the Cabal, as the most powerful leaders of their faction inevitably surrendered their position to enter hibernation, lest they wither and die.

The vampires were in a rush to awaken their ancient ones. They feared that the growth of the other factions would eventually lead to all the Cabal having greater power. If the vampires were going to dominate, they needed to awaken the old ones as quickly as they could. Other members of the Cabal reluctantly went along due to the need to compete with the Network.

In the case of Sydney, the Bankstown transformation zone was not ideal for vampires. They were highly resistant to most forms of damage, but fire was one of those that had a greater effect. This meant that while the flowing lava streams weren't a wildly dangerous hazard, they made for an unnerving environment.

This did not bother Franklin especially. He was a peaceful man who did not share the ambitions of many others in the Cabal and had never been dissatisfied with the way things were. He only spent as much time in the transformation zone as was necessary for his role in the Cabal, which is why he was unhappy to have been made manservant to the arisen ancient one.

Franklin had become sedentary over the decades, which had been costing him more and more in recent years. First, there was his nephew. As much as Franklin had despised the boy, Clinton had been the last family Franklin had. The end of his bloodline. Many vampires considered the other vampires they turned their children and Franklin had long considered this path, but again, his sedentary nature meant he had not gotten around to it. Another regret.

When Craig Vermillion had come to him, Franklin belatedly realised that he should have gone with him. Afraid of change, Franklin had declined, not realising that there was no staying the way things were. Change was coming. It was a matter of choosing which change to involve himself with. He had quickly come to realise that he had chosen poorly.

Like many vampires, Franklin had considered himself a living witness of history. He discovered how naïve he had been when confronted with a member of the British Empire born in the early years of the 16th century. Every moment was now filled with regret that he had not disappeared with Craig and the other Cabal members with the foresight to see what was coming.

The transformation events had changed the buildings of Bankstown into stone, usually very different from the ones that had been before. The Cabal had taken over the largest and most refined of them, a large stone manor, largely free of lava streams, with a luxuriously appointed interior. It was the single aspect of the new world of which the ancient vampire, Lord Willoughby, unreservedly approved. There was no longer any utility infrastructure, but that hardly concerned a man who had been hibernating in a sarcophagus since 1794.

One of the things he most disapproved of was modern clothing. A small army of Cabal members had been dispatched to find something more acceptable. As Willoughby lounged in a sitting room, in what no one dared tell him was women's underwear, a parade of clothing was presented. Each person presenting hoped that they wouldn't be the next one thrown into a hard stone wall when the lord's patience wore thin.

"My Lord," Franklin said. "I humbly recommend a more considered approach. The world has undergone many changes during your slumber. The essence magicians have grown powerful in your absence and—"

"Considered?" Lord Willoughby roared. "I have already considered the state of this miserable world and found it wanting! Jumped-up colonials thinking they can throw off the yoke of the Empire? Upstart sorcerers who would challenge the supremacy of the world's hidden rulers? The clothes alone are a travesty."

Franklin didn't voice his doubts on the degree to which the Cabal were ever hidden rulers directing human society from the shadows.

"My Lord, even the mortals have developed in ways that may come as a surprise. The capabilities of modern technology—"

"Are worthless in the face of overwhelming magical power," Willoughby cut him off.

"My Lord, I am merely making the humble suggestion that rushing to act before taking the time to learn may have unintended consequences."

"Do you think me a fool, Franklin? An ignorant buffoon, lost in time? Even in my day, we knew that if a servant kept insisting he was humble, he was anything but."

"I apologise, my Lord."

"Of course you do, you gormless peasant. Have the glory devices been prepared?"

"We've prepared the cameras, my Lord."

"Good. The Cabal of these modern times is a fallen beast. If magic is no longer hidden, then there is no excuse for the world not being under our heel. We shall begin with essence magicians and then the colonial government. The world shall see the glory of the new empire."

Willoughby's eyes lit up as someone brought in what looked like actual colonial-era garb.

"Excellent, finally."

"Costume shop?" Franklin asked.

Having escaped the mad British Lord, Franklin was in a car with Nathaniel, the man who had brought in the approved outfit. Nathaniel was an ogre, when not in human form, and a long-time friend of Franklin and Craig Vermillion.

"Theatre costume department," Nathaniel said.

"Smart," Franklin said. "Unlike me. I should have taken the advice of our mutual friend."

"He betrayed the Cabal."

"Did he? Or is he trying to save it?"

"Be careful who hears your words, Frank."

"Oh, I am, Nathan. I don't have a way to contact Craig. I made sure of it, in order to protect him. It means that I am unable to express the degree to which I regret my choice. It also means that I can't tell him that I could potentially arrange access to the reality core storage, should anyone be looking to get in there while a certain vampire lord was indulging himself in raiding the Network headquarters."

"You're taking a risk telling me this, Frank."

"I've lost too much by leaving everything around me to stagnate. It's time I started taking some risks. Is that something you can help me with?"

"I would never betray the Cabal," Nathaniel said. "Of course, if I just happen to run into my friend Craig, who knows what might come up in conversation."

Inside Jason's cloud palace, floating on the ocean, the friends and family of Kaito, Greg and Asya were taking the chance to say goodbye. They had nine final hours, which proved a boon, as it took some more time to accept what was happening than others.

Jason had created a large hall within the palace and once the ritual to call up the spirits of the dead was complete, he started modifying the cloud-stuff in the hall to fill the empty space with furniture. It was only moderately amazing to the group, most of which were getting their first exposure to the power of cloud constructs. After the ghostly souls of their loved ones returning, even the room transforming around them was only a mild wonder.

The event was essentially a wake, with two exceptions: the deceased were both present and cognisant and there wasn't any food. Although the food shortages of the monster wave months were slowly being remedied, the chaos following the transformation events was interfering with food distribution.

In that environment, Jason was not going to store a supply of food for entertainment purposes when almost everyone in his company was an essence user. Emi alone needed to eat, and only while she was outside of Jason's spirit vault. His soul realm suspended normal biological necessities, which left Jason both curious and glad. Curious, because he wondered what impact it had on the ageing process. Glad, because no one was going to the toilet in his soul.

Jason himself stayed quietly out of the way of the reunions, to the point of using subtle aura manipulation to push himself out of everyone's attention. A lot of the people present blamed Jason for the three deaths. He didn't want them wasting the last time they had with their loved ones on recrimination for him. That could wait until after.

Jason's gaze fell on Erika, speaking with their mother. She hadn't been back into his spirit vault since he killed the heroes in Venezuela, and he suspected that she was as uncertain as he was about whether she even could. It felt like the unconditional trust it took to enter might not be as strong as it once was.

As he watched everyone say their mournful goodbyes, he reflected on the people he had killed. From the beginning, he had worried about it becoming too easy and that had come to pass. Jason couldn't muster up any remorse for the people he massacred in Venezuela, only grim satisfaction that no more of his friends and family had been lost.

Jason waited as everyone else took their turn, sitting in a chair at the edge of the room until Farrah approached him.

"You're not being considerate," she told him. She sat on nothing, trusting him to create the cloud chair that rose up underneath her.

"What do you mean?" he asked.

"You're telling yourself that you're being considerate and letting everyone else spend the time with them. The truth is that you're scared. Scared to face them; scared that they'll blame you. Scared that they won't."

Jason looked at her and then gave a slight nod.

"I suppose I am," he acknowledged.

"Don't waste the time you have," she told him. "Who gets this kind of chance? Don't squander it."

"You're right."

"Then why are you still sitting here with me?" she scolded.

Jason nodded, his cloud chair sinking into the floor as he stood up. He made his way over to where people were surrounding the three dead guests of honour. Things grew quiet as Jason arrived near Kaito, whose soul was using Shade as a vessel. His body was dark and semi-transparent, looking every inch the ghost that he was.

"That's some pretty rough sad face you've got there, little brother," Kaito said. "Who died?"

Jason was taken aback by the flippancy of his dead brother, unable to find words to respond.

"This is what's great about being dead," Kaito said cheerfully. "No one will tell you how bad your jokes are."

"Your jokes suck donkey balls," Jason said.

Kaito burst out laughing.

"There he is. Excuse me, everyone; I need to have a private chat with my adorable little brother."

"Adorable?" Jason asked as they headed away from the others.

"I'm dead, so I can call you what I like."

"And here was me thinking that being dead might turn you into less of a tool bag," Jason said. "I guess the afterlife isn't turning into some enlightened being."

Kaito's image glitched like a television with a briefly interrupted signal.

"Probably best to steer away from that particular topic," Kaito said, looking queasy.

"Sorry," Jason said. "Good thing Aunt Marjory isn't here."

Kaito laughed again.

"Did you know that she thought you were an angel?" he asked Jason.

"So I heard," Jason said. "I wish I'd been there when she found out it was me."

The brothers sat down, facing one another.

"I'm sorry I couldn't protect you," Jason said.

"That was never your job," Kaito said firmly. "Your job is saving the world, so don't bugger it up. My wife and kids are on it."

"I'll do my best to see them safe," Jason said. "even if the world falls."

"It won't," Kaito said confidently. "Just make sure you and my wife don't comfort each other, reconnect, and get married," Kaito said.

"Oh, fuck you."

Kaito's laughter erupted through the hall, drawing all eyes.

"And here I thought that avoiding bad language was the one thing you did learn from Mum," Kaito said.

"You're an arsehole."

"You can't call me an arsehole. I'm dead."

"I should take out a sandwich and eat it in front of you."

"Why would eating a sandwich annoy me?"

"Because you're dead and you'll never get to eat a sandwich again."

"Oh, you're right. That would be a dick move."

"You seem pretty happy for a dead guy, but I won't ask how that works."

"I appreciate it," Kaito said. "You seem pretty cut up over me. It's nice to know you cared."

"No, I'm cut up over the other two. I'm faking it with you so Eri doesn't yell at me."

Kaito laughed before taking on a more sober expression.

"She's worried about you, Jason."

"I know."

"You killed a bunch of people on TV?"

"They were coming for all of us, Kai. As a publicity stunt. I had to drop them fast before they loaded themselves up with magic PCP. I didn't know it would kill them, but I'm glad it did. I won't let what happened to you happen again."

"Did you tell her any of that or did you just go all emo and broody on her?"

Jason bowed his head, not meeting his brother's eyes.

"That's what I thought," Kaito said. "Jason, you've always done whatever you set out to do. You have a way of looking at where you are, looking at where you want to be and finding the path between. A lot of people can do that, but not everyone has the resolve to pay the price it takes to go from one to the other. Hell, you got together with Amy and she's been in love with me since she was twelve. It wrecked you, yeah, but you got it done. It's pretty bloody intimidating, little brother."

"It's not always me who pays the price," Jason said, his voice breaking as he looked at his dead brother.

"I know. You need to watch out for that, but don't let it stop you. It's what makes you special. It's why I'm sure that you're going to save the world. If I'm being honest, I think it's why I did what I did to you. With Amy. You always had this determination, like nothing scared you and nothing was impossible. I never had that kind of courage. I think… I think I wanted to prove that I could overcome that. That I was better than you. Amy, I think was trying to escape it."

"You mean escape me?"

"Yeah. They were crappy reasons for the crappy thing we did. I'm sorry, little brother."

"Well, I did get you killed by an exploding wizard," Jason said with a smiling mouth and sad eyes. "Your thing is still worse, but since this is the end, I guess I can forgive you."

"Thank you, little brother. That means a lot."

"Just to be clear," Jason said, "forgiveness is about me being the better man, not you actually deserving it."

"Oh, you arsehole." Kaito laughed, then once more, he turned serious.

"Jason, I have something to ask you. Call it a belated dying wish."

"If it's a sandwich, I really can't do anything about that."

"It's about the guy who's going to save the world."

"Well, that's me. Unless you know something I don't."

"I know it's you. I just want it to be the right you."

"What are you talking about? Do I have an evil twin Mum never mentioned?" Jason asked, then scowled. "I bet she likes him more," he muttered.

Kaito grinned.

"This is exactly what I want," he said.

"Your dying wish is me ragging on Mum? Done."

"Not that, you unfilial prick. I want the Jason who saves the world to be the one obsessed with terrible TV shows that are older than he is, not the guy with the dead eyes who kills without remorse. I know you've seen a lot of awful things. I know you've had to do some of them yourself. I need you to rise above that stuff instead of letting it drag you down. We kind of all need that because we're relying on you, little brother."

"It's not so easy, Kai."

"I know. But set out to do it and you'll do it. That's what you do. Are you going to refuse the last wish of your brother's ghost?"

"I don't even know where to start. The things I've done. The things I have left to do. It feels like I'm being dragged into a swamp and I'm not sure how to pull myself out."

"By letting people help you, idiot. Being a brooding loner never works out. Even TV vampires figure that out by the end of the first season."

"As if you'd know."

"I watched vampire TV shows," Kaito said defensively.

"What vampire show did you watch?"

"You haven't heard of it."

"Look at who you're talking to. You didn't watch any vampire shows. If you say frigging *Highlander*…"

"I thought that was a movie about wizards or something."

"You think *Highlander* was about wizards?"

"I didn't like wizards. I watched a vampire show."

"What vampire show?"

"*Forever Knight*."

"*Forever Knight*?"

"See, I told you hadn't heard of it."

"All these years and only after you die do you reveal you did watch old TV shows after all? I can see why, given your choice. *Forever Knight*? A TV show based on a TV movie starring Rick Springfield—who they couldn't even get back for the show! The guy who sang 'Jessie's Girl' was too busy for your terrible TV show."

"You realise that if you knew as much about magic as you did about American television from the eighties and nineties, you'd probably have saved the world already."

"*Forever Knight* was Canadian!"

On the other side of the hall, Erika had a tear in her eye and a smile on her lips as she watched her brothers loudly argue.

58

HIGH MAINTENANCE

IN THE MEETING HALL OF HIS CLOUD PALACE, JASON SAT ACROSS FROM THE spectre of his friend, Greg.

"I have no idea what to say," Jason said.

"Wow," Greg said. "I had to die to see it happen, but at least now I know what it takes."

"I was going to get you a greeting card, but I couldn't find one for getting you killed by a wizard with bomb fists."

"And there he is."

"I looked into some print shops for a custom card, but with everything going on, the wait times are egregious. As for online, you can just forget about it. Shipping delays are crazy."

Jason's smile was a pained rictus, a poor disguise for his obvious guilt and grief.

"I don't want you mourning for me," Greg said.

"You're dead," Jason said. "You don't get a say."

"At least put aside the guilt. I chose this."

"I gave you the choice."

"And the alternative is what?" Greg asked. "Do you even remember how miserable I was when you came back? I was never much more than an adequate lawyer and I'd been all but pushed out of my father's law practice. I was staring down the barrel of a long, mediocre life. I lived more in the last six months than in the six years before it. Running around, fighting monsters with my magic powers. I got laid so much."

"Mate…"

"I know, but I totally did. I met beautiful women from other dimensions and played board games with a vampire. I had magic powers. Steampunk magic powers. I got killed by a supervillain and died fighting to save the world. Jason, if you told me everything that was going to happen—every single thing, even the end—I'd have made the exact same choice. I'd have jumped at it."

"Greg…"

"Don't you dare pity me. You made my life a triumph. My death too, for that matter. Don't you ever try and take that from me by thinking you made my choices for me. I died a hero, Jason, not a victim. You don't get to turn me into one inside your head."

"You seem pretty determined to not let me get a word in edgeways."

"That's because you'll just talk some crap. Look, we've been putting up with edgelord Jason for a while now, but it's time to knock off the melodrama. You're not Darkwing Duck, so stop swanning about pretending you're the terror that flaps in the night. You're a god damn chuuni. You were a chuuni in school, you were a chuuni when you got back from magic land and you're such a giant bloody chuunibyou right now that you don't even realise you're more chuuni than you've ever been in your life."

"Please stop saying chuuni."

"Jason, you need the chuuni power."

"Chuuni power?"

"The Cabal is digging up an army of ancient vampires. You think popping out of the shadows doing a Batman voice is going to help against that lot? They've been pulling that trick since Constantinople; they're going to be better at it than you. If you want to beat them, then you need to run your game, not theirs. Play to your own strengths."

"Which are?"

"A vampire is basically an ancient super chuuni. And in the land of the chuuni, the genre-savvy man is king."

"So you're pretty much talking out your arse," Jason said.

"Yep," Greg said with a grin. "Sounded good, though, didn't it?"

"Not even a little. You just said chuuni about thirty times. You were babbling nonsense."

"Well, you gave babbling nonsense up to go all edgelord drama queen. Someone had to pick up the slack."

Jason ran a hand over his face.

"Is this what it's like talking to me?"

"It used to be," Greg said softly. "Back when you were actually fun. Yeah, things have gotten bad. You've lost people. But if you lose yourself, then everyone on Earth is completely buggered, so it's time to stop moping and put on your big boy pants. The floral print ones."

Jason and Greg looked at each other and both started laughing.

"You are really bad at the final guidance from a friend thing," Jason said.

"It wasn't that bad."

"It was pretty much you just saying chuuni and edgelord over and over."

"Take a look in the mirror, guy. You've been acting like a chuuni edgelord over and over."

"Harsh. You're way better at making me feel bad than your dad, although he's giving it a good go."

"Don't worry about him. He's blustering because he's worried people will realise he's just happy that I was the one who died and not my brother."

Jason turned to glance at his mother across the room, in a group speaking with Kaito's spectre.

"Yeah, I know that story," he said, then turned back to Greg. "I'm going to miss you, brother. I'll think of you every time I play a new board game you'll never get a chance to try."

"Oh, you prick."

"You shouldn't have called me a chuuni so many times."

The streets of Sydney were much less congested than normal, in the wake of the transformation events. Government restrictions and business closures led to little enough traffic that the fleet of vehicles, mostly vans and SUVs, were able to sweep rapidly to the Sydney Network branch's building.

Cabal members poured out of the vehicles, human forms transforming into a menagerie of bizarre creatures and mythological beings. At the head was the vampire lord, Willoughby. Oddly, there were what looked like ordinary humans operating camera equipment.

The Network branch's lower levels were largely filled with ordinary humans, many of whom had only learned the true nature of their organisation when magic went public. These were the administration offices for the businesses that had been both the source of funding and operational cover for the Network over the last half-century.

The lower floors became a bloodbath as the Cabal stormed the building. They had clashed with the Network numerous times over reality cores, but this was different. The Cabal had invaded the Network's home, intent on pulling them out root and stem. This was not a fight for riches or power but for survival. The Network's tactical squads swiftly descended from the upper floors to engage the invaders.

Willoughby was startled by the resistance the Network put up. He had been warned repeatedly, but he was not a good listener. Surprised was not the same as being defeated, however, and the vampire's might was not to be overlooked. When a powerful conjured machine gun ripped holes in him, streams of blood flowed out of the wounds and through the air like ropes. They entangled the man with the huge gun and dragged him into Willoughby's waiting embrace. Draining the silver-ranker's blood rapidly restored his health and he pushed deeper into the building.

Shade was the vessel through which Kaito, Asya and Greg were projecting their souls and he had control of how realistic those projections were. He was keeping them ghostly to prevent their loved ones from thinking the soul projections meant that resurrection was possible, although some still hoped in spite of assurances otherwise.

Shade's control meant that as Jason sat close to Asya, holding her hands in his, Shade could make them more solid, feeling like her actual hands instead of insubstantial ephemera.

"Greg and Kaito both told me I need to pull myself together," Jason said. "Is that what you're going to do as well?"

"Do I need to?" she asked. "Trust me to find such a high-maintenance boyfriend."

"High maintenance?"

"Oh, please, Asano. I love you, but you are an absolute pain to deal with."

Jason's eyes went wide and she squeezed his hands.

"Yes, I said it," she told him. "It's not like I'll get another chance. I know you didn't get there yet, but you would have. I had no intentions of letting you go."

She tried to smile but didn't do a great job.

"I guess that's out of my hands now."

"I'm sorry."

"For what? I hate to break it to you, Asano, but not everything is about you. You weren't a part of my life when I joined the Network. I made the choice to stand up and protect the world from whatever magic threw at it. I didn't want to die, but at least I died fighting for something worthwhile."

Jason nodded.

"I'm not going to tell you to pull yourself together," Asya said. "I'm going to tell you to stay focused. Keep your eye on what we died for, not the fact that we died."

"You don't want me going after the gold-ranker," Jason realised.

"Yes. All that gets you is revenge and that's not for us. That's for you, and you have more important things to be getting on with. Don't take stupid chances that cost you everything and get you nothing."

"He killed you."

"And killing him won't bring me back."

She poked him in the forehead.

"High maintenance. I'm dead and I still need to stop you from doing something stupid."

"I wasn't going to go after him," Jason insisted.

"No?"

"No."

"Really?"

"Yes, really."

She gave him a flat look.

"I mean, if he came looking for me…" Jason admitted.

"Then you run. Run and hide like a scared little boy."

"What if I can lure him into—"

"No. Promise me, Jason."

"Fine," he grumpily acquiesced. "I won't fight the gold-ranker. It's not like I was going to anyway."

"Oh, please."

Jason bowed his head.

"I don't know if I can do it, Asya," he said, his voice barely a whisper. "Everyone on Earth is relying on me, whether they know it or not, and I'm just making it up as I go."

Asya's ghostly form grew more substantial and she lifted his face with her hands, resting her forehead against his.

"You always have been, for as long as I've known you. How many times did I yell at you for insufficient debate prep? But it's gotten you this far."

"I've died," he said. "Kind of a lot, and the world is coming apart at the seams."

"And you're going to save it. Then you're going to be obnoxiously smug about it, but try and tone it down. You're going to have trouble finding another girl willing to love all this."

She leaned back and gestured at him with a sweeping hand and he grinned at her.

"Is that so?" he asked.

"You should listen to Greg and your brother," she said. "Be the crazy weirdo I fell for."

"I really want to kiss you," he said, "but I would actually be kissing Shade. I'm pretty sure making out with your own familiar is crossing some kind of line."

"I don't care."

The deadline for Greg, Kaito and Asya's visitation drew close. Jason, Dawn and Farrah were meeting with them for the last time before handing them off to their families for their final goodbyes.

"You need to keep this guy in line," Asya told Farrah. "He's not as strong as you; he's just good at faking it."

"I know," Farrah said.

"Hey…"

They made their last goodbyes and then the three ghosts went off to their loved ones, Jason heading towards Erika and the rest of the Asano family with Kaito.

"I love you, brother," Kaito said as they walked.

"I'm going to bang your wife and raise your kids," Jason whispered. "I'm going to make all three call me Daddy."

"Oh my god, you're an arse."

As they waited out the clock for the three ghostly figures to reach the end of their time back on Earth, Shade quietly spoke to Jason.

"Mr Asano, there is a situation."

Jason wandered free of his family to speak with Shade in private.

"Something at the village?" he asked. He had left one of Shade's bodies at the village in case something happened while his family were all in the cloud palace.

"Not the village. The Cabal has initiated a full assault on the Network headquarters in Sydney. They are live-streaming it and the news stations have picked up the feed. The military has been called out, but this is far beyond them. The Cabal has one of the ancient vampires."

Jason looked over at Kaito, Greg and Asya, talking with their families. Asya was keeping an eye on him and wandered over when she saw his expression. Kaito, Greg, Dawn and Farrah spotted her and followed.

"You have to go?" Asya asked.

"Yeah," he said.

"What is it?" Farrah asked.

"The Cabal and their old vampire are live-streaming an all-out attack on the Network headquarters in Sydney."

No one suggested not going. For all that they had fallen out with the Network, they all knew people there.

"Alright," Asya said. "Go save the day."

"Kick some arse, little brother."

"Just remember to play the hero, not the villain," Greg said.

Jason looked at them all for the last time.

"Whatever it is waiting for you on the other side," he told them, "I hope it's amazing."

He opened a portal and stepped through. His portal ability was just strong enough to send three silver-rankers, allowing Farrah and Dawn to follow before the portal closed. Kaito, Greg and Asya turned back to the group, all of which were looking at them.

"He's coming back," Greg assured them. "He's almost definitely not going to leave you out here in the middle of the ocean."

59

TREACHERY OR COWARDICE

Nigel and his nine-person tactical section were retreating down a hallway on the fourth floor of the Network building. They had rushed downstairs in response to the Cabal's attack, only to encounter the people of the lower floors coming up, transformed into ravening ghouls. Undead monstrosities with a frenzied hunger for living flesh, they poured up the corridor like a wave, ignoring the gunfire slamming into them.

Becoming the undead had turned normal people into silver-rank creatures; they were far less powerful than even a weak silver-rank monster but still resistant to the attacks of bronze-rankers. The vampire lord knew this, so was surprised that the outnumbered tactical teams weren't immediately overrun.

Nigel's tactical team retreated in good order, despite only two members being silver rank. Nigel had been the tactical instructor for the Sydney branch prior to Farrah's arrival and had worked with her to develop a retraining program for existing tactical teams while Farrah focused on new recruits. Nigel's own team used a mixture of traditional Network methodology and Farrah's more ability-centric approach to good effect. They had come a long way since they escorted Jason into his first proto-space.

Their discipline leveraged their capabilities effectively, with Jonno and Nigel himself laying down fire from conjured assault rifles as they fell back. Thorny had grown an extra pair of arms and was firing four conjured pistols while Digit sent arrows downrange that exploded in blasts of fire and electricity.

Even with the gunfire laying waste to them, the ghouls kept coming. They wore the business attire of lower floor admin staff, with police and military uniforms mixed amongst them. The vampire lord had performed mass transformations on the dead killed by the Cabal, which was not limited to the Network staff. The police and military had been sent in as a response to the Cabal's brazen attack in the heart of Sydney, only to pay a deadly price at the hands of the vampire lord.

Nigel knew at least one of the teams that rushed down from the upper floors had been overrun. As his team had been pulling back in the face of a ghoulish wave, he had glimpsed the ancient vampire biting into the neck of another team's section leader and none of the team were responsive to radio checks. As far as Nigel knew, essence users couldn't be turned into ghouls, but he was worried they could be turned into something worse.

The ghouls broke past the gunfire, rushing Nigel's team. The team stopped firing and Cobbo dashed forward from the backline to meet them. He wasn't running but hurtling through the air, his spear set like a jousting lance. It plunged into a ghoul and Cobbo's magically enhanced momentum stopped dead. The momentum all transferred into the ghoul, who was sent tumbling back into the others before exploding, ripping apart the closest ghouls and scattering the rest. It gave Nigel's team a reprieve as Cobbo fell back and the shooters resumed fire at the ghouls.

They continued withdrawing to the stairwell, the elevators having been shut off to prevent the Cabal using them. The next time the ghouls drew close, Jonno dropped his conjured rifle and called up a comically large rotary cannon that mowed down the ghouls, ripped apart the wall behind them and shattered the glass on the exterior wall beyond. More of the seemingly endless ghouls came streaming into the hall, unintimidated by Jonno's absurd display of power.

"I'm glad to see you changed your mind, Frank," Vermillion said, shaking Franklin's hand. They were standing under a bridge, away from prying eyes.

"It was changed for me," Franklin said. "I should have listened to you, Craig."

"It may be for the best you didn't," Vermillion said. "Now we know your idiot ancient one pulled everyone off the storage facility to go attack the Network."

"Not everyone," Franklin said. "We're going to have to fight our way in and out. It's our own people, Craig."

"I know. But it's the only time security will be light enough for that to even be possible," Vermillion said.

"Yeah," Franklin said, resignation in his voice. "We need to go now. Our window is small."

"Alright," Vermillion said. "Let's go."

Due to the propensity of proto-spaces and transformation events, five full tactical teams had been on standby in the building's upper floors and had moved down to confront the Cabal attack. Without the magical interference of a dimensional space or transformation zone, comms worked perfectly and the teams were able to coordinate.

Unfortunately, the tac-teams arrived downstairs into the midst of chaos. The vampire lord had transformed an alarming number of the dead into ghouls and the Cabal was using them as cannon fodder. The Cabal members refrained from engaging the Network teams, who they let exhaust themselves against the ghouls.

The Network's Director of Tactical Operations, who the tactical teams called the Ditto, was Koen Waters. He had ordered the teams to make a slow withdrawal back upstairs, giving the people on the floors above time to reach the magical defences of the building's uppermost floors.

One of the five Network teams was hit by the vampire himself and wiped out, while another lost cohesion and was broken up by the encroaching ghoul horde. The silver-rank section leader fell back with a couple of team members as the others were cut off, either caught by the Cabal or the ghouls or managing to escape. Some shot holes in the exterior windows, the bronze-rankers willing to risk a four-storey drop over facing the wave of undead.

The remaining three teams, including Nigel's, successfully reached different stairwells around the building. They were all on the fourth floor and worked to secure the stairwell entrances before moving up. In the case of Nigel's team, this meant Darce hurriedly summoning her steam golem to serve as a bulwark for the door. As she did that, Orange crouched down and put his hands on the top stair leading down, using his ability to weaken materials on the stairs below.

When Orange was done, he stood up and Nigel gave him an inquisitive look.

"What?" Orange asked in his abrasive bogan drawl.

"Why didn't the stairs collapse?" Nigel asked.

"The stairs will seem fine until a few of them get on there," Orange said. "Then they'll collapse and drop those undead buggers like sacks of sh—"

"We get the idea," Nigel said. "Good job."

Leaving behind the trapped stairs and the large summoned entity made of what looked like brass, they made their way up as Nigel reported in over the radio.

"Ditto, we've secured the East stairwell at level four and are moving up."

"Evac of floors five through eight is proceeding smoothly," Koen responded. "Converge on the ninth-floor armoury; that will be our first fixed defence point."

The ninth floor was where the Network's emplaced magic defences began and their magical resources were stored. It was the place where the Network could best leverage their advantages to repel attackers. The only reason the tactical teams had descended from there was to protect as many people from the lower floors as they could.

The team continued moving up. The stairwell was located on the building exterior and had glass on one side, allowing the team to look out at what was happening on the ground as they ascended. After the Cabal's open assault on a building in the Sydney CBD, authorities had intervened, cordoning off a large area around the building. The team saw where the cordon had been pulled back and expanded after an unsuccessful clash with Cabal forces.

"Since when do you have the level of fine control with your abilities to trap the stairs, Orange?" Digit asked as they double-timed up the stairs.

"I'm gettin' good at me powers," Orange said. "I've been practising like Instructor Hot Stuff taught us."

"You're a pig, Orange," Darce said.

"I only call her that because of her volcano powers," Orange said. "Do I also want to bang her like a drum? Yes, I do, but I'm a gentleman."

"So that's the secret to having you put in the effort," Digit said. "Have a beautiful woman to tell you to."

"Mate, that's no bloody secret," Orange said. "Send a pretty girl my way and you can get me to do whatever you… oh, bloody hell."

Each member of Nigel's section was keeping their head on a swivel and spotted the danger together. People with grotesquely elongated limbs were climbing up the exterior of building, their bare hands and feet adhering to the glass.

"The outside of the building is pretty reflective, right?" Darce asked. "Do they even know we're in here?"

Nigel raised his rifle and aimed at the window.

"They're about to."

"My ghouls should have overrun this place by now," Willoughby complained. "What is taking so long?"

"Again, Lord Willoughby, it's the essence magicians. They're far more powerful than they were in your time."

"Every time is my time. Who even are you? Where's my manservant?"

"I'm Richard, my Lord. No one has been able to find Franklin since we arrived."

"Treachery or cowardice," Willoughby spat. "Either way, drag him in front of me the moment he's found."

Jason, Farrah and Dawn emerged on top of a tall building in the Sydney CBD, close to the Network building. Jason had first visited that rooftop to observe the building while still feeling out the Network, during his first days back on Earth. After getting their attention with his hospital faith healer stunt, he had Shade follow the people who had arrived to investigate. That had led him to this rooftop.

They were surprised to find they were not alone on the rooftop, finding an army sniper team overlooking the Network headquarters. Jason was worried about what their reaction would be until he felt a flood of relief from the soldiers.

"You're Jason Asano," one of them said.

"I'm wearing his underwear, so I hope so," Jason said.

"Thank god you're here."

"Aren't you meant to try and take me into custody or something?"

"Bugger that," the soldier said. "There's something down there. Something bad. It's killing people and turning them into some kind of fast zombie."

"Ghouls," Dawn said. "That will be people without magic that he's transformed. They're already dead and we can't do anything for them now but give them peace. It's the essence users we need to concern ourselves with. If he takes them alive, he can turn them."

"I fought a monster called a blood weaver," Jason said. "It vamped people up, but they could be cleansed if you got to them quickly enough."

"Lesser vampires," Dawn said. "You will be able to do the same here. The curse can warp the body and mind but not the soul, unless the soul surrenders to it. If you can get to them before the curse fully claims the body, they can be saved. Once their bodies have gone from living to undead, we can only put them down with the ghouls."

"How long do we have?" Jason asked.

"Hours," Dawn said. "If we act now, we should comfortably be in time. You just have to avoid getting killed while you work, but at least the curse will negate their essence abilities. You go through the building, finding and cleansing the lesser vampires. You will likely have to fight through ghouls and the Cabal to do it."

"We go after the head vampire," Farrah said.

"Yes," Dawn agreed. "I'm confident that I can outfight it, but even with fire powers to impede its healing, I can't deal enough damage to kill a gold-ranker. That will be your job, Farrah. I'll set up the strikes and you hit with maximum efficiency."

"Alright," Farrah said.

The trio moved to the edge of the roof and surveyed the area. The military and police cordon was keeping people away, while the street in front of the building was strewn with blood and destroyed cars. There were only a handful of bodies, the ones too damaged to be worth turning into ghouls. There were holes in the building's glass exterior. As for the inside of the building, both Dawn and Jason had aura senses powerful enough to examine the interior.

"Ghouls and the Cabal have the first three floors and most of the fourth," Jason said. "It looks like the Network is moving its people to the upper floors where they have magical defences in place."

"There's an armoury on level nine," Farrah said, knowing the building much better than Jason. "They'll set up their first proper defensive line there."

"Then that's where I'll go," Jason said. "I'll start at the bottom and make my way up. They're using the ghouls as meat shields, so I can hopefully catch the vamp minions from behind."

"We'll go straight for the old vampire," Dawn said. "The Network will fare better if we can keep him out of the fight."

"The aura those ghouls are throwing off is very feral," Jason said. "The vampire has enough control to stop the ghouls going after the Cabal?"

"From how quickly he created them all," Dawn said, "he is likely from a bloodline that specialises in creating servitors. That is good for us because that kind of bloodline is weaker in direct confrontations."

"How would I do against one of these vampires?" Jason asked.

"Your blood abilities won't be as effective on a gold-rank one as those of your rank and lower," Dawn said. "Your powers that impair resistances and ignore rank disparity means your blood magic will still be an advantage, but don't underestimate the vampire. Their attributes are similar to an essence user of their rank and they all have different blood powers, based on their vampiric bloodlines."

"How would you rate my chances?" Jason asked.

"If you used a vampire's minions to grow stronger before confronting a solitary vampire, you would most likely win. Without enhancing yourself, or against numbers, I would be far less optimistic."

"So I need to pick my battles," Jason said. "That's nothing new."

Jason had several means of stealing the strength of his enemies. He was able to stack health through various drain powers and if he had enough dead enemies he could compensate for the most dangerous disparity with gold-rankers, which was speed.

Ability: [Blood Harvest] (Blood)

- Spell (drain).
- Base cost: Low mana.
- Cooldown: None.

- Current rank: Silver 2 (04%).

- Effect (iron): Drain the remnant life force of a recently deceased body, replenishing health, stamina and mana. Only affects targets with blood.

- Effect (bronze): Affects any number of bodies in a wide area.

- Effect (silver): Gain an instance of [Blood Frenzy] for each corpse drained, up to a threshold determined by current rank. After reaching the threshold, gain instances of [Blood of the Immortal] instead.

- [Blood Frenzy] (boon, unholy, stacking): Bonus to [Speed] and [Recovery]. Additional instances have a cumulative effect, up to a maximum threshold.

- [Blood of the Immortal] (boon, healing, unholy, stacking): On suffering damage, an instance is consumed to grant a powerful but short-lived heal-over-time effect. Additional instances can be accumulated but do not have a cumulative effect.

From the beginning, Blood Harvest had been Jason's strongest recovery power, used to replenish himself after defeating enemies. Now it had a new purpose as a trump card for facing higher-rank foes. If he had the chance to eliminate enough lower-rank enemies first, he could compensate for a gold-ranker's speed by enhancing his own. He still wouldn't be able to match a gold-ranker, at least until he was much further into silver rank himself, but it would be enough to keep him from being wildly outclassed.

Jason, Farrah and Dawn leapt off the edge of the building, each sprouting wings. Jason, in the middle, had wings of night formed from the cloak he conjured around himself. To each side of him were women with wings of fire, gliding in formation towards the Network building.

60
COMELY WENCHES

Jason, Farrah and Dawn glided through the air towards the Network building. Twenty dark forms emerged from Jason, heading to the bottom half of the building. Shade couldn't penetrate the magically protected upper floors, but his incorporeal form could easily scout out the rest. Once Shade had bodies all over the building, Jason could shadow jump to any of them.

The vampires had naturally good aura control, if somewhat limited in scope. Jason himself had learned some tricks from Craig Vermillion. The ancient vampire was projecting his aura strongly, flooding the building with fear and dread. It made him easy to find, but he also sensed the approach of Jason and the others as they fended off his aura. Farrah needed to expend more effort than Jason and Dawn but still managed to resist the oppressive effects of the vampire's aura.

Jason headed for the ground while Dawn and Farrah went for the third floor. As they split up, Farrah used one of her powers on Jason.

- [Farrah Hurin] is attempting to use ability [Power Bond] on you.
- [Power Bond] will enhance some of your abilities for the duration of the bond and give [Farrah Hurin] access to your knowledge. This is restricted to your knowledge of concepts

external to yourself. This ability cannot read your thoughts or access your knowledge of yourself.
- [Power Bond] can be rejected or ended at any time by you.
- If you do not implicitly trust [Farrah Hurin], this ability will fail. Subconscious distrust will prevent this power from working.

Jason accepted the power.

- You have been affected by [Power Bond], connecting you to [Farrah Hurin]. You may end this connection at any time.
- [Power Bond] has used a random essence from [Farrah Hurin] to enhance one of your abilities at random. Ability [Sanguine Horror] has been enhanced by [Fire Essence]. While [Power Bond] is in effect, familiar [Colin] will be immune to fire and heat effects and inflict [Burning] when making attacks.

"Oh," Jason said, his dark hood hiding the wide grin on his face. "Oh, dear me."

Jason didn't bother to hide as he alighted on the ground outside the building, a half-dozen more Shades emerging from his shadow. There was a small group of Cabal members standing outside the door, none of them hiding their true forms. One was a cyclops, twice the height of a man, while the others looked like stretched-out humans with long, narrow limbs. The cyclops was silver rank, while the others were bronze.

When they noticed Jason's arrival, the Cabal members didn't move to attack. The long-limbed ones were fearful and the cyclops was angry, all of which Jason could read from their auras.

"Out and proud; I have to respect that," Jason said, looking up at the cyclops. "You're pretty awesome."

"Why are you here?" one of the Cabal members asked. "The Network betrayed you."

"That's why I put my trust in people and not institutions," Jason said. "I still have friends here and I'm not going to let your new boss eat them. Are you really okay with what's happening here?"

"Power always wins," the cyclops growled in a voice of rumbling thunder. "I want to test your power."

"I'm sure you do," Jason said, pushing the hood back off his head. "Once you have, though, you'll wish you hadn't. If the Cabal is willing to pack up and go home, I'm willing to let it."

The cyclops threw back its head to let out a booming laugh.

"You think you can kill us all?"

"Yes," Jason said.

"We never wanted to be part of this," one of the long-limbed Cabal members said. "You don't know how strong the vampire is. Can't you feel it?"

For all his aura's strength, Jason didn't have the power to suppress the vampire's gold-rank aura. His was too strong for the vampire to suppress in turn, even if it could. Only certain bloodlines possessed that aspect of aura control.

"I can feel it," Jason said.

He sent his own aura flooding over the building, overlaying it with that of the vampire. The domineering aspect of Jason's aura competed with the fear-drenched aura of the vampire. It wasn't exactly a positive sensation, but Jason's aura did include protective aspects. The Network members in the building were given a sense of being shielded from a monster by a tyrant as Jason alleviated the vampire's oppressive force.

The long-limbed Cabal members looked at Jason with even more fear than before. The vampire hadn't spared his own people from the effect of his aura, so now they were suffering both his and Jason's simultaneously. The results were purely psychological, but they were effective nonetheless.

"I have a thing about turning victims into the undead and me having to put them all down," Jason said. "If anyone but the old vampire and his ghouls choose to run, I won't chase. Go inside and tell your people."

"Don't you dare," the cyclops warned, sensing the fear from his minions. He had willpower to spare, impressively unintimidated by either aura.

"I don't want to get caught up in the middle of this," the long-limbed man complained. "Are you seriously alright with killing all these people?"

A beam of light shot from the cyclops's eye like a laser and the long-limbed man screamed as his flesh burned.

"Yes," the cyclops growled.

The man tried to run, but the beam tracked him until he fell dead to the ground.

Jason tucked his hood back over his head and wrapped his cloak around himself as identical cloaks manifested on the half-dozen Shades standing with him. Moving fast, it would be hard to tell them apart from Jason, especially with Jason's aura washing over them all.

Farrah's sword-whip lashed out to shatter the glass, allowing her and Dawn to fly into the third floor unimpeded. There they sensed the source of the vampire's aura. Unlike Jason, the vampire lacked the control to hide his location in an area flooded by his aura. Instead, he stood out like a beacon.

Dawn and Farrah touched down in a wide hallway full of ghouls. Farrah stomped the floor and a wall of obsidian rose up to bisect the hallway lengthways, swiftly enough to crush several ghouls into the ceiling. The wall then exploded into shards, shredding the remaining ghouls into bloody chunks, and the hallway fell silent.

The door at the far end of the hallway opened and a man entered, unfazed by the bloody horror Farrah had made of the hallway. Dressed like he stepped out of a period drama rather than the next room, he gazed at the women with a self-satisfied sneer.

"Finally something in this wretched modern world I can wholeheartedly approve of," Willoughby said. "A pair of comely wenches delivering themselves unto me."

"I don't think you're going to like what we're here for," Farrah said.

"I think I might," Willoughby said. "Women are no fun unless they struggle."

"I'm going to enjoy killing you," Farrah said.

"I'm going to enjoy teaching you to use that sharp tongue for… better purposes."

Farrah conjured her obsidian armour around herself as Willoughby dashed forward with the lightning speed of a gold-ranker, practically teleporting down the hallway. Almost instantaneous was not actually instantaneous, however, and while Farrah and the vampire traded barbs, Dawn had been muttering a spell incantation.

Just before the vampire reached them, magic circles appeared on each wall of the corridor, shooting out a net of flaming threads that Willoughby crashed into like a fly into a spider's web. His momentum was arrested as he was tangled in the burning threads, but he immediately started yanking himself free with his gold-rank strength. Farrah didn't waste the chance, though. Her whip-sword snaked out to wind itself around the vampire.

Farrah's sword, when unextended, was a jagged-edge greatsword made from obsidian. In its whip-sword state, the obsidian teeth separated and were strung along a flexible cord of red-hot lava, like shark teeth on a necklace. The lava joined the flaming threads of Dawn's trap spell in burning the vampire, but the damage was superficial. Willoughby strained against the sword wrapped around him. Farrah didn't leave it in place, knowing he would quickly burst the conjured weapon. Its flexibility and power were incredible, but its durability was a weak point.

When Farrah retracted her sword, the obsidian razors chewed up the vampire as if he was caught in an industrial accident. He rapidly healed, although the burnt portions of his flesh recovered more slowly. His regeneration was impeded as flames lit up from the corkscrew wounds left by Farrah's sword.

Dawn had been casting a second spell as Farrah clashed with the vampire. Steel rings appeared around Willoughby as he recovered. They immediately warped when the vampire flexed, but it bought time for the women to make more attacks. Farrah stomped and an obsidian spike drove up through the floor, piercing through the vampire's crotch to impale him. Obsidian spikes then stabbed out of his body.

It was one of Farrah's most powerful attacks, while also being very efficient in terms of mana cost to damage. The problem was that it was an easy attack to read and avoid, so it saw little use. Only when the enemy was large and slow or caught up by another ability was it useful, which made Dawn a valuable partner for Farrah.

Despite the power of the attack, it barely impeded the vampire. There was a sharp crack of stone from inside the vampire's body as he once more moved to the attack and the impaling shaft was broken. Farrah stood strong against the gold-ranker, fighting back as best she could. Their speed difference was on full display when her sword hit nothing but air while his clawed nails tore strips off her obsidian armour.

Farrah was not Willoughby's priority, however, as he had identified

Dawn's control effects as his primary impediment to killing them. The vampire kicked Farrah square in the chest, sending her flying back past Dawn and out through the hole in the glass where she had entered the building. She fell out of sight, leaving Dawn on her own.

Dawn targeted Willoughby's brief moment of imbalance after the lunging kick, seizing the chance to step up and place her hand against the vampire's chest. All the fire in the room vanished, from the remnants of Dawn's flaming threads to the burning effects Farrah left behind on Willoughby's body. Immediately after, an explosion under Dawn's hand sent the vampire hurtling back down the hallway. She followed up with a rapid series of hand gestures, each one causing a wall of flames to rise up one after another, blocking the path between herself and Willoughby.

Farrah flew back into the building, moving faster for having dismissed her damaged armour. Her flaming wings vanished and she conjured up a fresh set of armour.

"It's going well," she said, eyeing the flaming barriers sealing the hallway.

"It's far from over," Dawn warned.

Dawn was a control specialist, able to do some damage but nowhere near enough to kill a gold-ranker. Unfortunately, her silver-rank control effects only lasted moments against gold-ranker. The most she could do was buy critical moments for Farrah to land her attacks. Even so, Dawn's precision and judgement had allowed her and Farrah to largely control the opening stages of the fight, although the vampire's gold-rank power meant that everything could change in a moment.

Rather than rush through the sequence of flame walls blocking the corridor, Willoughby leveraged the advantage of his gold-rank physicality to smash through the walls of the adjoining rooms. Farrah and Dawn heard his approach as a rapid series of crashes. The vampire smashed his way back into the hallway, grabbed Farrah and kept going, battering her right through the opposite wall. After lifting her into the air by the neck, he slammed her into the floor so hard that they crashed through it, dropping to the level below.

Kneeling on top of Farrah, Willoughby looked around at what should have been a small army of ghouls. Instead, the ghouls were once more unmoving corpses, withered and dry as if they'd been dead for months.

His attention was drawn back to Farrah as she punched him in the ear.

He pinned her arms under his knees and grabbed the face of her helmet, the obsidian cracking as he broke the faceplate right off. He raised a clawed hand to bring it down on her face when a flaming rope from the hole above wrapped around his wrist. More ropes snaked around his other limbs and he was yanked through the hole and pulled up to the ceiling where the ropes were anchored. He was bound for only a brief moment before quickly breaking free.

In the moment he was tangled up, Farrah was still lying on the floor below but sent a stream of obsidian shards up to bury themselves in the vampire's body. They joined the broken shards still in his body from his earlier impalement, but like that attack, the obsidian did not noticeably impede him. He dashed at Dawn, who calmly evaded his attacks.

Unlike Farrah, who was at the beginning of silver rank, Dawn's avatar was closer to the peak. This meant that while her speed was no match for the gold-ranker, she was far better off than Farrah. The experience-born expertise of a diamond-rank essence user was enough to make up the difference with a vampire attacking like a feral beast, wildly swinging at her with clawed hands.

While he was unable to hit her, he was so fast and so ferocious that Dawn could do nothing but avoid attacks. Farrah leapt up from the floor below to attack the vampire from behind but was intercepted. As she arrived behind him, Willoughby snarled and blood spurted from his back, shredding his clothes. Rather than splatter over Farrah, it coalesced into a blood clone between her and the vampire. It looked identical to Willoughby except for its purple-red bruise colouration, reminiscent of Colin's silver-rank form mimicking Jason.

Both Dawn and Farrah sensed through the vampire's aura that creating the clone had cost him considerable power. As Dawn predicted, most of Willoughby's powers were related to creating minions, with little in the way of combat power. He had seen Farrah demonstrate that using ghouls was little use, while his freshly made lesser vampires had been blinked out of his senses steadily during the fight. It was a concerning development but one he could not turn his attention to as he fought the two women.

Willoughby needed to distract one of the women long enough to kill the other; their double-team tactics proved too effective. The blood clone was Willoughby's last resort, the creation that consumed a huge portion of his accumulated life force. Once he defeated the women, he would need to feed on them to completion instead of turning them into lesser vampires. Even then, he would need blood infused with reality core energy as soon as possible.

Unfortunately for Willoughby, a vampire's handful of powers paled compared to those available to an essence user. Farrah had a last resort of her own and, sensing Willoughby expend a huge portion of his power, slipped a gold spirit coin into her mouth. Her Limit Breaker power would greatly extend the time she could use the spirit coin boost to her attributes. The vampire swore as he sensed Farrah's aura grow sharply in strength.

When Farrah used her Limit Breaker ability to confront a gold-rank essence user, she had still been outmatched. This was not the case against a gold-rank vampire, let alone a blood clone that was an inferior duplicate. As she tore through it, Willoughby realised he was not going to win. He tried to flee, dashing past Dawn and aiming for the hole in the exterior wall.

Free of the vampire's attacks, however, Dawn was once again free to use her powers and a web of steel-like thread filled the gap. The vampire crashed into them, trying to force his way through, but they slowed him as Dawn cast a spell. More flaming ropes emerged from the floor, wrapped around the vampire and dragged him back inside.

After that, it was just a matter of time as Dawn continued to impede both the vampire and the clone. Farrah lay into them with power fuelled by the spirit coin she consumed. As a finisher, she transformed the many obsidian fragments she had left in his body into lava, burning him from the inside out. In the end, the vampire was left as a burned wreck, bound to the floor by conjured steel wires it no longer had the strength to break.

"Don't kill it," Dawn said. "Wait for Asano. There's something I want to test."

61
A LOT LIKE A GUESS

JASON STOOD IN FRONT OF THE NETWORK BUILDING, THE CYCLOPS AND other Cabal members still standing in front of him. The air stank of burned flesh from the one that had tried to flee and was slain by the cyclops for making the attempt. A dozen more remained. Jason stood flanked by Shades as he squared-off with the people in front of him.

The cyclops fired its eyebeam at Jason and one of the orbs turned into a shield to intercept it. The powerful beam swiftly annihilated the barrier, but the momentary delay was enough for Jason to step into one of the Shades and vanish.

The other Cabal members took the chance to scatter as the cyclops was focused on Jason, some dashing into the building while others ran into the streets or even started Spider-Manning their way up the side of the building. The cyclops panned its eye over the space in front of the building for Jason, blasting beams at the Shades and eliminating two of them before the rest vanished into shadows.

Jason rose up from the cyclops's own shadow, between it and the building. He immediately made a series of sewing needle dagger strikes into the towering creature's thigh while swiftly chanting spells.

"*Bleed for me.*"
"*Carry the mark of your transgressions.*"
"*Your fate is to suffer.*"

The cyclops didn't enjoy the balanced attributes of an essence user; speed was the price for its size and strength. It was fast for its size but still a brute, all power and no finesse. This made the creature easy pickings for Jason as he locked in his full suite of afflictions.

At silver rank, Jason's affliction array was more terrible than ever. Not only was he able to bypass immunities that had previously stifled him, but he also had more damage effects than ever. His special attack, Punish, had been one of his bread and butter powers from the beginning and continued to be a core technique.

Ability: [Punish] (Sin)

- Special attack (melee, curse, holy).
- Cost: Low mana.
- Cooldown: None.

- Current rank: Silver 2 (07%).

- Effect (iron): Inflicts necrotic damage and the [Sin] affliction.

- Effect (bronze): Inflicts or refreshes the duration of [Price of Absolution].

- Effect (silver): If the target has any instances of [Sin] they suffer an instance of the [Wages of Sin] affliction. If the enemy struck has no instances of [Sin] but does have instances of [Penance], they do not suffer [Sin] or [Wages of Sin]. They instead suffer transcendent damage from this ability in place of necrotic damage and suffer an additional instance of

- [Penance] and instances of [Penance] do not drop off for a short period.

- [Sin] (affliction, curse, stacking): All necrotic damage taken is increased. Additional instances have a cumulative effect.

- [Price of Absolution] (affliction, holy): Suffer transcendent damage for each instance of [Sin] cleansed from you.

- [Wages of Sin] (affliction, unholy, stacking): Suffer necrotic damage over time. Additional instances have a cumulative effect.

- [Penance] (affliction, holy, damage-over-time, stacking): Deals ongoing transcendent damage. Additional instances have a cumulative effect, dropping off as damage is dealt.

Punish was representative of the way Jason fought at his current rank. In the early stages of a fight, it added more necrotic damage than ever. Once Jason had cleansed an enemy, replacing the necrotic afflictions with the transcendent damage penance affliction, the special attack changed to support it.

The cyclops reacted to Jason's attacks, wheeling in place, but his size was an impediment when Jason stayed close. He kicked at Jason, who easily dodged, and tried to back off to leverage his eyebeam. Jason stayed underfoot, frustrating the monoptical giant.

One of Jason's orbs had been destroyed by the first eyebeam attack, but the other one was still floating around him. It moved to the cyclops and vanished as it applied the affliction that caused the cyclops to start spawning butterflies.

- [Harbinger of Doom] (affliction, unholy, stacking): Continually drain mana from the victim to conjure a butterfly that seeks out nearby enemies. The butterflies are incorporeal and deal disruptive-force damage in a small area when destroyed. Butterflies that contact enemies inflict one instance of each non-holy affliction present on the enemy it manifested from, including [Harbinger of Doom]. This effect cannot be cleansed while any other non-holy affliction is in effect. Additional instances can be accumulated. At the time of manifestation, one butterfly is generated for each instance of this affliction.

"Gordon," Jason said and his familiar appeared.

Four orbs manifested around Gordon instead of the usual six, with the two Jason had expended not yet recovered. Four was sufficient for Jason's needs, however.

"Open it up," Jason ordered.

One of the advancements Gordon had made at silver rank was the ability to use any of his abilities via one type of orb, instead of having different orbs with individual functions. Gordon could use all four orbs to fire resonating-force beams at the building. Resonating-force was a damage type with superior armour-penetrating qualities. It tore through non-magical concrete as easily as glass, opening the entire front of the building up as it threw out a cloud of concrete dust, obscuring Jason from the cyclops.

Inside the building, most of the Cabal forces were gathered on the ground floor as the ghouls forced their way up. The Cabal members had already become aware of the events outside after some of the long-limbed people fled inside. Now the wall was stripped away by energy beams that passed right through it and swept over them as well. They rushed outside even as Gordon vanished back into Jason's aura and Jason sank into the cyclops's shadow. In the meantime, butterflies moved from the cyclops in the direction of the emerging crowd.

Jason appeared from one of Shade's bodies on the second floor, in a small janitorial storage room. On the other side of the closed door, he could hear ghouls rushing about.

"Gordon, if any of the people outside decide to run for it, have the butterflies leave them alone," Jason said.

One of Gordon's orbs briefly glowed a brighter blue, signalling his acknowledgement.

"Mr Asano," Shade said. "Some Cabal members are climbing the exterior of the building and may circumvent the Network defenders to reach the people who have yet to reach the upper-floor magical defences."

"Many of them?"

"Only a few on each side of the building, all iron or bronze rank. Some are less interested in breaching the building as much as escaping the fight between you and the cyclops. I recommend deploying Gordon."

"How cool was that cyclops?" Jason asked. "That eyebeam?"

"I think, perhaps, you should try and maintain focus, Mr Asano."

"What do you say, Gordon? Want to play window washer?"

Gordon flashed a blue orb and passed right through the wall.

"What's the situation?" Jason asked.

"The gold-rank vampire seems to have scattered his new lesser vampires amongst the ghouls," Shade explained, having scouted the building as Jason confronted the cyclops. "The vampire's ability to directly control this many ghouls appears to be limited. I believe the lesser vampires are acting as sub-commanders to keep the horde under control."

"What am I dealing with on the other side of this door?"

"A number of ghouls led by one of the lesser vampires tried to ascend the stairs nearby, but the stairs collapsed on them. They are forming a pile and climbing up over one another. The lesser vampire I recognised from a Network tactical team. We've worked with him in the past."

"Let's go save him, then," Jason said. "I'm just sorry we can't do anything for the rest of them."

Jason opened the door and stepped out into an open office space full of toppled cubicle walls teeming with ghouls. Only the closest ones noticed Jason's arrival until he raised his arm, palm outward, and strafed the room with leeches that erupted from his hand.

This quickly drew the attention of the lesser vampire, easy to pick out for not being a twisted, animate corpse. The vampire dashed through the ghouls as Jason raised his other hand in his direction.

"Feed me your sins."

Nigel's tactical section checked the bodies of the long-limbed creatures sprawled on the stairs to confirm they were dead.

"What are these things?" Woolzy wondered out loud. "I thought the Cabal were all myths and fairy tale creatures and such. What's this meant to be? Once upon a time, Stretch Armstrong turned out to be a total prick?"

"Is anyone else feeling that aura?" Darce asked. "It dropped down on us just as we started shooting."

"Yeah," Nigel said. "Asano is here."

"You don't suppose he's chucked in with the Cabal, do you?" Woolzy asked. "I heard he was friendly with one of their vamps and we did kill his brother. And his girlfriend."

"That was the Seppos and their bloody cat-four bloke, not us," Orange said.

"Are you willing to bet your life on him making that distinction?" Digit asked.

"If Asano was against us, his aura would feel a lot worse than arrogant," Nigel said. "Jonno, Thorny, check the exterior for more of those things."

They had shattered the glass wall, attacking the things climbing up the outside. Thorny gripped Jonno's arm as he leaned out to check the exterior, only to duck back in. One of the creatures fell past the window, almost taking him with it. He poked his head out again, looking up to see a floating entity attacking the creatures clinging to the wall with energy beams.

"Asano's here, alright," he said. "I don't think we have to worry about the climbers."

Shade had scouted out each of the lesser vampires, which meant that Jason could jump directly to them. The problem was that after cleansing them of the vampiric taint, they were left weakened, confused and vulnerable, right in the midst of the enemy. He missed the assistance of Kaito, which would have allowed him to throw the essence users out the nearest window to be extracted by helicopter. Instead, Jason started locking them into storage cupboards, copy rooms and any other place he could find not overrun with ghouls.

The only place in the building Jason avoided was the section of the third floor where he could sense Farrah, Dawn and the vampire. The ghouls were pushing further and further up the building, with Jason appearing and disappearing as he needed. On the eighth floor, he encountered some of the Network defenders helping Koen Waters secure a stairwell being overrun with ghouls. Colin started at the top of the stairs and began devouring his way down, enhanced by the flame power he received from Farrah.

Once Gordon returned, Jason had him use his resonating-force beams to bore a hole in the floor from the eighth floor all the way down to the ground. The butterflies that had multiplied on the Cabal members of the ground floor used the hole to flood up through the building, going to work on the ghouls.

Jason arrived where Dawn and Farrah had what was left of the vampire. Farrah had called him over through the party chat, but he hadn't arrived until most of the ghouls were cleared out. Once the Network teams could move back down and retrieve their formerly vampiric companions he had stashed around the building, Jason sought out Farrah and Dawn.

"Why haven't you finished this guy off?" Jason asked after they exchanged stories. "If you think keeping him alive because he might be useful later is a good idea, you need to watch more movies."

"A vampire is not alive," Dawn said. "Its body is a vessel for stolen life force."

"Okay," Jason said.

"This vampire's stolen life force is infused with reality core energy. I suspect that if you drain the life force from vampires, you may be able to absorb that energy yourself, accelerating the advancement of your abilities."

"Hold up," Jason said. "You mean I can use this vampire like a monster core?"

"Very broadly speaking," Dawn said. "I'm not entirely certain it will work, but if it does, it will only be with vampires, who do not truly own the life force they contain."

"I don't want to do that. Monster cores mess up your ability to advance without using more monster cores."

"Reality cores have the same effect, when used for that specific purpose," Dawn said, "albeit to a lesser degree. In this instance, however, the vampires serve as a method of refining the energy. Their bodies should have already soaked up the elements that stain the soul and impede non-core advancement, like filters."

"Should have?" Jason asked. "That sounds a lot like a guess. You did just say the words 'I'm not entirely certain,' which do not fill me with confidence."

"There is a very good chance that there are more of these vampires than anyone realises," Dawn said, "and very few of them will be as weak as this one. If you can get even a little stronger, that may prove critical."

"No," Farrah said. "It's not worth risking your entire future over. Will he advance any faster than if he were using cores?"

"Almost certainly not," Dawn said.

"Then why bother?" Farrah asked. "Advancing through silver rank takes years. Eating a few vampires won't make a big difference."

"It does not have to be a big difference to be important," Dawn said. "You are both still at the early stages of silver rank, where your growth is at its fastest. Asano's abilities are strong against vampires. Advancing them even a little will be to our advantage."

"It's easy to tell someone else to cripple their potential when you're already diamond rank," Farrah said.

"That's enough," Jason said.

As the two women argued, his gaze hadn't left the scorched, helpless vampire.

"Yes, Dawn's asking me to take a crappy risk, but we all know what's at stake. What's the worst that can happen? I have to rank up using cores from now on? I'll trade that for keeping the world safe."

"You don't even know if we need to go around fighting vampires,"

Farrah argued. "Even if there are a bunch of them out there, how does that affect our objectives?"

"Perhaps not at all," Dawn said. "So long as you can convince Jason to not help people when there's an uprising of gold-rank vampires going on, we may not have an issue. Of course, if they learn about the door and its ability to access reality cores, they may come after us."

"It's my choice," Jason said, holding his hand over the vampire.

"Your blood is not yours to keep but mine on which to feast."

The life drain power was enough to finish the vampire.

- You have absorbed refined reality energy. It will be applied to advance your least developed abilities. The purified nature of the energy will not impede your ability to advance through non-energy absorption methods.

- You have absorbed insufficient energy to advance any of your abilities.

Jason's tense shoulders slumped with relief.

"All good," he said. "Looks like I might want to hunt some vampires, if I get the chance."

"See?" Dawn said to Farrah. "I told you it would be fine."

"And I bet the odds looked great when you weren't the one taking the risk."

"What's done is done," Jason said. "It was my choice and it worked out, so there's no point arguing."

"You shouldn't have let her pressure you into it."

Jason laughed as he gave Farrah a reassuring smile.

"Do you think that she's enough to force me into a choice I don't want to make?" he asked. "If I can stand up to the Builder and I can stand up to the Goddess of Knowledge, I can stand up to her."

Farrah frowned but gave a reluctant nod.

"Alright," Jason said, turning back to the vampire. "Let's see if I can shake the last bit of sauce out of the bottle."

He held out his hand and cast another spell.

"*As your life was mine to reap, so your death is mine to harvest.*"

The remnant life force within the vampire was drawn out and absorbed.

- You have absorbed refined reality energy. It will be applied to advance your least developed abilities.

- Ability [Verdict] had advanced from Silver 0 (93%) to Silver 0 (94%).

"Huh," Jason said. "I think I'll need to kill a lot of vampires."

62
IT'S OKAY TO LAUGH

Jason, Dawn and Farrah looked at the burned, drained remains of the vampire lord Willoughby.

"I still don't like the risk you took draining him," Farrah said. "Now that it's done, though, at least one of us has a path to advancement."

Since reaching silver rank, Jason and Farrah had both reached the limits of their early-stage growth spurt. Pushing into the mid and late stages of silver rank would be difficult so long as they remained on Earth. At lower ranks, confronting higher-rank monsters was a path to rapid advancement that Jason especially had taken advantage of, but that was less viable at silver.

Gold-rank monsters were too powerful to casually confront, even for elite essence users. More well-rounded and with fewer exploitable weaknesses, many such monsters were even more dangerous than less-competent essence users of equivalent rank. Without a solid team of elites, going after gold-rank monsters was too risky.

The traditional path to gold involved confronting many silver-rank monsters, ideally those who could pose a greater challenge than average. Gold-rank proto-spaces could offer silver-rank monsters in large numbers and had started to sporadically appear, but not often enough.

Jason and Farrah would need to monopolise those spaces, which they didn't have time for, even if they didn't have to compete with the

Network's strongest forces. After Makassar, even the fight over reality cores wasn't enough to distract the Network from descending on any gold-rank space with enough magically enhanced heavy ordnance to level a small town.

For these reasons, Jason and Farrah had given up on growing their power further until they returned to Farrah's world. The revelation that Jason could advance by treating vampires as monster cores gave Jason, at least, a means of advancement before then.

The biggest advantage of monster core advancement was that cores could be absorbed in larger quantities and slowly processed, compared to the constant need to seek out dangerous conflict. If Jason really could treat vampires like monster cores, then periodically hunting a few vampires before returning to the task at hand could pay off in half a year or so when his abilities grew stronger. Just ten or twenty percent further into silver rank would be a welcome jump in strength.

That did not mean they were about to go off looking for every vampire they could. Dawn and Farrah's victory was hard-fought, even with Dawn's diamond-rank experience and peak silver-rank power. They had the advantage of numbers and a lot of fire abilities, while the vampire's powers played little part. Other vampires would be stronger, which would make a hard fight even with the addition of Jason.

"We shouldn't go out of our way looking for vampires," Jason said. "We have our objective and I have a feeling that we'll be running into them one way or another."

"Agreed," Dawn said. "Future encounters are inevitable, if only because we are unwilling to conscience their behaviour."

"Mr Asano," Shade said, one of his bodies emerging from Jason's shadow.

"Yes?"

"The ritual effect in the palace has ended," Shade said. "They're gone."

Jason bowed his head, his lips pressed tightly together. After a moment, he nodded. The only three bodies of Shade's that Jason hadn't brought into battle were the ones being possessed by Kaito, Asya, and Greg.

"Thank you for setting this up, Dawn. And Shade, thank your dad, when you get the chance."

"The Reaper will not care," Shade said.

"I'd appreciate you doing it anyway."

***

Koen Waters, Annabeth Tilden and a tactical team stood on the eighth floor of the Network building, next to a neatly circular hole in the floor, some two metres across. It descended through the building, all the way down to the lobby.

"What do we do about the hole?" Koen asked.

"For now," Anna said, "we hope it didn't take out anything structurally necessary."

Anna's presence was the main reason for the security team since the ghouls had been eliminated and the surviving Cabal members had fled. A handful of ethereal blue and orange butterflies drifted up from the hole before dropping back down. They were overtly magical, with a glow to their vibrant colouration. There had previously been far more of the butterflies swarming the floors and reducing the ghouls to drained husks that were now scattered all through the building.

"How many dead?" Anna asked.

"We've only done eyeball estimates, but we're looking at maybe two hundred. Maybe more."

"That many?"

"We had a lot of staff on site with the extra shifts we've been running," Koen said. "We managed to evacuate a lot of them upstairs, but then there were the police and military. The Cabal killed quite a lot of them before they pulled back, and the vampire animated them all."

"Do we know where the vampire is? Or Asano? I'm assuming one killed the other."

"We think they fought on the third floor. Asano was brief when we encountered him. He told us about recovering our people and hiding them. The fight seems to be over because we can't feel either aura, so I've sent a section to check it out."

"How are we doing on getting those people back?"

"Our sweeper teams have found them and are bringing them up as we speak."

"Good," Anna said. "After what happened, we need to subject them to every medical test and magical healing known to humankind."

Koen's second-in-command, Manesh, was watching the hole and spoke up.

"Ditto, we have movement."

Koen went to look over the edge of the hole and then took several steps back. A dark figure swept up through the hole and landed in front of him. Jason arrived on dark wings, Dawn and Farrah quickly following with their wings of flame.

"G'day, Koen, Anna," Jason greeted as he pushed the hood of his cloak back.

"You beat the vampire?"

"No, the ladies were the stars of that show while I played ghoul janitor. Did you find your people that I stashed away?"

"We're bringing them back now," Koen said. "Thank you for stepping in, especially after how our organisation has treated you."

"No worries."

"Thank you," Anna echoed. She looked at Dawn curiously. "Last time I saw you, you were category zero."

"Coming back from the dead more powerful than ever is kind of our thing," Jason said. "How are you going to respond to the Cabal's attack?"

Anna glowered.

"We lost a lot of people," she said. "Your intervention prevented the loss of many critical personnel, so our ability to respond to proto-spaces is undiminished. Step one is to recover any isolated survivors while making sure we can still do our job. Protecting the country from proto-spaces and preventing monster waves is the first priority."

Jason nodded his approval.

"What we've lost," Anna continued, "is a huge portion of the administrative staff that allows an organisation as large as ours to function. A lot of our people died today and step two is counting the dead and securing our magical infrastructure. Also making sure that the hole in the middle of our building won't cause it to collapse."

"Maybe we can look at it as an opportunity," Koen's second, Manesh, said.

"What do you mean?" Anna asked.

"You could install an epic fireman's pole."

"Manesh, a lot of people just died," Anna said.

"Seriously, mate," Jason said. "I love a fireman's pole as much as the next bloke, but time and place."

"This coming from you," Farrah said.

"So, what's step three?" Jason asked Anna, forcibly changing the subject.

"After we make sure we're operational, it's time to clean house properly. I'm going to dissolve the Steering Committee and take charge personally."

"You can do that?" Farrah asked.

"She has the support of the tactical department," Koen said.

"Getting blindsided like this shouldn't have happened," Anna said. "It would take someone at the Steering Committee level to poke just the right holes in our security net without being noticed. We've been worried about the committee for a while, with some throwing in with the leadership faction and now others selling us out to the Cabal. The International Committee has already fractured, take in those local IC people who went against the leadership and restructure."

"That's bold," Farrah said.

"We're also going to work with some of the Cabal that split off because they don't want to work with the old vampires," Anna said. "Craig Vermillion is running his own splinter faction. Between us, him and the EOA members that left, back when they realised their group caused the monster waves, we're talking about a whole new group, with members from every major magical faction."

"That's oddly optimistic, in the middle of all this mess," Jason said. "Are there any more old vampires in Australia?"

"No," Koen said. "He came over with the earliest colonial forces. My family has been part of what is now the Network since long before they arrived. I have family records of his being a menace until he grew too strong and went into hibernation."

Koen Waters was an Aboriginal Australian, and Jason was startled to hear that the Network predated colonisation. He was curious as to how that worked given Australia's history of violence and oppression to the indigenous population, but it was far from the time for a history lesson.

"Our contacts in the parts of the Cabal not on team ancient vampire confirm that this vampire was the only one in Australia," Anna said.

"We're low priority compared to Asia and North America, but Europe has the strongest concentration. The southern hemisphere is mostly free of them, with the biggest concentration in South America."

"Small mercies," Jason said. "How are you going to respond to the Cabal?"

"It's too early to say," Anna said. "They declared war today. Hitting hard while they're on the back foot has emotional appeal, but as I said, our priority has to be preventing monster waves."

"The transformation events are bad enough," Koen said.

"We're certainly going to stop fighting over reality cores now," Anna said. "I suspect the Cabal will too, at least for the immediacy. The EOA have been the poor cousins in that fight, but it looks like the door may be open for them now, at least for a while."

"Great," Jason said. "They're using the cores to create boost injections, allowing their superheroes to juice up to gold rank temporarily."

"We know," Anna said. "We all saw your encounter with the EOA in Venezuela."

"You killed them with your brain," Manesh said. "It was scary as shi—"

He stopped talking at a glare from Koen.

"So, what about you?" Anna asked. "You never used that information I gave you."

"Too much risk," Jason said. "Too many variables. That's why no one else was willing to take a shot, right?"

"We thought you might be willing to try."

"I almost did," Jason said. "You gave it to me at my brother's funeral. Made me feel like I had to or I was letting him down. Kind of a prick move."

"I'm sorry," Anna said.

"No, you're not," Jason said. "I don't have to read your emotions to know that, although I can. It's time for us to go."

"Wait," Anna said. "I think Vermillion will want to contact you once he knows you're in the country. Are you still using a phone or did you ditch it?"

"I've still got my phone," Jason said. "The anti-tracking magic makes the roaming charges worse, somehow, but I still have about five million bucks left. I sank most of the cash from that gold you helped me flog off into building Asano Village, but I stopped paying attention to money a while back."

Anna took a notepad and pen from her jacket, scribbled a number down, tore out the page and handed it to Jason. "Vermillion's burner."

"Thanks."

A portal opened on the tower rooftop at the centre of Jason's cloud palace. Jason, Farrah and Dawn stepped through and Jason wandered to the balustrade, looking out over the ocean.

"They're gone," he said as Farrah moved up beside him.

"Yeah," Farrah said. "You alright?"

"I am," he said. "I'm kind of annoyed that they used their final message to the living to tell me to get over myself."

Jason and Farrah shared a look and started laughing.

"I don't know," Jason said. "I feel lighter, somehow. Getting to say goodbye. Maybe it's okay to laugh when you can, even in the dark days."

"I think that might be when it's most important."

Jason went and found all the people he had brought to his cloud palace, left somewhat at a loss by his departure. Some had gone off to explore the palace, although most remained in the hall where the ritual had been conducted. He rounded everyone up and then portalled them back to Asano Village before putting the cloud palace back in its flask.

The families of Greg and Asya were no longer as contentious towards Jason. That wasn't the same as forgiveness, but they'd been admonished by their dead loved ones and saw the magnitude of Jason's resources. It was one thing to see him on the news and another to experience it for themselves. Between the portal, the cloud palace and the ability to call up the dead, they realised that some fights weren't worth picking.

Once all the people were sent home, Jason wanted to leave before his presence called trouble down on Asano Village. Before that, though, he called Vermillion on the number Anna gave him.

"Oh, hey," Vermillion said, sounding distracted.

Jason could hear the roar of a car engine in the background. "You sound busy."

"Little bit," Craig said. "Didn't want to miss you, though."

"Anna gave me your number. Said you might want to hear from me."

"Definitely."

The sound of gunfire came through the phone.

"You aren't playing a video game, are you?" Jason asked.

"Uh, no, I'm not," Craig said. "I don't suppose you're anywhere near Sydney?"

63
DIGNIFIED MOMENT

"This is not going to plan, Craig," Franklin said, sitting in the front passenger seat as Vermillion was driving.

"You think?" Vermillion asked wildly as he kicked off what was left of the bullet-riddled driver-side door.

The streets of Bankstown had been transformed into a realm of stone and fire. The buildings were made from large bricks in dark shades of brown, red and grey. The cars parked on the street had been turned into stone carriages that a team of horses would be hard-pressed to budge. The car Vermillion drove, along with the ones chasing it, had been brought in from the outside.

The streets they drove on, oddly, were still flat asphalt. Due to Bankstown being abandoned by all but the Cabal, this allowed for the cars to take a breakneck pace as they belted through the streets.

"Bryan, did you find that stuff?" Vermillion asked.

"Come on, Vermillion," complained the vampire in the back seat.

"Seriously, Bryan? This is not the time!"

"But it's never the time, is it?" Bryan complained. Vermillion was about to fire back a retort when a fresh stream of bullets pierced the car, one of which hit him in the back of the head.

"Damn it, Bryan."

Bryan didn't say anything.

"Bryan!"

"You already have a cool vampire name," Bryan complained.

"I don't have a cool vampire name, Bryan. It's just my surname."

"Well, my surname is Slansky. No one is going to fear Slansky the vampire."

"My name's Frank."

"And nobody fears you, Frank."

"Oh, you might be surprised," Vermillion said.

"Why would I want to be feared?" Frank asked. "Have you ever tried to find four for a bridge game when everyone thinks you're going to eat them?"

An arrow shot through the gap where the back window used to be, buried itself in Vermillion's shoulder and then exploded, blasting the headrest from his seat and leaving his arm dangling from a strip of flesh. Blood spilled out, but instead of falling away, it transformed into flesh, restoring the massive wound in moments.

"God damn it, Bryan," Vermillion yelled. "Give me the damn stuff."

"I'm not responding to that name."

"Are you…"

Craig bit back his words.

"Night Stalker," he said through gritted teeth. "Can you please give Frank the stuff?"

"Of course, Vermillion," Bryan said, holding out a crude ball of what looked and felt like putty. "All you had to do was ask."

There was a thump as the roof bent inward under immense weight. A pair of huge, taloned claws pierced the roof as some manner of creature landed on it. Frank reached down by his feet and retrieved a sawn-off, double-barrel shotgun with glowing runes carved into the barrels. He casually pointed it at the roof and pulled both triggers, blasting most of the roof off. With a horrific screech, the gargoyle-like creature flew off with its long, leathery wings.

"Where did you get that?" Vermillion asked.

"One of those Network guys at the storage facility," Frank said. "Anyway, you're the one that stole their car. Maybe that's why those Network guys are chasing us so hard."

One of the reasons the car had held up under repeated magical attacks was that of all the cars they could have stolen for the getaway, they found and took the only magical one.

"What were Network people even doing there?" Bryan asked. "Shouldn't they be defending their headquarters right now?"

"I don't think those are Network people anymore," Vermillion said. "The Network is fractured as badly as us, maybe even worse. I'd heard talk of the higher-ups trying to recruit essence magicians, but I didn't think they'd have gotten anyone this strong. Are you still holding on to the stuff? Give it to Frank."

"What do you want putty for anyway?" Bryan asked, holding out the ball again.

"Frank's bloodline lets him absorb materials and pass their properties on to his blood," Vermillion explained.

"Why would you want your blood to be like putty?" Bryan asked.

Frank bit his finger, drawing blood that flowed out of the wound and over the ball in his hand. It was swiftly melted down and absorbed, even the spilled blood crawling back into his skin. Frank then bit his finger right off before plucking it from his mouth and tossing it out the window. When one of the pursuing cars drove over it, an explosion underneath sent the car rolling out of the chase. Frank's finger quickly grew back.

"You really thought that was putty, Bryan?" Vermillion asked.

"Night Stalker!"

"Night Stalker doesn't even sound like a vampire name," Vermillion said. "It sounds like a rapist from the eighties."

"But not an actual rapist," Frank said. "More like a rapist from one of those daytime TV movies where a housewife learns that handsome men are all terrible."

"You can both go fu—"

He was interrupted by Vermillion swerving the car hard, banging Night Stalker's head and smashing the car's last intact window.

"Sorry," Vermillion said. "That pothole had lava in it."

Jason, Dawn and Farrah stepped out of a portal near the border of Bankstown. Jason hadn't been able to send them to a familiar location like the airport because there were no familiar locations left. Bankstown had been transformed both physically and magically, down to the smallest particle.

"I think this is the right street," Jason said, extending his senses.

Dawn did the same while Farrah rolled her shoulders, shifting her body. She was still appreciating that she no longer suffered disorientation from teleportation after gaining the astral affinity of an outworlder.

"There they are," Jason said. "Oh, crikey."

Jason sensed a large number of magical auras moving at speed, along with a lot of overt magic being thrown around.

"Are those magic guns I'm sensing?" Jason asked.

"I believe they are," Dawn said.

"He must have some Network people chasing him," Jason said, tilting his head as if trying to hear a distant sound more clearly. "Yeah, those are essence abilities going off. Silver rank, damn. Who did Craig get cranky?"

"Maybe we should go find out," Farrah suggested.

"Yep," Jason agreed. "Shade, if you would?"

Five Shade bodies appeared from Jason's shadow and merged together, taking on the form of a huge, four-seater car. It had sleek, hypercar lines and a smattering of glowing white embellishments on what was, of course, a glossy black body.

"Okay, I'm going to get sued," Jason said. "This is a straight-up Batmobile."

"I could add non-trademarked badging," Shade offered, "but you would need a simple and elegant logo. Your personal crest does not translate into a clean, easily iconic symbol."

"Are you saying I need a superhero emblem?" Jason asked.

"It would help," Shade said.

"Can we please go?" Dawn asked. "We need to go catch up with them."

"Good point," Jason said, peering at the car. "Which part is the door?"

"Where exactly are we going?" Frank asked as the careening chase continued.

"Away," Vermillion said, swerving the car around a corner as they rushed through Bankstown's empty streets.

"I don't like 'away' being the most solid plan we have," Frank said.

An explosion to the right of the car tore up asphalt.

"You may have missed it, Frank, but even just 'away' is a high bar right this second."

"We don't even have the blood and cores, though," Night Stalker said. "We're the decoy car."

"They don't know that," Vermillion said. "Do you not understand what a decoy is?"

The gargoyle-like creature swept down once more but was met with a bloody mist that Night Stalker spat out and it backed off. Vermillion was about to turn the car hard into another corner, when he was startled by something popping up in the middle of his eyeline.

"What the hell?"

- You have received a party invitation from [Jason Asano]. Accept Y/N?

Vermillion moved his head to look around the obstruction, but it kept moving to the middle of his view and he almost ran the car into a stone carriage parked on the side of the road.

"What are you doing?" Frank asked.

"Yes, god damn it," Vermillion yelled.

"Yes, what?" Frank asked.

Missing the corner and then almost crashing had allowed the cars pursuing them to close in. Frank and Night Stalker were gearing up to fend off fresh attacks when a series of what looked like orange lasers started laying into the other vehicles, slicing them up like pieces of cake.

"What's doing that?" Frank asked.

Watching out the back window, Night Stalker saw the source of the attacks.

"It looks like a space cloud shooting lasers from on top of the Batmobile."

The lack of cars didn't entirely end the pursuit as the most powerful Cabal members and essence users who had been in the cars gave chase on foot, moving at speeds comparable to a car. There was also the large gargoyle creature still flying after them.

Gordon made short work of the non-magical cars, although the people inside proved more resilient as they sprang from the wreckage to continue pursuing Vermillion's car.

"I'm surprised Craig's car is still running," Jason said. "It must be one of the Network's magically enhanced ones, right?"

"I imagine so," Farrah said.

Vermillion's car was a wreck on wheels, missing two of the doors and most of the roof, the rest riddled with damage. The fact that all four wheels were intact was too much of a miracle to be anything but magic.

Jason and Dawn both snapped their heads to the left at the same time.

"That may be trouble," Dawn said.

"I'll deal with it," Jason said. "You two make sure our enthusiastic joggers don't run down his car. He almost crashed back there, so I'm not sure he's the best driver."

Farrah strained her senses and picked up what the others had already sensed.

"A conjured vehicle. Vermillion isn't the only one bringing in reinforcements."

Vehicle specialists were more common on Earth than Farrah's world. Many were flyers like Kaito and his helicopter, but land-based vehicles were more the norm, trading off the capability to fly for an increase in combat power.

Australia didn't have a lot of vehicle users, compared to China, who boasted a higher percentage of them than any other major nation. Combined with China's population, this made for a powerful force. Jason had occasionally seen them in action in large, multi-national actions like Makassar.

Because of Australia's deficit, Jason quickly guessed the identity of the silver-ranker coming his way in a huge, armoured personnel carrier. It wasn't someone he'd worked with personally, but Kaito's specialised training had been carried out by the senior vehicle specialist.

Jason opened the car door and hopped out, using weight reduction to drift a moment and slow down before dropping his feet to the asphalt. Gordon waited on his left, with Shade on his right. A short time later, a huge, futuristic armoured vehicle roared around the corner before slowing down to a stop.

"Jason Asano," an amplified voice boomed from the vehicle. "I have no quarrel with you. Please walk away and don't involve yourself in this affair."

"Andreas Kosmopoulos," Jason responded, his own voice booming in a trick of voice projection. "You're chasing a friend of mine. I'm not going to let that go."

"He stole from us."

"Putting aside that the goods in question were plundered from reality itself and that none of you have a right to them," Jason said, "he stole from the Cabal. Last time I checked, you were a member of the Network. Brisbane branch, if I remember rightly."

"These are dangerous days and the old order is breaking down," Kosmopoulos responded. "If the ship is sinking, you find anything you can that floats."

"You've grabbed an anchor, Andreas, not driftwood. Let go, before clinging to it drags you under."

"And what would you know, Asano? Running around the world, not having to watch everything you've come to rely on crumble and break. You were never in the Network. You never understood what it meant to be a part of it. How much was lost when it crumbled. Human civilisation is over; people just don't know it yet. Now it's about monsters claiming the biggest pile of the rubble that they can."

"I'm sorry you feel that way," Jason said. "I haven't given up quite yet and I'll never give up on my friends."

"I know you're powerful, Asano, but this is a bad fight for you. Only a fool fights a vehicle specialist on the road. My vehicle has no blood to poison or flesh to rot. It's shielded against teleportation and intangible creatures, so neither you nor your familiars can breach it."

A panel in the massive vehicle's roof opened up and a huge rotary cannon emerged.

"It has weapons you cannot endure," Kosmopoulos continued. "The matchup is bad for you, Asano. Leave."

"You're one of those people that sees a guy on the TV and thinks 'I could take him,' aren't you?"

"Very well, Asano. Bear the consequences of your actions."

The rotary cannon spooled up and spat bullets. Gordon turned into a swirling nebula and dashed away before reforming, while Jason ducked into Shade and vanished. The gun tracked Gordon, but six orange beams bore down on the weapon and sheared it off. A force field snapped into place around the vehicle and a new gun that immediately started firing was conjured in place of the damaged one.

Gordon sank into the ground, avoiding the bullets, and started popping up in random places to blast six blue beams at the force field, only to vanish into the ground as the gun rapidly swung in his direction.

The silver-rank bullets fired specialty ammunition that added disruptive-force to the impact of the bullets, ideal for an incorporeal creature like Gordon. Sensitive to the dangerous damage type, he used dashes to avoid them. In between dashes, he fired bursts of the same damage: blue beams of pure disruptive force that were highly effective against the force field.

The armoured vehicle started moving again, heading once more in pursuit of the other vehicles. As the force field collapsed, Jason appeared from behind a stone carriage and used his cloak's weight reduction to leap high into the air. His shadow arms reached out, grabbed the now-unshielded APC and dragged him to it. Its exterior immediately electrified, causing his body to jerk and twitch, tumbling, off the back to faceplant the street as the vehicle roared away.

"Not my most dignified moment," he groaned into the asphalt.

64

WHEN SOMEONE IS UNDER YOUR GUN

Jason pushed himself to his feet with a groan, his body still tingling from the electrical attack. The magical APC, looking like something from a sci-fi movie, had left him behind and was roaring around a corner in pursuit of the others.

"It's possible that you have been looking down on Earth's essence users too much," Shade suggested.

"I was thinking the same thing," Jason agreed. "If you would?"

Shade took the form of a motorcycle and Jason climbed aboard as Gordon disappeared into Jason. Two of Gordon's orbs appeared in his place and started orbiting around Jason as the motorcycle took off. The APC was fast, but the much smaller bike was both faster and more manoeuvrable, leading Jason to soon catch up.

A machine gun emerged from a recessed panel atop the APC and fired backwards. One of the orbs turned into a shield to intercept the bullets. The disruptive force added to the damage quickly destabilised the shield, but Jason started swerving left and right to buy more time before it collapsed.

The shield collapsed and the second orb took its place, although it, too, was swiftly chewed through. Bullets hit Jason and his cloak intercepted the attacks, but as with the shields, the disruptive force on the bullets was effective at negating much of his cloak's protective power. That left a good portion of the kinetic impact to slam into Jason.

Without a bunch of handy minions to afflict, Jason was at his weakest with both his physical fortitude and regenerative powers at their lowest point. That being said, at silver rank, the lowest point was still very good and Jason endured the barrage to draw closer to the vehicle.

"Let's give him some more targets," Jason said.

Six more bikes appeared alongside him, with Shade's bodies riding them. Jason conjured up starlight cloaks on each, and they started weaving amongst each other, making which one was him harder to pick out. The machine gun started spraying them all, but with the bullets more diffuse, the cloaks were better able to endure them.

Jason cast a spell at the APC, but as he did, the force field Gordon had torn down earlier snapped back into place around the vehicle.

"Bleed for me."

- You have afflicted target with [Blood From a Stone].
- You have afflicted target with [Necrotoxin].
- You have afflicted target with [Sacrificial Victim].
- You have afflicted target with [Bleeding].

- Target is fully shielded.

- [Blood From a Stone] does not take effect.
- [Necrotoxin] does not take effect.
- [Sacrificial Victim] does not take effect.
- [Bleeding] does not take effect.

"Bloody hell."

Jason had been spoiled by an aspect common to his spells, which was affecting targets directly, without an intermediary like a projectile. This was common in low-impact spells, the signature of affliction specialists like himself. Powers that provided comprehensive shields, however, were highly effective against such spells. Sadly for Jason, such powers were common, especially amongst healers. Jason had learned the frustration of that in the mock battles between his team and that of Prince Valdis of the Mirror Kingdom.

"Go again, Gordon."

The nebulous familiar appeared and jumped out ahead of the APC in a series of dashes before once more blasting the vehicle's force field with blue beams. The front-firing rotary cannon reappeared to harass him, preventing Gordon from constantly barraging the force field. Gordon also had two fewer beams, due to the orbs Jason had consumed as shields.

Seeing the limited effectiveness of his approach, Gordon instead fired two of his remaining six orbs at the shield. The orbs came into contact just before they reached it and exploded with blue energy. The powerful blast of disruptive force caused the APC's shield to collapse again, but Gordon was largely disarmed until his orbs recovered, which would take a minute for each. He fell back to be subsumed once more into Jason.

The APC had not been idle while Gordon worked. A roof panel slid aside and a stream of micro missiles fired up into the air before turning back and raining down on Jason and the Shades just as Gordon returned.

"Is this a bloody anime?" Jason decried as the bikes spread out.

Gordon's last two orbs manifested beside Jason and started firing orange beams to intercept the missiles, the pinpoint beams intercepting the ones tracking Jason himself. The bulk of the projectiles hammered down on the Shades, however, rocking them with explosions.

Inside the APC, Andreas Kosmopoulos watched the rear monitor where the chasing motorcycles had disappeared into a dust cloud as the missiles blasted the road.

"Did we get him?" asked the other person in the APC, a Cabal member named Javier.

"No," Andreas said. "There's no way that Jason Asano went down from that."

The driver's station in the APC was a futuristic command station with multiple screens and glowing control panels. There were no vulnerable windows in the vehicle, the exterior monitored through a series of external cameras. Asano was frustratingly hard to pin down, the vehicle's normally excellent tracking systems having trouble targeting him. Even his image on the cameras was something of a blur, and the heat tracking couldn't pick him up in the dust cloud.

Andreas glanced at the recharge time on the shield. One of his most critical defensive measures, it had now been rapidly brought down twice. His only consolation was that he was confident in the resilience of his vehicle. While Asano's powers were famously destructive to life, the APC had no blood to bleed and no flesh to rot.

The conjured vehicle of a true specialist like Kaito or Andreas differed from most conjured items. The APC was much more powerful than something like Jason's dagger, but it held commensurate weaknesses. It was critical to many of Andreas's other abilities that were either diminished or didn't function at all without it. The biggest drawback was that once destroyed, there was a considerable cooldown before it could be called up again. There were other conjured vehicles he could use, but these would only be lesser placeholders.

On the rear monitor, Asano emerged from the dust cloud. His decoy bikes were gone, but he appeared unharmed. Andreas was retasking the rear gun when the damage report monitor started flashing red.

"MULTIPLE ABNORMAL CONDITIONS DETECTED," came the APC's mechanical voice. "INTRINSIC NATURE COMPROMISED."

"Intrinsic nature compromised?" Andreas wondered aloud. His APC had been subject to all manner of attacks over the years, but this was something new.

"Andreas," Javier called out in a panicked voice. "What's that?"

A red liquid was leaking from between the spot where two wall panels joined.

"Some kind of mechanical fluid, probably," Andreas said. "Asano is using some kind of attack I've never seen before."

"ADDITIONAL ABNORMAL CONDITIONS DETECTED. INTRINSIC NATURE FURTHER COMPROMISED."

Javier transformed into a wolfman, occupying more of the interior space, but the APC was designed for moving groups of people. He sniffed at the liquid. Meanwhile, Andreas tried to get to the bottom of the continuing alarms.

"Define error 'intrinsic nature compromised,'" he commanded.

"Mechanical systems are now subject to biological vulnerabilities on multiple parameters."

"What does that mean?" Andreas asked.

"It means that your vehicle is bleeding," Javier growled with his wolf mouth.

"It doesn't have any blood," Andreas said.

"I don't think the guy who fought a zombie army with magic butterflies really cares."

Vermillion's stolen car was being pursued by multiple silver-rankers on foot. Three were vampires, including the one that had transformed into the gargoyle-like creature harassing them from the air. The other two were essence users, poached by the Cabal.

Vermillion's stolen car had endured a lot of abuse, but the pursuers had avoided using their most powerful attacks for fear of damaging the stolen goods. They hadn't realised those goods were not in the car at all. Finally, the car succumbed to a death by a thousand cuts. The engine gave out, the car slowing to a stop in the middle of the street.

A new black car dashed up, skidding to a halt in between the bullet-riddled car and the people chasing it. Dawn and Farrah stepped out, facing off against the pursuers. Seeing that Vermillion and the others in the broken car were not running, the pursuers slowed down to face off with the new arrivals. Vermillion, Frank and Night Stalker moved out to stand with Dawn.

"Farrah," Craig greeted. "It's been a while."

The two essence users and the two vampires on foot came to a stop. The gargoyle-like creature flew down and transformed into a naked man.

"Larry," Frank admonished. "Put on some damn pants."

"You don't get to tell me what to do, traitor," Larry said. "Besides, the ladies might like what they see."

Dawn and Farrah looked Larry up and down, shared a glance, and both smirked derisively.

"Hey…" Larry said, moving his hands to cover himself before turning back into a leathery monster.

One of the essence users hadn't shifted his gaze from Farrah.

"I've been wondering about you for a long time, Hurin," he said. "Coming here, acting like you're so much better than us. Teaching us how to use our powers as if we're ignorant primitives. You're supposed to be so great; I'd like to see it for myself."

Farrah conjured her obsidian armour and jagged sword.

"Happy to oblige," she said.

Farrah had never been plagued by Jason's self-doubt and fears of moral decay. If someone wanted to make themself her enemy, she would cut them down and sleep like a baby that night.

"It doesn't have to get violent," the other essence user said. "Just give us what you took and we can all walk away."

"The hell we can," one of the vampires spat. "You think they can just take from us and walk away?"

"Their vampires are second-grade weaklings," another vampire said. "Why make concessions when we are stronger?"

Each side had two essence users and three vampires, but the three Cabal vampires were silver rank, while Vermillion, Franklin and Night Stalker were only bronze.

"I hate to break it to you, but you got duped," Vermillion told them. "You chased the decoy. The blue blood and the reality cores are long gone."

"Enough talk," the first essence user said, raising his arm.

An obsidian wall raised up in his face, which shattered as the lightning blast from his arm struck it. The shattered fragments then rocketed towards the essence user in a storm of razor-sharp stone. Dawn timed the casting of a spell to activate right as the essence user was distracted; he didn't notice the magic circle appearing under his feet. As the stone storm passed, webbing shot up from the circle to swiftly mummify him. Farrah smoothly followed up with a spell of her own.

"*Fire bolt.*"

A blazing orb shot from Farrah's hand towards the essence user mummified in webbing. The webbing ignited immediately, throwing off an intense heat as it burned. Even so, it was being consumed slowly and kept the essence user bound as he had to force his way free.

"Oh, that's nice," Farrah said, admiring Dawn's spell as her fire bolt chained to the other essence user and the vampires. One quick spell was far from enough to deter silver-rankers, even if vampires were more vulnerable to fire. Their skin burning, they lunged into the wall that was Farrah and Dawn, the two women proving as impassable as a steel barrier.

One of the vampires was trapped in more threads that shot up from the ground, immediately igniting from Farrah's flames still burning on him. Another found Farrah's whip-sword wrapping around him, the obsidian fragments piercing his skin and the lava cord searing his flesh. Vermillion and his companions teamed up to fend off Larry, the flying monstrosity.

Bankstown was now supernaturally volcanic, which suited Farrah just fine. There was a pyroclastic flow running alongside the road and she dragged the vampire wrapped in her sword in that direction.

"This is going to be fun."

"Catastrophic system failure," the APC announced amongst a constant stream of warning messages.

"Your machine has a penchant for the obvious," Javier growled.

The APC was melting around them, the walls were dripping black, poisoned blood from panels starting to look more like distressed flesh than metal as it fell off in gobbets. Andreas was trying every weapon ability he had while feeding as much mana as it would take into the self-repair system. The APC continued to let out warnings.

"Self-repair has negated condition 'bleeding' and will resume normal function. Condition 'bleeding' has been applied. Self-repair system diverting resources to negate condition 'bleeding.' Self-repair has negated condition 'bleeding' and will resume normal function. Condition 'bleeding' has been applied. Self-repair system diverting resources..."

Andreas slapped his hand on the mute button. The rapidly degrading state of the APC was affecting the weapon systems, but there were still enough to hammer Asano with bullets, a flamethrower, and even the occasional rocket-propelled grenade. He watched in frustration and disbelief as Asano stopped avoiding the attacks. He only needed to periodically call up a new motorcycle as the one he was riding became damaged. Asano himself seemed invincible.

"Is that guy immortal?"

With afflictions applied and his Inexorable Doom ability continually stacking more, Jason's protective amulet was rapidly ticking over.

Item: [Amulet of the Dark Guardian] (growth, silver rank, legendary)

- Effect: For each instance of an affliction applied to an enemy, gain an instance of [Guardian's Blessing]. You may bestow all instances of [Guardian's Blessing] upon another person by touch.

- [Guardian's Blessing] (boon, holy): Instances are consumed to absorb damage from any source. Additional instances have a cumulative effect. For each instance consumed, gain an instance of [Blessing's Bounty].

- [Blessing's Bounty] (heal-over-time, holy, stacking): Heal over time. Additional instances have a cumulative effect.

Each affliction became a shield and each shield became a regenerative effect, which was boosted in strength by the blood robes Colin allowed Jason to conjure. Added to the formidable resilience of a silver-ranker and the diminishing attack power of the heavily damaged vehicle, Jason was no longer in any danger, although a large number of Shade bodies had been chewed through. It would take a lot of time and mana to replenish them, but for the moment, Jason had a fight to finish. From the back of his motorcycle, he cast a spell.

"*Suffer the cost of your transgressions.*"

Punition dealt damage for every instance of every affliction on the target. Jason sank extra mana into the spell and the APC's structure started to sag like a bouncy castle with a hole in it.

Ability: [Punition] (Doom)

- Spell.
- Cost: Moderate mana.
- Cooldown: 30 seconds.

- Current rank: Silver 2 (17%).

- Effect (iron): Inflicts necrotic damage for each curse, disease, poison and unholy affliction the target is suffering.

- Effect (bronze): Inflicts or refreshes the duration of [Penitence].

- Effect (silver): Damage per affliction can be increased by increasing the mana cost to high, very high, or extreme. This reduces the cooldown to 20 seconds, 10 seconds or none. Consecutive, extreme-cost incantations have truncated incantations.

- [Penitence] (affliction, holy): Gain an instance of [Penance] for each curse, disease, poison or unholy effect that is cleansed from you. This is a holy effect.

- [Penance] (affliction, holy, damage-over-time, stacking): Deals ongoing transcendent damage. Additional instances have a cumulative effect, dropping off as damage is dealt.

Maximising the mana cost also maximised the damage and negated the cooldown, turning the spell into a high-damage mana-sink. He cast the spell again straightaway, with the truncated incantation, then once more, the spell burning through his mana supply.

"*Suffer.*"

"*Suffer.*"

With each spell, the APC deflated alongside Jason's mana supply, but to his surprise and admiration, it was not yet destroyed. Unsure if it would even work, he cast another spell.

"*Feed me your sins.*"

Jason drained the accumulated afflictions from the APC, which apparently qualified as an enemy. He was unsure if it was because he'd been able to levy afflictions on it or because it was a special kind of conjured object. Either way, Jason was replenished by consuming the massive array of afflictions he drained from it, filling his mana and stamina well past full. They continued to rise, along with his health, as the enemy afflictions were converted into a stackable recovery buff.

The APC no longer looked like a stricken beast and more like the vehicle it was, albeit one that had been plunged into a lava pit. It was glowing bright with transcendent damage that cared nothing for active defence mechanisms and auto-repair systems as it chewed away at the metal. Jason cast the final spell.

"*Mine is the judgement and the judgement is death.*"

The two men inside the APC were surrounded in transcendent light and the APC finally succumbed. They fell to the road as the moving vehicle around them vanished as the conjuration ended. That was not enough to injure someone of their rank and they quickly jumped to their feet.

Looking around, they saw a dark figure walking towards them, the motorcycle behind him dissolving into a dark cloud and being drawn into his shadow. Silver eyes watched them from a dark hood as he slowly approached. With the cloak wrapped around him and his smooth steps, it was almost like he was floating. The intimidating visage was broken as Jason pushed the hood back off his head, revealing a face bloodied from a bullet that had hit him in the head.

"Hello, Andreas."

"Jason," Andreas said warily. "I'm sorry about Kaito."

"Not so sorry that you wouldn't try and kill his brother."

"You're protecting someone who stole from us."

"Reality cores aren't yours to possess."

"Only you get to have them?" Andreas countered.

"No one gets to have them," Jason said. "You're strip-mining reality. You think that won't have consequences?"

"We've heard your claims," Javier growled, still a hulking wolfman. "No one believes you're going to save the world, Asano."

"I know. I'm going to save it anyway. Go home, Andreas."

"You're letting me go?"

"Yeah. Do me a favour and remember that when someone is under your gun and you have a choice to make."

Javier looked from Andreas to Jason.

"You aren't just going to let this go?" he asked.

Andreas looked at the wolfman.

"He beat me at my best, and now I'm at my worst. You want to take him on, that's your business."

Javier turned to lunge at Jason, but Jason's aura came crashing down like a hammer. With just one target and nothing else to distract him, Jason could apply his aura at full force.

Title: [Giant Slayer]

- Overcoming a much stronger enemy has left a permanent mark on you that can be sensed by others. This may trigger a fear reaction from the unintelligent and the weak-willed if your aura is significantly stronger than theirs. Your actual rank being lower than theirs does not diminish the effect.

The wolfman froze, trembling like a prey animal.

"Take him home, Andreas."

Andreas looked at the stiff Javier and felt the fear drenching an aura hunkered down like a mouse under the gaze of an owl. He turned to look at Jason.

"Thank you."

65

WHEN, NOT IF

Farrah dragged a vampire out of the lava by the foot. He was still alive, or at least undead, due to his silver-rank fortitude. His normal vampiric healing was not kicking in, though, due to the burn damage.

"Why are you letting him out?" Night Stalker asked. "You should finish him."

"We came to save you, not to kill the people you robbed," Farrah said.

"What if they come after us again?" Night Stalker asked.

"Then you can lament your mediocre life choices."

"Leave it, Bryan," Franklin said.

"Forget this; I'll do it myself."

Night Stalker moved to grab the crippled vampire, only to find himself looking down the length of Farrah's sword.

"This is all very tense," Jason said from behind the group. No one but Dawn had noticed his arrival. The car Farrah and Dawn arrived in had turned back into a group of Shade's bodies, one of which Jason had stepped out of.

"G'day, Craig," Jason said.

"Jason," Vermillion said with a greeting nod. "Thank you for the save."

Jason looked around at a section of street marred by magical battle. There were scorch marks everywhere and a takeaway shop had what was left of Vermillion's stolen car sticking out of it. The two essence users were battered but alive, both strapped down to the road by webs that had the gleam of metal. There were three vampires, all severely burned and far too hurt to keep fighting. Vermillion and his companions had torn and bloody clothes, but their injuries had already recovered.

"This is Frank," Vermillion introduced. "And this is Night Stalker."

"Night Stalker?" Jason said. "Like the serial killer from the eighties?"

"It doesn't sound like a serial killer name," Night Stalker insisted.

"Yeah," Jason agreed. "It doesn't sound like a serial killer name. It *is* a serial killer name. There was a guy in the eighties who raped and killed a bunch of people in California. If you're a vampire and you're going to run around calling yourself the Night Stalker, I'm going to put you down now and call it a public service."

"It's fine, Jason. He's not running around killing people; he's just an idiot. How do you know so much about serial killers?"

"I went to school with this guy who collected serial killer trading cards. Greg and I used to…"

Jason trailed off, hanging his head.

"It doesn't matter," he said. "Craig, why are you chasing reality cores?"

"We're forming an alliance with members of the EOA and the Network. We have the numbers, but the leadership factions of each have most of the strongest members. We need to get stronger, fast."

"Are you going to be fighting in the transformation zones over cores?"

"Yeah."

"Don't expect further help, then. Reality cores aren't for anyone to have. That goes for you as much as your enemies."

"Our enemies are your enemies, Jason. Will you let them run rampant?"

"You're squabbling over who gets to be captain of a sinking ship, Craig, and you're throwing people overboard to keep it afloat. Look at the state of the world. The army is fighting mythical creatures in the streets of Sydney. America is on the brink of civil war because the Network wasn't careful enough with their secret coup. Europe is being taken over by vampires and China is reaching new heights of civic oppression keeping a lid on everything. Governments are turning tyrant or in danger of collapsing entirely. We're on the verge of anarchy."

"Our alliance wants to remedy that," Craig said. "Keep preventing the monster waves. Protect the people. But we need the strength to do that. Look, if you can tell me how to help you save the world or whatever, I will. I don't think I'm what you need, though. So let us do what we can and you do what you can."

Jason turned away, running a dirty hand over his bloody face.

"Craig," he said, his voice weary. "Going after reality cores is pulling down the roof to burn for warmth in winter."

"And not going after them is putting down your sword while your enemy is picking his up."

"It doesn't matter who wins if the world burns."

"But it does if you save it," Craig said. "That's what you're doing, right? Saving the world. We're trying to make sure it's still worth a damn when you do."

"He's not wrong," Farrah said.

"Whose side are you on?" Jason asked.

"Yours," she said. "Sometimes that means telling you to let something go and get on with the job."

Jason looked at her, his expression unhappy, but he didn't argue.

"People taking reality cores is a bad thing," she told him. "But do you think that telling Craig not to do it matters in the long run? You're frustrated that it's happening. We all are. But this is not the place to make that stand because it gets you nothing."

"Farrah's perspective on this is wise," Dawn agreed. "I likewise detest that the denizens of this world would ravage it for power, but you aren't going to convince them to stop. People will always ignore the greater dangers in pursuit of momentary concerns. Humans, elves, this world or another. It is true every time, in every reality."

"The only way to stop people from taking reality cores is to cut off the supply," Farrah said. "Which is a task we should probably get back to."

"You can do that?" Craig asked.

Farrah winced.

"I shouldn't have said that."

Craig shared a look with Franklin and they flashed into motion, grabbing a startled Bryan, dragging him to the lava flow and shoving him in, head first. Jason, Farrah and Dawn shared a confused look.

"Craig?" Jason asked.

The two vampires held Bryan under until he stopped moving, which didn't take long for the bronze-rank vampire.

"What was that about?" Farrah asked.

"Bryan was a plant," Craig said. "The faction of the Cabal loyal to the old vampires inserted him to infiltrate the new alliance forming against them."

"You're sure?" Jason asked.

"Yeah. We didn't give him a heads-up about hitting the reality core storage but brought him along so he would think he was in the inner circle. We were going to use him for misinformation, but we can't let the old vampires know you can turn off the tap. They'll make you their number one priority."

"I'm sorry," Farrah said. "I should be more careful."

"I didn't sense any duplicity from his aura," Dawn said. "Bloodline dominance?"

"Yes," Craig said.

"Which is what, exactly?" Jason asked.

"The dominus vampire bloodline allows those higher in the lineage to completely control those below it," Dawn said. "When a dominus vampire creates another vampire, they can control it, along with any more that vampire subsequently creates."

"Bryan was part of the dominus bloodline," Vermillion confirmed. "We're pretty sure that one of the old ones in Southeast Asia somewhere was controlling him."

"Bloodline domination functions rather like a star seed," Dawn explained. "Like a star seed, it is extremely difficult to detect outside of special circumstances."

"I had a bond with Bryan, using my bloodline," Vermillion said. "The bond was severed when the domination was put in place. That's how we caught it."

"A star seed hides so well because it infiltrates the soul," Jason said. "How does this bloodline get in?"

"Only lesser vampires are transformed in body alone," Dawn said. "Greater vampires —bloodline vampires—are changed body and soul. It is why they cannot be forcibly turned, unlike lesser vampires. They have to accept the change."

"We have to accept the gift," Franklin corrected.

"Mate, I'd return that gift," Jason said. "It makes you eat people."

After parting with Vermillion, Jason sent himself, Farrah and Dawn out to sea via portal and set up a cloud house. Distractions aside, they still had a node to repair and Jason needed to recover from the fight. A good number of Shade's bodies had been wiped out by the APC's weapon systems and it took most of Jason's full mana supply to reconstitute one. He had managed to replace a few using the mana he had after the fight, far above his normal maximum, but there was still work to do.

Jason went off to shower before he started meditating to replenish his mana as fast as possible. Midway through the shower, he swore out loud.

- Cloud flask supply of [Crystal Wash] has been exhausted.
- Supply additional [Crystal Wash] or an alternative cleansing agent to maintain cloud construct cleansing effect.

He was surprised it had lasted as long as it had. The flask had done an effective job of diluting the huge quantity Jason had fed into it. That didn't stop him from being aggravated when it finally ran out.

While Jason was showering, Farrah and Dawn went to the balcony to relax as they overlooked the Pacific. Farrah took the chance to ask some questions.

"I've been wondering about the vampires of this world. Do you know why they have so much more self-control than the vampires of mine? Is it the lower magic, somehow?"

"That is one of two factors," Dawn said. "Magically charged sunlight has a negative effect on vampires. In the short-term, this means their strength is greatly reduced in sunlight. In the long-term, it has a degenerative effect on their minds."

"Does that mean as the magic of this world gets stronger, the vampires will start losing control?"

"Eventually, some of them will, yes," Dawn said. "There is also the other factor to consider, however, which is strength of bloodline. The vampires of this world were spawned as echoes of other worlds. The oldest likely had the full strength of bloodline originators, so many of this world's vampires have much richer bloodlines than those of your world. It will shield them from sun degeneration."

"So, even the old vampires now being woken up can be reasoned with."

"Yes," Dawn said. "Although I would not hold out great hope. Their personalities may not have been warped due to their vampirism, but they will still be huge arseholes."

Farrah raised her eyebrows at Dawn's unexpected vulgarity and they both started laughing.

Jason trudged through the cloud house, where he encountered Dawn.

"Oh," he said, looking up. "Dawn, you don't know how to make crystal wash, do you?"

"I'm not an alchemist."

"But you could get the formula, right? Or something that works the same from another universe or whatever."

"Not while I'm in this avatar."

"But if we killed you off, though, you could grab the formula from wherever and bring it back when you made a new avatar. Then we just have to find a decent local alchemist… why are you looking at me like that?"

Dawn walked away.

"Is that a no?" he called out after her.

He continued on his way, finding Farrah on the balcony, lounging as she looked out over the ocean. He fell backwards as a deck chair made of cloud rose from the floor to catch him.

"All done?" she asked.

"Every Shade, present and accounted for. How goes the proto-space hunt?"

Finding the right nodes to repair required carrying out rituals in proto-spaces. As they improved their understanding of the process through trial and error, they had a better grasp of which proto-spaces would help them and which ones would throw out false positives. It allowed them to be more discerning in their activities, making the search for each individual proto-space take longer but ultimately saving them time.

"We had one hit, but it was a gold-rank space. You were still down a bunch of Shades and I thought trying it at anything less than full strength was a bad idea."

"You didn't tell me."

"Bad ideas are kind of your thing."

Jason chuckled.

"I suppose they are."

He pulled a silver spirit coin from his inventory and slipped it into his mouth.

"I miss cooking," he complained. "I really want to make a hazelnut dacquoise."

"I miss home," Farrah said. "Did you realise that I've spent more time in your world than you have in mine?"

He sat up, looking over at her.

"No," he said. "No, I didn't. But yeah, especially if you don't count all that time I was in an astral space."

"I've found your world as wondrous as you did mine," Farrah said. "I'm ready to go back, though. More than ready. I want to see hairy idiot Gary. Rufus is no doubt hopeless without me. I want to see my parents. My city. We were so eager to escape it and now I'm desperate to get back."

Jason's chair slid across the floor to arrive next to Farrah's and he gave her hand a reassuring squeeze.

"You'll get there," he said. "It's when, not if."

"I know."

"You're going to have to play tour guide when we get there, you realise."

"Oh, gods, no. I don't even want to think about the trouble you'll cause."

They both knew that their arrival in Farrah's world would not be a light, fun time, but they were happy, for the moment, to pretend. That their arrival would herald the worst monster surge in the history of the world was something to think about later.

66
NOT ENTIRELY ETHICAL

Jason emerged from the water, up the ramp at the base of the cloud house that led into the ocean. The swim had been pleasant and relaxing, although his silver-rank body was far too heavy to float. He didn't need to breathe, however, so he was as happy under the surface as on it.

Emi continued to splash about, under the supervision of her father, Ian, and discordantly youthful great-grandmother, Yumi. It had taken some convincing before Erika had allowed her daughter to go swimming kilometres out into the Pacific. Jason had to take steps to assure Emi's safety. He had put away the more modest cloud house and brought out the cloud palace. He configured it into a huge curve, forming an artificial lagoon, complete with underwater rooms that formed an artificial seafloor and a net at the lagoon's aperture. It formed a calm haven, safe from the ocean waves and any sharks foolish enough to come to the cloud palace in search of prey.

The cloud palace was a haven in more ways than one. In just the two weeks they had been working to identify their target reality node in Australia, the deterioration of world order had rapidly escalated. Australia itself was fine, in no small part due to an absence of the vampire lords making themselves known globally in even greater numbers than had been feared.

Several countries in Central America had already suffered total government breakdown, with several South American countries showing dangerous signs of following suit. America was a giant mess, already on the brink of mass civic conflict before vampires laid claim to Baltimore, Boston, and Philadelphia.

Using the two gold-rank essence users in their ranks, the vampires in Philadelphia were resisted and killed, but they lost many silver-rankers in the process of taking down eleven vampire lords.

China had been under a media blackout for months with the 'public protection measures' put in place months before that let almost no information out. The rest of Asia, as well as Africa, were both doing relatively well, with minimal vampiric activity, leaving the existing magical factions to continue fighting over reality cores. Russia and Europe were the exact opposite, suffering massive vampiric occupation.

Europe was the global hotbed for vampiric activity, with vampire lords laying claim to major cities all over the continent. Governments were working with the other magical factions, but Europe's Network branches had never been the powerhouses that China and the United States were. They would have trouble facing the vampires at the best of times, let alone in the midst of schism and factionalism. Russia faced similar issues but oddly minimal resistance, with rumours of government collaboration with the vampires rapidly spreading.

The entire European Union had declared states of emergency but no effective response had been found. The vampire lords were forming councils in the various cities they laid claim to and were difficult to respond to. With small numbers of extremely powerful individuals, the vampires were too strong to face with the Network's elite forces but too few to face with overwhelming numbers.

Overwhelming force was a response tried in several cities, but while the vampires were killed or driven off, the price was unacceptable. The vampires, with their small numbers, used the population and infrastructure as shields, while Network forces were forced to rely on magically enhanced ordnance designed to combat gold-rank threats. As a result, victory meant liberating a smouldering ruin, full of the dead.

Few nations were willing to pay that price after seeing the results. In many nations, the vampire lords were becoming de facto governments. Italy was the first nation to officially capitulate, in relatively bloodless fashion. France resisted hard, but the razing of Paris and the vampires' bloody reprisals in other French cities effectively wiped out the resisting civilian authorities.

In the wake of his final talks with Kaito, Greg and Asya, Jason felt lighter than he had since before the Broken Hill tragedy. He smiled, letting the sun dry him out as he watched Ian dive-bomb Emi, joining her in the water. Jason would take all the good moments he could get. Farrah came up to stand next to him, but instead of swimwear, she had the robust clothing she preferred to wear under her conjured armour.

"Another one?" he asked.

"Yeah."

"Hopefully, I can pinpoint the node today."

Farrah gave Jason the location and he opened a portal. He couldn't travel to the destination directly but could get within a hundred kilometres. During his time sweeping proto-spaces with the Network, Jason had travelled to a lot of Australia, and now his portal could range out to sixteen hundred kilometres.

They appeared in a small town still marred by damage from the monster waves. Shade bodies emerged from Jason's shadow and melded together to take the form of a helicopter. Other than being black, it looked exactly like Kaito's. Jason and Farrah boarded and headed for the proto-space.

Some of the nations worst-hit by the current chaos had largely eliminated any Network presence, leading to a reappearance of monster waves. Australia was mercifully spared that, at least for the moment, despite the chaos in Sydney and similar conflicts elsewhere. The leadership faction had moved to focus on reality cores, abandoning the old responsibilities to the larger but weaker faction, now going by the Global Defence Network.

One of the GDN teams entered a category-three dimensional incursion space, at which point the ritualist squad leader reported to the expedition leader.

"Sir, we've done the checks and the readings are way off."

"How so?"

"The anchor monsters are already gone and the integrity of the space is too high. It won't break down until as much as twenty hours after it should."

"Then it looks like we've got an easy one."

"Sir?"

"He's here. Tell everyone to pack it up. With how thin we're spread, we can be more useful elsewhere than in a space that's already been handled."

Jason got a fix on the node and managed a successful repair before returning to the cloud palace with Farrah. Afterwards, they sat on a terrace discussing their work with Dawn.

"As I spend more and more time working within node space," he said, "it feels like I'm getting a better grasp on astral magic. It's not like a skill book, imprinting knowledge, but more like being immersed in the primordial clay of reality is giving me a direct sense of all the theory I've been studying. Concepts that were abstract and hard to grasp make sense to me now."

"I believe the nature of your being also has an impact," Dawn postulated. "Normal physical beings have a perception of conventional reality that is a hindrance to understanding the higher concepts within astral magic theory. It takes an extraordinary mind or highly unusual circumstances to overcome that. Your being, like node space itself, is a gestalt of the physical and the spiritual, rather than two halves like Farrah, myself or this universe. Even someone with astral affinity will have trouble enduring it, yet you have no discomfort, do you?"

"No," Jason said. "There's an effect my abilities identify as dimensional discorporation, which sounds delightful. As you said, my unusual nature renders me impervious to it."

"It could be said that node space is more the place you are native to than normal reality," Dawn said.

"I'm not sure I like that," Jason said. "I mean, it's fine to visit, but I don't think I'd stay."

"The question is whether this improvement to your understanding of astral magic is improving your ability to identify and repair nodes," Farrah said.

"I think it is," Jason said. "It feels like it is, but I guess we'll see as we keep going."

"I ask," Farrah said, "because I'm worried about what happens when the ambient magic crosses the threshold where magic starts manifesting directly. No more proto-spaces will make identifying nodes harder."

"I don't know how that will go," Dawn said. "What Jason is doing amounts to pioneering a new sub-specialty of astral magic. Or, perhaps more accurately, he's exploring a field that has always been taboo. This kind of interference with the physical/astral boundary is exactly what the World-Phoenix, and I as its representative, have always sought to sanction."

"But you have to cut open that patient to perform surgery," Jason said.

"Yes," Dawn said. "If we haven't sufficiently repaired this end of the link between worlds before the magic here changes, we will find a new methodology. It will cost us time."

"I guess I should pack up the cloud palace," Jason said. "With how things are going in Europe, maybe we should have gone there before Australia."

"I don't regret it," Farrah said. "We cleared Australia's only vampire lord, which puts it in a good place. With how many vampires are coming out of the woodwork, it may be that Australia becomes a fallback position for humanity's magical forces. They're fractured and scattered now, but the vampire lords are just too powerful. The magical factions will need to stop fighting and come together."

"Assuming the Americans don't just nuke Venice," Jason said.

Five spears made of red crystal slammed into Jason, throwing him back and pinning him to the wall. One went through his gut, one through his chest and one each in an arm and a leg, immobilising them. One went for

Jason's throat, but he managed to dodge enough that it ripped a chunk from the side of his neck instead of piercing through the middle.

"You made a terrible mistake," the vampire said as it walked slowly towards him.

"I know," Jason said painfully through gritted teeth. "I should have changed before going out. This outfit is ruined. Which is ironic, given that you're the one in need of a wardrobe update. I'm sorry, mate, but if you think those lace cuffs are working for you, I've got some bad news."

"You are a fool."

"I'm a lot of things," Jason said. "Focusing on that one seems rude when there are so many options. I'm quite peckish, for example, which you'd know if you were polite enough to ask. I don't suppose you've got a sandwich on you? Probably not a sandwich guy, right?"

"I am going to turn you."

"Could you turn me into a construction guy? You're damaging a museum, here. You know they have Carracci's *The Choice of Hercules* here? I love that painting, although his choice should definitely be to put on some pants. I know the Mediterranean is a pleasant climate, but it would be nice to see one picture of Herc where he wasn't tackle-out. That's rough sunburn to get."

"I'm going to hurt you before I turn you," the vampire said as blood flowed from his hand, took the form of a sword and crystallised into a razor-sharp blade.

"I don't suppose you're talking about hurting my feelings?" Jason asked optimistically.

The vampire raised its sword to strike when webbing wrapped around it and yanked it backwards, sticking it to a wall opposite where Jason was pinned. The vampire immediately started yanking itself free, even as a fire bolt struck the webbing, setting it and the vampire ablaze.

The moment the vampire was pulled away, Jason cast a spell.

"Your blood is not yours to keep but mine on which to feast."

The red crystal spears in his body turned back into blood and were absorbed into his body, healing the wounds that they had made and freeing Jason. As the spell took effect, dark mist shrouded him, swapping out his bloody clothes as his blood robes and starlight cloak were conjured around him.

"You took your time," Jason said as the mist vanished.

Threads already on fire snaked in through a large hole in the wall, wrapped around the vampire as it pulled itself free and yanked it once more, this time right out of the building.

"He hit me through a wall with a sculpture of a naked guy hanging out with a naked little boy and some grapes," Farrah said. "It was more worrying than the vampire."

"I wasn't sure I could stall the guy out until you stepped in. If I'd tried to cast my spell with him right in front of me, he'd have stopped me before I could finish the chant. I couldn't even shadow-jump with those things in me. I think they stop teleportation."

"How did you stall him out?"

"Talked a bunch of crap."

"Then I'm sure you were fine. You played to your strengths."

Dawn came hurtling in through the hole, clearly not voluntarily as she went tumbling over the museum's display floor.

"Perhaps a little help?" she suggested, calm in spite of her dishevelled state as she lightly hopped to her feet.

Jason extended a shadow arm and smashed the ceiling light. There were more lights in the large hall and darkness didn't impede a vampire, but that wasn't his goal. The dim light and sculpture exhibits turned the area into a playground of shadows into which Jason melted as the vampire stalked back in through the huge hole in the wall where Dawn had pulled him out.

This vampire was stronger than the one they fought in Australia, able to turn its own blood into versatile weapons. With Jason added in, though, it was not as hard as the one Dawn and Farrah had faced without him. Dawn used control effects while Farrah staggered the vampire with blitz attacks. The final piece of the puzzle was Jason, taking the chances Farrah and Dawn provided to lock in his afflictions. Then Farrah and Dawn kept it off balance until the afflictions overcame it.

When the vampire went down, they were barely able to keep it alive. Fortunately, Jason's transcendent afflictions dropped off over time, allowing the gold-rank fortitude of the vampire to leave it barely clinging to life.

"I guess you drain it," Farrah said.

"Actually," Dawn said, "I would like to try something. Bring him and we'll go; he's not the only vampire lord in Naples."

"What do you want to try?" Jason asked as he grabbed the vampire's scorched legs.

"Something not entirely ethical," Dawn said.

67
AHEAD OF SCHEDULE

"You want me to use this guy as a battery," Jason said.

The cloud house had taken the appearance of an unremarkable and isolated farmhouse in the Italian countryside. The gold-rank vampire they had captured was locked in a cell from which they were confident it wouldn't escape. By silver rank, the cloud house was starting to show its diamond-rank potential as it grew more powerful and sophisticated. A single gold-ranker wasn't powerful enough to force their way in or out.

"Yes," Dawn said as they observed the vampire through a one-way window.

"You weren't wrong about it being ethically questionable."

"Vampires feed on people," Farrah said. "Seems fair that you do the same to them."

"And is that how we judge ourselves?" Jason asked. "By the standards of bloodthirsty monsters?"

"No," Dawn said. "We judge ourselves by our actions. Not just the momentary ones but the larger scope of what we do. With what we are trying to achieve and the obstacles in our way, draining one bloodthirsty predator to get any advantage is a morally acceptable act."

"And how far can we go?" Jason asked. "How many bad people is it okay to lock up and torture?"

"All of them," Farrah said.

"What about good people?" Jason asked. "How many can we sacrifice? Where's the line? What's the number?"

"There isn't a number," Dawn said. "Thinking there is some kind of objective value in all this that can be quantified is a fool's argument. Like all acts of morality, it's a matter of exercising judgement."

"Yeah, well…" Jason's shoulders sagged. "I'm not so sure I trust my judgement."

"Then it is good that you are not alone," Dawn said. "Miss Hurin was not sent to this world on a whim. She was sent so that you would have someone to rely on."

"You're saying I'm the sidekick?" Farrah pouted.

Jason looked at her thoughtfully, smiling as she grinned at him.

"Alright," he said. "Thank you. I'm still not comfortable just draining this guy over and over, though. Also, I don't think he's got a lot left in him."

The vampire was not in good condition. Between Jason's transcendent damage and the fire powers of Farrah and Dawn, even a high-rank essence user would have trouble surviving in his current state.

"We need to get some of the reality-core-treated blood they drink," Dawn said. "He can work as a filter for you to top off, drain and then top off again."

"You talk about getting at their blood supply like it's a simple thing," Farrah said. "There was a reason we didn't raid the reality core storage in America."

"It's not the same circumstances, though," Jason mused. "The vampires don't have the ritual magic to emplace defences and mundane security measures won't stop us."

"Don't be so certain about the magical defences," Dawn said. "The Cabal may have recruited useful Network defectors."

"Yeah," Jason acknowledged, remembering the silver-rank essence users they fought in Australia. "If they can get top tactical personnel on board, recruiting some ritualists is certainly possible."

"Especially given how badly the Network is struggling in Europe," Farrah said.

The vampire lords had repeated the attack on the Sydney branch all over Europe, with far greater success. Sydney suffered massive damage from one vampire, while in European cities, two, three, even six vampires had attacked Network branches to eliminate their primary rivals. The Network was holding on in backup locations and tertiary branches, continuing to shut down proto-spaces, but their efforts were growing desperate.

"I believe that the circumstances are different enough that the potential rewards outweigh the risks. Only the vampire lords themselves would be powerful enough to stop us and you've seen their pridefulness for yourselves. They will not be as diligent as they should. At least until someone gives them a reason to."

"A gold-rank vampire is only going to play guard if a stronger vampire forces them to," Jason reasoned.

"And they won't be happy about it, so they probably won't be too diligent," Farrah said. "Still, it's a big risk."

"We still have Jason's trump card, if something goes wrong," Dawn said.

Jason had a magic item in his possession that he obtained a long time ago, during the Reaper trials. It was a diamond-rank consumable item containing the power of sunlight, which Dawn confirmed would be highly effective, even against vampire lords.

"That's something I want to keep in my pocket in case we find ourselves in a bad situation," Jason said. "We only get to use it once."

"If we're going to use it actively," Farrah said, "we should do it right."

"What are you suggesting?" Jason asked.

"What if we track down the biggest storehouse of reality cores and vampire blood in Europe to hit. Except we leak that we're going to hit it, so the vampires are waiting for us. But instead of trying to sneak in, we come in force. Carefully recruit some Network people and hit them hard. Use the item and wipe out as many of the bloodsuckers as we can."

"In theory, that's good," Jason said. "There's a good chance that if we're recruiting, they'll catch wind of it, though."

"Then we let them," Farrah said. "The vampires are prideful and won't back down. They'll bring even more of their number to utterly crush any opposition and prove their dominance. The more we can hit with the item, the more we can wipe out."

"No," Dawn said. "That is getting too big. We're not here to kill vampires. Taking the chance to grow stronger when it costs us minimal time is one thing, but taking the time to organise a large-scale attack is too much of a distraction from our goal."

"You're right," Jason said. "I like the idea of making a dent in the vampire population, but that would be spending time we don't have to buy risk we don't need. I'm willing to spend days on this while we're waiting for the right proto-space to pop. That kind of operation would take weeks of active effort, though. In the end, cutting off the reality core supply faster will ultimately save more lives than killing some vampires now."

"Fine," Farrah said. "I'm keeping this plan in mind, though. If we see a good chance to try it, I want to revisit this conversation. Dawn, it feels like every time we're about to stage a great reality core heist, you throw cold water on it."

"Boldness is a requisite of achieving our objectives," Dawn said, "but to be bold is to walk on a foolhardy edge. We must be vigilant that we do not slip."

"We still require a supply of treated blood," Jason said. "We have to get it somewhere."

"We conduct a smaller operation than Miss Hurin suggests. Something quicker and safer. Rather than hit one of the core vampire territories, we choose a peripheral target and raid the blood treatment centre there."

"Will there even be one in a less important location?" Jason asked. "Won't they just distribute the blood from a central, secure site?"

"Even the weakest vampire lord is an edifice of power and pride. None of them would allow anyone else to hold them hostage with the blood supply," Dawn said. "Every vampire lord requires a regular supply of treated blood; otherwise, the low levels of magic will rapidly diminish their power until they return to a state of torpor. Given the enemies they are making of everyone, they cannot afford moments of weakness due to breaks in the supply chain. Reality cores they likely ship around, but none of the vampires will let themselves get too far from their blood supply."

"That's a weakness that hopefully gets taken advantage of when the time comes to deal with them," Jason said. "Unfortunately, the world has too much happening all at once."

"So we pick a city that's big enough to have vampire lords, but small enough that the stronger vampires are elsewhere," Farrah said. "That rules out going back to Naples, right?"

"Yes," Jason said. "It's too big and they'll be on alert after this guy disappeared."

They all looked in on the vampire, lying still in a miserable state.

Jason had used the cloud flask to produce its vehicle form. Previously, it had taken the form of a large tour bus, while now it was a medium-sized yacht, moored amongst other pleasure craft at a dock in Venice. The only reason anyone was using the boats now was to escape the city. The tourist boats around them were all empty, which their aura senses easily confirmed.

"I'm still not sure Venice was the best bet," Farrah said as they sat in the boat making plans. "Isn't this the very first city the vampires took over?"

"Yes," Jason said. "That's why it's the most damaged city. The Italian government hadn't thrown in the towel yet and supported the Network standing up to the gold-rankers. Those original vampire lords were also some of the strongest, though. They left a crumbling city for larger population centres."

"Vampires view population as a commodity, like herds of cattle," Dawn said.

Jason and Shade had already done some initial scouting of the city. He had likewise been sceptical of Dawn's suggested destination, but what he learned eavesdropping on lower-rank vampires validated her choice. Venice was a soft target that no one thought of as one because it was known that the strongest vampires had emerged from it.

"The original vampire lords here have moved on to larger cities, leaving the weaker ones to manage it," Jason said. "If you can call any of the gold-rank vampires weak. There are only two of them here."

"Which makes it a good target," Dawn said. "Venice is a symbolic territory for the old vampires, not a valuable one. This is especially true now that the fighting has caused so much destruction. There is no glory in ruling over ruins."

While Dawn and Farrah remained hidden on the boat, monitoring the grid for proto-spaces, Jason went back out to investigate the city. Shade and his many bodies were an incredible boon on that front, with one body left behind so that Dawn and Farrah could speak to him through it and he could quickly shadow jump back to the boat.

Roaming the city, he found that the streets and canals were largely empty. He sensed the people unfortunate enough not to have evacuated during the fighting huddled in their homes, only venturing out for food. The vampires allowed some remnants of civic authority to remain operating, organising food distribution stations, even importing food from other Cabal-controlled territories.

Almost everyone out on the streets was a Cabal member, and most of those were vampires. There was no shortage of lower-rank vampires ready to cast off the veneer of civility and indulge their thirst for blood. Jason spotted more than one group breaking into a home and sending the occupants running before hunting and consuming them for sport.

Jason itched to step in but unless he had some plan to liberate the city, all that would do is bring more trouble down on the residents. Even if he made just a few lower-rank vampires disappear without a trace, the gold-rankers would be unwilling to tolerate challenges to their authority and investigate thoroughly. The first one to suffer would be the closest innocent people the vampires could find.

Jason and Shade trailed the low-ranking vampires around the city, gaining a better understanding of the city's state of affairs. It was like territory captured by an enemy army, with only the occupying forces out in numbers on the mostly empty streets. Many bridges and buildings had suffered catastrophic damage, with some canals flooding after being dammed by rubble. The vampires were pulling people out of their homes and forming work gangs to clear them out.

The canals themselves were otherwise empty of activity. The famously filthy water was even running clear in the areas not stained by building debris. There were swans and Jason even spotted fish swimming about. It was an oddly bright point in a city that had otherwise become a dystopian nightmare. He hated that after years of wanting to visit Venice, this was the state in which he found it.

Jason and Shade were also able to glean more information about the vampire lords themselves. The lords needed more sleep than their less powerful brethren, despite the enhanced blood running through them. Vampire lords slept as much as twelve to fourteen hours, mostly during daylight.

Continuing to observe the lower-rank vampires, Jason learned of a growing rift between the vampires and the rest of the Cabal. The vampires were a minority within the organisation as a whole, but waking up the vampire lords had turned them into a ruling minority. There was growing dissatisfaction amongst the Cabal's many other factions, who were being edged out of positions of authority. There was also, from what he was hearing, a sizeable portion of the vampire faction that, like Craig Vermillion, did not support the old vampires.

Jason was scouting out the blood treatment centre set up in a medical clinic when Farrah called him back. He shadow-jumped back to the boat, arriving in the room where Farrah monitored the grid. It looked like the communications station of a spaceship, with screens and control panels everywhere. Farrah and Dawn were both watching different readings on the various monitors.

"You found a target proto-space?" Jason asked.

"No," Farrah said. "It's something else."

"Oh?"

"A transformation event had happened in a space that was already coterminous to a proto-space," Dawn said.

"Will they interact?" Jason asked.

"From the readings that the grid is throwing out, yes," Farrah said.

"What kind of effect is it having?"

"That is way beyond my understanding of astral magic," Farrah said.

She and Jason both looked at Dawn.

"I believe," Dawn said, "that this world has decided to end ahead of schedule."

68

OPEN WOUND

As they walked through an army base in Germany, a handful of male Network troops threw up fists as they spotted the huge and hairy figure of Jack Gerling. The Germans had been avid about expelling the American Network forces from their country until the rise of the vampire lords changed everything. The powerful US forces had been critical in helping Germany deal with vampires across multiple cities, leaving it as one of the least ravaged nations on the continent. In return, Germany was now the US Network's key staging point in Europe.

"Beer and titties!" they called out.

"Beer and titties!" he responded with a grin, pumping his own fist into the air.

His power and importance made him a recognisable figure on the base and he had gone out of his way to make friends with all the tactical teams. It cost him little to sow seeds that could potentially have him reaping a critical harvest in the future. He walked through the base, greeting various people as he went until he reached his personal quarters. The moment he stepped inside, the friendly expression on his face went blank.

Gerling was being more careful with his boorish façade, having let it slip too much in the wake of the fight with Asano. The leadership was still very tight with the reality cores and the last thing he wanted was to be seen as too capable to control.

The American Network's leadership had made a priority of advancing more people to category four, especially with the rise of the ancient vampires. It wasn't the disaster in the US that it was in Europe, but it was bad enough and only getting worse. The Network had been keeping a collection of people just short of category four and already reality cores had allowed two of them to cross the threshold.

This was in addition to the other category four who, like Gerling, had been woken up from stasis. Gerling was still the only one of the category fours the US Network had in Europe; the others were assigned to handle domestic problems. For the moment, Gerling was too valuable to be expendable.

Already, though, he had seen signs of the leadership becoming nervous about the category fours and the danger of them seizing power. Until he could be certain of a regular reality core supply, Gerling would keep leaning into his more self-indulgent urges, playing the hedonist thug.

His quarters on the base reflected this, being filled with personal luxuries he had obnoxiously demanded. His handler, Cleary, was more than happy to meet them, satisfied with the minor concessions he gained for providing them. Cleary, especially, had seen behind Gerling's mask and was looking to alleviate his suspicions. By being consistent with his self-indulgence, he would slowly but surely lead Cleary to dismiss any doubts.

Battling Asano and Hurin had been a startling wake-up call for Gerling. Although he maintained an outward display of hedonistic excess for his nominal masters, he quietly dedicated himself to growing stronger. The US had always had the best training programs, alongside China, and what Farrah Hurin had introduced to the Network had been used to refine them.

Gerling had gone through the same training as everyone else but had always coasted on the explosive potential of his abilities. Those powers were the reason he had been chosen as one of the first to raise to category four. It was only after the magical deficit forced him to be placed in stasis that he realised that he had also been chosen for expendability if something went wrong.

Now Gerling had a team of trainers helping him drive his abilities to new heights, refreshing the skills that had been drilled into him years ago and allowed to fall fallow. He kept his training quiet and his recreation loud, making sure to complain about the effort.

Inside his quarters, his personal assistant was waiting for him. He had two of them but only cared about one. Fiona was smart and ambitious. Gerling was confident that she knew that she would go further with genuine loyalty than reporting on him to Cleary. She did make those reports, but they contained exactly what Gerling wanted them to.

As for his other assistant, Gerling constantly amused himself by assigning the young man a series of lengthy and elaborate demands. To his surprise, his assistant's dedication and enthusiasm led to his unexpectedly fulfilling Gerling's often bizarre and indulgent requests.

Fiona handed Gerling a memory stick.

"This is everything I could get on Asano's encounter with the EOA in Venezuela," she said. "Several essence users were using that small town as a retreat, so there are quite a few testimonials there from people with magical and aura senses. There is also a lot of footage shot from phones."

Gerling took the memory stick, tapping it against his other hand absently, lost in thought. He had watched the news footage of Asano, killing the EOA's enhanced humans more than a dozen times. It was Asano's aura that concerned Gerling the most. Being a skilled essence user with excellent command of his abilities was something Gerling could accept. The raw power of his aura, however, overturned Gerling's understanding of what was and wasn't possible. What else was Asano capable of? Could Gerling obtain that power for himself?

"Anything new on here?" he asked, holding up the stick.

"Not any major details," Fiona said. "Additional confirmation that Asano killed them using his aura alone, based on what the witnesses were able to sense."

Gerling moved to a desk and plugged the memory stick into his laptop.

"Thank you, Fiona."

"What do you mean by the world ending early?" Jason asked.

He, Dawn and Farrah were still in the cloud boat, discussing the overlap between a proto-space and a transformation event.

"These transformation events are well outside of my experience," Dawn said. "This event is still ongoing, so no one can enter the zone to confirm anything until it completes its transformation and opens up again.

That being said, I have seen all manner of dimensional events and sufficiently unstable dimensional forces all have similar results."

"And?" Farrah prompted.

"Based on the readings we've been taking from the grid, I believe that something very dangerous is happening."

"Dangerous like a super monster wave?" Farrah asked.

"Far worse, I'm afraid," Dawn said. "Dimensional ulceration."

"Oh, that's bad," Jason said with a wince.

"Can someone explain that to the person not specialised in astral magic?" Farrah asked.

"Imagine an open wound in the side of the universe," Jason said. "That's very, very not good in a universe whose dimensional membrane is stable and healthy. In a fixer-upper universe like ours… I don't even want to contemplate."

"In the best case," Dawn said, "it will establish a second source of magic that will start feeding into this world."

"Like the dimensional link we're going to all this effort to fix," Farrah said.

"Precisely," Dawn confirmed. "Except that this source will be impossible to cut off. Normally, the World-Phoenix and her agents would work to remedy such a situation but Earth's dimensional membrane is like a thin sheet of glass, already full of cracks. Trying to repair it could shatter it entirely."

"That's the best case?" Farrah asked.

"The worst case," Dawn said, "is that the dimensional membrane rapidly collapses and this world is annihilated. That subsequently tears a chunk out of this entire reality, chaining into the universe completely breaking down. It's more likely the damage will be contained to your planet, or at least your solar system, but it may end this entire physical reality."

"So, worse than a super monster wave," Farrah said.

"Considerably," Dawn agreed.

"I'm assuming you have a plan," Jason said. "I'd really like to hear a plan."

"It may be possible for you to stabilise the effects," Dawn said. "During a transformation event, the entire area is sealed. I believe this is because the area is drawn at least partially into what you, Jason, have been referring to as node space. The dimensional changes taking place are being affected by the proto-space coterminous to that area, causing what is already a reality-shearing transformation to go out of control."

"You think I can use the Builder's door to enter the sealed space," Jason said.

"Yes," Dawn said. "The World-Phoenix personally sculpted a racial gift evolution that would make you the perfect living tool for resolving problems in dimensionally unstable space. Your presence alone will be a help."

"Hold on," Jason said. "You want me to go into a place that can't be entered and brave conditions that are completely unknown in an environment being torn apart and rebuilt at a level that makes subatomic particles seem shallow?"

"I know it seems too dangerous to—"

"Awesome," Jason said.

"Pardon?" Dawn asked.

"No piles of victims turned zombies. No saving who I can while the dead pile up around me. Just going to some crazy pocket dimension for some good, clean world-saving? Get it right and everybody lives?"

Jason nodded his head, grinning.

"I think I've needed this for a long time," he said.

"You will have to go alone," Dawn said. "No one else can reliably survive the conditions within an active transformation event, except for the people who are part of it, and they don't remember anything. They are, at the very least, unconscious. More likely, they exist in some kind of transitional state and you should avoid them as best you can. For your sake, as much as theirs. I was trying to tell you that it will be dangerous."

"You were also telling me that I have to do it anyway, right?"

"Yes. It needs to be done and only you can do it."

"You know that the transformation event will be crawling with people gearing up to snatch the reality core, right?" Farrah asked. "This will reveal Jason's door power to everyone. They won't understand everything about it, but the ability to enter transformation events is all they'll need. They'll start coming after him because they'll think he can give them a head start on core collecting."

"If only they knew," Jason said. "Reality cores are pebbles on the ground in node space."

"Unfortunately, there will be no getting past them unnoticed," Dawn said. "There will be considerable attention on the transformation space. You will need to enter swiftly, in case anyone attempts to intercept you before you do."

"Which is why you all need to stay here," Jason said. "You can't come into the zone with me and you can't hang about with all the others outside."

"We'll look after your family," Dawn said. "If the worst happens and you fail, I will make sure they and Miss Hurin are safely sent to the other world."

"You can do that?" Jason asked.

"If this world's dimensional membrane enters a state of irreversible collapse, I no longer have to worry about damaging it. I can intervene directly and take them away in my dimensional vessel."

Jason gave her a warm smile.

"Thank you."

Each transformation event had a tense prelude when the different magical factions arrived and everyone waited for the impassable barrier to drop so the search and fight for the reality core could begin. Fighting breaking out beforehand was more common than not. The rise of the old vampires had only added to the already strong position of the Cabal in these conflicts, as all their members grew stronger in transformation spaces.

There were places where the Network held the edge, however. In Europe, Jack Gerling was the single most powerful individual. The old vampires outnumbered him, but his abilities were specialised in devastating large numbers of enemies, levelling the playing field. Rumours spoke to similar circumstances in China, although very little information got out. No one was even sure exactly how many gold-rank essence users they had, although no one doubted they had at least some.

The transformation zone that appeared on the plains of western Slovakia was special because of the proto-space it formed on top of. This drew unusually large forces from every faction, all of whom could now tap into the grid. The EOA gained access when they took over Network duties at the request of several governments. The Cabal gained access more recently through Network defectors.

None of the magical factions had the understanding of astral magic that Dawn or even Jason possessed. They could tell that the transformation space was unusual, but most were postulating that the result would be additional reality cores, not an inexorable doomsday clock.

The transformation zone was currently a glimmering dome several kilometres across. A giant rainbow under glass, it swirled with bright, wild colours. In the nearby city of Nitra, Jack Gerling was sitting at an outdoor café, rather than hovering around the dome. Even if the event was unusual, it was unlikely to open up for days, like always. The estimations were that it would take more time than normal, not less.

Nitra was something of a blessed city, being too small to host any ancient vampires but large enough to warrant Network protection during the monster waves. It was now a major centre for the Network after the organization had been pushed out of Bratislava by vampires. As a result, it had weathered the magical tribulations of the past several years in far better stead than most, allowing the residents to maintain at least some aspects of their normal lives.

As he sipped at his coffee, Gerling's gold-rank perception allowed his eyes to pick out something moving through the air, despite its great altitude. It immediately arrested his attention as normal air traffic stayed clear of transformation zones. Also, not a lot of planes looked like someone had tried to turn a stealth fighter into a private jet. After months of investigating Jason Asano's behaviour, Gerling knew what it meant to see a strange black vehicle going somewhere it shouldn't.

"He's here."

THANK YOU FOR READING HE WHO FIGHTS WITH MONSTERS, BOOK FIVE.

We hope you enjoyed it as much as we enjoyed bringing it to you. We just wanted to take a moment to encourage you to review the book. Follow this link: He Who Fights With Monsters 5 to be directed to the book's Amazon product page to leave your review.

Every review helps further the author's reach and, ultimately, helps them continue writing fantastic books for us all to enjoy.

Want to connect with Shirtaloon?

Discuss He Who Fights With Monsters and more, join Shirtaloon's Discord!

Follow him on www.HeWhoFightsWithMonsters.com where you can find great HWFWM merch and other great content.

HE WHO FIGHTS WITH MONSTERS
BOOK ONE
BOOK TWO

BOOK THREE
BOOK FOUR
BOOK FIVE
BOOK SIX

Looking for more great LitRPG?

About the series: A progression fantasy epic set in a time-loop where planning and cleverness are as vital as swordplay, about a spoiled prince who discovers what it means to rule. Watch as he gains power, learns magic, forges alliances, and delves deeper into the mystery of the loop itself and the nature of his relationship with the ruthless antagonist.

Get Monarch Now!

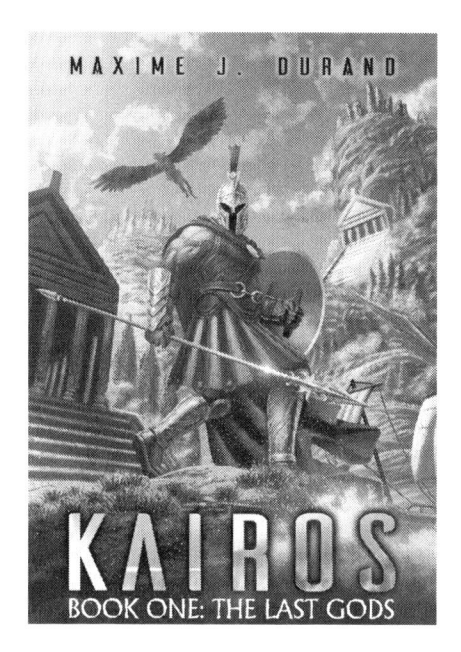

Divine power is not given. It is taken. It's been centuries since mortals unlocked the secrets of the Fate System and overthrew Mount Olympus, leaving the Old Gods dead and their thrones empty. Kairos, a young pirate with the ability to speak with animals, has dreams to ascend as the newest deity of a flooded world. Though it will take more than ambition, charisma, and a ship to do so. He must sail the endless sea, tame fearsome monsters, and conquer new lands. The challenges are many, but he will face them all. For Kairos is a cunning [Rogue] indeed...

Get The Last Gods Now!

About the series: Follow the path of a Xianxia cultivator in a LitRPG setting. See him increase his powers and carve out a new home in a hostile world out to get him. Rejoice as he spreads cultivation to those in need, each with their own story to tell. In this journey, wholesomeness and epicness go hand-in-hand.

Get The First Step Now!

For all our LitRPG books, visit our website.

AETHON BOOKS:
Facebook | Instagram | Twitter | Website
You can also join our non-spam mailing list by visiting www.

subscribepage.com/AethonReadersGroup and never miss out on future releases. You'll also receive three full books completely Free as our thanks to you.

Made in the USA
Monee, IL
27 September 2023